THE STRANGE HAUNTING OF JOHNNY FEELWATER

THE STRANGE HAUNTING OF JOHNNY FEELWATER

A Novel

Martin Brant

THE STRANGE HAUNTING of JOHNNY FEELWATER

Copyright © 2008 by Martin Brant

All rights reserved. No part of this book may be used or reproduced by any means, graphic, electronic, or mechanical, including photocopying, recording, taping or by any information storage retrieval system without the written permission of the publisher except in the case of brief quotations embodied in critical articles and reviews.

This is a work of fiction. All the characters, names, incidents, organizations, and dialogue in this novel are either products of the author's imagination or are used fictitiously. Confederate Square, a location mentioned in this novel, is a fictitious location and is used to depict the unique personality of Savannah, Georgia's many beautiful squares.

*Cover image from
Getty Images*

Printed in the United States of America

There are beings that have lived among us from the beginning of time, those that have gathered their matter in the bowels of the earth. They have evolved in human form with powers that cannot be explained or understood. The few of us who have encountered them are forever changed, never to view the world the same way again. Immortal by way of never-ending reincarnation, they have from us their sustenance and pleasure. They know inside many of us, hidden behind our religious beliefs and moral codes, lies a sleeping phantom of decadence.

Also by Martin Brant:

FIVE MARRIED MEN

THE PARTISANS

A SONG IN THE PARK

For Cathy
Who believes in me no matter what.

Prologue

Julian Mott entered the graveyard shortly after two A.M.

Not that the dead of night was of any consequence to one like him—for what he had to do, he preferred a shroud of darkness. A stray dog cowered as he strode through the maze of statuary and timeworn memorials. Shadowed by ancient oaks with sprawling limbs hung with Spanish moss, the necropolis lay before him in its everlasting wait. On he went, shovel in hand, his footfall silent across the dew-covered grass. He passed among those long since dead, a few he might have once known, thinking their existence had been a pitiful speck in time, their lives nothing more than insignificant dramas in the eternal scheme of things. He could not imagine passing into oblivion after a mere eighty or ninety years.

The warm night air lay over the old Savannah cemetery like an invisible fog. Hardly a leaf stirred in the limbs overhead. Beyond the black silhouettes of the high branches, an endless parade of iridescent clouds passed under the moon, one after another like ghost ships crossing the heavens. Scanning the environs as his short trek continued across the damp grass, the seconds, like somber increments of time, ticked by. Never hurried, not even on this most important occasion, he would find the fresh grave easily, even had he not come by to look after it earlier in the day.

As he anticipated, an indigent man was sleeping in the shadows behind a crypt, the same fellow he had seen that afternoon slinking into the cemetery with a bottle of wine hidden in a paper bag. The man awoke with a start, a premonition of someone's approach.

Trembling, his gaze moved upward over Julian's legs and chest. He shrunk back, ragged and terrified, looking up at the lone figure standing over him. Then, as if something pleasant had warmed the marrow of his bones, his fear melted away as he stared into the luminous crystal blue eyes. Within them rested a smile, omnipotent and disarming. The poor lost soul suddenly felt safe and protected. Falling prey to the authority of a powerful mind, not knowing or wondering why, he came to his feet and Julian extended the shovel. Aware he must abide this mysterious presence, the man took the shovel and followed as a duckling follows its mother. And on into the dark of night the two figures trod, the strong leading the weak, on through the maze of moss-covered headstones and tomes.

Ahead, barely discernible in the moonlight, a freshly turned knoll of earth came into view. Julian approached with a quiet sense of relief, not that he had found the grave, but that she had finally died. Cassandra Mott had lived to age ninety-two and had become quite impatient with her aged and crippled body. She never enjoyed those years beyond sixty—this time she had endured thirty-two of them. He looked down at the freshly turned earth, knowing several hours would pass before his decree would be fulfilled, the moment that for so long they had both waited. Soon everything would be put right once again.

Julian looked at the homeless man and nodded at the grave. The man started to dig. Standing a few away, his hands clasped behind him, Julian stared at the ever-expanding hole. A while later, just as the shovel struck the casket lid, he sensed someone's approach.

More accustomed to chasing teenagers out of the cemetery this time of night, the watchman figured it had been a good two years since he caught a pair of grave robbers. With stealth, the large man crept forward like an overweight cat. His eyes narrowed on the culprits as he drew near. Stepping out from behind a tree some fifteen feet away, he pulled his little-used revolver and drew an aim as the intruders went about their villainous trade.

"You don't look like no grave robber I ever saw before," said the watchman, piercing the quiet with his tense voice. He found himself discomfited by such a stylish man robbing a grave, wearing what looked like an expensive white linen shirt and matching trousers.

Julian turned and looked at the watchman, smiling inwardly, his hands still folded behind him. After so many centuries in Europe before coming to Savannah, he was still amused by crude dialect in this part of America. He looked at the watchman dispassionately, his vacant expression devoid of alarm or apprehension. The homeless man, wretched in his sweat stained and tattered clothes, stopped his work and stabbed the shovel into the newly created mound.

"What's you're name, Mister?" asked the watchman, his voice edgy.

Julian stood perfectly still, now amused by the watchman's sloppy appearance.

"You got big trouble here, Mister," the watchman assured him. "Best you answer me when I talk to you."

Julian stared.

"What's wrong with you?" asked the watchman, stammering. "Can't you talk?"

Julian sighed. Enough time had been wasted.

A foreboding came over the large man as he stared into the unyielding blue eyes. Reflecting needles of moonlight, they were cold and possessed by something he could not comprehend, like they were peering inside him, evaluating his soul. As the warm night air dampened face, he had forgotten the ragged man standing knee deep in the grave. His big hand gripped the gun. He aimed it recklessly at the intruder. His mind raced with conflicting notions and unease as he stared at a man too dashing to be a grave robber, sandy blonde hair, broad straight shoulders, a strange man standing erect and staring back as if he were looking at nothing more than a curiosity.

The watchman nervously fumbled for his handheld radio and switched it on. He listened for the familiar static, studying the intruder's face, struck by its beauty, its perfect symmetry and unsmiling lips. The radio was dead. A panic arose inside him.

"Why do you look at me that way?" he demanded, his voice thick with dread. He steadied the revolver in a direct aim, a feeble attempt to establish his authority.

Julian's eyes shifted to the gun.

It began to feel warm in the watchman's hand, suddenly hotter and hotter by degrees. Before he could think or had time to react, it had scalded his hand. He flung it away, standing like a large vulnerable child, staring at the intruder in mortal fear, his face strained and running with sweat as he rubbed his blistered palm. A sudden terrible pain invaded the watchman's belly. He buckled over and stumbled backward and fell against a tree. Doubled in pain, he looked up at the man standing near the grave and the image blurred in the moonlight. His head wobbled and then fell, his chin rested on his chest.

Julian turned and looked at the homeless man, who then reached for the shovel and continued his task. When the top of the casket was fully exposed, the man took a hold of one end and pulled it out of the grave. Julian stepped forward and leaned over it to search for the seam with his fingers. He ripped the top from its hinges as if it had been made of papier-mâché. A smile came to his lips. In the shadows of the small space, she lay peacefully within the satiny folds, lifeless once more.

He knelt and lifted her head. Her face had wrinkled and her body had become frail, and she had been angry that she had lived so long. He stroked the cold wrinkled cheek and then pushed his hands under her body to lift her and lay her on the grass. He stood, stepped toward his companion and placed two one hundred dollar bills in the man's shirt pocket.

The man didn't notice the money. As if by instinct, he knew his job had not been finished. At once he carried on with the chore.

By daybreak no one would know the earthen tomb had been disturbed. The watchman would have no idea why he had fallen asleep under the tree, nor what had blistered his hand. The homeless man would awaken near the spot where Julian had found him, two hundred dollars richer. He would not know why his back hurt, nor the source of the two hundred dollars, though he would set out to quickly spend it. The cemetery would appear to be undisturbed.

Julian lifted the dead woman close to his chest. It was a good distance to carry her, to the place on the river he had chosen to perform the ritual, but the task was hardly challenging. Cassandra was as light as a feather. It would take most of what remained of the night for what he had to do, but by daylight he would have her safely back in her own bed, youthful and vibrant once again.

Just why, Julian was not sure—it was not for him to decide such things; but it seemed Savannah had charmed Cassandra with its antebellum balls and abundance of eccentric personalities. She had simply decided to live another lifetime in the old southern city; and like any of her many whims, this was agreeable to him.

Yet he feared, beyond her love for old Savannah, she would bring into her new life a darker reason to return here; for she had died believing she had an enemy. On this Julian did not agree. He had gone into the man's bedroom before coming to the graveyard and found him sound asleep without a trace of malice in his heart or thoughts, or any knowledge of Cassandra Mott. Exactly why Cassandra hated him, he had yet to understand.

Chapter 1

Johnny Feelwater's eyes opened in the middle of the night. He lay motionless beside his sleeping wife for a long while, glancing this way and that, squinting into the shadows of every corner of the bedroom. A fine sweat had formed on his skin, though the tranquil night air seeping through the open window felt rather crisp. He had seen a movement of some kind just beyond the foot of his bed, he was almost positive. The same thing happened a few days before. He would have described it as a swirl of smoke zipping across the room like a fast bird. But the room was dark. Perhaps it had been a dream. He didn't know. Either way, it had robbed him of some valuable sleep and had left him with the oddest feeling.

Lying there, now wide awake, he looked at his sleeping wife. His thoughts shifted to the Globalcorp project, the reason he needed a good night's sleep. It occupied his mind most of his waking hours. He worked tirelessly on the project, everyday from early morning until well past the dinner hour. Landing such a big account felt like finding the pot of gold at the end of the rainbow. No one believed he could do it.

They deserved it, he and his wife, Marilee. It had been a long, arduous and debt ridden path they had trod together, but they had finally managed to get his small graphics design firm off the ground. The risks had paid off. Globalcorp offered him their cosmetics contract for the coming year's national advertising campaign. The sampling of ideas he had presented won them over. They promptly offered him the job for all the commercial artwork in the campaign; the first such contract ever awarded a small, black-owned firm by that company. The project had lionized his time for weeks. Its eventual completion not only meant a significant financial reward, it promised to elevate him to a prominent place on the list of who's who in the advertising world. As a result, he and Marilee had gotten their bills caught up. Only recently they had talked about renovating their small house there in Savannah's historic district.

He clasped his hands behind his head and stared into space. It wasn't the first time he had lain awake during the wee hours of the morning—his best ideas often came in the middle of the night. An hour or two passed before his eyes fluttered and sleep once again took hold.

When first light spilled into the room, his eyes opened again; this time prompted by a color scheme that came to him during the night. He wanted to try it on his latest design for a series of lipstick ads. Then his mind drifted to the dream that awakened him a few hours earlier. He remembered it clearly. How eerie it had been. Odd he remembered it at all, in that he rarely remembered any of his dreams or nightmares. Coming up on his elbow, he scanned the room, thinking it ridiculous that he had thought during the night that there had been something peculiar inside his house.

He turned his head and rested his eyes on the feminine contours beside him. She was still fast asleep under the quilt that he had flipped off his side of the bed before falling asleep. Though the early mornings were still cool, the quilt was a little too warm to sleep under, even though he had come to bed in nothing more than his usual silk pajama bottoms. Just how Marilee tolerated those heavy pajamas and confining underclothes in this warmer weather, he never understood.

Anxious to get the day started and get back to his project, he swung his legs off bed and hurried into the bathroom without so much as a thought for the toothbrush and razor on his way to the toilet. Then, back in the bedroom, preoccupied already. He pushed his arms through some shirtsleeves and pulled on his blue jeans, tucking in the shirt on the way to his drafting table in the garden room. An hour later, having finished a first cup of coffee and starting the second, Johnny sat hunched over his work, wondering absently who had shown up at the front door.

"Probably that damn preacher," he muttered, reaching up to scratch his chin, realizing the stubble his fingers scrapped across had gotten its start the day before. He had forgotten to shave, again. *Must be that preacher. Who else but the dashing Reverend Aragones would come calling this time of day?*

Johnny took a sip of coffee as his concentration returned to the graphics spread across the table. Reabsorbed in his work, he assumed Marilee had heard the bell, that she would answer the door; otherwise whoever was standing on the front porch would eventually give up and go away. The matter had receded into the back of his mind like a vague abstraction. There was work to do. A deadline to meet. The color scheme that came to him during the night had yet to find its way on paper. It might look like clutter to anyone else, but the graphics spread out before him represented Johnny's fondest dream, a long awaited achievement that cleared the way for a prosperous career, right here from his corner of the garden room.

The garden room, now also his office, had been their only major improvement to the house. After wading through a myriad of zoning restrictions and codes exclusive to Savannah's historic district, they had performed much of the work themselves: the walls nearly all glass, the floor carefully laid brick atop two inches of cushion sand. A cheerful, sunny space, it was Johnny's favorite room, tastefully furnished with lush potted plants, wicker patio furniture and a variety of mementos. Johnny had placed his coveted antique drafting table on the right side of the room, along with his business files, books, computer, and of course, in light of his growing business, a two-line telephone. The room not only created a perfect, year around environment for their tropical plants, it also served as corporate headquarters for Feelwater Graphics and Design, Inc.

Evidently Marilee had answered the door.

Johnny heard voices coming from the foyer and his shoulders tightened. The morning already off to a less than productive start, there wasn't time to suffer a half hour of small talk with Reverend Aragones.

The Reverend Aragones. There was something about this particular preacher Johnny didn't like. A handsome Spaniard, he had managed to recruit Marilee for a number of projects, almost from the moment she changed to his church a few months back. Her religious zeal had ratcheted up a notch or two; which didn't surprise Johnny all that much, though it irked him and had been the main reason for adding the second phone line. She wasted an inordinate amount of time chatting with various church members that never tired of pressuring her to bring her husband along, thereby prompting her to pressure him to attend Sunday services. One of these days Marilee would get it through her skull that there wasn't a chance in hell she could drag him out of bed on a Sunday morning to attend church.

In any event, it sure seemed the Reverend Aragones had taken an uncommon interest in her; and because of that, much to Johnny's chagrin, his wife's puritanical morality had been further enriched by her ever-expanding religious conviction. Turning his ear toward the door, Johnny didn't recognize the voice. An older man, an old-school type, in command of an old traditional southern drawl.

Must be a salesman. Insurance probably.

He looked at the graphics scattered across the drafting table, feeling a little antsy, not at all pleased with the way the day's work had progressed so far. But this was exactly how he perceived every phase of a project during the inception stages; so he would move lines here or there and change one color after another, and eventually the creation would take form. Eye-catching form actually, exactly the reason his work had accumulated significant recognition since he graduated from the Savannah Art Institute.

He had been twenty-one then, and smitten not only by Savannah's charming gardens and park-like squares, but also by Marilee, whom he met at the library one day after class. Applying for a job that day, she had dropped her courses at the Art Institute a couple of weeks earlier. After thirty minutes of exchanging surreptitious glances, Johnny worked up the courage to start up a conversation and ultimately invite her to dinner; which worked out well, though it took six months after that to coax her into bed. Shortly after she acquiesced, they were married and she soon fell into the role of dutiful wife. Undeniably pretty, she stood five-eight and walked around with a perpetual smile and brimming with innocent charm. There was a look of genuine propriety in the soft lines of her oval shaped face. Her African heritage provided voluptuous lips and smooth, creamy light brown skin, and she wore her hair boyishly short and straight. Feminine in stature with her small shoulders and smaller than average but nicely shaped breasts, it was the alluring flare of her hips that had captivated Johnny from the moment he set eyes on her in the library, the very feature that had compelled him to get her into bed way back then. Nine years later, her hips were no less provocative. What she might do with them had she a mind to, Johnny could only imagine; his fantasies were as foreign to her as her bible studies were to him. No one had ever criticized Marilee for being overly sexy.

Nevertheless, Johnny had become a contented husband. Though every now and then his mind might wander, his feet stayed well fixed to the ground. Considered attractive at age thirty-one, he had twice ignored some not-so-subtle hints cast his way by women he had encountered in the advertising trade. And that other little part of him, defined by a few misguided incidents with the boy across the hall in the school dormitory, had receded into the darkest corners of his mind.

So over the years he had convinced himself that a man didn't marry a woman for her sexual prowess. Those he knew that did were more often than not in the throes of divorce. But still, he believed a wife could have at least a little imagination, and he often wondered why his did not, attributing her modesty to the church. Marilee simply could not allow herself to do anything that others might construe as risqué, even in the privacy of her own bedroom.

Yet things could be much worse. Marilee wasn't a nag. She never complained. And she had created a warm and comfortable home. So Johnny, unlike those men that lead lives of quiet desperation, kept himself occupied with his work, certain the two of them were destined to grow old together.

He listened to the voices in the foyer for a moment; Marilee's more discernable than the gentleman's. It sounded like she was trying to explain that her husband was too busy to be interrupted; when in reality she was probably thinking her husband was not presentable in his worn out shirt and jeans. Johnny heard her inquire as to the nature of the visit.

True, he looked a mess, and could not have cared less. He had always been that way, despite what others might think. He grew up thinking he was different from other boys. From early on his mother had told him so, and he remembered agreeing with her because he had never fit in with the other kids at school, the black or the white kids, it didn't matter. To this day he walked with the private aloofness of a man that saw himself as one-of-a-kind, perhaps the very trait behind his motivation to start his own firm. He never thought of himself as stunningly handsome, nor did he cringe when he looked into a mirror. At six foot and slender, he walked with a casual gait on long graceful legs. Though not overly muscular, his upper body filled a shirt reasonably well for a man that never lifted weights. Most agreed his best feature was his beautiful skin. Several shades darker than Marilee's, it lay sensuously over the contours of his body like silky smooth caramel—the dark kind—accentuated with masculine patterns of black hair on his legs, forearms and chest. His facial features were more influenced by European blood—Spanish or Portuguese he figured.

Now the morning was slipping by, and it sounded like a bit more of it was to be snatched away by an unwanted visitor.

He heard footfall in the hallway, creaking over the ancient hardwood floor toward the garden room. Turning on his stool just as Marilee entered the sunny, garden-like space, he saw standing behind her a portly, rather sophisticated looking southern gentleman. The man stepped forward and bowed graciously and then extended his hand.

"Samuel McPhereson," he said as Johnny took his hand. "Glad to meet you Mr. Feelwater. I'm a lawyer, sir. I've come today with some news. I think it could be considered good news on your part."

At a loss, Johnny glanced between Mr. McPhereson and Marilee, wondering what on earth this was all about. Marilee shrugged and looked back at the lawyer, who continued his introduction.

"I represent a lady by the name of Cassandra Mott. At age ninety-two, she passed away not a week ago. She willed her only valuable property, a house facing Confederate Square, to you."

Johnny's loss turned into total bewilderment.

Samuel McPhereson saw the confusion in Johnny's eyes. "Let me try to explain." Adjusting his tie, he looked around for a place to sit.

"Here, Mr. McPhereson," said Marilee, pushing over one of the wicker chairs. "Sit here." She brought over another chair for herself.

"Let's see ... where to begin? Ah yes, your grandmother, Emily Hinton. She's your connection to Miss Mott. As you probably know, Emily descended from a slave owned by one Colonel Adam Mott, Cassandra Mott's grandfather. The Mott and Hinton families were very close since the days before the Civil War, and remained so long after. Your grandmother and Cassandra were born from their descendants and grew up together after the turn of the century. They became very good friends. Now, from what I understand, you've never met any members of the Mott family, have you, Mr. Feelwater?"

Johnny turned his head in dazed confusion. *I've inherited a house? Just like that? From someone I didn't know?*

Too dumbfounded to ask questions just yet, he instead pondered his family history, most of which lingered like unexplained shadows in his subconscious mind; but it seemed he did remember that his mother had mentioned that name. Yes, talking to someone over the phone one day. He remembered her mood grew foul as the conversation progressed; that he had listened in, tried to hear what it was about, but had caught no more than bits and pieces. When he inquired after his mother hung up the phone, her mood still bitter, she had refused to discuss it with him.

"No," said Johnny, stammering slightly, looking back at Samuel McPhereson, now thoroughly intrigued by the man's presence and his reason for being here. "I've never met any of them, but I've heard that name."

"Well, as I said, your grandmother and Cassandra Mott were very close." McPhereson cleared his throat and went on with his next statement slightly discomfited. "They were lovers, actually. Cassandra was very clear about that when she told me this story a couple of years ago. It's believed your grandfather was a Shakespearean actor from New York whose company performed in Savannah from time to time." McPhereson, clearly embarrassed by his own statements, cleared his throat again. "It seems he shared their bed when he was in town. Mind you, this would have been in the 1920's."

Spellbound, sitting several inches higher than his guest, his hands resting in his lap, Johnny's eyes drifted to the floor. Here was a man that apparently knew something of his grandfather, the grandfather his own mother disdained and never acknowledged. All of this fascinated him. Johnny knew his mother and grandmother were at odds with each other, but he never knew why. Obviously his mother didn't approve of Emily's lifestyle. Johnny's focus returned to McPhereson.

"Was my grandfather from New York originally?" he asked.

"No. He was an immigrant from Madrid." McPhereson studied Johnny's face for a moment. "That's probably where you got your prominent nose."

Johnny looked at Marilee and smiled. "I told you I have some Spanish blood running through my veins." Johnny was captivated, his mind running with questions. Hungry to know more, he looked back at McPhereson. "Do you know anything about him? His name?"

"Quite the adventurer I understand, but I know practically nothing about him. His name was Barnabas Muliama."

It all sounded wonderfully romantic to Johnny. He felt the strongest urge to learn more of his heritage. He resented his mother for keeping him and his grandmother apart; and he realized that he wished he had had the opportunity to meet Cassandra Mott.

McPhereson paused, as if to determine where to pick up his story. "Anyway, I got the impression that over the course of her long life, Miss Mott had never known anyone as important to her as your grandmother. Evidently they were quite ... shall I say *involved with each other*, and it seems your grandmother was every bit as eccentric as Cassandra, until you were born. Things changed for Emily then. She wanted to be part of your life, to be your grandmother; but as you must know, she and your mother were estranged. Emily became quite melancholy over that and died when you were a small boy. Cassandra remembered you for the rest of her life as someone special—her lover's grandson. I personally believe she felt responsible for the rift between your mother and grandmother; and having no heirs of her own, she bequeathed her house to you."

"Did she know anything about me?"

"A little. She asked me to make some inquiries about you and report back with my findings, which I did. Just a few generalities, mind you. She wanted to know where you live and more about your career in commercial art and whom you married. She was especially interested in learning more about your wife, Marilee."

McPhereson twisted himself to have a look at Marilee, who sat just behind him beaming with her usual gracious smile, though Johnny felt certain this story had severely impacted her moral sensibilities. Promiscuous sex was anathema to her. Add to that interracial couplings between two people of the same sex and her ears would begin to filter it out.

McPhereson returned his attention to Johnny.

"So I told her all I could about your lovely wife. I learned of her strong religious beliefs and her many civic charities."

Marilee looked at him in thought. "I remember one of the lady's at church saying something about a man making inquiries about me. Last month I think. Was that you?"

"Yes, my dear. I wasn't surprised to learn your friends hold you in the highest esteem."

"What does all of this mean?" Johnny asked.

McPhereson produced a folded document from his suit pocket along with a key. "Cassandra was bed ridden the last two years of her life; otherwise I believe she would have wanted to meet you. Nevertheless, she delighted in giving you her house." He unfolded the document and leaned forward to place it on the corner of the drafting table. "If you'll just sign on that bottom line, the house will be yours." He handed Johnny the key and added: "I'll take care of all the other paperwork and technicalities."

Johnny glanced over the document still in a daze. He picked up a pen and signed, and then handed it back to McPhereson. "You mean just like that—I own a house?"

"Just like that," McPhereson assured him. "It's yours as of this moment. You may have a look at it at your leisure. It's a large house, so I would assume you'd want to sell it. If so, Cassandra foresaw that possibility and made provisions for it with one or two restrictions."

"Restrictions?"

"Yes. Remember, I mentioned she's eccentric. She couldn't abide the house passing into the hands of a tax collector, a Yankee or a preacher."

Johnny glanced at Marilee, who looked miffed. As for himself, he had never been so intrigued by anything. He held up the key in the sunlight, which looked something of an antique itself, in use some fifty years at least.

Samuel McPhereson got to his feet and presented his business card. "You can reach me at that number anytime you have a question."

They shook hands again and Marilee escorted the lawyer back to the front door. She promptly returned to the garden room.

"It's a little overwhelming, isn't it?" she said.

Johnny was looking at the key.

"I wonder why she doesn't want you to sell the house to a preacher," Marilee said with indignation.

His gaze shifted from the key to her.

"What?"

"Why wouldn't she want you to sell the house to a preacher?" she repeated, feeling uneasy about the whole matter; not sure why, other than the fact her husband's heritage was linked to a woman of such low moral character. Or perhaps her queasiness had come about because it had all happened so unexpectedly. Whatever the cause of her misgivings, if they had inherited a house, it meant little to her, other than having some real estate to sell, which would provide money to finish renovating their own house.

"What does it matter?" Johnny replied. "Evidently Cassandra Mott didn't like tax collectors, Yankees or preachers. I think it's funny."

"It just doesn't seem ... appropriate."

"Let's go over there, honey."

Marilee's lips tightened. "I can't now, Johnny," she said, knowing he wouldn't like her reason why. "We're making Easter decorations this afternoon." She smiled haplessly, wishing she had not already made plans. Her husband asked so little, she hated to disappoint him.

"Huh! Can't they do that without you just this once?"

"I told them I'd be there. I'm responsible for the refreshments today."

"Goddammit, Marilee! We just inherited a house! Don't you wanna see what it looks like?"

"Of course I do, but I can go with you some other time."

He let out a sigh. "That's all you're interested in anymore. The church. Reverend Aragones. What about spending a little time with your husband?"

"Can't we go tomorrow?"

"Tomorrow!" He lowered his head and rubbed his brow. He knew it was useless. If inheriting a house wouldn't inspire her to change her plans, nothing would. He looked up. "I'm going over there. Right now. If the reverend doesn't need you for some reason, you and I can go tomorrow."

"I'm sorry, Johnny. If they ask about tomorrow, I'll tell them I have plans."

His frustration melted away as he hurried back to the bedroom. In the bathroom, he pushed his jaw toward the mirror. *Why shave just to look at a vacant house?* Heading toward the front door, he buttoned his shirt and yelled good-bye as he reached the foyer. His bicycle was where he left it, propped against the ancient brick wall, which was his usual mode of transportation in and around the historic district, especially this time of year when the weather was warming and the streets were clogged with tourists.

Fifteen minutes later he stood gaping at a two-story house, erected, so declared a small plaque mounted on one of the brick columns that supported the wrought-iron gate, in 1855.

Wow! Bigger than I imagined.

He fell in love with it at once, though the upkeep on such a grand house was far beyond his current resources. The tiny front yard was walled in. Not more than fifteen feet beyond the gate, five brick steps lead up to the front door. The house didn't have a restored look, like so many in Savannah; rather it appeared to have been perpetually maintained throughout the century. Everything about it, down to the door-knocker looked original and laid-over with a fine patina of age.

The wrought-iron gate creaked open with an effortless push and he bounded up the steps with the key in hand. The door towered before him as he pushed the key into the brass plate. He heard a distinctive click and the knob turned easily, yet the door would not budge. Pushing harder did no good. It seemed bolted from the inside. He took a few steps to a window and peered in, but lace curtains obscured the furnishings inside. The window was locked tight, as were the other three that were shaded by the covered front porch. After trying the door once more, he hurried down the steps and around the side of the house, his neck craned as he surveyed the fine architecture of the old house. He found all of the doors and windows locked.

It had to be the right key, he reasoned, it had turned the decades-old tumblers. Disappointed, he stepped backwards toward the front gate, looking up at the fine cornices and masonry of the front facade, thinking it might take a locksmith to get inside. Johnny crossed the street with a happy jaunt, turning frequently to look back at the house as he got further into the square. He wanted to see the effect of the house from a distance. Stepping backwards again, his eyes set in an enchanted gaze, he came upon an old lady sitting on a park bench next to the walkway. He glanced at her with a smile.

"Miss Mott isn't there anymore, young man," said the old woman. Johnny turned to look at her again. "You knew her?"

The old woman studied the enchantment in Johnny's eyes. He was obviously a personable young man. Her weary gaze shifted back to the house. "Yes, I knew her. She was a dear friend since we were very young girls. I was at her bedside last week, holding her hand when she passed away. No one lives there now."

A glorious scenario unfolded in Johnny's mind as he looked at the diminutive old lady. She and Cassandra Mott had lived in Savannah through nearly a century of enormous change. It occurred to him that she might have known his grandmother.

"Miss Mott had a special friend many years ago. A black lady. Did you know her?"

"You're talking about Emily." The old lady smiled with the memory.

"Yes. Emily. They say Cassandra and Emily were, uh ... they were ..."

"They were lovers," said the old woman. "Is that what you mean to say?"

"Yes," said Johnny, slightly wide-eyed. He had not expected the old woman to be so blunt.

"Of course I knew Emily. She was a dear friend, too. Died so many years ago."

"She was my grandmother," said Johnny proudly.

"Your grandmother? Then you must be Johnny Feelwater." The old lady's face brightened and became more animated. "My, my, how Emily talked about you. It was sad for her that she couldn't see you. I guess your mother couldn't accept her ways."

Johnny stared at the old woman, delighted to have come upon her. She had a slightly mischievous gleam in her eyes that he had seen before in seniors who have intriguing memories. And this lady seemed happy to talk about the past. He sat down in the grass across the walkway from her, smiling. "What's your name, ma'am?"

"I'm Arlene Landrum. Your grandmother and Cassandra and I all went to elementary school together. A small private school. At first they wouldn't let Emily in. You know how it was in those days. Maddening, I know, but seemed to be the way of the world. The Mott family intervened and that settled that." She closed her eyes and drew in a deep breath with the memory. "We all grew up together. How wonderful and carefree those days were. You'd be surprised at the adventures we got involved in. Now I'm the only one left."

Johnny's smile took on a touch of sympathy. "Did you know my grandfather?"

Her face brightened again. "Oh yes. A dashing man. Errol Flynn, I called him. Lava flowed through that man's veins."

"He was a Spaniard?"

"Yes. From New York. Called himself Barnabus Muliama. Why, I wouldn't know. I never believed for a minute that was his real name. He was an actor. I figured he took the name for that purpose. He was mesmerizing on stage, and a notorious lady's-man, not that I ever had a personal experience with him." She blushed as the memory unfolded in her mind. "He was difficult to resist. That much I will admit. I remember the first time I saw him naked." Her hand suddenly flew to her mouth as if she had spoken out of turn.

"No ... please, go on. I want to hear everything. Please, I'm not judgmental."

She studied him for a moment, detecting his eagerness to learn of his past. "Oh my, it's been years since I've spoken to anyone about those wonderful days, but at my age you don't think of such things very often."

"You were talking about the first time you saw him ... uh ..."

Mrs. Landrum smiled. "Yes. It was mid-afternoon. I walked into Cassandra's house and there he was, half way up the stairs, naked as the statue of David. He looked at me and that gleam formed in his eye. It was all I could do to get away. He chased me around that big house for ten minutes. I got away only because I beat him to the back door. I was out of breath by the time I got to the street; and there he was again, grinning at me through that gate right over there." She paused and shook her head. "Cassandra and Emily thought it was funny. They were both one of a kind, you know. Forever looking for absurd ways to amuse themselves. The things that went on inside that house provided some of the best gossip in Savannah."

Johnny was smiling at her, absorbing every word.

"I wasn't as daring as your grandmother or Cassandra. They were the instigators. I tried to keep up, but I promise you, that took a lot of energy and audacity. Afraid I may have a lot of explaining to do when judgment day comes."

"Please, tell me more."

Arlene Landrum gathered her purse into her lap and smiled at him. "I believe I will, but not today. These little outings tucker me out. I'm ready to spend the rest of the day in my rocker."

She came warily to her feet and Johnny jumped up to assist her.

"Let me walk you home, "he said.

"No need to bother. I live just around the corner and I'll be fine. It's the gray house, second from the corner," she said, nodding in that direction. "Call on me when you wish and we'll have a chat and some hot tea." She turned for another look at Cassandra's house. "Oh look! You left the door open."

Johnny's head snapped around. He stared at the house, gaping. To his astonishment, the door stood half way open.

Chapter 2

Johnny stared at the open door, distracted. Then he turned again to Arlene Landrum. The old lady had begun her slow walk home.

"See you soon, Mrs. Landrum," he called out.

"Johnny Feelwater, you call me Arlene," she called back, moving carefully along the uneven brick walkway with her cane.

He turned back to the house and stared at it a moment longer before starting toward it. It seemed impossible that he had opened the door without realizing it, having thrown his body weight against it without feeling the slightest budge. Perhaps someone was inside. But why would there be? And if so, how did they get in with the doors and windows locked? Johnny paused at the wrought-iron gate and tilted his head to look past the door—nothing more than mingling shadows and light.

A chill of gooseflesh raced over his forearm. Though there wasn't a superstitious bone in his body, a vague premonition prevented his next step, like a frightened voice imploring him to stay away from that door. He scoffed. How many haunted house tales had he heard over the years? Savannah was notorious for that sort of thing. This was a big, vacant house. Been around for over a century. An old lady recently died in one of the upstairs bedrooms. No wonder his imagination roared to life. Letting out a small laugh, he sucked in a breath and proceeded through the gate. He took the steps one at a time and approached the door this time with caution.

Johnny pushed the door wide open. He took one step inside and called out: "Anyone here?" Nothing but a faint echo. "Hello ... anyone here?" he called louder, then one more step forward.

Opulent beyond what he had imagined, the front foyer was an architectural masterpiece of nineteenth century craftsmanship: marble floor, elegant wallpaper, elaborate woodwork and trim. The octagonal entry offered archways leading to other parts of the main floor. A stairway, wider at the base, swept upward along the curved wall, narrowing as it reached the upstairs landing. The ceiling went all the way to the roof, circled near the cornice with windows. Johnny had seen this form of natural air conditioning before. The high windows, when opened, would create an updraft and pull fresh air through the windows of the entire house.

Can't believe I own this place.

He looked through the archways: the anteroom straight ahead, the dining room to the left, a smaller door to the right of the stairs that appeared to be a library. The rooms seemed well appointed, though the foyer was sparsely furnished with a narrow side-table against the wall adjoining the staircase. On it, next to a pewter art deco lamp, rested a silver dish filled with roasted peanuts.

Suffering the pangs of hunger from missing breakfast, Johnny moseyed over and picked up the dish and sniffed them. As fresh as peanuts could smell, they made his mouth water. He tilted his head back and let a fistful slide into his mouth. His stomach growled. The peanuts tasted better than he had expected, roasted, salty, a little spicy. Uncommonly delicious. He inspected them again as he swallowed the first handful.

Subtle at first, a lightheadedness came over him. He was suddenly dizzy. He wobbled and felt unstable. When it occurred to him to sit down, he stepped around the banister and took a seat on the bottom step. A wave of confusion blurred his mind. Then a chorus of voices flared in his ears. Startled, he nearly dropped the dish.

He turned this way and that, eyes darting, searching for the source of the sound. It had flared like a loud hum and then diminished into a vague chorus of young female voices, as if beckoning for something they could not have. Resonating through the foyer like a song on the wind, beautiful, yet sad and eerie in quality, it seemed to be coming from within the wall along side the stairway.

His eyes moved uneasily along the velvety wall, on up to the landing on the second floor. He stood and his heart quickened as he started up the staircase. Much like being drawn, one foot lifted after the other, one step at a time until he had half way ascended the stairs. He looked at the wall and then pressed his ear to it. The sound was more distinct. He listened, trying to distinguish what the song might be. Yes, a chorus of young girls, imploring, an indistinguishable melodic chant. A calm came over him as he listened. He suddenly felt very comfortable, almost euphoric, and he sensed it had something to do with being inside this house. The confusion in his head had cleared. As quickly as it had occurred, it had melted away.

No longer nervous or hesitant, he sat the dish of peanuts on the steps and proceeded to the landing, which narrowed into two separate hallways. On the wall near the head of the stairs, trailing down from the ceiling, a wire led to an electric light switch. He turned it before entering the hallway on the right. Opening one door after another, he came upon two bedrooms and what appeared to be a small private study, a linen closet and a room used for storage.

The other hall was much the same with one exception. Another door that would not open. It was at the end of the hallway. He turned the knob and threw his shoulder into it, but it wouldn't budge. A crow bar, he decided, would damage the woodwork.

Damn! His curiosity mounted as he stared at the door. *Might need that locksmith after all.*

On the way back to the stairs, he paused and held his hands up to look at them. His fingertips seemed uncommonly sensitive. He rubbed them together and could feel the fine lines of his fingerprints. He noticed a tingling on his forearms; the warm air felt good on his skin, as if his pores had come alive with the fragrances of early spring. Still in a bit of a fog, he looked over at the nineteenth century painting on the plaster and wainscoted wall. The feeling wasn't in any way unpleasant ... just strange. He licked his lips and could still taste the salt from the peanuts, though he had no appetite for more.

The floor creaked behind him, a distinct sound, like someone walking up from behind. The fine hair on the back of his neck bristled. He turned and his eyes were immediately drawn to a slithering movement on the floor at the end of the hall.

My God! A snake!

He shivered at the sight of it. The snake was quite large and moving quickly toward the locked door. His eyes lifted and his mouth fell open. The creaking sound had been the door. Standing rigid, he stared at a door now gaping open some several inches. The snake vanished behind it.

A jammed door opening on its own? It seemed irrational, though Johnny realized he was not as unnerved as it seemed he should be; but enthralled, and compelled to look inside that room. He stared at the gaping door, trying to make sense of the conflicts in his head. Something was vaguely telling him to get out of this house; on the other hand, far more compelling, his curiosity about the room. He took the first tentative step toward the door.

His eyes darted as he stepped closer to the room. He paused at the threshold and leaned forward to peek in. It was by far the largest upstairs room yet. Nudging the door with his foot, it creaked open another two or three inches. With a harder push, it yawed open and he scanned the floor for the snake before venturing inside.

He stood in awe of the opulence: paneled walls painted in pastel blue, intricately carved crown moldings, a private parlor appointed with elegant furniture, potted plants and paintings. A chandelier hung from the domed ceiling in the center of the room. To the left, a columned archway opened into a sitting room that overlooked Confederate Square. Next to that was a closed door. On the back wall to the right were three doors. A fireplace on the wall adjacent the entryway stood out as the focal point. Inside the fireplace was a grate stacked with fresh logs. Arranged comfortably in front of the fireplace, facing sofas upholstered in silk fabric flanked a coffee table. There were three or four chairs against the wall and a large wardrobe between the doors on the back wall. Johnny noticed a vibrancy in the room, an energy of some kind that he could feel on his skin. Assuming static electricity, he looked at his forearm and then heard a noise, muted, mingling with the silence. It seemed to be coming from behind the door next to the sitting room.

Johnny stepped further into the room. Still unable to identify the sound, he approached the door and placed his hand on the knob and leaned his ear against the smooth enameled wood. It sounded like running water, maybe a tub or a shower. He turned the knob and pushed the door open a few inches, dazzled by lavish paneled walls, gilded mirrors, marble counters, golden fixtures and ornate cabinet doors with glass knobs. A bathroom. Fit for a queen.

The sound was distinct now, though the partially opened door blocked his view of the back of the room and the source of running water. He pushed the door all the way open and froze, stunned by the unexpected.

His disbelieving gaze locked on a woman.

Her presence instantly escaped his mind as cause for concern—her beauty and nakedness had grabbed a hold of his every available thought. She had not noticed him, standing with her back to him under the showerhead within the marble enclosure, her head tilted downward, her red hair rich with lather that ran in soapy rivulets down her arms and legs. He stood dumbstruck, staring at the most exquisite female he had ever set eyes on. His life's experiences had never presented anything remotely like this. Such radiance in the soft light, pale skin smooth and glistening over a framework of ribs that narrowed and then flared into creamy white hips, a vision so alluring that those old sensations of a hormone-sated teenager formed between his legs.

A daydream of some kind ... must be, he vaguely reasoned. One he did not want to abandon. He had never walked in on a woman before, not in the shower, and certainly not one this beautiful; more accustomed to living with a woman that locked the bathroom door just to brush her teeth. It didn't occur to him to turn away, or avert his eyes, or do anything other than stand in a motionless stupor and watch the soapy water cascade down her long legs.

Then she turned off the water and stepped onto a towel, taking up another to dry her hair, still unaware of his presence. Wavering gusts flared through his nostrils as he stared and realized his body was starving, wondering what it would be like to take such a woman into his arms, to know the feel of her skin against his and the scent of her hair? What would it be like to lay with her, to feel the side of his face on those breasts, to feel those legs around his hips?

She leaned forward to blot the drops of water from her legs, then threw back her head and saw him.

"Oh my!" A look of surprise washed over her face, then curiosity, then a smile. She looked at him for a moment before starting in his direction. "I didn't know anyone was here."

Johnny tensed. A sense of panic came over him. His face flushed with embarrassment as his eyes shifted nervously, snatching quick glimpses as she neared. He took an awkward step backward, shamed by the guilt of a voyeur.

She stepped closer. No sign of modesty or alarm. She cast a smile one might construe as good fortune to have a man turn up in her bathroom. Her breasts, swaying under their own weigh, drew his eyes and his imagination, the nipples drawn into tight peaks.

His gaze followed the towel as it moved over her belly and then down between her legs. The thin swirl of red hair did nothing to hide her nether lips. He looked up at her enchanting smile when she extended the towel.

"My, my, an attractive man has found his way to my bathroom," she said, her voice sweetened with classic southern charm. "Dry my back, would you, darlin'?" she said, turning her back to him.

His hand felt limp as he held the towel and looked at her small shoulders. He lifted it absently and blotted away a few drops.

He was not the composed man of confidence that had entered the house a few minutes earlier—he had become a perspiring mass of disoriented male flesh. Even his most outlandish dreams had never occasioned a scene like this. It didn't occur to him to inquire why she was there, nor did he wonder how she had gotten into the house that he had just inherited. Nothing so rational entered his mind. His brain had disengaged from everything beyond the moment. Bewitched and muddled with embarrassment, an instant hunger possessed him, sending messages throughout his body, converging in rather conspicuous dimensions behind the strained buttons of his jeans.

When she turned to face him, she reached for the towel and tossed it aside. Standing in his gaze, she looked him over, a quiet, lengthy inspection, which to him was both awkward and undeniably pleasant. Then she turned and stepped in front of the mirror and picked up a brush to stroke her red hair, as if to suggest that his presence was perfectly agreeable and that her nudity was nothing more than happenstance. She watched his spellbound enchantment in the mirror, casually brushing her shoulder length hair like a seductress taunting a teenage boy, smiling inwardly at his statue-like gaze.

With her wet hair tangle free, she turned again to her visitor.

Johnny reflexively backed away as she stepped closer, stopping several feet into the parlor. She reached up to touch the side of his face in a way that seemed blatantly intimate. Without regard for the fact they were strangers, she held out her arms and struck a pose, smiling continuously as if she were delighted by his presence.

"Do you like my body?" she asked, turning so he could see front and back. "I love the way everything comes back to you after so many years."

He stood in want of something to say, of something to do with his hands, of someplace to settle his eyes. Finally his mind began to form questions. What did she mean: *everything comes back to you after so many years?* Who was she? Why was she there? His words seemed caught in his throat.

"Have something you'd like to tell me?" she asked with feigned interest, though her smile suggested a preference for the more provocative game of exercising pre-eminence over a man's composure and inferior moral defenses.

"Uh ..." He heard the sound leave his mouth, nothing more than an utterance that exposed his skewed sensibilities. He couldn't just stand there, but what could he say? His mind had gone blank. He finally managed a half-dazed reflection. "I saw a snake ... in the hall. It ... it came in here. Did you see it?"

"Good lord! A snake? Here in the house? My goodness no! Otherwise I'd be having a perfect fit. Surely you're not serious."

How could he not look at her when his entire lifetime prior to this moment had been reduced to insignificance? Though she seemed delighted by his errant gaze, which made looking at her harder to resist, in some vague corner of his mind he was beginning to feel pangs of guilt, like he was doing something that he would have to keep from his wife. But her smile, disarming and confident, seemed to reach right into the essence of his manhood. How comfortable she appeared to be with her nudity, which multiplied her affect on him in a number of confusing ways. If only he could think of something to say, start a conversation, something that might distract him from the tension building inside his chest.

"You're shy, aren't you, darlin'?" she said, stepping closer. "Except for teasing me about a snake."

He felt foolish. A snake, for crying out loud! Must have been his imagination.

"Maybe ... uh, maybe my eyes were ..."

"How did you happen to come here, darlin'?"

Her question registered, though no answer occurred to him. Her presence, her beauty, her nudity—all too unsettling. He could smell her freshly washed hair. He could feel changes inside his body. He couldn't stop glancing at her breasts, swaying and full, dropping slightly. Not easy to separate one's eyes from something like that.

She spoke again before he could respond.

"Are you a slave?" Her eyes widened. "Good lord! Are you? Seeking refuge from some awful foreman?" She reached out to stroke his face again. Her hand was soft and sensuous and spread electrical sensations across his cheek. "You've come to the right place, you know."

Johnny was mystified. *A slave? What the hell...* Her words bewildered him. And now that he was regaining his composure, more questions began to incubate. This wasn't a dream. He had felt her hand on the side of his face. He had dried her back. He could see her and hear her voice, though it seemed like something had gotten between his mind and reality. This entire scenario had invaded his consciousness like an unsettling dream.

Something distracted her. Her attention shifted to the middle of the room. Johnny turned and followed her gaze and his knees weakened. He stumbled backward toward the wall, caught thoroughly off-guard. A man was there with her, youthful, dressed in elegant summer clothes made of white linen, sitting on one of the sofas, legs crossed, hands clasped and resting on his lap. He was looking at the nude enchantress with intense blue eyes, his sandy blonde hair long and wavy and combed back, touching his collar.

Johnny glanced between them, even more bewildered. Though no words were spoken, it seemed she was listening to him. No sound came from him at all. Confused, Johnny watched them nervously, as if he sensed both the presence of something foreboding and something very exciting. When she turned to him, he felt certain some kind of communication had taken place.

"Silly me," she said. "Of course you aren't a slave. How absentminded I get sometimes when one era so quickly runs into another. Oh well, here you are and that's what matters, now isn't it, darlin'?"

The last thing Johnny expected in coming here was to feel like an intruder. He thought maybe he should leave, followed by second thoughts. Didn't he own this house? Besides, he was feeling more at ease. He wanted to know more about her. He wanted to find out why she was here; and now he was curious about the young man. They were intriguing, this beautiful pair. He wanted to understand what was going on in this room and inside his own head.

When he turned, the young man was gone. Johnny closed his eyes. What had become of his grasp on reality? He took a deep breath, wondering if he had actually seen the handsome young man, or if he had really seen that snake. On one hand it all seemed surreal; on the other hand the woman was too radiant, too sensual to be his imagination; though he realized *something* was affecting him. Nevertheless, in spite of the strange goings-on, he wanted to stay. Her trespassing didn't bother him, nor did her strange behavior, now that his heart had quit racing. Beyond his natural attraction to beautiful women, he recognized an especially intimate and personal contentment in looking at her, mainly because his lingering gaze seemed welcome.

He heard a whooshing, crackling noise. His eyes opened. The fireplace had come to a sudden blaze. The enchantress was standing in front of the fire, leaning close to the flames, letting her hair fall forward as she ran her fingers through the long strands to dry them. Johnny's throat tightened. In nine years of marriage he had never seen his own wife bend over that way. A sense of urgency rose in his loins and warmed the flesh between his legs and a spot of wetness expanded in his underwear. Nothing in his lifetime, no visual or female flirt had ever brought him this close to the brink. No woman he ever met had so thoroughly controlled what might happen next.

Then the young man emerged from the center door at the back of the room, apparently a closet, carrying a black satin dress. He approached and held the dress up so the woman could easily slip it over her head. It shimmered down and enveloped her body, clinging here and there, painting her sensuous form with a satiny sheen. When she turned to him, Johnny's gaze settled on a pair of nipples pushing provocatively at the sheer fabric.

"Shall we have a glass of wine?" she said, which prompted the young man to go to a side table near the wall and pour three glasses. Intrigued by his quiet demeanor, Johnny watched him, aware of something about him that evoked mystery, something undefined, something beyond his beauty and self-confident grace.

"Let's have a seat on the sofa, Mr. ... oh, you haven't mentioned your name yet, have you?"

"My name?" said Johnny absently, watching the man place the wine on the low table between the sofas. He felt captured by those blue eyes, bathed by them, naked.

"Why yes, darlin'. You haven't introduced yourself." She had moved between the sofas and stood looking at him.

Perspiration dampened Johnny's forehead. His clothes felt damp and seemed to cling. He thought for a moment before his name jumped to the forefront of his dazed thoughts. "Johnny Feelwater," he said, his throat dry and scratchy. He looked at the door. It occurred to him again that he should leave. Whatever was going on here, it wasn't good for a married man. All he had to do was start in that direction and go back down the stairs and out the front door. He could find a place to sit down, or walk over to the river, think this through and sort it all out. Instead, he looked the woman, standing in her satiny black gown, smiling. Then his gaze shifted to the man on the sofa.

He wanted to stay. Despite the fog in his head, despite circumstances all very strange, he wanted to know more about them. The sense of well-being that had settled over him was stronger than his shapeless suspicions. His misgivings had evolved into a rather pleasant mystification. That furtive voice that warned him to leave, to get far and fast away from this house, had foundered under the weight of overwhelming intrigue. He felt strangely comfortable in their presence and he wanted to stay, just for a while, just to learn more about this exquisite woman, just to look at her, to hear her voice, to feel her hand aside his face once more. It was unlike any calm he had ever known.

He walked over and took a seat on the sofa opposite the young man. The woman sat next to him and reached for her glass of wine. The man leaned forward and pushed a crystal dish filled with peanuts across the coffee table toward her. She took a few and pushed the dish closer to Johnny. He picked up his wine, took a sip and then reached for the nuts.

"Who are you?" he asked, letting a handful of peanuts slide into his mouth.

"Me?" She seemed surprised he didn't already know. "My goodness. You enter a lady's parlor not knowing who she is? How interesting."

"I thought this was my ..."

He paused, overcome by the same dizziness he had experienced in the foyer. He leaned back against the sofa. His head fell back. It was a weightlessness. His mind spun with sparkling flashes of red and blue and the most pleasant sensations melted through his arms and chest, like he had become a million particles floating in space where nothing was familiar and nothing mattered. He was aware of a growing enchantment with the two strangers who were behaving as if this house were theirs.

He lifted his head. The spinning passed like a summer rain and his mind began to clear. A moment later he looked at the woman and smiled.

"Are you all right, darlin'?" she asked. Her singsong voice, dripping with southern charm, danced about his ears like the chords of a harp. But he had detected more than that in her tone. Though lyrical, her words lacked authentic sincerity, as if spoken by someone with singular motives.

"So who are you?"

"Why, darlin', I'm Cassandra Mott. And you, Johnny Feelwater, are a guest in my house."

His eyes drifted to the coffee table. How could that be? Had he not been told that Cassandra Mott was a ninety-two year old woman that recently died? Had he not inherited this house? He looked at her, at the rose colored hues of her cheeks, the delicate features of her face, the feminine white shoulders set in contrast to the black silken gown, slightly less at ease with this odd course of events and his expanding bewilderment.

Johnny's eyes shifted to man. "Who is he?" he asked, staring at a man that appeared to be in his late twenties, uncommonly handsome, mysterious, elegant, a man that had yet to say the first word. Johnny stared at him. Handsome, yes, but better described as beautiful or radiant.

"He's my brother, Julian Mott," said Cassandra adoringly.

"He doesn't talk?"

"Of course he does, if he has something to say."

"You must be a ghost. Him too," said Johnny, not totally serious but amused by the possibility. It was as if his awareness had slipped past the defenses of his rational mind. If this is what it's like to be in the presence of ghosts, it was most agreeable.

"My word, you are such a delightful man." She reached out and took up his left hand and placed it aside her face. "Does that feel like the face of a ghost?"

He felt her smooth warm skin on the back of his fingers, her cheek soft and supple. A yearning came into his hands as the image of her washing her hair formed in his mind. A ghost? Hardly, though the feel of her skin set two minds at play: one insisting it was perfectly harmless to be in this lady's parlor, to be captivated by her, to be sitting so close that he could smell the fragrance of her skin; the other telling him it was dreadfully wrong to be sated with these thoughts while his wife was off contributing her time to the church. Yet, if she offered a taste of her lips, he would not be able to resist.

She smiled, a mischievous curling of the corners of her mouth that hinted she had read his thoughts. Her eyes shifted to his wedding band. "So you're a married man, Mr. Feelwater."

He withdrew his hand and as the smile in her eyes reflected a sensuous understanding of a man's libido, he fidgeted with his wedding band.

"I don't mind if you call me Johnny."

"Are you married, Johnny?"

"Uh, yes, married."

"Does your wife allow you to have personal adventures?"

"Adventures?" A shiver ran down his spine. He felt his shoulder blades gather closer to his neck.

She glanced at her brother, and then said: "Perhaps I'm too forward with my silly inquiries."

"No," Johnny said quickly. He felt anxious, his curiosity elevated. "I ... I just didn't ..." His gaze shifted to the bouncing motion of the leg she had crossed over the other. Distracted, his eyes followed the contour of her thigh. He pictured her stepping out of the shower, that swirl of red pubic hair etched on his brain. He had never put his hands on white skin before, never thought he would; but that brief touch, coupled with her beauty, had captured his imagination. "Not sure I know what you mean," he stammered, almost a plea.

"Debauchery, Mr. Feelwater. I'm sorry ... I mean Johnny. We're so informal these days. How I miss the forgotten formalities. That damn war ruined everything!" She sighed and turned to look at Julian. "Such a charming era ... don't you agree?"

Mesmerized by her feminine aura, though confounded by nearly everything she said, Johnny wondered what she was talking about. She had spoken of adventures and debauchery and another era. Her statements seemed both nonsensical and erotic. How was he to know what all of this meant, or what she might be getting at?

"What era?" he asked haplessly.

"Those wonderful summers before Sherman and those awful Yankees came to Georgia and ruined everything!"

He looked at her for a moment. Had she forgotten that she was talking to a black man, that he would take no pleasure in harking back to the days before the Civil War? Why was she talking about that era, anyway? It was as if she remembered it. Still, how could her naiveté offend him, enchanted as he was by her beauty and charm? If anything, her eccentricity served only to enhance her most alluring character.

"How silly I am today. Just ramblin' on without allowing you hardly a word."

His brown eyes raked over her before their eyes met again.

"We were talking about debauchery, weren't we?" she said, lifting his hand again to look at the wedding band.

"Uh ... debauchery?" Johnny reached up to scratch the side of his jaw. *Debauchery.* The word seeped into his skin like a tingling ointment, not unpleasantly so, though her reason for using the word eluded him. He looked at his hand in hers, unable to keep his legs from coming together as she ran her fingertip over his knuckles. "I don't know what you ..."

"The pleasures of the *nine gates*, Mr. Feelwater." She smiled and looked into his eyes. "Are you familiar with those, Johnny? I'm thinking of the *ninth* gate in particular."

Chapter 3

"The ninth gate? I ... " Johnny stopped mid-sentence, frustrated. He felt gullible, like an innocent boy. Cassandra Mott, obviously a woman of the world, was saying things that flew right over his head.

Her quick smile took on a hint of mischief and her eyes shifted to her brother. "Perhaps Julian would be willing to show you the ninth gate."

Like a lost lamb cowering between them, Johnny turned his gaze to Julian. Their eyes locked. Unnerved, he felt as if he were being looked at caged and unclothed. Staring into the crystal blue eyes, he saw something he could not identify, not wicked, not threatening, but puzzling. He drew from them a premonition, a kinship on some obscure level, and the feeling it caused ran through him warmly. His curiosity ran wild. He recognized an urge to know more about him, to hear his thoughts.

Johnny watched him come to his feet. His eyes followed Julian's hands to the buttons on the white linen shirt. When Julian lifted it from his shoulders and laid it on the sofa, Johnny realized that he intended to disrobe. He sat spellbound, his gaze fixed on the twitch and flex of a masculine chest. Mired in disbelief, he watched Julian's hands move to the front of the white linen pants and unfasten the buttons one at a time, while Cassandra remained attentive to Johnny's unsuspecting reaction.

A different kind of unease came over him. He tried to deny the sudden desire welling inside, a desire to see Julian's body. Feeling stimulated by this was wrong. A man undressing should be perceived with indifference, but the promise of Julian's nudity was unfolding before his eyes as a visual treasure. Facing the laws of right and wrong, he *should* be indifferent, yet he was eager for it to happen. It was as if a long dormant urge had been lying in wait. He wanted to see Julian undressed, to see his body, his muscles, all of him. But why? Why all of a sudden? Why this sharp desire that he had so easily denied all these years. Why did this seem like a reawakening? Whatever the reason, he could feel the long forgotten urges between his legs and in the pores of his skin.

The pants slid fluidly down Julian's legs. He stepped out of them, naked, his skin bronze, his forearms and legs and chest patterned with golden blond hair, his genitals inflamed and pendulous between muscular legs. Julian walked around the low table, looking down at his guest, a man that had become a taut mass of nerves and anxiety.

He stood close. Distinct odors mingled with the smell of burning logs in Johnny's nostrils, a man's underarms, the perceptible smell of a man's loins, nudging him with an undeniable message. Johnny's eyes lifted and met Julian's, a mutual gaze, and he realized the path he had been walking for nine years had veered in another direction. In spite of his bewilderment, he was aware of something he had vowed to never acknowledge again: that desire for a man—this man standing before him now, looking down at him with similar thoughts, the one that had suddenly cast him into a freefall of confusion and conflict.

"He's beautiful, don't you think, Johnny?" said Cassandra, her voice remote in Johnny's ears.

Johnny's eyes dropped to Julian's penis, substantial in size and no longer drooping heavily between his legs. It had taken on weight and was lifting outwardly. Its veined sheathe, darkened by arousal, formed a fleshy hood that covered the glans, which Julian pulled back to expose a glistening, walnut shaped meat. A gold ring protruded from the tiny hole, perhaps a half inch in diameter, circling back and entering the urethra through a piercing just behind the glans.

Johnny remained transfixed. Resting stiffly against the sofa back, a fascination with the gold ring took hold. *What's it there for?* he wondered, adjusting his weight on the sofa.

Then Julian abruptly turned around.

Johnny's shoulders tightened when Julian leaned forward and reached back to grasp his gluteal cheeks, parting them, laying open the two halves to reveal that which no man should share with another man, so close an unmistakable musk entered Johnny's nostrils. Unsettled, Johnny sank lower on the sofa, one hand fidgeting with the other, his eyes fixed on the umber gathering of tightly pinched skin, pursed like small lips, flexing, causing sensations Johnny could hardly ignore. The room felt warm. Perspiration filmed his face. A thousand spiders crawled over his skin. Currents tensed his haunches and legs. Forgotten urges raged. His eyes would not abandon the anus.

He stared at the shadows and scatters of blonde hair, fraught with the recognition of unwanted genes. So close was the anomaly of dark flesh and the danglings between taught and parted legs, it roused that old conflict between opposing minds. Yet he dwelled upon this display of male design as he might an exhibit of forbidden art; rapture not lost on Cassandra.

"There, Johnny," she said, sliding her arm behind his head, "the ninth gate. There, limited only by your imagination, is where you can find untold pleasure."

She looked at him with the knowing smile of a seductress. *I have you now, don't I, Johnny Feelwater? I have you to do with as I wish. You have no idea how long I waited.*

He lowered his head and closed his eyes, his emotions like a maelstrom of caged birds, swirling and feathered with guilt. How did something like this happen to him? How did this beautiful pair so quickly awaken his demons? He should stand and rush to the door and not look back. But no ... not just yet. Not when he so liked being near them. Not with his legs in this weakened state.

"Does your wife enjoy the pleasures of the ninth gate, Johnny?"

"My wife?" he said absently, turning to look at her. It seemed strange to talk about his wife, or even think about her. No two women could be more polar opposite than Cassandra Mott and Marilee.

"Yes, Johnny, your wife. Do her lovely cheeks tighten when you push your finger in her ninth gate?"

Marilee? A woman who finds it unthinkable to make love with a light on? *"God, no," he sighed, finding it impossible to even contemplate that scenario with Marilee.*

Johnny's eyes shifted back to Julian, who had crawled up on the low table, poised on hands and knees. "The ninth gate," he whispered, thinking he had never seen a human anus before. Certainly not Marilee's. Nor the boy's he had spent an occasional night with in school. No one's—other than his own with the awkward use of a mirror. Would it have occurred to him to straddle his wife, push his thumbs into her crack and pry her open for a look? Not likely, not when he could predict the outcome—the shrieks of protest and then finding himself exiled on the sofa.

He was looking at one now, a human anus, a man's anus, nearly hidden within damp blonde hairs. It was as if it had some irresistible power to draw his eyes. Yes, he had left the rational world behind when he entered this house; one hardly expects to walk into a carnal fairytale that strips away moral restraint. He knew everything here was inherently wrong, yet he had lost all desire to leave. He liked the odd feeling that had settled over him, the refreshing freedom from restraint. Beyond his unquenched curiosity he felt comfortable being near them, even comfortable with their erotic intrigues—until Cassandra took it to another level. Her voice came like a whisper from a siren's lips.

"Want to touch it, Johnny? I'm sure Julian wouldn't mind."

"Touch it!" Johnny gasped on a disbelieving breath. "Oh, no ..." he pleaded, staring at the anus half dazed, aware as he turned his head and looked at her radiant face that she could persuade him to do anything. "...please, I can't."

"Then I shall." She leaned over Johnny's lap. Her soft white hand reached out, a fingertip lit as it might upon a budding rose. Julian's cheeks tightened, the anus pinched at her finger. Without the slightest hesitation, she stroked and caressed it.

"It's warm, Johnny. Velvety." She leaned back to observe his reaction, her voice maddeningly seductive. "Wouldn't you like to see for yourself what it's like to touch it?"

He glanced at her, his eyes panicky, his hands lost and unsettled. Having assumed control of his self-esteem, she clearly intended to see him accept the dare. He felt like a small boy, taunted by the older children to do something he shouldn't do, something that threatened his masculinity. Consumed with dread, his eyes returned to Julian.

"Don't be nervous, Johnny. Only the three of us are here. No one else will know."

"I can't. I can't touch a man there. I'm not gay," he pleaded, closing his eyes, his jaw tight. "Oh God, I'm not gay, I'm not."

"Of course you're not, Johnny. That doesn't mean you can't touch my brother if you'd like to. We're all curious about such things, aren't we?"

Julian's knees were planted some two feet apart on the table, his back arched as he reached back and pulled his cheeks further apart. Johnny was breathing erratically. He lifted his hand as if it were weighted, slowly, index finger extended, shuddering as it ventured forth. He closed his eyes, all too aware that it was a man's anus warming the tip of his finger.

Yes, he had wondered what it felt like—he had been able to summon no will to resist. Now he knew. Pressing lightly, he knew the viscous texture and warmth, the small pinching that felt like a tiny kiss. Now there were different sensations going through him, well defined in every muscle of his body, powerful enough to change him inside. That very moment, brought on by this primordial intimacy, it gave new life to the forbidden curiosities of his youth, all of which for so many years had slept soundly in his subconscious mind.

Until now.

Johnny's eyes opened. Silken hairs lay across the twin mounds like golden, windswept grass. Julian had released his grip, which allowed the two muscular halves to tighten reflexively on Johnny's finger—everything past the second knuckle had disappeared. Lightheaded, he pushed ever so slightly and felt the finger's capacity to push through. He would have declared it impossible, this act, this all-consuming mystification, had someone told him what could happen in this parlor. He withdrew his hand and slumped against the sofa as if he had gone through an ordeal, emotionally drained. "Quite nice, isn't it, Johnny?" Cassandra said immodestly. "Nice how sensitive men are down there, don't you think?" She rested her hand on his upper thigh. "They're always damp there, aren't they, Johnny. No matter how cool it is in the room, men are that way, aren't they? Damp and receptive. ...You what I'm talking about, don't you, darlin'? Those parts of your body you love to have touched and caressed. Those places that make you smell like a man. Why, it makes me giddy just thinking about it." She fawned over him with her knowing smile. "Does your lovely wife get that way, too? Does she get carried away when she smells you beside her? Do her fingers find all those naughty places?"

Johnny was listening, looking absently at Julian's bare feet. He turned and looked at her, astonished such words were coming from the lips of a woman. When Julian stood up, Johnny looked at him, distracted by flexing muscle as Julian stepped around the low table and took his place on the facing sofa. Their eyes met again. No one, no woman and certainly no man had ever looked at him that way before, with eyes filled with want and adoration. To be looked at this way laid waste to long held convictions and any desire to leave this room. His gaze drifted over Julian's toned muscle and sun-bronzed skin, as he wondered what it would be like to lay with him, to taste him, to hold and be held by him.

Johnny's gaze rested once again on the cock ring. Fantasies, like freed lions, leapt from his imagination. The little voice telling him to leave had gotten lost in a fog, along with his rational thought. He pictured his finger hooked in that ring, drawing Julian near. He felt the want in his hands to roam over Julian's body, to know the texture and weight of that large cock in his hand. How they crawled on him, these images born in the reemerging shimmers of lost fantasies, knowing how difficult it would be to resist if such a proposition were put forth.

Johnny retreated from the dreamy illusions and turned to look at Cassandra. He wondered if he had been drugged or hypnotized. "What've you done to me?" he asked.

"Have I done something to you, Johnny?" her rich southern charm toned with innocence.

His weary gaze shifted to the low table. "I feel strange. I'm ..."

"Maybe you're warm, darlin'. It's getting warm early this year, don't you think?" Cassandra tilted her head back to rub her neck. She stood and crossed the room, her satiny gown clinging suggestively to the nuances of her body. She picked up a Japanese fan from the wall table to fan her neck, turning then and coming up behind Julian. She folded the fan and set it aside, then leaned forward and ran her hands down over her brother's chest.

Johnny found it difficult to fathom such closeness between a brother and sister. But why not? Why should that be considered strange after everything he had seen since he entered this parlor?

"Do you like massage, Johnny?" she asked, her eyes pouring over him. "Julian does. He'd have me doing this for hours if I were willing."

Watching her hands, Johnny recalled the one time he had gone for a massage. How quickly that hour passed under those masterful hands. The masseuse had been nothing at all like Cassandra, rather more like a female drill sergeant, rotund and blunt in manner. Though he remembered feeling self-conscious lying naked on her table, a small towel draped over his hips, she had imparted with her fleshy hands a true nirvana.

"Yes," he admitted with reservation, "I do like massage." He contemplated Cassandra's hands venturing over his body, fearing she intended to suggest it. He knew where something like that could lead.

She moved from behind her brother and came up behind him, taking hold of the tendons adjoining his shoulders and neck. She kneaded and massaged them and her hands eroded his resolve.

"My bedroom's right over there," she said, nodding at one of the doors on the back wall. "Would you like one now?"

Rolling his head, he closed his eyes. The suggestion had entered his ears like the sweetest of songs. What could he possibly want more? She made him feel like a man deprived, like he had been waiting his entire life for something like this, some small adventure apart from the mundane routines of his monotorious life. How, with his shoulders given over to the sensations of her hands, could any man resist?

Yet he did resist. There was but a single element planted in his consciousness that equaled Cassandra Mott's power of seduction—guilt. Challenged by circumstances like these, only the vibrancy of a married man's guilt could empower him to say no. Always lurking, always ready to spring, it was guilt that poisoned the temptations a married man should not abide. It was guilt, like a thorn pricking the soft flesh beneath his fingernails that caused him to fear this mysterious woman, despite her allure, her beauty, her ability to manipulate.

"I have to go," he said with stammering conviction, before her hands drew him into a state helplessness.

"So soon?" *I have you, don't I, Johnny Feelwater? Just wait. You'll see how I can turn your world upside down.* She leaned forward and he felt the breath of her whisper on his ear. "Then perhaps another day," she said. "Soon, I hope."

He swallowed dryly and came to his feet and started toward the door, turning to look at them as he reached the threshold. What could he say when nothing here made sense, when being with them seemed like a dream? He needed time to contemplate this encounter. They had changed him. They had made a dream become real. Had he not felt Cassandra's breath on the back of his neck? Had he not bitten into forbidden fruit the moment he touched Julian? They had reached inside him and learned things that he himself did not know. Real or imagined, it didn't matter. Either way, he felt the strongest urge to get outside, to figure out how to deal with this most unusual occasion, to decide if he should ever set foot inside this house again.

Then he remembered something important. "Uh, my wife wants to come here tomorrow. I, uh ... I think it's best if ..."

Cassandra smiled. "She won't know we're here, Johnny."

Johnny hurried down the hallway and then down the stairs. He pulled the front door closed behind him and turned to lock it. Anxious for a breath of fresh air, his dazed stride down the steps and across the small yard began to bring him back into a world it seemed he had left a lifetime ago. It was a fine spring day. Hazy shafts of mid-day sun stabbed down through the boughs of ancient oaks draped for eons in Spanish moss, and warmed the side of his face. He proceeded through the wrought-iron gate and turned to look at the house. He stared, caught for a moment in a kind of warp. Windows obscured by curtains, blinds drawn, the imposing structure appeared as vacant as he had first assumed it to be.

But it wasn't.

On across the street and back into Confederate Square. The fog in his head cleared a little more with each step. He sat on the brick ledge that encircled a threesome of bronze Confederate soldiers. They were forever reloading a cannon, the angst of war eternally etched on their faces. Here and there walked the tourists, snapping pictures, pushing strollers, sniffing out every square foot of historic Savannah, all blurs in his peripheral vision as he focused on the house.

His gaze shifted absently as he recounted the morning's events. He remembered waking up with that dream, feeling uncomfortable and then passing it off. It was routine after that, fretting over the graphics for Globalcorp that refused to take form. Then that lawyer showed up. Up until then, he was still Johnny Feelwater. Who was he now? Who was this man in Johnny Feelwater's skin, so strangely different from the man he had been an hour before?

Maybe they were ghosts. Maybe they were intruders, stealing the identities of eccentric personalities from the past. Whoever they were, they made him feel he had not inherited the property at all, that it still did and would always belong to Cassandra Mott. Now that his mind had cleared, the whole encounter seemed too far removed from reality: a woman that called herself Cassandra Mott, walking in on her in the shower, the affect on him seeing her nude, her provocative words; and even more peculiar, the one she called Julian, his silence and haunting eyes, his golden hair and magnificent body. Real or otherwise, they had captured his mind.

He lifted his hand and held it in his gaze. He brought it closer to his face. Then he passed his fingers before his nose, drawing from them the odor of Julian Mott. This was no dream, this ill-gotten smell on his fingertips, this lingering evidence of a most damning act. Unsettling—the beautiful pair were not ghosts. He closed his eyes and drew another breath. The smell passing through his nostrils crowded his mind with a more complicated and more compelling issue. He knew, as his eyes shifted from his hand to the house, in spite of the bitter aftertaste of guilt, in spite of society's relentless damnation, that he would put his finger there again. If the fear welling inside was to be identified, he would first have to admit that he had succumbed to Cassandra Mott's world of debauchery.

His eyes shifted to the next house and then the next. They were all stately houses facing Confederate Square. He wondered what had gone on inside them during the span of so many forgotten decades. Savannah's history—how he loved it because of, not despite, its immoral flaws. He had come to Savannah years ago, to be part of her many flavors, to explore her architecture and walk the sidewalks from era's past. Was he now, by way of wandering into one of her timeless parlors, to believe he had stumbled upon Savannah's past? Had he witnessed shadows of days gone by? Had he consorted with personalities that heretofore lived only in whispers? Who were these people, after all, that called themselves Cassandra and Julian Mott?

He looked again at his hand. It had not turned to stone, nor had it dissolved away at the wrist; though through it had come sensations he had never known. He could not shake the notion that Cassandra Mott indeed lived again, and that his destiny was somehow linked to the inexcusable scent on his finger.

Johnny scanned the brick fence for his bicycle. It was gone. He had intended to take it into the house, but by the time the door opened he had forgotten, and now it had been stolen. Oh well, a small loss on the heels of an astounding revelation. Starting afoot across the square in the direction of his house, it dawned on him that he felt suddenly alone in the world.

There was no one with whom he might relate this most unusual encounter. Who would believe his suspicion that an eccentric twosome from the past inhabited the house he had just inherited? Who would not show contempt for what he had allowed to happen with Julian Mott? He shoved his hands into his pockets and watched the sidewalk pass beneath his feet, wondering what to tell Marilee.

Debauchery, the enchantress had said. Was it the word, or the way it sounded flowing from her lips that gripped him so? Hearing her say it had sent chills down his spine. He felt the tingles even now, on the back of his neck and across the pores of his skin. His chest swelled with doubt as he strode homeward, pondering her invitation to come back. Somewhere in his mind he might have known that he would go back, but outwardly he questioned his nerve to ever walk through that wrought-iron gate again. Cassandra Mott had initiated a seduction. She would assume that he had returned to go forward with her notions of debauchery. Would he be able to resist her again? Risking his marriage, including his peace of mind, seemed far too costly a proposition. He couldn't imagine being in Cassandra's bedroom, getting a massage, though he wanted to know more about them, to find out who or what they are. He couldn't deny that he liked being with them.

He continued on, passing the facades of old storefronts and restored houses. He loved walking these streets, through these snapshots of Savannah's past; perhaps more so now that he had felt a breath from the past on the back of his neck. This was, after all, Savannah, where countless stories lived on about bygone eras and ghosts from the past. So if he wanted to go back, why not? He had nothing to feel guilty about, not really, nothing more than a fantasy or two that any married man might have. He had not entered that house with wrongful intent, nor did he stay when temptation threatened his conscious. What he did with Julian ... well, that he would keep to himself and perhaps one day forget it ever happened.

The sun was on its way into the western sky by the time his house came into view. The task at hand was finding a way to deal with Marilee. She would have questions about the house. He would have to respond without showing signs of guilt. Perhaps he could keep her from going there, though it was beyond him just how that could be accomplished. He entered through the front door and called out, then listened but heard no response.

Still at the church... Figures. She's involved with the Holy Ghost, I'm involved with the ghost of a seductress.

In the kitchen he went to the refrigerator for a bottle of beer and then plopped down at the breakfast table. He took a sip, staring across the room at nothing in particular, weighted by the day's events. He thought about the locked front door, how it seemed to have opened on its own. He thought about his conversation with Arlene Landrum, and the chorus in the foyer, and first seeing Cassandra in the shower. He wasn't sure how much time had passed by the time Marilee walked in with a bag of groceries, but what remained of his beer was warm.

He looked at her, felt guilty as sin.

"Didn't think you were here," she said, placing the groceries on the counter. "Your bicycle wasn't on the front porch."

"I know," he said distantly.

"It wasn't in the garage either," she added.

"It got stolen."

She turned to look at him, thinking that explained his distant behavior. "Think it'll turn up? We can't afford a new one."

His eyes shifted. *Always the practical one.*

He watched her put away the groceries, realizing that he understood her less after all their years of marriage than he had come to understand Cassandra Mott in the span of an hour. It seemed remarkable that in every imaginable way two women could be so different. Even more striking than the color of their skin, were their perceptions of life itself. Marilee lived on the surface of life, a life defined for her by a self-righteous few. Everything was simple. Everything could be accepted and explained as God's will. Whereas Marilee faithfully disavowed the pleasures of the flesh, Cassandra immersed herself in the essence of life and openly indulged her natural urges.

Cassandra Mott. Johnny had yet to figure out who she was. Cassandra's ghost? Not likely. He certainly never imagined a ghost to be so fleshy, so vibrant, so reeking of a most tantalizing female scent. If she was a trespasser, she had taken on the roll of Cassandra Mott with great flare, along with her beautiful male accomplice. Johnny's toes curled just picturing him sitting naked on the sofa.

Marilee's voice roused him back from his thoughts.

"I'm not used to seeing you in the kitchen," she said. "You must be caught up on the cosmetics ad." She opened the refrigerator to put away a carton of milk. "Oh yes, I almost forgot. Someone from Globalcorp called right after you left. They're hoping you plan to overnight the next layout by the end of the week."

Johnny was perturbed. They had inherited a house—she hadn't even asked about it yet. "Uh, I'll call them in the morning."

"We finished up the children's costumes for the Easter play today. They sure are cute. Reverend Aragones reminded me to make sure you attend the play." She fixed her eyes on him. "Remember? You promised you'd go since you missed the Christmas banquet."

He looked down at the table, rubbing his forehead with his fingertips. *Shit!* It was the downside of being self-employed—he couldn't say he had to work late.

"How about I sniff a cat-box instead?"

"That's disgusting, Johnny!"

"When is it," he asked in surrender.

"Two weeks from Saturday night. It'll only last two hours."

Two hours! A lifetime! All those parents fawning over their adorable children. All that chit-chat when the damn thing is over. But he couldn't deny the commitment. He remembered promising that he'd go to the Easter play, a good idea at the time, he thought, to get out of the syrupy Christmas festivities. At least he had two weeks before the sentence commenced.

Marilee joined him at the table and her face brightened with curiosity.

"So what did the house look like?"

The house. Finally. This, he had to give some thought. He stared at his wife for a moment before looking down at the table. What on God's earth was he to tell her about that house? Right away he felt antsy talking about it.

Well honey, met someone new there. The most gorgeous red head I ever saw in my life. Sorta fell into a trance watching her take a shower. There was a man there, too, almost as beautiful as the woman. I touched his anus.

The thoughts thrashing in his head were much like a bull raging a small room. His eyes lifted from the table and met hers.

"It's a nice house. Worth quite a lot of money, I'd say. Big. Lot of detailed woodwork. Guess we got the antiques, too."

"Antiques?" she said excitedly.

"Yeah. It's full of elegant old furniture. All of it like new."

"I can't wait to see it. Let's go first thing in the morning."

He nodded absently. So many *what ifs* flooded his head his stomach started to churn. Marilee would never be able to deal with Cassandra and Julian Mott. Nevertheless, Johnny couldn't imagine finding a way to avoid showing her the house. Maybe Cassandra would keep her word and stay in the parlor. Then all he had to do was keep her from going into that room.

That night Johnny went to bed early, exhausted. Marilee was in the kitchen, on the phone with someone from church. Thirty minutes later, in the dim glow of his reading light, he watched her cross the room and head straight into the bathroom. He listened as she turned on the shower behind the closed door, wondering what a day's perspiration might smell like between her legs. The only scent he had ever identified on her body was soap, not that his nose had ever been positioned that close to her more intimate areas, though the thought germinated another round of fantasies about Cassandra Mott. He was certain she shaved down there. Exposed as her nether lips were, the effect had seared prominently on his brain. He pictured himself wiling away the afternoon nuzzling her shaven lips.

But she didn't ask me to touch that, did she?

It seemed to Johnny that there was line dividing the mores of the world. Most people lived on one side, the side of Godliness and self-imposed morality. They were the masses, he among them, and they never stepped across the line. But Cassandra Mott, or whoever she is, dwelled and flourished on the other side. It wouldn't occur to her to venture across, though she was quite good at extending her hand and drawing someone to her side. Today, evidently, she had chosen him. So, he resolved, now that he was thinking clearly, that no matter how pervasive their seductive antics might be, he had no choice but to face the challenge. After all, they were in his house. They could not expect him to simply walk away; nor could he, not with his overwhelming curiosity to know more about them. The matter was settled. He would befriend them, find out who they are, and then deal with evicting them in due course.

A soft cast fell over his half nude body from the reading light. The spray of water from the bathroom droned on. A moment or two after he lifted the news magazine to resume reading, his eyes shifted back to the ceiling. The image of Julian Mott still loomed in his mind. The stirring between his legs returned, along with noticeably increasing and very pleasant phallic weight. He slipped his hand beneath the sheet, and then under the waistband of his pajama bottoms. It felt warmer there than usual and the additional size filled his hand handsomely. Picturing himself seated in Cassandra's parlor, he realized a carnal storm had passed harmlessly overhead by virtue of his will to resist. He could do it again. He knew he could resist them, though he wondered as he stared at the ceiling, his hand gathering the warmth of his penis, what it might have felt like had he pushed his finger a fraction of an inch inside.

He closed his eyes with a sigh, and then lifted the magazine, letting it fall with annoyance back to the bed.

Okay then ... so he was not have a moment's peace. So these absurd fantasies were going to linger inside his head. So be it. Is that what Cassandra wanted, to see his finger disappear into her brother's anus? Maybe that was why Julian bent over and laid himself open. So what? So why was he lying there now, that moment, wishing he had? Where, for God's sake, did this vile curiosity come from?

Though he tried to shift his thoughts to the Globalcorp ad campaign, Julian's image continued to displace the boring graphic designs. Johnny's attention returned to the hand inside his pajamas. He gave himself a squeeze, thinking it remarkable and a man's good fortune the way the loose skin slid so freely up and down. Marilee would be in the bathroom another few minutes. A rhythmic motion guided his hand as the image of Julian's parted legs blossomed in his mind. Then the sound of water stopped. She would be out in a matter of seconds. Johnny's hand moved faster. That familiar warmth began to spread through his body as the rhythm intensified. Then, precisely at the wrong moment, the bathroom door swung open. His hand jerked from his pajamas and his tense weight slumped in frustration on the sheet. He quickly pulled up the sheet. No sticky mess this time. No worrying that Marilee would notice a funny smell.

Marilee came out of the bathroom in her terry cloth robe. It brushed the floor with her stride. Underneath, her usual flannel pajamas. She took off the robe and hung it on a hook just inside her closet door, then crossed the room to get into bed. Watching her, Johnny wondered if anything a woman might wear could be less flattering. Even a potato sack would at least leave her arms and legs exposed. She crawled into bed and acknowledged him with a brief smile; and from that moment forward he might as well not have existed. He looked back at the ceiling, thinking about the software vendor he recently had lunch with. The man had replied, when asked if his wife slept in pajamas, that they sleep in the nude, adding they fit together like spoons when his wife backed up close to his chest. The reply had made Johnny envious. He remembered Marilee's reaction when he related the story that evening. One would think he had told her the vendor had confessed to roasting the neighborhood children for dinner.

He sighed and lifted the magazine once again. The words were there, the photographs and captions, but his concentration was like a skittish fly that wouldn't light. Some two hours later, a weary yawn. He fell asleep with the unread pages resting on his chest.

The morning came an eternity later. The night had been an unending drama of nightmares, tormenting images that caused a fitful night of groaning and tossing on sheets damp with perspiration. He awoke fretting over a pressing challenge, having relived it a dozen times during the night in a reoccurring dream. In a haze of chaos, he had seen two women in a confrontational exchange, Cassandra Mott and Marilee Feelwater. Marilee, listening, aghast, finally pressing her palms to her ears to prevent hearing more. The challenge, he surmised—to make sure they never find themselves facing each other.

He tried to think of a reason his wife should not see the house. It was hopeless. She was excited about seeing it. At best he might think of a way to delay her visit; but not for long, and that would only delay the agony of the inevitable.

She was already up, brushing her teeth. He swung his feet off the bed, his white silk pajama bottoms still damp. Reaching down to relieve a morning itch, he noticed the pajamas were wet near the fly and a bit sticky. One of the dreams must have taken over where his hand left off. The phone rang and he hoped it might be someone from the church, reporting an unforeseen emergency with the bunny costumes that would require Marilee's undivided attention until Easter.

No such luck. It was the terror of Atlanta—Marilee's mother, probably inquiring again about the money they had borrowed to buy the new van. The woman couldn't simply keep her mouth shut until the next advance on his Globalcorp project came in.

He hooked a thumb in the waistband of his pajamas and stretched them outward and glanced down. Ah, there it was, the primary culprit in a few of those dreams he had suffered during the night. How guiltless it looked inside the pajamas, resting with flaccid innocence between his legs; when in the dreams it had participated so eagerly in a number of unpardonable sins, misadventures that were invariably found out by Marilee—the one component that turned an otherwise blissful dream into a nightmare.

He rubbed his face with both hands. Was he losing his sanity? He pictured himself holding out his arms and tiptoeing over the edge. The thought brought a smile to his lips. Wouldn't that be the perfect reason to avoid going to the house, if instead Marilee had to drive him to the asylum? *Sure my love, we'll go see the house, just as soon as the doctor says I'm well enough the take the straightjacket off and leave the hospital.*

But then, there was nothing comical about it. His life had been interrupted by something that couldn't be explained, something he certainly couldn't share with his wife. It would be a while before his mind would let him think about anything else.

He lifted his elbow and sniffed his underarm and detected the smell of stress. But why question his sanity? Just because the temptation he had considered the day before would have meant cashing in of all the chips he had acquired thus far in his life? Or maybe because, for the first time in his married life, he found himself at odds with his own sexuality. Or was it because he had heard voices singing from a wall, or had seen a snake disappear inside an upstairs parlor, or had been mistaken for a slave, or had touched another man's anus—or maybe because all of these events had melded into an unraveling ball of chaos inside his head. Was it insanity or pure bliss?

Insane or not, he faced a trying day.

Marilee hung up the phone, frustrated as usual after a conversation with her mother. The wretched woman considered tormenting her daughter an accomplishment. She had turned her ability to do so into an art form. Marilee came out of the bathroom and went into her closet for something to wear, at which time Johnny hurried into the bathroom to relieve his bladder. With that done, he stepped in front of the mirror and sucked in his belly. He liked the white silk pajama bottoms. They were light and airy, and he was partial to the way he looked in them, comparing himself to the carefree Bahamans he had seen in a travel ad on TV. After he brushed his teeth and shaved, he made sure Marilee wasn't looking before he lifted his hand to sniff his finger. Julian's scent had been displaced by toothpaste.

Marilee had breakfast ready by the time he entered the kitchen.

"What did your mother want?" he asked when she joined him with a plateful of pancakes.

Marilee shook her head, agitated. "She was complaining about the Easter play again. She doesn't give up. Keeps insisting a church play should be more theological than kids performing in bunny costumes. It doesn't matter we did a religious program last year."

"She didn't mention the money?"

"I hung up on her," Marilee stated frankly.

A doubtful grin came to his face. "You did what?"

"Well, it wasn't exactly like hanging up on her. I told her I had to get off the phone."

"Ah."

"You don't just hang up on your own mother, Johnny. You know that."

"Yeah. Especially when you can hear her screeching all the way from Atlanta." He forked some pancakes onto his plate and took a bite of bacon. "So do you still wanna go see that house?" he asked with his mouth full.

She was surprised he asked. "I can't wait to see it. It didn't seem real at first. We actually inherited a house."

He nodded and looked down at his plate.

"What are you thinking about?" Marilee asked. "You've seemed preoccupied ever since you got home yesterday."

"Just thinking about the creepy feeling I had when I got there. Kinda like the place is haunted."

"Haunted?" A fork-full of pancakes stopped short of her mouth.

"When I walked through it yesterday. I felt a chill or something. Like something evil. I'm not sure I'd go back in there if you didn't want to see it."

She stared at him, gaping. "Evil? What do you mean, *evil?*"

"I don't know exactly." He paused for a moment for affect. "Maybe something evil happened there, ten years ago, maybe a hundred. That could be it. Just didn't like the weird feeling I got." He waited a moment longer before asking: "Sure you want to go?"

Her eyes drifted to the table, then jumped back up. "Of course I do. You've let it get to you, all those stories we've heard about Savannah's haunted houses. You were alone in a big empty house. That's all. It affected your imagination." She resumed her breakfast.

It had been his best shot, but he didn't really expect her to change her mind about seeing a house they had just inherited. His imagination? Well, there was every possibility that Marilee would find herself listening to Cassandra Mott's opinion about that.

Chapter 4

Johnny noticed, as they walked through the wrought-iron gate, that his haunted house story had affected Marilee after all. She hesitated as she looked up at the house, wide-eyed.

"Change your mind about going in?" he asked.

She shook her head meekly.

He felt a bit depressed, rooted in guilt, standing next to his wife, the one person in his life that trusted him unconditionally. The things that passed through his mind the day before, here at this house. It was the first time he harbored a secret he couldn't share with her.

She still seemed reluctant to ascend the porch steps.

"Why are you standing there?"

It dawned on Marilee that they had not inherited a house so much as a windfall. She had not allowed herself to believe they would ever have a lot of money, not even when Johnny landed the Globalcorp account, but that notion was creeping into her mind now. "It's so big," she said, scanning the façade somewhat overwhelmed. "How much is a house like this worth?"

"A lot." He placed his hand on the small of her back and encouraged her toward the stairs.

The key worked as intended. The lock popped open. He turned the knob, pushed the door wide and followed Marilee's tentative steps inside.

Alarmed at once, his head snapped in every direction. The house was as empty as the day it had been built. Not a stick of furniture anywhere. Though he had mentioned a houseful of beautiful antique furnishings, Marilee didn't notice right away. While she leaned forward, twisting her head this way and that, he tried to sort out his sensibilities. When his weight shifted backward, he placed his hand on the wall for balance as he scanned the rooms he could see from the foyer.

She took three or four more steps, leaning cautiously forward, craning her neck to peer through the broad archways that led to different parts of the house. Her gaze then shifted upward toward the landing.

"Is all the furniture upstairs?" she asked. Her voice echoed in the empty house.

"Marilee ... I don't get it."

She turned and looked at him.

"Something's happened to the furniture," he said nervously.

She stared at him, at a loss.

"This whole house was full of furniture yesterday," he insisted, spreading his arms for emphasis.

Her face washed over with bewilderment.

"I have no idea what happened to it." He said glanced around as if he could not believe his own eyes. "Maybe it belonged to someone else. Maybe Cassandra Mott left it to a friend and they came by to pick it up. I don't know, but it was here yesterday."

"They picked up a whole big house full of furniture since you were here yesterday?" she said doubtfully.

"I'm losing my mind here, Marilee. This house was full of furniture yesterday! I saw it myself."

"Call Mr. McPhereson when we get home. Maybe he knows what happened to it."

"Yeah. He'll know. That's what I'll do."

She shrugged and looked into the dining room. "Shall we start downstairs?" she said, venturing in that direction.

He wiped his forehead on his sleeve and glanced up at the landing, shocked by what he saw. Cassandra, at the railing looking down at him, smiling. His eyes shot in Marilee's direction and then back up. It was his worst fear. If Marilee found out what happened yesterday, she would never forgive him. She would have expected him to leave the moment he realized a woman occupied the house, especially having walked in on her in the shower. Now, beyond explaining the missing furniture, he faced the possibility of a confrontation between Marilee and a seductress that might find it amusing to disclose the regretful details of yesterday's visit.

What now? Did Cassandra plan to come down? Did she plan to wait for them to get upstairs, then maybe have a little chat with Marilee? He closed his eyes and drew a deep breath and then set out to find his wife.

Johnny followed Marilee though the rooms on the lower floor. She seemed more comfortable now, taking her time, awed by the intricate woodwork and the rare craftsmanship of days gone by. He was certain she would want to see the second floor and he could think of nothing that might discourage her. Never had he wanted to get through anything as badly as he wanted to get out of this house. When they got back to the foyer, Marilee turned to say something, disturbed at once by the angst on his damp face.

"My God, Johnny! You look ill?"

"I'm telling you, this house is haunted! Do we *have* to go upstairs?"

"Honey, it'll only take a few minutes." She stepped forward and placed her hand on his forehead. "I wonder if you're allergic to something in here. Maybe the fabric in these old drapes or the carpet."

He let out a breath of defeat and glanced up at the landing. "C'mon, let's get it over with."

A sense of dread crawled up his spine as he climbed the staircase. One step at a time just behind Marilee, staring intently at the wall, wondering if he had actually heard the chorus of young female voices the day before. Then, craning his neck as they neared the landing, he looked toward the parlor door. It was closed and there was no sign of Cassandra Mott.

Marilee wandered into the hallway opposite Cassandra's wing. Entering one room after another, her pace quickened now that they were upstairs. Perhaps she was concerned about Johnny's nervousness, or perhaps she had developed her own reservations about being there. He waited near the doorway of each room as she perused the elegant but empty spaces, continually watching the hallway for unwelcome appearances. Finally, with that wing assessed, Marilee started for the last section of the house, Cassandra's wing.

Johnny's heart was thumping as she ventured into and out of the first couple of rooms. When she entered the third room, Johnny paused at a door he didn't remember opening. He turned the knob and swung it open. A linen closet. His eyes were drawn to a hissing sound from the floor. *"That snake!"* he gasped under his breath.

It lay coiled in the corner, its eyes like needles looking up at him.

He closed the door quickly as Marilee came up behind him.

"What's in there?" she asked, reaching for the knob.

"Don't open it! There's a dead rat in there," he said, holding his breath for composure.

Her hand recoiled from the knob. She shivered. It was all she needed to know.

She looked at the door at the end of the hallway. "That looks like the last room," she said stepping toward it.

"Haven't you seen enough of this place already?" he pleaded, shoulders narrowed.

Marilee, standing in front of Cassandra's door, looked at her husband for a moment. "I've never seen you like this before."

"I don't like being here. Can't you understand that?"

"You actually look scared."

"I am." He folded his arms over his chest as if he were cold.

"But you've not superstitious," she said, finding it difficult to take his trepidation seriously.

"I am now! This house is haunted."

She turned and looked at the door. "Well, this is the last room. It'll just take a minute to look at it. Okay?"

Johnny closed his eyes and nodded.

She turned the knob, pushed the door open and looked in before stepping through the doorway. Johnny held his breath, picturing his wife's high-strung morality colliding with Cassandra's free-spirited immorality. He saw Julian reclined on the sofa, naked, the absent expression and the crystal blue eyes. Marilee would not be amused by his cock ring.

She had disappeared inside the room. Johnny listened. He heard no voices, no cries of surprise. He hurried down the hall and walked into a barren room, the same intimate parlor he remembered so well—just empty. When Marilee opened one of the doors along the back wall, he took a quick look inside the bathroom. No towels, no robes hanging from wall hooks, no Cassandra Mott.

Though relieved, he was also disoriented. How had she managed this? And why ... why would she move out all of the furniture? Just because he intended to bring his wife today? Did Cassandra want no one but him to know they were living there? And where were they? He had just seen Cassandra on the landing. Did they leave, or were they still somewhere in the house? It was difficult to manage a coherent thought.

Standing just outside the bathroom, head bowed, rubbing his eyes, Johnny looked up when he heard Marilee's voice.

"This must be the master suite," she said, approaching him.

"Yeah. That's what I figured," he said, casually as possible.

"There's two bedrooms back there and a large closet."

He looked at the doors on the back wall, remembering he had wondered what they led to yesterday.

She reached up to straighten his collar. "Your shirt is damp!" she said, laying her palm on his forehead again. "You don't have a fever. You can't be that upset just being here, can you?"

"Yes. Let's go."

She looked around his shoulder, into the bathroom. "Is that the bathroom?"

"Yeah," he said wearily.

She stepped around him and went in, dazzled.

"I've never seen such an elegant bathroom," she said, running her fingertips over the marble countertop and golden fixtures. "Mrs. Mott must have had this room renovated."

"Probably."

She turned and looked at him and decided he had been patient long enough. "Are you ready?"

"Yeah, I've been ready," he said, hurrying her out of the bathroom, on through the parlor and down the hallway.

His pace didn't slow until they reached the sidewalk on the other side of the wrought-iron gate. Marilee started toward the passenger side of their new van.

"Wait!" Johnny called out.

She turned, standing in front of the van.

"You drive the van home. I feel like walking. Need some fresh air or something. Just a walk."

She looked at him quizzically. "Johnny ... you sure you're feeling all right?"

"I'm fine. I just feel like walking." He stepped forward and handed her the key.

She took it skeptically and started for the driver's side door, turning to look at him again.

"Maybe you shouldn't walk home. You look ill."

"I'm fine, really. I'll be home shortly."

She looked up at the house, not at all certain about how she felt about owning it, then turned reluctantly to unlock the van.

He stepped back up on the sidewalk and watched her get in, start the engine and pull away from the curb. He didn't move until the van turned the corner and was out of sight. Then he started toward Arlene Landrum's house. His hands stuffed in his pockets, he crossed the street and entered Confederate Square, stopping half way through to turn and look back at the house. Upstairs, from the sitting-room off the parlor, he saw a figure step back from the window. A chill ran down his neck and he turned and kept walking.

The maid answered the door. Johnny introduced himself. Suggesting he wait in the foyer, the maid took her leave to inform Miss Landrum of his visit. He fidgeted, breathing deeply to calm his nerves, rubbing his hands together to temper his hunger for information that Arlene Landrum might be able to supply. Questions. A dozen or more of them waited to jump off the end of his tongue; and in his current state of mind, he worried they might fly at the old woman like an interrogation. He had to calm down. He quit wringing his hands and pushed them back in his pockets as he surveyed the sitting room adjacent to the foyer. It was a comfortable room, reminiscent of another era with its lace adornments and rockers and a delicate tea service tarnishing on the bureau. He leaned on the doorframe and his head fell back against it.

The maid returned a few moments later to let him know the dear lady was feeling well enough to see him on the veranda. Pulling his weight off the doorframe, he followed her down the hallway and through a den, to a pair of French doors that opened on the veranda. Arlene Landrum was sitting contentedly in the mid-morning sun, a blanket spread across her lap. She seemed glad to see her unexpected guest.

"I wasn't expecting you to come by so soon," she said as he took a seat in the rocker beside her.

"Glad you're feeling well today, Miss Landrum."

"Call me Arlene, young man."

"Yes ma'am. Uh ... I was hoping you'd feel like talking about Cassandra Mott. I'd like to know more about her."

"Of course, dear boy. You seem upset."

Johnny glanced at her with a forced smile. The smile evaporated as he glanced out toward the garden, feeling like he was about to burst. He didn't know where or how to begin.

"You have something troubling you, it seems," said Arlene, evermore curious about the young man's visit.

Johnny took a deep breath and looked at her.

"Do you believe in ghosts?" he asked with disquietude.

"Oh my yes, not that I've ever seen one that I know of. But you can't live in Savannah as long as I have and not believe in ghosts."

"Do you think it's possible a ghost can look and feel like a real person?"

Arlene's brow lifted. "Well, that's something I couldn't be sure of, but I guess it's possible. I must say, you've confused me. What does that have to do with Cassandra?"

"I think she's come back as a ghost."

Arlene looked at him, amused.

"Well, a ghost or something else," Johnny went on to say. "You knew her. Do you think that's possible?"

"Cassandra?" Arlene pondered this for a moment, then said: "I suppose if anyone came back as a ghost, it would be Cassandra." The old lady shifted her gaze out across the small back yard as if her mind had traveled back and captured a few cherished memories. "She loved life. The dear girl had a passion for living like no one else I ever knew. She always had to be involved in something, something exciting, even daring."

Johnny sat upright, his torso twisted toward the old lady. "So you think maybe she loved life so powerfully that she was able to come back in one form or another?"

Arlene looked back at Johnny with a touch of misgiving. "You're talking as if you've seen her."

"I'm not sure what I've seen, Miss Landrum ... Arlene. I just know I have an overwhelming curiosity about Cassandra."

Arlene adjusted her blanket in thought, then said: "It's quite possible she loved life that much, young man. You see, for most of us there comes a time when we're resigned to death. Our bodies get old and tired and we think back over our lives with a sense of satisfaction. We're ready when it comes. Not Cassandra. It was painful to visit her the last few years. She hated being bed-ridden. Even hated getting old. Called it God's curse." Arlene paused and looked at her arthritic hands before she went on. "A ghost? It's funny you ask. I remember we used to talk. Gossip, you know. A few thought Cassandra must be reincarnated from the past. Ridiculous, I know, but she used to say things. Things that made you think she must have lived other lives in the past."

Reincarnated. Johnny was fascinated. "Did you hear those things yourself?"

"Why yes, yes I did. One time she planned a costume party. A young gentleman came dressed as Napoleon. Cassandra took offense to it. She actually berated him for his costume. She told him he was too tall to be Napoleon, that his hair was all wrong. Said Napoleon would have never worn the kind of boots he had on. It stunned me. It was as if she had known Napoleon personally."

"Did you question her about it?"

"No. She realized she said something odd. She dropped it, like it never happened. I figured she must have read a book about Napoleon."

Johnny hung onto every word, distracted when the maid came out to serve hot tea. He waited for the young woman to place the tea service between them before quickly getting back to the conversation.

"I hope you don't think I'm a basket-case," he said with a disarming smile.

Arlene Landrum laughed. "I've always rather liked Savannah's basket-cases."

"This thing about reincarnation. Do you think it's possible someone can come back as the same person they were before they died?" he asked, not sure how reincarnation could explain the exotic young woman that had so easily softened his resolve.

"I've never heard of such a thing," said Arlene Landrum. She still seemed amused by their intriguing conversation.

Johnny turned his head in thought, remembering how Cassandra thought he might have been a runaway slave seeking refuge in her house, as if she were momentarily confused as to what era she was in. That tied in with what Arlene Landrum just told him. Still, it didn't explain her reappearance as her youthful self so quickly after her death. He knew only one thing with certainty: he was drawn to a woman that called herself Cassandra Mott, enchanted by her, and very possibly in love with both her and her brother.

"Did you know her brother?" Johnny asked.

"You're talking about Julian. Yes, I knew him. He was a quiet boy. Maybe the handsomest young man I ever knew." Arlene smiled thinking about it. "Before he died, I remember wishing he was a bit older and not related to Cassandra, thinking I could seduce him." She turned to look at her visitor as if she had allowed a slip-of-the-tongue. "I didn't embarrass you by saying that, did I?"

"Oh, no. Please go on."

"You want to know about Julian," she said with light in her eyes. "Then, simply put, you should know a handsomer man never walked the face of the earth, nor a man with more passion. When he was only fourteen they caught him in bed with an older man, a banker. The two of them were caught naked and fondling each other. It was quite an embarrassment for the banker."

"Did they prosecute him?"

"The banker? Lord no! No one that rich got prosecuted back then. Besides, everyone quietly assumed Julian had been the culprit, not the other way around. When I heard the story, I was told Julian wasn't remorseful, only angry they had been interrupted."

"And he died young?"

"Tragically young. Twenty-six years old. Cassandra went into a terrible melancholy for a long time when she lost him. Not nearly so terrible as when she lost your grandmother, though."

"How did he die?"

"They said it was consumption."

Aware *consumption* explained a good many deaths in that era, Johnny wondered what had really caused Julian's death, if there was a death.

"I must say, you do seem uncommonly interested in all of this. You said earlier that you thought Cassandra has come back as a ghost. I can't help but ask why?"

He wondered how he might explain his situation to a little old lady. He looked at her. "I don't mean to alarm you, but I have a feeling Cassandra is back in that house."

"Oh my!"

"Do you have any idea of what happened to all her furniture?" he asked.

"Yes I do. Cassandra borrowed money from the bank. Her beautiful furniture was used for collateral. The bank picked it all up the day after she died."

Johnny's eyes widened. "When?" he gasped.

"Two weeks ago, the very next day after she died."

Johnny's gaze shifted out toward the garden. Two weeks ago... He had seen a house full of furniture the day before, furniture that had been taken out two weeks earlier and was now gone again. Stupefied, he feared he might leave Arlene Landrum's house more confused than when he arrived. He himself had seen that furniture just yesterday; he had touched it, even sat on it.

"Did you think her furniture was part of your inheritance?"

He looked at her. "No. Not at all. I was just curious." And also in a state of panic. He stood up. "I have to go, Miss Arlene. Thank-you for seeing me."

She seemed surprised by his abrupt departure, but in view of her long imbedded southern decorum, she smiled and took his hand. "Please come by anytime you wish. You're such a delightful young man."

He nodded and turned and hurried toward the French doors. Passing through the den, from the corner of his eye, he saw a dozen or so framed photographs on the fireplace mantel. Pausing to look, their aged patina drew him closer. They appeared to be portraits of old friends and family, some dating back to the Civil War. Moving slowly along the mantle, he came to a photograph that weakened his knees. His eyes locked on an old picture of three people, two of them chillingly familiar. Seated side-by-side, both dressed in formal gowns, were two women. One was an exquisite, youthful black woman. Her eyes, even in the old photograph, gleamed with enchantment. The other, equally lovely, was Cassandra Mott. Behind them stood Julian. There could be no mistake. Other than the 1920's style of clothes and hair, it was exactly the same woman now living in his newly inherited house. He reached for the pewter framed photograph as if it might be hot, holding it in both hands, staring at it as he would a pair of eyes glowering from the shadows.

The maid came through and noticed his cold trance. Setting aside her feather duster, she approached with concern.

"Is something wrong, Mr. Feelwater?"

Johnny didn't hear or see her.

"Mr. Feelwater, are you all right?"

He glanced her way, but then his eyes returned to the photograph as if he had looked through her. Shaken, he returned it to the mantle and then looked absently in the direction of the hallway that led to the foyer. Overwhelmed with a sudden need to get outside, he started for the front door, followed by the maid, who closed it with concern after watching him walk unsteadily to the street.

Reaching the sidewalk, he bent over and braced himself on his knees, breathing hard as his equilibrium began to return. He stood upright and looked in both directions to confirm, at least outside in the fresh air, the world still appeared to be normal. He took solace in the tourists strolling the sidewalks, the school kids on their bicycles weaving through traffic, the people talking and getting in and out of their cars. Nothing was different, no one concerned about ghosts or strange reincarnations. No one was staring at him as if he had just escaped from an asylum, though the turmoil inside his head could easily be mistaken for insanity. He felt oddly apart from the world around him as bits and pieces of the challenges he faced began to come together in his mind. He was determined to figure out what was going on in the Mott residence.

He started toward Confederate Square, remembering vaguely that Marilee would be looking for him soon. The thought left him as soon as he reached the corner. The Mott house had come into view, standing like a stately relic from the past, beckoning with its mysteries like a siren. He crossed the shaded street and entered the square, his eyes fixed on the house, shifting from window to window for signs of her presence. Nearly falling over a bench, he stepped around it and sat down, staring at the house that loomed not fifty yards away. Without realizing it, he had withdrawn the key from his pocket and found himself rubbing it between his fingers, a small metal object that had changed his life overnight, that had drawn him into a world he couldn't explain or understand, a world he wanted to know.

It was her in that picture. She's in there and she knows I'm out here. She wants something from me. I can feel it.

He stared at the house as if it and its connection to him were all that existed. He wanted to find out what had happened to the furniture, to know her, to once more look upon her radiant red hair and soft pale skin, to understand how she could be in a photograph taken in the 1920's; and all of these years later not look a day older. Was it her beauty, or the unspoken messages from her eyes that captivated him? Did she intend to arrange another intrigue with Julian, an even bolder dare that would serve no purpose other than to amuse her? Just thinking about it set his mind sailing as he pondered the nuances of Julian's body, the masculine intricacies and his manly smell, giving rise to his deepest primordial instincts and a tightening in his loins. The images played out again in his mind, the talk of debauchery, Julian's casual presentation of the *ninth gate*—it all came like an entrapment of his soul, both wanted and unwanted, like an irresistible attraction that a shrinking part of him knew was wrong.

I can't keep that house. I have to sell it.

But how? How, he wondered, could he sell a house occupied by an apparently immortal seductress and her brother? Who would Cassandra Mott permit to live there? It seemed, for now at least, that the house and its occupants had become a part of his life in a way he would have never expected, that he stood on the threshold of some kind of inexplicable adventure. As he stared at the house, it occurred to him that he wanted to go back inside. It seemed a inner voice was telling him to be secretive, to step forward, urging him toward an end he could not grasp, instilling a hunger that two days before he would have vehemently denied.

Such was the power of Cassandra Mott, that he would plot a compromising measure with a most beautiful and beguiling pair, for his armpits were damp with the sweat of temptation. An anger rose inside him. He was angry at himself, angry that the important things in his life had been clouded by this vexing snare, angry at the hollowness of his marriage—nine years and his wife had never once stepped out of the shower and handed him a towel to dry her back. A small panic settled in his hands. A beleaguered awareness crept into his mind—he could not throw away the promise of Cassandra's enchantment, but throw it away he must.

He stood, ready to leave the square, ready to go home, ready to find a rational context in which he might discuss the Mott house with Marilee. He glanced one more time at the house, taking it upon himself to ignore the conflicting voices inside his head, those silent whispers trying to wrench his mind from the predictable middle-class life he had always known. There were no signs of Cassandra in any of the windows that trapped his eyes. She was there but couldn't be seen, not from here anyway. Yet the need to see her had rendered him unable to walk away from the square. He had to know. She was there, on the upstairs landing an hour earlier. She must be in there now. If so, couldn't she explain the missing furniture? Perhaps even explain what had happened to his rationale the day before.

He set out toward the house. Fragmented sunlight splashed his face through the leafy voids overhead. The noises around him merged into muted clutter in his ears as his pace quickened: the cries of children at play, birds fluttering from branch to branch overhead, cars entering and leaving the square. And as the ancient brick walkway passed beneath his feet, his determined momentum brought him closer and closer to the house.

Chapter 5

Johnny gasped the instant he stepped through the door. He stared as if he had turned to stone, his heart pounding away in his chest. Before him, wearing a flowing white dress, peering up at the landing, stood the young black lady he had seen with Cassandra Mott in the photograph at Arlene Landrum's house. Exotic to a fault, she was perhaps the most beautiful creature that ever filled his eyes, more so, disquietingly, than Cassandra herself. His mouth fell open when she spun around, setting alive inside him everything that made him a man. Were she to step forward to stroke his face, were she to smile and place her fingertips upon his lips, she could have him renounce anything he had ever considered essential.

Instead, her eyes widened as the soft texture of her face contorted with surprise and alarm. One step backward, then she turned and hurried into the dining room. Stunned, he followed, at once beset with the need to know her. She moved swiftly through the dining room, then disappeared through the kitchen doorway. By the time he got there she was gone. His eyes darted in a furious search as he hurried from room to room, frantic for another glimpse; but she seemed to have vanished into thin air.

It dawned on him then that the furniture had been returned to the house. His head swung in one direction and then another. The furnishings were intact, just as he remembered them. He wandered aimlessly back into the dining room and leaned against the back of a chair, glancing around the room in thought, no longer astounded the furniture had been replaced. Such things must be a matter of due course in this house. Surveying the room, Johnny realized his presence put him at risk. Just how wasn't clear, but it had to do with the occupant's mind-boggling power.

She's here.

He looked through archway into the foyer and could see the bottom of the stairs. Starting in that direction, resigned to whatever might happen, it dawned on him that Marilee was not to be allowed inside Cassandra's alien world, which explained the missing furniture. Apprehensive, he entered the foyer, noting that even the peanuts had been replaced. He took up a handful, tilted his head and let them fall into his mouth, chewing, swallowing, aware again of their uncommonly delicious taste. He looked up at the landing and started for the stairs, feeling dizzy by the time he reached them. He sat down on the first step.

His ears filled with voices, not the chorus of young girls, but the murmur of a small crowd. He closed his eyes and rotated his head. The noise emanated from all around him, as if he were sitting in a crowded room without knowing why. People were looking at him and talking and he wanted to leave. He felt a chill and realized he was naked. There was nothing he could do; there were no doors, no windows, nothing but white walls and noise.

The chaos gradually evolved into a warm feeling that spread through his chest and belly and down into his loins; he was rocking and rubbing his inner thighs. He opened his eyes and realized it had been a hallucination of some kind. The dizziness receded. A feeling of calm took its place. He felt quite comfortable being inside this house and with Cassandra Mott's sovereignty over it. Whatever had just happened to him had passed. He wasn't concerned. The demons had defeated the saints. His questions had evolved into an overwhelming desire to see her, to be near her and Julian, to be part of their mysterious realm. The world beyond the front door would go on without him.

He came to his feet and ascended the stairs, eager for the first glimpse of her door. Stepping up on the landing, he turned and walked toward it and placed his hand on the porcelain knob. Vague second thoughts stirred at the back of his mind, not nearly as potent as the desire that welled throughout his body. He pushed the door wide open. There they were, brother and sister Mott, facing each other on the sofas, eating sliced fruits from a silver tray, Cassandra dressed in an oriental sarong, Julian draped in an untied robe.

Johnny scanned the room. Everything was intact, the furniture, the paintings on the wall, everything; including the addition of a narrow, upholstered table centered in the space between the sofas and the bedroom doors. Beside it a porcelain washbasin and folded towels had been placed on a small wooden table.

"My goodness ... Johnny Feelwater has come to see us today," said Cassandra, licking the juice from a slice of fruit off her finger, her smile inviting and as provocative as he remembered, the smile he had envisioned again and again in his dreams the night before.

He looked at her a long while, absorbing her beauty and sensuality, acutely aware of her supernatural power.

I know you, Cassandra Mott. You don't fool me. You knew I would come.

"I think Julian was quite taken with you yesterday, not to mention the few little fantasies of my own you inspired."

His eyes shifted to Julian.

"You seem quiet, Johnny. Something on your mind?"

"*You* are on my mind," he replied, looking back at a woman as purely beautiful as any goddess man has ever created, her long legs crossed, her ankle bouncing, her shoulders bare and delicate in the sarong.

"My, my, such flattery from such a handsome man."

He stepped into the room and closed the door. "I saw a lady downstairs. I think she might have been my grandmother."

Cassandra's expression immediately turned cold. Watching her with concern, Julian glanced between her and Johnny as she uncomfortably adjusted her weight on the sofa. Almost instantaneously, she regained her composure and charm.

"I'm afraid that's impossible, Johnny. Your grandmother died many years ago."

"She was beautiful, wasn't she?"

As if he had caught her off guard, Cassandra became distraught. The subject obviously troubled her, one that she would rather avoid. "Yes ... your grandmother was beautiful," she said, her tone wistful and weighted with many years of mourning. "Think about a long span of time, Johnny, three thousand years. All those centuries, no woman walked the face of the earth as beautiful as Emily."

Three thousand years. Was she saying her world exists without limits, that time passes with no significance?

A tear formed in the corner of her eye. "Do you want to know about your grandmother, Johnny?"

"Yes," he said, taking a couple of steps forward.

"We grew up together you know. Emily was the bravest woman I ever knew, as brave as Joan of Arc. Yes. As audacious as Lady Godiva. As seductive as Cleopatra. She was all of that and more, Johnny Feelwater. She was also vulnerable. You wouldn't know that, but your mother knew, and that was Emily's downfall."

"Her *downfall?*"

"That's right. You'll understand that in time," said Cassandra.

"And you loved her?"

Julian looked at his sister with heightened concern. He seemed uncomfortable with the way this conversation impacted her.

Cassandra closed her eyes, her face etched with a painful memory.

"You loved her?" Johnny persisted.

Cassandra nodded distantly. She reflexively covered her lips with her hand.

"Do you get something from me that reminds you of her?" Johnny asked, wondering why she had brought him into her world.

Cassandra opened her eyes and looked at him. She came to her feet and approached him, placing her hands aside his face. "I loved her, Johnny, and I love you because you're a part of her." She took up his hand and caressed it adoringly. "I love you because your skin reminds me of her." She looked deeply into his eyes and reached up to stroke his lips. *I hate you because you destroyed her!*

Pieces of the puzzle were beginning to fit together in Johnny's mind. "That phony inheritance. You arranged that so I'd come here. You knew I would come back today."

Cassandra looked at him with no reply.

There were a hundred things Johnny wanted to know, but it was obvious Cassandra was in no mood to answer questions. He broke from her and approached Julian. He scanned down a statuesque body only partially covered by the robe. Their eyes met.

Why don't you speak to me? Tell me what you're thinking. Tell me why I'm drawn to you. Tell me why I had those dreams about you last night.

Julian stared back at him with a gaze so erotically daunting, Johnny's heart quickened. He closed his eyes to avoid letting his urges overwhelm him entirely. Issues of fact were becoming clearer in his mind, things he had to admit, things he had to face. He was beginning to understand that they had mastery over him, yet it failed to frighten him. In fact, he felt comfortable with them, safe, protected. He reached out to stroke Julian's sandy hair and the silken texture awakened the sense of touch in his fingers. From no more than that sprang the urge to devour him, to be devoured by him—did they have him there for that purpose? His eyes again drifted downward. The robe lay open, a strong brown chest and muscular thighs exposed, a man in casual repose, legs outstretched and resting on the low table, one resting upon the other. They were toying with him. Just why, he didn't know. They were different. It was like what they were meant to do, their nature. It was up to him to resist.

I was just a kid then. I don't do that anymore. I'm married.

Johnny sensed that Julian could hear his thoughts, his silent plea. Still no response. He shouldn't be tempted like this, yet his thoughts betrayed him as he stared at the parted robe. Bolder initiatives threatened to rise in his hands. He averted his eyes, aware of the long repressed inclinations stirring in his loins, and he looked at the upholstered table standing a few feet from the sofas.

He walked over to it and ran his hand over the soft vinyl-covered padding. Cassandra approached from behind and he turned to face her. She had regained her effervescent presence-of-mind, smiling, her eyes suggesting her immodest thoughts.

"It's for you, darlin'," she said reaching for the buttons of his shirt. "A massage you'll never forget."

He looked down and watched her deft fingers undo one button after another. Both what he feared and had hoped for was beginning to unfold. Years of pent-up frustration issued from every muscle and pore. It was not in him to stop her. And besides, a massage seemed innocent enough. Finding himself being undressed rendered his voice useless. He felt his body surrender. He stood in her aura with no control, wordless as he looked up and stared into her beguiling eyes. The shirt fell open and she lifted it from his shoulders. In an instant she had taken him across a bridge he would have never set foot on.

It was too real to be a dream. She was too warm to be a ghost. Whatever was happening here had gotten inside him, had become part of him. His will to resist had succumbed to the touch of a beautiful seductress.

Leaving the robe behind, Julian stepped forward and took Johnny's shirt from her hand. He draped it over his bare shoulder and went down on one knee. First the sandals, then the buttons of his fly, fingers nimble as they went about their purposeful task, a soft hand caressing the side of his damp face. He felt the jeans slide down his legs. He shivered, not as he might in the cold, but with a rush of nirvana that accompanied the feel of sudden nakedness. He stepped out of the jeans, aware of Julian's hands coming up the back of his calves, then his thighs, then higher, much like a blind man learning the shape and texture of another man's flesh. Then Julian's fingers found their way into the waistband of his briefs, and Johnny's face warmed as they too came down his legs. His cock sprang free, enraged and erect, twitching in response to Julian's hands. He lifted his feet so that Julian could free them from the underwear. He stood naked before them, his gaze captured by Cassandra's mesmeric eyes.

Tingles crossed his skin in waves and his breath came in gasps, as if he had been plunged into icy water. He felt an urge to cover himself and a profound sense of euphoria, standing before them this way as cool air settled over his moist skin. It was thrilling on a breath-taking scale, the breeziness about his swollen genitals, the sense of deliverance and the vulnerability of standing naked before a fully dressed woman that had given over her undivided attention.

Cassandra's fingertips brushed over his lips, sending chills down his back. She stepped back to allow her eyes a full sweep. "My my! What have we here?" she said, pinching the meat of his glans which caused his stiff penis to jump from her fingers.

She moved to the other side of the upholstered table and extended her hand, inviting him to lie down. Johnny stepped forward and climbed on and lowered himself on his belly. There came the sensation of her hands gliding over his legs, an altogether different kind of euphoria. If a man had to wait a third of a lifetime for this, it was worth the wait, he reasoned, drifting on the way her fingers electrified his skin and delivered sensations that melted into his muscle and bone. Her hands moved up his leg inch by inch, kneading taut muscle and exploring the contours and creases of his lower body. Never had he imagined being this exposed, sharing these forbidden places, having them explored by such curious feminine fingers. She had put him at ease, oblivious to the workings of a complicated world, oblivious to the wife at home waiting for him.

With no idea of how much time had passed and no muscle ignored, he felt the breath of her whisper upon his ear. "It's time to roll over, if you can, my beautiful, delicious man."

And he did, closing his eyes as her hands found his shoulders. He felt her fingernails trail down the length of his torso, pausing to comb his pubic hair. He felt the fondling and the weighing of his testicles on a warm palm. His penis flexed and discharged a drop of semen. The pearly white fluid snaked down the tar-like color of his sheath, the workings of a man's body familiar and noticed by Cassandra. *I'm dreaming*, he thought when she took the semen on her finger and smeared it on his lips, smiling down at him, leaning forward, licking it off. His lucid eyes drank her in. How easy it was to belong to a woman that would do such things.

The blissful minutes ran together as he drifted on the wiles of her sensual skill. She crawled up on the table and straddled him and came forward over his chest. Resting her knees aside his shoulders, a damp heat moistened his chest. He lifted his head slightly and peered into the shadows between her legs, and his head fell back, his brain sopped with images he had always assumed he would never see. Her weight lifted and he tilted his head for another glance and, to his astonishment, Cassandra had pulled the sarong up over her hips.

The red swirl of hair had emerged from the shadows, so near a fragrant humidity lay upon his face. He saw creamy white legs spread wide, their inner tendons stretched taut from her pubic mound into the flesh of her inner thighs, the rift between the folds so close that a slight tilt of his head would dampen his nose, so alluring he could hardly swallow. The fragrance was pungent and gripping, the pussy glistening and wet. He stared, the image powerful enough to bring his legs together, to tell him without a word spoken what a man's purpose was there. Then, beyond anything he would have dared to imagine, she placed her fingertips inside and pulled the lips open.

You like this, don't you, my puppy? You belong to me, my helpless little boy. Yes, yes you do.

She felt the quivers in his body and enjoyed it immensely. She arched her back and spread herself further, intending to take him to the edge.

From the wet folds came a squirt of fluid splashing his face. Odorous and warm, the taste was strong on his lips and the magic of her pheromones set him licking. He drew a breath, aware and disbelieving—his seductress had squirted him with urine. His eyes opened just as the golden flow issued fountain-like from within the pink folds, drenching, setting his mind reeling with the most perverse, intensely erotic sensations yet. A useless struggle ensued, his body pinned under her weight, his head turning from side-to-side to avoid the splash.

He found himself drawn to it, impelled to open his eyes and witness the translucent cascade that was drenching and warming his face. His mouth opened to the erratic stream, the odor steamy and unmistakable, as if within him a desire had awakened for the aromatic taste. The prominent smell engulfed him, drew him further and further into carnal oblivion, lapping as he was at the warm yellow fluid. And as the final squirts issued forth, she reached behind his head and pulled his wet face into her, smothering him in her heat and slippery secretions, relishing the sensation of his eager tongue.

The carnal storm had not passed overhead as it did the day before. Instead, it had swept him into a unexplored sea, from which there was no return to the mundane life he had always known. Now schooled in acts of debauchery, the euphoria had lightened him and made him feel weak as he lie aching for resolve, aching for something yet named. Suddenly he was aware of her body moving back toward his hips.

Her knees planted on both sides of his ribs, she lowered her weight, sodden with female emollients and lust. Impaled, she undulated and rhythmically maneuvered her hips, her wet tissues clinging and sliding on the cock. She watched his chest rise and fall, his writhing groans, the tendons of his neck growing taut as her inner muscles tightened and gripped.

Short-lived were these pleasures of the flesh—that quickly he came to the brink. His toes curled and his hands turned into fists and the spasms drew his body into pleasurable knots. The welling within his loins erupted with pulsing intensity, an endless spurting of pent-up fluids which laid waste his last remnants of strength.

More than pleased with her masterful seduction, Cassandra got off the table and stood next to the washbasin, lifting her dress to attend to the residues between her legs.

Johnny, lying on the upholstered table in a decadent fog, soiled and wet, his mind floating in drug-like haze, lay sexually spent in naked submission. No part of him would be denied the beautiful pair; no humiliation could motivate his will to resist. Then, like the next chapter in a dream, Julian stepped up to the end of the table. He took a hold of Johnny's legs and pulled his lithe body closer to his belly. Johnny raised his head and saw Julian, positioned on a small stool, lift his legs and rest them on strong bronze shoulders.

Through the fog came the reality of being taken by another man. *No! Not this! Please!* An awful torment stabbed through his mind. Was it not a surrender of his masculinity to lie there passively? Was it not an abomination to allow himself to be violated this way? Could he live with the indignity of such an act, giving over his manhood like a boy handing a prized possession to the schoolyard bully; though at that moment, intoxicated on the potent chemistry of his body, the real question was whether he wanted to live without it? They were urges as distinct as the sun's warmth and flowing from his very center. The attraction was absolute. Why deny the man who, by the mere sight of him, had given rise to undeniable desire, the man now positioned between his legs, touching him so lovingly?

He closed his eyes with a passive sigh.

How quickly he realized nothing equaled the feel of one's testicles in another man's hand, malleable as they were, and vulnerable, being pulled and fondled and squeezed. Rhetorical mores aside, what could be wrong with something that felt this good, a man sharing his body with another man, when the body willingly cried out for it? How the intimacy quickened his breath, this ongoing masculine caress, delivered by one that knew precisely how it felt. Julian's hands moved up Johnny's ribs and swept over his chest, pressing the sweetest intensity upon his nipples, pinching and pulling and turning them into small peaks, before the hands once again moved downward. Then, from the tip of Julian's finger, a chill of lubricant touched Johnny's anus. It shrank into a small kiss, a reflexive protest to the sudden intrusion. Teeth clinched, he felt the finger push deeper.

The rude shock evolved into a pleasant shimmering throughout his body, reaching his shoulders and the bottoms of his feet. The intimacy of it welled in his consciousness like the petals of a flower opening to the morning sun. Julian's finger pushed deeper, probing, stoking the slippery inner walls and setting alive countless nerve endings heretofore dormant. His hips writhed and his anus clung and pinched on the finger as it moved in and out, mingling the smell it released with the other odors in the room.

This was beyond what he could have imagined. He had given himself to a man and nothing that he could remember had ever been so disturbingly overwhelming. Other than those naïve investigations in the dorm room, nothing this perverse had ever settled over him so naturally.

Cassandra stepped up beside him with her knowing smile. She placed her hand on his hair that was still tainted with her urine.

"You made me like this," he said, looking up at her, holding his breath with another deep stab of Julian's finger. "You peed on me ..." He closed his eyes, sailing on the sensations of the finger while struggling to retain his voice. "I swallowed it ... as if it were nourishment."

"Did it nourish you, Johnny?" Her soothing tone melded with his growing calm.

"Yes," he sighed, his lips slightly parted, "... oh yes." His voice trailed in the throes of anal pleasure.

"That's good, Johnny." She ran her hand over his chest. "And now you know the pleasures of the ninth gate. Tell me, Johnny, do you like what Julian's doing?"

His eyes opened reflectively. The smell of her urine heightened the effect, the taste of it still bitter on his tongue. "Yes," he sighed. "Oh God, yes."

"Debauchery, Johnny. The province of wonderful madness."

He looked at her, yearning for understanding through pleading eyes. *Why me? Why have you chosen me?* An indoctrination of some kind? A vile, perhaps random torture? Whatever the circumstances that brought him here, it was real, as were the tingles in his underarms and nipples.

He felt Julian lift his testicles out of the way. Tilting his head, his eyes widened on Julian's cock. It suddenly grew forth in length, writhing like a snake, alive in his grip like something apart from him that must be restrained. Johnny stared in dazed horror, not believing his own eyes when a snake-like tongue flicked from the tiny hole. He had heard of these kinds of illusions in school, a kind of implausible imagery one experiences when involved with hallucinogenic drugs; but he had not taken drugs and this looked so very real.

Johnny's head fell back. *Drugged. Why do I feel drugged?*

He felt the snakelike phallus nudging at his anus. For want of reason, his thoughts shifted to the growing urges inside his belly. He wanted it; he wanted to feel it inside him. His anal flesh was mellow and slippery, the small hole gaping from Julian's finger. Then came the first push, the diameter much, much too large. His jaw fell open and his body tensed and he cried out. The ripping pain screamed out for this to stop and radiated through his entire body. His legs came together against Julian's neck, and he bore down, his jaw clenched, his hands clutching the table. The writhing cock had pushed through, a forced dilation that seemed unimaginable; though the want and anticipation still lived in his bowels.

Julian plunged deeper, stretching the small hole beyond what seemed its limit. The pain screamed, then gave way to surrender, then exquisite pleasure. Such a sweet depth, a satisfying, perfect contentment. Johnny had not done this with the boy in college. It was new to him, provoking a whole new field of thought, an act unlike what he had imagined, this sweet plundering that set electrical currents racing across his skin. More than the act itself, more than the thrusting and the slow pulling out, it was a taste of the forbidden, the having this thickness inside that redefined him. It was the fine mist that had settled over his skin, the dawn of a profound emotion born only in the coupling of two men, one aching to deposit his seed, the other aching to receive. It was the bond beyond all else, the emotional gratification, unique in man from all walks of life, a closeness brought on by the synchronization of two minds in search of one end. And yes, the pleasure, the way he could lay there and savor it, pondering the revelation of another man's penis thrusting inside him.

Johnny felt it writhing inside, just as it had in Julian's hand. An aberration? So what? It could not keep him from loving this beautiful man—nothing that felt like this could be corrupt or be defined as evil. And there was more. Johnny sensed, by looking into those haunting blue eyes, that to be loved by Julian was to be protected by him, and somehow that seemed immeasurable. No longer fearful or doubting, Johnny pictured the cock protruding from blonde curls, like a reptile vying to escape, now probing his sweetest depths. In time he might come to understand, to know who or what Julian might be, with his silence and piercing blue eyes and snakelike phallus; though for now and for whatever reason, he had been made a part of this world and he found it agreeable. He closed his eyes in pleasant thought and turned his head to the side; his body jarred by a fine rhythm, his buttocks squeezing on each thrust.

Finally the inevitable. Julian tensed and pounded harder. From his throat came a guttural moan. His hips, purposeful and unrestrained, drove forward as if he were desperate to get further in. Johnny clung to the edges of the table and grit his teeth, his body slammed hard again and again. White arms locked tight around black legs and seconds later the thrusting became a desperate push.

Johnny's legs ached in the powerful embrace. A man's body was pressed against the back of his legs, his cock pulsing and spewing, etching on his psyche the discovery of an unfamiliar new horizon, the path there forbidden but impossible to resist. What he had seen in his dreams the night before had come to pass, and now it was over. He lay in a carnal stupor, tainted with the perfumes of sex, every muscle sore or in want of rest. When Julian pulled free, he went to the sofa to recline. Johnny rolled onto his side, rendered useless, his cheek resting in the remnants of urine that had pooled under his head. He lay despoiled in this realm of decadence, breathing in the odors about him, only beginning to realize what he had done.

Cassandra approached with a towel and blotted away the urine. She cleansed him as she might a small boy, using a damp washcloth to wipe his face, his neck and shoulders and chest, moving further down to blot away the residuals of sex.

"Lift your legs, Johnny," she said cannily, as if she had foreseen the outcome of his visit. She held his testicles aside as she swathed through his crack.

He winced, the muscle there sore to the touch. As she methodically wiped away the secretions and semen, he watched her through particles of incomplete thought and questions unanswered. Had he expected any of this to happen? Did he know in the back of his mind why he came back instead of going home? There were these questions and more.

"Where did you go earlier? Nothing was here when I brought my wife. Where was all the furniture?"

She turned her back to him and dropped the washcloth into the porcelain basin.

"You're not Cassandra Mott. She died two weeks ago. A ninety-two year old woman. She left me this house. Who are you really? What have you done to me?"

She turned a deaf ear to his questions.

"How can you make me forget who I am? I have a career and a home ... and a wife." He went silent with a somber pause. Marilee's image had formed in his mind. His eyes drifted helplessly toward the ceiling as a wave of guilt set in. "I betrayed her," he said, the words spoken in angst.

Cassandra turned with her disarming smile and touched his lips. It was obvious she did not intend to reply. In frustration, he turned his head and looked at Julian.

"Why ..." he whispered, "why do I love a man who hasn't uttered a single word?"

"Not all questions have answers, darlin'," she said. That lack of seriousness was in her voice, as if life and everything about it was for nothing more than amusement.

He turned back to her. "What are you? You speak of centuries as if they were seasons of the year, but you aren't a ghost. I opened my mouth when you peed on my face. I didn't resist when Julian lifted my legs. I don't understand. Why have you brought me here?"

Her smile lingered. "Why seek answers to the obvious, Johnny? Didn't you receive pleasure from my brother? Didn't it come easily for you? Life is quite simple, darlin'. Destiny has many unexplained twists and turns. We don't have to question why. Everything is here for us to enjoy ... or oppose."

"I can't come back here, ever," he said. Something in his mind prevented true conviction, yet he went on with his unconvincing attempt. "I'll find a way to explain to my wife why I can't sell this house. I'll tell her that neither one of us can ever come back."

Cassandra's smile broadened. "You'll come back, Johnny. Part of you is here, always waiting, the part only Julian and I understand? Look at you. You're naked. You like it when I look at you. You like being touched."

"Oh God ..." he moaned. The emotional chaos wouldn't clear from his mind; but he knew. He knew the urge to return would loom out at him again. He knew with the same certainty of his need to breathe that he would come back to this parlor. Corrupted and foul, though hardly disposed to hide his nakedness, Johnny realized again how comfortable he felt in the presence of this beautiful pair, aware that he should go, though his reluctance to do so was pervasive.

He watched Cassandra stroll around the table and on toward Julian. She knelt and dropped the left strap of her gown, exposing her breast. Julian sat up and leaned forward and took the breast in both hands. He engulfed the nipple with his mouth and began sucking it like a newborn calf. In his eagerness, milk ran from the corners of his mouth and dripped from his chin. Johnny looked on, entranced.

Cassandra's attention shifted to Johnny, her face radiant and flush with nurturing passion. Her cunning eyes fixed on him, the message clear, an invitation, a dare. Johnny forgot that Marilee would be worried. He got off the table and slowly approached the sofa and sat down, his shoulder and leg pressed against Julian's, their contrasting skin lost on everyone except Cassandra. When she lowered the other strap, his thoughts went blank but for the nipple—it had gathered and was supple and irresistible. She cupped the breast as an offering, drawing him closer. He leaned forward and his mouth closed on the nipple and he sucked with the instinct of a new babe.

Enraptured by two men side-by-side at her breasts, Cassandra placed her hands at the back of their heads and held them close. Her milk flowed over their tongues in streams. Bittersweet, they went at it like gluttons.

"Yes," she whispered. "That's it ... that's how it's done. Fill your bellies my lovely boys."

Their enthusiasm finally waned. Her breasts were barren. She wrapped her arms around them and pulled them tight to her chest and stroked the back of their heads. A long moment passed before Johnny pulled free. A cramp had formed in his belly. He leaned forward and hugged himself with his arms. He weaved and yawed and rolled onto the floor. A kaleidoscope of colors and images flashed in his mind, liquid colors flung from a spinning top. His knees drew up and he wrapped his arms around them. A sense of freefalling swept over him accompanied by almost maddening indescribable pleasure. He rocked and floated on the sensation, let it carry him like a leaf in the wind. He could feel Cassandra's eyes and the exhilaration of his own nakedness.

When it passed he sat up, realizing vaguely that he had to leave, that his wife would be worried and awaiting him. Through a mental fog, scanning the area for his clothes, he spotted them on the other sofa where Julian had folded and placed them. He came wearily to his feet and began to dress.

Julian took a position next to his sister. Sitting side-by-side, the beautiful pair watched Johnny step into his sandals and walk toward the door. He stopped and looked back with a long, fixed gaze.

"Tomorrow, Johnny?" Cassandra said.

"Tomorrow?" Johnny looked down at the floor in thought, then back up. "I..."

"A friend of mine will be here. He arrived today from Germany. He's planning to spend a few days in Savannah. You might be interested in meeting him."

It was a game to her. Johnny could see that, despite his skewed presence-of-mind. A game of intrigue. Her invitation for him return, her tone—it all suggested that she knew he would come, that he would be curious about meeting one of her friends.

One of her friends?

Johnny turned his head in thought. Was this strange world comprised of more than just the two of them? Fascinated for a number of reasons, he wondered what sort of person, other than himself, she might bring into this house.

He looked at her. "From Germany?"

"Yes. Gerhard Trent. I've known him a long time."

A long time? How long ... a year, a decade, a century? "Why me, Cassandra?"

Her knowing smile brightened. "Because, darlin', I'm sure you would be charmed by all of my friends. Especially a man like Gerhard, knowing your penchant for massage. He's a masseuse. He specializes in sensual massage."

Johnny's eyes drifted back to the floor. The notion of seeing others here from the outside world had not occurred to him. He glanced back at her, wondering if this man was as peculiar as the brother and sister Mott.

"When?"

"Tomorrow afternoon."

Johnny felt an urge to defy her. He turned and walked out of the room without another word said. He had not replied to her invitation, believing that a small intrigue of his own, a tiny defiance, but defiance nonetheless, might preserve his will and what was left of his manhood. But at the back of his mind he knew a reply had not been necessary. He knew the suggestive nature of her invitation would crawl on his skin like ants; that try as he might, now that she had claimed a significant piece of his soul, he could never gather the will to resist one of her whims.

Chapter 6

Stepping from the curb into Confederate Square, Johnny started toward a bench, beleaguered by what was happening to him. He staggered and collapsed, catching his weight with his hands. The shaded grass felt cool on his palm. The warm spring air felt clean and vibrant as it swirled through his nostrils. Maybe the fresh air and humidity had affected him. Maybe that's what caused the roiling to return in his stomach. He considered crawling to the bench; but instead sat up and clasped his arms around his knees, rocking back and forth while the demons cleared from his head and belly. He opened his eyes and noticed a young couple staring at him in passing. Yuppie types, he called them, their cameras ready and summer clothes perfectly pressed. They stared at him as if he were an indigent, most likely depraved on cheap wine. Here and there across the square, others were staring as well.

He didn't care.

Nor did he care what time of day it might be, or whether he had important things to do, or what anyone thought of his wretchedness, including Marilee. After all, where in her tiny world could he find solace? A sense of isolation settled over him. He had no one to talk to, no one to confide in, no one that could explain the goings-on inside that house. Who would believe or not scoff at what he had to say? Who could salvage what the beautiful pair had left of him, now that he had been exposed to Cassandra Mott's world of debauchery?

Johnny's eyes lifted and rested on the house.

Born in the remnants of pain still radiating from his rectum, images emerged in his mind as he pondered the ramifications of having sex with another man. It had come over him like a need. The wanting of it had massed in the crease of his buttocks. Why? He wasn't gay. Those fleeting incidents in the past hardly justified lifting his legs for Julian—he had been young then, and curious, and single. They had been naïve episodes, a boy exploring ion. Stepping out of the tiled stall, he felt more like himself, cleansed, as if the shower had transported him back from a supernatural world to his own. He walked into the bedroom, blotting his face with a towel, startled when he looked up and saw Marilee sitting on the edge of the bed.

He wrapped the towel around his waist, feeling the weight of her troubled expression. A painful silence filled the room. It wasn't anger sniping from her eyes, more like indicting concern. The walls that had comforted him were closing in. His toes pinched at the carpet as he stood in the glare of the late afternoon sunlight that spilled in through the window. Guilt had crept from his blindside and covered him like unwanted oil. He felt it coating his tongue and on the palms of his hands, promising a torture he felt loathe to bear. He had betrayed his wife, and though she didn't know, a near equivalent of that kind of hurt came through her eyes and scorched his face. Nothing entered his mind that might direct them away from the unwieldy silence that had iced-over the room.

"Where were you?" she finally asked.

"I was going to ask you the same thing," he said in want of a rational defense.

"I went out to look for you. For an hour, Johnny, worried sick. I couldn't find you."

"Don't ever go out looking for me again," he snapped. It was a reflexive burst of anger, surprising even himself, followed by immediate frustration. Her face jumped from concern to shock. He backed up to the wall and let his head fall back against it. "It's just that ..." What could he say? Her shock transformed into hurt and stabbed his heart. "I'm sorry, Marilee. I didn't mean to yell. It's just that there for a second it seemed you didn't trust me or something."

"Trust? How could you think it's a matter of trust? What if something happened to you? I was worried sick!" A tear ran down her cheek and she reached up to wipe it away. "So where were you?"

He had never lied to her before, but he could not tell her he had gone back into the house. That alone would not account for the time he had been gone, and would likely lead to difficult questions. "I went down to Factor's Row. Drank a couple of beers and watched the boats on the river. The time got by me, that's all."

"You couldn't call me?"

"I'm sorry."

"Why take a shower this time of day? You never do that."

He looked at her, frustrated. She wasn't about to let it go. "How do you know what I do in the afternoon? You're gabbing on the phone half the time, or out doing something for the church."

"Johnny ... that's not true."

"So I took a shower. It's warm out today. The walk made me feel sweaty."

Her eyes shifted here and there as she tried to comprehend his odd behavior. Marilee sensed something was wrong, not just because of his nervous demeanor, but also in how he had spent the afternoon. It was the first time she could remember that he wasn't obsessing over his project. It didn't make sense that he would wile away the better part of the day on the riverfront.

Johnny averted his eyes from his unsettled wife, feeling the consternation of breaking mankind's most sacred vow. More so than ever before, he felt the distance between them. His anger, that subconscious wall thrown up to protect him from the ravages of guilt, had begun to fade. Or perhaps the anger had made an inward turn. He felt out of place in his own home, like he was some kind of contaminate ruining a field of daisies.

But he wasn't the only one here contributing to a dysfunctional household. Marilee's religion was getting on his nerves. Everything about her righteous persona collided with what he had learned about himself in the last two days. If only he and Marilee knew how to talk to each other, he would sit down beside her, tell her that something very powerful had taken a hold of him, something paranormal that caused him to do things he would never do. Yes, paranormal. What other explanation could there be? Again, he felt utterly alone in the world. If only he had never entered that house. But he had and there was no going back. To hope for her understanding, to hope that she might help him break Cassandra's spell was useless. Marilee would interpret the whole scenario as nothing more than a husband gone astray, coupled with the fact that she simply couldn't deal with such things.

There was no reason to try to talk to her about this. The outcome all too predictable. The sin of adultery was well defined in the Bible, and in Marilee's mind. There was no wiggle room when it came down to sins of the flesh. Not with her. It wasn't a matter of being spiritual—she needed her faith confirmed by something tangent, the bricks and mortar of a church. It never occurred to her that there were thousands of religions in the world, many radically different from her own, and all of them concocted at some point in history by man. Rather than use the brain God gave her to interpret the world around her, solutions to life's problems could only be found by way of her complete confidence in the church.

"I just felt like I needed a walk, a little fresh air," he said, piecing together his part of the conversation from a thousand flecks of thought. Under the circumstances, it was difficult to reassure her that there was nothing to worry about. "You know, with these deadlines and all, I feel a little burned out."

"You got another call from Globalcorp. Evidently you forgot to call them back."

Shit...! Johnny had forgotten about that. Nodding with resentment, he looked at his wife and said: "That's what I mean. The pressure never stops." He wondered if he had the motivation to get some work done before dinner, but the thought of scooting his stool up to the drafting table seemed like an unwanted burden.

"Shouldn't you call them?"

He released a sigh. "Yeah. I'll call them."

Funny how awkward he felt in the towel in front of his own wife, when he felt at ease with Cassandra looking at him completely naked. He went the closet for clean clothes. When he returned, he stood near the bed watching Marilee tidy up the bathroom. She picked up his soiled clothes and paused as if she had noticed something. She looked at the bundle for a moment, and then brought it closer to her nose. Holding the shirt up with one hand, she inspected it, then shrugged and pushed it all into the hamper.

Johnny breathed a sigh of relief. *I'll have to be more careful.*

A few minutes later, hunched over the unfinished work spread before him, Johnny sat staring at the phone near the back of the drafting table. When he came back around to matters-at-hand, he picked up a pencil and tapped it on the wooden surface, yawning. He moved the sketches and graphics around, looking for a place to start. It all seemed like a thankless, superficial task. His head nodded. Suddenly he could barely keep his eyes open. The pencil fell from his hand and rolled onto the floor. He lowered his head and rested it on folded arms atop the papers, sound asleep seconds later.

The smell of roast beef wafting from the kitchen awoke him at six o'clock. Lifting his head, he glanced across the unfinished work and then looked at his watch, realizing the day had passed without so much as a pencil touching paper. His computer had not been turned on all day. The full belly he had leaving Cassandra's parlor was growling with hunger. The high-strung executives at Globalcorp could wait. He'd call them later. He stepped down off the stool.

Marilee placed a salad in front of him when he took his place at the table.

"What was Globalcorp calling about?" she asked when she joined him.

"Oh, uh, I figure they want to know how the graphics are coming on their cosmetic line. Thought I'd call 'um after I get a little more finished."

She had been shaking pepper on her salad. Her hand stopped and her eyes lifted with concern. He still had not returned their call. She looked at him a good while before her eyes shifted to the table in thought. Dinner proceeded quietly after that, as did the evening they spent together in the den. For two hours he stared at a movie on TV, unaware of what it was about. He didn't notice Marilee looking at him from time to time.

He drifted into the bedroom a few minutes after Marilee went to bed, turning the light on in the closet when he went in. There was a stiff dry stain inside the fly of his white silk pajama bottoms that showed through when he held them up to the light, the byproduct of last night's dreams. He draped them over his forearm and took a clean pair from the shelf, and then took the soiled ones into the bathroom and stuffed them into the hamper. Scratching himself absently, he stepped up to the sink to brush his teeth.

Johnny studied his reflection in the mirror. He still looked the same, but he felt older, less naïve, changed. This time he was looking at a man harboring secrets and unsettled emotions. Then it dawned on him that he was about to get into bed with the woman he had betrayed, that she would be lying innocently beside him, still believing in him, still loving him. Nothing could hurt her more than to learn what he had done. He also knew he was looking at a man that would assuredly do it again. Reaching into the drawer for his toothbrush, it occurred to him that his willingness to participate in such vile acts must be rooted in his genes; that it must have been a part of him all along. How is it, he wondered, one doesn't realize these things?

♦ ♦ ♦

Johnny awoke unsettled. Marilee had scooted close to him and slept with her arm draped over his chest. He looked at her stiffly, unable to remember the last time she slept that close to him. They had gotten through his misdeed the day before, though it had caused him to recognize something about their marriage. There was distance between them, and he still felt it as he carefully moved her arm and eased off the bed, then went quietly into the closest for his robe.

After making a pot of coffee, he went into the garden room and sat staring at the full cup until eight o'clock, the hour he hoped Cassandra Mott's lawyer would arrive at his office. Sifting through the papers atop his drawing board, he found the calling card Samuel McPhereson had left. Below the phone number were his office hours—nine to four o'clock in the afternoon.

One more hour. He released an impatient sigh.

Marilee had gotten up and set about doing the laundry. She had not ventured into the room. *Probably still pissed-off about me yelling at her.* He walked to the French doors and stared across the back yard, oblivious to the fact that it was his favorite time of the year: everything green and fresh, the morning sun warm and inviting. He turned to make sure he was alone before pushing his hand into the pajama bottoms. He reached between his legs and touched the tender flesh around his anus. It was still sore, a reminder of whom he had become. *It doesn't matter. Besides, no one has to know, do they?* It wasn't like Cassandra Mott planned to broadcast his indiscretions to the entire world. He let his forehead rest against the glass. So he had willingly lifted his legs for another man, so what? It happened. His real problem was figuring out just who or what Cassandra and Julian Mott really are.

He dialed Samuel McPhereson's number at nine o'clock. An electronic message came through the phone.

"Sorry, this is not a working number."

Johnny's fist tightened on the receiver. The phone moved several inches from his ear. He sat staring at the wall for a long while, not expecting this; but in thinking about it, he wasn't surprised. He hung up the phone and then dialed the number again. Same electronic answer. That feeling of solitude settled back over him. Then his eyes settled on the phonebook. He grabbed it and began tearing through the pages, looking for Arlene Landrum's number. Her maid answered and Johnny waited as she took the phone out to the veranda.

"Hello."

"Thank God. Uh ... Miss Arlene, do you know if Cassandra Mott has any other personal friends? Anyone who's known her for a while?"

"Johnny Feelwater ... is that you?"

"Yeah, uh, sorry, it's me." Johnny replied eagerly.

"Good mornin', young man. Nice to hear from you. I really enjoyed our last visit."

"Yes! Me, too. Please, do you know anyone that knew her personally?"

"Is something wrong? You sound upset."

Johnny cupped his hand over the receiver. He closed and rubbed his eyes. *Calm down, dammit.* He drew a deep breath and put the phone back to his ear. "No, ma'am. Nothing's wrong. Guess I'm still curious about Cassandra. Figured I might talk to others who knew her personally. A gardener or a maid, maybe. Anyone that might've known her."

"Well, let's see ... I'm afraid she didn't have many friends, not in her later years. Time passes so quickly, you know. Most of our friends are gone."

"Anyone at all. Maybe she mentioned a name when you were visiting."

"I met her doctor one day when I was there. Called himself Basil Salazar. I remember thinking it an odd name. A dreary, stooped little man. Seemed he really didn't want to be there that day."

Johnny scribbled down the name.

"A local doctor then?" he asked.

"That was my impression, yes," said Mrs. Landrum. "Seems I remember him saying he planned to close his practice and leave Savannah."

"Thank-you," said Johnny, pulling the phone book closer. "Hope I wasn't a bother this early in the day."

"No bother, young man. I'll be looking forward to our next visit."

Johnny hung up, thinking about Samuel McPhereson. The man had played a convincing role as a lawyer. Maybe he *was* a lawyer. Maybe he was somehow in cahoots with Cassandra, hired to cover the legal side of protecting her house until she could come back and take possession again. Johnny thought it might be a good idea to stop in at the records building and see what he could find out there.

He jumped. Marilee's voice had startled him.

"Who were you talking to?" she asked.

He spun around. "Good lord! Didn't know you were there." He scratched the top of his head, thinking fast. "Did I tell you about Arlene Landrum, the little old lady I met in Confederate Square?"

"No."

"That first day I went to see the Mott house. She and Cassandra were lifelong friends. She lives alone. I called to see how she was doing."

Marilee stepped up beside him. She glanced at the phone book and his cup full of cold coffee. "I'm worried about you."

"Why?"

"Look at you. You're fidgeting. You tossed and turned all night."

He wasn't even aware he had slept. "I don't know what it is, Marilee. Hope I didn't keep you awake."

"It didn't bother me. I just don't like seeing you this way. You'd tell me if something's bothering you?"

"Sure."

She nodded at his cup. "Can I get you some more coffee?"

"I'll get some later."

She turned and started for the door, wondering why her husband seemed so antsy, turning back before leaving the room. "I put that message from Globalcorp on your drawing board. Upper left hand corner."

"I saw it."

She stared at him for a moment, doubtfully. "Don't forget to call them."

"I'll call them. Don't worry about it."

He grabbed the phonebook the second she disappeared, leafing through the pages. *Salazar... Salazar... ah, there it is!* He jotted down the address and stood off the stool, looking at the unfinished work sprawled across the drawing table. *I'll get some of that done as soon as I get back.*

Hands in his pockets, he approached Marilee, who was wiping down the counter in the kitchen. The phone rang and he watched her move toward it. "I'm going out," he said just as she picked up the phone, glad it rang. She would want to know his reason for leaving. The call took away her chance to question him. "I'll be back in a little while," he said over his shoulder, half way to the front door before she could think to respond.

The phone did not make it to Marilee's ear. She held it in her hand, suddenly oblivious to the call, staring dumbly toward the hallway. She heard the front door slam and then stood at a loss for a long while. Not thinking to hang up the phone, she set it on the counter and headed for the garden room. There she saw the unfinished work spread across his drafting table, his phone book resting open atop the graphics, the message from Globalcorp still exactly where she had taped it. She backed up, dazed, and sat down, staring at nothing, trying to fathom her husband's very sudden, very strange behavior.

Johnny found the address in an area heavily populated by professionals, mostly medical related. Basil Salazar was in an older restored building. His practice was located on the second floor. Johnny stood at the base of a stairway looking up at a door with Salazar's number on it, thinking the hallway looked dimly lit for a doctor's office. After ascending the stairs he entered a small, rather melancholy waiting room. There was a doorbell button on the back wall next to a sliding window. Johnny approached, unable to see through the frosted glass. A buzzer behind the wall sounded when he pressed the button.

"Who's out there?" The voice belonged to an older man with a foreign accent, perhaps Austrian.

"My name's Johnny Feelwater," Johnny called back.

"I'm taking no new patients, Mr. Feelwater," the doctor's blunt reply.

"I'm not here for that. I'd like to talk to you for a moment." Johnny didn't like shouting through the closed window.

He heard a shuffling sound and then a door three or four feet from the window opened up. Out stepped a drab, paunchy, older gentleman. His sagging expression suggested he didn't appreciate the interruption.

"Are you Dr. Salazar?"

"Of course I am. Who else would I be? And I'm not interested in buying anything, so if ..."

"I'm not a salesman," Johnny interrupted. "I've come to ask you about Cassandra Mott."

Chapter 7

Basil Salazar stiffened. An unmistakable fear came into his eyes, as if Johnny had threatened to drill holes in his teeth.

"I was told you were her doctor before she died," Johnny explained.

Salazar squinted with suspicion. A moment later his eyes darted about the room before settling on his unwelcome visitor. He was fidgeting. "What does that have to do with you?"

"I inherited her house." Johnny no longer believed this, but he wanted to establish his connection with Cassandra.

Salazar studied him for a moment. His expression softened by a degree or two, as if this had given Johnny's visit some legitimacy.

"Well," he said gruffly, "she died of natural causes in her own bed. Old age more than anything, I'd say. There had been a few problems with her heart."

Johnny stared at the doctor as if he expected to hear more.

"What else do you want to know?"

"Uh, I hardly know anything about her. Did you know her well?"

"She was a patient and an old woman. A demanding old woman. I shan't miss her."

Johnny's curiosity surged. Salazar obviously knew her quite well. "Were you her doctor long?"

Salazar's patience seemed to have already run out. "Look young man, I'm busy. I have nothing more to say about Cassandra Mott."

Johnny sensed the old doctor was deliberately holding something back, as if he had a reason for evading questions about Cassandra. If so, Johnny wanted to know why. He was determined to hear everything Salazar knew about the Motts, determined to stay until he did. He would not be put off so easily.

"Suppose her ghost still lives in that house," he stated frankly.

The look of fear returned to Salazar's eyes, more vividly this time. It appeared he might swoon. He staggered across the small room and took a seat on one of the well-worn chairs, staring straight ahead in thought. His eyes finally shifted to Johnny.

"Why would you say something like that?" he wanted to know.

Johnny took a deep breath, not certain he wanted to say it, thinking Salazar might pass him off as a nut. He decided to take the risk. "Because I've seen her."

Salazar's gaze drifted down to the floor. His mental presence seemed to have left the room. "She's back," he said, a thought spoken out loud. "Already."

"What do you mean, *she's back*? I don't understand. Do you believe her ghost has come back?"

"She has no ghost, young man. She doesn't need one."

Johnny's puzzlement increased. "She doesn't need one?"

"I want you to leave. I told you I have nothing to say about Cassandra Mott."

Johnny looked at the old man, put off by his rude defiance. He wasn't about to go. He had come here to learn about Cassandra and he intended to choke it out of the old doctor if necessary.

"Mister, I'm in turmoil here. I've come to you for some answers. You'll tell me what I want to know or else I'll stay here all day."

Salazar looked at him, appraising a serious young man quite large enough to issue a viable threat. Salazar also recognized Johnny's desperate need to know, proof positive that he very well may have seen Cassandra Mott. He folded his hands and leaned forward and looked at the floor for a moment. Then he looked up, his eyes sharp and direct.

"You did *not* inherit that house," he stated flatly.

Johnny looked at him for a moment before asking: "Her lawyer said I did."

"That's a laugh!"

"Go on, tell me more."

"You're asking about a woman who ruined my life. God knows what she'd do if she found out I was talking to you."

Johnny studied him. Salazar seemed like a man treading water in a bottomless sea. "Then I'll go out of my way to mention it to her, if you don't explain what you're talking about!"

A look of defeat reddened Salazar's face. "Tell me, how old is she?"

Johnny turned his head in thought. "Middle twenties."

Salazar's face reflected an old sadness. Then he opened up, as if all of a sudden a lifetime of pent-up frustration needed to pour out. "Ah yes, a great beauty no doubt." He seemed to be picturing her. "She was closer to forty when I first met her, though she looked much younger. I was just out of college, ready to start my own practice. She financed it. Became one of my first patients. I realized there was something extraordinary about her during her first examination. To my amazement, she was lactiferous. I knew she wasn't pregnant, never had been. Anyway, not long after she seduced me with her money, she seduced me with her body. For a while I felt like the luckiest man on earth ... for a very short while. I've spent a lifetime paying for it, catering to her whims. My intentions were to get out of Savannah before she came back." He looked up at Johnny. "So you think you inherited her house? You'd do well by forgetting that notion. If she's decided to stay in Savannah, she'll live another lifetime there. She'll never leave that house."

"But her lawyer delivered papers to my home. Legal and binding documents."

"Sure they were," scoffed Salazar. "Her lawyer you say? I met that pompous old fart shortly before she died. I couldn't get a straight answer out of him; not even where his office is located. The inheritance must have been a ploy to keep the house out of probate or something. Believe me, she's using the both of you to preserve her precious house. My only question is: why did she choose you?" Salazar's eyes raked over his visitor. "I bet she was attracted to your black skin."

"There's more to it than that. My grandmother and Cassandra were lovers."

Salazar' jaw dropped. "Your grandmother? Emily Hinton?"

"Yes."

"Well, that explains something. Just what, I wouldn't know."

It was all piling up in Johnny's head like unwanted weight, still making no sense to him at all.

Salazar could see his discomfiture. He felt a twinge of affinity for the young man, thinking it likely that he too had fallen prey to the ageless seductress.

"I still don't understand what you're talking about," said Johnny.

Salazar nodded at the chair across from him. "Sit down and I'll tell you what I know about her. But first give me a minute. I'll be right back."

The old doctor came to his feet and disappeared into the back room, returning a couple of minutes later with a book in his hand. He handed it to Johnny.

"That may answer some of your questions. Most view what is written in that book as pure fiction, except those few who know otherwise. You and I for example." He plopped again in his chair, tilting his head in thought, combing through years gone by. "Well, let me just say that I had intended to become a great surgeon; but what am I? More or less a gynecologists, and a pill supplier to some of Savannah's most illustrious personalities, thanks to the woman in question."

Johnny was still lost in a confusing muddle of words. He looked at the book, *Unexplained Facts About the Supernatural*, and then looked back at the doctor.

"She reincarnates herself. There's much I don't know, and most of what I believe about her came from that book you hold in your hand. It was written by a man named Dr. Brian Fowler. I've pieced certain things together over the years that match what Dr. Fowler has written from his studies on the subject. You'll see what I mean when you read it. The best I can make out is that she has reincarnated herself some thirty to fifty times over two or three millennia."

Salazar produced his first smile, though it came weighted with regret. "I see you're a little stupefied, Mr. Feelwater. Consider this: She mentioned during the course of one of our conversations something Julius Caesar once said in a political speech, as if she had heard it with her own ears, which I believe she did. Then she changed the subject when I questioned her about it. That was one of the first clues. She lets her guard down, unintentionally of course, like the time I heard her talking about how beautiful Pompeii was before Mount Vesuvius buried it. How far back does that date her?" He shrugged with irony. "Funny; I've known her all these years and most of what there is to know about her is still a mystery."

The old doctor paused in thought, shaking his head as if he himself found all of this implausible. Then he went on. "Dr. Fowler believes their power increases with each reincarnation. I don't know about that, but I do know she has incredible power. I'm certain she has at least some control over matter, such as making things disappear." He paused again before going with his next thought. "For whatever reason, she doesn't use her powers casually. Maybe because they're exhaustible, or maybe because unexplainable acts makes it difficult to assimilate in human society, I don't know. But when you're in her presence, be wary Mr. Feelwater. She *will* know what you're thinking."

He stared at Johnny for a moment before asking: "Do these things surprise you?"

Johnny shifted his weight in the chair. Surprise him? Shock would be a better word. Trying to sort through what Salazar had been saying, his response was slow in coming. "Uh ... yeah, it does surprise me. How is all of that possible? I've been trying to come to grips with the possibility she's a ghost of some kind. You make her sound like an all-powerful witch."

Pursing his lips, Salazar nodded thoughtfully. "I suppose she could be called a witch. After all, the rather broad definition of the term fits, doesn't it? But I assure you, not a witch like those found in American folklore. Woe is the Salem forebear that had tried to burn Cassandra Mott at the stake."

Johnny was staring at a cluttered magazine rack, contemplating what he knew about Cassandra, combining that with what Dr. Salazar had revealed about her. It all seemed like a new twist on Savannah mythology. How could such an exquisite, sensual woman be evil, or be described by such words as Dr. Salazar was using? But, despite his inclination to disbelieve these outlandish assumptions, it added up. Had she not made a houseful of furniture disappear? Had she not taunted him, made him desirous of acts he would have otherwise never considered? Had she not lived early in the last century when that photograph on Arlene Landrum's mantel was taken? The questions were complicated and numerous. Would he be able to resist her power? Would he want to, now that his body was sending messages that could not be ignored; when what he felt was not fear or revulsion, but something much closer to adoration, though her own doctor had rationally called her a witch.

"So tell me, Mr. Feelwater, what has your experience been with this woman thus far?"

Johnny looked at him. It was a question he couldn't answer, for what had transpired between him and Cassandra and Julian could be confided to no one.

"We're, uh ... I guess you could say we're acquaintances."

"I'm sure!" said the doctor a bit too sarcastically. He let out a sort of mocking laugh. "Don't worry about getting her pregnant. She's infertile. Nevertheless, you don't have to tell me. If you've been inside that house for as long as an hour, I already know."

Johnny swallowed what felt like a lump. His thoughts shifted to Julian. "Did you know her brother?" he asked.

"You're speaking of Julian?"

"Yes."

"He died a young man shortly before I met Cassandra. I never had a chance to meet him."

"He's there with her now," said Johnny.

Salazar looked astonished. "He's there? I don't understand. If he's capable of coming back, why didn't he do so during her last life? She grew old. Lived all alone in that monstrous house. If he has the power to reincarnate, why didn't he join her when she was old and frail?"

Of course Johnny had no idea what the explanation might be. He shrugged. "All I know is he's there."

"What does he look like?"

Johnny sighed as Julian's image formed in his mind. "A little shorter than me, muscular but not bulky, maybe twenty-five, blonde. He has blue eyes that seem to look right through you, and he never speaks. I'm not sure he can."

The doctor listened thoughtfully. Then his eyes widened with a revelation. "Of course ... her house boy! I never gave it much thought, perhaps because she prevented it, but your description matches the houseboy she had until a few years ago. I remember thinking there was something strange about the arrangement, but then passed it off. That must have been Julian!" Salazar's thoughts carried the theory even further. "After that there was a yardman. It seemed he was always in the shadows. I never got a good look at him. I'd bet my mutual funds that both the houseboy and the gardener were Julian." His contemplation continued. "I wonder ..."

Johnny waited but Salazar didn't finish the sentence. The conversation seemed too bizarre to be credible. "So you think Julian reincarnates with her?"

"Who knows, for God's sake? But what about this: Just before her death she instructed me to make sure her body wasn't moved from her bed until a scar appeared just above her belly. I was stunned. I remember her frail hand lifting her nightgown to show me exactly where it would be. She issued a warning: Anyone who tried to move her before the scar appeared would regret it. It horrified me. But think about it. Could that be Julian's purpose, to remove something from her body, an organ or internal tissue that would be used as a catalyst for her reincarnation? How does a scar appear without someone cutting her open?"

"Oh God!" Johnny cried softly.

"What's wrong, Mr. Feelwater? Beginning to doubt your judgment in coming here?"

"I can't stand the confusion," he said, almost pleading. "You're resentment raises more questions than answers."

"Uh huh. I can see you're attached to her. You reject the notion she's evil."

"She's not evil!"

"There, you see."

"She's not evil!" Johnny insisted. "Maybe she does have those powers. Reincarnation? That's no longer too difficult to believe, but she's not evil. Satan is evil."

"Where do such powers come from, if not Satan? Ask yourself that, Mr. Feelwater." Salazar glanced at Johnny's hand and back up. "I see a wedding band on your finger. How has your acquaintance with Cassandra Mott affected your relationship with your wife? Are you still inspired to mount your wife after a taste of one of the most sensuous women that ever lived?"

Salazar's question hit home. A taste? Yes, he had been given a taste. The memory of it was still vivid on his tongue. Prior to knowing Cassandra, he had already lost most of the physical attraction that he once had for his wife; but yes, knowing her would most certainly impact his marriage. It already had. Not that Marilee wasn't lovely, she was—it was just that their love making had become a thankless task. And those occasions were rare. Her righteous indignation served only to stiffen her body. Seducing her meant lowering her pajamas no more than pragmatically necessary. Enter Cassandra Mott, a woman whose smile, whose suggestive eyes, whose every nuance inflamed a man's desire.

Johnny sat uncomfortably. It was anything but clear whether this conversation with Dr. Salazar had resolved his questions, though it had certainly created multiples of those still unanswered. He tightly clutched the book in his hand, as if it were a lifeline.

Salazar's expression took on a sad, reminiscent cast. "I married my high school sweetheart," he said looking at and rubbing the ring finger that bore no ring. "Her name was Betty. Our lives together began with many wonderful dreams, none of which were compatible with Cassandra Mott's aspirations. You see, if she wants you in her life, there's no room for anyone else. She wants you all to herself. I believe to this day that Cassandra arranged for my wife's death."

"My God!"

"It's true. I believe it sincerely."

"What happened to her?" Johnny asked.

"Struck down by a car while crossing the street. I'll never forget the gleam in Cassandra's eyes when I told her what happened."

Johnny believed that the doctor, in loving memory of his wife, must have embellished the cause of her death over the years. He had literally called Cassandra a murderer, simply too much of a stretch, especially since Salazar seemed ready to blame Cassandra for any bit of bad luck that had ever befallen him. He looked at the stack of packed boxes waiting to be carried out. "Where will you go?" he asked.

Salazar shook his head. "No living soul in Savannah will know that."

"You really are afraid of her, aren't you?"

"As you should be," Salazar said bluntly. "But you don't know that, and you don't believe me. I can see it in your eyes. No doubt you will go to her as soon as you leave here."

Johnny studied him for a moment. "You seem calmer than when I first saw you."

"Ah," the doctor smiled, "I suppose I owe you debt of gratitude. Never had the opportunity to have this conversation before. It's refreshing to talk to someone who doesn't automatically write me off as a lunatic. You become reclusive. You can't identify with anyone else. This chat has lifted a burden I've carried silently for a long time. Even though you don't believe everything I say, I finally feel like I have a little sympathy. I wish there was something I could say to help you, to prevent your demise, but I know better. You're skeptical. You think I'm a cynical old man, sour because my life didn't turn out the way I wanted it to."

Johnny released a sigh. "I don't know what to believe, Dr. Salazar, but I appreciate you taking time to see me."

"There's something else I'm curious about, Mr. Feelwater. How much do you know about your grandmother, Emily Hinton?"

"Very little."

"So I have assumed. She and your mother were at odds. You see, I know because Emily was also a patient of mine. She spoke to me about these things. I remember providing a shoulder for a very depressed young woman. It's true she was every bit as eccentric as Cassandra, but she was also human, with human emotions. It tore at her heart that she couldn't see her own grand baby."

Johnny's eyes had become watery.

"Sorry if I distressed you, young man, but I thought you might like to know. Emily wasn't like Cassandra. A prolific sinner, yes; but very human." Salazar looked at his palms in thought. "I must say, the two of them were a striking pair."

"Wish I could have known her," said Johnny.

"Of course you do." Salazar glanced at his watch, and then studied his visitor for a moment. "Whatever you choose to believe about what I've said today, believe this: Cassandra Mott didn't leave you her house. She drew you into her life for some reason. I think it's because you're Emily's grandson. I can't help but believe there's more to it than you being a virile, handsome young man. Handsome young men are a dime a dozen in her world." Salazar looked at him for a moment. "Yes, she had a reason." He paused with a cynical laugh. "But in actuality, Cassandra's motives are anyone's guess."

Johnny thought about it for a moment. He felt he could confide in the doctor at least this much: "She did tell me I remind her of my grandmother. Obviously you know how close they were."

"Close! That's an understatement if ever I heard one. They were like two individuals operating under the influence of one very bizarre mind. They had a physical attraction for each other the likes of which I haven't seen again in my lifetime. Obsessed with each other to the extent it could be embarrassing to be around them. Their passion for living was boundless."

Johnny could envision such passion in a woman like Cassandra. It saddened him that their great love came to a premature and tragic end. It saddened him more that he had not had a chance to know his grandmother, that his mother never spoke of or acknowledged her.

He came to his feet.

"I've taken enough of your time, Dr. Salazar. Thanks for seeing me. And thanks for the book. How will I get it back to you?"

Salazar waved it off with his hand. "Keep it. It's yours. I've memorized every word in it."

"Thanks again," Johnny said, starting for the door. He turned with a look of concern just before stepping out.

Salazar smiled and nodded. "God speed, young man."

Johnny turned and hurried down the stairs, squinting in the sunlight when he reached the street. It had been a long walk to that part of the historic district. He decided against a cab, stopping in the first square he came to. There, on a shaded bench, he looked hard at the well-worn book cover. Inside, the table of contents listed three sections: *The Myths of Vampires*, *The Spells of Witches*, and the last section, *Unexplained Elements of the*

Paranormal. The book was written by an antiquities professor at an eastern university, a Dr. Brian Fowler. Apparently the man was also a medical doctor, as mentioned in his bio inside the back cover.

A bit queasy in reading it, Johnny did not want his mind contaminated by superstition, rejecting out of hand that Cassandra Mott was evil. Yet he could not avoid reading it; and as he glanced over the words in the third section, he began to realize that Dr. Fowler might as well have been writing about Cassandra. The professor referred them as *entities*, not ghosts, describing a theory about how they rejuvenate themselves time and again over hundreds, even thousands of years; a process akin to reincarnation. Within the dog-eared pages, Fowler claimed to have come upon two such entities, and had studied them inconspicuously over a long period of time.

Johnny read on.

Fowler theorized about how these entities create great wealth from one life to the next, how they become adept at protecting it, how they take on the same personality with each new life and establish themselves among succeeding generations of the human populace, sometimes very nearly replicating a previous life, while at other times establishing themselves in completely different parts of the world. Evidently uncertain whether the entities could evolve into different body types or into a different race or sex, Fowler *was* certain of their supernatural power, documenting his suspicions that these powers increase with each reincarnation. The powers included the ability to read minds, extrasensory perception, the ability to make solid matter disappear, or at least make an observer believe something has disappeared, and the power to generate fire.

Drawn in with great interest, Johnny stretched his feet out and continued to read.

In another chapter, Fowler claimed to have observed in his two entities a voracious sexual appetite, which he believed also evolved with subsequent reincarnations. The forms of sex they engaged in were all encompassing, including self love, same sex love, multiple partner marathons, and stalking and seducing anyone they should find physically attractive. Observing one in the parking lot of a supermarket, Dr. Fowler wrote that he had witnessed his female entity lift her dress and masturbate to a dramatic climax before getting out of her car to go into the store. He added that they must be unable to restrain their sexual appetites, that they would deal with it by whatever means available at any given moment; i.e. they would duck into an alley if better accommodations weren't convenient. He also believed sex might be used by certain entities to create or enhance wealth.

Fowler concluded by writing that there seemed to be no reason for mortal fear of the entities. They were self-indulgent, wrote Fowler, though they did not appear to be inherently evil or dangerous, unless they were threatened. Under menacing circumstances, they could be ruthless without remorse. Back such a powerful entity into a corner and the outcome would be rather predictable.

Johnny's mouth had gone dry. He closed the book, holding it in his lap, looking around vacantly at the sightseers and unhurried passers-by. The world around him, the world he had lived in for so long and took for granted now seemed one step away. He felt different from those passing through the square; different, he supposed, from practically everyone else that walked the face of the earth; for he had entered a realm in which almost no one knew existed, nor would believe were they to be told.

A delivery van had pulled up to the curb across the street. Johnny watched the driver walk to the back of the van and begin unloading packages onto a dolly. Wearing a t-shirt and blue jeans, when the man leaned forward to adjust the stack of boxes, Johnny noticed that he filled out the jeans nicely. He wondered what the man smelled like, aware that delivery work this time of year would make a man sweat. He wondered if the man smelled like Julian.

Staring across the shaded park, rubbing the back of one hand with the other, he noticed an enhanced sensitivity on his skin. It made him think about the one single element in all of this that had moved to the forefront during the last couple of days. Somehow that carnal appetite Dr. Fowler described in his book had been instilled in him, too. It was as if he had missed out on something all these years, that the forces inside him were no longer willing to rest while his life trickled by.

As he stared absently across the square, he reasoned that Cassandra had been the cause. But was her beauty that pervasive, to the degree that two visits had changed him, even though the visits had been extraordinary? Or was it a lifetime of privation, given the layers of bedclothes his wife slept in every night?

His gaze drifted back to the delivery man. Perhaps Cassandra had not caused it at all, but had merely sparked an awakening of something that had been lying in hibernation. Either way, he was different than the tourists walking to and fro through the neighborhoods of old Savannah, different in that he was privy to one of the world's darker secrets, carnally different in that his appetite had taken on the forbidden wantonness inspired by the shadows and damp creases of a working man's jeans.

Johnny stood up, not thinking about the piles of unfinished work spread across his drafting table, not thinking about a wife waiting at home. Instead, a certain German by the name of Gerhard Trent was on his mind, the man Cassandra had mentioned yesterday in parting. He might have looked at his watch, had he bothered to put it on; but what difference did it make anyway, when the unproductive passing of time paled in comparison to what he might learn. One should take chances in life, he reasoned, or else lie down and die. He felt energized, and all too aware of how the fresh air of a lovely spring morning could revitalize the body's urges; which likely meant for him, were he to pay Cassandra Mott a visit, a most pleasant and inexcusable solution.

Setting out in the direction of his newly acquired house, that is to say, Cassandra Mott's house, he strode with a rising anger, brought on by his underlying but relentless guilt. *Dammit! Why should I feel guilty about anything? Haven't I worked my ass off all these years? Haven't I been devoted in spite of everything, and tolerant of her endless religious zeal? After nine years, why can't I have an afternoon for myself? Just one lousy afternoon without feeling guilty?*

It was shortly after twelve noon when Johnny approached the Mott house. Would he remember the time of day he arrived? Not likely; though there was much about his previous visit that he *did* remember, and those images flooded his mind when he pushed open the wrought-iron gate. Still, he found it impossible to approach the front door without that feeling of apprehension that drew up his shoulders and tightened his neck. He paused on the porch, looking at the book Dr. Salazar had given him.

She can never know I read this.

He looked around for a place to stash it and found it would fit inside the mailbox attached to the wall near the front door.

In the foyer, he half-consciously took a handful of peanuts and ate them as he scanned the landing overhead. The house was quiet as usual, no sign of a guest. That familiar churning came into his belly and quickly spread through him like something giving off heat. An uneasy step forward. Then he clutched his belly with his forearms and bowed his head, wondering if it was caused by tension. More a queasiness than pain, the sensation quickly passed, leaving him lightheaded as he wobbled toward the stairs. The lightheadedness had evolved into a calm by the time he reached the landing, dulling the edge of apprehension as he proceeded toward the parlor.

He opened the door and peered inside. Instead of Julian or Cassandra, he saw on the sofa a stocky, middle-age gentleman with graying hair and slightly sagging jowls. The man looked up from a magazine as Johnny stepped into the room, his wide face awash with surprise, then recognition, and then an analytical gaze.

"Is Cassandra here?" Johnny asked, somewhat disoriented by seeing someone other than his secret lovers in the parlor.

"She'll be here shortly," said the man. His eyes drifted over Johnny once more before he spoke again with his thick German brogue. "I'm Gerhard Trent." He smiled. "And you must be Johnny Feelwater."

Chapter 8

Johnny stared at the German with wide-eyed curiosity. "Yes," he said absently as his gaze drifted to an added fixture in the parlor, a rather elaborate contraption on the far side of the room. It stood like a medieval invention of some kind, in the same spot the massage table had been the day before.

Gerhard turned and followed his gaze. "Would you like a closer look at my massage bench, Herr Feelwater?"

Johnny looked at him. The German, though powerfully built, appeared to be a sophisticated gentleman with the demeanor of a congenial doctor that effortlessly put his patients at ease. Preoccupied with his own thoughts, Johnny approached the machine. It was unlike any massage table he had ever seen. Centered within a cube shaped metal framework, an upholstered bench slanted slightly downward from one end to the other. From each corner of the overhead framework hung a leather strap. It appeared one would lie on the bench with the straps dangling over his shoulders and feet. Johnny circled the device and scrutinized it with interest.

"Cassandra spoke quite eloquently about you," said Gerhard. "I understand you respond well to erotic massage."

Johnny was still distracted by the device. Something about the complexity of it electrified him. It was as if he were sticking his toe into a pool of warm milk, itching to know what it would be like to submerge his whole body. Most intrigued by the dangling straps, they seemed to represent an element of risk and Johnny could not avoid wondering about their purpose. Was he to place himself in this man's hands, set his stride on yet another unknown path? His eyes shifted to Gerhard Trent. Johnny had heard the German's statement, and yes, as he had learned the day before, he indeed responded well to erotic massage.

He nodded.

"Then shall we proceed?" asked Gerhard lifting his hands to Johnny's chest.

Johnny looked down, taken aback by the thick fingers undoing the buttons of his shirt.

"Ah ..." said Gerhard with frustration. "I'm so awkward with this. Perhaps you will unfasten these buttons."

"You want me to take my shirt off?" Johnny's curiosity melted into misgiving.

"You must be completely undressed to receive my massage."

Johnny swallowed dryly, taken swiftly by the momentum of his imagination and Gerhard's eagerness to begin. "I don't know you," he said, placing his hand on his shirt near his collar.

"It's not necessary to know me, Herr Feelwater. Your pleasure is my only interest. Besides, not knowing me will only amplify the intensity of what you're submitting to."

Johnny stood staring at him for a moment. Reluctance thickened his fingers as he began to unbutton his shirt. Hardly at ease undressing in front of a man he had never seen before, he took off his clothes in a mechanical daze. As his garments fell one by one to the floor, he stared at the apparatus awaiting him not more than an arm's length away, severe with its iron and leather. The German observed, one hand propped his elbow, the other propped his chin, as if he were a scientist in the throes of an experiment with a new subject. Johnny hesitated, standing in his white cotton briefs, suddenly aware of the chill of refrigerated air on his skin. He looked at Gerhard Trent, his eyes casting doubts.

"The underpants, Herr Feelwater," said the German, nodding at the briefs.

Johnny drew a breath and looked down. A wet spot had appeared on the absorbent cotton. The anticipation of his own nudity had caused his penis to swell against the fibers. He reluctantly leaned forward and pushed the underwear down his legs, then stood upright, overwhelmed by a rush of lightheadedness standing naked before a strange man. He responded to Gerhard's thick, outstretched hand by lying down on the padded bench, his head at the lower end, immediately flooded by second thoughts. There had not been time to think this through. His questions about the machine had not been asked.

But wasn't this why he was here? Indeed, he had expected something out of the ordinary. Relax, he told himself. Relax and let it happen; have yet another adventure to relive in his dreams.

Not completely surprised when the German began to fasten the leather straps to his wrists and ankles, Johnny tightened with alarm by what occurred next.

He fought an impulse to resist as Gerhard Trent stepped around the framework and pulled the straps taut one at a time. The effect drew Johnny's hands and feet toward the four corners of the frame. His limbs suspended high above his prone body, he lay spread-eagle and helpless. Every part of his body was exposed. Straining and squirming did nothing to address the sudden indignity. Just that quickly he had found himself in a predicament that at once thrilled and unnerved him and sent chills racing across his skin. He felt quivers in his arms and the tendons of his inner thighs tightened. Certain Cassandra would enter the room at any moment, an overwhelming nervousness knotted his stomach. She would see him this way! She would have him vulnerable and exposed and helplessly disposed to her whims.

"Comfortable, Herr Feelwater?"

As Johnny's adrenaline rush began to recede, he felt a debilitating containment that relegated him to a world of tension and humility. Aware of everything said, of everything going on around him, he was hardly prepared for pleasantries exchanged or thoughtful interactions. His response did not come in the form of a reply, rather a tightening of fists and thighs and gluteal muscle. *Comfortable?* How does one get comfortable, or even force a faltering smile while positioned this way, with his anus exposed and his genitals splayed over his pubic mound?

"The bench is designed to maximize your pleasure," said Gerhard Trent, stated mechanically as if he had said it a thousand times. "You'll be amazed by sensations you weren't aware your body was capable of."

Was it panic that laid the fine sweat over his body, that made it difficult to reply or engage in undistracted conversation; or was it the chill of air on his nipples and between his wide-spread legs? That and more, more than the jittery madness of anticipation, more than the smell of stress from his own underarms, more than the tension in his neck—it was also the pleasurable and intensely erotic sensations creeping into his loins as Gerhard Trent continued his preparations. He felt his testicles draw closer to his body, felt endless tingling across his skin. Bound and squirming, his desperation grew as to Cassandra Mott's whereabouts.

His words sounded like panic. "Where's Cassandra and ...?"

Gerhard Trent looked at him and smiled at his unease. "And who, Herr Feelwater?"

"Julian," Johnny said on a gust of breath.

"She's with her guests in the garden behind the house. Julian is with her of course. Such an unconventional lady. I dearly love the woman. A true one-of-a-kind."

"She has guests!" Johnny gasped, plunged into a whole new kind of torment. His arms and legs strained reflexively against the straps, brought on by a sense of urgency, a need to get free and get dressed before it was too late.

Gerhard Trent ignored the struggle. "Three of her friends came to visit," he said complacently, visually exploring the minutia of Johnny's body. "Such marvelous spring weather. Probably why the ladies decided to have their mint juleps in the garden."

Johnny's chest sunk in. Any minute the door would open. He would be in their presence, Cassandra's and her three female guests. The certainty of being shamelessly exposed transformed the tingles across his skin into rampant stress. And from this revelation sprung a dozen more. If Cassandra had come back as her youthful self within the last week or so, a young woman no one in Savannah would know, how could she already have friends coming to visit? It also opened a question about the German.

"Have you known the Mott's long, Mr. Trent?"

"Please, call me Gerhard."

"Have you?" Johnny insisted.

Gerhard looked at him and smiled. "Cassandra told me you're an inquisitive young man."

"Please ... how long have you known her?"

The German looked at his watch, and then picked up a towel to wipe his hands, as if he had not heard the question.

Johnny gave up. He would not ask again. Apparently, in this house, it was standard procedure to avoid questions.

Johnny tugged at the straps with another shiver of second thoughts. "I'm not sure about this," he stammered, ignored once again.

Gerhard Trent reached out and ran his hands down Johnny's legs, seemingly captivated by the masculine texture of hairs and flesh. "I don't have many Negro clients in Germany," he said, allowing his eyes a lengthy study of Johnny's legs. "None actually. I have to say, I'm looking forward to your massage." His hands came down the front of Johnny's thighs, then over his belly and chest. "Lovely," he said, "just lovely. Your skin has a wonderful feel."

The caressing feel of Gerhard's touch made Johnny's heart race faster. His second thoughts had multiplied several fold. "What kind of massage is this anyway?"

"Ah, I see Cassandra has left you in the dark. Be that the case, allow me to enlighten you." Gerhard Trent's eyes drifted over him again. "The process is called *milking*. I intend to milk you, Mr. Feelwater. Over a period of time, by performing various forms of stimulation, I will exhaust your seminal fluids. Think of it as a prolonged climax without the intense muscular contractions. You'll find it exquisite, I assure you."

Johnny heard the words—they had fallen over him like flecks of ice. It was a matter of determining their meaning. *Milking?* The ramifications intensified the quivers in his outstretched arms. He had never heard of such a thing. Breathing hard and deeply as the German moved between his legs, he tried to imagine what it might be, this bizarre massage called *milking*. Not fear, not even alarm—what he felt, beyond fading confusion over Gerhard Trent's intent, was the sudden distraction of thick fingers spreading his ass cheeks. Just that quickly his awareness shifted from the mental to the physical as Gerhard's finger raked over the small pinched gathering, which spread electricity across his thighs, coupled with another rude reminder of the bindings when his legs flexed against the straps. Johnny lifted his head and saw Gerhard Trent inspecting his anus.

It was not a massage at all, at least not this part of it; rather an extraordinarily intimate caress, a delicate, continuous touch. It set him floating and inundated his mind with a blur of fantasies about milking. He wondered what those *various forms of stimulation* might be. Then, with the back of his head resting on the padded bench, Johnny shuddered when the finger produced a small push. His buttocks muscles tensed. His testicles retracted even closer to his body. He felt his penis lift off his belly and twitch. If the intent was to relax him, Gerhard Trent was failing miserably.

Unaware of how much time had passed by the time the hallway door swung open, Johnny had been adrift. He tilted his head to look. Framed in the doorway stood Cassandra in a mid nineteenth century dress. Form fitting and frilly above the waist, it cascaded over her hips in folds and ruffles and untold layers of petticoats. Her focus turned immediately to him. She entered the room, sporting that mischievous smile, followed by, to Johnny's horror, her three female guests, all dressed in kind. As if they had stepped out of the eighteen-sixties, the four women swept across the carpeted floor toward what was to be, he had the sinking feeling, their afternoon entertainment. They neared just as his one last struggle against the leather straps gave way to defeat. He closed his eyes, rendered complacent, reduced to a visual novelty for four idle women. A feeling of falling through space overwhelmed him.

Seconds ticked by. Johnny felt every pore on his body. No embarrassment could be more profound, no humiliation more complete. Their collective gaze came like a thousand needles pricking his skin. He wanted to draw his legs together, to crouch somewhere, to cover himself and escape the intimate scrutiny of these aggressive female eyes. The bindings mocked him, demanded unconditional surrender. His masculinity had been reduced to so many pounds of sweat and quivering flesh, splayed for the frivolous pleasure of four women. He looked desperately at Cassandra, who acknowledged with little more than a gleam her eyes.

"A Negro, Cassandra?" said one of them. "You didn't mention that."

"You *are* one for surprises, aren't you Cassandra," said another.

"How marvelous," said the third. "I'm afraid my husband would have a perfect fit if he knew I was looking at a naked Negro," she said, stepping forward. "Such beautiful black skin," she added, running her fingers over Johnny's belly. "Oh my, his skin is so satiny. Come on over here, Janette. Feel how smooth he is."

Janette skimmed her fingertips over Johnny's thigh. "I never imagined," she cooed, a tall brunette in a blue dress, her hair sculpted in curls. "How nice. Is he a slave, Cassandra?"

"Ladies ... please!" insisted Gerhard Trent. "Please, take a seat if you intend to observe."

The women collected chairs from the back wall and arranged them in a semi-circle near Johnny's feet. They chatted and carried on immodestly about what Cassandra had planned for them to see.

Resigned, chest heaving, head dropped back, Johnny stared at the ceiling. *What am I doing here? Why did I let this happen?* They were eccentric and frivolous and dressed as if they belonged in the past; but foremost, they were fully clothed and he was naked. He had lapsed into fog of erotic madness. He quit resisting the straps. His flex and squirm was nothing more than involuntary reactions to their sighs and whispers and their most inquisitive eyes.

Gerhard leaned close to his ear.

"Ignore them, Herr Feelwater. Evidently they believe your milking will amuse them. Perhaps it will, but I assure you, their presence will make you exceedingly aware of your body."

Exceedingly aware! It was a humorous understatement. He had never been more exceedingly aware of his body in his life, laid open this way before an audience of women, his maleness displayed like some kind of curiosity. *Exceedingly aware.* It could have gone without saying. His nudity tingled like an icy consciousness that had frosted onto his body.

He bore the humiliation and waited. Each slow passing second brought deep intakes of air that expanded his chest. Gerhard Trent had spoken of sensations that he was unaware his body could produce; but without the first application of any form of massage, it was exactly those kinds of sensations that were tormenting him now. Feminine voices reverberated in his ears. He could hardly believe the words he was hearing.

"I do detest those Union soldiers setting up their camp in Colonial Park Cemetery," one woman said.

"Why, I've heard they're defacing the lovely memorials," huffed another.

"Those loathsome brutes."

"Sherman is nothing short of a criminal. He simply wants to humiliate us."

A dream? Blissful insanity? Four women reliving the Civil War, for God's sake; while he lay bound and naked and frolicking in a garden of fantasy while the German worked his nipples into small peaks. His eyes closed and his head back, Johnny felt the masterful hands travel down over his belly. A hush fell over the women.

"You're still tense, Herr Feelwater." Then his hands returned to Johnny's nipples. "Ah yes, these caresses are torment, aren't they my good man; but nothing compared to what you are about to experience." His thumbs moved into the recesses of Johnny's underarms and he kneaded the soft damp flesh. "Feels good, doesn't it?" said Gerhard as his fingers traveled lightly up Johnny's inner arms. "I'm sure you're beginning to see why the restraints are so effective, aren't you, Herr Feelwater?" He glanced down past Johnny's belly, which was rising and falling on each breath. "Ah, I see we're having the desired effect already. You have a fine erection."

Gerhard moved in between Johnny's suspended legs. Twitching involuntarily, Johnny's cock emitted a drop of semen. He heard murmurs from the women. Then Gerhard took the penis between his fingers and thumb and milked out another drop. A creamy white pearl trickled down the ink-colored shaft and into the void between Johnny's legs.

"Quite a good start, I would say," said Gerhard. He reached under the table and brought out a pair of clips, then attached them to a pair of swollen, already sore nipples.

Johnny let out an audible gasp. "Oh God!" he moaned, tossing his head from side-to-side. Again the female voices, though he could no longer make out their words; nor did he care, suffering this unexpected torture on his chest. He felt fingertips on the head of his penis, drawing lightly over it again and again. The pain in his nipples gave way to a reflexive shudder of pleasure. He felt an ache welling in his belly, an ache short of spasms. The caress was just enough to take him right to the edge. Then another pearl formed and dripped from the tiny hole.

Gerhard's attention had shifted to Johnny's testicles. Using both hands, he rolled and kneaded them, which produced tormenting pressure. Johnny's legs tightened against the straps. He heard the sound of Gerhard's voice, like the sound of a foghorn late at night from the sea.

"Madam," he said to the belle nearest him, "if you would do this for me, I shall proceed with his prostate massage."

She rose reservedly and stepped forward, her antebellum petticoats rustling and sweeping the floor. Attentively, she took the pliable egg-shapes into her softer, warmer hands.

"Madam," said Gerhard sternly, "allow yourself a bit more enthusiasm for that."

Johnny winced with the sudden squeeze, then shuddered when Gerhard artfully and repeatedly milked his penis. The welling in his loins had turned into a need, a desperation as another emission trickled down through the rift between his ass cheeks.

"Now madam," said Gerhard, "see how this is done? Take it like this, your thumb here on the urethra. Then a slow stroke up to the tip." She released Johnny's testicles and Gerhard helped her correctly position her fingers at the base of Johnny's penis. "That's correct. Finesse, madam, more finesse." He watched her for a moment, then said: "If you will stand more to the side and give me a little more room."

The pleasure was maddening. Johnny was aware of smoother, more dexterous fingers stroking him, slow and deliberate, delivering the intended effect. Only the straps prevented his knees from coming together.

"It's called prostate massage, Mr. Feelwater. That's what you'll endure next. You'll find it quite stimulating."

If ever he was to endure anything, it was now. They had brought him to the brink. Every muscle was taut and shuddering. His humiliation had turned into a need unlike any he had ever known.

No longer passive or demure, the woman made use of both hands, captivated by Johnny's breathless reactions to the dark pleasure she took in manipulating and squeezing his swollen organs. She watched his face tighten in response to her aggressive fondling, his wincing as she squeezed harder by degrees, his straining to close his legs.

God, that feels good!

Johnny felt the welling fluids migrate through the inner vestibules and trickle from the tiny hole. He had not known it could be drawn out like this. The time was now. The ache was unbearable, a climax mere seconds away. Now, for God's sake! Now! Why deny his body its desperate need for release?

They're watching. They're watching it drip out and run down between my legs.

His eyes opened in a daze. If only he had known this was going to happen. He could have thought it through, been mentally prepared. Yet the shock of it, the anguish, was beginning to fade. The thrill of being exposed, of being naked and humiliated before four fully clothed women, of being toyed with sexually, had set a pleasant chill on his skin. He lifted his head and saw Gerhard Trent apply something that glistened to his finger. He watched the German position himself and then felt a deliberate stab. His head fell back and he held his breath as the thick finger pushed further in. An intensely gratifying sensation spread though him. His toes curled. His anus flexed on the finger.

What's he ... no ... that feels ... Oh God, that feels good ... who is he? ... how does he know these things?

"Ah, there it is," said the German, his finger imbedded well past the second knuckle. "About the size of a walnut I'd say. Look at his face, madam. See what can be accomplished when you caress a man's prostate gland. A gentle swirling motion. Press just hard enough so he can feel it." Gerhard Trent looked at Johnny. "How does that feel, my glorious suffering friend?"

Afloat on the harmony of his body, his words were locked behind clenched teeth. His jaw thrust upward, his neck muscles tight, his buttocks flexed and his anus locked on the finger. He moaned, a whole new and unimaginable level of human pleasure. *How does it feel? Are there words that can describe how this feels?*

He bore the pleasure as a defenseless captive, his hands clutching the straps, arms aching from the strain, drawn in as if Gerhard Trent's finger was an opiate. And on it went: the manipulation and fondling, unending it seemed, as one-by-one pearls of semen dripped from the end of his penis. Nothing could have prepared him for such prolonged pleasure, nor had he ever suffered such unbearable urgency for a release. Had he been able to observe from another part of the room, he would not have recognized himself, the prudent and honorable man he had always been now lost in the throes of debauchery.

"There, Fraulein, do you see?" Gerhard said to the woman that had stepped up for a turn between Johnny's legs, his tireless finger at work on the sensitive gland. "By depleting him this way, we are giving him immense gratification. Since I'm occupied here, I shall depend on you to masturbate him." He used his free hand to position hers on Johnny's penis. "That's right, all the way up and then down. Set a quick rhythm and we shall see a male climax without ejaculate. Very good, my dear," he said, watching the delicate white hand work the satiny black sheath. "A firmer grip, if you will, Madam. Yes, that's it. A bit faster perhaps."

The young belle, surprisingly adept at having a penis in her hand, followed Gerhard Trent's instruction. She squeezed and delivered faster strokes, setting the testicles slapping about. Within seconds the tendons and muscles of Johnny's legs constricted and his shoulders grew taut. The spasms he had ached for welled and burned through his body. His penis raged and pulsed; and though one might have expected to witness several streams of semen, this climax was dry. His onlookers watched in awed silence the shuddering and the draining of a man's last ounce of strength. Gerhard Trent's milking had been successful. There was nothing left. The body's mechanics had come into play though nothing spurted from the small hole.

It was over. In less than an hour, by way of humiliation, leather straps and a gathering of female voyeurs, Gerhard Trent had presided over more intimacy and sexual pleasure than Johnny Feelwater had experienced in all of the previous years of his adult life. His arms and legs hung limp in their bindings.

Cassandra stepped forward and began to unfasten the straps. When he was free of them, she leaned close to his ear and whispered: "Julian's waiting for you in the bedroom, darlin'."

His eyes opened on her. The fog in his mind yielded an image that seemed to have stepped from a dream, a celestial harlot, the loveliest of creatures schooled in all things prurient. She took the clips from his nipples, which were aching and sore; and he covered them with his hands as he rolled onto his side, drawing his thighs up toward his belly. He had become her plaything, plain and simple—she could do with him as she pleased. And today she had arranged to have his body ravaged. She looked upon him now with a gleam of satisfaction, her lady friends in their southern finery to her right and left. Having witnessed the male workings of his body, they were staring quietly at what was left, a spent mass of male flesh, damp with his own sweat and curled in fetal nudity.

An enlightened and wretched self-discovery came over him. He realized their presence during the ordeal had indeed heightened the pleasure. Their eyes had sweetened the torment. Even now, lying so pitifully before them, it was a sensually rich kind of euphoria. The instinct to cover himself had faded away. Time would tell how much this had changed him; and whether this, too, was a part of him.

Eventually he got off the padded bench and made his way into the bedroom, where Julian lay naked on the bed. Johnny paused just inside the doorway, merging his thoughts with the image. Of course. It was obvious. Had he not been primed to crawl into bed with this perfect man, to lay in the halo of his warmth, to be held and taken by him? Was that not a part of him as well, to breathe the fragrances of two men making love?

Johnny moved forward, oblivious to aching shoulders, to sore wrists, to the smell between his legs. With barely the strength to crawl onto the bed, he scooted close, mindful of the silent affinity between them. He lay on his belly and turned his face to Julian, his senses alive with being in bed with another man. Where their shoulders touched, he stared at the contrast of their skin, which heightened his awareness of the moment. Then Julian rose up and got to his knees and drew his hand down the rift of Johnny's damp back. His hands rested for a moment on Johnny's buttocks, as if he were contemplating mankind's most sumptuous taboo; and then, using his thumbs, he parted the fleshy rounds. Nothing was said. No words were needed beyond Julian's caressing lips, his tongue wet and cleansing, his nostrils flaring with the smell of masculine loins, his thumbs insistent and determined.

Johnny lay perfectly still. Chills ran through him as the side of his face settled on the cool sheet. Once again a man's hands were upon him. He realized at once the difference between Gerhard Trent's hands and Julian's. The

German had performed an unemotional act of manipulation. Julian's hands delivered a precise message. Through his touch came an unspoken urgency hinting at what was to come. Now positioned between Johnny's legs, his momentum reflected an escalating, all-consuming need. Johnny closed his eyes and raised his hips and felt the heat of Julian's thighs against his inner legs. His eyes stayed closed with anticipation, the feel of it different this time, different because there were no doubts, different because he recognized a distinct void in his life, different because he had lain awake the night before with the blissful memory lingering in his bowels. He had thought about it through the wee hours the night and dreamed about it when he finally slept. Yes, it was different this time, because the time before had explained away so many years of uncertainty.

His mental oblivion was soon accompanied by pain. He bit down on his lip and held his breath. His consciousness became an extension of his body. Deep inside, sensations passed over every nerve-ending—first like a storm and then a pleasant breeze. Then the motion of one man upon another, the jarring and the hunger, the gasps and the hands turned into fists, the seed given and received; and finally, the long sigh as the eyes gently closed.

An hour or so later, Johnny awoke locked in Julian's gaze. It vaguely occurred to him that he should go home. But no. Not just yet, he decided as he looked at Julian sitting beside him yoga-style, thinking how nice it would be to look at him a while longer. He sat up, staring into Julian's crystal blue eyes, depleted of the will to leave. Whom had he given himself to, he wondered, man or ghost? Could a man of this world have dangled these temptations that had caused his legs to go limp? Man or immortal, either way, what he felt was love.

Johnny reached out to stroke his lips. "Why don't you talk to me? ...Can't you speak? You know I dreamed about you last night. I think about you constantly. You know what you've done to me, don't you?" He got no reply, though he saw the silence answer in Julian's eyes—they were adoring.

In the parlor, Gerhard Trent, Cassandra and her friends were nowhere to be found. Gerhard's iron apparatus stood ominously with its padded bench and dangling leather straps, as if awaiting its next prey. Johnny stared for a long while at the straps, rubbing his wrist where they had been attached, before he looked around and found his clothes. They had been folded and placed on the sofa. He stepped into his jeans and pushed his arms through the sleeves of his shirt, leaving the buttons undone and the tail draped over his hips; wondering, as he stared at the apparatus, what it meant to have so willingly embraced this ungodly world. What seeds had lain dormant inside him that rooted the moment he set foot inside this house? He pondered the consequences. The seeds, it seemed, had grown into entangling vines and threatened to ensnarl his soul, had they not already.

He stepped into his sandals and walked to the door, pausing to look back across the room. Would he lie down again inside that seductive framework, he wondered, knowing what was in store? ...Yes, for having done so had made him aware of his own body for the first time since the hormones of his youth had gone to sleep so many years before. Yes, he would undress and recline on that narrow bench, and he would watch his hands and ankles buckled into the straps, knowing that the most undiluted form of pleasure was about to bring life to every nerve and fiber in his body.

His eyes shifted to Cassandra's closed bedroom door, beyond which she must have taken her friends to experience a few of Gerhard's talents. Then Julian appeared in the frame of his bedroom door. The two of them looked at each other for a moment, before Johnny turned and walked out of the house.

Chapter 9

Johnny paused next to the mailbox to retrieve the book Basil Salazar had given him. He stood staring at the softbound cover. It was curled and creased, the pages yellowed. Beneath the title was a picture of an Egyptian pyramid, in front of which, wearing a robe, stood a lone woman, looking away from the pyramid as if she were looking through time. Below the picture was the name Doctor Brian Fowler.

A wisp of smoke suddenly rose from the binding, followed immediately by a burst of flame. The book fell from Johnny's hand and he quickly ripped off his shirt to smother the fire. He picked it up and inspected it, the back cover now slightly charred. Slinging the shirt over his shoulder, he hurried down the steps and on through the wrought-iron gate, pausing again on the sidewalk. He looked at the book in disbelief. Then his eyes lifted to Cassandra's upstairs window, where she stood with her familiar, knowing smile. Backing away from the window, she blew him a kiss and then disappeared from view.

My God! She knows I have this book! He looked again at the book and cringed. *She must know what this man has written.*

The real world moved in around him: car engines, people out strolling, kids at play in the square. Marilee stepped from the shadows in his mind when he thought about going home. She'd be upset, have questions. *What do I tell her?* Even though the haze in his head had cleared, he had not yet contemplated the consequences of his actions. He remembered walking out when she answered the phone, just like that, without telling her where he was going. He had not intended to stay out this long. So be it. He had savored the rewards—now the punishment. His shoulders grew small and guilt tightened his jaw. *She'll want to know where I went. Why I've been gone so long.*

By the time he walked two more blocks, his mind had gone in a dozen directions. Splashes of sun filtered through the overhead boughs and checkered the street. His shirt felt damp from the afternoon heat. The remorse had turned to anger, a pent-up anger, like an angry lion suddenly freed. *I've paid my dues!* His eyes were fixed straight ahead, unyielding. *Does she explain every time she leaves the house?* The time had come for a small escape from the mundane, from the endless toil at his drafting table, from the day-to-day existence that ran one day upon another, always duplicating the day before. His chest rose on a determined breath. *That's what I need, a vacation*—though a visit to Cassandra's house would be better described as a reprieve from lifeless, half-hearted sex and weeks of abstinence.

Asserting his independence brought on a grand sense of elation. As he strode closer to his house, even his footfall on the timeworn sidewalks of old Savannah was more resolute. *Why be in such a hurry to go home?* He would go somewhere else, though just now he had no desire to. *Maybe I'll stretch out in the den ... watch a movie on TV ...eat some cold cuts and cheese. Maybe have more than one beer. Why not? Why not have just one day to do anything I want?*

His house came into view. His stomach felt queasy as soon as he walked through the front door. The bluster that had expanded his chest during the walk home had flared out like the falling sparks of spent fireworks. A deep sigh brought the smell of home, representing all things right in his life, familiar and comforting, increasing tenfold the agony of his guilt. He found Marilee in the kitchen, sitting at the breakfast table, her face puffy and wet. Johnny walked past her, to the refrigerator for his first beer. Her eyes bore on the back of his head, tangling his resolve with more guilt. He turned and leaned against the counter and took a swig, waiting for the eruption of verbal spears lying in wait just behind those bleary eyes.

"Globalcorp called while you were out," she said as calmly as her somber mood would allow.

"Well, shit!" He took another swig of beer.

It was difficult for Marilee to look at him. The man that had walked into her kitchen looked like her husband, but there was nothing else about him that resembled the man she had known for nine years. He had never walked out of the house without telling her where he was going, let alone stay gone the better part of the day. He had never strutted across the room with such a flippant attitude when she was stricken by despair. It felt like a cold hand had gripped her heart, his leaving the house that way, then returning so many hours later in the form of a stranger. Yes, a stranger—she could see it in his eyes and the way he was looking at her, cold and defiant.

At first she had been angry, but as the eternity of each passing minute fed the hissing cats of her anxiety, it turned into the worst day she had ever lived. Her anger had been pushed aside by bewilderment and hurt and fear. More than once she had come to the point of screaming. Each attempt to occupy the time, her mind, her hands, had been futile. No magazine or TV show distracted her. Her futile attempts to go on with the day's housework led to nothing but frustration. She had answered the phone only because it might have been Johnny. Now it hurt to look at him, with this strangeness emanating from him that caused even more alarm.

"Johnny ... what's wrong? Why are you behaving this way?"

His anger emerged. He exhaled a gust of exasperation. Any other day he would have taken her into his arms, comforted her, assured her everything would be okay. Today it wasn't a wife-in-need that he saw, rather a blithering female, a woman that had occupied nine years of his life with her misguided morality and self-righteous posturing. There was nothing earthy in their sterile, properly lived lives, no private nuances exchanged, no glimmer of eyes with concurrent thoughts, no magic in bed at night. His life had become maddening.

So she wanted to know what was wrong with him. He looked at her for a moment and through his frustration and anger, he realized she had a right to some kind of explanation—she deserved as much, though of course it couldn't be the truth. What then? Concoct a lie? What could he tell her that would satisfy her pathetic, sobbing curiosity? "I'm sick and tired of the way things are," he blurted in lieu of an explanation, instantaneously recognizing a bad start. "No ... actually I'm not sick and tired of the way things are—everything is fine, most everything anyway." His words reflected the chaos ranging in his head, which increased her bewilderment. He averted his eyes from the hurt etched on her face, pondering a new tact. "It's me," he said, nodding affirmation. He looked back at her. "Think about it, Marilee. What have I done with my life? What have I accomplished ... personally I mean?"

"Johnny, how could you say that? You're an artist. You're accomplishments are outstanding. You've started a company and convinced Globalcorp to—"

"No!" he shouted.

Marilee froze, all but frightened of her own husband.

Johnny lowered his head and rubbed his brow with his fingertips, and then looked up. "There was a guy on CNN the other morning who sailed a boat around the world. Alone for God's sake. Some guys ride bicycles across the country, or hike the Andes, or write books. What have I done? Sit in there and draw pictures! Wait for you to get home from church! Then what do we do? We eat dinner. And if you aren't talking on the phone, we watch TV. Then we go to bed with you dressed like an Eskimo. Have you ever noticed there's usually two feet of space between us when we go to sleep? Doesn't that bother you? It does me. I'm tired of living such a sterile life." Staring angrily at the sink, he took a swig of beer, and then looked at her. "So that's it. As of now, I want some time for myself. Time away from this house and that endless pile of work in there. I'm tired of deadlines and telephones and monthly payments and ..." *You! I need time away from you!* "I need a break, that's all. Something different. Damn it, Marilee, I wanna feel like I'm still alive."

It was such a sudden and perplexing change in him, Marilee sat in a painful stupor, trying to bear the chill of his eyes. All of this must have been lying under the surface. Now he was letting it all out at one time. Clearly, there was something wrong that she had been unaware of. She had no clue where to begin, let alone how to resolve it, though his comment about their sleeping arrangements rang in her ears. A dreadful possibility jumped to the forefront. "Is it me? Are you tired of being married to me?"

He stared at her, trying to restrain his anger while the rage continued inside him.

"I don't know what to do," she pleaded.

"Hmm," he vented with a tone of indifference. "Well ... let's talk about it, Marilee. Let's talk about what you've *never* done." Oozing from his internal rage came the sarcasm rooted in long festering resentment. "Let's see ... oh yes, the church. The all-important church! Have you ever woke up on a Sunday morning and decided you'd rather stay in bed with me than go to church? Or when Reverend Aragones calls to recruit you for another program, have you ever told him you'd rather spend more time with your husband?" Pacing the kitchen, his glances her way were like blind gunshots. He avoided her eyes, with their power to turn his rage inward. "And why not talk about intimacy while we're at it, yours and mine. Have you ever suggested we get in the shower together? No! You close the damn door! You don't want me to see you undress. What kind of a marriage is that?" He took another swallow of beer and continued to look at her. "What if I wanted to go to a nude beach, or watch a dirty movie? You get new ideas by doing that, you know? Not you. You'd have a heart attack. Remember that time I tried to make love to you in the living room? You froze up like a nun trapped with a flasher. Dammit, Marilee, there's more to it than spreading your legs a few inches when your husband comes to bed with a hard-on. You don't even try to enjoy it. You treat sex like a wifely duty, like you'd rather be reading a magazine." He rubbed the back of his head in frustration. "Don't you wonder why we rarely make love these days?"

Glancing at her just long enough to see another tear streak down her face, he turned to the sink and tilted his head for a long drink of beer. More was seething just under the surface. Now frustrated enough to get it all out, his tone continued to reflect his discontent. "Aren't you curious about your body, the pleasure it's capable of? Haven't you ever wanted to push my head down between your legs? I could make you wet that way, and I don't mean because my tongue is wet either. Lord no! We don't do things like that. We use KY Jelly. Get it over with quicker." He stared at her for a moment. "Hard for you to fathom, isn't it? Hard to imagine how turned-on I'd get watching you take your panties off and squatting over my face? Goddamn you, Marilee! You're pretty enough to turn any man's head, but you're oblivious to what he's thinking. You say you believe in God, but you're perfectly content to deny His gifts. We're married. It's something you and I could share. But no! For you it's a task. Something to be done with. That just doesn't make sense."

Marilee was stunned. Tears had dampened her entire face. If not for the desperation in his voice, it would have seemed like an attack.

"It's that fucking mother of yours! What'd she do, cram your head with anti-sex propaganda from the moment you were born? ...You don't have to answer. I know she did. I saw that book she keeps on the shelf in case we ever have a daughter ... yeah, like I'd let her get close to my daughter. You don't know what it's like to take a breath of life because of all that crap your mother bombarded you with."

He looked at her long and hard. This was not what he wanted. He had gotten nearly a decade of frustration off his chest at her expense, without the slightest bit of tact. As a result, another familiar emotion rushed into his chest and displaced his rage—more guilt; not just vague culpability, but full-fledged raging guilt. He had been harsh with her, the woman he loved, and now she was sobbing. He found the wherewithal to step over beside her and pull her head into his belly and stroke her hair; yet he could not let go of what had turned rancid in his heart.

"I'm worried, Johnny," she whimpered. "You've changed overnight. You never talked to me like this before." She used the wadded tissue in her fist to blot her eyes. "You've never disappeared for a whole day without telling me where you're going. You never ignored your business affairs before. It's like that's not important anymore. Globalcorp called three days ago. You still haven't returned their call. Now you're talking about things I don't think I can do. I ..." she took a deep quivering breath before attempting to go on. "I could try, but ..."

It's too late, damn you! Cassandra Mott has made it inconsequential.

"Marilee, listen ... I've got some things to think through. I plan to spend some time alone. Don't ask me about it. I don't intend to explain everything I do. You found personal fulfillment with Reverend Aragones and the church; it's time I find mine."

"What are you saying?" she pleaded. She looked up at him, realizing she didn't want an answer. His words, his attitude and behavior, it all added up to another woman. She had to know. "Are you leaving me?"

"No!" he blurted. His jaw tightened. He looked at the door to his office, and then glanced at the clock over the stove. There was still time to call Globalcorp.

"I never wanted religion to come between us. What do you want me to do, Johnny? I want so much to be a good wife. It's important to me that you think I am."

Quit the church! Call your mother and Reverend Aragones. Tell them to get screwed!

"Do what you want, Marilee. Do what inspires you. You always have."

He walked out of the room, brushing against the broad leaves of a large potted fern as he rounded the door heading to his drafting table. He grabbed the telephone book and flung it across the room in a fit of anger. A few minutes later he took up the phone and dialed Globalcorp.

"Johnny Feelwater here ... Yeah ... Sorry I didn't call sooner. It's been a bad couple of days for me ... Not a problem. We're ahead of schedule ... Sure ... By tomorrow afternoon. I'll overnight the next set ... Good-bye."

He looked at the layout before him, everything in disarray. After putting the graphics and drawings back in order, he set his laptop on the table and turned it on, clicking on his graphics software when the icons came up.

I can do this. I can finish this series. Get it shipped out and have it out of my hair for a couple of days.

Glancing at the book given to him by Dr. Salazar, he resisted picking it up. Instead he reached for his pen and started in where he had left off on a preliminary concept, the same he had been working on when Samuel McPhereson showed up at the front door to convey Cassandra Mott's house.

Ha! As if she'd let anyone other than her to own that house!

McPhereson's visit seemed like a decade ago. It was a different world and he was a different man. Since then he had learned the bittersweet smell of the earth's unsavory breath, that it came from the lungs of an enchantress, swirling about his ears in whispers and drawing him into a world no one else could see—Cassandra Mott's secret world of debauchery.

She had tainted him as a husband. She had seduced him. She had mystified him and set lava running hot in his veins, all beyond reason. For the first time in nine years, he had placed his own emotions before Marilee's. Where he had once obsessed over color and shapes coming together on paper, he now obsessed on those green eyes glistening with life, those pale white fingertips skimming down his chest, those hips lowering so sensuously and engulfing him. How could he envision a color scheme for a magazine ad when his mind was fixed on that tuft of red hair melding with his black curls, and those folds, wet and fragrant, engulfing him with body heat? His gluteal muscle tightened. He could still feel Gerhard Trent's finger, and those female eyes intently perusing every inch of his splayed body. How could he work when images like these owned his mind?

All of this while his wife foundered in despair in the next room.

It was a fruitless effort. The strokes conveyed from hand to paper seemed tight and uninspired. Cassandra Mott might as well have been standing behind him, whispering in his ear. Yet he labored on, late into the evening, trudging into the bedroom around eleven o'clock.

Marilee was in the bathroom. Odd. She had turned off the TV in the den an hour or so earlier. He had assumed she would be asleep by now, weary as they both were. Coming out of the closet in his white silk pajama bottoms, he crawled into bed and laid on his back, determined to finish that set of graphics first thing in the morning.

The light in the bathroom went off. Marilee came out and stood beside the bed, nude, caramel brown skin radiant in the soft glow of his reading lamp. He stared at her, dumbstruck, wondering what on earth was going on in her mind. He had assumed he had offended her earlier with his blunt statements. Evidently he had inspired her instead. There she stood, daring and naked.

"I waited in there until you came to bed," she said, demure and vulnerable and unsure of herself.

Johnny said nothing. Nine years of sleeping next to this beautiful woman, wasted. She was as beautiful as the day he married her; her breasts rather small though alert and very feminine, enhanced with large nipples several shades darker than her skin. Now they were swollen, exposed as they were to his eyes and the fresh night air. Her feminine curves conspired to steal his mind, a body that seemed a pity to conceal, never flaunted in a bathing suit, never used to set fires in the privacy of their bedroom. Yet there she stood, gazing timidly down at him.

Contemplating her motive, he couldn't help but look at her—she had never presented herself nude, not intentionally anyway. Lost in thought, he stared at her hips, rounding in such a way the lost years angered him. They were curves that a man's hands ached for; though he, her husband, had never delved between the shapely halves, nor plunged his face there for basking. Her skin, silky smooth and the color of light coffee, was flawless, precisely what made the thick shock of pubic hair so visually prominent, as if by design to trap a man's eyes as his were now. Why weren't they lovers? Why was having her like having a rich chocolate cake, but denied even a small slice.

"Well?" she said nervously.

His eyes lifted to hers. "Well what?" She took heart in what he had said in the kitchen and had set out to prove him wrong, he could see that.

"Think I'm still pretty?"

"Yeah. You're beautiful."

She folded back the sheet on her side of the bed and laid down on her back, tensely, delivering her next surprise—she didn't hide her body with the sheet. It all seemed rather awkward, like two teenagers taking peeks at each other for the first time; though where would it lead? How could it repair their lost years now that he had been decadently mingled with Savannah's history and indoctrinated by the city's most notorious and skilled seductress? Yes, this was awkward, way out in left field as it was for someone like Marilee. How was he to react to the demur church mouse, lovely as she was, lying uneasily beside him now?

"Are you going to do it?" she asked, shrinking into the bedding, breathless. Such gall from her own lips.

He sat up and folded his legs, looking at her, laboring for a way to talk to her about something they had never talked about before. He had no idea of what went wrong, only that they had fallen into a pattern and that his frustration with it had redoubled over the years.

"Marilee, it's not a matter of 'doing it'. That's not what it is. We vowed to grow old together. We make love, not *do it*. We make love because it's a wonderful way to express our feelings for each other. It's sharing something the rest of the world is excluded from, a bond. It's knowing each other in ways no one else ever will."

Her eyes were wet. It dawned on her that she had never heard anyone, not even Reverend Aragones, speak so eloquently about their beliefs. "I'm sorry," she said, wanting to get past the doubts that had been laid bare in the kitchen. "I didn't mean to make it sound demeaning."

"I know you didn't." His tone had turned patient and compassionate.

"I'm trying." One hand clasping the other, she rested them on her belly. "I want so much to please you."

He paused again, gazing at her. Suddenly it was one of those times when he realized how much he loved her, despite her religious zeal, despite the fact that it was also the first time after nine years of marriage she had presented herself undressed, as a wife, as a woman trying to get in touch with the essence of marriage. Her hands were shaking. It was as if any second she might fold up under the weight of his eyes, though her labored breath hinted resolve. It was also the first time he sensed that another Marilee lived inside her beautiful skin, one that was ready to experience a more earthy part of life. Lovely to look at and a near perfect homemaker—did she sincerely want to set free her sexuality?

"You look nervous," he said.

"I am. Very." To stop fidgeting with her hands, she folded her arms beneath her breasts and hugged herself.

"Wanna cover up?"

"No."

"It's not just a matter of pleasing me, you know. Husbands want their wives to enjoy making love as much as they do."

"I know. I just don't know how. But I'll try."

Johnny sighed. His shoulders fell. Another crossroads—perhaps the most significant milestone of their nine-year marriage. He was actually talking to Marilee about sex, as if she suddenly wanted to travel that road with him, not just as an unwitting accessory, but as a vibrant, willing partner. It took considerable adjusting to. As he stared at her, the images from Cassandra's parlor that had so thoroughly possessed him seeped from his thoughts like melting wax. His wife's presence in bed, which had not distracted him for so many years, now did so profoundly. A tidal-wave of debauchery or a fountain of innocence; given the choice it surprised him how captivating innocence could be.

He took her hand in his. She had taken upon herself the act of a wife and it had given him a break from the insane choices he had made. He had traveled through a swamp, silted with the rawest form of pleasure, only to end up in his own bed facing an unexpected revelation. Had Marilee looked at him this way before, had she given herself over to an intimate evening, perhaps it would have diluted Cassandra's ability to snatch away his mores. His defenses would have been nourished and keen. He looked at his wife, naked and waiting, and found himself absorbed in the aura about her that was falling over him like a warm summer rain. It was real. He saw the anticipation in her eyes, which made him wonder about the limits of her resolve.

"How do you feel?" he asked.

"I'm not sure. I feel tingles all over my body."

"Does it feel agreeable?"

"Yes."

"What if I asked you to come to bed without the shower?"

She looked at him straight on. "Why would you?" she asked, curiosity more than aversion.

"Because I like the way you smell without the soap."

"But ..."

"But what?" he interrupted. "You shower every morning. You don't get that dirty in one day. Things don't always have to be pristine and perfect."

She nodded uneasily. "I ... I would come to bed that way if you asked me to?" she said, exercising effort to overcome her reluctance.

The struggle in her eyes melted his heart. It also intensified the pangs of guilt. He knew that, even if this was the beginning of a new chapter, he could not deny what had happened in that house. Whether it had awakened dormant genes, or exposed a simple weakness, or whether it had been a spell cast by those that Brian Fowler described as supernatural, the reason didn't matter—an irreversible temptation rested just under his skin. He loved his wife, and even if they could somehow breathe life into their marriage, he faced a dilemma. Like a moth drawn to light, he would again be drawn to the house on Confederate Square.

Marilee closed her eyes for a moment with a hard swallow, and then looked at him again. Her voice wavered slightly. "Those things you said in the kitchen ... I want to try. You said a man can make a woman ..."

"Wet?" he injected, his voice tinged with sarcasm.

She looked away. Her knee came up and she crossed it over her thigh. "Yes. I want you to do that to me."

Johnny could hardly believe his ears. He thought he had stepped over the line with her in the kitchen. He had assumed he had offended her, that she would be hesitant to even share his bed anytime soon. But the opposite was true. She said it with sincerity, on a breath hinting resolve and genuine desire rather than a concession to his challenge.

"You sure, Marilee? You're not doing this just to make me happy?"

"Oh, Johnny. I want to be your wife. I want to show you how much I love you. I'm just nervous, that's all."

He ached for her and wanted to comfort her. At the same time, he couldn't let go of holding her responsible for their empty marriage. He leaned forward with a gentle kiss, a caress of her lips with his. It evolved into a kiss unlike any they had ever experienced together, unhurried, emerging from the shadows of their love, a mutual and passionate promise of what was to come. Shifting his head, he kissed her belly, her heart beating so furiously that it had warmed her body. She stiffened, a reaction born of desire, not dread, her skin luxurious to his lips, soft, silky, inviting. He kissed the fleshy area around her navel and drew his hand up her leg and rested it on the curve of her hip. His kisses trailed up her abdomen and he nudged her left breast with his nose, breathing the fragrance of her skin as the tension in her body slowly began to recede. He licked and sucked one of the nipples, dark and covered over with tiny bumps, moving then and pausing upon the other before kissing his way back down her belly. She resisted the urge to draw her knees together when his nose brushed her pubic hair, where he lingered in the musk of her arousal, allowing her a moment to adjust to an intimacy she had never known. Then she gasped at the feel of his tongue.

Her breath quickened as his tongue became more assertive and her hips lifted off the sheet. There was no resistance when he coaxed her legs further apart. It came to him that she truly wanted to be his lover, to give of herself and take from him in return; his harsh words must have blown the cobwebs from her mind, for her body had grown damp and pliant and receptive to the slightest touch. Her legs widened voluntarily when he came between them on his knees. Her head turned to the side as his hands brushed up her inner thighs, and her mouth fell open with a moan when his fingers massaged the hidden folds, parting them, exposing the dark pink petals tinged so provocatively in black, the clitoris swollen and awaiting his touch.

On each breath as he leaned forward, her subtle fragrances entered his nose. He kissed between her legs and his tongue flicked at the supple flesh. What seemed unthinkable just an hour before had become part of the night—he found himself devouring his wife. She squirmed and used her hands to press his head closer and she wrapped her legs around his back. Her wetness had dampened the sheet. Indeed, her eagerness surprised him and made him hunger for her. She had taken his hand and started willingly on this path. All reluctance was lost. The fact that it was happening was a revelation to be considered later; for now he couldn't get the pajama bottoms down past his hips quick enough.

Her legs tightened around him and they fell in sync with the rhythm of their bodies, her hunger as fierce as his desperation for the shivers of release. He thrust hard again and again and from her came a shriek, a cry of sudden recognition of that which can build and explode in one's body. The sound caught him by surprise. Had it actually come from Marilee, his wife, the woman that locks the bathroom door before taking her clothes off? That too he would ponder later, as the throes of passion had overtaken him, racing from his loins, up his spine, and set his mind reeling; and what had come in endless dribbles as a result of Gerhard Trent's talented finger, now spewed forth with abandon deep within the contractions below his wife's belly.

They lay entwined, sweating, man atop the woman, both in awe of this turn of events. He felt her breasts pressed against his chest, her arms about his neck, her breath upon his ear. He lifted his head and looked at her face, and there he saw the glow for the first time, the glow that made a man feel worthy, that look beyond words that could lock him to her forever. It was a precise kind of communication, feminine in nature, found only in the eyes of a woman expressing her love, powerful enough for an enduring grip on a man's heart.

He pulled free and sat up beside her, his lower legs still tangled in silk. She turned onto her side, resting her cheek on her forearm, looking at him. There was a gleam in her eyes, as if she had met and conquered her life's greatest challenge, a look that said she had come to know her husband.

Marilee broke their long silence. "Did you think I could do it?"

"Why have we waited so long?"

Looking down at the bed, she pondered the question. "All my life I believed decent women behave in certain ways. There're things we shouldn't do." She took a deep breath. "I did them tonight and I'm a little embarrassed."

"Embarrassed? Why?"

"It's like a stranger entered my body. It feels ... well, it feels nice. I'm embarrassed because I'm afraid of what you'll think of me."

"Are you kidding? All this time you've locked me out. You've been a cocoon. Tonight, just like that, you turned into butterfly."

Her face flushed. She took a deep breath and then displayed a playful smile. "It's your fault, you know."

"What do you mean?"

"You never told me. You never made me understand, until tonight, in the kitchen. You forced me to see."

Johnny sighed. He looked away in thought, then said: "Nine years. It gets by you in the blink of an eye." He looked at her. "We forgot what's important. We got caught up in getting our lives started: my career, paying off bills. We were stuck in a routine. Nine years go by and we never stopped to talk." He formed a confused smile. "I thought you hated me after I yelled at you in the kitchen!"

"It made my stomach turn. It hurt and it did make me mad. It also made me want to be your wife more than I ever realized."

He looked at her for a long while. "Has it taken us all this time to fall in love?"

"Maybe it has," she said. "Or maybe it's taken this long to recognize it."

"Oh God, Marilee! I've always loved you, but it became a confused, tormented kind of love. Now I realize I love you madly. I wouldn't want to live without you."

She hesitated before she responded, the words caught in her throat, her eyes welling with tears. "Well, it's only been only nine years," she said, wanting to close that long chapter. "Shouldn't be too hard to make up for lost time."

His chest swelled. Here they were, naked in bed together, talking, really talking for the first time since they were married. It revived his desire to spend the rest of his life with her. He resolved to forsake his enchantment for Cassandra Mott. And those episodes with Julian? ... well, maybe that was a part of him, but hasn't it always been? Perhaps, but he had kept it buried since college. He would do so again. He would never again jeopardize his marriage.

Her eyes shifted to between his legs. "I like looking at your penis. It was just hard to admit. Sometimes, when you're asleep, I'd look at the shape of it under the sheet."

"Marilee ... I ..."

She smiled and wiped away a tear with her finger. "You look funny with your pajamas halfway down your legs."

"Couldn't get the damn things off at the key moment."

"I know. Almost made me laugh."

He leaned back on an elbow and pushed the pajamas down his legs with his free hand. Marilee pulled them from his ankles and flung them to the floor. He liked being in bed with her this way, talking, just simply enjoying each other's company.

"Was it hard for you, Marilee? I mean, after all this time, was it hard to let go?"

"Not as hard as I thought it would be." She released a long sigh. "I really did believe you'd think I'm wicked if I behaved that way."

He gazed at her. An eerie feeling came over him and settled in his hands. It was easy enough to renew his vow, but lurking in the back of his mind was doubt. Cassandra Mott was alive on his skin; he knew it and it scared him. It was like he could feel her presence, a connection of some kind, consuming and mystical. It not only threatened his marriage, it threatened his sanity. Like heroin controls a man's soul, Cassandra had addicted him. She would reach out and offer another fix. Looking at his wife, he saw the day-to-day routines of his past life fading like a fine mist in the summer sun.

Please bear with me. Please, Marilee, give me time to find a way to break free of this. Know I didn't ask for it, but I love another woman; and heaven help me, a most beautiful man. I don't know what to do. I don't know how to ask for your help.

An overwhelming loneliness set in. He lied down on his side and rested his head on the pillow. Marilee turned over and backed up to him. Placing his arm over her, their bodies locked and warm, he silently berated his newfound weakness. He had uncovered a secret world that seemed unreal and complicated, and he realized that no matter how close he and Marilee lay together, the bother and sister Mott were between them. It wasn't just his misdeeds from earlier in the day and the days prior; it was the hold he felt on his soul. It wasn't just his introduction to debauchery and the pleasures of the ninth gate, nor Cassandra's great beauty, nor her fondness to display it; it was the drug of her persona. And, even more daunting, it was the magic of Julian's embrace. Johnny feared his willpower amounted to little more than a trifling snag.

He detested himself. How could he hurt the woman lying so devotedly, so sensuously in his arms; the woman that will awaken at first light and prepare his breakfast, and then wash his soiled clothes; the woman that encourages and inspires him, even after he had disappeared for a whole day, only to come home and yell at her? If she ever found out, she could never love the man he had become.

When Marilee fell asleep, he rolled onto his back and stared at the walls most of the night, their warmth mingled beneath the sheet, loathing himself, wondering what was to become of his marriage, his future, everything he held dear.

Chapter 10

Marilee awoke feeling effervescent. She sat up in the bed, looked down at her nude body, then looked at Johnny, still sleeping. She drew up her knees and ran her palms up the back of her legs. Waking up naked felt naughty, and energizing. She got up and put on her robe, the elation from the night before tainted with concern over Johnny's recent behavior. As she looked at him, Globalcorp came to mind. It seemed he had lost interest in his work. He had changed and it had something to do with that house.

Thinking her unanswered questions would spoil the morning, she decided to keep it inside and focus on what had transpired the night before.

She was preparing toast and scrambled eggs when he came in for breakfast. Her vibrant mood was infectious. As he watched her go about her morning chore, a pleasant tranquility fell over the kitchen, their fleeting smiles hinting at what had transpired between them. With a plate of toast in hand, she joined him at the table.

Her demure morning radiance suggested that she might be a bit self-conscious, considering the way she had let herself go during the night. Lifting a forkful of scrambles eggs, Johnny watched her reticent manner.

"Any regrets?" he asked.

"No," she said, passing the toast.

"How do you feel this morning?"

"Different."

"Oh? In what way?"

She looked at her plate, ill at ease with a subject she had never talked about before. "When I came out of the bathroom last night, I liked the way it felt when you looked at me."

"I liked it, too. You have a beautiful body."

"I didn't know it was supposed to be like that. Didn't know it *could* be like that."

"That was your first climax, wasn't it?"

Her face flushed.

"Was it?"

"Yes."

"Think you'll let out that little scream every time?"

"Johnny! Don't embarrass me!"

He smiled at her reluctance to discuss it, thinking about her resolve when she came out of the bathroom. "Having a hard time talking about it?"

"Yes," she said quickly.

He wondered what she was contemplating. "What are you thinking about?"

"What you mentioned in the kitchen last night. I don't know if I can do things like that."

He remembered the challenges he had fired off at her. Now they were talking openly about their sexual relationship, though Marilee was a bit reserved. It would take some getting used to. "You mean squatting over my face?"

Her eyes shifted to the stack of toast. She reached for a slice in want of something to do with her hands, her lower lip held nervously between her teeth. It troubled her, not what he was asking, not that such acts between a man and a woman went beyond the mores of her upbringing; but that she suspected other wives did these things.

"You don't have to feel pressured to do that. I'd never expect you to do anything that makes you uncomfortable."

Her eyes lifted. "But I want you to be glad you married me."

"That doesn't have to include something you don't want to do." With a disarming smile, he reached across the table and gave her forearm a squeeze, which gave her a sense of relief. "I might fantasize about it though."

She reached for the butter dish. Everything hit all at once: his outbursts the night before, his odd behavior, Globalcorp, her misgivings over the Mott house. Just now, just when their marriage had crossed a new threshold, everything seemed unstable. A solemn look came over her.

"I don't understand what's happened," she said, absently buttering the toast. "Your anger. Your behavior. Something's happened." She looked up. "I thought about it all day yesterday. It's like you've lost interest in your project with Globalcorp. They leave messages and you don't to return their calls. You haven't done that before."

His shoulders fell.

"I felt closer to you last night than I ever have," she went on, "but something's come between us. You disappear all day and come home angry. I'm worried, Johnny. If you need a break from your work, I understand."

The weight of his guilt settled on him like wet cement.

Marilee had wanted the morning to be free of stress, but her concerns were too disturbing. "It has something to do with that house. You didn't want to take me there. I thought it was because you wanted to work, but that wasn't it, was it? You really didn't want to go back inside that house. You felt uncomfortable while we were there, and so did I. Then you went back for some reason. There must be something about that house that's caused you to change."

Panic tightened his chest. She was inching closer to the truth, a truth she could never accept or understand. But he owed her an explanation of some kind, something to justify his irrational behavior. It was more than a fascination with Cassandra Mott, more than an urge to be with Julian; it was a hold of some kind, and he had yet to figure it out. He simply could not walk away from that house.

She could see his crestfallen demeanor, his reluctance to answer. "You don't want to talk about it?" she asked.

"No." He rubbed an eye and slumped against the chair-back. "I need a break, Marilee. Every day's a carbon copy of the day before. I'm tired of that."

Some part of him wanted to tell her everything, to let the words pour out and then ask for her understanding and help. He wanted to take her hand and let her lead him from this darkness. If only he could; but not this. The thought of a confession made him cringe. To confess the decadence he had been involved in, the pleasure he had taken from acts she could never grasp—that he would surely be drawn to it again—made his stomach churn.

"Last night was wonderful, Johnny," she said resolutely, the voice of a woman remarkably changed from the day before. "I enjoyed being your lover. I also want to be someone you can talk to, the one you turn to when you need help. I can be the wife you want me to be, so I'll wait. I know something's happened to you, something from outside our home. I'll wait until you decide to tell me what it is. I'll wait as long as it takes."

He wanted to scream, to go running from the house screaming at the top of his lungs. He didn't know what to say to his own wife, who was desperately reaching out to him. He knew only that he loved her; and that, in spite of the promise of the two of them sharing paradise, he also loved the one that never spoke. A thousand times yes, he loved her; but his love could not diminish what had awakened inside him. Even if she wanted to, she could not lessen the ache, when only a man could do that, a man called Julian Mott.

"Please, Marilee, bear with me. I know I've been preoccupied. Just bear with me while I work it out."

Her eyes shifted from him. "I'm sorry. I didn't mean to pry."

They finished breakfast somberly.

"Are you going out today?" she asked apprehensively when Johnny got up from the table.

"No. I plan to finish that set of graphics and get it out to Globalcorp this afternoon."

He didn't notice the sense of relief that washed over Marilee's face. It was just part of her concern, but a substantial part nevertheless. If he lost the contract that he struggled so hard to get, if the checks from Globalcorp stopped coming in, they would lose all the ground they had gained during the last few months, not to mention the damage to his credibility. They would fall further behind on their bills and it would be that much harder to pull ahead again. She stared at the table, suddenly realizing a credit rating paled in comparison to losing her husband.

The first hour at his drafting table passed. Johnny had glanced at Brian Fowler's book several times, *Unexplained Facts About the Supernatural*, resisting the urge to pick it up, though it lay within reach like a pack of cigarettes tempting a smoker trying to quit. But it wasn't as simple as facing down the Medusa of nicotine—it involved the onset of a deep seated fear, that which could not be explained, that which had changed him, when printed within the book's pages might lie some answers. But to pick it up and read it now would mean missing another deadline. He couldn't afford to test the limits of Globalcorp's tolerance.

Another hour passed. The midmorning sun spilled into the room and the potted plants were healthy and fragrant. He had toiled with his drafting pens and had pecked on the keyboard of his laptop, searching for the right perspective for the ad. Then he heard Marilee start the vacuum cleaner in the other room, and he suffered even that. Propping his elbows on the drafting table, he buried his face in his hands. How many men would give everything to have a wife like her, a wife that provided an impeccable home and managed a most difficult budget; a wife that had supported his decision to quit a good job and start his own business, and then never complain about the hardships it brought on?

He shuffled through the papers spread before him. There had been some progress made on the project. He turned and looked at the wall clock, fairly certain he'd be ready to ship out this phase for Globalcorp's approval by three o'clock or so that afternoon. It was the first time his work seemed like labor, the first time ideas did not flow from his mind the moment he perched on the stool. Even choosing color schemes seemed trying. Yet he labored on, and by three o'clock a proposal for selling cosmetics through magazine ads had taken form. He printed out the last of the graphics, and then gathered it all up and sealed it in bubble-padded envelope.

Marilee was in the den, sitting at her easel, sketching with charcoal on a fresh canvas. With the large envelope in hand, Johnny stepped over behind her. It was the rudimentary sketch of her next still-life. That and composing flower arrangements in pastels was her hobby—her therapy, as she liked to say. She was quite good at it, having sold a few pieces during the last couple of years. Johnny loved her creations, though it had caused him some unspoken grief when she declared her talent a gift from God, thereby donating her sales proceeds to the church.

"Thought I'd walk this over to the overnight drop," he said, lifting the envelope. His emotions had finally calmed by midday, primarily because worrying about Cassandra Mott and Globalcorp and losing his wife had simply worn him out. Around noon, shifting his focus to the turn of events the night before had had a positive and productive effect. "Wanna walk with me?"

Her smiled warmed his heart. "Love to," she said, brushing her fingers together to dust off the charcoal.

They were a half block down the street when Johnny took her hand. "I heard the phone ring several times today," he said.

"Yes, it did."

"People from the church?"

"Yes, and one telemarketer selling carpet."

"You didn't talk very long. I'm used to hearing you gab most of the afternoon."

"I've got more important things to think about right now," she replied, glancing at him as they crossed the street and entered a shaded square.

"Like what?"

"You ... that's what. I bowed out for a while, including the Easter program. I'll be at home until whatever is bothering you is over with. In case you need me."

He was watching the ancient brickwork pass beneath their feet. Though he complained from time to time about how much time she spent on the phone, and how much time she spent at church, he never meant to interfere with things that were important to her.

"I'm not sure that's necessary, Marilee."

"It is to me."

They walked the lovely sidewalks of old Savannah in silence, reaching the Federal Express office a few minutes later. Emerging from the pristine lobby, Marilee had an idea.

"We're just a few blocks from the market," she said, looking at her watch. "Would you like to walk over there? We could pick up something special for dinner."

"Are we celebrating something in particular?" he asked, tongue-in-cheek, glancing at her breasts.

She slapped his shoulder. "You must like embarrassing me."

"No," he replied with a smug smile. "I'm just wondering if our celebration has something to do with getting those graphics in the mail, or is it because of last night?"

"I'll go with the second reason. You want to?"

"Sure. Maybe they'll have some good steaks, huh?"

They started in the direction of the market.

Everything was within walking distance in the historic district, which is one of the reasons he loved living there. Their favorite markets, a variety of shops, the bank and a few good eateries were all close to their neighborhood. Johnny's barber was only two blocks from their house. From the Federal Express office it was less than a ten-minute walk to the market.

Approaching it, Johnny stopped in his tracks.

Perusing the fruits and vegetables displayed on the sidewalk in front of the store was Cassandra Mott. Julian stood just behind her. Johnny stared as if he had seen something that frightened him. Seeing Cassandra out and about happened to be the last thing he had expected; but there she was, like anyone else, quite lovely in her flowing summer dress, placing vegetables in a basket that dangled from her forearm. As if she had not noticed him, she didn't turn with an acknowledgment; though he felt certain she was aware of his approach.

"What is it?" Marilee asked, looking at his glazed eyes.

"Uh ... nothing. Just thinking about something I might have left out of that envelope."

"Well, if you did, we'll just have to send it separately."

"Yeah," he said absently, staring at the enchantress.

Johnny's pace seemed involuntary as they started toward the store. Nearing the entrance, he said: "Go on inside. I'll be in after I take a look at what they have out here."

With Marilee safely inside the store, he drew a breath and edgily stepped up beside Cassandra.

"Why, it's Johnny Feelwater," she said gaily, feigning surprise. "Out for a stroll with your lovely wife today?"

He was looking at Julian; predictably dressed in his off-white linen shirt and pants, hands in his pockets, relaxed. His eyes ... interpreting the message in them took little imagination. Johnny lowered his head. The mere sight of him confirmed his addiction. Julian's masculine symmetry had turned Johnny's eyes to the sidewalk. One glance is all it took to start the chemical changes, and the feelings that produced immediately collected in his loins. He lifted his head and tilted it sideways, unable to deny his own thoughts. Their eyes locked. Both knew it was a matter of time.

"Darlin', I'm so glad to see you before Friday," Cassandra went on to say as she observed the magnetism between the two men. "Julian and I are planning an evening out that night. We'd be delighted to have you join us."

His eyes shifted to her, sweeping over her, a glance that reminded him once again of the power of her charm. Friday night? An evening out? What on earth could she possibly have in mind? He rather doubted they intended to see a movie.

"Nothing fancy," she added. "Just dinner and a nightclub. A place I've heard about only recently."

He looked at the vegetables in her basket, wondering what to say, thinking that if he could resist her invitation he might break the spell they had over him. Then he turned and looked at Julian again, all too aware of the limits of his resolve.

His eyes shifted back to Cassandra, her red hair falling in curls about her neck, lustrous in the late afternoon sun. *Read my mind, Cassandra. Tell me what I'll do. Tell me if I can resist anything you want of me. Tell me if I can even wait that long to be with Julian.*

She smiled and turned to Julian. "I believe he'd like to accompany us, little brother. Won't that be fun?" She turned her attention to the sky and then looked at her forearm. "Oh my! Shall we return to the house, Julian? You know how quickly the sun burns my skin."

Setting the basket of vegetables aside, she raised her parasol and took hold of Julian's elbow. She looked at Johnny and drew her tongue across her upper lip as her eyes drifted down the slender length of his body. She winked, and then they turned and started toward her house. Johnny stood dumbly, staring at the basket of vegetables she had left behind, wondering why she happened to be here, just now, just when he and Marilee walked up. His gaze shifted and he looked after them, both wary and captivated by what she must have planned for him Friday night. And as he watched Julian escort her down the block, that familiar ache found its way into his hands.

Collecting his wits, he turned and went inside the store, where he found Marilee at the butcher's counter, awaiting a burly woman behind the counter to cut two steaks.

"New York strip sound appetizing?" she asked when he approached.

He nodded, watching the woman slice two steaks off a large slab of beef.

Marilee saw the distance in his eyes, one of his recent nuances that was difficult to get used to. "Did you pick out some vegetables?"

He shook his head.

"We'll get some frozen carrots then, and some green leaf for a salad. That should be enough for dinner, don't you think?"

"That's fine," he said.

Marilee watched him discreetly, wondering what might be going on behind his absent gaze, a little nervous now that his behavior changes seemed to strike so unpredictably. Having considered many possibilities, she had decided the cause might be a chemical imbalance, perhaps brought on by overwork or his approaching middle age. What else could explain such bizarre behavior? Little did she know his mind was reeling, that his imagination had been set afire, that she faced a worrisome night speculating on his whereabouts, come Friday.

The butcher handed them a package of steaks and they picked up a few other items before leaving the store. Back home, while Marilee prepared dinner, Johnny sprawled in a wicker chair in the garden room in distant thought. When Marilee appeared in the doorway to let him know dinner was ready, he didn't seem to notice her standing there, or that she had changed into one of his favorite outfits: blue jeans and a red, bare-midriff blouse.

"Did you look to see if you left something out of the envelope?" she asked.

Responding to her voice, his head turned in her direction. "What?" he said as if he had dropped a thought.

"Did you leave something out of Globalcorp's package?"

He stared at her for a moment. "What are you talking about?"

She paused in thought and then shrugged it off. "Never mind. Dinner's ready."

At the table Marilee remembered something she had thought about off and on all day. "Mother called this morning."

Johnny looked up.

"Her doctor told her it was time for the hysterectomy. He's checking her into the hospital Sunday night."

Johnny pondered the very little he knew about this operation.

"She'd like me there with her," Marilee continued. "I promised I'd come and spend the weekend with her, and be there when she's in the hospital."

He had been thinking about the way Julian looked at him in front of the market. This news returned his thoughts to that.

"I'll drive to Atlanta Friday afternoon, if that's okay with you."

He looked at her again. "Sure," he said, a bit antsy. "Uh, that's a serious operation, isn't it?"

"Well, yes, it is. I think she'll be a little more relaxed about it if I spend a little time with her before she goes in. Will you be all right while I'm gone?"

"Me? Sure. Just go. Don't worry about it."

She had forgotten the salad dressing. Getting up for it, she felt his reaction had been uncharacteristic, considering the conversation was about her mother. He actually displayed a little compassion, when Marilee had expected him to morbidly calculate the odds against her mother's survival, insinuating that the world would be a better place if her mother didn't make it off the operating table.

The two of them disliked each other intensely, her mother being especially opinionated concerning anything Johnny said or did. Marilee had long since given up being concerned about it, having gone through emotional hell for a couple of years before she realized it would never change. She had even developed a sense of humor about their relationship, born one year at the state fair. Stopping to get out of the sun for a while, she and Johnny went into a big barn where a hog show was in progress. While they rested in the bleachers, two of the male hogs got into a vicious fight, at which time the attendant pushed a piece of plywood between them. Unable to see each other, the hogs forgot what they were doing, thus ending the fight.

Marilee had laughed, wondering if a piece of plywood would be as effective on Johnny and her mother.

He seemed preoccupied all through dinner and the rest of the evening. When she came out of the bathroom after showering and brushing her teeth, she found him in bed, lying on his back, staring at the ceiling. She eased in between his arm and ribs, pulled the sheet over her lower body and rested her head on his shoulder. Coming to bed nude had not been as challenging as the first time. She liked the feel of his eyes; and then being held so intimately through the night had been one of the most exhilarating experiences she had ever had. Fifteen minutes later, when she fell asleep, he was still staring at the ceiling.

During the rest of the week Johnny's mood swings continued, though he flared in anger only once, on Thursday morning.

"Goddammit!" she heard him yell over the hum of the dishwasher, followed by shattering glass.

Hurrying to the garden room, she stopped in the doorway. He had spilled coffee all over his work. The coffee was dripping off the edge of his drafting table. The shattered glass had been the mug he threw against the wall in anger.

"Why are you just standing there?" he blurted irritably.

"I thought you might be hurt," she said, more concerned about his irrationality than offended.

"I'm not."

"I'll get some paper towels."

"Yeah," he said curtly. "Good idea."

Marilee returned to the kitchen for a roll of paper towels, wondering how to approach him. She had been thinking about a psychologist. This was not the man she had married and had lived with for nine years. He needed help, professional help, she had concluded, having agonized over it for two days. The problem was finding a way to talk to him about it. He seemed to be unaware of his mood swings, probably because she had quietly tolerated them all week. Moody or quiet one minute, he could become playful the next, as if nothing at all bothered him.

That night Marilee decided to take a long warm bath, thinking it would ease the tension in her neck. She had avoided her husband most of the day; he had sulked through redoing the work the spill had ruined. After lighting several candles, she turned off the light and lowered herself into the luxuriously warm water, which immediately began its relaxing effect. She pondered leaving Johnny alone for the weekend. A trip to Atlanta just now would be out of the question if it weren't for the seriousness of her mother's operation. She *had* to go, though she would worry about him every minute she was away.

The bathroom door swung open a few minutes later. Johnny stepped in and his gaze settled adoringly upon her. There was no distance between them now, nor did he seem tense or preoccupied. He had walked in purposefully, as if there was something he wanted to say; but as he stared, whatever had been on his mind seemed to melt away. Still feeling a little reserved, Marilee resisted an urge to sink further into the water. Her eyes shifted as blossoms of gooseflesh spread across her skin and overwhelmed her ingrained sense of modesty. It pleasantly surprised her, the thrill of his eyes raking over her body, so quickly stimulating her imagination. "There's room in here for two," she ventured, remembering the challenges he had issued earlier in the week. She knew now to suggest daring ideas without thinking about them. That way it sounded more natural and lessened the chance of changing her mind.

Johnny stepped forward. His mood had softened; he looked like a man walking through a dream. Still not used to indulging himself with her nudity, he stopped a few feet from the tub. All those puritanical years of housecoats and locked bathroom doors; he never expected to see her sitting in the tub, her skin awash in the golden glow of candlelight and glistening with steam. She had asked him to join her, something just a few days before he would have scoffed at as utterly improbable. His shirt fell to the floor and then he stepped out of his jeans.

All week Marilee had snatched glimpses when he undressed. Lady-like or not, now that she had discovered the more intimate aspects of marriage, she couldn't resist looking at him; and just now she intended to have much more than a glimpse. When his leg came out of the jeans, she stared brazenly at the fleshy danglings between his legs, hardly blinking when his leg lifted over the edge of the tub. Their eyes met when he lowered himself in. She had noticed it had been his testicles that touched the water first. Yes, she enjoyed looking at him, she realized, aware of the flutters below her belly when his feet slid in between her hips and the two sides of the tub.

"Are you still angry with me," she asked.

He looked at her quizzically. "Angry?"

"This morning, when the coffee ruined you work, remember? You snapped at me. You were quiet all day."

"I'm sorry."

"Did much get ruined?"

"Let's not talk about that right now."

She smiled, splashing her chest. "I have to leave for Atlanta tomorrow?"

"I know."

"Will you miss me?"

His adoring expression answered her question. She watched his eyes drop to her navel. Instead of bubble-bath she had chosen fragrant oil, which left nothing below the water to one's imagination. She drew up her knees and parted them, and her breath stopped for a moment when his eyes dropped lower. It beleaguered her, now that her marriage had taken flight, to have it unraveling at the same time.

For Johnny, sharing the bath with her was freedom from the brother and sister Mott, a thorn removed from his consciousness. He would not go there Friday night, he resolved looking at the woman that had evolved from a religious zealot into a sensuous wife. Even though the beautiful pair had been on his mind all week, even though images of their encounters paraded through his brain constantly, he would stay home. If he could just get past that overwhelming hunger, past that fascination with their prurient lifestyle. One moment he felt free of them, as if they had come and gone like a whisper in the night; the next minute they owned his every thought; which always seemed to lead to another walk down that upstairs hallway. That's when it frightened him—their power to summon him and his inability to resist. That's when he could look at his wife, as he was now, and vow to cut himself free. That's when he feared, down deep inside, what was to become of him.

Friday morning was met with gloom. Having shared a night of affection and intimacy, Marilee awoke to see him sitting on the edge of the bed, leaning forward, staring at the floor, preoccupied again. Would he mope around the house not knowing what to do with himself? Would he pull the stool up to his drafting table only to get frustrated and storm out of the house?

She sat up against the headboard and pulled up the sheet, staring at his back, drawing on her courage. "Johnny, what's wrong? Why can't you talk to me about what's bothering you?"

He lifted his head and sighed impatiently. "Nothing's bothering me."

"Yes, it is," she stated flatly. "You're carefree one minute, then moody the next. We had a wonderful night last night and now you're staring off in space again. These highs and lows—it's like you're depressed."

"What are you getting at, Marilee?"

"I'm worried about you ... about us. Maybe you should see a doctor," she said, throwing it out and holding her breath in anticipation of his unpredictable response.

He turned to face her. "A doctor? Why? I'm not sick."

"You know I don't mean that kind of doctor, Johnny."

"Say what you mean then," he shot back.

It was as if he had dared her to go on, but she was in no mood to back down. She came out with it. "A psychiatrist."

"You're kidding, right?"

"Surely you're aware of your mood swings. They're getting worse. We have to find out what's bothering you; maybe run some tests. For all we know, you may have developed a chemical imbalance of some kind."

"Mood swings?" he huffed. *I can't be that hard to live with.* He couldn't pretend—he knew exactly what she meant. Only the magnitude of his unpredictable behavior eluded him, which Marilee had been suffering quietly for days. Truth of the matter, he had considered a seeing shrink, disinclined only because he knew the diagnosis. No psychiatrist would believe what he had to say. If only he could talk to Marilee, the only person that cared, that might believe him, though it was a straw he could never clutch. She wouldn't see the acts he had participated in as something that had happened to him, that he was a victim—he wasn't certain himself. Whether it was a mystic power that drew him to that house or his own weakness for what he found there, he would as soon cut off a finger as devastate her with his vile secret.

"I'm sorry, Marilee," he said, trying to be reassuring. "I know I've been edgy lately. Guess that damn project's weighing on me. It'll pass. You know how long it's been since I've had a break. I'm burned out. You can understand that, can't you?"

"Yes," she said, defeated. He obviously wanted to divert the conversation from seeing a psychiatrist. Maybe he was burned out on the Globalcorp project, but that wasn't the problem. If anything, it was caused by the problem. The sheet fell lower and she watched his eyes drop to her breasts.

By one o'clock Marilee was in the bedroom packing a bag. She would be in Atlanta four or five days. Shortly after two o'clock, Johnny stood on the front porch, watching her back the mini-van out of the driveway. She waved from the street and then drove off. He stood in a daze for a moment, contemplating five days without her; then he turned and locked the door.

Chapter 11

Johnny started toward Factors Row. The riverfront would be crowded with tourists this time of year; he didn't care, he loved going there anyway. Nowhere was Savannah's history richer than the row of old four story buildings that once housed the offices of prosperous cotton factors.

He turned down a steep alleyway between two buildings, a precarious descent to the riverfront cobbled in ancient ballast stones. Inside a small store, he bought a bottle of beer. Outside, an elderly couple vacated a bench overlooking the river. There he sat and sipped the beer. The smell of fish and marine oil wafted from the river. The sun warmed his outstretched legs and glinted on the murky surface. Tourists walked by in endless numbers. Raucous, misbehaving children and parents taking pictures of them busied the park-like walkway; which indicated, as far as Johnny was concerned, that the world was vastly over-populated.

He sat in contemplation, feeling apart from the humanity surrounding him. A massive tanker passed along the waterfront, its great hull dwarfing everything it neared. His eyes shifted north and settled on the graceful suspension bridge spanning the river: highway 17, which connected Savannah to South Carolina, the tiny cars like ants crossing over a twig.

Everything about his life seemed different and vague: career, marriage, even his perspective. He had lost his grip on what was real and unreal. His life's history seemed like magazine pages flashing quickly in the wind. Yet the house on Confederate Square was alive and fresh in his mind, as if he were part of that world, as if the beautiful pair were more like family than acquaintances.

A small gust stirred the dust and gum wrappers near his feet. It made him feel alone, like someone living on the street, people looking through him in passing. If any one of them were to hear what he was thinking, they would be wary of anything he had to say, fearful, disbelieving. They would not understand his encounters with the unknown; that within him, within everyone, lie a hidden and most compelling fascination with carnal pleasure.

Five days alone. A gift? A gratuitous opportunity to indulge himself in Cassandra's fountain of decadence; or a companionless eternity to fear? All he could do was continue his contemplations, try to rebalance his life; and in the end, hope he didn't lose everything. It just seemed there was too much to face.

The brother and sister Mott had endeared him. Cassandra had reached inside him, found the void in his life, shown him pleasures he had never imagined. He had never sensed the slightest sign of danger in their presence. Yet he feared them. It occurred to him, as he watched the tiny specks of traffic crossing over the bridge, that he and Marilee should pack up and get out of Savannah, maybe move to Charleston ... no, too close. California would be better. San Francisco. Start over a continent away from the beguiling seductress and her Pandora's Box of surprises. In time he would forget. His desire for Julian would eventually fade, slowly, like an addict's fading need for drugs. He could bury that side of him, again.

A tantrum-throwing child distracted him. Johnny laughed, shook his head. The idea was ridiculous. Marilee would not want to move to California, too far from her mother, her friends. He would never be able to tell her why they should leave their wonderful home. Besides, he himself planned to grow old in his beloved Savannah, spend his last days hobbling over her charmed sidewalks, and gazing out over the river just as he was now.

He leaned forward, bracing his elbows on his knees, staring at the pavement beneath his feet, the bottle of beer dangling between two knuckles. Thinking about his connection with Cassandra Mott, he smiled, intrigued that his grandmother and Cassandra had been lovers. So he had not really inherited that house—had he instead inherited a place in their world? Maybe that's why Cassandra was toying with him. Maybe the time had come that he be initiated, that he be made a permanent part of the goings-on in that house. It was perplexing, feeling as he did like nothing more than a pawn, a plaything, vulnerable and naive, gullible enough to be exploited by an eccentric enchantress whose very existence could not be explained. Rhyme and reason were as elusive as a wisp of smoke. So why was he sated with this fascination, this obsession to figure it out? Why, when his marriage had reached a promising new dawn, was he compelled to be near them, to look at them, to disrobe and lift his legs for Julian as if he were a woman?

He finished the beer and went for another, then sat on a step near the river, ignoring the tourists as he observed the myriad riggings of passing vessels. It was an ache and today the ache lived. It had set his body alive with need; an ache that hardly abated as the afternoon wore on and the sky grew weary with the day and the shadows grew longer around him. He stood, made his way through the tourists and ascended the steep alleyway. Confederate Square was just a few blocks away.

Knowing its occupants, it occurred to Johnny as he approached, that one might expect to see something remarkable about the house: glowing eyes peering from darkened windows, mysterious vapors seeping from the eaves. But nothing. Nothing other than stately serenity, standing, by anyone's definition, in old Savannah splendor. He climbed the steps and his heart quickened as he turned the key and pushed open the door.

All quiet as usual.

Inside, he glanced here and there, wondering if he would ever see the exotic black lady again, his grandmother, her beauty etched on his brain forever. He longed for a few minutes with her, to stroke her face and feel his heritage through his fingertips. Those bits and pieces he had collected about her—did they explain his sexual anomaly or his newly discovered affinity for carnal decadence, tapped so easily by a woman calling herself Cassandra Mott? Had he been imprinted by way of his grandmother's genes, to be drawn to a place like this house, to hunger for one like Julian? Likely it seemed, that he sprang from seeds that had evolved over the eons; that he was like her, with the same needs that now rested in the hollows of his body. What other explanation could there be, he wondered as he reached for a handful of peanuts.

Half way up the staircase, feeling faint, he sat down. From the wall beside him came the chorus of young voices. Closing his eyes, he swayed with their forlorn song, drifting on the haunting rhythm. He pictured himself in a forest, dancing naked among the imps and fairies in never-ending merriment, the air ripe with the smell of moss and fragrant flowers, the lush overhead boughs luminescent with sunlight that pierced through in long golden shafts. How sweet they were, these sensuous images; to escape, to forget one's trials and futile existence. Could he not simply frolic here forever, dance and be chased by the elves and watch the fairies at play, then curl up in the cool beds of ivy to sleep away the long wait for yet another day of wonder?

His eyelids lifted slightly. Diamonds of light interspersed with the images flickering in his head, and it all began to fade as his eyes opened further, falling like glittering dust into oblivion and forgotten as quickly as a dream. His eyes shifted upward, dazed, and followed the remaining stairs to the landing.

The distance seemed further to Cassandra's door as he stumbled and swayed down the hallway. Simply breathing the air in her house must have this effect on him, this dizziness, this sense of euphoria. It took a conscious effort to connect his hand with the knob.

Turning it slowly, he hesitated. His head lowered, his eyes closed, he felt his pounding heart. It was not too late to turn back, to flee this house and get back to the security of his home. But the knob had turned. The door, predisposed by its own weight, swayed open. Assaulted at once by a cloud of cigar smoke, he stepped inside the parlor and froze. His shoulders fell as he stared with incredulous eyes.

Across the room, on the far side of the sofas, sitting around a table he had not seen before, were four Confederate soldiers. As real as anything he ever set eyes on, they were playing cards. He heard murmurs and grunting at raised bets. Mingled with the pall of smoke, the unwashed odor of their soiled and sweat-stained uniforms assaulted his nostrils. Seemingly unaware Johnny had entered the room, their game continued, eyes fixed on tight knits of cards clutched in calloused hands, each of them intent on a pile of paper currency centered on the table.

When Johnny stepped further into the room, one of them glanced his way.

"You here to fetch more beer, boy?" The voice of a southern youth, so tainted with drawl a longer sentence would have been difficult to understand.

Drawn by pure fascination, Johnny slowly approached the table. The uniforms were too dirty, too weary, to have come from a costume shop. Their side-arms were weathered, well-worn flintlocks. They had leaned long rifles across the back wall. Their strong cigars, rolled irregularly, would not be found in modern day tobacco shops. On two of them, beards and long drooping moustaches hung from smudged faces, natty from the fats of past meals. With each cautious step, Johnny grew nearer, their odors angry and moldering in his nose. He stopped in awe a few feet from the table.

"That nigger must be def," said the young soldier.

"He ain't no slave, Hank. Them clothes he's wearin', too fancy."

"Could be a houseboy," said the older man, squinting at Johnny. "You Cassie's houseboy, sonny?"

"She ain't said nothin' to me about no houseboy," said the forth. "Figure Julian sees to her needs."

The young one laughed. "Now don't we all?"

Their loutish guffaws fell contemptuously on Johnny's ears. He stood dumbstruck.

"I reckon he's def," said the youth. "Cain't talk neither."

Julian emerged from his bedroom. He paused just inside the parlor, staring at Johnny. He glanced at the soldiers, then rounded the table and reached out to stroke the side of Johnny's face. The crude presence of the soldiers bled from Johnny's mind as Julian's longing blue eyes captured his gaze. When he leaned his head against Julian's palm, Julian locked his hand on the back of his neck and pulled him close. Their lips met. Their mouths became devouring and wet, much to Johnny's astonishment and that of the young soldier.

"I'll be dang," he said. "Never figured Julian to be partial to black boys. Sure takes to kissin' um, don't he?"

"Careful what you say there, Hank. Heard tell of a fella's nose once't shrinkin' up right on his face after getting' crossways with Cassie's brother."

"Ain't fer me, men gittin' that way with each other."

The older man leaned back in his chair and looked across their faces. "Ain't somethin' any one of you boys is likely to turn down one day," he said. "You out in that field long enough, see one man have a go at another. Gits to ya out there two months at a time, prayin' the Yanks don't run ya over with their dang cannons. A man can take to it right smart when he gets scared and lonely enough. Seen one or two git partial to it."

"Ain't somethin' a man wants to admit to, is it?" said the lean one.

"I thought on it once," admitted one of them. "Heard if you close your eyes, it's like a real tight woman." He laughed. "Jus' don't smell as good."

"Reckon you'd wanna pick a little bastard," said the youth, "so's he don't stomp ya 'fore ya git a little."

The embrace ended. Julian turned and looked at the four soldiers as if their presence was a simple matter of due course. Johnny stared at him for a moment. He had not expected the embrace, feeling a little overwhelmed by it. Their passion had been one thing, but a kiss? Passionate, yes, but the kiss was something else—more affectionate, more intimate than their couplings had been. Reeling with a momentary sense of ardor, he looked back at the Confederates.

He felt safe with Julian there. His curiosity returned as he stepped closer to the table, circling it, pausing behind one of the soldiers. The money on the table had been issued by the Confederacy. This close, their odors were more distinct—Johnny wondered if people from that era simply got used to it. Their hair was oily and stringy, their clothes tainted with oils and the grime of war. The aura about them made him lightheaded.

"Move on, boy. Don't cotton to no nigger standin' behind me when I'm playin' cards."

Hearing the word stirred mixed emotions; though, from the lips of these brutes, it came with an odd, historical slant. Johnny continued to circle. Earlier intrigued, now amused, he couldn't imagine how Cassandra had managed to bring them here. Had she plucked them from the shadows of history, four men on furlough, biding the precious minutes of a short reprieve from their hopeless war? Truly from another time, they were men that had lived in a tiny world, their minds confined to issues of no consequence beyond their call to arms. Their reeking bodies and foul mouths defined the limits of their imaginations—had he ever been addressed as *boy* or called a *nigger*? Hardly, though these ragtag Confederates had given him a bitter taste of what it must have been like in his great grandfather's day. But then, Johnny was no longer certain his great grandfather was black, at least on his mother's side.

How could he not come back to this house? There was more here than his hunger for Julian, much more—there was Cassandra Mott's imagination. How could he, or anyone, resist stepping into a lifelike page from the Civil War? What, he wondered as he moved closer to Julian, or who might appear in this parlor tomorrow, or the next day, or a week from now? These things were gifts from Cassandra's world, these delicious and vibrant assaults on his senses. Tomorrow, he felt certain, would come the curse.

Cassandra emerged from the bathroom. It was as if a light had brightened the room. Wearing a bawdy red dress, apparently from the era of the Confederacy, she looked like a proverbial saloon girl. Cut low and tight, the dress flowed over her narrow waist in satiny folds and amplified the curve her hips. Her breasts, two fleshy globes pressed into impossible confinement, called out for one's eyes like bonfires. Red hair piled in swirls atop her head left small delicate curls tickling her ears and neck. Her face was dappled with abundant color, lips bright red, cheeks rosy. Light and airy, she cut a lively swathe across the room, responding with delight to the vulgar chorus of catcalls and whistles erupting from around the poker table.

"You're somethin', Cassie!" called out one of the soldiers.

"You gonna be back by the time we finish this here poker game?" the voice of another.

She whirled around the table, mussing their oily hair and snatching up a Confederate five-dollar bill, stuffing it into her bosom.

"Hey, I'm losin', Cassie," he cried in protest. "Get some of that pile Hank's got stacked up over there."

"We've been missin' ya, Cassie. Don't be out too late, hear?"

"We'll see," she teased. "Just remember, you boys have each other if I don't get back by the time you're ready for a little fun."

"Ah shit, Cassie. Ain't none of these fellas smells like you."

She continued around the table and came to a stop in front of Johnny, stroking the back of his head, gazing deeply into his eyes, her smile as charming as any he had ever seen.

"I'm so glad you decided to come. I'm sure my dear brother is too."

You own me, lovely lady. You know you do.

Her smile broadened. "Are you ready to go for dinner?"

"Any time you say," said Johnny, smiling complacently, bewitched by the gaiety her presence brought to the evening.

She held out her arm to be escorted to the door, and the three of them strode out to the street, drawing second takes from those in passing as they started toward the restaurant. Hardly a soul could resist staring at her nineteenth century shamelessness.

Amused by those gawking, Johnny almost wished the soldiers had come along. *Take a good look one and all. This, you bloody tourists, is old Savannah.*

It was a warm Georgian evening, the stars bright and twinkling in the sky. The sound of ship's horns carried mournfully from the river on the calm night air. The threesome strolled casually on the sidewalks of Savannah, just as its southern residents did a hundred-fifty years before, the carriages replaced by cars, the humid cross-breezes through open windows replaced by air conditioners. Nearing a corner, Johnny spotted one of the stepping stones used by the ladies of that era for stepping up into carriages, and he wondered if Cassandra had ever used this very one for that purpose. Their eyes met. Aware of what he had been looking at, she smiled. On they went, passing gardens and wrought-iron gates and restored houses befitting the grand old city, coming finally to Cassandra's restaurant of choice, one in which Johnny had never ventured.

The maitre d' seemed to take in stride their unusual appearance, his half-hidden smile rather smug. Glancing around the dining room, Johnny saw a collection of the matronly and the frivolous, the wealthy and a smattering of Savannah's finest eccentrics, wearing everything from Armani suits to crew-neck sweaters and sandals. No need to fret over his blue jeans and wrinkled white shirt, he decided.

Garnished in elegance, the space looked like a hotel dining room from the 1940's, obviously pricey. Cassandra snatched from her bosom the Confederate note and handed it to the maitre d', bringing another indulgent half-smile to his face.

"Something cozy," she said, casting her eyes on a table in the corner of the room, the direction the maitre d' then led them.

It occurred to Johnny, as the maitre d' properly placed a white linen napkin in his lap, that the dinner would generate a significant tab. He remembered Samuel McPhereson saying Cassandra had gone through her fortune and had died in poverty, save the deed on her house. Would he be expected to pay the bill, or just his share? He had very little cash and Marilee was certain to notice a credit card charge on the statement. Then, inexplicably, Julian placed his hand on Johnny's forearm and nodded at Cassandra's neck. Johnny looked at her, puzzled for a moment. Of course, the necklace, an ostentatious display of diamonds that must have cost a fortune. It dawned on him, as he stared at the sparkling colors of refracted light, that Julian had read his mind, that he shouldn't worry about the bill. It reminded him of Brian Fowler's book. Fowler had written that immortals have great wealth and hide it masterfully.

An extraordinary level of service came into play. First the wine, then appetizers, then a three course of dinner, more wine, and finally dessert. During the course of the meal, Johnny watched those coming and going, the elegance and pretentiousness involved: old men with young, gorgeous women, and matrons dripping in jewels. It was a world apart from average Savannah, though as much a part of it as anything else, these eccentrics of the old south, rich and beautiful, all more than willing to join Adam and Eve for their bite of the apple.

Sated with wine and rich food, Johnny relaxed against his chair back, watching Cassandra, of which he never tired. His thoughts reeled through the evening's gauntlet of images, the Confederate soldiers awaiting her return, the way they looked at her as she swept across the parlor. Did she plan to bed the four of them later in the night, to let them contaminate her with their stench, to take their wretched minds from the war with the kind of feminine wiles that war-weary men dream about? He no longer questioned her motives or tireless imagination, or her ability to lend pleasure no average person could conceive. Even her ability to wrest lovers from the past didn't surprise him, for it seemed anything must be possible within the four walls of her parlor.

Johnny had stopped wondering why she had chosen him, settling for the explanation that his grandmother had been her lover, and that she had no other heirs and felt, in her own way, an affinity toward him. It no longer mattered if the old lady that died in that house, the ninety-two year old Cassandra Mott, had intended to come back and use him to retain the house. Like Dr. Salazar suggested, perhaps the inheritance meant nothing more than settling the nuances of the law. None of that mattered. In Cassandra's farcical world, logic was illogic and conventional mores were to thumb one's nose at. For what were days and nights meant, if not simply to live, to seek pleasure and indulge every whim?

A waiter presented the check. Johnny stared at it as if it represented the national debt. From the corner of his eye, he noticed Julian's hand rising from under the table. Johnny's eyes shifted from the check to a fistful of one hundred dollar bills. The waiter watched Julian lay two of them on the table. He then scooped them up and sauntered away.

"My, my, I couldn't have taken another bite," said Cassandra, blotting her lips with the linen napkin.

Cassandra had mentioned a nightclub. Savannah's nightlife, notorious in its own way, was something else Johnny was not familiar with. As Julian stepped behind her to pull out her chair, he wondered what kind of venue had aroused her curiosity Moments later, strolling again in the night air, they started in a direction opposite the section of town in which most of Savannah's nightlife was located.

They walked for fifteen minutes, past the fringes of the historic district and on into a neighborhood not well lit and neglected, continuing toward an even seedier area. Stopping on a corner under the halo of a street lamp, Julian nodded at a narrow side street lined with mostly vacant buildings. After a brisk three block walk down the deserted street, one more turn delivered them into an alley lined with motorcycles, a dead-end. There, two men loitered in front of a dimly lit doorway.

The threesome approached; Johnny far less enthusiastic about this idea than his female companion. Tight with apprehension from the moment they turned into the alley, he stared with a sense of dread at two burly men dressed head to toe in leather, baldheads, large forearms hideous with tattoos, eyes lingering ominously upon Cassandra. She approached them jauntily, without hesitation, as one might the bellmen of a fine hotel.

Has she lost her mind? Johnny pushed his hands into his pockets. The humidity lay over his face like a damp cloth. Or was it a sense of misgiving that had dampened his face? The dark and littered alleyway was a horror. This, he feared, unlike the sanctuary of her parlor, was the real world where real dangers exist, a place they shouldn't be. Maybe their long walk had taken them in the wrong direction. Maybe she had approached the two brutes to ask the way. How fragile she looked standing before the larger of the two, a human bear; and how vulnerable wearing that taunting red dress that was certain to set his juices stirring. The brute's eyes narrowed as he contemplated his unexpected good fortune.

"Pardon us, gentlemen," she said, looking at the larger one that stood blocking the door. "May we go inside?"

Johnny could hardly believe his ears. Could this ungodly place be the nightclub? But then, what had he expected? He looked at Julian, whose quiet focus remained on the heathens. The man stepped aside, scrutinizing each of them as they brushed against his belly passing through the door.

The first assault came to his ears, a blaring, pulsing rock and roll. The first odor Johnny recognized was marijuana. The door behind them closed and the threesome paused in the darkness. The smell of stale beer and male sweat lingered in the damp, smoke filled air. No public restroom smelled this foul. No zoo housed such ungodly creatures. Surely Cassandra would realize her misguided choice. She would not want to stay.

Here and there were candles, centered on small round tables, their small flames setting dim glows on faces, motionless men with peering eyes. As Johnny adjusted to the dark, he made out human forms in expanding numbers, all wearing various configurations of black leather. He saw draping chrome chains and tattoos, exposed chests and shaved heads, pierced nostrils, ears and lips. Masculine forms all, sitting behind pitchers of beer; no women, no mouths graced with a smile. Making their way further into the crowded room, another male image near the back wall took form, a dancer of some kind, wearing a pair of black leather chaps that covered his legs and nothing else. Was it a dance, those wild undulations, that semi-flaccid penis whirling like a propeller?

They took seats at an empty table, suddenly available in the center of the room. Lost in a surreal state of unease, Johnny watched the approach of a man carrying a pitcher of beer. Cursed with body hair, the rotund, bare-chested waiter set the beer and three glasses on the table, turning to leave after Julian handed over a hundred dollar bill. The music loud enough to dampen conversation, they sat quietly with their private observations, standing out like lambs among lions in a hungry den: Cassandra, twisted in her chair, watching the dancer's twirling penis; Johnny, his breath quick and shallow, glancing this way and that, reluctant to predict the outcome of this adventure; Julian, his hands folded calmly on the table, watching the man that had come with them, the man fidgeting with a napkin, the innocent and unsuspecting man he had come to know as Johnny Feelwater.

His eyes now more adjusted to the dark, Johnny saw a scattering of women, also dressed in leather, bound and laced so tightly they seemed intent on punishing their own bodies. He found it unimaginable, such extreme diversity of the human mind, all too aware they had ventured into the bowels of society. Though his eyes had adjusted, his nostrils still objected to the tainted air, his breaths shallow and impatient. He decided that Cassandra must be amused by this hellhole.

They drew glances from all around, the whites of eyes like muted flashbulbs across the room. Cassandra, with no apparent concern, poured three glasses of beer. Julian rubbed his lower lip, disconnected from it all, for it was just one more of his sister's whims that he would not deny. Johnny, with the smell of decadence tainting each breath, drank down half the glass of beer, thinking a little alcohol might settle him a bit. His eyes flitted about the room, averting from those staring at him, as he wondered what kind of thinking weighted the minds of those that would collect in such squalor.

As he scanned the cave-like environs, he sensed something strange, an unpleasant perception suggesting the room was alive with a carnal undertow. *Must be my imagination.* He tried to ignore it, but the presence seemed to feed on itself and grow. He sensed it, like something emanating from those milling about and from those seated nearby ... they were waiting. He glanced from face to face, concentrating, hoping against hope that the feeling crawling up his spine was in his head; yet minute by minute the energy grew stronger.

They're waiting. Why? For what?

A stab of dread chilled his neck. Those around them were now staring openly, heathens all. Johnny's eyes shifted to Cassandra. Had she not seen what she came to see? Was it not time to go?

A dizziness came over him, as if some kind of a drug were shuffling his thoughts. He looked at the half-full glass of beer. Of course. Were the three of them not out of place here? Were they not intruding upon this clan of lost souls? A place like this—entirely appropriate for them to drug three hapless strangers, a lesson of sorts for unwanted outsiders.

His mind reeled. His head fell back. His skin felt like a grassfire of tingles. The timbre of the pounding music slowed, entering his ears like yawing noise in a cave. Everything entered a realm of slow motion. Lifting his head, he shuddered with the sensation of electricity pulsing across his skin.

The rush in his head passed, leaving him calm and relaxed. The heathens nearby stared with interest. He closed his eyes, bearing the authority of enormous pleasure. Though part of his brain remained aware of the real world, everything around him seemed surreal, just beyond reach, just beyond his ability to comprehend. He opened his eyes, realizing that whatever they had put in his beer had put him at ease; and this he found agreeable; for if Cassandra intended to stay, he did not want to feel his heart go on thumping. Slumped a bit in the wooden chair, he looked at the remaining beer in his glass, no longer leery of consequences. He picked it up, tilted his head and drank the rest of it down.

One of the heathens approached and singled out Cassandra. Sunken eyes, hair long and stringy, a mouth impoverished with scorn, he towered over her, an aberration of humanity, reeking, glowering like a Neanderthal in the throes of pondering a new woman. Long, muscled arms hung from a leather vest-like top, baring a tattooed chest and belly. Like an invisible mist, his stench settling on Johnny and those close by; yet Cassandra returned a seductive gaze. She turned in her chair to face him, sitting attentively; her every inflection suggested permissive thoughts. Across the table, Julian sat calmly, watching like a cat, with a keen intensity that advised caution. One wrong move on the part of the uninvited guest, whether he realized it or not, would be at his own peril.

The heathen lifted his hand, passing it down over his chest and belly, landing it on his crotch. He unzipped the leather fly and pried out his cock, thickly veined and jutting forth, and then presented it to Cassandra like some kind of treasure. Taken into her gaze, she reached out, her fingers skilled and uninhibited. She pushed back the foreskin to expose the sheen of mucid glans, then leaned closer and took it into her mouth.

No! You can't let this happen! For God's sake, Cassandra, not even you can be willing to do something like that!

Beside himself with disbelief, Johnny witnessed Cassandra's degradation, her gluttony and receptive throat, her nose buried in a mass of pubic hair. The contrast was more than his mind could accept; her sophistication and great beauty fastened by way of her lips to a subhuman beast. The drug. Maybe it had affected her and made her behave this way. Yes. It had to be the drug. Johnny looked at Julian, wondering why he had not put a stop to it.

Like a vulture from a high perch, the heathen peered down on his prey. Furrowing his fingers into her red hair, he took a hold of her head as if to hold her in place, as the act drew heightened interest all across the room. Like vampires alerted to the smell blood, they looked on, a brood of unwashed males and their clinging females. The carnal undertow grew palpable, a human mass in sway. All around the small table were moving shadows, a stirring of air and the sound of scooting chairs. As if an awakening had taken place, a closing nearness of vague male forms pressed an invisible weight on Johnny. A nervous dew dampened his face. Shrouded in dark, he could not make out the texture of the walls, which seemed not so far away; yet they, like the mob, were closing in on him.

The color of raw meat, wet and glistening in the near nonexistent light, the cock disappeared again and again down Cassandra's throat. Johnny looked on, transfixed, the drug's effect seemingly negated by this turn of events. His emotions welled and took a physical presence in his arms and hands. An urge to protect her came over him, to stand, to vanquish the abuser, to chide her for such irrational behavior, take her arm and drag her from this ungodly room, though he stayed fixed to his chair. His mind labored over the bits he had pieced together about her: her own doctor believing she had walked the streets of ancient Rome; Brian Fowler describing in his book exactly this kind of sexual appetite. Had she, before the time of Christ, performed this same act on ancient Romans, conquering warriors perhaps? Were they, with their bloodied and muscled bodies, the men that taught her how such things were done?

Johnny felt himself swelling. Disturbed that Cassandra's defiling had aroused him, he reached down to adjust the sudden misalignment in his jeans. Another, even more sinister fear crept into his consciousness, not so much disquiet for life or limb, as for the descent of his own moral character. He looked through the shadows at the door, aware he could stand and bolt through it and not look back; yet something held him to the chair, as if he, too, were waiting.

Julian, his presence a lifeline, appeared little concerned about possible danger, and amazingly tolerant of what Cassandra had become involved in. Johnny watched the keen way Julian surveyed the elements around them, glancing from face to face. Then Julian's eyes locked suddenly on something just behind him. Johnny turned slightly, immediately aware that one of the heathens had come up close behind; too close in fact, for if his head tilted back barely an inch, it would rest upon a belt buckle.

Another stepped forward and positioned himself at Johnny's side, this one shorter than the other, sporting a belly carpeted with hair. Johnny closed his eyes. His teeth clamped together. He did not move, other than forcing a hard swallow. *It's not happening... it can't be!* He had never been more nervous in his life. *Ignore 'um. Don't look. No eye contact.* He felt the leaden weight of unparalleled fear. On his own, so it seemed, he had become the focus of the two now looking down on him; though Julian, in his white linen clothes, sat across the table like a beacon of security.

The man behind Johnny grabbed the back of his chair and spun him around. The one now in front reached for his fly. A rush of adrenaline flooded through Johnny, steeling him for flight, an option, he realized, that had suddenly vanished. *Oh God... I can't pray... I can't... not here.*

Johnny opened his eyes, cowering before the heathen's dull red cock, wishing for the love of God that he had stayed home. He tried to stand, thwarted from behind by the rude grip on his shoulders. His heart was thumping again. He found himself gaping at a cock large enough to hang below a mule, a tongue's length from its tiny hole. Resisting the meaty nudge against his taut lips, his breath flared through his nostrils and he cringed when the man behind took hold of his head, viselike, directing his face toward the cock. A sour fog had escaped the unzipped leather, a rogue's mix of the distinct odors that molder in a confined and unwashed crotch, a smell that leapt into Johnny's nostrils like vaporous nettles. Fraught with helplessness, the sinews of his neck strained, Johnny's head pounded with the chaos around him. No resistance could defy the unyielding hands. The cock's owner grew impatient with waiting, more aggressive. Johnny hissed and sputtered as the cock forcefully parted his lips.

"Open your mouth, mister." A crude voice from behind.

Unable to turn his head or resist, Johnny's mouth slowly opened. Upon his tongue came a warm and pungent taste.

"Suck it, boy. Suck it or I'll damage your balls."

The menacing queue closed in around him to watch the misplaced soul take on the task. Resigned, Johnny's reluctance began to fade. His mouth filled, his eyes found Cassandra, who was looking on with those hulking around her. *She knew this would happen. She's testing the limits of my sanity.*

Goaded, Johnny's lips plowed over the rippled veins, his mind a scattering of particles with one purpose—he sought the heathen's release. Like the changing wind of a gale at sea, his angst evolved into abandon. As dreadfully it began, he found himself drawn in, his fervor increasing by degrees. To avoid a fiery pit, he had entered a garden of thorns; so were the circumstances of this dreadful act. Now caught in the throes of drugs and decadent sex, he slathered the cock with growing resolve; and as the large hands held his head in place, finally it came, the spewing ropes of milky fluid. He closed his eyes and forced much of it from his mouth with his tongue. Then he swallowed and melted against the chair-back, a remnant of the man that had walked in a few minutes earlier, realizing the second half of the glass of beer had taken effect, the stripping of one's mind and his very soul.

Johnny felt himself lifted from the chair, raised into the air, carried, his feet gangling some distance from the floor. Hands came upon him, tearing at his shirt and fussing impatiently at his fly. He felt his jeans and underwear slide down his legs, his shirt torn open. He had become weightless over a turbulent mass of humanity. He felt crude hands groping and fondling and his testicles compressed within a fist. It muddled him, this disassociation with gravity, this sensation of floating, of being transported midair upon shoulders and palms to some different part of the room. They flopped him on a pool table, on his belly, his face against the dirty, beer sodden felt. His sandals were pulled from his feet, his jeans and briefs, the mob a roiling blur, grasping at him, prying open his legs. He moaned, wretched in his lost will to resist. He lay naked, resigned, writhing with the certainty of his indoctrination, reaching out as if someone might help him as he lie helplessly in an unwanted kinship with these slovens of the earth.

Above the chaos of heads and shoulders was nothing but darkness and smoke floating on pale light. His ears throbbed with the harsh anti-rhythm of blaring drums and shrieking guitars. He felt the cool shock of a gelatinous slathering behind his testicles. It was an ungracious and sudden moment of truth, receiving two brutish fingers at once, the pain at once sharp and maddening and exquisite. He winced as the fingers worked in and out, stretching him roughly, preparing him as they were for a taste of their world.

Restrained, he wanly lifted his head and twisted it left then right. He beheld a ruthless mass, an undulating monster with uncountable arms and many heads and bellies. They were on the table and around it and between his legs, some naked, some unzipped with cock in hand. Charged with the indifference of unbridled lust was the first searing lunge, a plowing through his anus that delivered pain so acute he nearly passed out, a merciless rape, performed without compassion or care, jolting his body with immediate pounding. His legs tightened. His fingers clawed at the felt. God, it hurt. It hurt as if he had been had torn, the pain searing down his legs and up his spine, radiating through his body like a fast flow of lava. There came hands gripping his thighs, then spasms, and finally a phallic spewing coupled with the howl of an animal. And no sooner did the first abandon his bruised rectum, yet another pushed his legs wider, grasped his gluteal cheeks and pried him open with another plundering. What manner of men with such huge cocks use them this way, mocking another man's masculinity, violating that small hole, that most intimate place on a man's body, that, if given over at all, should be given willingly?

The second one felt enormous, searing, ramming with the fervor of a bull. In this vague sphere of odors and shapes and muted color, the monster took form with its many penises; naked men shoulder to shoulder above and beside him, those above charged with the desperate rhythms of masturbation. And from the man between his legs, thrusting hard again and again, a final thrust and a guttural moan of spent lust.

They rolled him over, yet another position of vulnerability, spreading his legs like mere objects in the way. Johnny opened his bleary eyes on an ogre with one eye scarred shut; the other eye glazed with drunkenness and cast down below his belly. Then his legs were hoisted upon a pair of thick shoulders, and on it went. One by one they maneuvered between his legs, until the world outside seemed a distant memory. Atop the table, a man knelt near Johnny's head, retracting a brooding hood of foreskin, exposing a swollen and glistening walnut-shaped meat. No longer put off by such visual and odorous assaults, the cock rested in his semi-conscious gaze, the smell distinct, a sour bouquet that curled into his nostrils like wisps of smog. Thumping the exposed glans on Johnny's lips, the brute inched closer on his knees as Johnny lifted his head and took it into his mouth like an obedient child. The feel of its heat on his tongue branded on his awareness like something he had hungered for.

Above his head the primordial images came like a menagerie of male legs, thick and darkened with hair; of genitals pierced and adorned with small rings; of squatting asses probed by the fingers of other men. He had lost the boundaries between right and wrong, between moral and immoral, reveling in this filth and willingly sinking deeper into the wanton depths of degradation, no longer repulsed by the semen that rained down and ran in rivulets across his shoulders and chest. And as he squirmed his altered mind began to dim; he grew more and more oblivious to his ravaging. Teetering on the verge of obscurity, he saw a man standing over him, a phallic grip, a tiny hole aimed at his chest. There came a splattering of warm fluid, drenching his face and chest. His head rocked miserably from side-to-side as another joined in, their golden streams, odorous and warm, pooling beneath his shoulder blades and running like miniature rivers across the table.

Johnny's consciousness left him. How many had masturbated or urinated on him, or rammed their cocks into his anus, he would never know; though he realized with his last flickering thoughts, that he had been changed in some significant way. The peace of mind and self-confidence he had always known, that came to him so easily and had been a part of him from his youth, would never be the same again.

Chapter 12

Johnny's eyes fluttered when morning's first light filtered through a small window that had been painted over with thin black paint, engraved by fingernails with phone numbers no rational person would ever dial. He stared at the ceiling, at cobwebs as old as the sagging black acoustical panels. Lying on his back in the gloom, his calves and feet hanging off the edge of the table, the foul air crawled through his nostrils and returned the nightmare to his conscious thoughts. He was still there, still lying on that pool table, left to fend for himself by the beautiful pair. So it had not been as it had seemed—a painful, deplorable dream.

He shuddered, then lay perfectly still. A simple twitch of muscle reignited the pain his body had endured. He searched his mind for an answer, some rationale as to why Cassandra brought him here. The drug, in spite of its potent effect, allowed him to remember it all, everything; only now the humiliation had evolved from those vague, surreal images into the very real and injured emotions of a mind still sane. Surely the drug had made him susceptible to those vile acts; though this was worse, lying there alone, naked and wretched and in pain, retrieving images he'd rather forget as he lay sprawled upon the unforgiving surface of a filthy pool table. Yes, this was much worse, waking in despair, facing his misdeeds head-on, realizing he would have to live with the undistorted memory of what had happened. What could he do about it after the fact? How could he ever again face Marilee?

They had waited. Then they came at him like a pack of wolves, their carnal appetites inflamed by his forced subservience. They swallowed him into their world and they neutralized his will and his masculinity. Why did he allow it to happen? Where in the shadows of a man's psyche, he wondered, hide those dark urges that had surfaced in this room? What drives a man to take one more step toward his own destruction? Now he lay on damp green felt, his body putrid with urine and semen, spewed and ejaculated by heathens.

How it sickened him.

Lifting his head, squinting, his eyes shifted about the shadows. He was alone. Drawing up his legs, he groaned, taking his lower lip between his teeth in response to the pain radiating from his rectum. Images reeled through his mind, resistant to his plea to stop, like flashing frames of a nightmare: faces reddened and twisted with lust, necks drawn taut, fleshy, tattooed arms prying his legs further apart. Johnny reached down slowly, gently, to appraise his sore testicles—how they ached. How those malicious hands delighted in gripping and pulling and slapping at them, though the agony resting in the flesh behind them was even worse. Had they torn him during the rape? He was afraid to know, for it felt like a hot ember had been pushed inside. He cringed as his gluteal muscle squeezed together, aware of a lingering sticky wetness, fearful it might be his own blood.

He closed his eyes tightly, bitterly, on the verge of a scream, trying desperately to shut out what could not be denied. What had he become but a withering, pathetic human receptacle, violated by phallic dimensions of unimaginable size, by unwashed men bearing down on him with their rancid weight and discharges, heathens predisposed to brutal sex and leaving behind the torn souls of their victims? And as he pondered the ramifications of what he had done, another thought crept from the dark of his mind. It came like a fowl breath on his face, a revelation born in a swamp of immoral pleasure. Had he been raped, or had he been their willing whore?

Heaven help me ... I didn't try to resist. Oh God, please don't let me be drawn to this place again.

He loathed himself. He prayed that this too had not become a part of him, that the mesmeric pleasure was no more than a drug-induced byproduct of circumstances never to be repeated.

The welling fear of what he had become collided with the sanctity of his marriage. He pictured Marilee coming out of the bathroom, unsettled with her nudity, trying for the first time to be the wife he wanted her to be. Why could he not simply end his enchantment for Cassandra, or renounce his addiction to Julian? But he knew, even now as he lay shivering and naked, that he would be drawn back to them. Though he might convince himself the massive rape had been forced, even now, as he suffered its aftermath, he could feel the allure of Cassandra's spell. He could not deny her. And besides, what could he blame her for? She had not forced him to leave Factor's Row.

She had not forced him to enter this despicable place. It was simply his lack of will to resist. So who, in the end, could he blame but himself?

Johnny turned slightly on his side. Bracing his weight on an elbow, he reached back and drew his fingers through his crack and brought them before his eyes. He had felt no torn flesh. He saw no blood mingled with the semen and bowel secretions, and he sighed with small relief.

Slowly he sat up and braced himself on a palm. He glanced down, then averted his eyes from his defiled body, nauseated.

Why did she leave me here this way?

As he caught his breath from the effort of lifting his own torso, he pondered his fluctuating sentiments for Cassandra. Should he loathe her now? Should he hold her accountable for what she had led him into? ...No. Not possible, not really, no matter that she had left him at the mercy of brutes. He was certain the evening had been, in her mind, no more than simple amusement. After all, she had forewarned him of her world of debauchery. Even if she knew the extent of what was to happen to him here, he would forgive her even then.

A movement caught the corner of his eye. His head turned in that direction and his heart sailed. Julian stepped from the shadows and Johnny's eyes closed with elation.

He stayed. He didn't leave me this way.

Julian came up beside him, gleaming with affection. He placed his fingertips just under Johnny's chin, lifting it, a gesture that eliminated any need for words. His sharp blue eyes drifted down over Johnny's tainted body and his expression changed to compassion.

"You stayed," said Johnny, warmed by the sudden appearance of a most welcomed friend, struck at once by two thoughts: that Julian had abandoned his guardianship over his sister; and that with Julian, he did not feel humiliated by his naked and filthy body. "Cassandra didn't mind if you stayed?"

Julian shrugged and placed his hand on Johnny's knee.

"You defied her? She allows that?"

Julian tilted his head with a smile that suggested his sister did not decide all things for him.

"Julian, why? Why me? Why do you care for me?" Johnny looked down at the white hand on his knee. His affinity for Julian increased and he yearned to know more about him. "I think I'm beginning to know you, even though you don't speak. I believe you have eternal life. I believe you can change into other forms. That snake I saw in your house was you. It's true, isn't it? You have the power to do these things." Their eyes met. "Why would someone like you choose me for a friend ... or a lover?"

Julian's smile melted into a silent sigh, but no further answer.

"I felt safe with you here last night. Should I have? Could you have stopped them if our lives were at risk?"

Julian's eyes locked onto his. The words seemed to pass from them into Johnny's mind. *Yes, you were safe. If not, I would have stopped them. No real harm could have come to you. But the evening belonged to Cassandra. My place was to watch over what she intended for you to endure.* Julian looked at him for a moment, then: *You must ask no more questions. Do you understand?*

Johnny was shaken. For a moment, he had forgotten his presence in the bowels of Savannah's decaying neighborhoods, his wretchedness, the pain radiating from his loins. Nodding in awe, he hardly believed it had happened. Not only did it seem like he heard the words verbally, but the process had cleared his head of a nagging ache, as if his mind had been purged of pain and clutter, purposefully so and instantaneously, perhaps to receive Julian's disclosure. Johnny looked at the hand on his knee, daunted by the man it belonged to. He would have given himself to Julian then and there, willingly, but he was filthy and it would be too painful. But in time he would heal and their moment would come. This he knew intuitively. This urge could not be ignored.

Julian stood by as Johnny inched himself off the pool table. Then, as he closed his eyes and took a few quick breaths to ease the agony in his body, Julian knelt and picked up his soiled clothes. He handed Johnny the white briefs, still damp with stale beer, as were his shirt and jeans. Johnny took the briefs and looked at them, then flung them over his shoulder.

"I'll leave them a souvenir," he said sardonically, taking the torn shirt from Julian and pushing his arms through the sleeves of what was left of it. He reached for his jeans and lifted his leg, leaning sorely against the table as he stepped into them, a simple task that had never been so arduous. He stood upright for a moment to allow his body to regain equilibrium, the damp jeans clinging in an irregular way, his shirt hanging from his shoulders like a damp rag. He looked at the door and then back at Julian.

"I'm going home. I want to be with you, but ..." He lowered his head and rubbed his eyes. "I should go home. I feel weak. I have to get something to eat ... and figure out what's become of me."

Julian nodded and offered his help to the door. Johnny draped his arm over his shoulder, soiling the clean white linen shirt as he limped closer to the exit, profoundly aware of where he ached and how it bothered him, though he assured himself it would heal. Then the morning light pierced his eyes when Julian opened the door. Momentarily, he stepped outside and glanced around the littered alley. He would never come here again, or even near it, and his strongest hope was that the night's events would eventually fade from his memory.

Standing just outside the doorway, Julian watched Johnny start toward the street, a beautiful black human male whose mind had been toyed with, limping away with his hands pushed into his pockets, his head down, his shoulders narrowed and small. Julian thought about how he had opposed Cassandra's objective when she arranged to bring this man into their lives, but her hatred was fierce and she had been resolute. Now, as he watched Johnny Feelwater trudge from view, his regrets redoubled.

Johnny's pace quickened as the abuse began to retreat from his body. He desperately wanted to be home, to be shut away from the eyes of the world, to submerge himself in warm water and wash away the stench and be alone. Entering the more refined streets of the city, he walked briskly, head down and eyes fixed to the walkway just beyond his stride. He passed among Savannah's pedestrians, looking at not one of them, but feeling their eyes, as if he were something subhuman trying to slink as invisibly as possible through the streets of civilization. One block fell behind, then another, a pace that quickening his breath.

His head still down, he finally turned the last corner and was on his own street, glancing sideways at the neighbors' houses, hoping none of them would see him; not that he cared what they would think, but feared what they might say to Marilee. Reaching the sanctuary of his front porch, he pushed his key into the lock and opened the door, melting quickly into the entryway. He leaned back and rested his shoulders against the closed door, breathing a sigh of relief. From there, he started directly toward the bedroom, stopped cold in his tracks in the den.

On the sofa, beside Reverend Aragones, sat Marilee. Shaken, Johnny gaped open-mouthed at the two of them. He had watched her drive away with his own eyes. What was she doing here? A silence passed, an awkward exchange of disbelief. Awash in shame, embarrassed, then angered by this unexpected surprise, his shame turned into rage.

Marilee had heard the front door open and was looking in that direction when he walked in. Seeing her husband enter the house in this condition, she gasped. Her eyes fixed on the ghastly image, having worried about him throughout the night. She found herself at a complete loss as to his tattered, filthy appearance; never-mind where he had been the entire night. Her eyes jumped to meet his when his anger broke the stiff silence.

"What are you doing here?" he demanded.

She stared at him, alarmed. Her sensibilities skewed, she hardly knew how to react or respond, stiffened in frozen silence beside the preacher.

"And *you!* Why are *you* here?" Johnny wanted to know, glaring directly at Reverend Aragones.

Marilee found her voice. "I ... we were worried about you, Johnny. I called Reverend Aragones early this morning when you still weren't home. We were about to call the police." She tried to stay calm though her heart pounded fiercely. Her eyes combed over him, appalled as she was by his appearance. The odors he brought into the house had permeated the room, elevating her anxiety. "I didn't know what to do," she said helplessly, struggling with her tears. "I had to call someone."

"Mr. Feelwater, has something happened to you?" asked Reverend Aragones, his brow fixed high with concern.

"Yeah. I was mugged. Left for dead in an alley. Too bad I lived through it, huh, Reverend Aragones? Appears my wife won't need all that consoling after all."

The reverend remained calm and tried to stay aloof of Johnny's innuendo. "We should call the police and report the crime."

"Ha! Lot of good that'll do now! Why interrupt their coffee and donuts?"

"I think you're upset, Mr. Feelwater. Maybe we should ..."

"Aren't you just a little too handsome to be a preacher?" Johnny interrupted.

"I beg your pardon ..."

"You heard me! What, are you on call for all the distressed wives in your congregation? Is that it, Reverend Aragones?" He spat the words from his mouth as if they were dirt. "Move over Don Juan, the Reverend Aragones is here to save the day!"

"Johnny," Marilee pleaded, "what is wrong with you? Why are you saying those things?" She scooted forward on the sofa, not certain if she should stand, go to him, try to calm him. Her shoulders felt weak. She folded her arms vulnerably beneath her breasts, lost as to why their lives were careening out of control, barely able to look at the man she had lived with for the last nine years.

"I thought you were going to Atlanta!" he shouted.

"Oh God," she moaned, at wits end. She ran her fingers across her forehead, staring at him in horror, trying to gather the mettle to explain. "Mother's operation was delayed for two weeks. I came back home. Johnny ... you weren't here. I couldn't stand the worry."

"Shit!" he muttered, staring at her, trying to ignore the damage he had caused. *Just my luck, isn't it? Your mother! Probably made up the whole affair just to get you to Atlanta for a few days. Bet she threw a fit when you decided to come home to that worthless man you married.* Trembling, his eyes fell from her pathetic expression and searched the floor in shear frustration, beside himself with shame and anger. He was destroying himself, his marriage, everything, yet his rage roiled on.

The reverend sat quietly, looking at the wall behind the madman that had so rudely entered the room, absently rubbing the back of his neck. Marilee came to her feet, wanting more than anything to go to her husband.

"Don't get up!" Johnny yelled. "I'm gonna take a shower while you two visit. Sorry I interrupted."

Dejected, Marilee slumped back onto the sofa.

Johnny stormed out the room, oblivious to the pain still crawling through his body; but more than aware of the emotions splitting his brain into fragments of confusion.

The Reverend Aragones turned to look at Marilee, placing his hand gently on her knee. "You poor dear. I had no idea you were living with that kind of man."

Caught off guard by his statement, Marilee looked at his hand for a moment.

"Do you need someone to stay with?" he asked.

"What?" More words that did not sound just right.

"Mrs. Hutchinson. Her husband died last year, you know. I'm sure she'd be happy to have you stay with her."

Marilee's mouth fell open. She looked at the wall, dazed, thinking about Johnny in the bedroom. "But he's my husband," she said, distracted.

"You don't have to live like this, Marilee."

She turned and looked into his brown eyes, realizing they seemed devoid of genuine sympathy. It dawned on her that he had offended her, the man she had for so long looked to for guidance and support. If there was anything she needed to hear at this particular moment, it was not someone passing judgment on her husband. A calm came into her hands. As if by sheer force of will, her emotional state leveled. His hand lifted from her knee as she came to her feet and looked down at him.

"I believe the situation is in hand, Reverend Aragones," she said, making no attempt to hide her indignation. "Thank-you for coming. Now you may leave."

He stood and reached for her hands, which retracted. A puzzled expression washed over his face as she extended her hand toward the front door. She followed, then closed the door behind him, having acknowledged his best wishes with no more than a curt nod.

She turned and looked toward the bedroom, pausing before taking that first step. Her husband's behavior wasn't caused by burnout, or pressure from the deadlines he had to meet—it was caused by something far worse. Something was dreadfully wrong with him and it scared her. A disorder of some kind. The word *insanity* crept into her thoughts, rejected at once. He wasn't going mad—he couldn't be, not the rock-stable man she had known for so many years. Her heart raced as she closed her eyes, resigning herself to get through this. And now, after that episode with Reverend Aragones, she realized that her so-called friends would become hyenas feeding on gossip. She and Johnny were alone in the world, just the two of them, for no one else would empathize with the sudden trials in their marriage, or exhaust the effort to try.

Marilee heard running water as soon as she stepped into the bedroom. She walked resolutely toward the sound and found him sitting on tile floor in the shower stall, still wearing his tattered clothes. The shower spray rained down on his head, drenching him, creating a pitiful image. His bluster had turned into despair. He was sobbing like a small boy that had lost his way. She saw anxiety and torment and she wanted to take him into her arms and never let him go. Instead, she sucked in another breath of resolve and knelt beside him. After pulling the drenched shirt from his shoulders, she turned off the water and coaxed him to stand. Without a word said, she unbuttoned his jeans and got him to step out of them after pushing them down around his feet. Ignoring the odor, she took the jeans and the torn shirt to the wastebasket. Returning, she turned the water back on and adjusted the temperature, then watched it cascade over him for a moment, his tall lean body cowering like a forlorn prisoner-of-war standing naked in the rain. She reached for the soap.

He stood emotionally drained and despondent; his body lathered thoroughly, the residues from the night before began running down his legs in streams of soapy water and swirling into the drain. She scrubbed him like a mother washing her first grade son, noting a wince when her soapy hand came up through his crotch, concerned, but not enough to allow her imagination to wander. Finally he was clean. She drew him from the shower and blotted him dry, kneeling to dry his legs. When she looked up, he was staring at her.

"How can you care for me like this? How can you still love me?"

She stood and looked at him squarely. "How, Johnny? How can I not love you? You're my husband. Nothing is more important to me than you."

"Marilee, you don't know me anymore. I don't even know myself. I feel like I'm losing my mind."

"That's nonsense. I know you quite well, finally. You're not losing your mind. Look what you've been through, all the business pressure. It's taken a toll."

She went about drying his legs. Her response sounded more like a defensive justification, a confirmation of her love to assure herself and him that she was prepared to protect their marriage.

"You know it's more than that, don't you?"

"I know you weren't mugged. You make a poor liar, and I love you for that, too."

"You're not going to ask what happened?"

"No."

"You don't want to know?"

"Only if you want to tell me."

"You're not even angry," he muttered with dismay.

"Oh yes I am, Johnny," she said, standing and facing him. "I've never been angrier in my life, and one day I may punch you in the lip for all of this; but right now I'm more interested in hanging onto my husband. It's pretty simple really. I don't want to live with another man, not after living with you. And I can't imagine sleeping with anyone else. Don't even want to think about it."

Tears ran down his cheeks. She blotted them with the towel and then led him to bed and turned back the sheet. "You hungry?" she asked, pulling the sheet over his chest after he lied down.

"Yeah."

"I'll bring some toast and milk. Then you can sleep. Maybe some rest will make you feel better."

He sat up when she returned with the toast. She sat beside him, watching him eat, handing him the milk after he swallowed the last bite of toast.

She watched his Adam's apple rise and fall as he gulped the milk, loving him with the unyielding determination of a woman. He had developed a mental disorder, she reasoned, something temporary, something that came on suddenly, which she could adjust to until it passed. Marilee looked at him closely, ruling out the possibility of another woman; for those were the husbands that sinned with unfaltering secrecy, who worked late nights at the office and took sudden business trips; not husbands slipping off a cliff in a free-fall, or husbands whose eyes are fired with confusion and fear.

"Is it time to see a psychiatrist?" she asked calmly.

Tears again welled in his eyes. Were the questions tormenting her worse than the truth? ...Unlikely. Either way, it was not in him to hurt her more than he already had, nor could he believe she might view his involvement with Cassandra Mott as the result of a mystical influence on his will to resist. Again, and more so than before, he felt alone in the world.

"No," he answered, forcing a swallow.

"What if these are symptoms of a nervous breakdown?"

He handed her the empty glass. "That's not it," he said, closing his eyes in an attempt to settle his guilt. "If it was, I wouldn't know whether I was here with you or on Mars. I'm not that far gone."

Marilee listened closely. He seemed resolute. No psychiatrist, though she heard doubt in his voice, perhaps an underlying plea for help. "Why won't you let me in? I'm your wife. I want to understand you, Johnny."

His eyes shifted to the end of the bed. "You *wouldn't* understand," his voice trailed off with defiance and despair, "...that's the problem."

"You don't know that!" she shot back, exasperated, then let out a breath. She wondered if it was her, or if they had simply lost the ability to communicate. "Can't you see how this is affecting me? You're shutting me out."

The demons gnawing at his brain expanded his loneliness. He wanted more than anything to confide in her, but how could he? How does a man tell his wife that he allowed a mob of heathens to use him as a whore? He *allowed* it to happen—that's what ate at him. It was disturbing to admit he had felt a certain exhilaration descending into that swamp. And it must have been by choice; otherwise would have defied them; he would have fought his way to the door. Marilee would never accept it. He had been violated and he couldn't tell her. There was nothing he could say that would justify his going there.

"Yes, I can see," he said, feeling angry and alone, hiding it as best he could. "I'm worried, Marilee." His voice was distant. "I've never been so worried in my life."

She sensed he was on the verge of opening up to her. "Then talk to me ... see a doctor. People don't become someone else overnight, Johnny. Something's wrong."

He pictured himself in a psychiatrist's office, describing the goings-on at the Mott house. "It's no use. No psychiatrist would take me seriously," he said, thinking about the Confederate soldiers in Cassandra's parlor. "Within ten minutes they'd start writing prescriptions." His eyes shifted from the end of the bed to her. "Or slap me in a straightjacket."

Her head cocked inquisitively. "Take you seriously?"

Everything he said seemed to rouse her curiosity.

"Try me," she said. "See if I take you seriously."

His resolve to stay silent was written on his face. But there was more, a convoluted mix of defiance and shame, revealed by eyes unable to settle, fidgeting hands, edgy body language. A number of scenarios had passed through her mind, but it occurred to her as she looked at his hands, that his anxiety was within—it had nothing to do with her.

"You're involved in something you're ashamed of, aren't you? Something you don't want me to know about."

His jaw tightened.

The reaction confirmed her suspicion.

What could affect him this way, she wondered, scanning down over the sheet? What would keep him out all night and then cause him to come home in that condition? What put this kind of fear in his eyes? Then it dawned on her. *Gambling.* Why not? He's always been a risk-taker. Perhaps it started innocently enough, a simple diversion. Maybe he had gotten in over his head. Marilee had read accounts of men gambling on credit, only to find themselves left for dead in an alley for shirking their debts.

He looked at her with a growing sense of urgency, wary he had said too much. Clearly, he had to tell her something that would ease her mind a bit, and thereby his own; but what? He pulled the sheet higher up his chest, at an utter loss, ridden with guilt, while Marilee reacted with patience and devotion. What could he say that would not heighten her curiosity? Walking home from that hell-hole, blustery and defiant, he had resolved to never see Cassandra and Julian again, that he loved his wife and it tore his soul to jeopardize her love for him. Then he realized all over again that he knew better. He knew it was more than a physical ache to be with Julian, more than a quirky bisexual urge. It was an inexplicable and powerful form of mind control, and Cassandra would use it to call to him again and again. She would take him to the heights of ecstasy one minute, then plunge him into the depths of despair the next, all for her amusement. That was the way she played. All he could do was try to prevent it from wrecking his marriage.

His helplessness felt like weight pressing on his chest.

"Marilee, you're right, I *am* involved in something. And I *am* ashamed of it; but just now I can't tell you what it is. You have to give me a chance to deal with it myself. I know that's not fair. No one would blame you for being angry with me, but I promise I'll tell you when I figure out how to get it out of my life."

She looked at him for a long while. That was it—all she was going to get. Loathe to press him further, she knew his mood swings of late and they frightened her. His eyelids grew heavy as she watched him. The weariness from his mysterious all-night ordeal had set in. His hand moved and rested on her lap. His eyes fluttered and closed and his head nodded to the side.

I'm scared, Johnny. I'm afraid of what's happening to us. Marilee wanted to scream, to shake him and tell him not to do this to her, but a battle of wills would only divide them further. It angered her that he would allow something outside of their marriage to affect them. And it happened so suddenly, like he had ingested something that altered his mental stability. It brought her to the verge of a headache. As she stared at him, an image came to mind: it was in his hand when he came home the other day, a book. She remembered being curious about it then and still was now. Easing gingerly off the bed, she rested his limp hand on the sheet.

The morning sun still glared through the windows when she walked into the garden room. The book would be in here, where he kept most of his personal things. She found it on the drafting table, near the back edge, as if it were meant to be as convenient as a reference book. The title delivered another assault to her sensibilities. *Unexplained Facts about the Supernatural.* Her gaze lifted from the well-worn and charred cover. She stood for a moment, frozen in time, staring at a grouping of potted plants, her imagination whirling with things absurd. Her eyes drifted back to the cover of the book.

That house!

The more she thought about it, the more she remembered how uncomfortable he had been inside the Mott house. She remembered feeling queasy as they toured the rooms, recalling a chill at the back of her neck. Marilee had never been superstitious; now she was considering things she would have called absurd a week earlier. Something had happened to her husband. A psychological problem or chemical imbalance couldn't have turned him into a different man this quickly. Strange as it seemed, it was beginning to add up. It wasn't gambling; he was too rational to fall into a trap like that. Johnny's personality change began immediately after his first visit to that house.

A page had been dog-eared near the back of the book. Reading it brought no relief, for it described the shocking sexual appetite of some kind of a supernatural being. She read on, holding the book as if it were something infectious. Bleeding into her reluctant consciousness were concepts of reincarnation and extrasensory perception and supernatural powers. Skimming through the chapters, she saw words like *vampire* and *ghost* and *witch*, and she allowed herself to consider for a moment, at odds with her most basic instincts and reasoning, the possibility of such phenomena. How truly difficult it was to believe her husband had been affected by something supernatural; though at the moment it was the only glimmer Marilee had, and it seemed far better than facing insanity. She closed the book and returned it to the drafting table.

Still, it was like grabbing onto a thread, a half-hearted possibility that offered little consolation. Even if something so outlandish were possible, how did it connect to that house? What was there that could transform a man, a man both ordinary and extraordinary, into a frightening Jykel and Hyde?

She could no longer simply mill around the house waiting for something else to happen, nor sit and fret. Glancing back at the book, an idea came to her, not so much a revelation as a gutsy course of action.

Back in the bedroom, standing next to the bed, she gazed down at the sheet over her husband's long lean frame. He seemed peaceful, sound asleep. She stepped quietly to the dresser, where Johnny emptied his pockets at night: his money clip, car keys, a package of gum. No key to the Mott house. Then to the wastebasket in the bathroom where she dug out his wet jeans and wrinkled her nose when the odor blossomed in the air. Judging by the smell, he had gotten drunk, probably passed out and then wet himself. Her reluctant hand went into a pocket and came back out with the key. The other pockets were empty, which meant he must have left the house with no more than this one key. At the sink, she laid it on the counter and washed her hands. Her heart raced with what she intended to do.

She took one more look at him before leaving the bedroom, his eyes aflutter with dreams, hoping he would sleep until she returned.

Chapter 13

The moment she turned the corner, the house loomed like the only structure facing Confederate Square. Pulling up to the curb, she switched off the ignition, her eyes glued to the house, glancing from window to window across the front facade. The wrought-iron gate creaked open and she stepped through, continuing with tentative steps up to the porch. The key fit the lock easily and she closed her eyes and took a deep breath before turning it. One step inside, her mouth fell open and she froze.

Not more than six feet beyond her reach, staring up at the second floor landing, wearing what looked like a 1930's era gown, stood a beautiful black woman, perhaps in her early thirties. The young woman turned with a start and stared at Marilee for a second before she turned and dashed into the dining room and on into the kitchen. Marilee's hand flew up to her throat, her mind reeling. She let go of the door and it closed behind her, as if a breeze had swept through the foyer. Her heart pounded as she gathered her thoughts, her eyes fixed in the direction the young woman had gone. Seconds later, after she had calmed a bit, she was more determined than ever to pursue the mystery of this house.

"Hello," she called out and then awaited a response. Her voice, weak and dry, echoed through the empty house. She listened, but no answer came. "I didn't mean to intrude," she called out, taking a step or two toward the dining room, tilting her head in order to see the kitchen door. No sound came, no reply from the young woman. She ventured into the dining room, alert, scanning the empty space, the windows and walls and shadowy corners. Moving toward the kitchen door, her heart quicken again. Being there took more courage than she had assumed.

She entered the kitchen and remembered it had never been updated, its old tile counter tops and wooden cabinet doors the same as installed perhaps a hundred years earlier. Of the furnishings, only an old gas stove rested like a forgotten memorial against the wall.

"Hello," she called out again. "Are you still here?"

The kitchen remained silent.

That couldn't have been my imagination.

Her eyes drifted to what appeared to be a pantry door. She approached cautiously, trying to convince herself the tightness in her neck would pass. The smooth porcelain knob, cool to the touch, turned with a squeak and the door opened to a dark, closet-sized space, the walls lined with empty shelves. Marilee sighed with relief, still queasy, still not reassured her fears were unfounded. If not a figment of her imagination, who was that beautiful young woman, and where did she go?

Contemplating the strangeness of it, although her power of reasoning soundly rejected the notion, it occurred to her the woman might have been an apparition. She had moved that swiftly, like a swirl of dust blowing across the road. It was all Marilee needed; to be relegated to that special group of screwballs who see ghosts and flying saucers, those adamant souls that rant sightings no one else ever believes. But one thing was certain: the lady, who or whatever she was, had vanished without a trace.

That chill came again to the back of her neck as she explored the kitchen. Why, with such certainty, did she feel like something in this house had caused Johnny's behavior change? Though she couldn't realistically believe the lady in the foyer was a ghost, the possibility loomed in her mind and frightened her. She wanted nothing more than to leave, to get back into the van, lock the doors and drive away as quickly as possible, never to see Confederate Square again. Yet she was determined to stay. What compelled her, what frightened her more than an eerie house was the destruction of her marriage; and if the way to prevent that could be found here, she could hold on to her resolve and look.

All at once a chorus of voices wafted into the room, a mournful sound, much like the background melody of a tragic song. Marilee reasoned it must be a neighbor's stereo turned up loud enough to permeate the old walls around her. The repetitive lyric persisted as she opened closets and cabinet doors, all the shelves and wall-hooks empty. Within ten minutes not a single pantry or nook remained unexplored on the first floor. Marilee started back toward the foyer. Nearing the octagonal room, the chorus grew louder, more distinct, stopping abruptly just as she reached the arched doorway. That chill gathered in her shoulders. There for a moment it sounded as if the chorus was coming from this room. Her vigilant eyes shifted with each step as she entered the foyer.

Superstitious or not, her imagination found fertile ground for a dozen unsettling scenarios. Her stomach had knotted. Her resolve had waned. She stood meekly at the base of the stairs, her eyes ascending them, dwelling for a few moments on the landing some twelve feet above her head. She did not want to believe the chorus she distinctly heard came from this room, but was almost certain it did. Or perhaps it came from upstairs. Children's voices, a chorus of three or four, mournful, eternal, as if they had been singing the same chords for decades and would be singing them as long as this house stood.

Marilee's focus shifted to the front door. An urge rose inside to dash for it, to get through it as quickly as possible. She closed her eyes and drew a breath that swirled audibly through her nostrils. Wringing her hands, she noticed they had become cold and clammy. No. Not yet. Not when the answer might be upstairs. Fists clenched, she resolved to stay, to ascend the stairs for a closer look at the second floor. She would not leave without doing so, or else defeat the purpose of coming here. She could get it over with now and *never* come back.

Half way up the stairway, drawn by a high-pitched hum, Marilee's eyes shifted to the wall. Barely perceptible, it was eerie enough to threaten her resolve. She backed against the railing, tense, drawing erratic breaths. Trying to deny the superstitious clutter filling her mind, she took another step, staring at the wall as if something from it threatened to reach out and grab her. The hum suddenly flared in her ears. She gasped. Her eyes widened on a wall that seemed alive with some kind of unseen horror. Then, as quickly as it had flared, the sound faded away and left behind a deafening silence. Sidestepping as far from the wall as possible, her rear haunches slid along the rail as she continued her slow ascent. With a quick glance at the landing, she turned and scurried toward it, her feet not getting her off the stairway fast enough.

A few feet onto the landing, she stopped, closed her eyes, leaned forward, braced herself on her knees and took a few deep breaths. She was stronger now. She would leave this house a stronger woman than the demure and fragile Marilee that had entered it. Having the courage to stay surprised her, for the mysterious woman she had seen in the foyer had been real, whatever else she might be; and that chorus came from the foyer as surely as her knees were shaking now. If there really was such a thing as a haunted house, this was it, with its elusive females and its choruses emanating from nowhere. Had it transformed a skeptic into a believer? Perhaps—there was certainly less doubt; and she fully intended to read every word in Johnny's book of unexplained supernatural facts, read it as reverently as she had ever read anything.

That is, if her heart lasted the duration of this misguided adventure.

She was less terrified now, retracing the steps she and Johnny had taken together a few days before, confident in her newfound valor to face-down perhaps even Satan himself, should he happen to appear in one of these Godforsaken rooms. Frightened? There was no doubt; though a sense of anger had shouldered aside her fears, in that she had been intimidated by an empty house. Now she believed, more so than before, that something here had changed her husband.

Just as she remembered, there was nothing remarkable about the wing leading off the staircase to the left. Those rooms sat vacant, as if given a reprieve from the hulking weight of pretentious bedroom furniture. It had been the wing leading to the left that Marilee remembered so vividly—the parlor at the end, it being the one room that made her feel uncomfortable.

She paused on the landing, looking down the dimly lit hallway, fanning the dying coals of her courage. Here, the wisdom of second thoughts took on greater significance. But then, had she not come with the goal of helping her husband, of gaining some insight as to what might have happened to him; and hadn't this visit already awakened her to suspicious goings-on that, heretofore, she would have never believed? What if the answer awaited her in that parlor? Steeled again, Marilee started down the hall, opening every door, looking over every room like a detective looking for clues, combing over every wall ... looking for what? A portal to another world? A mold that could have affected her husband's thinking? What? She didn't know.

At the parlor door, she turned the knob without hesitation and pushed it open.

At once she lurched back.

Centered on the floor in the empty room, coiled, its cold eyes fixed on the intruder, was a snake, its tongue flicking. She looked at it in horror as she gathered the courage to lean forward just enough to grab the knob and slam the door. Then she slumped against the wall with quick breaths and a fast beating heart. She noticed the gap beneath the door, realizing immediately it was high enough for the snake to slither through and come at her. A shiver came up her legs and her feet came together as she pressed her back against the wall, her eyes fixed for a long moment on the gap. Surely there were snakes in the river; but how one could have gotten inside this house and into that room was a mystery. It was almost too much ... but not quite. When her heart calmed, she opened the door again, cautiously this time, leaning in to see as much of the room as she could without stepping inside.

The snake had disappeared.

She felt bold again. The snake should have sent her screaming for the front door, though it didn't, most likely as afraid of her as she was of it. A small sense of elation boosted her resolve. She had more guts than she would have given herself credit for and it made her feel good. One more room, her most oppressive challenge yet, the parlor and its several doors. On high alert, she stepped into the room as one might venture into high grass. With each step, her eyes swept the floor as if her foot might inadvertently come down on the snake. The parlor, with its connecting bedrooms and bathroom took about ten minutes to explore. Most unsettling were the two or three pockets of chilled air that she passed through, and an area in the bathroom that felt statically charged and lifted the fine hairs on her forearms. This could not have been her imagination. The snake she had seen—it was horribly real. So if the static and the chilled air meant the presence of ghosts, it was hardly enough to set her running for the van. They would need to do more than produce vague hints of themselves if they wanted to make her hair stand on end, now that she had acquired the nerves of a veteran adventuress.

After one last look around the parlor, she started back toward the stairway, feeling good about facing down the challenge of Cassandra Mott's house; though she would leave without a clue as to the reason for her husband's behavior.

Marilee made it back to the wrought-iron gate quickly and without further incident; only then completely overwhelmed with jitters. She didn't look back at the house until she was inside the van with the doors locked, her hands quivering on the wheel. She did it! She followed through, though she firmly believed she could not go back inside that house for all the gold in Fort Knox. Nevertheless, for some reason, the effort seemed worthwhile— just why, she wasn't sure yet. But she *did* know that going into the Mott house had opened up possibilities she could have never before taken seriously. Did she now believe in ghosts? She took another look at the house. Yes. On that issue, she and Johnny could agree. But how had a haunted house affected him so? He had become paranoid and irrational and unpredictable, and that was still a mystery.

She looked up at the parlor window.

What's in there that turned my husband into a stranger? ...Maybe that book will have some answers.

Chapter 14

By the time Marilee pulled the van into the garage, she was determined to get her husband to talk. That he would not confide in her was simply too unsettling. She had grown weary of the rollercoaster emotions: feeling beautiful and loved in his arms one minute, not recognizing him the next. She had become his willing lover—it was time to become his confidant.

She found Johnny in the garden room, sitting naked in the wicker rocker with his legs crossed yoga style, hunched over that book. She paused in the doorway, looking at him, surprised by his nudity. She had never seen him outside of the bedroom without some form of clothing. The midday sun bathed him in warm light and heightened the sheen on his skin. He sat with his elbows resting on the chair-arms, his head bowed in concentration, the book in his hands, his genitals splayed on the cushion between his legs. A week or two earlier she would have been embarrassed or even indignant. Today, seeing him in the middle of the day, naked in the sunlight, she was aroused.

"You look comfortable," she said from the doorway.

"You went over there, didn't you?" he said without looking up.

"How did you know?"

"I couldn't find the key," he said, glancing at her. He then turned his head with a gaze toward the garden.

"You gonna quit wearing clothes now, too?"

"Maybe."

"I can live with that, as long as you at least put on your pants when you go out for the morning paper."

He looked at her. The smile wasn't on his lips so much as in his eyes. "We can compromise then. I'll agree to put on my underwear for the paper. Pants only if I go more than one block from the house."

"Agreed," she said, and why not? Like it or not, her life was different than it had been a week ago—what seemed like an eternity. She could never go back to the church; not certain, after much contemplation, if she even had a desire to. And she knew now, when a woman parted her legs for her husband, that she could do so with the same desire that compelled him to come between them; not to mention the pure joy of feeling his eyes down there.

He looked at her for a long moment. "Are you changing, Marilee?"

"I have changed." She watched his eyes drift down her front. He was still somber. "Does that worry you?"

"I don't know," he said, shifting his eyes back to hers. "Only if your feelings for me have changed."

"They have. I love you more than I ever have. I love you so much I can't think of anything else."

"I don't know why."

"Because you taught me, Johnny. You taught me the joy of feeling like a woman. I realize how rare it is to have a unique husband. You taught me how to be a wife and love someone so deeply that nothing else matters."

He turned in thought, staring at the floor. He could hardly believe these words came from Marilee, words that leapt at him like knives of guilt.

"I've changed in other ways, too; but it shouldn't worry you, except you'll have to adjust to a full time wife."

"I'm not worried. I've waited for it nine years."

"And that includes Sunday mornings," she added.

"Sunday mornings?" He looked confused.

"Would it surprise you if I took a hiatus from church? And no more endless telephone conversations."

"It would shock me."

"You'll just have to get over it. Fact is I intend to take care of you, in every way you can imagine. Let's hope you don't get worn out."

He stared at her for a moment, almost a stupor, contemplating the meaning of her statement. Comments dripping with innuendo. It was difficult to believe, after living with her for nine years, that she had buried within her not only the ability, but also the initiative to be provocative. It was like another person inside her had awakened and vanquished the old Marilee. "What do you mean, *worn out?*"

"Hmm... Never mind." Her focus shifted to the book in his hands, which he had lowered. It now blocked her view of his genitals. "I want to read that when you're through with it."

"This," he said, holding up the book. "It's pretty interesting. I'm not sure you'd buy into it though."

"Maybe I would."

He was staring at her again, keenly, like he was seeing her for the first time, listening to her with increasing interest. He found himself excited by her, not sure if he still knew her or not. And in thinking about it, it had been a while since he heard her chatting on the phone with someone from the church.

"Going to the Mott house have anything to do with wanting to read this book?"

"Funny you should ask," she said.

"So you actually went inside?"

"Yes."

"See anything interesting?"

"Just a very beautiful young woman," she said, intentionally keeping her tone casual.

Another revelation Johnny could hardly believe. His eyes drifted leftward and fixed in space. Had Cassandra revealed herself to Marilee; and if so, what could that mean? His eyes shifted back.

"A woman? Was she black or white?"

"Same skin color as yours, actually. Quite beautiful. Every man's fantasy, I'd say. She didn't hang around for coffee though."

He nodded thoughtfully and then said: "That was my grandmother."

"That thought crossed my mind," Marilee said, stepping into the room. She sat down on the wicker chair next to him. "She looked real though. She disappeared so quickly. I never heard a sound. No footsteps across the floor, no doors closing, nothing. That's when it dawned on me she was a ghost."

"Then you know strange things are going on over there?"

"Yes, I know," she said nodding. "Very strange things."

"Where was she when you saw her?"

"In the foyer."

"Looking up at the landing?"

Marilee looked at him. "How'd you know?"

A calm came over him. It seemed Marilee had climbed up on the horse with him; and on this particular horse, having her close to his back felt good. "Because that's exactly where I saw her. Then she disappeared in the kitchen before I could catch up with her. I think she's doomed to stand in the foyer for eternity, longing to go upstairs to be with her lover, but can't. She's just a ghost fixed in a moment in time forever."

Marilee's curiosity went into high gear. "Why would she think her lover is upstairs?"

"Because her lover *is* upstairs," Johnny said, feeling comfortable plunging into some of the occurrences inside the Mott house. He had come to believe, by virtue of her visit there, that Marilee was prepared for the full rogue's gallery of its occupants. "Cassandra Mott occupies that suite at the end of the hall to the left, with her brother Julian. She came back after she died and started her life over again. She's young now, twenty-five or so. Julian's a little younger." He looked at his spellbound wife and gingerly shifted his legs out in front of the rocker, moving a bit like an old man to avoid wincing at the pain in his rectum. "I think I figured out what she is. She's human, maybe a mutation of some kind, but Julian's another story." He released a sigh. It felt good to talk to her about this. "Was the furniture there?"

Marilee's mouth had dropped open. It took a moment to register his question. "The furniture? Uh, no, there's no furniture there."

"Evidently not when you're around, but it's there."

"But nothing was there. Nothing in that suite upstairs either, except a snake."

"Oh yes ... the snake. I think you met Julian."

Knocked back to square one, Marilee was dumbfounded. She thought the house divulged all of its spooky little secrets during her visit. It seemed she had only been teased, unless Johnny had imagined these things or had dreamed them. And that was Marilee's problem—the scenario was too far-fetched; and though he obviously believed it, she could not. She was still laboring to believe she had actually seen a ghost. Had it not been for the mournful chorus in the foyer, and the fact that the beautiful woman had disappeared so mysteriously—which could easily have some explanation she hadn't thought of yet—Marilee would never have seriously considered she had seen a ghost. Her head was spinning. Johnny was saying things that were simply too fantastic to believe.

Then something else occurred to her. She looked at her husband, who had folded his hands over his naked belly and was staring across the room. In view of his state of mind, coupled with his errant behavior, it wouldn't matter if those things were real or not. It only mattered that he believed they were. She had seen some strange happenings in that house—what if he had seen the same things, but in him it triggered his imagination and caused these other delusions, people and furniture that were very real to him? Maybe that explained his personality change. Maybe he felt threatened in some way by these absurd notions.

More questions flooded her mind: Where did he go when he thought she was in Atlanta? To that house? All night? How does that explain why he came home in a rage and reeking of filth? Or did he sit in a bar and get drunk, then wile away the hours on the riverfront, wandering around all night trying to deal with an overactive imagination? Maybe he passed out in the squalor of some ally. At least that would explain how he got so filthy.

This new scenario unsettled her. None of it added up. The more Marilee tried to figure it out, the more frustrating it became. She slumped against the chair-back and rubbed her eyes. The mystery seemed to be growing and feeding on itself. She had seen the beautiful lady and there was nothing at all rational about her: her elegant but outdated dress, her odd behavior, her ability to disappear without a sound or trace. Maybe she *was* the ghost of his grandmother. And that chorus. Marilee heard it with her own ears. Had someone told her these things, she would have scoffed and rationalized, but she had experienced them herself. But how did Johnny turn a vacant house that might be haunted into a house full of furniture with two people living upstairs?

It gave her a headache.

Johnny was watching her. "You look troubled," he said. Her body-language gave him a sinking feeling.

She looked up at the ceiling, taking the back of one hand into the other, resting her joined hands in her lap. "I am. I was worried about you going crazy, but I think it's me."

"I love you, Marilee," he said, as if it were something he wanted her to remember.

Her gaze turned to him. It felt odd seeing him this way, sitting naked in the garden room, dwelling on a brother and sister no one could see but him. *I love you too, my beautiful man ... my perfect, hurting man. I love you more than you'll ever know.*

Johnny looked away from the bewildered concern that had washed over her face. Her enlightened mood had evaporated. She may have witnessed a small phenomenon on her adventure to Confederate Square, but that had not prepared her for the complete truth. She was not ready to hear about the beautiful pair. He closed his eyes and rested his head against the chair-back.

"I don't know what to think," she said distantly. "My mind is blank." She looked at him. "One minute I feel strong, like you and I can deal with anything. The next minute I feel helpless, like I'm falling into a bottomless well. ...Why would you want to go back there, Johnny? Neither one of us should. We should sell it and be rid of this nightmare. It never seemed real, anyway."

Loathe to say more, Johnny felt the tension in his neck migrating to his head. He had to make her to believe, but how? She knew something wasn't right at the Mott house—how could he make her believe he had gained entry to a secret world? He had hoped, since she acknowledged the possibility of supernatural phenomenon, that they could build a dialog on that; but her mind-set limited her imagination to nothing beyond the strange noises in the foyer and a lady that may or may not be the ghost of his grandmother. It was an impossible wall to breach; and now she wanted to get rid of the house they never owned in the first place. "I have to go back ... whether I want to or not. There's something I have to resolve."

"See what I mean? You say things that don't make sense. You make it sound like something terrible is happening to you. It scares me. We must sell that house, Johnny, or give it away, I don't care. We need it out of our lives?"

"We can't sell it, Marilee, ever."

His statement made her skin crawl. She had not expected him to sound so ominous. "We can't? Why not?"

"Because it's not ours to sell."

Her mouth fell open, incredulous. "But you inherited it!" she said, a desperate appeal.

He looked at her and took her hand. One more thing he couldn't explain. Speaking in a somber monotone, he tried. "That was a ploy to get me there. The Mott house never changed hands. No one could buy that house, Marilee. No one could live in it and survive."

Her face went blank for a moment, her curiosity muddled with confusion. "The other day you said that lawyer, Samuel McPhereson, planned to help you find a realtor. You talked to him on the phone."

"I lied. That was Cassandra Mott's doctor, Basil Salazar. He had the misfortune of having her as a patient during her lifetime." His eyes shifted from her as he muttered: "...her previous lifetime."

"Stop it Johnny. You're frightening me." His account seemed awfully elaborate to be a figment of his imagination. "...What did you mean when you said *you have to go back*?"

He closed his eyes with a defeated sigh. He had strewn her life once again with unnecessary litter.

She stared at him a long while, her eyes fixed, pleading. He was looking across the room, distant, holding on to that book between his legs. She looked down at her sandals and pushed them off with her toes and rested her feet on the sun-warmed brick floor, the comforts of the garden room lost on a swirl of apprehension. She had not loved him this way before, not this powerfully. Nine years, and until these last few days, their marriage seemed so superficial. This was a kind of love that took hold of her, more earthy, a love that reduced everything else to insignificance, a love she could feel in every fiber.

No, she didn't want to hear more about Cassandra Mott, or that house, or about furniture that disappears; not just now, not when what he already said had frightened her so out of hand. She needed a break from thinking about it. It had been a trying morning. She wanted to make believe, for a little while anyway, that everything was as it should be in their lives. She wanted to hold him and pretend.

She glanced at him, struck by the cast in his eyes. His expression had softened. He was taking deeper and quicker breaths. When his eyes dropped to her chest, she glanced down and saw his erection.

There had been moments she doubted his sanity, and moments his behavior left her stunned, but just now, there were no doubts about the message alive in his eyes. Looking into them affected her profoundly. She felt a flutter, a welling sensation that spilled warmth down through the soft flesh between her thighs. She knew if she put her fingers there now, they would get wet. Did she love him more because of his trials and enigmatic behavior? Or because he had awakened her long dormant body? Or maybe it was that inexplicable fear of losing him to the sudden darkness that had invaded his mind. Whatever the reason, just now it didn't matter, now that she realized what his eyes could do to her after all these years.

He stood and looked down at her. Her legs drew together, squeezing the sensations within her thighs up into her body. Chills raced across her forearms when he reached down to touch the side of her face. She took a long account of his masculinity, another stride toward recognizing the wonders of her own body, to see him nude in the sunlight, to be this close, to see his penis swollen with need. When she came to her feet, his hands closed on sides of her face and he drew her head closer to his.

Their lips came together, their mouths open, a kiss as warm as the sun-warmed room, a lingering reaffirmation of their bond, evolving finally into a fury of tongues and wet lips. He found the buttons of her blouse and in seconds it fell to the floor, joined seconds later by her bra. On his knees, breathing the scent of her belly, he unfastened her jeans. Down her legs they went, along with her panties, her legs warm on his palms, her scent bewitching in his nostrils. She stepped out of what had become a jumble of denim and nylon encircling her feet. He took up her panties, fresh as they were with the bouquet between her legs, and pressed them to his face and drew the scent into his nose.

Marilee had heard men did such things—she had held such acts in contempt; but seeing her husband's face buried in the panties she had been wearing inflamed her even more. Then his hands came up the back of her legs, a firm grasp of her buttocks, and he pulled her close enough to bury his tongue.

Together they went to the floor, a tight embrace on the soft oval rug, bodies joined by virtue of instincts that refused to abide further delay. Engulfed in heat and sweat and motion, confirming their desire had finally escaped nine years of prison, they locked themselves together as if this were to be their last coupling. Marilee tossed her head from side-to-side, her neck taut, and from her came a scream, eliminating her husband's ability to hold back. He wrapped his arms around her, pulled her close as their bodies shuddered and pulsed. Then, their passion spent, they melted into a useless heap, their arms and legs entwined. Their love, weighted and put to the test, expanded and filled the room.

A long moment passed before Johnny attempted to move.

Wobbly on his feet, he walked out the patio door and dropped his depleted body into a chair that overlooked their small back yard. Shrouded from the neighbors by foliage and the high fence that enclosed the yard, he sat for a long while, spell-like, his elbows propped on the wooden armrests, his long legs stretched before him. Air warmed by the noon sun lay humid on his skin. Slumped in the chair, he leaned his head sideways and rested his cheek on his knuckles, thinking about Marilee.

It would take some getting used to, this adventure with a woman he had not really known all these years. Naïve and young, he had married her for the conventional reasons a man takes a wife, not expecting the wiles of an exotic lover, though they had just devoured each other like sex-starved newlyweds. Astonishing, after nine frigid years, that it came to her so naturally, the essence of giving herself and taking from him. And that scream, uninhibited, fired with passion, still tingled on his skin like the last chord of a perfect song. How could that much energy have burned inside her so long and not found a single occasion to surface? Thinking about it, he figured it had been his fault more so than hers. After all, he had waited nine years to voice his thoughts, evidently the catalyst that had awakened that part of her, though he had hammered his frustrations at her in a tempestuous fit. But that didn't matter. They had crossed the bridge together. They had found the magic of being a man and a woman in love.

So why now? Now that the phantom of guilt had become his adopted brother? Now that his need for Julian Mott gnawed at his vitals?

Guilt. It dampened the thrill of pure joy, just when Marilee had become a wife any man would envy. And there was more than her newfound passion. Did she not provide for him and their home? Had she not taken a part time job to help pay the bills when he quit a good job to found his own design firm? Had she not forsaken the church so that she could love him with undivided affection? All put at risk by a need, a physical ache for Julian and Cassandra Mott and their vexing mystification.

Two words, *guilt* and *need*, irksome by nature with their invisible nettles; perilous for the otherwise innocent husband when imposed by such forces as the beautiful pair. Two words. They defined him now, did they not? *His* need above all else. *His* guilt as a result. How could he, a successful artist with a beautiful and dedicated wife, allow a seduction to work such decadent treachery? He had betrayed everything he stood for. It made his stomach turn with self-loathing.

Pondering it brought both anger and fear. What good did it do to resolve to break Cassandra's spell, to vanquish her hold as if it were as impotent as a fine mist in the sun, to feel his chest swell with commitment, only to have the urges recompose and crawl out on his skin like spiders? And that secondary issue—his sexuality, or bisexuality so it seemed, long ago discovered and until now ignored. It was like trying to ignore the trolls perched on one's shoulders that never tired of stabbing at one's ears with long sticks. It was palpable, his hunger for Julian, even now as his rectum throbbed with the abuse that made it uncomfortable to sit. Could he still deny, after all these years without the scent of a man in his nostrils, the written work of his own genes, a power that even dwarfed Cassandra's mystification?

An hour passed. Johnny had lost awareness of time. The hour brought no answers. His thoughts had returned to Marilee, though not her newfound penchant for squeezing the breath out of him. He thought of her as a beacon of hope, for she had begged him to let her in, to let her help battle his demons and destroy them; devotion that, he was still certain, would go up like a puff of smoke if she knew the full scope of his degradation. Though she had in her the ability to cut loose with the most sensuous scream he had ever heard, it was not in her to understand or forgive the nature of his sins. And therein lie his most unbearable fear—that he would he lose her; that now, just when their marriage had taken wing, she might learn of what he had been involved in and leave him.

He sighed. It was a beautiful spring day, hot, the air still, the kind of day that one could almost feel Savannah's past lingering in the humid air. Johnny reached up to rub his damp neck. It was a day of respite from deadlines and a reprieve from the temptations of debauchery, a day he could spend in quiet harmony with his wife. He looked at his hands. A pleasant feeling came over him. He was free of Cassandra's control, at least for the moment, a freedom he could feel like a blissful void in his chest. Together, he and Marilee could wile away the hours, exchange a few of those knowing glances, touch each other from time to time, and perhaps later on watch a movie from pillows stacked against the headboard in bed. It was the kind of day that turned one's home into a private paradise, undisturbed by the goings-on outside the parameters of their own self-contained world.

It was also a day that preceded tomorrow. Come a new dawn, he could very well awaken with a heart cold to everything but the unexplained, driven by the unseen, induced from his home in pursuit of something that reached out from an entirely different world.

He needed help. Help beyond any that he could scrounge from within himself, and beyond that which Marilee so desperately wanted to provide. But how could he hope to find someone that believed in the supernatural, someone that would be nonjudgmental and emotionally neutral?

Arlene Landrum?

Johnny contemplated his conversation with her. The old lady had enjoyed sharing reflections of her youth; but even as one of Cassandra's dearest friends, she had witnessed no more than glimpses of the real Cassandra Mott. Though Mrs. Landrum harbored vague suspicions about her old friend, she was old and fragile, not one he could look to for help.

Dr. Salazar?

No. Even if the paranoid doctor was the only man alive other than himself that knew the real Cassandra Mott, he had most likely fled Savannah in mortal fear. Even if he were here, would he have the fortitude to reach beyond his own crippled soul to help someone else?

So who? Who could he call upon to talk to and seek help? Who would have the devices to break Cassandra's grip?

It came to him like a thunderclap.

Johnny sat up with a sense of elation, alert, clasping his hands over his belly. Brian Fowler! Yes, the college professor that wrote *Unexplained Facts about the Supernatural.* Who better than the man that studied the immortal, *entities* as he called them, those like Cassandra and Julian Mott? *Entities.* Fowler had described them perfectly in his book. The more Johnny thought about it, the more excited he got about the idea. No one, anywhere in the world, would believe him or know more about his mystification than Professor Fowler.

He heard the French doors open and turned his head. Marilee was bringing out a tray of sandwiches for lunch, though the sandwiches were not what drew his attention. She had stepped back into her blue-jeans, but wore nothing above the waist, nothing to cover her breasts. Johnny stared at her, awed by yet another facet of her metamorphosis. His wife, whom a week earlier would not have come to bed without three layers of bedclothes, was exposing skin that had never known the sensation of direct sun. It didn't matter if the backyard was obscured by shrubs and a fence, she would have argued a few days before. Today she had actually walked into the open-air baring her breasts. He couldn't figure out what had gotten into her, or how a woman could have become so effervescent overnight.

After getting dressed and making the sandwiches, Marilee had paused for a moment near his drafting table, where Johnny's work on the Globalcorp project lay sprawled and neglected. Her jaw had tightened with concern. They would soon be calling again and her husband seemed oblivious to it. She would not mention it, not today, not after what they had been through during the last twenty-four hours, not with their moment of passion still tingling between her legs.

She had watched him through the window, feeling like a teenager in love; and feeling helpless, shouldering an array of emotions that felt like physical weight. Though she wanted to believe him more than he knew, the scenario he painted of Cassandra Mott and that house was too much. If only she could understand what was happening in his mind. Then she would know what has caused him to believe such things. Earlier in the day, she had touched the fringes of panic by just thinking about it. But enough of that. She would get her husband back, eventually. She would wait it out, look for a way to help him without allowing these waves of madness to erode the foundation of their marriage.

Before she went out, she set aside the sandwiches and looked down at her clothes, wondering how much nerve it took to walk outside undressed. Her tentative fingers went for the buttons down the front of her blouse. Off it came and her chest heaved and her legs instantly felt rubbery. Standing just inside the French doors, she looked down at the jeans. She reached for the fly, only to have her fingers freeze on the zipper—not quite that bold. With tray in hand, she opened the door with a hard swallow. Emerging from the house half nude would have to be enough.

"Your mouth's open," she said, setting the tray on the small table near his elbow.

"Uh ..." He thought of nothing to say as his eyes followed her across the patio to her gardening table, where she picked up a small tilling fork.

"Warm out today, isn't it," she said, turning back into his gaze.

"Yeah ... summer's getting closer."

She saw his eyes fall to her jeans.

"You're wondering why I didn't take off my jeans," she said, as a nervous flurry of words welled and inadvertently spilled out. "Well, I couldn't. I couldn't just walk out here naked. I tried, but I couldn't." She scanned across the trees as if she were checking the shadowy limbs for gawkers. "I know the back yard is enclosed and nobody can see, but I can't do everything you want me to do ... not all at once anyway." She looked at the gardening fork clutched tightly in her hand, and then sighed. Her arms fell limp at her side. "I give up. I can't explain things like this to you." Her motor seemed to be running as she looked over at the garden and then back. "Besides, you're a man. Men can do things. Women can't ... they don't have the courage ... some women anyway."

"You're fine, baby," he said, scratching his head without a clue as to what she expected him say. "Everything's fine."

Her nostrils flared with a deep, emotional breath. She had taken on a small challenge that made her giddy; in that she was bawdy enough to do it; and well worth the gamble in that her husband was so obviously enchanted.

"Did you know the warm sun would turn your nipples into little peaks?"

Her face flushed. "The sun didn't cause that," she said, resisting the urge to fold her arms over her breasts. She fidgeted for a moment in his adoring gaze before adding: "Anyway, thought I'd do a little gardening this afternoon."

He nodded. "Good day for that," he said, inclined to tease her a little more, but thought better of it. She was frazzled enough already.

She stared at him for a long moment in thought.

"Something on your mind, gorgeous?" he asked.

Her reply hinted concern. "Johnny ... don't be upset with me, but I was wondering ..." She looked at him a moment longer, second-guessing her question before venturing: "I was wondering, do you think it's possible you imagined some of those things in that house."

The smile in his eyes diminished as he released a breath. If only she could feel his rectal suffering for two minutes, she would know his imagination was not conjuring the young and beautiful Cassandra Mott.

"Marilee, let's not talk about it anymore today," he said calmly, as if all of that was a world away.

"I'm sorry. I ..."

"I know. Just not today."

He shifted his weight in the chair, taking a sandwich as he watched her walk across the backyard, her stride so feminine and lovely across the cool grass. She knelt at the edge of the garden and plowed the fork under a weed, her dark skin radiant in the sun, a stunning contrast to the colorful perennials swaying beyond her bare shoulders. Leaning forward, he ate the sandwich and crunched a few chips, watching her fork and till the soil, pulling weeds and placing them into the basket she had taken with her. He was falling in love with her all over again, more powerfully even than the day he first saw her in the library so many years ago. Instead of the shy young girl that had cast those coy glances his way, he was falling in love with a woman. Just how she was putting up with him, he didn't know. But she was; and even though he had never needed her before, that too had changed. He couldn't imagine needing her more than he did now.

His thoughts returned to Brian Fowler. It meant a trip to Boston, a few days off, but what could be more important in the scheme of things The day's calm didn't fool him; he could see himself in a determined stride to Confederate Square. It waited inside him, perfectly still like a toad awaiting a fly, a constant awareness, unyielding even as he watched his partially nude wife; that need that promised to draw him back into Cassandra's world of debauchery. So he would travel to Boston, find Brian Fowler and seek help. It equaled no less than the salvation of his marriage and his sanity.

Johnny picked up the tray and took it into the house, pausing by the drafting table when he noticed Brian Fowler's book. Not today. He would not call the university until tomorrow. First thing in the morning, get Brian Fowler on the phone and arrange a meeting. He turned and looked through the glass, at Marilee on her knees in the garden. Today he would spend with his wife and savor his time with her, unencumbered by what might come with a new day.

After putting the tray on the kitchen counter, he went into the bedroom and slipped on his favorite pair of cutoff shorts. A size too large, they were frayed around the legs, faded and comfortable, salvaged from the bottom drawer for more summers than he could remember. He then joined Marilee in the garden. She had gone for a pair of shears and was cutting dead leaves from the flowers and plants. A smile lit her face as he approached with the hoe in hand.

Together they went about tending the garden, ridding it of weeds and turning the soil, comfortable with the silence born in the time-honed informalities of their nine-year marriage. It didn't matter that such a mundane activity occupied their time, not as long as they were close. Like nutrients for the soul, these precious moments provided the time to cherish the good fortune of simply having each other.

Wiping a light sweat from her brow, Marilee looked over at his backside when he got on his hands and knees to pull some grass that had grown in from the yard, a temptation too delicious to resist. Swept by mischief, she quietly reached over the few plants separating them and snuck her hand up the leg opening of his shorts, far enough to give him a good nip; then fell back in hysterics when he yelped and nearly jumped out of his skin.

"Marilee!" he blurted with feigned indignation as he turned and plopped down on the freshly tilled earth. "That was *not* very ladylike!"

"Oh?" she said, blotting a tear, "Are you expecting ladylike behavior from the woman you turned into a shameless hussy?"

A silence came over them. Their eyes filled with the knowledge of what the other was thinking. Marilee put the garden tool aside and stood and stepped over the plants between them, the freshly turned earth swallowing her feet. She got down on her knees and sat back on her calves and lifted her hand to his cheek. A film of perspiration glistened between her breasts, like dew on the petals of a rose. Her eyes sparkled with the joy of the afternoon, belying that ever-present hint of discord that reflected lives changed and minds tormented by the unknown. How easy it was, for a while, to pretend their problems did not exist, that she lived with her husband in a carefree

Utopia. How essential it was, if for just one afternoon, to pretend their lives were not unraveling.

Chapter 15

Johnny awoke the next day and found himself sitting on the edge of the bed, wringing his hands, thinking about the day before. It had evaporated so quickly, a dream turned into a memory. Marilee had forgiven him for staying out the night before, then coming home like a cowering dog freed from the sewer. They had made love and napped and awakened in each other's arms, and then a casual dinner. They had stayed up late watching a movie. Not once did she mention a psychiatrist, or question him, or bring it up in any way. Why did he have the urge to abandon her?

He got to his feet, shoulders tight, that familiar tension in his hands, like a faint but nagging electrical current running through them. He turned to look at his wife, still sound asleep, her hips prominent under the sheet. For her, not just for himself, he would phone Brian Fowler.

The bruised flesh around his anus had healed; there was no more pain. His buttocks squeezed in response to some vague anticipation; and as his body relaxed, he wondered if women experience these same sensations.

His shorts lay crumpled a few steps across the room. He leaned forward to pick them up, stepping into them on his way down the hallway, buttoning them as he entered the garden room. The first glimmer of sunlight had fallen across the drafting table. Outside, shadowed by the luminescent leaves of the neighboring trees, a mockingbird greeted the new day.

Positioned on the stool, Johnny reached for Bryan Fowler's book, convinced the man that had conducted years of research into the supernatural was his only hope. After staring at the charred cover, he set the book aside and leaned on his elbows and buried his face in his hands. An hour passed as he contemplated what he might say once he got Bryan Fowler on the phone, vaguely aware Marilee had gotten up and had started her routine in the kitchen. Some few moments later, the room quiet and filled with sun, he felt her eyes on the back of his head.

"Breakfast is ready," she said from the doorway, noting the distance in his eyes when he turned. "How do you feel this morning?" she asked hesitantly as he approached.

"I'm Fine," he said, absent the enchantment in his eyes from the day before.

An underlying tension followed them to the breakfast table. Watching him furtively as she buttered her toast, Marilee had become alert to his demeanor during the past few days. His mind this morning was elsewhere. She would not inquire further; she assumed the ill-gotten notions that had pervaded his life was the reason for his quiet mood. She would not bring up her concerns or risk an emotional maelstrom, not when his ability to cope seemed so fragile. Instead, she remained silent as she toyed with her scrambled eggs, letting her anger roil inside, regretting his sudden transformation had overshadowed her memories from the day before.

When he got up from the table to go back into the garden room, she prayed he intended to work, that he would meet the next deadline on the cosmetic campaign for Globalcorp. She stared at the food he had left on his plate, trying to deny that creeping doubt about what his agenda for the day might be.

Back at his drafting table, the phone book before him atop his unfinished work, Johnny leafed through the well-worn pages for Boston's area code. After getting the university administration's number from information, he dialed it in a near sweat, hoping that Brian Fowler would be available to take a phone call, and receptive to meeting with him as soon as possible.

A receptionist answered.

"Is Professor Brian Fowler available?"

"What department is he in, sir?"

"Uh ..." Johnny quickly opened Fowler's book to the back page and scanned his short biography. "He's a professor of antiquities."

"Just a moment please," said the voice.

He listened to a long silence before the next voice came through the phone, another woman.

"May I help you?" she asked.

"I'm trying to reach Brian Fowler."

"He's not here at the university, sir."

"...It's important. Could you tell me where I can reach him? Maybe his home number?"

A silence followed that seemed like reluctance. "Sir, even if I could give out his home number, which I can't, it wouldn't do you any good. Professor Fowler has already gone to Africa."

"Where?"

"Africa. He goes every summer. He left earlier this year since he had no second semester classes."

The phone nearly slipped from Johnny's hand. A sense of despair washed over him and left him incapable of a response.

"Sir ... are you still there?"

"Africa?" Johnny said, faltering.

"Yes. Where he does his research. I believe it was Kenya this year. He works with the people there, the Maasai I think he said."

"Works with people?"

"Practices medicine. He's a medical doctor, too, you know. Donates his time and medical skills. Says it's his way of repaying the Africans for allowing him to work in their country."

"Uh, can he be reached there?" Johnny asked.

"Oh Lord no," she said with a small laugh. "He stays in those remote villages, you know, the kind you see in documentaries. There's no electricity, let alone telephones."

"It's importance that I reach him. There must be some way to get in touch with him."

There came another reluctant silence. "Are you a friend of Professor Fowler's? You know how much he hates to be disturbed."

"I'm familiar with his work. This pertains to his book. I'm certain he'd want to hear what I have to say."

"May I have your name then?" she asked.

"Johnny Feelwater."

"Mr. Feelwater, we do have a number where he can be reached, an acquaintance of his in Nairobi. A tour guide or something like that."

"Yes," Johnny said anxiously, "may I have that number?"

"He's an Englishman," she went on to say, apparently in the process of looking up the number. "I spoke with him last summer, after Professor Fowler's father died. Ah, here it is." She recited the number.

Johnny scratched it down on the opened page of Fowler's book.

"Mr. Feelwater ... I've taken a risk by giving you that number. I hope you don't call it without a very good reason."

"I understand," said Johnny. "Don't worry. It's more likely he'd be upset if you hadn't given me the number."

"Well then, good luck in reaching him," she said, and then hung up.

With the sound of the click, Johnny's heart sank. Africa. How could anyone be more difficult to reach? A sense of urgency stiffened his neck. He rubbed his face with his hands, having allowed himself the optimism of getting his life back through Bryan Fowler. Why not Mars, or the moon? What difference did it make? In frustration, it dawned on him that he forgot to ask when the professor planned to return. But what did that matter, when in all likelihood he will have already stepped over the edge by then?

Africa. He looked down at the phone number. Fueled by a sense of urgency, his mind sailed on an impossible idea.

Why not? If he'd been in Boston, wouldn't I have gotten on a plane to go there? Aren't there flights to Africa as well? It's just a longer flight.

A feeling of stress overwhelmed his plotting. No, he couldn't afford to go to Africa for a dozen reasons, not the least of which was the lady cleaning up the breakfast dishes in the kitchen.

But it's for both of us, our future.

Images from the day before passed through his mind. He wanted more days like that. He wanted to cherish those moments with Marilee for the rest of his life. Their future was threatened. He had to go to Africa. There was no other way to fight Cassandra Mott's spell.

The other line rang as he dialed the number in Nairobi. He ignored it, thinking Marilee would answer the call, not caring either way. A Mr. Doug Stanton answered the phone. Johnny introduced himself and inquired about Brian Fowler.

"Aye, I know the bloke. Dare say the orneriest S.O.B. I ever came across in me life."

Johnny lowered his head, pressing his fingertips into his brow. Getting the impression that no one liked Brian Fowler, he also wondered if he had gotten the right man on the phone. "The lady I spoke with at the university said Mr. Fowler's acquaintance in Nairobi is English. You sound like an Australian."

"I *am* Australian, mate. She ain't the first to mistake me for an Englishman."

"That doesn't matter anyway. ...Mr. Stanton, it's very important I talk to Mr. Fowler. Do you know where he is?"

"Your voice sounds distant. Where you calling me from, mate?"

"The United States. Savannah, Georgia."

"Ah, you're on the wrong side of the world to talk to Brian Fowler, mate."

"I'll come there. Can you take me to him?"

"'Spose I can, mate. That's 'ow I make my livin'."

"How do I get in touch with you when I get there?"

Stanton gave out an address, then added: "No need to try to find me. Just call this number when you get to Nairobi. I'll meet you."

"Okay then. I'll make the arrangements and let you know when to expect me."

"Fine, mate. Just call me. Make it fast though. Got some bookings comin' up."

Johnny hung up, drawing a deep, nervous breath. His heart was beating abnormally fast. He felt a sense of desperation, like Cassandra had sent vapors crawling through the streets of Savanna, seeking him out, finding their way into his belly. He sat staring at the phone. His hands had knotted into fists. Was it him? Did he simply lack the will to resist a beautiful enchantress? Was it an inherent weakness that ignited this irresistible temptation for a beautiful man? If it were only that simple; for it felt more like a summons, not heard or seen, something with an unyielding grip. He folded his arms across his stomach, closed his eyes and leaned forward to rest his forehead on the cluttered drafting table, silently begging the feeling to pass.

A few minutes later, Marilee walked into the room. When he turned to look at her, his heart fell again. Something had happened. She looked away from him in despair, her eyes welling with tears, and she slumped into the wicker chair as if her knees suddenly lacked the will to hold her up.

Johnny watched a tear run down her cheek. The tightness in his neck moved into his head in the form of an ache. That call he had ignored. It dawned on him that she must have answered it in the kitchen. Now, with premonitions emerging from the corners of his brain, the morning loomed like a monster waiting to devour them. Marilee finally spoke.

"That was a lawyer from Globalcorp," she said, laboring with the words as if she had just learned she faced a dreaded disease. "They weren't happy with that last presentation. They're exercising their option to take the contract elsewhere." She looked at him as if their future had just been snatched away. "We lost it. Just like that. I tried to talk to him but he hung up. I wanted to tell him you'd design another set and send it out immediately. I pleaded for more time. Promised there would be no more delays. He just hung up. He hung up before I could explain."

Johnny agonized for the woman he loved. She seemed even more distraught than the morning he came reeking into the house after being gang-raped. He wanted to get to her, to take her into his arms and assure her that they would get through this just fine; that really, he would much rather work for smaller, more independent firms than those assholes at Globalcorp; but he made no move to comfort her. The bombshell that he had yet to explode weighed heavy in his hands. It would demoralize her more than that phone call had.

Blotting a tear with a wadded tissue, Marilee sat like a lost child alone in the world, her knees together, her free hand resting limp upon her lap. Her agony stabbed at his heart. He wondered, beyond her predictable reaction to the news he was about to deliver, if his own sanity could survive telling her, when already the foul breath of madness chilled his neck. Should he beg for understanding, plead that she indulge an idea that she's certain to perceive as lunacy? Should he bring it up when the light on the horizon seemed so distant, when the uppermost concern in her mind right now was next month's mortgage payment?

His concern shifted to the ramifications of that call from Globalcorp.

So that's the price of loving an enchantress and her brother. Beyond unraveling his moral fiber, beyond the chaos she had strewn in his life, Cassandra had cost them the contract with Globalcorp. He knew that last presentation was substandard when he mailed it, as he had not found that special magic in his hands to create his usual work. And even in realizing that working for behemoths like Globalcorp brought little satisfaction, he had needed that contract to set him free to pursue the projects he truly loved. All of that was gone. His eyes closed with the thought. *Gone.* Gone as if it never existed, along with all the glorious opportunities that were sure to follow, along with the sweet bliss of financial security.

Marilee's eyes shifted and came to rest on him. "What're we going to do?"

His jaw tightened. He reached down deep for a way to explain why he wanted to meet with Brian Fowler, and found nothing. There was no good way to tell her, no fabrication he could weave that might justify his scheme in some small way, especially since she believed he had already stepped over the edge. His only option—state his plan and get it over with.

He looked at her long and hard, breathing as if he could not get enough oxygen, trying desperately to gather the courage to get the words out. One last deep breath, and then he simply said: "Marilee ... I'm going to Africa."

Chapter 16

What did he say?

In their fast approach to the moment in time they could scarcely afford a movie, did he say *Africa*? Sitting in her robe, staring across the room as if she did not recognize her own house, Marilee's dazed eyes shifted back to her husband. He was staring at her as if awaiting a response.

The statement had stabbed into her ears and was splaying about in her mind like a loose hose spewing folly; so distracting her sensibilities lapsed into disarray. For all the good her brain was doing her now, she might as well have been thumping melons at the supermarket. Wasn't it ludicrous to believe that he had actually said something like that when their world was flying apart? Evidently not, attested by his forlorn expression, his quite serious facial appeal. She slowly began to realize that this, based on the direction their lives had taken, was exactly the kind of thing that could come crashing down from the sky. And why not, when in the twinkling of a couple of weeks her life had become unrecognizable and she had been body-slammed into a realm of madness? So far fetched it was, she could not be angry, just stupefied. Yes, he had stated it clearly. His unexpected and incomprehensible plans to go where? ...of course, Africa. How utterly appropriate. If he intended to knock her for a loop, what else could he have come up with that would have been more effective?

Johnny lowered his head. Telling her this felt much like swinging a sledgehammer. It caught her thoroughly off guard. He glanced up and saw her staring at him in an odd state of distraction. Then, to his chagrin, a vague smile curled near the corners of her lips; not a smile really, more of an ironic realization of a crumbling world, the kind of expression that follows hopeless defeat. She seemed to be looking right through him. There was nothing to do but go forward, he reasoned, ransacking his mind for the right words to justify his going to Africa.

A long awkward silence passed. The duel onslaught of losing Globalcorp and her husband's increasing irrationality had jolted all emotion from Marilee. Incredibly, she found herself thinking with a clear head, as if chaos itself had become a normal state-of-mind; and in this house an art form, except for more than a few unanswered questions. In fact, questions about this trip to Africa seemed to be multiplying in her mind like the redoubling cells of a fast growing amoeba. She watched Johnny get off the stool and walk to the French doors, where he stared out across the patio in silence. Considering first the question of money, she thought she might suggest they had no funds for a trip to Africa, though that seemed rather mundane in their expanding world of turmoil; so her first statement evolved into a calm and simple query.

"Why are you going to Africa?" She immediately felt silly for asking. Though he must believe that he had a good reason for wanting to go, didn't he realize on some level that his notion of actually going there was not only illogical, but simply absurd?

Johnny turned to her. "Because that's where Brian Fowler is," he said, as if in his mind that explained everything.

"I see," she replied, exasperated, feeling much like a mother having to make a sixteen year old son understand that he wasn't old enough to marry that fourteen year old girl. He didn't seem to realize that she had fallen into a fast flowing river and was foundering on its roiling currents. "Who is Brian Fowler?"

He nodded at the drafting table. "The man who wrote that book."

Her eyes shifted to the book. Of course. That house. She should have known. His intent to go to Africa was not a baseless notion that came to him in a dream, not total loss of reason; but instead, he was reaching out for help. Whether the idea had merit or not, obviously Johnny thought it did. Whether his obsession with that house was based in reality or not, to him the anxiety was real. That, she realized, concerning a trip to Africa, was square one. She could deal with it now on a more rational level.

Marilee pondered this turn of events for a few moments. It came down to keeping her eye on the horizon and staying the course. So their lives were careening in outlandish directions. From the moment she realized an invisible hand had turned Johnny's soul inside out, she had resolved to endure the ride, to hang on and face each day as best she could, awaiting the moment she would get her husband back. Now, in looking at him, it was like seeing him in a deep pool of water, beneath the surface and looking up at her with fearful eyes, foundering for air. How she wished her arms were long enough to reach down and take a hold of his hand.

"We could lose the house," she said, not bitterly or accusingly, but as a matter of fact.

He looked up from the floor. "Honey, I won't let that happen. If we get behind on the mortgage again, I'll talk to the man at the bank. Let me resolve this in my own way and I'll find new clients, better clients than Globalcorp. I'll work my ass off to get us caught back up. You'll see."

"Still refuse to see a psychologist?"

He looked at her for a moment, thinking he would see a psychologist to appease her, if they had the money. But they didn't, so why heap expenses on top of bills that were already going to be a struggle to pay? "Marilee, you went inside the Mott house yourself," he pleaded. "You saw my grandmother's ghost with your own eyes."

"I'm still debating that."

"You heard the chorus in the foyer. You've seen strange occurrences there."

"I know what I *thought* I heard. There could be some other explanation."

Frustrated, Johnny gave up. He came to the conclusion that Cassandra had no intention of allowing his wife into her world. "I know I've said some incredible things about that house. I know you'll never believe me." ...*It's probably best this way. You'd leave me if you knew the whole truth, anyway.* "Please, just try to understand, even if you think it's all in my head, I really believe Brian Fowler can help me find a way to ..." *To what? Tell her what I'm trying to break free of?* "...I think he can help get these hallucinations, or whatever this is, behind me."

She absently looked round the room as she sorted out her thoughts. Then her weary gaze found him again. "How long will you be gone?"

"No more than a week or two."

She didn't have to inquire about the money, knowing a trip to Africa would max out their credit cards again. It meant talking to her mother about the car payment, and then listening to a rant about her irresponsible husband. So be it. She had invested her heart and soul in this man. Nine years equaled no more than a down payment on a lifetime vow, and she intended to make every one of the installments, even if making this one threatened to cost them their home. Though it angered her that he refused to see a doctor, she loved him, now more than ever, and she would wait for him to come out on the other side. If their finances were to be exhausted and they had to start over again, that too could be endured; for nothing, absolutely nothing, was nearly as awful as losing him.

He turned and looked at the unfinished graphics on his drafting table, almost relieved. They represented his first taste of the rat-race. The whole affair left a bitter taste on his tongue. Never again would he kowtow to faceless, overpaid corporate executives like those at Globalcorp. One by one he picked up the sketches and color separations, waded them and dropped them in the trashcan. Marilee came up behind him. She had said everything she intended to say. She kissed him on the back of the neck before turning to leave the room. When the drafting table was free of clutter, he quietly sought her out, pausing in the hallway near the bedroom door, where that invisible hand once again tightened its relentless grip on his heart. He could hear her sobbing.

He lowered his head and rubbed his eyes with his fingers. Instead of going to her, he returned to the garden room and perched solemnly on his stool, wondering how much longer Marilee could abide a marriage that out of the blue was spiraling toward disaster. Was this a woman's nature, to love a man no matter what, to cope with anything he might throw at her, and then resolve it quietly on her bed with tears? He could hardly stand the feel of his skin crawling with such helplessness.

♦ ♦ ♦

"How do you know what to pack for a trip to Africa?" Marilee asked, rummaging through a dresser drawer filled with underwear and socks.

He glanced from the open suitcase on the bed to the back of her head. His eyes traveled down to the small of her back. It might have been easier if she had thrown a fit and ranted about the cost. Instead, she was helping him pack. How much could she take? Two days had passed. Not once did she question him or express a single doubt. Now she planned to drive him to the airport in Atlanta.

"I looked on the Internet," he said, rubbing the back of his neck. "It's not as hot in Kenya this time of year as people think."

"Will you need a jacket?"

"No."

Two nights had passed since he declared his plan to go to Africa—two abbreviated lifetimes; during which they held each other for long moments in silent contemplation, husband and wife in a state of transition, evolving from two souls lost in their own endeavors into a bonded pair. It was a kind of quiet security in an insecure world. Whereas the void in their lives had provided a need for his endless ambitions and her religious zeal, that void no longer existed. They had noticed each other smile for the first time, really noticed; which made them instinctually aware of life's important elements. At least on this level they were not alone; though both, even as they shared body heat during the night, held reservations for the future. Their world was crumbling.

Marilee tucked three pairs of socks and three pairs of underwear under her arm. She pulled open the drawer where he kept his shorts, silently dreading his long absence.

"Are the seasons there reversed, like Australia?" she asked. "Might be too cool for shorts."

"It's right on the equator," he said, pausing at the door of the closet. "It's always mild there."

She turned to look at him, teetering on the verge of tears. "Isn't Kenya a dangerous wilderness? What if you can't find Brian Fowler?"

Johnny looked at her, aware of her struggle to be brave. "That guide in Nairobi knows where he is."

"How do you know he'll talk to you? What if he's some kind of a nut? Or one of those academic eccentrics that won't find time for you, or care you traveled all the way around the world to see him?"

Watching her, a finger pressed against his lower lip, Johnny realized Marilee's tone reflected more concern than doubt. If she broke down now, he was not sure he could comfort her, not with the butterflies fluttering in his belly. Fretting over the same negative scenarios, he replied with as little concern as possible.

"I can't be certain he'll see me, but I bet he will. He's interested in the supernatural. He'll want to hear what I have to say."

She turned back to the dresser, emotionally drained. She took out two pairs of shorts, crossed the room and folded them into the suitcase. Johnny, watching her, released a sigh and walked into the closet. The brown and black hiking shoes he bought when Globalcorp's first check arrived in the mail were on the top shelf. He remembered feeling rather affluent when he deposited the check. That night at the mall, after he and Marilee celebrated with a bottle of wine at dinner, he saw the shoes in a store window and they became his one small indulgence. He didn't know then that he would find a practical use for them.

There had been something remarkable about the day, though he tried to avoid thinking about it. Not once, not even when he awoke, had he felt Cassandra's reach. Standing under the light in the middle of the closet, he looked at his hands, turning them, aware as he absently rubbed his palm with a thumb that he felt no sense of urgency. The feeling, when present, was much like the second day after he had quit smoking, when all he could think about was a cigarette. Just one more. Just one more visit and he would never go back; knowing, in the back of his mind that he would.

Yes, he would go back, because her aphrodisia was more potent than nicotine, more difficult to understand. Like the day before, when he awoke it was like she was lingering in the bedroom, a lion watching a gazelle. He had even scanned the room to assure himself she was not. And later, he felt her presence again while driving to the bank, where he planned to arrange for another extension on their mortgage. The real difficulty came a few blocks from his destination.

It was as if her breath had touched the back of his neck, feeding an irresistible urge to turn toward Confederate Square. His hands felt clammy and were knotted on the wheel. All rational thought scattered. He wanted to be with them, just for a while, to look at them, to be close. He pictured Julian stretched out on the sofa, nude. Yet he resisted. He had pulled to the curb and lowered the window, his preoccupation with Africa overshadowed by desire for Julian, as were the excuses he planned to present to the banker.

A quick visit, the demon whispered in his ear, *just one breath of her hair*. But he knew it would not stop there. Cassandra was calling him for Julian. She had caused the fever in his belly, the tingles that tightened his legs and set him squirming on the warm leather seat behind the wheel. Those walking by looked in on him with curious concern, as he took long deep breaths of fresh air, hands clasped between his legs, forehead pressed against the wheel. And when it finally passed he drove on. By the time he ascended the front steps of the bank, his brow had relaxed and he remembered the tale-of-woe he planned for the banker.

With a couple of shirts and his never-used hiking shoes, he came out of the closet and watched Marilee place his shorts in the suitcase. When she turned he saw taut lips and weary eyes that were creased with stress. She took the shirts as he drew near and began folding and packing them.

There was something unsaid on her mind. He could see it in her demeanor. He could feel the tension in the room.

"What are you thinking about?" he asked, sitting on the edge of the bed.

She handed him a pair of socks to wear on the plane. "How much I love you. That's what I'm thinking about. That's all I've been thinking about for two days. I've tried not to burden you with how nervous I am about you going to Africa, but I am. I'm scared to death something might happen to you." Her chest rose and she closed her eyes, as if stating what bothered her was difficult. "... I'm afraid you'll never come back."

He looked at the socks in his hand.

"And why shouldn't I worry?" she went on. "Look at what's happened to us since you inherited that house. I'm sorry, I just can't help it." She sat down beside him and rested her hand on his leg.

He set the socks aside and wrapped his arm around her shoulders and drew her near. Surely she knew that nothing on Earth could keep him from returning home to her. No man ever had a better partner or loved his wife more. He would he be back, soon, hopefully with the knowledge to stop their lives from unraveling.

♦ ♦ ♦

It was a somber drive to Atlanta. At the airport, they made their way to the counter and collected a ticket and a boarding pass after a short wait in line. Johnny's stomach felt queasy when he laid their credit card on the counter, the fare with all the connecting flights so steep. After checking in the suitcase, they went to the security area where he and Marilee were to part. Johnny looked at her, turning his face aside with eyes and lips tightly closed, drawing back his composure. They found themselves locked in a hug that neither wanted to break.

After passing through security, Johnny started toward the gate. A short way down the corridor, he stopped and looked back and smiled. His wife was waving good-bye. How fragile she looked surrounded by throngs of people and the electronic barriers that separated them. It felt like he was stepping from a dream they had shared, into another which offered no predictable end.

Chapter 17

Johnny didn't remember walking onto the plane, he realized as he sat strapped into a seat by the window, thinking he must have been preoccupied. He gazed down at the activity on the tarmac, seeing not men and machines, but the mental image of Marilee waving good-bye. It would be a long flight to London and already he missed her. In London, he would lay over a couple of hours before boarding another plane to Cairo, where he would change planes one more time before landing in Nairobi. Sitting on the plane brought on the full impact of his challenge.

Africa. The circumstances could have been vastly more desirable—perhaps a celebration to share with his wife had the Globalcorp project worked out. Nevertheless, he was actually going to the great continent, the homeland of his forebears; and, the reason aside, it was thrilling.

The huge craft lifted into the air a short while later, a phenomenon that Johnny found unnerving, which usually left him gripping the armrests and holding his breath. This time, instead of images of aircraft falling from the sky, his thoughts drifted to the moment he would set eyes on Brian Fowler. He pictured a scenario of unusual surroundings, filled with exotic and carefree Africans and the endless savannahs of Kenya. A myriad of faces formed in his mind's eye as he tried to imagine what Professor Fowler looked like. A white man most likely, perhaps tall, sophisticated in stature to match his academic accomplishments. What will the man's reaction be, Johnny wondered, to have been sought out from half way around the world?

Weariness crept over him as the jet rose and fell on a series of annoying air pockets. Two sleepless nights with Marilee and the unending tension had caught up with him. Not ten minutes passed before his head wobbled and leaned against the window, and vague dreams began to mingle with his fleeting awareness of droning engines. And as he sank into deeper and sounder sleep, images of leather clad brutes formed around him and his legs were pried apart and the humiliation was like sinking in quicksand. Then, as he lay in this wretched state, a hand took a hold of his shoulder. He looked up and saw Marilee. But it wasn't Marilee seeing him that way, he realized as he adjusted his weight in the seat, but the flight attendant trying to awaken him for dinner.

He sat upright, blinking, wondering how long he slept. The lovely young woman positioned the tray and served his dinner. Disoriented, he lowered his head and rubbed his eyes with his fingertips.

"What would you like to drink, sir?" the flight attendant repeated patiently.

I'm in a plane, going to Africa. The countless small muscles in his face relaxed as he looked up at her with a drowsy smile.

"Coffee," he said, his mouth breathy and dry.

Unraveling a fork from the rolled napkin, he craned his neck to look forward, then aft. The flight attendant had gone to the front of the plane. The couple across the aisle was sound asleep. The confined space between the high seats provided a bit of privacy in the dim light. He sucked in his belly and pushed the napkin under the waistband of his briefs to blot away the stickiness that had occurred during the dream. With that done and unnoticed, he slumped against the seat back and closed his eyes, wondering how Cassandra found a path into his dreams, even here, thirty-five thousand feet over the Atlantic Ocean.

A few moments later, Johnny picked up the fork and poked at the food: a scoop of potato salad, a slice of baked ham and green beans. The plane dipped rudely on an air pocket and he looked out the window. Now well past sunset, a black void lie beyond the glass. The moon reflected on the swells far below. Johnny imagined a number of potential disasters. It occurred to him that this heavy aircraft could very well plunge into those unimaginable depths, then sink and merge with that black, weightless world. The cabin would fill, a dreadful watery death; a thought that affected his appetite, he realized when he looked back at the rather bland food he had been served.

Wonder what I'll be eating in Africa, he was thinking as he lifted a forkful of potato salad to his mouth. He looked about the cabin again, at those sleeping across from him, then glanced at those behind, turning again to scan the numerous fair-haired passengers in the front part of the plane; a mix of light-skinned passengers who were likely ending their travels in London. He surmised the mix would be somewhat darker on the plane to Nairobi.

He had eaten a few more bites before his eyes fluttered again. The rocking and monotonous drone of jet engines compounded his weariness. His head tilted to the side, resting lightly against the seatback, and he slept until the jet began its descent into London.

Heathrow was even busier than Atlanta's Hartsfield International. After getting through customs, Johnny wandered through the disquieting throngs, assaulted by bright lights and echoing noise after the long flight in the quiet womb of the plane, realizing somewhat wide-eyed that he was actually in London. After picking up a magazine to pass the time, he found his next departure gate and took a seat holding the magazine and a small bag of chips, oblivious to the comings and goings around him as he pondered meeting Brian Fowler.

Who would learn from whom in this exchange between two men in the heart of Africa? Fowler described his supernatural subjects as *entities*. He has studied them for many years. But Johnny had experienced events far more dramatic than any of those outlined in Fowler's book, so it seemed that he might be relating tales Professor Fowler had yet to imagine. In contemplating Fowler's revelations, there remained only one important question: Does this man know enough about the immortals to advise how to purge them from one's life?

The magazine remained unopened by the time Johnny boarded the jet to Cairo. Buckled into his seat, he noticed a more Arabic flavor aboard the plane, and a scattering of travelers from other parts of the world. As he had assumed, the composition of passengers had gotten darker nearing Africa. He sat as if he were staring at something invisible during much of the flight, his thoughts bouncing about like a lopsided ball. The flight over Europe, he noticed gratefully, was less turbulent than the one over the Atlantic, though he avoided the window when the pilot announced they had entered airspace over the Mediterranean Sea. Somehow crash and burn seemed less ominous than sink and drown.

Cairo brought a rather unnerving wait in getting through Egyptian customs. Here, Johnny had far less time to connect with his next flight. His eyes jumped anxiously back and forth between a clock on the facing wall and the line ahead of him, which crept forward ever so slowly. Finally, after a struggle to answer a dozen questions posed to him in broken English, he stepped away from the dissection of a pair of narrow, scrutinizing eyes, and walked no more than a few paces before breaking into a run. Following in a near panic those few signs posted in English, he found his way to the right gate, where the passengers bound for Nairobi had already boarded. Fumbling through an array of documents, he found the ticket and stepped up quickly to hand it to an attendant that was looking at her watch. She casually handed him a boarding pass.

His heart finally settled a few minutes into the air. It dawned on him that he had just landed, and had become a nervous wreck, and had flown out of a country in Africa; but then Egypt didn't really fit his perception of Africa. From his earliest reflections on the Dark Continent, he had conjured images of giraffes and savannahs and Swahilis, not camels and pyramids and Arabs. As far as Johnny was concerned, Egypt simply did not represent his ancestral homeland, but where this plane was heading did.

He settled into the seat, this time among passengers with far darker skin; and this time, when he ducked under the low doorway to step off the plane, he would be stepping onto true African soil. Nairobi, Kenya. He could not help but feel giddy, though he harbored no idea of what to expect.

Distracted by a couple not much younger than himself in the seats ahead of him, he focused on their fawning and lively banter. They gave off an air of mutual love and an eagerness driven by hormones. Watching them through the gap between the seat backs, their display sparked a touch of homesickness; it reminded him of the day he had spent with Marilee in the garden. Much like the pair in front of him, he too knew the joy of having someone to love, albeit a rekindled love formed on the foundation of many years. He wished Marilee were in the empty seat beside him now, that he might reach for her hand and savor her presence on this adventure.

The flight had been longer than Johnny had anticipated. Making his way through customs and then the airport itself, his stomach knotted. He followed the throng of departing passengers, listened to dialects he had never heard before—it all seemed like harried confusion. Having located the baggage claim area, he found his suitcase with little problem; and then, with no idea of what he was doing, he stepped up to a bank counter to exchange a few twenty-dollar bills for local currency.

He walked back through the lobby and found the front doors, which opened on the busy street fronting the building. He stepped out and stood in the glare of sun, looking down at his new hiking shoes, aware they were planted on a sidewalk in Nairobi. As his mind took hold of the fact that he was in Africa, all five senses came into play: the visual activity around him, the noxious smell of auto fumes, the blaring horns and the roar of jet engines streaking into the sky, and the sun warming his face. They were the familiar elements of urban life, but different in a less affluent way, strangely different, he sensed, as defined by the mind-sets and perceptions of those passing in cars and those walking in and out of the terminal. Odd, he thought, being among the people of a foreign country that view the world through different eyes.

Holding the suitcase firmly in his hand, Johnny watched a myriad of black faces: porters, cab drivers, men and women of various concern entering and leaving the airport. He had always thought of himself as an African American, but he realized, as he studied the goings-on around him, that here he simply felt like an American. It seemed an unsurprising revelation, actually, as the notion formed and mingled with that vague kinship he felt with this land; though the people here would certainly see him as a foreigner.

He sighed and took from his pocket the clump of documents, sorting through them for the one on which he had scribbled Doug Stanton's address. Instead of phoning, he had decided to take a cab to Stanton's office and make immediate arrangements for the last phase of this journey, the trek into Africa's vast wilderness to locate Brian Fowler.

The cab entered what looked like slums: filth in the gutters and on the sidewalks, poverty-stricken pedestrians, aging vehicles baking in the sun. The traffic was heavy and seemed unorganized and impatient. Small busses and delivery trucks routinely blocked traffic. Johnny leaned forward when the taxi pulled to the curb in front of a rather seedy storefront; quite certain he would not want to do any driving in Nairobi. He saw Doug Stanton's name embossed on the front window. Staring at it, he reached into his pocket for the fold of local currency he had picked up at the airport. His eyes shifted to the meter and then to the currency that he had fanned out in his hands, at a total loss as to how much to pay. Johnny looked at the man as he reached back with a firm pinch and tugged at two of the bills. Reluctant to loosen his hold, Johnny scrutinized the driver, whose face expanded into a smile of assurance, which moved his suspicious passenger to release the money.

Suitcase in hand, Johnny stood on the sidewalk as the cab sped away, perusing the weathered brick façade with its large plate glass window and door framed in aging wood. So tour guides, this one anyway, were on the meager end of the economic scale. What difference did it make, when all he wanted was a Jeep ride into the wilderness. Besides, had the office been lavish, so too would be Stanton's fee.

Johnny opened the office door and stepped inside. The air was stale and a little too warm. Setting his suitcase on the wooden floor, his eyes raked over a fairly large and untidy room. Among a few aged leather armchairs, he saw end tables piled with well-worn magazines, ashtrays spilling over with crushed cigarette butts, and two large lamps with frayed, yellowed shades. The aged brown leather upholstery was splitting open in places. Overhead, a tired ceiling fan creaked and swayed with its endless labor. Everything in the room seemed covered in dust, not the fine filaments he was accustomed to in Savannah, rather a gritty sand that was light tan in color. Hither thither across the walls were enlarged photographs of various expeditions, mostly camera shots of Kenya's exotic wild animals. Among the adventurous tourists posed in the photographs, was the image of the same man sitting behind a desk at the back of the room. Walking toward him, Johnny ran his fingers across the surface of one of the wooden end-tables, inspecting the grit that had collected on his fingertips before brushing it off on his jeans.

"Might just get me an air conditioner one of these days, mate," said the man, his voice familiar. "Could keep these windows shut and keep that dust from gettin' in here."

Johnny looked at him with curiosity. Scraggly, he perfectly fit the mold of a swashbuckler with his long and unruly hair, sandy in color and apparently unwashed for days. Wearing khaki, short sleeves and shorts, sweat stained and wrinkled, he sat with his feet propped casually upon the desk. Stopping in front of the desk, Johnny detected an odor akin to a man that had just unloaded a truck.

"I'm Johnny Feelwater."

A grin formed on Doug Stanton's face. "Ah yes, the bloke who would travel around the world to have 'is arse reamed by Doctor Fowler."

Johnny had already gathered that Brian Fowler might not be a personable sort. He got right to the point. "I'm anxious to leave as soon as possible."

"You Americans! Always in a hurry."

"It's important," Johnny stated with no hint of humor.

"Of course it is, mate. Why else would you come? Have a seat there," Stanton said, nodding at the wooden chair in front of his desk.

Johnny sat down on the edge of the chair.

"How about we settle the question of my fee?" Stanton lifted his feet off the desk and sat upright, leaning forward to rummage through what looked like a stack of notes. "Let's see ... ah yes, you want me to take you to see the good doctor, but you didn't say anything about me goin' back out there to pick you up."

"I'll need a ride back, but I don't know when my business with Fowler will be finished."

"He has a radio in 'is Jeep, mate. You can't call him on it because he never turns it on unless 'e wants to call out. You can use it to let me know when to pick you up."

"Okay," said Johnny, ready to reach into his pocket. "How much to get me out there?"

"Five hundred, American," said Stanton matter-of-factly. The glimmer in his eye suggested he knew he could name nearly any price. Johnny's hand stopped short of his pocket. His mouth fell open slightly. He had anticipated fifty, maybe a hundred dollars; why, he didn't know. But this price stunned him. It was beginning to seem it would take the rest of his life to pay off those damned credit cards.

"Uh, I didn't know it would cost that much," he said dumbly.

"Is that a lot, mate?"

"Well, I figured ... that is I ..."

"I never charge more than a bloke is willin' to pay. I figure you're willin' to pay five hundred, since I'm the only man in Africa who knows where Brian Fowler is and can take you to him."

"Uh ... you take credit cards?"

A frown formed on Stanton's oily, sun bronzed face. "You don't 'ave cash, mate?"

"Not that much."

"Then I take credit cards," said Stanton, taking from a drawer an ancient credit card machine and plopping it on the desk.

From the cards he had banded together, Johnny fished out a Visa and handed it to the Australian.

"There's a hotel two blocks down the street, mate. Get yourself a room for the night and we'll set out first thing in the mornin'. Seven o'clock sharp."

Feeling financially raped, Johnny nodded and picked up his suitcase and walked back out into the glare of the sun. Somewhat dazed by growing debt, he strode solemnly toward the hotel, his attention drawn just ahead by a group of children at play. They were an impoverished lot, as were the men and women going about their simple, but seemingly busy lives. There was a certain harmony about the people he passed, as though they were unaware of their poverty and took from life its small pleasures. Their smiles and nods reinvigorated Johnny's morale.

A few minutes later, Johnny walked into the hotel. A short walk from Stanton's office, it was situated in the immediate outskirts of central Nairobi, a neighborhood interspersed with commerce and the residential poor, teeming with traffic and people afoot. After entering his room, his feet soon blissfully free of the sweaty hiking shoes, Johnny sat down on a sagging mattress covered with a threadbare blanket. The old steel bed frame creaked as he sprawled back on the blanket and looked up at the lethargic swirling fan blades, relieved the room had cost only ten dollars. It was sparse even for that amount, the air as stifling as that in Doug Stanton's office. There was no air conditioning, no bathroom, no carpet on the wooden floors, and no peace from the noise which came through opened windows. He could hear on the street below people yelling and trucks grinding gears and car horns honking at children. But it was Africa. With the small taste he had gotten so far, it was beginning to feel much like what he had imagined Africa to be.

He folded his hands behind his head, exhausted by the time zone changes and the trip. Within a few minutes he fell asleep, awaking fitfully in the wee hours of the night with a full bladder. He crawled off the bed and considered peeing in the porcelain washbasin, deciding it best that he venture the few doors down the hallway to the privy. Stepping cautiously in the almost non-existent light, groggy, he nearly tripped over a man that apparently had not made it to his quarters, laying curled near the wall a few steps from Johnny's room. The man rolled over and groaned as Johnny stepped around him and continued to feel his way along the wall. He stopped at the door that smelled like the right one; and thankfully it was, for in taking a hold of the knob, the image of walking into someone else's room flashed in his mind and awakened him fully.

Inside the dank room, standing barefoot, his knees nudging the rim of the piss-trough, trying to ignore the puddle he was standing in, he wished he had put on his shoes.

I can live with this for ten dollars.

An hour later, he still had not gotten back to sleep. Lifting himself once more off the sagging mattress, he strode to the window and looked down on the street. In the dreary light cast from a single streetlamp, there wasn't much to see. Across the street were the peeling facades of storefronts and offices. On the corner below, another man had not made it to his quarters, sitting bowed and asleep against the lamppost. Johnny sat down on the sill and leaned back against the window frame and his eyes followed the occasional passerby. It occurred to him, as he watched the few nocturnal souls walk by, that Doug Stanton was one of the very few white men he had seen since leaving the Nairobi airport. To be the same color as almost everyone else seemed strange to him; stranger still, that here, even among all these black Africans, he still felt like a loner, poised just slightly on the outside, just short of being part of the whole; like at home at social gatherings predominately white, or among those of his own color who thought of him as a white man in black skin.

Ah, where the mind can wonder in the middle of a lonely night, he thought as he rubbed his arms chilled by the night air, arms that seemed to know the great distance separating him from Marilee. How dearly he missed not having her there to crawl in bed with.

He thought about something else as he stared down on the forlorn street—another day had passed without menace from the beautiful pair. Was he too far away from them, he wondered, or had he been too preoccupied or simply too weary to draw their beguiling summons? Either way, the demon had slept through the day. Maybe, just maybe it was the first sign he had embarked on the right path.

Rolling his head, he felt stiffness in his neck. Reaching back to rub it, he felt grit. He ran his tongue over his front teeth, felt grit on them, too. A dry film coated the lining and roof of his mouth. Loathe to venture back to the privy for a pitcher of water, which he could use to brush his teeth, he decided it would keep until daybreak. *Why worry about it?* he blustered silently. *I'm in Africa!* Does a man alone in Africa concern himself with the poor condition of his mouth? *Hardly.* And in thinking about it, he would gladly make it worse, much worse, if only he had a bottle of beer and a cigar.

At seven o'clock, after a sleepless second half of the night, Johnny was standing in front of Doug Stanton's office, thinking there must be a market nearby. There were a number of people walking past him carrying bags of produce and meats and sundry items newly purchased. He watched them with interest, the women followed by small children, old men with canes, elder daughters out running errands, and the older children in their tattered clothes on both sides of the street, playing and shouting and chasing each other, much like he imagined they would be doing anywhere. Only this was Nairobi. Everything interested him, the colors, the smells, the people of every age and size and shape, content it seemed with their impoverished plight. It was still hard to believe he was among them. Scanning one end of the street and then the other, Johnny figured most of the buildings in the area must be residential, low rent naturally, for those walking to and fro seemed poor indeed, poor but hardly pitiful or down and out.

Doug Stanton was twenty minutes late. He pulled in at the curb and piled out of the battered Land Rover like a man without a care in the world. Johnny was certain his rumpled khakis were the same he had on the day before. Hands casually in his pockets, he spoke Swahili to the scruffy young boys playing near the curb by his vehicle. It looked like he might be warning them to stay away from the Rover. Then he looked at Johnny and pulled a set of keys from his pocket.

"G'day, mate. Still in a hurry, I see," he said, stepping across the sidewalk to unlock his office door.

Nonplussed by the wait, his tone of voice exposed his impatience. "Good morning, Mr. Stanton."

"Drop the *Mr. Stanton*, mate. My mother called me Douglas. You can call me that or Doug. Settles easier in my ears."

"Okay, and feel free to call me Johnny." Johnny followed the Australian into the office.

"That I will, mate."

Stanton walked straight to a gun cabinet, unlocked it and selected a rather large rifle, leaning it against his shoulder as he went to his desk. He pulled open one of drawers and took out a pint of Jack Daniels, then held it up with a sort of man-to-man grin.

"For emergencies," he said, shoving the pint into his back pocket.

Johnny hoped he had not hired an overpriced drunk.

"How far do we have to go?"

"About two hundred kilometers, I'd say. Fowler is working in a permanent Maasai settlement in the Great Rift Valley just east of the Serengeti Plain. Beautiful country over that way, mate."

These were names of places Johnny was familiar with. To hear them spoken in reference to his destination raised goose bumps on his arms. But for the cost of coming here, it almost made him glad Brian Fowler had not spent the summer in Boston.

"Book most of my safaris on the Serengeti," Stanton went on to say as he rummaged through a stack of papers on his desk. "Mostly photographers though. Shows 'ow the times are changin', don't it?"

"What's the rifle for?"

"Poachers. Two men crossing the plain alone, they might decide we'd make good target practice." He looked up from the papers. "I like to shoot back."

"That's reassuring," Johnny said flatly.

"You ready to go, mate?"

"Anytime."

With the rifle slung over his shoulder, Stanton locked the front door when they stepped out on the sidewalk. Johnny believed, perhaps in want of confidence in the man that had extorted five hundred dollars from him, that the Australian's physical appearance fit his job description appropriately: the rifle draped across his back, the khakis and sun-bleached hair and weathered face. He noticed Stanton looking at his suitcase.

"Anything in there that could get me arrested, mate?"

"Like what?" asked Johnny, doubting that socks and deodorant were illegal in Kenya.

"Drugs ... marijuana."

"I don't use drugs, Doug. We're okay, unless toothpaste is against the law here."

"Toss it in the back, mate, and get in."

Stanton drove quickly through the streets of Nairobi—Johnny felt a little too quickly—weaving the top-heavy Rover around anyone not driving fast enough to suit his fancy. They were leaving the outskirts of the city twenty minutes later, and Johnny was glad. The ever-present exhaust fumes tended to burn his eyes. He marveled at the differences in Nairobi from American cities, the different feel one had in being there, as if a rugged individualism and undying will to survive permeated air. It was a city where people walked and rode bicycles everywhere; of thoroughfares congested with cars of earlier vintages than he was used to seeing at home; a city that looked like it had been there forever even though most of it had grown up during the last fifty years. Stanton sped away from the city on an eastbound highway. Through the opened windows came a buffeting wind across their faces. The cool that hung in the air during the night was dissipating in the morning sun.

An hour outside of Nairobi, a few kilometers after the highway veered north, Stanton turned off the pavement, heading west.

"Don't mind a shortcut, do you, mate?" he said, taking the steering wheel with both hands.

The Rover now bouncing and bounding over raw land, Johnny gazed out over the vast savannah ahead. He had seen it countless times in documentaries and movies, the unending vistas of the African plains, the windswept grasses and distant plateaus. But seeing it on television equaled not seeing it at all, compared to driving through it. Johnny felt reduced to insignificance by the grandeur and enormity of the distant panoramas and endless sky. Being there was being part of it, by feeling it on one's skin, by breathing the scent of its earth and grasses. The sun, now behind them, strew warm yellow light across the plain like a velvety liquid, casting hues and shadows across a land that set a man's imagination soaring. They were heading into the land of the Maasai, a land of giraffes and lions and wildebeests, a people little changed over the slow grinding of untold centuries.

A short cut? Did he mind? So mesmerized by Africa's timeless beauty, there were long moments Johnny hardly remembered why he was there. He glanced at Stanton, a carefree man bouncing happily in the well-worn driver's seat, gripping the wheel as if it were keeping him from bouncing out, peering through the windshield as if he were seeing country he could cross a thousand more times and never tire of it.

Johnny looked down between Stanton's legs, made out the distinctive bulges. He wondered about the organs confined and sweating in the shorts. What did he do with them, a man living alone in the prime of life? Masturbate? Ten dollar whores? Johnny vaguely shook his head. Why he was having these impulsive mental diversions, he didn't know, but they were very typical of the strange thinking he had been doing these days.

"I don't mind," Johnny said, thinking about how incredible it must be to live worry-free like Doug Stanton, fleecing outrageous sums from those who want to see this beautiful land. How marvelous to deal with people that happily pay his price, while living utterly free of responsibility or obligation.

"So tell me, mate, why you'd come all the way around the world to see Brian Fowler?" Stanton asked. They were thirty minutes into the savannah. "Are you in the medical profession?"

"No. I'm a commercial artist. I came to see him regarding a book he wrote."

"A book!" said Stanton. "He writes books, too?"

"Yeah. Well, at least one anyway."

"Must be a darn interestin' book."

"It is," said Johnny.

"He's a strange one, that professor Fowler," said Stanton, throwing his head back and forth between Johnny and the terrain in front of the Rover as he spoke. "Seems to get along better with the Maasai than 'is own kind. They generally don't take to white men meddling in their affairs, but he's won 'um over. Can't say I blame 'um though, the Maasai I mean, the way government types and outsiders make it their business to show 'um how to live. That's par, don't you think? Bloody college blokes, sucking fine warm milk from the government tit. They come out here to tell the Maasai how to live, when they've been doin' just fine without any help for a thousand years." Stanton craned his neck to see the terrain just ahead as the Rover dropped down into an arroyo. They were on what might be called a goat path, though it often seemed to disappear. "Gotta hand it to our friend Fowler. That's why they accept him. He respects their way of life."

"You said he's strange," Johnny said, looking at Stanton. "In what way?"

"Never seen the man in a good mood. He's an arrogant bastard, that one is. Deals with you like he's toleratin' the worst form of stupidity. Strange? Well, I remember taking him some supplies a couple of years ago, to a Maasai camp down near Kilimanjaro. Walked up behind him and heard him talking to one of the elders about reincarnation. Now that's strange."

Not so strange as you might think, Mr. Stanton.

"Before that," Stanton went on, "oh, I don't remember exactly how long ago, he got involve with a Maasai girl young enough to be his daughter. My God, she was the finest female creature I ever laid eyes on. Spent the summer with her. I know because I carried out 'is supplies every two weeks. All I ever saw them do was swim in the river and sit around naked in the shade, playin' the card games he taught her." Stanton paused in thought. "Come to think of it, 'e was rather personable that summer."

Doesn't sound that strange to me, Doug, at least not any stranger than you.

At Stanton's unnerving rate of speed, clouds of dust billowed off the wheels as the Rover took them further into the Great Rift Valley. Entering the lower elevations, where the earth had split apart over untold millennia, the terrain became more rugged and distant cliffs enhanced the panorama both to the north and south. Johnny watched the terrain and the vistas reverently, nary blinking as they passed through this life-sustaining land, the very land from which sprang the origins of mankind. Never in his wildest dreams had he envisioned himself in one of these rugged vehicles, leaving behind the so-called civilized world to blaze across such an exotic Eden. He had pondered countless times the continent that had sustained his ancestors and their way of life, and now found himself warmed by just breathing the same dry air they had breathed.

As the journey grew long, and as they got closer to the Maasai village, Johnny continued to think about Brian Fowler. He had conjured a million concerns, not the least of which being the fact that the professor might not be where he was expected to be. Though it remained unclear to him how Kenya related to Professor Fowler's research. Evidently, as a doctor, his medical calling could take him to any number of Maasai villages along the Rift Valley. What if he had moved on since his last communication with Doug Stanton? What if he was busy and refused to see him? Johnny had heard enough about Brian Fowler to believe he could be extraordinarily stubborn. Was it possible to travel all the way around the world to see a man that would invite him to leave without so much as a *How do you do?* And there was certainly the possibility that Fowler himself might be at a loss in dealing with Johnny's mystification.

The thought of returning to Savannah empty-handed, having exhausted his and Marilee's credit, made him cringe. He tried shifting his thoughts to more positive light, though it was difficult to not worry, having longed for the opportunity to talk to someone sympathetic to about his dilemma, someone that would not think he was a basket case when he described the feeling that so often came into his hands. There was nothing to do but hope this expensive endeavor would pay off.

Progress was slow as they entered the lower elevations of the valley, the terrain ever changing and far more rugged. The northern cliffs had closed in on them, creating the effect of a canyon wall, leaving only the open vista to the south. Bouncing and swaying more violently than before, the durable machine groaned on. Shortly after Stanton maneuvered the Rover across a narrow riverbed, they came to what could be identified as a road—two parallel ruts made by the wheels of an occasional vehicle. Their pace quickened.

"Now there's a piece of luck," said Stanton a few kilometers later, nodding toward the southwest.

Johnny followed his gaze and set his eyes on a herd of grazing zebras.

Stanton pulled the Rover to a stop. "Probably migrated over from the Serengeti. It's warmer and dryer this year and the grass'll be a little better over this way."

For a moment Johnny forgot his concerns, enchanted by the zebras. He had always been fascinated by them, intrigued that a creature could look so much like a horse and be so different in nature. It was another of those moments he wished Marilee could be there to share with him. Zebras, far too many to count, grazing casually not more than two hundred yards away.

"Don't see anything like that over your way, do you, mate?"

"Maybe a raccoon rummaging in the trash every now and then, but no, nothing like this."

"Could be a lion laying in wait in that tall grass," Stanton said, shifting the Rover back in gear. "If you weren't in such a hurry, we could give it a while and see."

Johnny looked at him. "How far are we now?"

"Maybe an hour."

Stanton followed the primitive road's north-westerly direction. It gradually led into higher ground, where the grasses were greener and the thorny acacia trees stood in small groves with their graceful, umbrella-like crowns. It seemed to Johnny they were climbing into foothills, the large green knolls rising before them, the air perceptively cooler. Stanton veered the Rover off the road and followed a chortling mountain stream as the elevation grew gradually higher.

Nearing the settlement, Johnny saw first a herd of cattle. He spotted a child surrounded by goats, a little girl perhaps eight years old, her head shaved, her thin body draped in a red-orange, sack-like dress. Then he saw the mother kneeling beside one of the goats, milking it. He gawked, struck immediately by their raw beauty. They both looked up as the Rover slowly passed. There were more cattle in a small meadow at the base of a series of rolling hills. Rising one after another, the hills, like a pan of dinner rolls rising and baking together, seemed to go on for miles, scattered with grass and scrub. Among the cattle stood a man, perhaps the father, wearing a flowing ochre cloth that draped from his shoulder to below his knees. With staff in hand, he looked at the Rover, his tall lean stature erect with stoic pride.

"Africa," Johnny whispered in awe as he and the man stared at one another. *Are we visitors or intruders?*

Seeing the zebras had etched the reality of Africa on his soul, but his first glimpse of the Maasai charged him with even higher energy. They were the real people of Africa it seemed to him, primitive, at one with the earth as were his own ancestors.

Johnny's heart was pacing by the time Stanton pulled in next to the only other vehicle in sight, an open-air Jeep parked just outside the Maasai settlement. The compound was a circular collection of huts, small and rectangular in shape, shaded by the high sprawling crowns of acacia trees and plastered over in what appeared to be mud.

"Doesn't the rain wash the mud off their houses?" Johnny asked, the first he suspected of what were to be many questions.

"That's cow dung, mate, mixed with mud. Pretty durable stuff. No shortage of it around here either."

Johnny could not take it in fast enough. Children of varied age immediately surrounded the Rover.

Both men got out and stood among them. Stanton, with his jovial manner spoke to them in Swahili, then opened the back door of the Rover and began handing out candy bars from a full box. The children reacted with extended hands and grins, their dark round eyes alive with eager anticipation. It was like Santa Claus had arrived, though Johnny doubted they had ever heard of that portly old gentleman. They were an unwashed lot, poor in their dusty and tattered robes that hung about their knees from bare shoulders. The girls, slightly timid in their approach, reached over the smaller boy's shoulders, naked above the waist in their long skirts, some of them smeared over with what looked like glistening red grease paint.

It was indeed another world, both primitive and enchanting, these warmaking people complacent and content. Johnny stared at them across the compound, picturing the images from documentaries of them standing on a rise, shoulder to shoulder in an endless line, emboldened by their elaborate feathers and paint, shields and spears fixed and ready. His and Stanton's sudden appearance had drawn much interest among the men and women, young and old, all engaged in various activities throughout the circle of mud-like huts, almost all dressed in draping red or ochre garments, individually tied and cut in a variety of styles. They were a tall and lean people, as Johnny had imagined, and obviously in harmony with their isolated world, their skin shades blacker than his own, their arms, necks and ears adorned with beads of flamboyant colors and styles.

They maintained a casual air with their visitors from the outside world, in that if the children were happy with this unexpected visit, so then were the adults. Plus it seemed they recognized Stanton. Some of them continued to stare while others resumed their chores. Yearning to learn more, much more, Johnny found himself drawn by the simplicity of an ancient lifestyle that promised to seep into his heart like new rain on a parched earth.

An older man swathed in a heavy tan blanket approached, a long walking stick in one hand, a flyswatter made from the tail of a wildebeest in the other, his hair short and graying, his ears hung with silver rings and strands of beads. His earlobes gaped with a hole dramatically stretched over decades as large as an infant's fist. Exchanging words with Stanton in Swahili, the conversation appeared to be a bit stunted; and then the older man looked at Johnny.

"It seems Fowler is involved in some kind of medical procedure," said Stanton. "This old man is one of the elders. His Swahili is a poor second language, so I couldn't make out everything he was trying to tell me. He'll take us to Fowler. He's assuming you must be his assistant or something. I didn't tell him different."

The elder strode with authority, swishing the wildebeest tail about his face and shoulders to shoo the flies. Johnny followed behind Stanton across the settlement to one of the huts on the far side of the compound. There, the elder held out the bushy tail before an entryway with no door.

"Go ahead, mate," said Stanton, rubbing his chin skeptically. "I'll wait out here. If Fowler tells you to get lost, you can ride back to Nairobi with me. No extra charge."

Chapter 18

Apparently just steps away from the man he had traveled halfway around the world to see, Johnny squinted against the daylight at the darkened entryway and released a sigh. To be able to take these next few steps had decimated his finances; and as he stared into the darkened void, the fear of failure grew volatile in his stomach. Next came a rush of adrenaline. Ducking out of the glare through a small passageway intended to keep out nothing but the wind, he turned left into a rudimentary alcove and paused to let his eyes adjust. The house smelled of straw and manure and the faint sweat of humanity. Beside him was a tiny room with a straw covered floor that housed three calves, stirring as if there might be for them some significance to his sudden appearance. Looking at them standing side-by-side at their gated doorway, he sensed a somber gloom, the silence broken a moment later by a dire groan from what sounded like a young girl.

He moved forward two or three steps into the main room, where he saw in the glow of a kerosene lamp three people huddled near the back wall. Squinting, he could not make out their purpose for being there, though it was clearly some kind of dreadful activity. Taking another step, he saw the anguished face of a young girl not yet fourteen years old. Behind her, sitting braced against the wall, an elderly woman with withered arms held onto her, a constraining, nervous embrace. Kneeling before them, his back to Johnny, a man with broad shoulders and wearing nothing more than a pair of khaki shorts went about some indistinguishable task.

Johnny took another cautious step forward. The young girl was naked and in agony, her legs sprawled wide before the man. Johnny assumed he must be Brian Fowler, most likely assisting a birth. Awkwardly out of place, Johnny surmised that he should announce his arrival and then wait for the professor outside in the compound.

"Professor Fowler," he said finally, his voice ungainly and dry.

"My God, man!" Fowler roared, not looking back to see who had imposed. "Can't you see I'm in the middle of something here?"

Johnny's jaw tightened. "Uh ... I came to ..."

"Whoever you are, get out!"

Absorbed by the needs of his patient, Fowler remained engaged without so much as a glance Johnny's way. Johnny stared at the back of Fowler's head, with his long hair combed back and resting damply on the nape of his neck. Shocked and humiliated, armed with no appropriate response, Johnny stood on the verge of gasping for his next breath.

"Be off with you, Mister. Be off to wherever you came from and don't bother me here in this village again."

"I'll just ... I'll wait outside."

"Be off with you I said!" Fowler boomed harshly, his voice a commanding, deep rich baritone, unforgiving.

Confused, his heart racing, Johnny took a few angry breaths as Brian Fowler proceeded to ignore him. How was he to reverse this unacceptable beginning? Perhaps in his mid forties, Fowler was a stout-bodied man, his hair graying prematurely. It looked like it had been combed back with his fingers. He seemed fit in the dim light, and eccentrically casual in his wrinkled shorts and crudely made sandals. Between the girl's legs, his knees rested on a woven mat. Beside him sat an opened medical bag and a basin of water.

"Professor Fowler ..."

"You don't hear well, Mister!" huffed Fowler. "American, aren't you?" His hands went about their purposeful work. "An *African* American," he scoffed, glancing over his shoulder. "Now there's a real folly if ever I heard one. You, sir, are no more African than I am. Cast among these Africans, you'd go running back to your affirmative action and your quotas like a squalling lost child."

Stunned, Johnny continued to stare at the back of Fowler's head. His worst imaginings had not prepared him for this, though his determination to stand fast prevailed in both his feet and his mind.

"What are you doing here, anyway?" demanded Fowler, his voice magnificent, though authoritative and exceedingly offensive to Johnny.

Johnny's anger and disappointment threatened the better of him, though beneath the brawn of these emotions, he realized he could make a bad situation worse. Gripping the fist of his left hand with his right, he took one more deep breath, staring daggers at the back of Fowler's head.

"I read your book," Johnny stated flatly, his tone hardened with indignation.

A long silence followed. It had been all that need be said. A palpable thoughtfulness came over Fowler as he went on tending the girl. Moments later he spoke, his voice more accommodating, though still tinged with his wariness for Americans in Africa.

"Step over here in the light, Mister. If you're going to intrude on the Maasai, you might as well see the kind of thing some of them have to endure."

Johnny stepped forward and his eyes widened in horror. He reeled backward, overwhelmed with an urge to wretch. It took a conscious effort to avoid throwing his hand to his mouth. The girl's genitals looked like raw meat. She sat in a pool of blood, her young gangly legs quivering, their inner tendons straining to draw them together, her thighs and lower belly and Fowler's hands covered in blood. Fowler continued his awful task, soberly, with a scalpel in one hand and gauze in the other, slicing off precious fragments of flesh and then blotting away the blood. The girl's head thrashed from side-to-side against the old woman's breasts, her teeth clamped on a small piece of wood to avoid screaming.

"What's your name, Mister?"

His throat dry, Johnny attempted to answer, preceded by a hard swallow. "Johnny Feelwater."

"Well, Mr. Feelwater, this girl has suffered a circumcision gone bad. Infection set in. I'm cutting away the tissue that's showing potential signs of gangrene."

"She couldn't have been anesthetized first?" Johnny asked incredulously.

"Americans," Fowler laughed. "Don't forget where you are, Mr. Feelwater. The elders allowed the use of antibiotics, but grudgingly. I didn't bother to plead for the use of anesthesia. Where you come from, my friend, this is called genital mutilation. Here it's a sacred rite of passage. This girl is in the process of becoming a woman, and pain is part of that process. This kind of infection is rare, thank God, something the Maasai don't bargain for, but it does happen." He set aside the scalpel and picked up a needle and thread. "Here, you see, I'm using sutures that will dissolve as she heals. That way she won't have a man such as myself invading her privacy again."

Johnny stood as if he were frozen in time, numbed by the girl's torment. He averted his eyes. This was something beyond his ability to comprehend.

Though the blustery Brian Fowler may have expressed sympathy for a time-honored tradition, to him any form of traditional or religious desecration of the body was nothing short of brutality. The girl's agony had plunged him into a stupor.

While Fowler completed the meticulous sewing of the girl's wound, Johnny stepped back and allowed himself the distraction of making out the sparse environs of the room. As his sensibilities began to recover, it occurred to him that he was standing in someone's home. To his left, there was a stall-like room, its earthen floor covered with a woven mat similar to the one now soaked with the girl's blood. In the shadows near the back wall, he saw pots and sundry cooking utensils. From hooks on the nearest wall hung a robe and two or three of the faded red, toga-like garments. It defined by any standard the unimaginably simple life led by its occupants.

He glanced at the girl as his mind cast thoughts in a dozen directions. Africa. How it had taken a hold of him as so much more than simply a place where he might take stock and learn from a man called Brian Fowler. They were life's colors here, clarified by perceptions he had never conceived of, its hues and textures and smells, its primordial plowing of hands into ancient superstitions as if the superstitions were as real as freshly tilled soil. Such were the far-reaching abilities of the human mind that could bring on this kind of bravery from a desperate girl.

His eyes shifted to Fowler. *You son-of-a-bitch. The gall to treat someone so rudely after traveling so far to see you.* Johnny smiled inwardly. How quickly Fowler's tone had changed with the mere mention of his book. *Ha! Now you're curious. You're wondering why someone traveled thousands of miles to see you after reading your book.*

Johnny's thoughts drifted to his walk with the elder and Doug Stanton through the compound. "They cover themselves with red makeup," he had whispered to Stanton. "That's animal fat tinted with ochre powder," Stanton had said. "Traditions die hard out here, mate." Johnny had seen contentment on the faces that were looking back at him. Just by walking through the compound, he had witnessed an exotic simplicity, a way of life so remote, so foreign to everything he had known that it shadowed his agenda for being there.

His mood had evolved. He felt an overwhelming reverence for yet another unknown, a way of life he had never contemplated beyond the two dimensions of the Discovery Channel. It was Africa, a dramatic distraction from matters at hand. His eyes shifted hither about the shadowy room. So far removed from the plastic-wrapped sterility he left behind, it was as if Africa had stolen him from Cassandra's grip. He sensed a wonderful discovery lie just ahead, determined to learn all he could about the Maasai and their ancient ways on God's most diverse continent. Being there, among them, breathing the uninhibited smells of humanity and casting his eyes on diversity he had never seriously contemplated, settled over his skin like revitalizing steam.

Brian Fowler had rinsed his hands in the basin and had gotten to his feet. The girl, grappling with the difficult stages of puberty defined by the small swells on her chest and the first hints of pubic hair, had drawn her legs together and sat sobbing and huddled in the old woman's arms. The woman was stroking her head. Now, with the girl's legs folded and hiding the unthinkable wound, the pair became an image of natural beauty, separated in age by decades, brave in facing their ordeal. Remarkable was the affection that made them of one mind.

Fowler was looking at him, sizing him up, guessing at the inspiration forming in Johnny's mind that shown so obviously in his eyes. Fowler bent over and closed his medical bag, picked it up and looked back at Johnny.

"Shall we go outside, Mr. Feelwater, and leave these two alone?"

A couple of paces ahead of the professor, Johnny ducked through the doorway, blinking into the brightness before turning to confront the man he had come to see. They stood eye-to-eye for a moment.

"I wasn't expecting an asshole when I decided to come to see you, Mr. Fowler. Or a racist."

Fowler stared at him for a moment and then reached up to rub his chin. "An asshole, yes; a racist, no."

"You damn sure sound like one to me," Johnny shot back.

"How many racist do you know who come to Africa to provide the Maasai with free medicine?"

"Then you just hate American blacks."

"No, sir. I hate American politics." He paused in thought as his eyes raked over Johnny. The lines of his face seemed to release a tightness that Johnny thought might have been innate. Then Fowler added somewhat lightly: "Ah, but what do I know about politics."

"That doesn't flush your commode, Mr. Fowler. I've never benefited from affirmative action or quotas, nor do I agree with them. I do, however, try to respect the opinions of those who do."

"Touché, Mr. Feelwater. Allow my frustrations in dealing with such a badly mangled girl as that one in there to be my excuse. Please accept my apology."

Johnny stared at him with diminishing contempt, looking down slightly at a somewhat shorter man who in another setting would have an air of obvious academic distinction. Here, standing naked above the waist, with his tanned arms and chest scattered with gray hairs, with his unshaven face and broad brow, and his sweat stained shorts slipping down below the slight paunch of his belly, he looked more like a vagabond. As Johnny studied his prospective mentor, all across the compound were fleeting glimpses and dark eyes staring outright.

Relieved their botched introduction had shifted course, Johnny detected sincerity in both Fowler's eyes and tone. "Apology accepted," he stated gladly, putting the matter to rest.

Doug Stanton had been sitting and leaning against the wall of the next house. He had gotten to his feet when they emerged. Fowler recognized him immediately when he approached.

"So you're the culprit who brings all manner of tourists my way. Don't make a habit of it, Stanton, or you'll find yourself clamoring for a new client."

Stanton slipped his hands into his back pockets. "Sorry, mate. Want me to haul him back to Nairobi?"

Professor Fowler looked at Johnny again. His eyes drifted from head to foot. He reached up and rubbed his mouth in thought. "You don't want to go back with this misplaced Australian, do you?"

"No."

Fowler's attention returned to Doug Stanton as he fished a folded paper from the cargo pocket of his baggy shorts. He handed the paper to Stanton, saying: "Looks like you're going back alone. Don't get lost. I need that list of medical supplies. Some of it will have to be ordered from my source in Boston. Have them airfreight it to your office. I'll get you on the radio in a week to see if it's arrived."

"You got it, Doc. And no more tourists. I promise." He nodded at Johnny. "Pleasure doin' business with ya, mate." He turned and strode back through the compound toward his Land Rover.

Fowler watched him for a moment with humored patience, then turned back to Johnny. "How much did he take you for?"

"Five hundred dollars."

Fowler laughed. "He saw you coming."

"Thought I might walk back. I can't afford Nairobi cab fare."

It dawned on Johnny, as he looked at the fine creases and casual deceptions of the professor's face, that the man had taken an unspoken interest in him, that the two of them were standing among a people that lived beyond the fringes of civilization with something very much in common. Exactly how that might benefit either of them remained to be seen, but Johnny had the deepest sense that a mutual enlightenment awaited. He sensed also, from the moment of Fowler's apology, a prospective rapport between them.

"So you read my book?" said Fowler.

"I'm *living* your book would be a more accurate way to put it."

"I see. The book consists of three sections, doesn't it?"

"The third section," Johnny said, still at odds with the conjecture about vampires and witches laid out in the first two sections of Fowler's book, though now he felt prepared to believe anything.

"That section, my friend, happens to be the one I've had personal experience with. It's the other reason I'm here in Africa, which I'll tell you more about later. For now, I'm interested in hearing your story."

Tongue-in-cheek, Johnny said: "I'd like to get a bath and freshen up first."

Fowler's expression turned incredulous. "A bath!"

"Just kidding."

The professor's expression evolved into a smile. "I just might end up liking you, Mr. Feelwater." He wrapped his arm around Johnny's shoulder. "There, let's have a seat under that shade tree."

When they started toward the tree, an older woman walked past with a gourd in her arthritic hand. She entered the hut from which the two men had just emerged.

"Blood," said Fowler. "Drawn from the neck of an unblemished bull. The girl will drink it. They'll believe that's what healed her. Not the antibiotics." Brian scanned the compound. "Due in part to my medical reputation in the Rift Valley, they allowed me a few moments with her, mainly to hedge their bets. It seems the girl has been promised to one of the more charismatic warriors here. Of course that raised the level of importance that she live. Thus the gamble with an outsider. Sometimes things have to get pretty desperate before the Maasai are willing to trust a white man."

They took a seat in the shade, on the well-trampled grass. Johnny wrapped his arms around his knees, reflecting on the settlement. He had entered a day in the life of a people that lived in another era, much the same as their ancestors had lived a thousand years before. There were those among them, Johnny had learned from Doug Stanton, that had never seen a light switch. Almost all of Maasai wore clothing one shade or another of red. The toga-like garments, many no more than sheets of cloth hung from sinewy shoulders, flowed down over lean bodies and personified a sense of casual freedom. A few of the seniors, their arms and legs frail, their fingers long and bony, wore blankets, some of which were patterned with striped designs. The young children frolicked naked.

Curious, thought Johnny, were the shaved heads covered with ochre colored powder. Curious were the pierced and gaping ear lobes, adorned with beads and silver rings of every size and description. Some of the younger girls wore disc-shaped necklaces made of beads that lay heavily on their shoulders and draped over newly swelling breasts. More flamboyant still were the young warriors with their hair plaited and dressed with ochre-tinted animal fat, their legs smeared with the same, which looked pale pink against their black skin. Some had drawn their fingers through the greasy paint to create zigzagging patterns and stripes. As if a visual orchestra was playing out before his eyes, Johnny watched with fascination the daily labors rooted in the consensus of hundreds of years of history.

"None of them are overweight," said Johnny, glancing from one villager to the next.

"That's right, my friend. The Maasai were ahead of us on the low-carb diet. They invented it hundreds of years ago."

Fowler was amused by Johnny's enchantment. He leaned back against the acacia tree, watching his new acquaintance take it all in. In return, the two men drew curious glances from those going about their routines across the compound. The children at play maintained a respectful distance, though a few appeared hard-pressed to restrain themselves from a closer look at their foreign visitors.

One young girl in particular, Johnny noticed, seemed to have taken an uncommon interest in him. Perhaps the stirrings of her youth brought on her distraction, a strange man from a strange place, stealing her from a conversation with her friends. She stared, her head shaved, her lower face swathed in red up to the rise of her full lower lip. Red stripes ran up both cheeks and another ran from her forehead to the tip of her nose. Large beaded rings hung from her ears, through gaping holes in her lobes and smaller piercings near the top. She wore one of those colorful, disc-like necklaces, its weight rising upon youthful breasts. She stared without reservation or shyness, displaying an expression that belied her youth and provided little doubt of the thoughts behind her dark, imaginative eyes.

"Are you wondering, Mr. Feelwater, if your distance relatives might have lived in a settlement like this?"

Johnny turned his head to look at the man he had come so far to see. "Actually, that question *has* crossed my mind."

"No, my friend, they didn't. Your ancestors were from northwest of here, around the Ivory Coast I would think; and judging by the bone structure of your face, you had at least one forefather from Europe, probably Spain." Fowler followed Johnny's gaze and noticed the girl's silent communication. He nodded at her. "That one would be yours tonight with a well-timed smile."

Johnny shifted his eyes. The suggestion made him uncomfortable. "Even if I wasn't married, Professor Fowler, that girl is much too young for me."

"Doctor Fowler would be more appropriate, Mr. Feelwater. But there's no need for formalities here in Africa. Please call me Brian."

"I will, and you can call me Johnny."

Brian looked back at the young temptress. "She has a reputation for being a little too promiscuous. Because of that and her beauty, any warrior who lays claim to her will face sharing her with his friends. The warriors share all of their possessions with each other. It's not uncommon for them to share their women. One of a thousand unwritten laws long established by the Maasai." Brian watched him for a moment, then added: "The more you learn, the more you realize how incredibly different things are here from the so-called civilized society you and I come from. Doesn't take long to feel that urge to learn more about them, does it?"

"No."

"You bring along your preconceived notions about Africa's dynamic from what you've seen on television; but when you're here, you really see it. You breath it. Feel the grit on your skin. You're not in your easy chair, my friend. You're here, sitting in the middle of a Maasai settlement. If you stay a few days, sleep among them, share their food, they'll get into your heart and soul."

"Do you sleep with the young girls, Brian?"

"Ah, your curiosity is as direct as my own." He glanced at the young beauty staring at them. "Yes, she's a temptation all right. I can't deny a similar temptation I was unable to resist. About five years ago in a settlement much like this one. Picture a group sitting in circle around a fire for dinner. I sat down beside her. Not as young as that one over there, but she *was* very young. She told me her father had been killed by a lion. Said her mother died of heartache shortly after. My God, she was beautiful, and the smells coming from her burned in my nostrils like a sweet rage. That night, after she helped pen the calves and young goats, I watched her walk to her father's house, where she slept alone. I was sitting under a tree, much like you and I are now. She paused in her doorway and looked back at me. Her thoughts came through her eyes and I found myself going to her. Before that night passed, I was so enamored that I considered giving up all of my earthly possessions and donning a red robe. I considered spending the rest of my life with her."

"But you didn't."

"No. Just the better part of the summer. You'll understand why after you know me better. You see, I'm driven. Years ago, when I first came to Africa, I came to explore what I had heard about the supernatural. As a doctor, I began to treat various injuries and maladies during my travels. That soon became a part of my summer sojourn. Now it's my primary reason for coming back. My research is secondary. I've been smitten by Africa, my friend, specifically Kenya. I wouldn't go back to Boston every fall if it weren't for the financial considerations. Nevertheless, even though these young girls are here and some are available, a blissful life with one of them is not in the cards for me."

Johnny looked at the girl. He could envision laying with her, breathing in her earthy scent; but he could not, no matter how blissful it may appear to be, envision such a life. His thoughts were interrupted by the sound of Brian's voice.

"What's your story, Johnny? What's in my book that inspired you to come to this side of the world?"

Johnny rubbed his lip with the back of a finger, wondering where to begin. He glanced at Brian and then started in with his eyes locked on a spot of earth just beyond his knees.

"I've encountered a woman. An extremely enchanting woman. Claims to be Cassandra Mott, a woman that died of old age in the same house a few weeks ago. It's like she controls me. She plays with my mind as if it were so many particles to arrange and rearrange at will."

Fowler was watching him closely. When he heard this, he shifted his weight and his brow furrowed. The statement, coupled with the underlying desperation in Johnny's voice, and the fact that he related this experience to specific details in the book, suggested he may indeed be involved with an entity.

"This woman, did you just happen upon her?"

"It all started when I inherited a house," Johnny began, going on from there to relate events as they had happened. Over the course of the next few minutes, he took Fowler through his first encounter with Cassandra, on up to the night he had been gang-raped in the bar, omitting, for reasons of his own shame, certain details.

The tale, with most of its carnal elements, was now in Brian Fowler's hands. Johnny slumped back against the tree and allowed himself to relax.

Fowler contemplated what he just heard for a long while, finding the story extraordinarily unique in his long study of supernatural entities. He had yet to come across anyone so directly and profoundly affected by one of the immortals; and he had never heard of Cassandra Mott, which caused him to wonder again just how many of them inhabited the face of the earth. He immediately realized, by virtue of Johnny Feelwater's unexpected appearance, that this was an unusually lucky day.

"So now you own this woman's house, this Cassandra Mott?"

"That's a laugh," Johnny said cynically.

"I don't follow. I thought you said you inherited it."

"That was a ruse."

"A ruse? How so?"

"She'll own that house forever, or at least as long as she wants to own it. No one could ever live there. Her brother would never allow it. God knows what he'd do to someone who tried to take possession of it."

"Her brother?" Brian shifted his weight again, growing evermore absorbed in this story. "This woman has a brother?"

Julian was the part that Johnny had omitted. Aware Julian's role was critical to Brian's understanding, Johnny still felt reluctant to talk about it. How could he admit to his affinity for Julian when the shame of it gnawed at his self-esteem and put in question his masculinity? He glanced at the sophisticated gentleman beside him and found it difficult to look him in the eyes, averting his gaze back to the spot of ground before him.

"Yes..." Johnny said distantly, temporarily possessed by his emotional tie to Julian, feeling like a schoolboy about to confess a misdeed to the headmaster. "Julian. He's part of it ... a big part. He watches over Cassandra, like her protector. His kind isn't described in your book, but he's as much a part of that world as his sister. Enormous power, even more than Cassandra I think, and he does her bidding without question."

Brian Fowler's eyes drifted from Johnny and on across the compound as if they were following something invisible. He was stupefied. Until that moment, he had assumed the entities exist as individuals, unaccompanied by others of their kind. His mind ran with a number of unfathomable theories. Momentarily, his attention returned to Johnny.

"You seem reluctant to talk about her brother. Is there something distasteful about him?"

"No. It's the part that's not easy to talk about. I'm not proud of it, either." *But it's...* he could think of no other word to describe it but *wonderful.*

"Then you've had personal involvement with him, too, the one you call Julian?"

"What do you mean?" Johnny said defensively.

Brian looked at Johnny with great interest. "Your whole demeanor has changed," he said with curiosity. "Tell me why you're so defensive all of a sudden."

Johnny stared straight ahead. He felt humiliated. Julian had made him feel like a woman. He had lifted his legs and taken him as if he were a woman. How could he confide these transgressions to another man, especially since the man listening was so powerfully masculine? The indignity tightened the tendons in his neck.

"You can talk to me, my friend. Remember, I know how formidable they are. I know how beguiling they can be."

His jaw clamped, Johnny looked at him, and then looked away again, before plowing on with this part of the story. "He ... Julian ... and I ..." Johnny couldn't bring himself to say it. He drew his legs closer to his chest and the fine muscles of his jaw was twitching with tension.

Brian was beginning to get the picture. It didn't surprise him; he knew human beings were vulnerable to supernatural seduction. Obviously, though he may have been powerless to prevent it, a sexual experience with another man troubled Johnny. "I can see you find this difficult to talk about?"

"He fucks me," Johnny said quickly, simply, not looking from the ground in front of him.

"Hmm ..." Brian replied as his mind engaged an unexpected dimension. He wondered if he was sitting next to a man that was coming to grips with his own sexuality, or if Johnny had been under the influence of some kind of drug. "Well ... let's see. You've mentioned you're married, and I see the ring on your finger. Are you by any chance bisexual?"

"No!" Johnny's response came like a pistol shot, though he knew it wasn't true. Then his knee began to bounce nervously. All those old emotions long since buried, now and again tingling on his skin, here recently had become a constant breath on his neck. He blamed Julian. Admitting it to himself was one thing; talking about it openly with another man was quite another. "I didn't ... not since college..." He had not anticipated how difficult this part of his mystification would be to explain.

Brian reached over and squeezed his shoulder. "Relax, my friend. It's nothing to be ashamed of. I personally believe we're all bisexual to some degree or another. I can see how Julian affects you and no doubt you haven't had anyone to talk to. Your wife would be beside herself and anyone else would think you've gone off your rocker. But you can talk to me. Rest assured I won't be judgmental about anything they have involved you in." Brian studied him for a moment, concluding that Johnny desperately needed a confidant. "You said earlier the house seems to draw you to it, that Cassandra neutralizes your will to resist. Does it seem like Julian is somehow involved in this?"

"Yes," Johnny said, pausing in thought. He found it nearly impossible to describe the physical urge to return again and again to that house. "It's like a summons. At first I thought it was Cassandra calling me, and maybe it is, but I eventually realized I'm summoned for *him*. When I'm there, she taunts me. Julian watches, like he's waiting for my clothes to come off." Johnny paused, disheartened, and shook his head. "It doesn't matter where I am ... it's like a need, like I could stop breathing if I don't go to him."

"In other words, you and Julian have an ongoing physical relationship. The two of you routinely engage in ..."

"Yes. And I don't understand it. I'm happily married. Have been for nine years. Since all of this started, my wife and I have fallen in love all over again. She ... well, she changed. She's trying to be the wife I want her to be. I feel like a bastard every time I look at her. You wouldn't believe how guilty these things make you feel. I don't deserve her, not when I'm capable of that kind of betrayal."

"So of the two, Julian affects you the most?"

"Yeah," Johnny said dismally.

"I see. I assume Julian appears to be a normal human male."

"Yes and no. I can't explain it, but when he's near, you sense he's different. I mean different from you and I, like he's something else in a man's body. But when he touches me, all I can think about is how good it feels to be close to him."

"Does he show affection?"

"In his own way, he does. He never speaks, except one time. I asked him a few questions and he answered them, but not with words. He uses telepathy or something. I understood him clearly. His reply seemed to come from his eyes directly into my mind. Then he warned me to ask no more questions."

"My word!" Brian was flabbergasted.

"There's something else," Johnny said, reflecting on his first coupling with Julian. He paused, as if he had discovered telling his secrets had begun a healing effect. "It's about Julian. The first time we had sex, he was between my legs. I looked down at him before he entered me. His penis had taken the form of a snake. It still looked like a penis, but it was long and writhing. A snakelike tongue flicked from the pee hole. I felt it writhing inside me. At first it frightened me, but the pleasure was so intense I didn't care what his penis looked like. I didn't want him to stop."

Brian stared at him dumbly, trying to fathom the revelations that were raining down upon him so freely, after so many years of tireless, exhaustive research, snatching fragments of knowledge here and there about these most illusive creatures. He had traveled the world to interview those who had made some vague contact with the entities, those who had read his book and likened it to some encounter or personal experience; but he had never come upon anyone with anywhere near this level of involvement. Having listened to Johnny like a child clinging to every word of a ghost story, Brian gathered his sensibilities as quickly as he could, so he could delve further into this treasure-trove of discovery.

"Uh, a snakelike penis you say," he said, trying to some degree to mask his excitement and maintain his academic facade. "Could that have been your imagination?"

"I thought it *had* to be, until I felt it inside. But it happened that way only once. Julian's penis usually looks normal, except it's huge."

Brian wanted to distinguish the factual elements of Johnny's account from what might have been his imagination. "When you visit the house, do you ever eat or drink anything?"

Johnny thought for a moment. "No, nothing I can remember. You mean like lunch or dinner?"

"Anything at all while you're there?"

Johnny remembered the peanuts. "Oh yes, there's always a dish of peanuts in the foyer. I've eaten them."

"Did they taste like peanuts?"

"Yeah, they did, except they're flavored with something other than salt. A spice or something. They're delicious."

"They might not be peanuts, or they may have been laced with a drug," Brian said thoughtfully. "A drug-induced hallucination could have produced that image of a snakelike penis."

"Even the way it felt inside me?"

"Yes, I believe even that. The entities often use drugs to seduce human partners, usually administered in the form of food. If the peanuts were tainted, it'd be difficult to determine where their natural powers leave off and their drug-induced enchantments begin. And I can promise you, my friend, we won't be sitting them down for an interview any time soon, though I'd give all I own for such an opportunity."

A scraggly dog wandered by, stopping to sniff Johnny's pants leg. It slunk away when he reached out to stoke its head. Johnny realized in talking to Brian that he suddenly felt lighter, like he had been freed of a terrible weight.

"And Cassandra. You have a physical relationship with her, too?"

These were specifics that for Johnny were even more difficult to describe. What could he say—that she had splashed his face with her urine, that he had relished it, that he had suckled her like a newborn babe? How does a man admit these things? Yet he realized it was important Brian know as much as possible, so he told him. His new confidant sat spellbound, listening in complete amazement.

"You and Julian at the same time?"

"Yes. He was beside me and Cassandra's hands were on the back of our heads."

While Brian contemplated this extraordinary account, Johnny, feeling emotionally purged, scanned the settlement. It was a duel onslaught on his senses: talking openly with Brian Fowler about his mystification and doing so in the heart of Africa, in a Maasai village where the people and the earth were at one, where the value of time meant the here and now as much as the past and future. Fascinated with the harmony around him, he watched mothers holding their babies, cooing and smothering them with affection, and small boys chasing one another with leafy branches, swatting at each other's legs. Across the way, a half dozen young girls sat around an elderly woman, listening attentively to the old woman talk as if they were in a classroom. Now and then, those in passing would nod a fleeting acknowledgement and continue on their way. He watched the young men Brian had referred to as warriors, intrigued by their peacock-like adornments, their mutilated ears weighted with beads and pierced with sticklike jewelry. Adorned more elaborately than the others, they strutted about with their egos displayed as well as their beaded belts and jewelry. Split down one side, the bright red togas swayed on their stride, providing the contrast of red against naked black thighs and hips.

"It makes you wish your own life could be as simple," Johnny muttered.

Called from the obscurity of his concentration, Brian glanced at his companion and then followed his gaze. Johnny was staring at two warriors engaged in horseplay for the benefit of a couple of seemingly disinterested girls.

"They have their challenges, my friend. But yes, I know what you mean. They're free of material bondage. If the rest of the world would leave them alone, we could come back in a millennium and see them living just as they are today."

Johnny looked at him. "What am I going to do, Brian? How do I get Cassandra out of my life? She's tearing it apart and destroying my marriage."

Brian leaned back and looked up through the graceful branches of the acacia tree. Inside of an hour his hapless new friend from Georgia had tripled his body of knowledge about the immortals. How he was to help him in return, he was not yet sure.

"My friend, you've made me giddy with this story you brought from Savannah. But I'm afraid what you've told me so far raises more questions than answers. The most intriguing aspect is Julian. What is he and where does he fit in? I have to think about that. In all my years of research, I've not known the entities to exist in pairs. As secretive as they are, it could be something I've missed. But we don't know where they come from, do we? We don't know if they procreate or if they come into existence by some other way. Perhaps Cassandra and Julian are a breeding pair. I'm also intrigued by the fact that she allows, or perhaps induces you and Julian to consume her breast milk. Is there a significance here? Is it a means of control, or does she simply indulge herself with bizarre fantasies? Whatever her intent, I think there must be something to it. Maybe it nourishes Julian, or even sustains him."

Considering the magnitude of Brian's research, Johnny believed he must have a basis for considering these possibilities; but he himself had assumed her dalliances were motivated by something far less complicated. "It seems she does these things just for the pleasure of doing them. She talks about debauchery like it's a way of life."

"Of course that could be her motivation. I learned early on they have insatiable sexual appetites and they frequently seduce humans. In your case, I have a feeling there's more to it than that. This woman has taken you into her confidence, and I believe there has to be a reason beyond her penchant for debauchery."

"How many entities have you come across?" Johnny asked.

"Three. One here in Kenya." Brian turned his head and looked out toward the green and brown hills rising just south of the settlement. "A half day's walk beyond those hills. He lives on a mountainside. Meramo they call him. From what I can determine, he's reincarnated himself at least five times. This I've learned from things he's said that can be matched to specific circumstances in history."

"You just go to him and talk about these things?"

"Lord no. I visit him under a more or less religious pretense. A younger man simply visiting an older man for his wisdom. He's considered a spiritual leader and people come from near and far to confer with him. But after hearing your story about Julian, it makes me wonder. He also has a constant companion. A teenage boy. Like Julian, the boy never says a word. He's there, quite beautiful and naked in the sun, seemingly at the old man's beck and call. I've watched the boy bring him water and attend to his needs."

"You know for sure the boy doesn't speak?" Johnny asked. "Have you tried to talk to him?"

"Yes. He just stares at me with his beautiful black eyes. Maybe a nod, nothing more, usually when I greet him. Meramo informed me the boy is mute." Brian paused in thought, muttering: "Those eyes." He glanced at Johnny and then rubbed his mouth. "You know, now that I think about it, the boy looks at me as if he knows exactly who I am, as if my charade hasn't fooled him in the slightest. How odd I only realize that just now. Guess my focus has always been on the old man."

"Maybe I've inspired a new chapter for your book," said Johnny.

"Ha! My friend, you've inspired an entire revision. Tell me, are you in a hurry to get back to Savannah?"

"I told my wife I'd be gone a week or two."

"Ah, good. That'll give us ample time to explore all of this. I also think it'd be a good idea the two of us pay Meramo a visit. Perhaps we could approach him with some questions."

Along with a sense of curiosity, Johnny felt uneasy about confronting another entity, knowing, with their ability to read minds, how difficult it would be to visit under pretense. He looked at Brian, doubting the professor had truly succeeded in not giving himself away on his past visits with the old man. Then his thoughts shifted to his own ordeal. It seemed there was so much to talk about, and even the smallest details concerning Cassandra interested the professor. Time. Yes, time is what they needed to merge their knowledge and better understand these entities. Maybe they could sort through it all. There had to be a way to deal with her, to keep her from completely contaminating his soul.

Johnny wrapped hands around his knee and looked around. During these initial moments of his visit, he had come to recognize something else missing from his life. Contentment. Pure contentment. The kind he could see on the faces of the Maasai. It seemed to emanate from them like a soft glow from a light bulb. He wanted to learn about this kind of contentedness, to learn how to achieve it for himself. These people were living lives elevated above material whims. They had molded poverty into riches. They lived with a peace of mind beyond need for superficial luxury, an asset that could not be stolen, or rust or rot, or crowd a city landfill.

"I'll speak to Pakopai later," said Brian. "He's the highest ranking elder here. Owns the house I'm staying in. I'm sure he won't mind another guest." Brian looked at his watch and smiled. "The Maasai love these watches, but only because of the shiny gold surface and the constant ticking. They think watches are useless for telling time, when you have the sun's position to tell you the same thing. That's why I wear an inexpensive Timex. I give so many of them away.

"Anyway, it's three o'clock. We have a couple of hours before Pakopai's wife has dinner ready. Hope you like beef." Brian's weight came off the tree. "By the way, your timing is excellent. Tomorrow you'll see a time honored ceremony. A couple of hundred young men are rising to the status of junior elders, which is one step up from warrior. A few will be from here and the rest from neighboring settlements. It's called Olngesherr. I've seen one before. They're fascinating."

Johnny's mind was elsewhere.

"What are you thinking about?" Brian asked.

"You said you personally know about three entities, the old man here in Kenya and two others."

"Yes. The other two are far more elusive than the old man. I'll tell you about my first encounter, the incident that got me interested in all of this fifteen years ago. She's a socialite in Boston, beautiful and extremely wealthy. I came across her at a dinner, a fundraiser sponsored by the university. She was there in all of her glory. First captivated by her beauty, I observed her discreetly, then became intrigued for other reasons. She didn't realize I was watching her set out to seduce a young faculty member. Such things in those circumstances aren't really all that extraordinary, except for her overt forwardness in going about it, coupled with the way he reacted. It was as if he had become oblivious to his whereabouts and was prepared to disrobe and take her down to the carpet. The two of them had moved off to a secluded part of the room. I can still picture it clearly. The star-struck young man was so charmed you could see the rising elevation of his fly. They disappeared into another part of the house, and no doubt he still dreams about it to this day. I sought him out a couple of weeks later on campus and quizzed him about her. All I could gather from his evasive responses was that it had been a one-night stand. And that's what intrigues me about your case."

"That it's not just a one-night stand?"

"That's right. As I've said, I've known from the beginning the entities indulge themselves with humans, but you've been taken into Cassandra Mott's world for some reason. That young man at the party believed he happened upon nothing more than a good lay. Cassandra has revealed who she is. I find that incredible, and I can't help but wonder what her reason is."

Johnny believed he might know the reason, but he decided to wait until Brian finished his story to relate it.

"So later that night, the next thing I noticed was her position in a rather heated discussion on the French Inquisition. She passionately argued certain points as if she had firsthand knowledge, a certain priest for example. She called him by name, mind you, speaking of him as if she were speaking of an acquaintance. I had inched my way closer to her small group of listeners and heard every word she said. I couldn't believe my ears. Doubtful the others noticed it, they were too drunk; but I was completely taken by her determination to make a point about an issue that should have been presented as an opinion.

"Well, all of that was trivial compared to what I saw next. By then my eyes never left her. Seemingly oblivious to my covert observations, she cast a glance around the room. Satisfied no one was watching, she caused the smoldering logs in the fireplace to burst into flame, not with a poker, my friend, but with a quick, rather vicious gaze. I was stupefied a good while after seeing that." Brian drew in and crossed his muscular legs and shifted his eyes in thought, as if the incident still haunted him.

Johnny smiled. What had astounded Brian that night would be child's play for the enchantress he had come to know so well.

"I was hooked," Brian went on to say. "I followed her at every opportunity, like a stalker, always keeping a safe distance, always wary she might be on to me. Even went out of my way to secure an invitation to another party, which I found out she planned to attend. You might laugh, but I plotted to make myself available for one of those *one-night stands* my young colleague had confessed to." Brian grinned. "For investigational purposes, of course. Alas, I wasn't the dashing sophisticate I am now, so I failed to arouse her interest and the night passed without further incident. She's the woman I wrote about in my book, the one whom I eventually observed masturbating in a supermarket parking lot. Over the course of time, I carefully selected acquaintances of hers to interview in sly and indirect conversation, asking questions I hoped were unlikely to raise suspicion. I managed to gather more evidence, mostly about her prolific sexual appetite.

"All of this honed my ability to recognize the signs. As a result, I've grown suspicious of extraordinary people. You see, the entities have a natural ability to prevail over human beings, that is if they so choose, which seems to be rare. They can compete with powers we can't possibly comprehend. Case in point: my third sighting, a gentleman, a rather famous stock trader on Wall Street. You may be familiar with his name: Ken Wells."

"I've heard of him," said Johnny.

"It struck me as odd, his uncanny ability to pick remarkable stocks. I looked into it and my investigation lead to some news articles and a good many stocks trades dating back to the eighteen-seventies. I struck gold when I found a couple of old photographs of him in some old newspaper archives. My jaw nearly hit the floor when I came across those pictures. Evidently the entities can reincarnate themselves into any person in any part of the world they wish, including the same person they were in a past life, which is what Cassandra Mott and Ken Wells are doing. His stock manipulation goes back to the early days of the railroads. In one picture I found of him, he was standing behind J.P. Morgan. Obviously he's found a way to preserve his wealth from one lifetime to the next, which must be getting more difficult to do in this electronic age of ours. "Naturally, because of those pictures, I became obsessed with him. My focus shifted from the socialite in Boston. Next thing I knew, my colleagues were asking why I was spending so much time in New York. I followed him at every opportunity and witnessed his voracious appetite for sex. Man or woman, doesn't matter to Ken Wells. He haunts the streets with a vengeance, incognito. He's devised some rather inventive disguises, which he dons before setting out on the hunt. I've followed him a number of times through some of the sleaziest alleys in New York. I've seen him administer drugs to his, shall we say victims, with a hypodermic needle. I've seen him plunge his face into the crotches of the most deplorable prostitutes. All of this from afar, rest assured, and usually with high-powered night-vision binoculars. He's like a vampire, prowling for sex instead of blood."

"Did you ever make yourself available to him, too?" Johnny asked, again tongue-in-cheek.

Brian laughed. "I might have, my friend, but I've become too familiar with the ravages of AIDS with my work here in Africa. I wouldn't know if the entities are subject to such viruses, but I elected to avoid the risk. Anyway, it's easy enough to conclude that our immortal friends have enormous sexual appetites, including now of course Cassandra Mott. But I'm still at a loss why she's so careless with you."

"Maybe I know why."

"Tell me, man."

"My grandmother and Cassandra were lovers. Whether she's lived just two lifetimes or a hundred, I get the impression she valued her relationship with my grandmother more than any she's ever had."

Brian was looking at Johnny as if he had an invisible tongue hanging out to hear more. "How do you know this?" he asked excitedly.

"Cassandra's lawyer told me. My wife heard it, too. Cassandra herself acknowledged it."

"Go on, man. Out with the whole story."

"I don't know that much," Johnny confessed. "I never knew my grandmother. She died not long after I was born. She and my mother had a falling out over her lifestyle with Cassandra. They became estranged. I was told my grandmother died of heartache because of it. Cassandra gets emotional talking about it. Apparently, she took my grandmother's death as an enormous loss." Johnny glanced at him and saw a man hungry for every detail. "Her name was Emily Hinton. I believe she exists today as a ghost. I've seen her in the house, at least I think I have, downstairs, longing to go upstairs to be with her lover, but can't."

"A ghost?"

"A beautiful ghost actually."

Brian looked away absently, as if he were stricken with information overload. "This ghost," he finally said. "We'll go into that later. I want to hear more about Emily's relationship with Cassandra. It's hard to imagine Cassandra having some sort of grandmotherly affinity toward you."

"Oh God no. It's nothing at all like that. Cassandra wouldn't recognize a maternal instinct if it slapped her. I must remind her of my grandmother, skin color or something. At least that's part of the reason she's interested in me."

"Fascinating."

"There's something else I wanted to ask you. Do you believe the entities can bring people back from the grave? For temporary visits? People they knew in previous lives?"

"Why would you ask that?"

"I think Cassandra has the power to do it. Or maybe Julian has. I've seen them in her parlor. They might be ghosts, like my grandmother, but they seemed real. Especially the Confederate soldiers." Johnny paused in thought and then went on. "Julian must be behind that. Nothing about him surprises me."

Brian looked down and rubbed his brow. He seemed truly dumbfounded. Then his eyes lifted and rested on Johnny. "We have a lot to think about, don't we?"

"Yeah, we do."

Chapter 19

Johnny leaned back against the tree with his legs stretched before him. He clasped his hands together and rested them on his lap. Both men sat contemplating the new path they found themselves on, vaguely aware of the scenes around them.

"I must say, this all is a bit frightening, isn't it?" Brian finally said.

"Frightening!" Johnny said, sitting up, incredulous, looking directly at Brian. "My life's been taken from me. Tell me, Professor, have you ever been strapped naked in a contraption with your arms and legs suspended and restrained by leather straps? Then receive a prostate massage from a German you never seen before, while three gawking women, right out of the eighteen-sixties, set aside their concerns for southern misfortunes in the Civil War so they can observe your humiliation? Have you ever walked into a room occupied by four Confederate soldiers sitting a table, four foul smelling men playing poker, who think you must be a slave? Have you ever been so mystified by a woman that you'd allow her to lead you into a den of leather clad sub-humans, who strip you naked and lay you out on a table and pee on you and force your legs open so they can take turns ramming their cocks up your ass? Frightening? Yes, I'd call that frightening. But you know what's really frightening about it? It's not living through those episodes as much as realizing you actually have the capacity to be drawn to them, that they might be part of who you are."

Johnny let out a long sigh and his shoulders dropped. These were the particulars he had been reluctant to admit. It came out in a fit of frustration. The images in his mind had turned into words and spilled out in an angry cascade, an exhausting release of pent up resentment showered on his sympathetic companion; though getting it out seemed to have had a neutralizing effect on the acids churning in his belly.

Brian Fowler sat speechless. Hearing such a bombardment of detail from the lips of a man that had personally encountered those things surpassed his every experience. Everything he knew and had written about the entities had been reduced to a novice's understanding by this first hand account from a hapless victim. Brian shifted his gaze across the compound, and ran his hand over the scattered gray hairs across his chest as he contemplated this unfolding wealth of enlightenment. Here was a man that, by virtue of his own misfortune, could very well open the door to the secret world of the supernatural.

A small group of children came running and yelling by, followed by a barking dog. Brian hardly noticed. He leaned forward and wrapped his strong arms around his knees as his thoughts grew long. He glanced at Johnny, his eyes reflecting what he knew to be truth. A reverence for the unknown had long since found a place in his heart; and now, with this unexpected new acquaintance, that reverence was more profound than it had ever been.

"I'm glad you found me," he finally said, as if the revelations Johnny had confided so far had brought him to a crossroads. His research had grown stagnant. Now, just like that, it was revitalized and set on a new, far more illuminated path.

Both men sat quietly for a while in the shade of the acacia tree. The flies were bad. Johnny wondered how the children playing a few yards away ignored them crawling on their faces and legs. He felt calm. His thoughts shifted to the vibrant scene surrounding him. He sat in wonder of a people dependant on nothing more than what they could get from the earth, awed by the diversity of mankind, awed by the diversity of nature itself. It had not been that long ago, had someone approached him with such a fantastic tale, that he himself would have disavowed them; but why? Why, when the earth's diversity included so many things yet to be discovered? The world was rife with untold secrets, divulged in grudging increments by the plodding explorations of mankind. Why not things supernatural? Why not a place for these entities in such a vast and mysterious world?

A feeling of cleanliness had come over him, though not in a physical sense; on this third day without a shower he had caught an occasional whiff of his own underarms. More like a spiritual freshness. Whether by way of his confession to the man sitting next to him, or by being so far away from the beautiful pair, he didn't know. Perhaps it was simply the magical aura of being among the Maasai. Either way, it came bearing tranquility. There had been relief in talking to Brian, sharing a dialogue tempered with the stability of two men whose perspectives were in sync. Now it was a matter time, of musing and further talks, of fitting the complicated pieces together.

Enough had been said for a while. Awash in a kind of post-climatic calm, both men recognized and reflected on how the day brought change into their lives. Mingled with their thoughts were the visuals around them, the routine undertakings of the Maasai. A woman entered the compound across the way, her head shaven, her ankles ringed with silver bracelets, her breasts not faring well the battle with gravity. Hunched forward, she carried on her back an ungodly load of dried limbs that had been chopped for firewood. She passed three young girls that were giggling and fretting with each other's adornments. On the far side of the compound, a young man sat naked on a rock, his head patiently bowed as a friend plaited his hair and styled it with ochre-tinted animal fat. Johnny and Brian watched these comings and goings, two men caught in the throes of transition, losing themselves in private thoughts juxtaposed with Africa's exotic images: long legs, naked or partially naked, set in graceful strides; faces illuminated by a perfect ambiance with the colors of life. Their thoughts and the images blended well, inspiring both Johnny and Brian to believe that which comes without explanation can be explored and perhaps one day understood.

An hour passed by way of casual conversation. Capturing Johnny's imagination, Brian had been telling him about the Maasai, explaining their ways and time-honored traditions. Johnny watched them as Brian spoke, wistfully picturing himself as one of the warriors, perhaps much like one of the pair he was watching now—the taller of the two that stood lean and sinewy as the other smeared his upper back in ochre power. Johnny pictured his own hair longer and dangling in plaits, glistening with fatty red dye, his earlobes gouged and stretched and draped with strands of beads. Would he find himself enamored by the young miss that stood in observance a few feet away, giddy with the message in the warrior's eyes, much like that day in the library when he first set eyes on Marilee? Only here, her head would be shaved and covered in ochre, her neck and arms adorned with beads, her lovely chest exposed beneath a drooping disc-like necklace. Could there be any doubt that his thoughts that day nine years ago were not exactly the same as these young warriors'?

As the notion grew warm in his shoulders, he tried to imagine living in a world that existed no further than the horizon, where a man concerned himself with nothing more complicated than straying cattle and killing the lions that ate them. Though it swelled in his heart, he knew it would never meld with his psyche, for his contaminations were permanently ingrained on his soul: computers and air-conditioners and running water. Yet he was glad to have these few days. The experience would live in his memory like an elixir, to be used when the voice of a bill-collector came over the phone, or when the mail grew thick with bills he could not pay, or when Cassandra's summons knotted his fists. He could, on any of those unwanted occasions, close his eyes and travel back to Africa and slip into that warrior's crude sandals.

When Pakopai approached, both men stood up. Unfamiliar with the local dialect, Johnny listened to the odd intonations and quick syllables of Swahili. After presenting Johnny formally, Brian spoke with Pakopai for two or three minutes. As the laibon, Pakopai was the most feared elder, the spiritual leader, the diviner, the one considered expert in all things. He stood proud in his flowing red toga, a long silky flyswatter slung over his shoulder, his wrists and ears and neck festooned with beads and intricate ornamentation. High self-esteem lay confidently on the aged landscape of his face, his head shaven, his cheeks broad and full, his eyes reflecting the wisdom of many years. Though his full lips generated an easy smile, one looked upon him loathe to second-guess his authority or patience. He pronounced Johnny welcome to live among his people for a while, which came with an invitation to sleep in his house.

They gathered next to a cook-fire on the ground in front of Pakopai's house, and they were served beef sliced from a large roasting slab. Handed a gourd, Johnny sniffed at its contents.

"Honey beer," said Brian, sipping from his own gourd. He swathed a forearm across his wet lips. "It's made of honey, water, sausage fruit and roots. The concoction ferments for two weeks near a fire and is then strained through a piece of cloth."

Johnny took a gulp and nodded, finding its honey flavored taste agreeable. Serving the three men were two teenage girls and Pakopai's wife. Their servile task completed, the two girls followed the woman into the house.

"Are they Pakopai's daughters?" Johnny asked.

"Adopted daughters you might say. They lost their parents to fever at a young age. Pakopai took them in. Another of the unwritten codes. No Maasai child will ever want for adoptive parents."

"Won't they join us for dinner?" Johnny inquired, glancing at Pakopai. The elder seemed amused by Johnny's obvious curiosity.

"The women eat inside the house," Brian explained, his mouth full of beef.

After dinner, a half dozen girls close to the age of Pakopai's adopted daughters gathered and went inside the house.

"They'll be in there an hour or so, listening to Pakopai's wife talk about the old days," said Brian.

"Does Pakopai know where we're from?" Johnny asked.

"He knows there's another land across a big sea, but I think the notion is a bit vague to him. He likens America to Nairobi." Brian looked at Pakopai and explained that Johnny was from America.

"Amar-eeka," boomed Pakopai, followed by a good belly laugh, the reason not quite clear. Perhaps he pitied those that lived outside of the savannahs and hills of Kenya.

Later that night, when the girls emerged from the hut to return to their own families, the men, having smoked a couple of pipes of strong tobacco, got up to turn in for the night. Pakopai's house was the largest in the village. Johnny entered behind Brian with first-hand knowledge of what to expect inside a structure made of limbs and cow dung. Passing through the open doorway and turning right, there was the usual small room where the owner kept his youngest calves. Beyond that, the house consisted of a main area with a hearth centered on the floor, a kitchen area and three sleeping stalls. Meant to take away the night's chill, a fair blaze in the hearth cast dancing yellow light across the room, smoke wafting up through a vent hole in the roof. The rudimentary kitchen occupied the back wall: a table upon which sat a large calabash of honey beer, and a few shelves where various utensils were stored. The beds inside the semi-private stalls were no more than woven mats spread over the earthen floor. Soft hides comprised the bedding.

Aware the men were ready to go to bed, the two girls got up from a game they were playing on the floor, pulled their togas over their heads and hung them on wall hooks. Of an age American girls are most ill at ease with their changing bodies, these two were not. Johnny watched them step naked into their small sleeping area, marveling at their natural lack of modesty as they cast giggling glimpses toward their two male guests. Next to the girl's stall, Pakopai's wife awaited her husband in their tiny room. Pakopai disrobed before he went to her, exposing a well-fed belly, one of the few ample physiques in the settlement.

"They wear such carefree clothes," Johnny said, scanning the colorful garments hanging on the wall hooks.

"The Maasai don't care for western styles," said Brian, stepping out of his shorts. "Too confining. They'll point out that our clothes don't allow the breeze to blow away unwanted odors."

Johnny looked at the hanging clothes again. Apart from this more practical aspect of Maasai apparel, he wondered if the breeze might be the extent of their hygiene. He watched Brian hang his shorts on the wall. Thickset by nature, fit, the professor stepped toward the stall that the two of them were to sleep in. His chest and belly and legs shadowed with hair, he was notably masculine and well proportioned for a man approaching fifty. Brian got down on his knees and leaned forward to adjust the bedding, a position that redefined the contours of masculine symmetry and allowed for a rather conspicuous dangling between his legs. His thoughts stolen for a moment, Johnny's mind registered a man that was hauntingly attractive.

Johnny eyes shifted. He glanced around the room in reverence for a rare way of life. The contentment that had graced the Maasai faces during the day now permeated the warm air inside Pakopai's small house. Even as they lie falling asleep, their well-being seemed to fill the house. If only he could scoop some into his arms to take home with him. Johnny took off his clothes and found an empty hook. Standing quietly in the flickering light, he paused to look around one more time, as if to bathe in the quiet aura of tranquility and let it mingle with the skittish sensations of nakedness on rarely exposed skin.

Now exhausted by the intensity of the day's emotions, Johnny ducked barefoot into the stall and crawled onto the mat beside Brian. Positioned, he pulled the soft cowhide up to his chest as he lay back. He groaned inwardly, his belly still bloated, having eaten far too much beef. The night air, warm and laden with certain distinct smells, lay luxuriously on his face. They were earthy smells, a variety of odors that crept identifiably through his nostrils: the cowhide that covered him, the calves and their manure not twelve feet away, the wisps of smoke from the flickering fire, and the dank smell from the earth itself. Johnny also detected the smell of the man lying on top of the hides beside him, the unwashed odor of male underarms and loins. Absorbed in thought, he stared up at the shadowy ceiling. He had never reclined in such close proximity to such masculine smells, nor had he ever contemplated a night that he would sleep so near another man. Not ten inches separated them.

He thought about his purpose for being there, somewhat amused by the preliminary fears and conjecture he had suffered, only to find himself sharing a primitive bed with the man he came to see. It seemed that a friendship had sparked, that they had taken a mutual interest in each other beyond their individual distinctions with the supernatural. By just talking to Brian, by being taken seriously by someone who listened with concern, he felt immense relief. And in the bargain, an adventure, though much dampened by the devastation of his finances, this journey into Kenya, this once in a lifetime opportunity to learn about a new land and its people. Unintentionally they had drawn him in, the Maasai and their realm, for he felt like a young boy peering into the mouth of an unexplored cave. Now he lay engulfed in its spellbinding assault on all five senses, both physically and spiritually, realizing that somehow he would be changed. And it had given him a reprieve from Cassandra Mott. Though not yet certain how Brian Fowler could help him deal with Cassandra's manipulations, Johnny believed he and Brian could find a way, that he could return to Marilee with a better understanding of what had invaded their lives.

Brian opened a book that he had retrieved from beneath the bedding, having lit a candle that protruded from a bottle next to his head. As Johnny stared quietly at the thin, crisscrossing branches in the ceiling, he heard in the vast silence a page turn from time to time. Perhaps thirty minutes had passed when he heard the rich, sophisticated eloquence of Brian's voice reduced to a whisper.

"I can't sleep."

Though Johnny felt calm and relaxed, he knew sleep would be allusive for him too.

"It's too incredible," Brian said, resting the book on his chest. "How many have seen or experienced what you have?"

Johnny was aware that Brian was looking at him.

"Shame you're not bisexual," said Brian, a sudden and unexpected whispering of his thoughts.

Johnny turned his head and their eyes met.

"Forgive me, my friend, but I'm no longer inclined toward the fairer sex, even to these frequently available young girls. I would consider myself inappropriate for them anyway. But now I'm in bed next to a man, quite an attractive man I might add, and it occurred to me that a little mutual affection is nourishing for the soul." Brian shifted to his side and faced Johnny, bracing himself up on an elbow.

Caught off guard, Johnny glanced down at his companion's torso, a candlelit display of shoulders and a chest thick with muscle, of dark hairs mixed with gray that curled about a pair of nipples and ran a wide path toward a sunken navel. The glance ventured downward, over strong hairy legs, then upward, fixing on genitals flaccid in the warm air, dropping with generous weight from a dense swath of salted pubic hair, fleshy and splayed atop a muscular thigh. It was no more than a glance, the entirety of which lasted the bat of an eye, though it sparked the fires of adrenaline.

Oh, the power of such a visual to set one's imagination stirring, Johnny realized, not much to his surprise as he twisted his head upward and returned his gaze to the shadows. It all came rushing back as if the image had opened a floodgate of memories from his confused youth. Those fleshy organs— were they not an anomaly of the male form, peculiar in shape and so much darker than the rest of the body? Were they not an inconsistency in the fluid contours of muscle and limb, hanging from the body at the apex of one's legs like something alien by virtue of their odd design? Perhaps it might seem, but for that inborn consciousness of their purpose, and in being male with the same fragile effects, accompanied always with that sublime awareness of their ever changing weight. Oh, those daunting colors, dark and purposeful, like magnets drawing one's eyes, like streaking meteors that suddenly exclude all other thoughts. And those masculine odors lingering in the air with his own, born of errant drops of urine and yesterday's sweat and last night's involuntary seepages from that tiny hole, mingled with those living with aromatic vibrancy between damp gluteal cheeks. He was thinking about all of this as he stared at the ceiling, his face fixed with a dreamlike gaze, thinking there was even more to resist: the warmth of a man lying so close, the warmth he could feel on his face, the feel of that same man's breath on his ear. What was it, but a universe of two men, a symphony of maleness within the parameters of a small space, offensive perhaps to some, though more akin to euphoria for two certain men on a warm Kenyan night.

As his eyes moved about the ceiling, his thoughts of Africa and the Maasai and Cassandra Mott lost in flight, his mind traveled back to his first days in high school, where he first saw the dangle and sway between the other boy's legs. He had snatched glimpses of the side-to-side bounce as they strut from the showers to their lockers, and he had watched those darker colors yawing about with the vigorous blotting of a towel. How he had perused his own at length, turning this way and that in the mirror, learning the sensations of a well place grip; but not until that first day in the gym had he discovered, by seeing it dangle between another's legs, the undeniable flights of fancy that came through the eyes and flashed through the body like comets on a midsummer night. And that boy across the hall in the college dorm.

How timorous they had been with their awkwardness and naiveté, and that awful fear of getting caught. What would he do now—he had contemplated a hundred times since—given the opportunity to have one more night with him? What would he do but savor that maleness with his eyes and fingertips and tongue? What would he do but devour him and lock the memory of the night among his most private thoughts forever?

So had Brian's proposal fallen pleasantly upon his ears? It might have, to be sure, had the stirrings inside his body not been displaced by the nervous dampness of his hands brought on by guilt. He had suppressed for a decade those thoughts born in adolescence, which had blossomed into a physical tryst in college. He had buried all of that permanently on his wedding day, and he had endeavored to ignore it every day since, save Julian. But that was not his fault. Not his choice or his doing—that had been Cassandra Mott's mystification. Only the power of her curse could have awakened these forbidden urges.

And awake they were. This time without curses or drugs. Facing yet another dilemma, another thorn in his fragile peace-of-mind, Brian's proposal brought on a new and different kind of tension, in that he, a professor, was simply a man, albeit an extraordinary man, but a man nevertheless, devoid Julian's supernatural ability to bring this tingling across his skin. Could he truly deny his bisexuality, Johnny wondered, considering his indiscretions with Julian, considering this attraction now creeping into his soul for the man lying next to him? Could he deny it, considering the odors swirling through his nose were utterly masculine and stimulating the sweetest of physical reactions? Could he ignore the instantaneous ache or the irrefutable messages from the most sensitive parts of his body?

His breath had become shallow. Perspiration dampened his neck and warm feelings settled inside his thighs, a warmth not caused by the hide covering them. What, just this moment, could be more agreeable, or more likely to bring about a memorable night than placing his hand aside Brian's face?

But no. He would not. He simply could not let it happen. This wasn't, after all, a supernatural spell. It was nothing more than a temptation that a husband so far from home must resist. So no, even if he couldn't deny his attraction to this interesting man, no matter how keen it might be, he would not know the pleasure of Bryan's touch. He would not feel Bryan's warm breath upon his lips, or know the fleshy weight of that handsome cock within his hand, not this night, not ever. He would abide this fitful wakefulness and eventually fall asleep with his commitment to Marilee intact.

"Another time and place, Professor, but not in this lifetime."

"Of course, I understand. Please forgive my forwardness."

"No apology necessary."

Johnny rolled over. He could feel Brian's gaze. He had said the appropriate words for a man in his position, and had stated them with resolve, though they left a wake of lost opportunity. What was there about this man, closer to his father's age than his own, that had so thoroughly captured his imagination? Johnny realized, as he stared into the flickering yellow light just outside their tiny room, that Brian's appeal went beyond the sense of security he felt by having someone understand his dilemma with Cassandra Mott. He folded his arms beneath the hide and hugged his chest, lying a great distance from sleep, thinking about that strapping man with the shadowy contours and masculine patterns of gray hair, the damp muscular rifts and creases that sweetened the air and secretly turned his hands into fists. He lay there thinking that he had found a moment's peace from Cassandra's spell, only to face something equally, perhaps even more daunting.

Johnny stayed awake for a long while, promising himself that he would not turn and further risk temptation, listening to the occasional popping ember, the stirring calves and the snores from across the room. Finally, with thoughts fading, a weary sigh accompanied an irresistible hint of sleep. The secure womb of Pakopai's house closed in on him and his eyes fluttered, relegating his trials to oblivion.

They stirred at dawn, lying sprawled and restless, their bedding askew and dampened by fitful dreams, their bellies empty and their bladders full, that urgency disclosed by halfhearted morning erections. Johnny's eyes opened first, the cowhides he had fallen asleep under now bunched between his legs.

Africa.

The first thought born on a new day, accompanied by a mindfulness of firm earth beneath his back as his bleary gaze took focus on the woven branches and mud of the ceiling. A yawn came as he turned his head and his eyes settled on Brian.

Still asleep, his long hair in disarray on the rolled up hide that he used for a pillow, Brian lay on his side, hugging the pillow as a child hugs a stuffed bear, one leg extended downward, the other drawn toward his belly, the knee mere inches away. They were strong hips and legs and shoulders, those of a man at peace with himself, an image that once again took hold of Johnny's mind. He stared, damning his duplicitous psyche. No, he would not rest a hand on that magnificent shoulder! He would face it down, just as he had these many years, and get on with the business at hand.

After a breakfast of cornmeal mixed with water and sour yogurt, Johnny and Brian took a walk outside of the compound. Situated on a shaded rise of a grassy meadow, the settlement overlooked a panoramic valley to the north. To the south, foothills textured in green and brown rose to the distant horizon. The two men strolled across the meadow among cattle grazing in the morning mist. They paused where the land began meandering toward the valley, and sat on the trunk of a fallen tree. There they watched a group of young warriors throwing spears near the glint of a fast stream. Some hundred yards away, animated with youthful antics and horseplay, the young men strutted like peacocks with their plaited red hair, their faces smeared with ocher and their lean torsos flaunting all manner of beaded finery. Instead of red togas, they had on short, skirt-like wraps that were tied at the waist. They laughed and cajoled each other, erupting in cheers when the occasional spear precisely hit its target.

"Your visit's had quite an affect on this beleaguered professor, my friend," said Brian as he watched the young warriors. "I woke up during the night thinking about Cassandra Mott."

Johnny looked at him.

"One single question keeps pounding in my brain," Brian went on to say. "Why? Why has she allowed you in? The fact that you're her ex-lover's grandson, I'm afraid doesn't reconcile it for me. I've come to know their nature quite well. I've never detected the slightest sign of sentimentality. They live and thrive on the pleasures of life. Cassandra has a purpose, I feel it."

Johnny's brow furrowed.

"Oh, a barrage of theories arose in my mind as I lied there last night." Brian scoffed through his nose, as if to suggest his theories were nothing more than a maze of ever-expanding conjecture.

"Like what?" Johnny was hungry for any reasonable conclusion.

"Well, consider the fact that we have no idea of where the entities come from or how they procreate. Are they born into this world from the womb of a hapless mother, perhaps with mutated genes, and then mature with supernatural powers?"

Johnny's gaze returned to the spear throwing and camaraderie near the stream, though his mind was absorbing every syllable of Brian's evolving scenario.

"I don't want to alarm you, my friend, but consider this: What if from time-to-time they set out to create another of themselves? Could that be Cassandra's purpose? What if those ordeals she is putting you through is an initiation of some kind, or a test of your qualifications to become one of them?"

Johnny cringed. His eyes shifted back to the professor, wide with horror at the thought. "You think she intends to turn me into an entity! My God! You may not want to alarm me, but you're sure doing a damn good job of it."

"Ah," said Brian, passing it off with the wave of his hand. "Just shows you how my mind works."

"But how would I fight it, if that's her purpose?"

Brian considered the question for a moment. "The only weakness I ever observed is their astounding sexual appetites, but there must be other weaknesses as well. Have you ever noticed anything about her, anything at all that seems to make her vulnerable?"

"Only when she tries to read my mind. I've learned I can prevent it by force of will."

"So perhaps your force of will is your primary defense against her. Maybe you can strengthen it further and use it as a defensive weapon. Does she know what you're doing when you block her?"

"I don't know."

"Experiment with it when you're around her. Try different methods. Push it hard. See if it angers or frustrates her when you're doing it." Brian paused. His eyes shifted aimlessly as he sorted through his thoughts. "The more I think about it, the more interesting that is. I've known a long time they have at least some ability to read minds, but I didn't know it could be thwarted by human willpower." He turned to Johnny and placed his hand on his shoulder. "We have such a short time to spend together here in Kenya. That's only a beginning, considering all we have to explore. You and I will be keeping in close touch after you return to the States."

Johnny smiled. He already thought about his return to Savannah, that it meant giving up the reassurances of Brian's friendship. He liked the idea of keeping in close touch.

The sun inched higher in the morning sky while they talked. Johnny described the Mott house, its rooms and the parlor, and Confederate Square. He went on to describe the historic district, the fine old houses and shops that surround Savannah's lovely squares. Brian spoke of Boston and his years at the university and carried on about his love for Africa. Then he broached the incident the night before.

"Say, listen, about last night ... " said Brian, rubbing his jaw.

"Forget it," Johnny interrupted, a bit snappishly. He looked down at his knees, regretful, recognizing the defensiveness of his reply. He didn't expect this subject to come up. A brief but awkward silence descended over them. Johnny thought about the ongoing conflicts with his bisexuality. Why continue to deny it? To convince himself maybe? To hold on to the fallacy that he wasn't really attracted to men? What a laugh, having coupled with Julian without the slightest protest. It was one more thing screwing up his life, but it was also a simple matter of fact. It dawned on him, as he stared across the valley, that he wanted to talk about it, to get it off his chest and be free of it at least to that extent. So why did he feel reluctant? Especially with someone like Brian, a man like himself that understands what it's like to be attracted to other men.

"It's just that ..." Brian continued, trying a little too hard to express his regrets. It was the first time Johnny heard him falter with his words. "Well, I should have never suggested ..."

Johnny looked at him sharply. "Listen, don't worry about it. I'm flattered you find me attractive." They stared at each other for a moment, in more of a stunned silence this time than awkwardness, broken when Johnny added: "Plus it makes you seem a little more human ... maybe a little less infallible."

"Guess I thought," said Brian, pausing, wanting his words to come more freely, "...well, that thing between you and Julian, I thought maybe..."

"Was it that, or your intuition about me?"

"I shouldn't have made assumptions," said Brian, looking at his somewhat dejected companion, thinking it seemed his new friend had more to say on the subject.

Johnny let out a sigh. Just one more thing that he had no one to share his feelings with. His gaze landed on the sparse grass a few feet from where they were sitting. "I think it was your intuition, Brian. Couldn't have been too difficult to piece together my little secret, not after I confessed my sins with Julian. I've been trying to pretend it was all part of Cassandra's mystification. She knew. All she had to do was expose me to a little temptation." Johnny leaned forward and rested his elbows on his knees. "You know, it's funny how something like that can rear-up again at my age and haunt you the way it does. I thought it was a phase, a teenage thing. Now I know I've been doing a lot of pretending for a long time. A hunk in tight jeans—I catch myself staring. You wonder if his ass is hairy or smooth. You wonder if his dick is bigger or smaller than yours. You wonder what it would be like to get close to him in bed." He released a self-mocking laugh. "So I pretend; I guess because I'm married, not to mention I was brought up believing it's wrong.

"But Cassandra knew. Then she confirmed her suspicions when she had Julian undress in front of me. I may have been drugged, but I was fully aware of what was going on. It wasn't so much a transformation of a happily married man, as a confirmation of what I had buried inside, waiting to surface. She awoke the phantom when she had Julian bend over. I was ..." Johnny paused and looked at Brian. "You sure you want to hear the whole story?"

"Nothing has ever intrigued me more."

Johnny studied him for a moment before going on, struck by the notion that he, Brian, would give his eye-teeth for a similar episode with the entities. "I was sitting no more than three feet behind him, nervous and scared. Then he bent over and exposed his anus." He blew a small ironic laugh through his nostrils. "Cassandra knew I wouldn't be put off by that. She was right; I wasn't. Something pleasant spread through my whole body. She reached out and stroked it with her finger, and I watched, nervous but curious, wanting to do it, too. I was determined to resist, but Cassandra saw what she was looking for in my eyes. She wouldn't take *no* for an answer, so that gave me an excuse to touch him there." Johnny drew a breath and released it. "It's hard to describe. You have think about a drop of dye hitting a pool of water, how the dye spreads and changes the color of the water. Something like that happened to me. It was like something passed through my fingertip and spread through me like that dye." He lifted his hand and looked at his fingertips. "I touched it, stroked it, pushed on it. It left a smell on my finger. I didn't want to wash my hand that day."

Brian shifted his weight on the tree. "My God man! An incredible story. If I were ten years younger, you'd find me masturbating in the bushes."

"The point is that was the first time I tried to use my willpower. I tried to deny the urge to touch him. It failed." Johnny looked at Brian and smiled. "You see, I'm surprised it didn't fail when I used it last night with you."

"You used it quite effectively, my friend."

"I suppose I did," said Johnny, suddenly distracted by a cow passing in front of them, close enough to reach out and touch.

"So you're reluctance last night was based on the sanctity of your marriage. That I understand and respect."

Johnny looked at him. "I was tempted. More than you know. But if we're to sleep that close together, we can't…"

"Of course," said Brian. "It's a matter of honor. I've always tried to live as an honorable man, at least when it matters. Sometimes it's a struggle; but when I lay in bed at night, thinking about my own existence and doubting its value, at least I have the satisfaction of knowing I've made it through another day without degrading my integrity. Do I want to feel like a rodent crawling into a hole because I have violated a woman's trust while she waits at home for her husband? I want no part of causing your guilt."

Johnny stared at the ground, his face drawn and somber. "My guilt is already well established." He rubbed his right temple with his fingertips. "I know it's not real love, but I feel close to Julian, and safe. The sex … there's no doubt in my mind I'd do it again."

"So now you've told me. It's quite obvious you're suffering the consequences. But you did it under the influence of a most unusual form of mind control. You can't be held responsible."

"Nobody held a gun to my head when I lifted my legs for Julian," Johnny replied.

"A gun, no. Something far more persuasive than that. Call it supernatural hypnosis. You were correct earlier. Your will *was* neutralized, my friend. Nothing could be more obvious. As for you and me, here in Africa, it's a whole different set of circumstances. Here we're making our decisions with sound minds. We've laid our cards on the table. We have something in common beyond our immortal friends. But you have a wife. Because of that, nothing can justify going any further with our little fantasy."

"It's funny," Johnny said, exasperated, "something like this happening. When I first saw you, I wanted to kick your ass. Last night, I wanted to…" He shook his head and let out a frustrated breath. "Before I got here, I didn't know what to expect. Sure didn't anticipate being attracted to you."

"Ah, a real dilemma for a man who loves his wife," Brian said with irony. "Certainly a dilemma for the poor soul sleeping next to that man. You're a fine specimen, Mr. Feelwater."

"I really don't understand it, Brian," Johnny agonized. "Everything Marilee and I have accomplished during our nine years together began to unravel overnight. It's not just because of Cassandra and Julian Mott; it's what I've discovered about myself—the potential to be completely irresponsible. I had important phone calls to return and kept putting them off. Our only source of income is gone. Now this. When you took your shorts off last night, I wanted to look at you. Even if nothing could come of it, I wanted to look. I won't have a wife if I ever tell her what's inside me."

"Tell her what? We haven't done anything." Brian looked at him. "Or are you talking about your victimization? Cassandra imposed that on you. You have nothing to gain by telling your wife about that. Instead, let's find a way to deal with Ms Mott and get it behind you. And since our mutual attraction has been precluded by your marriage, there's nothing there to feel guilty about either. It seems neither of us can abide betrayal." Brian rested his hand on Johnny's shoulder. "You demonstrated that quite effectively last night. When I made that little proposal, I bet you started thinking about your wife."

Johnny closed his eyes and nodded. "Yeah. I did. I haven't said much about Marilee, but here recently, after nine years together, we've fallen in love. It's like it took adversity to bring us together. I mean *truly* fallen in love, after what I've put her through during all of this. She's in the dark about Cassandra, yet she hangs on to her faith in me all the same. Believe me, telling her about my plans to come here was a real blow, not to mention how it affected our meager finances, but she accepted even that." A tear formed in Johnny's eye. He stopped talking for a moment to regain his composure, wiping away the tear on the back of his hand. "I can't stand what I'm doing to her. That other side of me was buried inside a long time. Question is, can I bury it again?"

"Rest assured, you aren't the only married man on earth who has a little cache of secret fantasies."

"I'll just have to try," Johnny said, staring at the ground, oblivious to Brian's last words.

Brian looked at him for a moment, seeing a man internally at war on two fronts.

Johnny paused in thought, watching the tireless young warriors. "You're my only hope, Brian. No one else can help me deal with Cassandra Mott. I have to get my life back before it's too late."

Brian was still staring at him, already determined to do everything he could; though, at the moment, at a loss for a solution. Until now he had been more caught up in what he might learn from Johnny's ordeal. He realized he cared, that he wanted to find a way to help his new friend. "We have to figure out what she's up to. Why has she singled you out?" Brian looked down at his feet, and then back at Johnny. "That's what she did. She singled you out. Then she caused you to betray the woman you love. That must be tough."

"It's fucking miserable. Your stomach never stops churning." Johnny turned his head away from Brian, his lips pressed together, collecting his thoughts. "She's toying with me," he said, turning back. "I know her. She's doing it because it amuses her. She uses men like playthings. Doesn't matter to her if it destroys their lives. She calls it debauchery. That's Cassandra's purpose. I just happened to be the one she chose this time."

Brian was doubtful. "That could be it, certainly, but you and I can't narrow our minds to only one scenario. Let's stay open to any possibility."

"Do you think they're dangerous?" asked Johnny.

"Dangerous?" This had been one of Brian's concerns from early on. He had drawn some conclusions. "No doubt they can be, if it comes down to self-preservation. Beyond that, I'm convinced they mean no harm. Not even in your case, even though they've disrupted your life. I don't think harming you is Cassandra's intent. I've observed them for a long time. I'm certain they exist among us in peace, that our world and theirs intermingle in many ways. If they were dangerous, they couldn't coexist in secrecy for as long as they have. Greed, lust and self-absorption, certainly; but I've never witnessed pure evil. They indulge themselves with riches and sex, thereby involving us on different levels. Cassandra surprises me only because she actually took you into her confidence. That surprises me. As far as our friend Julian is concerned, I have no way of knowing if he's dangerous or not. We don't even know how he's different."

Johnny's eyes shifted in thought. "Sometimes it seems like I could walk away from Cassandra. But not Julian. I think she planned it that way to insure my subservience." He pondered the thought for a moment and then continued. "They reach out for me. I feel it physically. It's like a headache setting in. You know it's coming. Starts in your neck and gradually moves into your head. It's like that, only this starts in my hands. When I wake up in the morning, I can tell by the feeling in my hands that I'll end up going over there."

"That sounds psychosomatic," Brian put in.

"Maybe so, but I feel it nevertheless. It's hard to explain. If I try to resist, it starts knotting up in my stomach. It's unbearable. I've doubled over because of it. Then it stops as soon as I start toward Confederate Square."

"I've always known they can be seductive, but what you're describing goes beyond all my years of research."

"I'm sure Julian didn't instigate any of this. Cassandra did. She must have a fondness for seeing two men together. She loves watching us. She knows I can't resist him. I can't explain exactly how or why I love him, but I do. I ache for him ... and I also fear him. I don't have to ask you if he's dangerous. He is. He seems reluctant to use it, but there's no telling how much power he has. He's the one who makes the furniture appear and disappear, I'm sure of it. I believe he can turn himself into a snake." Johnny paused in thought and then added distantly: "Sometimes I think he's a form of Satan."

"Good lord!" said Brian. "That *would* be remarkable. Not only find Satan really exists, but actually know him."

"But why does he pair with Cassandra?"

"Ah, the questions come without end, don't they? And each must be examined." Brian had been listening intently, listening for clues that might help define what they were up against. Having his head cocked toward Johnny caused his neck to stiffen. He rolled his shoulders and then said: "I thought a lot about our friend Julian last night. We know he's different, most likely not human. Like you said, he seems Satan-like. He's why I intend to cut my summer here in Africa as short as possible. I am most anxious to get to Savannah and see him with my own eyes."

Johnny was delighted to hear this. "You're coming to Savannah?"

"Soon as I can. Julian intrigues me. How difficult will it be to observe him?"

"At the house, impossible. I can't imagine anyone being anywhere near that house without him knowing it. But Cassandra likes to step out and he always accompanies her. Maybe then. You'll have to be careful, Brian. Even from a distance there's a high possibility he'd be aware of you. You'd have to be patient and use stealth. Maybe then you could get away with it."

"Hmm. Okay then, to avoid unnecessary risk, most of my observations can come through you."

"That'd be best," said Johnny, thinking about Brian's sudden plans to go to Savannah. He felt a sense of relief in having an ally in Savannah; though beyond the risk to Brian's safety if he were caught nosing around in their world, there was another consideration as well: dealing with the temptation he had struggled with the night before. Brian's presence in Savannah would set up the close proximity of a man in his own home town that would keep him lying awake at night. "I wasn't expecting you to come to Savannah."

"I realized last night just how intrigued I am with Julian. We can learn more about him if I'm there. Cassandra, too. I'm anxious to get a look at her. I'll rent a small apartment somewhere. Then you and I can figure out what they're up to. You game?"

"Yeah, I'm game. I'm glad you're coming."

"What do you know about Julian's mind-reading abilities?"

"I believe he hears everything you're thinking," said Johnny. "Since he communicates with mental telepathy, you have to make that assumption."

"I agree, and that's certainly not pocket-change when it comes to supernatural power. You'll have to be mindful of what you're thinking about when you're around him." Brian swiped across his nostrils with the back of his finger. "Damn allergies." He looked at Johnny with a thought. "Maybe you can experiment with him, too. Try thinking about how thirsty you are. See if he brings you a drink. Try things like that."

Johnny wondered if it was foolhardy to entertain ways to toy with Julian or uncover his secrets. One could learn the folly of doing so the hard way. He looked at Brian and then followed his gaze toward the warriors.

"Think of it," said Brian. "I never believed all the religious propaganda about Satan, but if Julian is some form of Satan-like creature, think of what we could learn from him. All of that religious history about devils and Hell could have come about because of his kind. Imagine, all the questions about Heaven and Hell, all the mystery surrounded the after-life, cleared up just like that."

"Don't get your hopes up, professor. Even if you find yourself in Julian's good graces, he doesn't answer questions. You'd stand a better chance getting those warriors to dance the Nutcracker."

"No doubt, my friend. We'll see soon enough."

Lost in thought, they watched the Maasai warriors for a while.

"Look at them," said Brian. "The fun they're having. I've watched scenes like this for hours on end. On a hunt, those spears are thrown in earnest, perhaps at a lion that's been eating their calves. They're beautiful aren't they?"

"Yes," said Johnny, mindful of being privileged to observe a day in their lives. His gaze went skyward. The pale morning blue had deepened as the sum climbed higher. Lucent white clouds passed in a feathery armada on their never-ending easterly drift, migrating like grass-eating African beasts. Before him were miles of windswept grasses, splashed with muted shades of gold and yellow, rising in a distant upward sweep toward the haze and hues of far-off mountains. Johnny had not imagined such natural beauty, or the sentiment of seeing it with his own eyes—so vast, so enduring.

Did he anticipate Africa getting into his heart? Perhaps, but not so completely. It was a true awareness as he gazed across the panorama, a world much different than his own. It seemed to instill its silent chant into his soul, this mysterious land and its people. How they whooped and bounded upward into the air as if their feet were fixed with springs, the young Maasai warriors cajoling each other and throwing their spears, living lives devoid of material want. How he loved being among them, watching them, envying them as he did, these men and women that owned both nothing and everything. What better way, if only for a few days, to escape a nightmare?

"They're wearing skirts," Johnny said, looking at the towel-like brown cloths wrapped around their waists.

"Casual wear," said Brian. "Equivalent to the blue-jeans you're wearing or these shorts I have on," he pinched a bit of the fabric off his leg and added, "that need to be washed. Wait until you see them later on, when the Olngesherr ceremonies begin. Pakopai told me they intend to initiate upwards of two hundred new junior elders." Brian nodded at the warriors. "Those young men will be wearing their best finery, as will the warriors from neighboring settlements. They'll be a magnificent sight to behold." He put his hand on Johnny's shoulder and said: "So my friend, it seems you and I are like two small boys facing Halloween for the first time. Quite a lot to think about, I'd say." Brian looked out across the savannah and came to his feet. "Let's walk."

The morning passed as two men, lost in the enchantments of Africa and the challenges they faced with Cassandra Mott, strolled down through the meadow, kicking back and forth their theories on the supernatural, often distracted, as they walked along the stream, by the magnificent endowments of the land.

Chapter 20

That afternoon some five hundred people from neighboring settlements had gathered in Pakopai's compound. By that time, the girl Brian attended to the day before had improved to the extent that she managed a few smiles when Pakopai entered her hut for a visit. Having learned her fever had broken during the night, Pakopai elected to give Brian's medicine the credit instead of the bull's blood, which earned Brian and Johnny the status of honored guests during the Olngesherr ceremony. Nearly two hundred men, too old now to be warriors, were to leave behind their days of tracking lions and rounding up stray cattle, and be elevated in status to junior elders. It was a great honor for them, and for Brian and Johnny, who were invited to join Pakopai and the other important elders on a grassy knoll to watch the proceedings.

From the beginning the ceremony promised to be festive, a raucous gathering of Kenya's finest pagans. Tall and lean, they were wrapped or draped in various styles almost exclusively one shade or another of red. Some wore togas tied with beaded belts. Others wore sheet-like wraps emblazoned in an infinite variety of stripes. Extravagant they were in their jewelry and adornments, limited only by each individual's imagination: ears pierced top and bottom and hung with trinkets and strands of beads, lobes skewed with silvery stick-like ornaments. They wore necklaces and bracelets and anklets, and draped strands of beads about their foreheads and chests. It was a constant coming and going no single pair of eyes could pursue in entirety: the chosen junior elders animated with anticipation, women ambling through the throngs with heavy calabashes and pouring more honey beer, children and their dogs interspersed among the many long legs. Strutting with spears and gathered in groups, relating lively tales of recent hunts, the warriors were the most fascinating to watch.

Flamboyant to a fault, they dispensed unending flirtations and cleverness as they moved like celebrities through the crowd. Costumed in beaded neckbands and flumed crowns, their long legs painted in stripes, they presented a glorious show, standing in threes and fours around the coy young women while the younger boys looked on. They gave off an aura of adventure, a fearing of no man or beast. And when entering a young woman's gaze, a warrior's smile came easily, as if he were picturing himself having her and sharing her ultimately with his friends. The emanations given off by these virile young men included promises of great value: that every man, woman and child could live without fear of predator or injustice imposed by mankind; promises nourished by thousand-year old laws and ingrained on vibrant hearts, shouldered with style by these cocky and fearless young men.

The men chosen to become junior elders were easy to spot, collecting as they were in groups near the carcass of a bull that had been suffocated for use in their initiation, their black skin glistening in the sun, all wearing sheet-like, pale red cloth that hung from shoulder to knee. They and their friends and families for the first hour milled about, trading news and gossip while some three dozen women prepared for the ceremony. For those on the threshold of adulthood, it was the same serendipity found anywhere in the world, young males and females skittish with unsettled hormones, letting go their blustery and blushing displays of mutual attraction. And throughout the hour of renewed acquaintances and anticipation, many of the guests approached Pakopai as he sat with his legs folded on the knoll among the elders, to show their respect and express appreciation for his hospitality.

Provided with pipes and strong tobacco, Brian and Johnny sat slightly to the right of the group of senior elders, sucking on the long stems and puffing out small clouds of smoke. Johnny watched the camaraderie in a fog of enchantment, stolen away from the unending torment of his haunting. He had been granted a short reprieve by the sensory deluge of color and commotion of a Maasai celebration.

Joining the laughter came chanting and song; joining the to and fro came dance. As if he had been allowed into a kingdom of wonder, his head turned this way and that as his curiosities rose one upon another and his questions sprouted like dandelions in the morning sun. It was a world the polar opposite of his own, this earthy way of life, an unfolding of images to be collected by his eyes and stored forever in his mind.

He leaned closer to Brian. "What are they planning to do with the bull?"

"It's part of the tradition. They chose a pure white, unblemished bull. After cutting a two-foot slit along its dewlap, they'll pull back the skin to form a basin of open flesh. The bull was suffocated so it wouldn't bleed out. The blood will pool in the gash. Each of the new junior elders will kneel for a drink. You'll see them add honey beer from time to time to insure each one of them gets a drink. Since Pakopai donated the bull, they'll show gratitude by asking him to go first."

Johnny's nose wrinkled. "Almost sounds like an initiation at a college fraternity."

Brian laughed. "Rest assured, my friend, there's a significant philosophical difference."

When the time came, Pakopai got to his feet, grunting with effort, being one of the very few overweight Maasai. The colorful crowd parted as he made his way to the dead bull. He knelt and pulled the lip of flesh further back; and as his face neared the pooled blood, a hush fell over the crowd. On the hush came a slurping sound. Then, lifting his great baldhead, his tongue emerged and lapped over his reddened lips as his eyes raked the crowd and rested on Brian and Johnny. He waved and called out to them, summoning them to go next, which gained quick popular support from a boisterous, approving crowd. Johnny stiffened, staring with dread at the bull. Brian stood and extended his hand.

"No getting out of this one, my friend," he said, feeling Johnny's reluctance as he assisted him to his feet.

Johnny followed his companion through the crowd, most of them taller than himself. He found himself standing over the bull, his toes nearly touching the bull's nose as he cringed at the sight of the blood-filled gash. He looked up and scanned the dozens of animated faces that were enchanted by this unexpected turn of events. They were aware that city dwellers, deprived of such sacred rituals, were somehow put off by them; and this strange, black *A'ma'ree'kan*, his face twisted with aversion, struck them as humorous.

Brian knelt, lapped at the bright red pool and came up with a bloody chin. Then, by decree of Pakopai's authority, Johnny knelt, leaned forward, closed his eyes and breathed in the warm, aromatic bouquet of blood. Scattering the flies from the carcass, he placed one hand near the bull's shoulder, the other upon its jaw and then leaned closer. As the blood's warmth collected on his face, he resisted the impulse to draw back, ignored the flies swarming his nose and ears, pursed his lips and hesitantly sucked up less than a thimble-full. Swallowing in one miserable gulp, he shrank back and rushed the back of his hand across his lips. The crowd, delighted with Johnny's stiff apprehension, parted so the two visitors could return to the knoll. He fought an urge to wretch, receiving a few back-slaps as he followed Brian back to resume the less daring roll of spectator.

After the last junior elder took his turn, several of the men tied the hooves together and by means of a long pole, they carried the carcass into an enclosure the women had erected earlier. It was a secluded area about forty feet in diameter, walled off using stiff tanned hides fixed to poles to form a fence. There, they sliced the carcass into long strips and laid them over a network of green branches erected over a bed of coals. While the beef roasted, the mouth-watering smell wafting through the settlement, and the initiates collected inside the enclosure where they would have their foreheads rubbed with the fatty meat. They would be the first to eat.

It was a time of waiting. Puffing their pipes, Johnny and Brian continued to observe the activities from their positions on the knoll. Johnny's reprieve held. There were no omens in his hands. Locking his fingers around a knee, he sat comfortably, the pipe clenched in his teeth, his shoulder and neck muscles tension free. While the elders next to him spoke among themselves of their important concerns, Johnny continued his private study of Maasai contentment. He watched young mothers with newborn infants at their breasts, tiny babes engulfed within loving arms and gazes. A toddler emerged from a forest of long legs, wailing. So distraught was his small face that Johnny's heart felt a pang. The child had lost his mother, not yet old enough to know there was no safer place on God's earth he might be. The younger men, the warriors, stood in small groups, conversing and comparing adornments and body paint. From them came no shortage of teasing; for it seemed where go the warriors, so go the girls and the catcalls and flirting.

Johnny had been watching one of them in particular. A young man who would be king, Johnny surmised as he leaned forward and stared, resting his forearms on his knees, letting his hands hang limp. The warrior, shouldering no more than twenty-five years of life's trials, stood an inch or two taller than his companions; a stature enhanced by a magnificent, horseshoe-shaped headdress, feathered with stuffed orioles and kingfishers. Flaring nearly as wide as his shoulders, he wore it like a crown. Chalky white paint formed a raccoon-like mask around his eyes and strands of beads crisscrossed his forehead. Set in the perfect symmetry of a longish, oval-shaped face, his eyes shone with self-confidence and arrogance, his nose long and broad with large nostrils, his lips a voluptuous, omnipotent smirk. Tied at the back of his neck, a bright red cape draped down over his torso to his knees. It hung loosely open down the back, which allowed shadowy hints of rich black skin and the masculine contours of his lower back and buttocks.

The shadows had drawn Johnny's eyes and his imagination. Not surprising, now that his self-recognition was out in the open and clear. Why not allow for one opportunity to savor male beauty? He sighed as he stared at the uninhibited warrior as if no one else were there, with little doubt about what had claimed his eyes, mindful of the tingles that warmed his inner thighs. He wondered what went through the young man's mind, displaying himself that way, so freely allowing one and all to behold his sensual beauty. Reflections accompanied Johnny's dream-like gaze that unmistakably defined his evolving vulnerability, enhanced each time the animated warrior turned this way or that, or a wisp of air stirred the red cape.

Such perfect form, that gluteal flesh, as if by design that part of the body was meant to reduce one's thoughts to flights of fancy: two mounds separated above strong and graceful legs by a tantalizing rift. So specific were Johnny's thoughts as he stared at these umber and tar-like colors, the image took complete hold of him. Yes, he knew. It was nothing less than another confirmation that rose out of his not-so-subtle gaze. Now he fully recognized these duplicitous urges. He was in touch with his need to enjoy such fine male sculpture, and enjoy it he would; for it was the one part of him, upon leaving Africa, forever destined to live in poverty.

As if the dead leaves had been raked from his consciousness, so many things were clear. He finally realized how often over the years his head turned for a second glimpse at a man in passing, those subliminal occurrences that went back to his earliest memory. Incubating inside him since birth, it had drawn its first breath that day in the gym. All those boys. How naked they were in the shower, that pageant of genitals and male flesh every which way he turned, those gluteal contours that cast a spell every time one bent down to wash his legs. No, he had not been simply curious about the other boys' penises that day—he had lain awake that night wondering what it would be like to take one in his hand, as his mind sailed with the infinite varieties of color and shape. So was it all buried on his wedding day? Hardly. Nor could he blame Julian; after all, Julian had not infused him with this propensity for firmer flesh and masculine smells—Julian had simply looked into his mind and responded to a fantasy already there.

The tireless warrior did not hesitate to impose his lively antics upon the young women, teasing them and lifting their chins as if he were inspecting their faces, while the other warriors stood near and looked on with awe and envy, passively acknowledging they stood in the presence of a man with whom they could not compete. Spellbound by the warrior's charisma, Johnny drifted on reverie as his eyes revisited again and again every glorious detail. On his fingertips lived the desire to touch; on his tongue the desire to taste; within his arms the desire to hold. Involuntary were the flexing muscles of his buttocks and legs, and within his loins lay a yearning for the penetrating warmth of another man's need. Such was power of human genes, the instincts and desires that are called upon from within those dark creases and landscapes of flesh, those subtle nuances that connect the world's like-minded men. Such was the power of one man to own another man's mind.

Encroaching on his wistful thoughts came the deep resonance of Brian's voice.

"That's Seto."

"What?" Johnny asked, jolted from his daze.

"His name is Seto," Brian repeated.

"Who?" asked Johnny, turning to him.

"The one you're staring at. He's the one connected to the girl I was treating when you first arrived. Now that she's recovering, she'll become his third wife. He and the men he's with have been out stalking some goat-snatching hyenas. ...Quite captivating, wouldn't you say?"

"Captivating?"

"Apparently you agree. You've been staring at him the last ten minutes."

"Yes, I agree," Johnny replied, looking back at the enigmatic warrior. "Three wives. That's hard to fathom."

"No kidding, when just one can be a handful. These men can marry as many women as they wish, and a young man like Seto has little difficulty attracting them. I'd say at least one or two of those gazing at him now are hoping to be his fourth wife."

"Brian ... how can you feel worthless one minute, I mean really worthless, not worth the cost of the bullet it'd take to kill you; and then feel justified to indulge yourself the next, because you've worked every day of your life and not once enjoyed a personal reward for the effort?"

"Sounds like guilt. Bet I could guess what was going through your mind when you were looking at Seto."

Johnny stared at his companion without a reply.

"I thought so. Well, this isn't an occasion to lose behind a blindfold of guilt, my friend. Take stock of what's before you. Isn't it obvious Seto has put himself on display? So why not enjoy looking at him? He represents God's finest work. Why deny yourself the pleasure of such perfection?"

The young warrior turned suddenly and caught Johnny staring at him. Their eyes locked for a moment, Seto's gleaming with humor and curiosity. He broke from his friends and started toward the knoll, his prankish gaze lit with hints of mischief. His friends followed, stopping behind him as he stood towering before Johnny, looking down at what likely seemed to him a rather plain looking, city dwelling black man, confined in a white shirt, blue jeans and sandals. The elders on the knoll stopped their conversation and watched with interest.

A nervousness settled over Johnny. He felt antsy becoming the sudden focus of Seto's attention.

"Iloridaa enjekat," said Seto, grinning. Laughter erupted from the elders.

"What did he say," Johnny asked, aware the words had been directed at him.

"It's a reference to your jeans," said Brian. "It means 'Those who contain their farts.'"

Johnny looked back at the young man, who then barked a command in Swahili.

"Well, my friend," said Brian, "seems you've become a potential source of entertainment. He wants you to stand up."

A chill rushed up the back of Johnny's neck. With no small reluctance, he came to his feet, feeling diminutive in the presence of an exotic Maasai warrior standing two inches taller than his own six foot, one inch frame. Seto looked him over, thoughtfully, head to toe. He then reached out and took a hold of Johnny's collar, issuing another command.

"He wants you to take off the shirt," Brian translated.

Johnny looked at Brian meekly. "I'd rather not."

"I'm afraid he's expecting you to be a sport."

An anxiousness tightened Johnny's chest as he turned and looked into the dark eyes peering at him from the chalky white, raccoon-like paint. He glanced at those behind the tall warrior, their faces set in anticipation; then he hesitantly went for the buttons of his shirt. Handing it to Brian, he watched Seto's hands come forward and the long black fingers rake down over the hairs of his chest.

"He's intrigued by your chest hair," said Brian. "I'd explain the European influence in your genes, but I'd lose him in the translation."

Galvanized, Johnny stood stiffly as Seto stepped around him to survey his upper body. Then came the next command. Johnny noticed Brian had bowed his head and was rubbing his eyes.

"What did he say?" Johnny asked, growing jittery at Brian's reaction.

"He wants you to disrobe."

Johnny's jaw tightened. *Disrobe? Entirely! In front of all these people!*

"You're in an awkward position, my friend. But look at it this way: The Maasai aren't as stigmatized by nudity as we righteous Americans are. It's inconsequential to them. Be advised: Your new friend isn't inclined to take 'no' for an answer."

Incredulous, Johnny looked back at the impatient warrior.

"But ... " he stammered, feeling a creeping inevitability.

Seto grabbed the waistband of Johnny's jeans and gave it a firm yank, implying compliance with his demand.

Like the smaller boy bullied by the bigger boys in an alley, Johnny found himself unbuttoning and unzipping his jeans, in want of nothing more than to get this episode over with. Lightheaded, a breath of resolve flurried through his nose as he pushed the jeans down his legs. Nothing at all like the surreal humiliations imposed by Cassandra and her decadent retinues from the past, here he felt conspicuously and utterly exposed, like in that awful dream when one finds himself vulnerably naked in public. His jeans bunched around his ankles, he kneeled and pulled off his sandals and then stood upright and stepped out of the jeans. With the breeze tingling on his bare skin and gooseflesh racing across his forearms, he stood before a dozen pairs of eyes, nude, desperate for something to do with his hands.

Seto knelt for a closer look at his hairy legs, brushing over them with the palm of his hand. For Johnny, it had become intoxicating, his nostrils drawing air in large, audible volumes. His face flushed when the young warrior casually lifted his penis and then looked back at the others, displaying it so they could see that Johnny had been circumcised, which prompted nods of approval among the men. Seto then addressed one of the young women, who turned abruptly and hurried away.

The elders had fixed their attention on the tall black, now naked American visitor, obviously amused by Seto's toying with him. A small queue had formed around Seto, faces adorned with beads and tinted animal fat and lit with amused curiosity.

"What's going on, Brian?" Johnny asked pointedly.

"He seems to have taken a liking to you. He wants to see you dressed like a Maasai. Perhaps he feels a kinship of some kind."

Johnny closed his eyes and let out a sigh as Seto inspected and sniffed at him. Charged with a bewildering array of awkward sensations, Johnny's tense shoulders fell with submission. It was, after all, Africa, an adventure; and in this particular Maasai settlement, he was apparently destined to experience it as few tourists ever do. He stood resigned to whatever might happen, resolved to endure Seto's whims; even this affront, which was, all things considered, really no affront at all. He had already begun to mentally record memories of Africa, its land and its people, the sentiment of being included in a day in their lives. Why not this? Why not make the best of it before these many eyes and join the revelry of Maasai life? So no, he decided his imposed nudity was not a humiliation; rather a Maasai-style welcoming, and a way in which he might have yet another taste of his own heritage.

Seto drew him from the knoll with an outstretched hand. Johnny, still clinging to his composure, stepped forward, now exhilarated by his unsolicited interaction with a Maasai warrior. Those behind and around Seto had grown keen with interest in what might unfold between these two men. The tall warrior stood before him on the flatter ground in front of the knoll, grinning, his hands placed confidently upon his waist. He abruptly extended a leg and planted his right foot on the ground between himself and Johnny, pointing then at Johnny's right foot.

Johnny caught on to Seto's proposal. A contest of strength and balance. An immediate rush of adrenaline steeled through him. Instead of feeling intimidated by the young buck, the challenge came over him as an opportunity, even if Seto happened to be the stronger man. Seto extended his hand, his elbow cocked, his fingers upright and curled, inviting Johnny's grasp. Johnny stepped forward with his right foot. Now combatants, their feet planted side-by-side in the dirt, Johnny reached out and had his hand taken in a vise-like grip.

Both men tensed.

Though his sudden nudity had drawn hardly a glance, this contest grabbed widespread attention. Oblivious to the gathering crowd, Johnny braced himself with determination. With their hands locked together, they pulled and pushed at each other, more forcefully by degrees, their bodies contorted this way and that with increasingly precarious balance. Johnny's determination held fast. It would not be strength by which he would win, but wit, beginning by proving himself a little more than Seto had bargained for. The struggle intensified, Seto's eyes now gleaming with a bit less bravado.

Johnny suddenly feigned a near-fall, catching Seto off guard, and in that fleeting instant he pulled hard, bringing the surprised warrior onto his knees.

There were gasps among the crowd and quick murmurs of conversation and even some laughter from the older men. From his knees, Seto looked up at his foe and a magnanimous grin slowly formed on his lips. The gleam in his eyes took on a hint of admiration. He stood and laid his arm around Johnny's shoulders, nodding accolades and respect.

Elated, Johnny stood at Seto's side, at one with his victory and his close proximity to the one he had vanquished. From the warrior came odors forged in pursuit of hyenas, the grit and sweat of untold days in the brush, both sour and sweet, though not so very disagreeable as potent and masculine and laden with the pheromones of youth. Sweet was the honey beer tainting Seto's breath. Sour was the damp wafting from beneath the warrior's arm, draped admiringly around Johnny's shoulders, so close as to conquer the earthy smells of smoke and roasting meat and the countless human bodies sweating in the sun.

The young woman returned a few moments later. In her arms she had a red garment and beads and a gourd of liquid. Seto himself did the honor of draping the sheet-like cloth down over Johnny's head. Knotted at the shoulder and split down the side, it left one shoulder bare and flowed down just below Johnny's knees, billowing slightly on the westerly breeze. Seto lifted it from the bottom and wrapped a beaded belt around his waist. He fixed bracelets of silver and beads to Johnny's wrists and ankles. He tied a beaded necklace around Johnny's neck. He took the lid off a small, hand carved wooden box and took onto his finger a daub of chalky white paint, applying it in a series of stripes down the side of Johnny's face. Finally, from the gourd he poured a mixture of liquefied fat and ground ochre on Johnny's head, working it through his short hair with unhurried fingers.

Then Seto stepped back to admire his creation.

Palms up, Johnny stretched out his arms and looked down at himself. Seto's careful blandishments set his mind sailing. The onlookers witnessing his transformation stood smiling. Johnny turned to look at Brian, who sat looking back with tongue in cheek. The young woman produced a small mirror, which Johnny took and held before his face. His eyes set in a disbelieving gaze, it took a moment to recognize the man in the mirror as himself. A tingle went through him as a wispy breeze shifted the flowing garment and fluttered the fabric across his skin. He released a reverent sigh, not just fascinated by his transformation, but feeling quite nice. An aura of delight had descended over him, temporary though it might be, in that he was having fun; that opposed to leaving these citizens of Africa as strangers in passing, he had found himself embraced and befriended by them.

Seto turned to take a broad survey of the compound. Johnny's eyes swept from the breadth of his shoulders to the small of his back, where he had a fixed leather patch to his belt, another of many adornments. It was square in shape and beaded in a colorful design. Pulled tight to his skin by the belt, it rested in the concave of his back, just above the flare of his rump. Here, in response to the chanting women across the way, were muscles set in motion. Here, flawed by not so much as a blemish, the color of dark cocoa and glistening with imbedded particles of sand, were firm rounds of hairless flesh and long hairless legs giving rise to dance.

Seto danced a few steps forward and added his voice to the women's rhythmic chant, soon joined one-by-one by the other men around him. The mantra grew louder and contagiously gathered more and more voices across the compound. Perhaps heard for miles, the timeless chant filled the early afternoon with sound, repetitive as it was infectious, evolving into a collective refrain. Seemingly pressed on their souls by the ancient mysteries of Africa, the ceremonial sound surely resonated across the land as the mass of men and women began to lose themselves in the primordial rhythm. Up and down they went, then forward and back, all in unison with their gyrations and sway.

This is me, thought Johnny, enchanted as one with front-row seats at the Bolshoi, already caught up in the rhythm when he heard Brian's voice from behind.

"You're dressed to join them, my friend. Don't forfeit your one opportunity to dance with the Maasai."

Johnny studied the movement and listened to the chant a moment longer, falling in tentatively at first. Invigorated by their growing fervor and enticed by the infectious rhythm, he found himself in harmony with the crowd. Jump he did, as did the throngs around him, though not so high as the Maasai men, who sprung into the air like arrows shot from the earth. Then back he stepped in unison, then forward as part of the whole, until the throng tightened like one massive creature with many heads before stepping back again. It was a glorious natural high. Never before had he felt so alive, so enriched by human sound and movement and smell, so free of life's shackles and embraced by a people; and for at least in this blinking of an eye, his trials with Cassandra Mott were lost on the energy of a mesmeric mantra.

The day passed with feasting and song. There were no more encounters with Seto, as the young warrior's attentions had returned to the young women. How easily he set hearts aflutter, plying them with his displays of charisma and irresistible charm. *A natural showman*, thought Johnny, whose eyes found him often as he politicked and flirted during the course of the day.

During the late evening, Johnny sat down by himself on the knoll to watch the day's events draw to a close. Brian was across the way talking to an elder. The Olngesherr ceremony would continue the next day and conclude by day's end. He had danced and he had joined the chanting; now memories that left him feeling pleasantly mellow as he reminisced back over the day.

Distracting him from his thoughts, a girl approached. He realized it was the same girl that had stared at him when he first arrived in the settlement. She was staring at him again, and he wondered if his painted face and beads and ocher-tinted hair might have heightened her interest. She sat down on the knoll beside him and he stared back without restraint, her dark eyes reflecting the moonlight, her round face adorned with draping strands of beads. From her eyes came a communication any man from any part of the world could understand, and he found himself wondering what she looked like circumcised, finding that one tradition he couldn't abide. He smiled at her, remembering a time in his youth when she would have been impossible to resist. Then his gaze shifted wistfully from hers to the ground.

I have missed you, Johnny Feelwater.

Johnny shuddered and closed his eyes with a sense of dread.

Stunned, he looked up. There could be no doubt. He looked at her face in horror. She had issued the words from her mind as surely as moonlight glinted upon the moisture of her succulent lips. She reached out to stroke the side of his face, and he knew at once that he had not escaped the beautiful pair.

"Julian ..." he muttered, staring into the girl's eyes, aware Julian had displaced her consciousness with his own.

A long silence followed, during which time Johnny was drawn back into a world he had assumed was thousands of miles away. It was clear, they were his masters, they owned his soul. And another fear came over him when he noticed Brian walking toward them—his new friend could be in peril.

The girl got to her feet and walked away when Brian approached, leaving Johnny staring after her as if he had seen a ghost.

Brian studied him for a moment, and then turned to look at the girl. At a loss, he sat down beside his companion. An ill-omen settled over him as he pondered Johnny's grim expression.

"You've gotten quiet all of a sudden," said Brian, taking a handkerchief from his back pocket to blot the perspiration from Johnny's face.

"They're here," said Johnny, bowing his head, rubbing at the pounding in his temples.

"They?"

"I don't understand it," Johnny said, his tone stressed. "How did they find me here in Africa?"

"What are you saying, Johnny?"

Johnny looked at Brian as if he were pleading for help. "Cassandra is here. Julian just spoke to me through that girl."

Brian looked at the girl again. She had joined others her age, engaged in spirited conversation. Nothing about her appeared to be amiss. Brian thought it might be Johnny's imagination, that the excitement of the day had exhausted him and made him vulnerable to the tricks of a weary mind; though something about Johnny's certainty dismissed such wishful logic.

"Said he misses me," Johnny muttered.

Brian rubbed his chin in thought. Of course it was possible, given their supernatural power. He had been anxious to travel to Savannah, to see Cassandra and Julian Mott for himself, to study them, to better understand their extraordinary encounter with Johnny. Caught between exhilaration and foreboding, Brian looked at his forlorn friend. Was he to have his chance to observe them right here in Kenya?

"That feeling was in my hands this afternoon. I ignored it. Didn't seem possible they could find me in Africa."

Chapter 21

Brian stared at the ground a long while, wondering what to make of it. Then he got to his feet. "I'll be back shortly, Johnny. Just stay there."

He retrieved a bar of soap from his duffel bag and sought out Pakopai's wife for a pan of water. By the time he returned to the knoll, those from the neighboring settlements were spreading blankets on the ground across the compound, preparing for a night's sleep under the stars. Johnny was still somber. Brian set the pan and bar of soap beside him and took from his belt the towel that Pakopai's wife had given him and draped it over Johnny's shoulder.

"Thought you might want to wash up."

Johnny looked absently at the soap and water.

"I'm afraid I'm exhausted, my friend."

"Me too," said Johnny.

"That's good soap. You should have no trouble getting that dye out of your hair."

Their eyes met: Johnny's solemn; Brian's pensive and somewhat lost.

"You sure they're here?"

Johnny nodded.

"Should we expect to see them?"

"I don't know," Johnny answered, getting on his knees to wash his face over the pan of water.

"Want me to wait out here with you?"

"Nah, go ahead and turn in," said Johnny. He watched his companion turn and start for Pakopai's hut. "Brian," he called out. Brian looked back. "Thanks for the water and soap."

Brian eyes crinkled with a smile and then he took one more broad look around the compound before ducking inside the hut.

After Johnny washed and dried his hair, he blotted his face and looked around. He could see the numerous silhouettes of those already asleep on the ground. A mongrel dog approached and Johnny looked at it suspiciously.

"Julian?" he whispered quite seriously.

The dog cocked its head, and then wagged its' tail when Johnny sat back down and ventured his hand. The dog sat on its haunches and welcomed the head rub, absentminded as it was as Johnny gazed into the night. He looked down at the cape Seto had given him. The open seam on the side fell between his legs when he raised his knee, which exposed his right leg. He had never worn anything quite this sensual. He scanned the dozens of prone bodies on the ground, silhouetted by moonlight, still trying to fathom a lifetime wearing these kinds of clothes, tending cattle and fretting over hyenas and lions.

The dog inched forward and rested its chops on Johnny's leg. Kneading the soft skin on its neck, Johnny stared into the night, wondering where they were, wondering if they intended to show themselves, or involve him in some kind of carnal intrigue. All he could do was wait.

His mind drifted. He though of Marilee, this coupled with the image of Brian inside Pakopai's hut, lying naked on the soft hides. Perhaps he shouldn't have married her—he had known even then, on some level, what was inside. He would soon be home to face her, as a man in the grip of his own innermost fears, those yearnings he had refused to acknowledge since his emotionally conflicted days in school. Perhaps he should not have sought out a woman to grow old with, to build a home, to sit across from at dinner, to walk hand-in-hand with, his love on display, hiding his defective genes. Was it a gift or a curse, this duel sexuality, this attraction for one's own gender, this bittersweet agony that put his peace of mind and his marriage on a bed of thorns?

So where were they? Waiting for everyone to fall asleep? Why did they come to Kenya? Indeed, they were here. He felt their presence on his skin as surely as felt the cool night air. Johnny looked absently at the mongrel dog, at a loss as to how they had found him in such a remote place. Why had he not seen them yet? It had dampened his optimism that he and Brian could work as a covert team and find out why they would get personally involved with someone like him. If they could find him in the wilds of Africa, surely they could thwart any human endeavor to be rid of them.

Johnny got to his feet, took a few calming breaths of the dry night air, then trod dispiritedly to Pakopai's house. The moonlight lit the way. The loose fabric of the cape bushed his skin with each stride. The dog followed, pausing a few feet away when Johnny ducked through the doorway. Inside, soft flickering light from a small yellow flame in the center hearth danced on the shadowy walls. Pakopai and his family were asleep. Brian, sitting on the hides, his back against the wall, watched Johnny pull the red cape over his head and hang it on a wall hook.

"You were out there a long time," he spoke softly. "You okay?"

"I'm fine."

"Did you see them?"

"No."

"Hmm. Guess we'll see what happens. It's funny how this has turned out. I was thinking about it while you were outside. You've come to me for answers, and I've learned more from you about the entities than you'll ever learn from me."

"It doesn't matter," said Johnny. "Just having someone believe what I say has done me a world of good."

"I really think we can make some headway in Savannah. We'll find a way to deal with them. I have a good feeling about that. Cassandra's let you in and that's significant. I can't help but believe it can lead to wider understanding. I'm excited about it. I'd return with you if I didn't have such important commitments here the next three or four weeks. AIDS medication. A significant shipment. It's taken three years to arrange for it and I have to visit the stricken settlements to show them how it's administered."

"I understand," said Johnny, reclining, fixing his gaze on the ceiling.

"I see the soap did the job," said Brian. He reached over and drew his hand over the damp silkiness of Johnny's hair.

Johnny's jaw clenched. *Oh God, Brian. If you only knew what's gone through my mind today.* He had looked forward to this night, and dreaded it at the same time. He liked to look at Brian. He wanted to touch him and be touched, and breathe the smell of his skin. He wanted to be close.

Brian noticed Johnny's tight reaction. "I won't test your good will, my friend." He withdrew his hand.

Johnny turned his head and looked at him in the flickering light, sitting naked atop the cowhide like a king in his own private world, a fine feast waiting to be devoured, an image that got inside him like a kind of electricity. Johnny thought about their contrasting skin, and Brian being older, factors that seemed to intensify the stirrings within.

"Ah, what a day," Brian said casually. "Fine showing from Seto this afternoon. Can't say I've ever seen a finer male specimen. ...Hmm. All that perfection given over entirely to young girls. They'll never know how to truly savor it." Brian paused, as if he were drawing visual gratification from the image in his head. "Be nice to have him for a week on a deserted island."

Of the many things Johnny had been curious about during the course of the day, one of them came to mind. "Are there homosexual Maasai?"

"I've never pursued the matter," said Brian. "But I think it's safe to assume in any population, in any country, anywhere in the world, given a small population of men, you'll find a few attracted to each other. One in three."

Johnny looked at him with a smile. "One in three! Are you saying a full third of the male population is gay?"

"One third have admitted it, one third have denied it, and one third aren't sure. Perhaps they're the ones who see it both ways. As far as Maasai men are concerned, you and I weren't the only males looking at Seto today."

Johnny's eyes returned to the ceiling. *Little consolation for a man whose wife is waiting for him to come home.* His guilt was heightened, despite the religion and the empty years, by the fact that Marilee was his best friend.

"Listen to me, would you!" said Brian. "A middle-aged eccentric with a paunch, captivated by a young buck wearing beads and a red cape. A teacher, for God's sake! I should resign my honored position in Boston society."

"What they don't know won't hurt 'um, professor."

Brian smiled at Johnny's reassurance. "Thank you for that," he said, spontaneously reaching over to take Johnny's hand. His mood softened as he ran his thumb over the knuckles. "A remarkable contrast, don't you think? Our hands together like this." He turned Johnny's hand to look at the palm. "I've rarely seen such a troubled man as you, Mr. Feelwater. I'd like to hold you tonight."

Brian noticed his tense reaction. "Don't worry, my friend. I know you're married. I shall respect that as long as I draw a breath. I envy it actually. Rest assured I want no part of hurting a woman. The thing is ..." Brian looked down at the bedding in thought for a moment, and then looked back up. "Well, the thing is, here we are, two human beings starving for a well-suited friend. I see no harm in sharing the comfort of each other's arms. I would love to hold you tonight."

They were persuasive words and they quickened Johnny's heart. The sensitivity of Brian's fingers on his palm traveled the length of his arm and relaxed the muscles in his neck His breath was deeper and more pronounced.

At that moment nothing existed he could possibly want more than to be held by the man sitting beside him. The want was in his arms as powerfully as any hunger that ever tormented him, so desperately his soul needed nurturing. He had agonized over the lost opportunity the night before. Tonight he would not deny what he had contemplated all day, though the risk of being so close yielded unknowns that threatened to poison the thorns of his guilt. But yes, the world be damned—tonight he wanted to be held; and this he wanted to say, though his throat had become too dry and raspy to respond. It was in his eyes, his wet and passive gaze, the only reply his companion needed.

Brian moved closer and lied down and lifted his arm. Johnny shifted onto his side and inched his back up against Brian's chest, a subtle and quite harmless maneuver, yet a glaring declaration of his ambivalent sexuality. Perhaps it was a form of surrender, but the warmth between them melted into Johnny's body and made him feel safe. A sense of nirvana spread through him when Brian draped his arm over his shoulder and pulled him closer, and he lifted his knee so Brian's leg could settle between his. Now, with the rise and fall of a soft belly against the small of his back, and the warm breath on the nape of his neck, the day had come to an end and the night would pass with two men at peace with their intimacy.

The next few moments brought complete silence. The center fire diminished and the shadows grew darker around them. Both men drifted peacefully on the luxury of their closeness. For Johnny it was a moment to reflect, to recognize that it was a man's leg between his legs, a man's genitals pressed against his flesh, a feeling as agreeable as he had anticipated it would be. They lay quietly, contemplating the tingles on their skin and the harmony of two men with like minds, thoughts that drifted in pleasant increments into a realm of impossible dreams.

Johnny awoke during the night with a start. The nightmare had been all too real. He rubbed his eyes as if he were trying to abrade images from them. In the near pitch dark, the fire long cold, a movement caught his eye. He stared in into the void, thinking, hoping, that one of the young girls had gotten up for some reason. All at once, as if struck by noiseless lightening, the fire burst into a roaring blaze. His eyes widened in horror. Then he saw her. Not two feet from the angry flames, statuesque and radiant in the yellow light, her eyes fixed on him, stood Cassandra. Angelic in her summery cotton dress, it fell about her knees in floral pastels, the thin strings tied behind her neck seemed inadequate to support her breasts. As she stepped closer, the fire behind her died down to a gentle flame, and he stared as if he were caught in an unpredictable dream. She knelt at his side and his eyes shifted to her lips; upon them a delightful, empathetic smile.

He emerged from a muddle of languor and shock. His heart, having jumped to his throat, seemed to be calming. Why, he wondered, should he be surprised about this, when it had been so very predicable? Then he remembered, as the reality of Cassandra's visit settled in his mind, the others who were asleep in the house. Surely the sudden fire had disturbed them. He lifted his head and listened, staring in the direction of the other stalls. No one else was awake. Brian had rolled over and now lay peacefully asleep, his breath rasping through his nostrils.

"Don't be concerned, darlin'," said Cassandra, her voice as subtle as her hand coming aside his face. "Julian made sure no one in this charming little village will awaken tonight."

His head dropped back to the pelt he had rolled for a pillow. He felt pangs of anger—was there to be no part of his life to remain undisturbed? But the anger was short-lived, transformed into a sense of wonderment as his eyes drifted from the red swirling hair about her ears down over her exquisite form, for he loved her in the strangest of ways and no anger could flourish for long. He found nothing to say, certain the night's agenda had been predetermined.

She lowered the soft hide that covered his chest. "Have you enjoyed your trip to Africa so far, Johnny?" she asked, teasing his left nipple.

Their eyes met again.

"I've missed you. So has Julian."

He watched her eyes shift to Brian.

"Who's your friend?" she asked.

As if you don't already know. He had not tried to resist her will to hear this thought, and her smile led him to assume she had.

"Does he know about me, Johnny?" she asked, reaching behind her neck to untie the strings. She came to her feet and allowed the dress to fall from her shoulders, underneath which she wore nothing. Drawn like a child's eyes to candy, he stared at her creamy white body, an alluring and stark contrast to the flickering shadows behind her. She kicked aside his covering and lifted her foot to straddle him. Then she lowered herself, coming to rest upon her knees, and he felt her moist heat on his abdomen.

"Has he told you all about me, Johnny? Does he think he knows who we are?"

"How did you find me here?" Johnny asked, his voice slightly bleary with sleep as his mind faded into the sweet chills crawling across his skin.

"Why, Johnny! ... were you hiding from me?"

"No," he replied vaguely, like the word had been lost for a moment within the pleasures swelling in his mind. "I'm trying to understand you. To understand what you're doing to me."

"I'm making love to you, my beautiful black man. Look how lovely we are together."

He lifted his head and saw the soft rounds of her hips and her thighs widened over him and the feathery red flames of her pubic mound licking at his belly. Arching her back deftly, she inched back and ground her pubic bone onto his and his legs tightened beneath her. Then, unexpectedly, she reached over and ran her fingers through Brian's unruly hair.

"Look at him, sleeping like a baby. Tell me, Johnny, shall we allow him to wake up in the morning, or shall we have him sleep for a hundred years?"

"Don't hurt him, Cassandra," he said, swallowing hard. "Don't destroy my love for you."

"Oh, Johnny. I would never hurt him, not a man who comes here to help these people. Why, the rest of the world thinks he's a fool. Why would I hurt him? No one seriously believes what he's written in his book."

"You know who he is?"

"Did you miss me, Johnny?"

She leaned forward and her breasts swayed heavily before his face. He hungered for them instantly, for that gnawing they provoked had awakened in his stomach. She cupped them, as if weighing them with her hands; the nipples, dark red and swollen, beckoned with succulent peaks.

"Do you miss what I have to give, my lovely man?"

She squeezed one of them, from which squirt a thin stream of milky fluid, spattering Johnny's face and chest. Drawing his tongue across his lips as she leaned closer, his head lifted reflexively and his neck strained as the offering neared. Then his mouth engulfed the nipple. He took a hold of her arms, holding them firmly as he lapped at the nipple and drew tentatively from her at first. Then his thirst for her, disobedient and unrestrained, erupted in a storm of passion. His hands locked hard on her arms as he shivered with the first swallow; and he closed his eyes and drew her close, lost as he pressed his face into her breasts, and warmed as the milk traveled down to his belly. Gripped by the need for more, he sucked the nipple in earnest, emboldened by the silken nourishment flowing abundantly over his tongue, ravenous in his biting and sucking, her arms aching in his grasp, her nipples given over like helpless birds to a hungry cat.

"Harder, Johnny. Bite harder," she begged, her breast pressed to his face, the nipple swollen and sore from his unmerciful aggression. She gasped. Her head fell back. Her knees clamped hard against his ribs. She moaned and whimpered when he released an arm and grasped her breast. A ruthless grip, squeezing from it all it had to give, a pain so ravishing it set within her nether lips a sumptuous flow. Taken to the edge, Cassandra lifted her hips to allow his stiff penis to breach her wet folds, then felt its satisfying diameter push through.

Lost to everything but the here and now, her hips undulated and her pelvic muscle tightened—it was quickly much more than Johnny could stand. His neck grew taut. His face was streaked with rivulets of milk. His head twisted aside and his grip clamped hard on Cassandra's breast. She shrieked and squeezed her loins as he throbbed and spewed his pent-up fluids inside her. And then a pause: muscles spent, legs weakened, bodies filmed with sweat. Their breaths came in small, quick pants. Finally their eyes met. She wanly looked down at her breasts and lifted the one he had released, noting the red marks left by his fingers, the same marks she found a moment later impressed on her arm. Another smile formed, a gratified and subtle curling of her lips.

"You were hungry tonight," she said with her knowing smile, "weren't you, my lovely boy?" She examined the other breast and found bite marks on the creamy white skin near the nipple, and then ran her thumb over the severe impressions as if to savor the memory. The sore breast slipped from her hand and she looked at him again, then reached forward to touch his milk-sodden lips.

He felt dizzy, pleasantly so, like his body was floating some few inches above the hides. He closed his eyes, quivering, certain the sensation was brought on by a belly sated with her milk. An unbearable warmth spread through him and left a sense of well-being in its wake. His heart had quit pounding. His breath was no longer labored. He was comfortable with her weight resting on his hips, his penis still inside, her hands braced on his chest.

How could he want to be rid of her knowing the emptiness that would surely follow? How could he deny himself her unique form of sustenance? Did it matter if someone might be left behind, if someone were betrayed or forsaken, when this need for her sang from every fiber and the hunger she imposed was absolute?

His eyes opened tranquilly. "Where's Julian?"

Cassandra nodded toward the middle of the room. Johnny's head twisted in that direction. There, dressed in white linen on the far side of the fire, hands clasped behind his back, stood the most exquisite man on earth. What was he, really, that beautiful compilation of warm flesh and earthy smells now standing beyond the gentle flames? A man called Julian Mott, or some mysterious, omnipotent creature? But why would that matter, when the sweetest depths of his loins had been so thoroughly corrupted; when his buttocks tightened just by looking him, poised so beautifully in the form of a man, waiting patiently, wantonly, in the yellow glow of the small fire?

Cassandra reached for her dress and came to her feet. Julian stepped from behind the fire, reaching for the buttons on his shirt. It was off before he reached the bedside. Cassandra stood a long while in the entryway, looking down at Brian as she retied the strings behind her neck, her eyes narrow and her lips tight with unrestrained hostility. It sent a chill between Johnny's shoulder blades, though his thoughts and his gaze, just now, belonged to Julian.

The muscles of Julian's back flexed with redefined symmetry as he leaned to pull the slacks free of his feet. Disrobed, he stood beside the bed, looking down, his eyes gleaming with adoration and need. He read the fantasy that had formed in Johnny's mind.

"Oh, God ..." Johnny murmured, watching Julian's foot pass over his face and come down on the other side of his head. Staring up between Julian's legs, his metamorphosis began as the image came closer to his face. He had not expected Julian to straddle him this way; nor could he have anticipated the affect it would have on him. His eyes were alive with a whole new perspective as the damp male flesh settled like warm mist on his cheeks, lush with the smell of a man's most intimate body heat. His tongue feasted with a renewed and different kind of hunger, until Julian broke free and crawled to the end of the bed. He came up on his knees between Johnny's legs and lifted them to his shoulders.

Accompanied by pain came the first nudge. Johnny winced and took two fistfuls of cowhide, gritting his teeth as the walnut-sized glans pushed through. The pain tore through him like a fireball, an agony so complete, so rude, his fists twisted the hides. Oh the premium to be paid for giving over the hollows below his belly to a lover's desire. His jaw quivered through the pain as he squirmed for that euphoric relief when the agony mellows into bliss.

His legs taut, his toes pinched, the pain slowly abated. Johnny closed his eyes and his head rolled side-to-side as the pain evolved into pleasure. He felt a void as the cock slowly withdrew, leaving a shiver across his belly, and then Julian rammed into him again. Then again and again as he lay on his back like a passion-sopped whore, his legs willingly propped upon strong shoulders, his loins slippery with bowel secretions and semen. With the jarring his air came in gasps, the thrusts forceful and pounding, bringing on a voyage less baggage and all things worldly, the pain displaced by endless waves of pleasure. Emerging from his languid thoughts, the notion that he could live these next few moments and then die not wanting more, having experienced life's ultimate gratification.

At the point of no return, Julian's hard and fast rhythm ceased with a sense of immediacy. He withdrew and pressed himself hard against the back of Johnny's legs, taking his testicles in one hand, stretching them downward and grasped his pulsing cock with the other. Strings of semen fell over Johnny's chest and belly like hot wax, followed by the distinct odor that blossomed in the small space.

Johnny, his chest heaving, his body filmed with sweat, contemplated the ingrained motives that had weakened him with the essence of pleasure. At peace with his need to love and be loved by another man, he lifted his head and saw a man spent, just as any man would be. He saw the cock diminish and slip from his fingers as Julian shrank back on his haunches, head bowed and shoulders small. Could this fleeting moment of recovery be Julian's one moment of vulnerability, Johnny wondered, a moment in which he forfeited his powers, having exhausted himself within another man's loins? Perhaps, but it hardly mattered. Who would be foolish enough to test him, even now, as he slumped on his knees like a small boy that had been pushed down by a bully?

Johnny turned his gaze to the man sleeping beside him, not at all astonished that his companion had slept through it all, as did everyone else in the house; though Cassandra's scream might have, under other circumstances, awakened the dead. Such was the power of Julian Mott, which Johnny could not guess the extent; but he knew intuitively the consequences of challenging him were certain.

As he lay in a contented fog, Johnny's drifting thoughts turned philosophical. He wondered how the two of them came about. Not of God, certainly—the Almighty would not have placed such creatures among His human children to toy with and humiliate them. Their inception would have been rather more sinister than that. However many there might be, those like Julian and Cassandra must have assumed their matter in the fires of Hell and had found, at some point in time, a way to ascend and dwell among the unsuspecting souls on the face of the earth.

    He turned to look at Cassandra, who stood near the fire in the front room, peering at the two young girls sleeping soundly in the next stall. Johnny wondered what might be going through her mind—surely her world of debauchery did not include the likes of such youthful innocence, their immature bodies devoid of sensuous shadows and the perfumes of adulthood. Yet she peered at the two as they slept, her face set in wonderment. Did their youthfulness intrigue her, simply that? Did they remind her of being their age? That must be it. Perhaps she had lived too long as an adult and their youth reminded her of another form of beauty, one of optimism and boundless energy. Perhaps their chaste put her at a loss, something she could no longer comprehend; though who knew what went through her mind from her perspective of three thousand years? Besides, why bother with teenage girls when the world at large teemed with an abundance of far more corruptible adults?

    Lying wretched and sore, Johnny's thoughts began to fade. He rolled onto his side and drew up his knees, too weary to remain concerned over the unexpected visit. As he watched Brian's chest rise and fall in the dim light, his eyes fluttered, losing their focus on the man he had come to know and admire. Lost in soon forgotten dreams, he was unaware the beautiful pair had disappeared into the night.

    When dawn spilled first light through the entryway, Johnny awoke. He knew at once that none of it had been a dream. The pain resulting from Julian's fervor was real. He lay wondering, as he listened to Pakopai's family stirring about, what it was about Julian that so effectively neutralized his will, when all he had to do was say *no*. His arms and legs felt weak, his head seemed full of muck. Though events from the night before were clear in his mind, the state of mind he had fallen into was not. What came over him during the night, that had affected him like some kind of drug, that had allowed him to believe his purpose was Julian's pleasure. What had caused him to lap at Julian that way and lift his legs with abandon, whereas he had been able to resist the man sleeping beside him?

    Pakopai and the others had left the hut by the time Brian awoke. He coughed, then groaned, and finally lifted his head with bleary eyes and came up on an elbow. "Feel like I've been sleeping for a week," he grumbled, rubbing his eye with a fist. He sat up and pushed his arms into the air with an audible yawn that sounded like a bull elephant. He folded his legs and looked at Johnny, prone atop the cowhides, quiet and introspective. Brian's expression changed as he stared, from quizzical to concern.

His eyes raked over Johnny's chest. "I'm almost afraid to ask what that is all over you."

Johnny was relieved Brian was safe. He wearily lifted his head, winced, and looked down at his chest. He remembered feeling chilled during the night and realized he failed to cover himself before he dozed off.

Brian reached across the small space between them and ran his thumb across Johnny's cheek. "And it looks like you spilled something on your face."

Johnny reached up and felt the dried remnants of Cassandra's milk. He could still taste it in his mouth. It still warmed his belly, though he no longer felt its intoxicating effect.

"It's on your neck, too. What is it, man?"

Johnny looked at his befuddled friend with resignation, grateful that he happened to be with someone that would believe what had happened. Johnny swiped his hand across his face and held it out palm up. "Cassandra's breast milk. Guess I was a bit zealous with her last night." He looked down at his chest. "That's Julian's semen. He wanted me to see his climax. I figure that image will stay in my mind forever."

Brian stared dumbly. A mixture of alarm and confusion troubled his eyes. He leaned for a closer look at Johnny's torso, a tentative investigation before his eyes shifted back to Johnny's.

"Good lord ..." his astonished response.

"You're surprised they showed up last night? Well, I wasn't," Johnny stated flatly. "She has no intention of letting me go."

"Did you tell them you were coming to Kenya?"

"No."

"How did they ..." Brian stopped short of completing the question, suddenly overwhelmed by the magnitude of an event he had slept through. He stared at Johnny in bewilderment for a moment.

Johnny's eyes were fixed on the interwoven branches overhead, his face drawn and resigned.

"Why here? What did they want with you here?" Brian asked uneasily.

A sad half-smile reshaped Johnny's troubled expression. His head shook with irony, once again feeling alone in the world. "I can't expect you to understand," he muttered, turning toward his companion. "Even you, Brian. How can you or anyone understand why I fear the most exquisite pleasure a man can experience? But that's exactly it. Pleasure is her method of control, even here. Yesterday, I felt their presence, even before Julian spoke to me through that girl. They were here, waiting. When I woke up in the middle of the night, I saw them walking across the compound. Thought it was a dream, but it wasn't. I felt her presence in this hut before she ignited the fire. And then I saw her. From that moment nothing else mattered. I would've chosen what followed no matter the consequences."

"Her hypnotic effect on you is more powerful than I thought. That much is clear enough."

"It's like being high, except you're fully aware of who you are and what's going on. I think you're right about the peanuts in the foyer. They must be drugged. Cassandra's breast milk has the same effect, only more intense." Johnny paused to contemplate the emotional state they imposed. "You feel submissive. You have an overwhelming urge to please them. They make you feel safe and you want to be with them. Around them, you feel sensuous and always aroused. You want sex with them—not just traditional sex, but passion in any form. It's like everything you value has been sucked into an all consuming form of desperation." Johnny paused, rubbing his hands as he continued. "You know you aren't yourself, yet you believe it's who you really are. It's only after the drug wears off, when they release you, that you realize how destructive it is."

Brian had stared at him as all of this poured out. Then, at a complete loss, his gaze landed on a vague spot past his knees. Fifteen years of inquiry and research and he still felt like a novice. His heart bled for his new friend … the companion he held in his arms the night before which brought on a most luxurious sleep. He immediately longed to know more, to understand the extent of the entity's power and why Cassandra used it to manipulate Johnny's life.

But there was more to it than that. He wanted to come to terms with them, to befriend them, to ally them with the human race in harmony and in scientific quests yet to be imagined.

His eyes lifted.

"I shall drive into Nairobi and make some phone calls. I intend to find someone to finish what I have to do before I can leave Africa. Then you and I will return to Savannah together. Somehow we'll learn what there is to learn about our immortal friends. We can't make the world believe, but at least we can try. And we'll find a way to break your bondage."

Brian's burst of enthusiasm did little to lift Johnny's morale—in fact it troubled him. "I'm worried, Brian. I'm afraid of what she could do to you."

"You keep saying that."

"She knows who you are. The way she looked at you last night scared me."

Because of his published work, Brian was only slightly surprised Cassandra knew him. Concerned for other reasons, he pondered Johnny's unease, wondering, since he was a fairly light sleeper, why he had not awakened.

Johnny continued: "It was like she was trying to decide what to do with you."

"Ah," said Brian, making light of Johnny's foreboding, "Cassandra Mott knows I'm no threat to her."

"Damn you, Brian. How does she know that? For chrissake, you've written a book trying to expose her and her kind to the whole world. You say you intend to keep trying."

"Rest easy, my friend. I won't antagonize them, nor ask of them anything they don't wish to give, short of getting them to break their hold on you."

It was little more than a glimmer for Johnny, though it opened the dark closet that he had not yet spoken to Brian about, the secret fear that he was just beginning to understand; something that, if dwelled upon, made him feel the cold hand of insanity. Certainly he would give anything he owned to be free of his ache for Julian, yet not at all sure if he would then give even more to have the both of them back. He had pondered the day Cassandra would tire of him and cast him aside, leaving him a lifetime to yearn for her. It seemed entirely possible to grow empty and blind to everything but having her back, and having Julian just one more time. He could see losing Marilee, his career, even his will to eat. Even now, in the company of a trusted new friend and free of drugs or spells, he perceived his love for them, the kind of love a child feels for an invisible friend, invented to side with him against the world's challenges, which made the road Johnny must take a difficult choice.

He quietly looked at Brian for a moment, the one person who believed him, feeling the distinct aura of solidarity between them. It was a comfortable feeling. He thought of the long while he had lain awake with Brian's arm around him, how secure and sensuous it felt to be held by him. So why would it matter? Why would it really matter if he had rolled over and had come to know this lovely man in a more intimate way? Why did he not set himself free to make love with him, when he had given himself so freely to

Julian? Why would it matter, when, the night before and even now, he so wanted to?

Johnny released a sigh. They were damnable thoughts, wrought with confusion and conflict, for they were thoughts inevitably challenged by his love for Marilee. It seemed so unjust, as if he were all of a sudden doomed to forfeit something important one way or the other; and for the life of him, he could not understand why that kind of choice should befall a man trying to live with integrity. It wasn't the great distance that separated him from his wife that loosened his resolve, that allowed him to be tempted by the warmth of another man—it was the discovery of himself, that which was born in him, though long suppressed. He not could blame Cassandra for causing it, only causing him to recognize it. Such basic elements inherent in human nature could not have been induced by her potent milk.

Johnny rolled over on his belly. The morning air felt cool and exhilarating on his skin. Turning his head and laying his right cheek on the soft hide, his eyes again rested on Brian. His gaze drifted over a stout and handsome professor in deep thought, masculine beauty enhanced by the minor changes of age revealed by his nudity, the creases across his belly, the salty hair across his chest. Had Brian awakened with an appetite, were he to lean forward with so much as a breath upon his ear, Johnny knew he would not be able to resist. Yes, he was married, and though nary a soul would condone his thoughts, he was clearly affected by an attraction to this man; and it smoldered within him on this early morning. Whether Julian had planted the original seed, or whether it had accompanied him into this world, it made no difference now, for that resting in his eyes and nostrils lie aching in his arms and lips.

Not lost on the sedate radiance of Johnny's face, Brian's contemplation shifted back to the man lying like an ebony siren not two feet away on the tawny bedding. He reached out and his hand came down cautiously on the back of Johnny's leg. He felt the leg tense and saw a pair of dark eyes close, as if the man that saw through them was resigned to what might come next. It was an attraction Brian found irresistible that prompted this moment of weakness, in which he allowed his hand to slide up the back of his companion's leg, brushing lightly over the soft dark curls and setting his palm alive with tingles. Near the rise of Johnny's buttocks, his finger traced over the crease where the leg joined the body. It wasn't a big slice of chocolate cake that Brian wanted just then—he knew that was forbidden; but what harm could come from licking the bowl? His hand ventured up over one of the gluteal mounds, cautiously, caressingly, tempting as they were to one so predisposed, fleshy and firm and divided by that most tantalizing rift.

"A blind man would look at you this way."

"You're not blind," Johnny replied, nothing in his voice implying a reason to stop.

"All the same, it's a nice way to look." With a final squeeze, Brian removed his hand. Johnny winced, causing Brian some concern. His eyes shifted from Johnny's tight face to the fleshy mounds, and he came up on his knees.

"Lie still, my friend," said Brian. "I'll just have a quick look at you." Parting the gluteal cheeks for examination, he saw evidence of Julian's visit—the anus still slightly distended and tainted with bowel secretions and semen. He also saw a spot of blood. As a doctor, Brian never attached himself or his emotions to those he cared for, until now. Now he knew that even a professional man could be distracted from matters at hand when the right circumstances come together, when his hands find the texture and warmth of the right flesh, when his nostrils detect in a rising musk the right aphrodisia, when his eyes rest on a visual that steals him away from rational thought. Oh that small anomaly hidden within the crease; this one swollen and sore in the damp confines of dark flesh, hidden away from the eyes of the world but the one that would be this beautiful man's lover.

"You have a real mess down here." Brian released his hands and collected himself to address the issue. "Looks like Julian might have damaged you," he said, the assured resonance of his voice belying the flutters of distraction inside his head.

"It'll heal," Johnny stated matter-of-factly, believing Julian would have never left him seriously injured.

Brian reached for his backpack and took out a box of tissue and a small bottle of water. From his medical bag, he found a jar of salve. Hovering over Johnny on his knees, he parted his buttocks and gingerly wiped away the sticky mess before applying the salve.

"Roll over," said Brian, reaching for another tissue.

He wet it and wiped the dried milk from Johnny's face and neck. Johnny watched his hand move downward to blot away the semen from his chest and belly. Then his eyes shifted to Brian's rugged face, studying the intent creases across his forehead and the unruly brown hair streaked with gray and swept back. Brian tossed the tissue aside and looked at him.

"You look drugged," he said, pushing Johnny's left eyelid up with his thumb, looking closely into the eye. "You *are* drugged, my friend. Did you ingest anything besides her breast milk?"

"No."

"That's quite an effect it has on you. It's just one more thing, isn't it? She's lactiferous without the stimulation of a pregnancy. Incredible. I wonder if that's incidental, or if it fits the scheme of things. Either way, her milk is obviously quite potent. No doubt she has little trouble tempting you with it?"

"Her breasts are irresistible."

"Hmm. I can tell you what's irresistible, and rest assured it's not Cassandra Mott's breasts." Brian watched him for a moment, not sure what Johnny was looking at. "Is something wrong?"

"Your hair's sticking up on top."

Brian raked his fingers back through his long hair in thought. "You know, I don't sleep that soundly. I'm surprised their visit didn't wake me."

"World War III wouldn't have awakened you. Julian saw to that."

"I see. A drop of something on my lips maybe?"

"I don't know how he does it," said Johnny. "By force-of-will I imagine."

A silence passed as the two men collected their thoughts, having a long look at each other.

"Well, shit," said Brian. "Talk about irresistible. As tempting as you look right now, I guess I'll have to demonstrate how to ignore Cassandra's breasts by ignoring the suggestions passing through my mind right now." He sat back on his haunches and looked down at himself. "Look at this... an erection. Those don't come at the drop of a hat for me these days." Brian looked at his companion with playful suspicion. "I wonder what caused it."

Johnny's eyes drifted downward and he cracked a smile, feeling amiable for a number of reasons in Brian's company. They had joined on the same path; and though they may never consummate their mutual attraction, he thoroughly enjoyed the like-minded camaraderie. The closeness they had shared during the night had been wonderful. It actually had had a therapeutic affect and seemed to have restored his sanity. Though it kept them focused on what they could not have, he simply liked the banter and innuendo. In itself, it at least provided a kind of relief.

Looking at his endeared friend, Johnny remembered the way Cassandra looked at Brian during the night. That worried him. He fully believed, upon her whim, Julian would cosign Brian to the ice age. He reached for Brian's hand and then examined it, thinking it felt smooth and silky for a man that led such an adventurous life. A sun-bleached river of hair flowed down Brian's masculine forearm, forming a delta on the back of his hand. Veins protruded at the wrist. Turning the hand over, grazing his fingers lightly over the palm, Johnny felt at peace with their small intimacies, thinking he could spend the entire day naked with this magnificent man, looking at and touching him as he was now. But the day was meant to bring other diversions, so Johnny would wait for the night, when they could hold each other again.

"You probably just have to pee," said Johnny, nodding at the condition between Brian's muscular legs.

"You think I don't know the difference, my friend? What about yesterday, when the same thing happened while I was watching you dance? But that's my luck, isn't it? I have a hair-trigger with a certain man I've run across, and he's married."

Johnny looked back up at the interwoven limbs of the ceiling and exhaled through his nose.

"Well, enough schoolboy behavior for one morning. We best get ready for the day's events. Since Pakopai invited us as his honored guests, we're obligated to attend the entire ceremony. It'll end late this afternoon. Tomorrow, we'll take that walk into the hills to see Meramo. I think I'm about ready to ask him a few pointed questions. If there's enough daylight left when we get back, we can take my Jeep into Nairobi so I can make arrangements to leave Africa with you."

Johnny pondered their conversation about Meramo, the Kenyan entity that had lived five lifetimes or more.

"Be careful with that, Brian. If that boy watching over him is like Julian, he might take exception if he thinks the old man is being antagonized."

Brian didn't hear the warning. His mind was elsewhere. After a moment he looked at Johnny and knuckled his shoulder. "C'mon. It's time we go out and have breakfast."

Johnny came uncomfortably to his feet. He stretched his fists outward with a yawn, as the low ceiling permitted no stretching above a standing man's head. Thinking about Julian's eagerness the night before, he reached behind and drew his fingers up through his crack and had a look. His anus was sore, but no more blood. He planned to tell Julian to be more mindful of his phallic size.

Johnny stepped tentatively around the wall. Next to his shirt and jeans, hung the scarlet toga Seto had given him. He chose the toga, looking around in the dim light as he lifted it over his head. The primitive quarters, sparse by any definition, were quiet but for the skittish calves in their stall by the entrance. Brian stepped up behind him.

"You're limping. Evidently Julian is quite the stallion."

Johnny shrugged with a hapless smile. "A good metaphor there, Brian."

"You hungry?"

Johnny rested his hand on his belly. "Lord no."

Even this intrigued the professor. "Seems it takes an inordinate amount of time to digest her milk. You would have been done with cow's milk by now."

"That's okay," said Johnny, moving his hand behind his right hip. "I feel fine, except for that soreness back here."

"We'll keep an eye on that too, my friend."

The two men stepped out of the hut, the sheet-like cloth flowing down Johnny's lean body. He had become less inhibited when it shifted with his stride or if the breeze threatened to lift it. Stepping out into the compound, they saw the elders had already taken positions on the knoll and were smoking their long stem pipes. Brian spotted a slab of beef on a stone next to a fire and went for a slice of it before he and Johnny joined Pakopai and the others.

Chapter 22

The sun had brightened in the eastern sky by the time Johnny and Brian approached the knoll. Draped in red and stripped blankets, their tobacco pouches and wildebeest tail flyswatters at hand, the elders nodded as the two men took their earthen positions. Johnny drew his shoulders up with the good feel of the morning. The early haze, golden and dissipating in the sun, cast the day in a drowsy infancy. Lush with familiar cattle and human smells, the air lay pleasantly warm on his skin.

A kind of euphoria had settled over him, a feeling he was more conscious of than the calm he had felt the day before, and he wondered if it might be an aftereffect of his episode with Cassandra and Julian; or more likely, the aftereffect of sleeping in Brian's arms. He had thought about that quite a lot during the night, both before and after Cassandra's visit. The experience of being held by a man had affected him more than he had anticipated. Though he had convinced himself it was a harmless gesture between two men a long way from home, it produced a new wave of guilt nevertheless; different from undressing for Julian, different because he realized that sleeping so close to Brian would be more difficult, if not impossible to explain to Marilee. Yet he could not regret agreeing to it—he had to know. He had to know, at this point in his life, if sleeping that way with a man was the postscript of the music he heard every time he looked at Brian—and it was. It was as if those strong arms and the warmth of being in them had melted the poisons from his soul. And there was something about it vastly more intimate than his couplings with Julian, something subtle that he liked, something he was thinking about again ... until the activities around him finally drew his attention.

Scanning the compound, he spotted Seto across the way, engaged in what appeared to be some kind of spear-honing demonstration for the benefit of a small group of adolescent boys. Johnny smiled, wondering what it would be like to walk a mile in his sandals, to live one week of Seto's life just to know, for it seemed to him that the tall warrior, all of the Maasai for that matter, were first cousins to the breezes that swept the timeless savannahs of Kenya.

The newly appointed junior elders had gathered for the first proceedings. Each shared a drink of milk from a gourd, after which they were presented a finger ring. These were made from the hide of the bull slaughtered for the ceremony the day before. Johnny scanned the faces of the younger men looking on, many of them warriors growing tired of their abundant responsibilities, likely thinking of the day when they themselves would be honored this way. After the junior elders had their faces smeared with a white, chalk-like paint, the senior elders moved from the knoll to supervise the heating of the branding irons.

"This is an important part," Brian pointed out as he and Johnny watched the junior elders place individual branding irons in the fire. "When the irons are red hot, they'll be placed in that pool over there," he said, nodding at a three foot wide hole in the ground, embanked with six-inches of earth and filled with what looked like dirty water. "It's cow urine. The women bear the task of collecting it for this ceremony. The junior elders submerge their irons in it and then pass them through the rising vapors, thereby consecrating each individual brand. For the rest of his life, each man's cattle will be distinguished by the brand he establishes here today."

Sitting in casual observance of a remarkable people, his arms wrapped around his knees, Johnny watched with interest, mindful of the breeze wafting the loose fabric of his toga and the feel of fresh air between his legs. Watching seemed much like a daydream, these Africans and their rituals, their realm of color and texture free of plastic and steel. What was it like, he wondered, to worry over a lion feasting on one's calves, as opposed to, say, fretting the next mortgage payment? What was it like to patch one's roof with fresh manure as compared to being gouged by a contractor? Was it a simpler life, or really just the same—who could say without an ample taste of both? It just seemed to Johnny that life came predictably for these people, that they faced a far less likelihood of losing control of their circumstances. He thought about the many occasions, despite his country's nettlesome politics, that he had thanked his lucky stars to be an American. Now he wasn't so sure. Had he been born to a woman like those he was looking at now, walking about and doting on the newborns at their breasts; had he grown up in a Maasai settlement with his hair plaited and dyed red and became a warrior, hunting lions like Seto, all but naked in his red cape, he could imagine thanking his lucky stars for being born a Maasai.

By dinnertime, the effects of Cassandra's milk had left Johnny's mind and body, which made way for his thoughts to stay more focused on his life back home. He had spent the better part of the afternoon thinking about his wife, watching a young woman that looked a lot like Marilee. He smiled. The young woman seemed frazzled by chasing after her three year old, who seemed determined to get away from her. Though he could visualize himself holding a spear as a Maasai warrior, it was considerably more difficult to picture Marilee rubbing dyed animal fat in her hair, and wearing in public little more than beads and a skirt. It wasn't difficult, but impossible to picture her following cattle around with a gourd to collect urine for the Olngesherr ceremony, as many of the women here had done the day before.

So his temptation for Brian had morphed into guilt; and for the time being it made him less vulnerable to making the one mistake that would make him feel small in Marilee's eyes. It seemed a matter of defeating that part of his identity, of focusing on Brian as a friend and nothing more, a partner joined in a mutual quest to learn more about the immortal. Easier said than done, but much easier than losing the one thing that would bury him in grief—the woman he loved.

Johnny's attention shifted to Seto, who was being chased by a young girl with a switch as he swatted playfully at her legs with a leafy branch. Laughing and jumping from side-to-side to avoid being hit with the switch, he seemed to be leading her out of the compound.

"Looks like he's after a young one tonight," said Brian, propped on his elbows on the knoll beside Johnny. "She's not old enough to be circumcised," Brian added, sitting up. He and Johnny craned their necks to watch the pair, now exhausted, turn and walk toward the foothills south of the settlement. "Look at his friends," said Brian. "The chagrin on their faces. They're trying to figure out how he does it."

Brian looked at Johnny and smiled. "Quite a life, huh? Pursuing hyenas one day, young girls the next." He stretched his legs out and rubbed his thighs. "I've gotten a little stiff sitting here this long." He nodded across the compound. "Looks like the women have finished cooking the meat. You hungry yet?"

"Famished."

They joined the queue around a roasting carcass and received portions a few moments later, which they took outside the compound to the felled tree that overlooked the valley. Johnny had learned the Maasai held in contempt almost anything grown from the earth, though recent history had grudgingly given them over to ingesting a bit of cornmeal. Nevertheless, it was beef for dinner, again, which happened to be the first bite of food he had all day.

He ate gluttonously.

Brian watched Johnny pull off a mouthful of the charred beef with his teeth, aware, as he had been all day, that his affection for Johnny had reached a near critical heartfelt status. The last thing he expected was to run across this kind of situation in the wilds of Africa, but he had simply never liked anyone as well. Suffering the intuition that yields previews of what might be, he had come to realize he liked being with Johnny and looking at him, especially after their nightlong embrace had awakened emotions that he had forgotten about. He could not remember ever being so physically affected by a man. It threatened to become a difficulty. Beyond the chemistry that overwhelmed Brian's sensory awareness, was the whole of this man: the occasional puzzlement in his dark eyes, the boyish optimism that survived beneath an unwanted pile of tribulations, the sensitivity he often displayed, like the night before, when he took off the toga Seto had given him and ran his fingertips over the tightly woven fabric.

So what was it that his intuition had spliced into his thoughts? Not the winding down of life and spiraling alone into old age, but a rebirth of being a man, a rejuvenation, woven with companionship and intimacy and joy, and sharing the promise of two men at one with the future. The futility of finding himself in want of this paradise was maddening. By all that's holy, Johnny belonged to someone else; so all they could share was his victimization at the hand of Cassandra Mott. And here Brian felt, equal to his other emotions in many ways, a kind of fatherly instinct to protect him.

Their bellies full, they sat in silence on the trunk of the fallen tree, contemplating their circumstances, waiting out the few minutes until sunset. When the golden yellows and reds born in the western sky had darkened on the mountains across the valley, and the late afternoon breeze had hushed, they stood and strode side-by-side through the sparse grass back to the close confines of Pakopai's hut, ready to turn in for the night.

Brian lay on his back, his head propped upon the bundled pelts, his wire frame bifocals resting low on his nose, reading by the light of the candle. All was quiet in the house but for the stirring calves and an occasional popping ember from the dying fire and the nasal sounds of sleep from other parts of the house. Sitting on the soft cowhide next to Brian, legs folded, Johnny stared down at the bedding with a lingering thought. Having glanced two or three times at Brian, the words he wanted to express had taken a while to form.

"You took care of me this morning," Johnny finally said.

Brian looked at him over the top of his glasses. "What?"

"You cleaned me up. I wouldn't have expected you to do that. You knew I was vulnerable after what happened last night, yet you didn't take advantage of it."

"That was nothing."

"Well, it was to me. I know what you were thinking. I could tell by the way you touched me. I was thinking the same thing."

Brian stared at him for a moment. "I told you I'm trying to be noble."

Johnny rubbed at the corner of his eye with his finger. "It's just that ... well, on one hand, it seems like something that belongs to me, you know, something apart from my wife and shouldn't affect my marriage. It's like there's two of me in the same body, two different men. Then you think about it for a while and it seems like simple adultery."

"What seems like adultery?" Brian asked.

"It doesn't with Julian. Not really. That's drugs or some kind of witchery, even though it seems like I'm doing it by my own free will. I think ... no, I'm sure he causes me to feel that way."

"What're you getting at?"

Johnny looked at him, frustrated. "I'm trying to figure out how to say it."

"Just say it then."

"The thing is, it's hard to be here with you like this and ... you know, not let go."

Brian turned his head in thought. Setting his book aside, he sat up. "Well, my friend, we have quite a dilemma, don't we?"

"It's different with you than Julian. With you ... it's hard to explain, but it's more than just an urge to have sex." Johnny rubbed his brow, his frustration elevated. "I don't know how to deal with it. I'll tell you Brian, if I had known this was going to happen back then, I would've never asked her to marry me, no matter how much I wanted her. Now, on top of everything she's put up with, she's faced with my feelings toward you."

Brian nodded with a woeful smile. "*Betrayal* might be a better word than adultery, an equal cancer on the soul. To be honest with you, my friend, I'd give more than you can imagine to have you here as a single man. But you're not. You're married and you love your wife, and you're fighting a pair of supernatural beings that neither of us fully comprehend. I've joined your fight, in part because you want to save your marriage. I can't forget that."

"And now I'm up against the way I feel about you," Johnny said dismally.

"Yes. And so am I ... and that's a fight we both have to win. We'll just have to deal with it once we get to Savannah. Ignore it." Brian shook his head. "Look at me, a man who spits in the face of society and relishes it, acting like an adolescent coping with his first infatuation. Frankly, I wasn't ready to step into that kind of quicksand. But no matter how dearly I'd love to set the night on fire, I can't be part of something that would hurt a woman I don't even know." Brian paused in thought and then said: "You know, God's punishing me for my cynicism. He's sent you to show me what I might've had if I wasn't the cynical bastard I've become."

Ignoring that analysis, Johnny drew a deep breath and released a sigh. "Brian, what if..."

"Don't say it. We can be companions, even close companions ... no more than that." Brian's jaw tightened as he looked at him. "Now, lay on your stomach. I want to make sure you're not still bleeding before we go to sleep."

Johnny complied, parting his legs and allowing his muscles to relax as Brian leaned over him.

"You have a bowel movement today?" Brian asked.

"Yeah."

"Notice anything?"

"No blood if that's what you mean."

"That's good."

Johnny knew why Brian had interrupted him before he said the words, words that under different circumstances might have set them both on a path of discovery. Now the words were resting prominently in his thoughts, simmering, fueling the ache throughout his body, shadowing the waiting jaws of guilt. His forearms folded his beneath his chin, he felt Brian's thick fingers prying him open, a single finger rake over his anus. He closed his eyes, contemplating the possibility of loving two people at once, each capable of answering a distinct need, neither capable of both, an emotional quandary that loomed with greater risk and heartache than any threat posed by Cassandra and Julian Mott.

A small breeze wafted through the entryway, fluttering the small fire in the front room. Johnny turned his head toward the front entry, wondering why the Maasai didn't fix some kind of barrier over the doorway. What if a lion smelled the calves just inside the door, or a black mamba slithered into the room in the dead of night? He laughed to himself, paradoxically. Here, instead of bill collectors invading one's home on the telephone, it might be a snake on the kitchen floor. But then a man can kill a snake—he can't kill a cold voice that comes relentlessly over the phone. Nor can he kill the emotions that slither into his brain.

"Is it still tender?" asked Brian, pressing lightly on the tender skin.

"No," said Johnny, as if it didn't matter one way or another.

Brian shifted his weight. He reclined beside him, propped on his elbow. "No real damage down there. No swelling and no sign of blood."

Johnny nodded.

"You ready to go to sleep?"

"Yeah."

Craning his neck, Brian blew out the candle, leaving only the small flicker from the center hearth. Johnny turned onto his side and Brian scooted up close to his back. Lying close, fashioned spoon-like, they lay in a sort of anti-climatic desperation, two men prepared to deny their instincts, two men most aware of their commingled heat. But this much, at least, was necessary, this closeness; and though it came tinged with guilt, it also subdued their loneliness and nurtured a broader part of them. So now, complicated by the boundaries they could not cross, they faced an endeavor with the unknown, a quest to challenge the secrecy of the immortal and no way to predict the outcome. With no glimmer of light on the horizon, Johnny took on faith that surely the day would come when his life returned to normal.

Just now their close proximity was foremost on Johnny's mind. He looked down at the arm draped over his shoulder, at the hand resting on his chest. He felt the muscle of his back pressed against the muscle of Brian's chest, skin damp, slightly sweaty. He breathed the un-perfumed smell of a man's underarms, distinctly masculine—it set changes happening in his body. He felt a breath on the back of his neck, the leg between his own, the fleshiness of male genitals compressed against his butt cheeks—it made his breath more physical, more pronounced. So maybe the embrace was beyond the boundaries of moral righteousness. Maybe at the back of his mind it evoked images of Marilee, her usually luminous face contorted with disbelief and mortification. Side-effects didn't mean that he could deny that the warmth of Brian's body was, for a number of reasons, exactly what he needed

... even if the electrified tingles caused by skin touching skin produced temptation and nearly irresistible urges.

No, he would not reach down. Instead, he tucked his hand beneath the wadded cowhide pillow and closed his eyes with a final sigh and waited for the next round of unwanted dreams.

When the sun glowed in the eastern sky, Brian and Johnny awoke entwined. Neither wanted to break free. They lie together in a rather lethargic and dreamy state, contemplating a number of unspoken thoughts that had occupied their minds during the night.

"Seems Pakopai's brood starts the day a little earlier than we do," said Brian, Johnny's back up against his chest. His hand slid down to Johnny's belly. "This is nice, isn't it? I've been so preoccupied with my work these last few years, I've forgotten how nourishing it is to sleep with someone. You become hollow and don't even realize it." He took a deep breath of the back of Johnny's neck. "This won't be easy to give up." His hand slid lower, his fingertips felt a tickle of pubic hair. "I owe you, my friend, for causing this miserable state-of-affairs."

"Brian ... how will I face her when I get home?"

"There, you see ... she's thousands of miles from here and still your wife is in bed with us."

"What difference does it make?" Johnny looked down at the white arm hugging his ribs, at the white leg wedged between his, a sensuous swirl of ebony and ivory on the soft hides. "What's the difference in not letting go and wanting to so badly? It's too late to avoid guilt. I'm already there."

"I suppose we both are." Brian squeezed him affectionately. "Funny, all those years of searching, oblivious to what I should've been looking for." He sighed. "I don't know the answer, my friend. I do know there's something here a man shouldn't live without."

A parade of *what ifs* had kept Johnny awake during the night, tempted him to roll over and face his companion and touch his lips. Now he wanted to languish all morning in this luxurious entanglement and savor the moment. Added to a compliment of many things that attracted him to a man fifteen years his senior, Brian's wistfulness endeared Johnny further. There were many things indeed, besides his manliness, besides his sophistication and intellect, besides the masculine smells that wafted so lavishly from his body—there was this, the way it felt to be held by someone that sympathized and believed him. He knew intuitively Brian would be an all-consuming lover.

"They must have seen us sleeping like this," Johnny said haplessly. "They must think we're a couple of foreign oddballs."

"Probably," said Brian. His hand ached to move lower. "I was just thinking about the line we established. We're not crossing it with my lips so close to your neck, are we?"

"My back's to you. I can't see where your lips are."

"Can you feel them?" said Brian, lightly brushing the nape of his neck.

"Yes. And your breath, too."

"Is it?"

"Is it what?" Johnny felt his will to resist diminishing by degrees.

"Crossing the line?"

"No," said Johnny, his voice reflecting weakened sentiment.

"How about this?" whispered Brian, stroking the thick mat of hair a few intimate inches below Johnny's navel. His lips opened against Johnny's neck.

"Why does it have to be so complicated?" He turned his face upward, denying Brian's lips his ear. "Crossing the line? You've given me an erection. So what do you think?"

Brian stopped. He rolled onto his back and looked up at the ceiling, exasperated. "I'm a silly old fool. That's what I think. I make light of it while I'm letting myself get emotionally addicted to a married man."

"It just happened. Neither of us expected it. So we're not made of steel."

"No, but we are torturing ourselves. Maybe that long hike into the hills will zap some of this surplus energy we seem to have this morning."

"I like being with you like this, Brian."

"Enough of that, goddamn you!"

"Right or wrong, it feels natural."

Brian sat up. "C'mon, get your sweet ass out of bed. We've got an interesting old man to go see."

Johnny sat up and watched Brian step into the center room, a glimpse of flexing muscle, that tantalizing bounce and sway, then the quiver of firm butt cheeks. He let go an audible yawn and got to his feet, suddenly feeling a bit amused by the odd pair that he and Brian had become. Standing in front of the wall hooks, he watched his companion hopping on one foot while trying to stab the other into his khaki shorts. Johnny stepped around him and lifted the red toga from a hook, unable to resist wearing it another day.

"It never ceases to amaze me," said Brian, reaching for his shirt. "Can you imagine living your entire life in a hut like this?"

"I can't," said Johnny, scanning the small confines of the room, thinking about how much he loved his house in Savannah. "Bet there's no mortgage."

"No mortgage. That's funny. Two goats a month for thirty years."

After strapping on their sandals, they ducked under the doorway and squinted into a glare of sun. Pakopai's wife had left them a couple of strips of beef on the large stone next to the fire.

"First thing I plan to do when we get to Nairobi is eat a salad," said Brian, wiping his mouth on the back of his hand after the meal. He reached for a small twig on the ground and used it for a toothpick.

They got to their feet. The morning sun had grown warm. The breeze, what few wisps there were, came like whispers out of the hills. The breeze fluttered Johnny's red cape, which caught Brian's eye and provided a distracting glimpse of dark skin. He thought about their confessions the night before. Despite the long day before them and all they planned to do, the cape promised to trump all manner of rational thought. Even now he was thinking about having year or so on a secluded beach with this beautiful man, with all of his eccentricities in tact, and those boyish, inquisitive eyes. He caught himself staring again, at the contours beneath the cape, visualizing that lean black body stretched out on white sand. Yes, at least a year, investing heart and soul in an intimate relationship with him, lost in a calendar of endless days.

"Damn you!" Brian muttered under his breath, scanning the compound, oblivious to the Maasai going about the business of a new day, but seeing his future.

The tropical island disappeared. Instead, he saw a small room, a man lying on the bed, thinking about the one thing he could not have. He saw himself having dinner with Johnny and the woman he would soon meet, looking at them, envious, lonely, facing forever what could not be. Instead of warm southern nights together, the two of them would be exploring the revelations Johnny had brought to Africa, those intrigues imposed by Cassandra and Julian Mott. Would that not be enough? Could he not submerge himself in that unknown world and relish the process of discovery? Especially now that he had a real chance to find out who or what they are and what their purpose might be? Of course he could work with this married man in Savannah, this would-be lover, this magnificent man wearing a revealing cotton robe. He could ignore these urges and endure a simple working relationship. Why not? After all, why should a cynical, middle-aged man be rewarded with life's most precious gift?

Pakopai's approach brought Brian back to matters-at-hand. Wearing his importance well, the elder offered a greeting, wildebeest tail flung over his shoulder, staff in hand, his weathered face fixed with a smile as he glanced over Johnny's cape. Brian bid him good day in Swahili.

"We're going into the hills to see the old man," Brian said to him as Johnny curiously glanced between them.

Pakopai nodded thoughtfully.

"How old is he, do you know, Pakopai?"

"Very old. Very wise," said the elder.

"The boy who cares for the old man. Do you know the boy's age?"

Pakopai thought for a moment, and then said: "The boy never ages. He was there when I was a young warrior, just as he is today."

Brian looked at Johnny as if he had just heard an ill omen. When he translated Pakopai's words, Johnny realized at once that the boy was like Julian.

Brian went on to express gratitude for Pakopai's hospitality, at which time the elder turned and walked away. Brian turned to Johnny.

"Settles the question about the boy, doesn't it?"

Johnny was staring after Pakopai. "So it seems."

"I have a couple of canteens in my Jeep," said Brian. "We'll carry 'um along. You ready to get started?"

Johnny nodded and then turned and scanned the hills they planned to set off into. Brian had described a rather arduous four-hour hike the day before, first across a rugged landscape of hills and rock, and then down into and across a valley. He wondered what they would learn from the old man, and he feared Brian's exuberance. The nature of the *pointed* questions Brian intended to ask worried him. The boy was surely the old man's protector, from the same family of creatures as Julian, and therefore dangerous.

Chapter 23

They started into the hills south of the Maasai settlement. The morning sun was making its slow rise into the sky. Sandals firmly tied, they trod over a crusty earth scattered with rock and dull green grasses, a constant ascent. They walked silently side-by-side up broad slopes, one behind the other through narrow trails and ravines, two men venturing into the unsettled and varying terrain of Kenya, contemplating their challenges and united by supernatural mysteries unknown by the rest of mankind. The desolation reflected their loneliness, in that they were alone in facing these mysteries. And their thoughts ran concurrently, though their broad visual sweeps across the African panorama remained silent. The pangs of a forbidden mutual attraction would time and again override the day's business. Even here, far away from the eyes of the world, the ogre of betrayal stood between them.

They entered steeper hills and followed narrow animal trails through low scrub and increasingly rockier terrain. Brian had been thinking about Cassandra's visit.

"You weren't surprised when Cassandra showed up, were you?" he said after nearly an hour's silence.

Watching the uneven ground before his feet, Johnny considered Brian's question. "No," he said. "I *was* surprised she knew about you. That still bothers me."

"It shouldn't," Brian said over his shoulder.

"Isn't it obvious, Brian? They want to live anonymously. You're the one man who threatens to expose them."

"Ha! Does the mouse threaten the lion?"

"Hope you don't learn the hard way how powerful they are." Brian didn't reply. "I'm serious," Johnny insisted, looking at the back of his head, wondering if his bluster was meant to hide fear. He wanted to scream. He had hoped this trip would provide answers. Until now, Brian had only managed to complicate his life further. And today he intended to prod one of them with questions—why not poke a sleeping bear with a stick? Yes, scream, and this was a good place to let it out—just tell the whole world to *get fucked.*

"I know you're serious," said Brian. The sinews of his muscled legs stretched as he stepped up to cross over a rock embankment, his sweat-stained khaki shorts clinging, desperately needing a wash, his shirt unbuttoned and hanging open. "But if she knows me, she also knows no one believes a word I say, whether I write books or shout it from the rooftops. Most of my colleagues think I'm an asshole gone bonkers. Those who still think I'm sane, believe I'm an asshole with an over active imagination."

"They're wrong," said Johnny. "You're just an asshole."

"An adorable asshole, wouldn't you say, my friend?"

Johnny was thinking about how Cassandra had stared at Brian as he slept the night before last. It still bothered him. What was she contemplating? What will she do if Brian becomes too aggressive with his investigation?

"Just don't get confrontational with this old man. That's all I ask."

"You're fretting over nothing, my friend," Brian said, gingerly climbing the loose footing of a stair-like trail. "I may be an asshole, but I'm no fool. I promise you, even if we learn everything there is to know about them, no one will believe a word of it. But just think—what if we can find a way to befriend them? Get them to join the fraternity of man. Imagine the science that could be resolved with their power and knowledge. Let your imagination expand on that, Mr. Feelwater. Think of what could come of it."

They walked another hundred yards in silence. Johnny's apprehension tightened its grip. Not so much a premonition that something was going to happen to Brian as a viable possibility—he seemed much too cavalier.

"The boy we're going to see. We know he's like Julian. He'll protect the one he looks after. He's capable of killing us. We'll be out here with him in the middle of nowhere."

On the other side of the embankment, they walked up on a group of vultures tearing away at a carcass. The huge birds seemed angered by the intrusion, lifting themselves into the air with their great wings and landing some few feet away, determined to stay close to the kill. They watched and fluttered as Brian and Johnny passed, the carcass indistinguishable, its torn meat glistening and dirty in the sun.

Brian had barely noticed the scene, preoccupied with Julian and the boy. "Our most pressing question." A thought spoken out loud. "They exist in human form, paired with immortals like Cassandra and Meramo. Who are they? What are they? Why do they interact and seek pleasure from us? Why are they subservient to less powerful entities?"

"I still think Julian is demonic." Johnny replied. "A descendant or an extension of Satan in some way."

Brian stopped and turned and looked at him.

"Why not?" Johnny insisted. "If Satan exists, it doesn't mean he has a pitchfork and tail. Julian's dick writhes like a snake, for God's sake! That was enough to convince me." Brian's doubtful expression exasperated him. "Don't you think the devil or his descendants could exist in human form? What else explains Julian's power? I think he's capable of anything."

"To take hold of that theory, you have to start by believing in Satan. Then you have to abandon conventional wisdom. Theology tells us Satan is evil. Neither of us believe Julian is." Brian had detected Johnny's sincerity about this subject. He stopped short of totally discrediting the premise.

"I used the word *Satan* for context," Johnny argued. "Not necessarily in a literal sense. A creature of that nature." Frustrated, Johnny absently scanned the knee-high scrub around them before he looked back at Brian. "No, Julian's not evil. I'll never forget he stayed with me that night I was gang-raped. He stayed to watch over me. He was gentle. Seemed like he disagreed with Cassandra's notion to take me there."

"That was the morning he communicated with you?"

"Yeah." Johnny swallowed with a tight throat.

Brian tilted his head and squinted at him. "Why are you so tense?"

"Figuring out what they are. I don't know ... sometimes it drives me crazy. I was thinking about it the other day. It occurred to me that beings like Julian might be the basis for our modern-day concept of Satan. Isn't it possible that two, three thousand years ago, whenever, someone encountered a being like Julian, maybe even Julian himself? What if that person got a demonstration of his power? Or what if the entity had taken an interest in an entire village? The people were scared and confused. They invented the concept of the devil to explain what had confronted them. Then the concept evolved over the centuries into our present day idea of Satan? Doesn't that seem possible to you?"

"Of course that's possible," said Brian, in thought, rubbing his grizzled jaw with the back of his hand, thinking about the present day Julian and Johnny's personal interaction with him. "That night he stayed to look after you. Obviously he feels a kinship of some kind. Maybe you could establish a deeper communication with him. Gain his trust or sympathy perhaps, whatever's necessary to get him to explain more about his kind and his association with Cassandra."

"We'd have a better chance of talking those vultures back there into giving up that carcass." Johnny was thinking about that morning he woke up naked on the pool table, of how caring Julian had been. He also remembered how Julian's final directive struck him as ominous. "We can't toy with them like that. They would know. It was clear that morning. Any future attempt to learn more about them would be unwelcome. He specifically told me to quit asking questions. I'll tell you, Brian, he has a way of making a believer of you."

"You're right, obviously. Rest assured, my friend, I'll be careful today. Even though they don't appear to be evil, you've convinced me they may be dangerous."

They resumed the climb. After another hour's walk, they topped the last of the hills and paused for a moment to look out over a broad, rock-strewn valley. Perhaps two miles across, the land lay before them gouged and jagged from untold millenniums of flash floods and wind, like an enormously wide ravine.

From their high post, they began the descent on a winding and rutted trail, at times so steep the laws of gravity quickened their pace. The morning sun that had felt good on their skin had grown hot. Brian's under-sleeves were damp and Johnny's toga clung to his perspiring skin. Buzzing flies lit annoyingly on their arms and faces. The great silence, disturbed by only their footfall on the crusty earth and the buzzing flies, seemed to amplify their thoughts. Stepping cautiously with poor footing, both slipping now and then on loose gravel and sand, they continued the descent as the fickle trail veered in zigzag directions. Following a few feet behind Brian, glancing at him from time to time, Johnny found himself at wit's end. It was like all of his tribulations had caught up with him at once. He had been thinking about his return home, facing Marilee with a growing list of secrets, when he slipped and nearly fell, which was all it took to set off an outburst of resentment.

"Goddammit!" he blurted, plopping down on a large rock.

A few paces ahead, Brian stopped and turned and looked at him. "What's bothering you this morning?"

The constant rage moldering in Johnny's vitals had fed on his conflicting thoughts, erupting in a verbal fireball aimed at Brian. "*You* for one thing. What is it with you anyway? Why can't I get you out of my head?

Why can't I quit thinking about sleeping with you? I'm looking at my watch every ten minutes to see how long it is to nightfall, so we can be close again. You're not even that handsome, for God's sake!"

"You're no Michael Jordan yourself, my friend," Brian shot back.

"Dammit," he seethed, coming around to realize his outburst had been irrational. "That's not what I meant. I know I'm no Michael Jordan."

"So what are you upset about? That you like sleeping with unattractive men?"

"I said I didn't mean that. You *are* attractive ... to me anyway. I just don't understand why this happened to me, after nine years of marriage." Johnny looked out across the valley, squinting in the sun, his forehead creased with unease. He shook his head in frustration. "I didn't come to Africa to confirm I'm gay. I don't want to be gay. I don't want to face my wife when she finds out. I just wanted to find out who those creatures are, and what they're doing to me, and why. I want to know why I woke up one morning and my whole life was fucked up."

Brian studied him for a moment, and then took the few steps to sit down beside him. "I know what part of your problem is," he said. "You've spent your whole life caught up in a world of clutter: credit cards, cell phones, owning the biggest SUV on the block. You've been immersed in a populace whose misguided values revolve around status and political correctness and belligerent moral intolerance, all of which displaces the purities of the mind and soul that make us human. Quite a contrast, I should think, to what you've experienced living among the Maasai these last couple of days. Give *them* a shiny new SUV and they're likely to see how many warriors it takes to turn it over."

Johnny's tight lips hinted a smile. Then he said: "I'm talking about you, and me, not our fucked-up society back home."

"Ah, yes. You and me. Think I have that figured out, too. Tell me, have you ever known a masculine gay man, personally known one. A guy you'd never assume was gay?"

"No."

"Until you met me."

Johnny nodded, staring at him directly.

"I'm not surprised. You made a defensive comment yesterday about a couple of gay men you know. I got the impression you were insisting you're not like them. You said they act more like women than men. Could be the root of the problem you're having with this. You're not effeminate and you don't want to be associated with effeminate men. Not because you dislike them. Not because they disgust you. You just don't want to be like them. So you suppressed your sexuality early on because you linked gayness with that kind of man. Then along comes our immortal friend, Julian. He makes you face what you've always known.

"Then another bomb explodes in your face—you travel to Africa and happen upon a man who's attracted to you. No big deal he's rather unappealing, he's as macho as they come, and that makes real what clicked inside you with Julian. With him, you could pretend it wasn't real. With me there's no pretending. We happen to be two men who find comfort in each other's arms. It made you realize you could express who you are without feeling effeminate. For whatever reason you're attracted to me, it forced you to face your sexuality."

"It's not who I am. You forget, I'm married and I love my wife."

"Of course, how convenient for a man attracted to both sexes to marry a lovely lady in an attempt to deny his bisexuality." Now Brian had become frustrated. "Rest assured, I haven't forgotten you're married, nor can I."

"That's not why I married her," Johnny protested, his anger melting into confusion. "I'm not using her."

"Not consciously anyway. No doubt you love her. No doubt she's your best friend. But she's also your unintentional victim, and I wish to God I had some kind of an answer to resolve that."

"So if I'm bisexual ..."

"If?" Brian interrupted.

"Okay, if you have to hear me say it, I will. I am bisexual. I know I'm attracted to other men ... to you. So what should I have done? I loved Marilee then and I love her now. Should I have ignored how I felt? Then spend the rest of my life trying to figure it out?"

"Wish I knew. No need to feel guilty about marrying Marilee, though. I don't think you recognized your bisexuality back then. The thing is, you *are* married, and there's no morally appropriate way deal with this other thing your body is telling you."

Johnny turned and gazed solemnly across the valley they had yet to cross. "That's just it, Brian. Does it matter if it's morally appropriate? I was thinking last night, about you and me. It seems ..."

"You don't have to say it," Brian interrupted. "I know what you're thinking." He paused, smiling as he glanced over the red toga billowing on the steadier breeze of the higher altitude, wondering, since Johnny had become so attached to it, if he planned to wear it for the duration. He continued: "You're thinking a secret affair is the only solution, and maybe it is. I know how it feels, those urges crawling through you like the sweetest kind of poetry. It would be a perfect scenario—for you. But for me? It'd leave me sharing someone I want all to myself." The front apron of cloth settled between Johnny's legs, exposing his ribs and flank. Brian's eyes, always thirsty, paused for a drink. A feeling of being plunged into warm water came over him.

An affair, he thought, appraising the sweep of dark knotted hairs across Johnny's thigh. Does a starving man decline dessert just because he's denied dinner? "Dammit, man, you aren't the only one racked with complications. We're both brimming with them and they're distracting us from matters at hand. Get up," he said, standing and extending his hand. "We have a couple more miles to go before you meet your next entity."

They made their way down the hillside and on across the barren and rocky valley, toward a range of high sandstone cliffs. There, Brian found a trail that zigzagged back into the higher elevations, all rock and sparse, desert-like flora. A plodding labor, the steep trail wound endlessly up through the unstable rock. Now and then stretches of it narrowed much too close to perilous drop-offs. They stopped for a drink of water and to steady their nerves, having just traversed a one-yard wide ledge jutting from a wall of rock, which fell away in a sheer hundred-foot drop.

"I dreamed about that ledge for a month the first time I crossed it," said Brian, craning his neck to peer over the edge. "More like a reoccurring nightmare." He turned his head upward. "Meramo is isolated here. He gets a fair number of visitors, but as you might guess, they usually have a very good reason to make this climb. He speaks English, by the way."

At the moment, Johnny was more concerned about the dangerous trail. "Any more sections like that?"

"The worst is behind us, my friend."

Thirty minutes later they reached their destination, a small plateau nestled against a wall of sandstone. Johnny likened it to living like eagles. The view provided a breathtaking panorama, across the valley and foothills to the hues and haze of distant mountains. A wind, like feathers tickling their faces, swept the plateau in gusts and howled through the higher cliffs above. The sun's glare set their eyes in a perpetual squint. A cave gouged in the sandstone yawed at the base of the wall. There, upon a large boulder like a primitive monk, sat Meramo.

Much like the preconceived image that had formed in Johnny's mind, Meramo was indeed an old man, though the true extent of his years would be impossible to guess. He sat on the rock wearing an ochre blanket. A walking stick leaned an arm's length away. His age showed mostly in his frailty, his temples shrunken and veined, his nose a humped prominence centered on his face, his earlobes, as if tugged at by gravity for decades, hung flaccidly with unadorned gaping holes. The skin of his bald-head seemed leathery, stretched tight over his skull and wrinkle free but for the horizontal furrows above his brow. He sat with an aura of mystery and wisdom, looking calmly at his sudden visitors with a pleasant gleam in his eyes. He greeted them with a nod.

Johnny's attention very quickly shifted to the far side of the landing. Some twenty feet from Meramo, near the edge of the landing where the mountain fell away in a bottomless plunge, was the boy. He was positioned on his hands and knees, stretching and staking out a zebra hide in the sun. With a sharp twist of his head, he fixed his eyes on Brian and Johnny the instant they appeared.

Johnny's first reaction: a momentary lapse of precaution. He simply stared. So youthful and lithe, so sensual his bent over form, so seemingly harmless was this naked boy, the image irresistibly fixed Johnny's gaze. Flawless bronze-tinted black skin, a teasing of underarm and pubic hair— the boy's adolescence glistened radiantly in the sun. Though his face and small shoulders retained a boyish quality, his genitals dropped with sexual maturity between long thin hairless legs. Johnny assumed his physical age to be just slightly past the last stage of puberty, though beneath his shaved head and astute brow, something within his eyes suggested an intellect far beyond his apparent years. Recognizing this, Johnny's wonderment lapsed into renewed and very real apprehension.

More accustomed to Maasai elders coming for Meramo's advice, the boy's interest in the sudden intrusion was visibly acute. He came up on his knees and sat back on his calves, his eyes lit with quick recognition of the white man known as Brian Fowler. Then his eyes shifted to Johnny, a man he had never seen before, a black man that looked somewhat out of place in the unconfined simplicity of flowing red cloth.

Brian paused for a moment to catch his breath after the climb. He then stepped forward to greet Meramo, who nodded and invited him to sit on the ground. Brian complied. Johnny joined his companion, sitting and folding his legs beneath the drape of the toga, his eyes still prone to fleeting glimpses of the boy. Only when the boy resumed his work on the Zebra hide, did Johnny's attention shift entirely to Meramo.

It seemed surreal to Johnny, this odd pair existing on a gritty, hot and gusty pinnacle, exiled one lifetime upon another and content with the vast emptiness surrounding them; when they could live anywhere in the world in endless luxury. What could be the motivation, he wondered, for such a bleak existence? Quite incredible they could find life's rewards solely by way of each other.

Brian began by telling Meramo about the large shipment of antiviral medications on its way to Kenya, which would be distributed to those villages and settlements most affected by AIDS. He told Meramo of their plans to educate people about protecting themselves from the disease, that he and his fellow doctors wanted to make the people of Kenya understand that there need be no stigma attached to the disease, which happened to be the biggest hurdle in reaching those stricken. To all of this Meramo listened with interest. He seemed saddened by the fact that so many Kenyans were suffering and dying from mankind's latest blight.

Meramo's eyes shifted to Johnny when Brian introduced him. Growing a bit anxious, Johnny suspected this detour in the conversation might be where Brian planned to venture those *few pointed questions* that he had come here so anxious to ask.

"He came all the way from America," Brian said, turning to look at Johnny, who sat fidgeting just beside him.

Meramo nodded, as if he not only understood the great distance, but that he also had a degree of knowledge about America.

Rubbing his left arm, Brian continued. "Meramo ... Johnny's had someone come into his life, a lady living in the body of a twenty-five year old woman, though she's very old. Cassandra Mott."

The boy's head twisted again. He bore an expression of heightened concern, an expression that strongly suggested a distinct awareness of the brother and sister Mott.

Brian plowed on, heedless of Johnny's earlier warnings. "We know she's lived many lives. We think she's been around for three thousand years or more. A young man called Julian, presumably her younger brother, lives with her. Do you know of these two, Meramo?"

The old man's eyes drifted back to Brian. The gleam within them reflected intrigue with the course of the conversation. Now alert, the boy got to his feet, perhaps anticipating a summons from the old man. Meramo glanced at him and then raised his hand, as if to let him know that everything was well in hand. Meramo remained silent, his contemplative eyes fixed on Brian. The silence stretched into awkwardness as Brian and the old man looked at one another. Johnny sensed danger. His hands had tightened and he was rubbing the knuckles of one with a thumb, watching for a sudden mood change in either of their hosts. Brian was taking far too much risk.

"I've come seeking your council, Meramo. Please enlighten us. Do you know of Cassandra Mott?"

A moment later the gleam returned to Meramo's eyes. He smiled and said: "You have affection for this man who came with you today?"

This tact distracted Brian, as if he had expected to hear one thing, but heard another. Johnny was all too familiar with their methods. Any question they wished to avoid was simply ignored. Brian glanced at Johnny, and then his gaze drifted to the ground as he regrouped his thoughts. Glancing discreetly between Meramo and the boy, Johnny wanted to tell him to back off, lest they find themselves seeking a crevice in the form of toads.

"Yes," said Brian, looking back at Meramo. "I do have affection for him. He's my friend. He wishes to understand the mystification Cassandra has imposed on him. We come to you for your help."

Meramo looked again at Johnny. A sadness came into his eyes, as if he saw something unsettling. Already, Brian's audacity had gotten everything into the open. Johnny's heart quickened as the boy approached him and Brian, his long fluid legs moving him forward with the grace of a dancer. The boy stopped directly in front of Brian, looking down upon him, scrutinizing him, staring into his eyes as if Brian's thoughts were spilling from his pupils in revealing torrents.

It felt like time standing still, a long silence deafening in the wind. Were they pondering the issue of Cassandra Mott, intending to help; or were they sizing up their visitors as threats which must be dealt with? Johnny's shoulders shuttered with dread. Had he and Brian not imposed themselves on Meramo's private realm? Had they not trespassed in want of knowledge that Meramo would likely find intolerable? Why should he and his mysterious boy allow any human to threaten their secrecy?

The boy then looked at Johnny and stepped before him, kneeling eye-to-eye, imposing the same scrutiny. Johnny felt his heart pounding heavily as the boy's hand came forward to stroke his face. The hand traveled downward, fingertips brushing lightly the fabric of the toga, and he took a hold of the lower seam and lifted it off Johnny's lap. Johnny tightened and held his breath as the boy's fingertips brushed across the hair on his thigh. The boy seemed fascinated by the hair on Johnny's body, as he lifted the toga a little higher to look at the hair trailing down Johnny's belly. Their eyes met again. Johnny sensed the probing of his thoughts. The boy rose a moment later and moved closer to Meramo, taking a position behind him.

Johnny feared Meramo would lose patience with these questions; or worse, feel compromised and alarmed that Brian knew who they were.

"Let it go, Brian," he said urgently. "Perhaps we shouldn't have bothered Meramo with this. I think it's time we leave."

Brian looked at him, recognizing the foreboding in Johnny's voice. It dawned on him at once, considering Johnny's first-hand knowledge of how dangerous the entities could be, that he in fact must have good reason to suggest they leave. A nervousness fluttered in his belly as he turned and looked at the old man.

"Forgive me, Meramo. I feel I've intruded on you today."

Johnny and Brian both got to their feet. Brian reached into his cargo pocket and produced a tin of sardines. He approached Meramo and extended the tin.

"I brought a gift. A symbol of our friendship."

Meramo nodded and took the tin graciously, handing it to the boy, who held onto it without taking his eyes from the two visitors.

They turned to leave, then heard Meramo's voice.

"I have lived sixteen lifetimes," he had said.

They turned with a start and stared at the old man as if they couldn't believe their ears.

Meramo looked at his two visitors with a stoic smile. "You've been aware of my multiple lives for some time now, Doctor Fowler. You've written about my race."

It took Brian a moment to collect his wits. "Does that anger you, Meramo?"

"You can bring me no harm. You will vanish from the earth before you ever do."

Brian's excitement welled within his chest. His gamble had paid off. Meramo had acknowledged a different race, something apart from humanity. Brian's fear evaporated. He could not resist betting every chip.

"Is it forbidden to inform the world of you and your power?"

"Do as you will, at your own peril," Meramo stated bluntly.

Brian did not hesitate to go on. "The boy. Is he one of you?"

"No."

"What is he?"

Meramo smiled. "He is of the earth and of the heavens. My companion. He has endured these many lifetimes with me. He comforts me. He nourishes and protects me."

"Yes, but what is he? What manner of being is he?"

Meramo smiled again, this time with no answer.

Johnny was astounded that the old man was actually responding to questions, at a complete loss as to his reason for doing so; and equally astounded by Brian's continuing audacity.

"I asked you about Cassandra Mott," said Brian.

"Yes, I know of Cassandra. She is one among hundreds of us scattered across the earth. One of many sisters."

"Hundreds!" Brian gasped. His eyes drifted for a moment as he pondered the enormity of their numbers.

It felt like a time warp to Johnny, like that moment when the condemned is granted a last cigarette before his short walk to the gallows. He watched them both carefully, Meramo and the boy, glancing back and forth between them, watching for the lifting of a hand, or a sudden inflection of the eye.

"Why has Cassandra taken my friend into her world?"

"We are peace loving, Doctor Fowler. We live among you, and you live among us in harmony, but only as the laws have been written for thousands of years. You have questions about evil. Evil is not in our nature, but in yours. In battle, humanity would survive—there are so many of you and your penchant for destruction goes beyond ours. For that reason, we live in secrecy. For that reason, we will be watching you."

"Yes, I understand and I believe you; but Meramo, please, tell me why Cassandra is interested in my friend."

The old man was silent for a few moments. The cause of his reluctance was unclear, though the boy seemed to know, seemed to hurt for the animosity this question caused Meramo. "We are not evil, Brian Fowler ... but we must abide the emotions that affect us. Surely you understand this. Cassandra's reasons are her own and are not known by me. I know only she is not happy with this man standing beside you."

This statement shuddered down Johnny's spine. His jaw locked tightly as the ramifications consumed his thoughts and stole into the very marrow of his bones.

"Does she intend to let him go?" Brian asked, his voice increasingly desperate.

Meramo stared at him for a moment, glancing once or twice at Johnny. He finally spoke. "You have done great deeds for the people of Africa, Doctor Fowler. I'm certain you will accomplish much more, provided your curiosity does not cause your final grief."

These words chilled even Brian, yet he could not resist one last question. "Meramo, you know I have no desire to bring you harm. I want only to understand your kind, nothing more. I seek no personal benefit from knowing who you are. This friendship you must allow. And I ask you to consider just one more thing. Consider the potentially fertile seeds of understanding between your race and mine, if your race would allow it. Such a partnership would benefit us all."

"Be careful with your ideas, Brian Fowler. Your race destroys what it does not understand. There is more of that kind among you than you could count in your lifetime. They would destroy us."

Brian's mind was swollen with triumph, and it shone in his eyes as he turned to look at Johnny, who wondered if the idealistic professor had heard the true message in Meramo's words; or whether he had spliced the meaning to fit his own ambitions.

"May I come to see you next summer?" Brian asked, turning back to the old man.

"Yes, my friend; but do not forget you were forewarned. Scan the high grass for snakes before you step forward."

The four stared at each other for a moment longer, as if each recognized something extraordinary had transpired today. Then Johnny and Brian turned and started their descent down the mountain.

Chapter 24

Gravity quickened Johnny's hurried pace. Brian, not quite as agile, labored to keep up, stumbling, grasping at scrub in his unsteady descent. Ahead, moving quicker than caution would allow, his sandals awkward on the precarious footing, Johnny moved with urgency to get away from the landing as fast as he could. His thoughts came like whirling saw blades, sucking him ever closer. It had already occurred to him that he alone, or even with Brian's help, might not be able to break Cassandra's hold, though he had time and again pushed that disturbing prophecy aside. Meramo's reluctant assessment dashed his last speck of hope. What had he done, he wanted to know, that had raised Cassandra's ire? Had he forfeited his life for her amusement or for something more sinister, something that Meramo was apparently ashamed to disclose? The consequences of being chosen by her had already piled one upon another, damaging his career and threatening his home and marriage. Was the ultimate cost his sanity?

"Hey!" Brian called out. "You're getting too far ahead!"

"Hurry, Brian. Let's get off this cliff."

Johnny's thoughts were a swirl of confusion. He stopped absentmindedly for a moment to let Brian catch up, wondering if Meramo had opened a door or cast a bit of light by anything he said. The trek had been worthwhile. Yes, the results both remarkable and terrifying. To have heard those words spoken by the old man, to have heard him confirm their existence as a separate race and admit to sixteen lifetimes. *And the boy. Of the earth and of the heavens. What did that mean?*

Johnny resumed his descent.

Indeed Meramo had confirmed their theories, but he also heightened Johnny's despair. That there were hundreds of them scattered around the world wasn't surprising, not really, not for one now prepared to believe anything; though it altered forever Johnny's perception of humanity as the superior race. It also cast a pall of suspicion on any great achiever.

Michelangelo, Aristotle, Caesar, Joan of Arc, even Hitler—were they outstanding figures in history, or immortals sticking their toes into an expanding pool of humanity, indulging themselves in mankind's abundant juices of good and evil? *Hundreds of them!* Just hearing their numbers knotted Johnny's optimism into a maze of impotence and turned his path back to a normal life into a treadmill.

But then, Meramo had spoken out. Even though he didn't tell them how to deal with Cassandra, perhaps Brian was right. Maybe Meramo's candid words were a sign their race might be receptive to a dialogue with their human counterparts. Perhaps Brian's drive to know and befriend them, despite their untold millenniums of secrecy, was some kind of predestined catalysts to breach their walls of silence. Would that not give him a way to bargain with Cassandra and free him from her grip?

Though more treacherous than either would have preferred, the descent was much quicker than the climb up. The unpredictable trail, with its steep inclines and uneven rock, imposed stretches racked with white knuckles and two men holding their breath. Unnerved and winded by the time they reached the valley floor, Johnny finally stopped and leaned forward and braced himself on his knees. He drew a few settling breaths as he continued collecting his thoughts. Brian dropped down to rest. He lay sprawled on his back on the crusty earth, breathing hard and shielded his eyes with his forearm from the glare of the midday sun.

"Kinda in a hurry to get off that mountain, weren't you?"

Johnny twisted his head upward and scanned the face of the mountain. Nowhere in the crags and jutting rock could he make out Meramo's landing.

"I'd say we opened a line of communication," Brian said triumphantly.

Johnny sat down beside him. "He didn't tell us much we didn't already know?"

"What we *assumed*, you mean. He confirmed what we had assumed, and I call that quite significant, my friend. If we can get Cassandra to talk openly like that, we'll make some progress. I can't tell you how elated I am."

"I'm sure you heard Meramo's not-so-subtle warning," said Johnny.

"I heard what he said. A request for respect. The wish to avoid being imposed upon by the chaos of the human world. Not a rejection of a thoughtful dialogue."

Johnny drew a long breath and let it out. Why did he doubt Brian's assessment and find himself at odds with his enthusiasm? The dialogue Brian sought could certainly be a means, if not the only means to his freedom from Cassandra. He came to Africa, after all, for Brian's help. Why resist it?

Johnny folded his arms on top of his knees and rested his chin. He gazed over the professor's relaxed form. Brian's shirt had fallen open. Johnny watched his belly rise and fall on each breath. Particles of sand clung to the salty hair across a sun-bronzed chest that glistened with sweat. He was in too good of shape for a man approaching fifty, a complication of a completely different nature that was making its way to the top of a growing list. The desire in itself was harder to deal with than actually coupling with Julian. It was real life, completely human in nature. Here, sitting on the hard earth under the sun in the middle of nowhere with this man, though his faculties to resist were fully intact, it was becoming increasingly difficult to deny his instincts.

He looked back up the mountainside and scanned the crags and barren cliffs, vast desolation that made him feel small. His gaze shifted to the distant hills across the valley. Implausible events had brought him to this isolated corner of the world; Africa of all places. *Why me?* How long had it been since his life was normal, when he awoke each day to face a day much like the one before, when everything was so utterly predictable? A lifetime ago. Now he was someone else, not at all the same man that labored day after day at his drafting table. All of that history, those years that he and Marilee had plowed ahead in grudging inches—it all seemed like a murky speck in time. Now the future loomed like an unpredictable void, each new day nothing more than a twenty-four hour contract with the unknown. How much weight, he wondered, could be piled on one man's shoulders?

"I need your help, Brian," he said, staring distantly at the mountains, as if a plea hidden in his mind had escaped through his lips.

Brian lifted his arm a bit to look at him. Concern creased his shadowed face.

"I can't go on not knowing what to expect."

Brian sat up, staring at him. His companion looked despondent. "Johnny ..."

"I could learn to live with Cassandra in my life," Johnny continued dismally, "...I could." His voice labored with futility. "Maybe I could talk to Marilee and make her understand. Maybe we could wait it out together. Cassandra will get tired of me eventually. But Julian ... how do I deal with that? What will he leave behind when he's through with me? How can a wife forgive a husband that takes pleasure from another man? Even if she could forgive me, it doesn't end there, does it?" Johnny looked at Brian. "There's you."

"You can't give in to defeat, Johnny. You're feeling vulnerable. It'll pass."

"No, Brian ... it won't." Johnny glanced up the mountain. "I don't think you saw. I slipped on some loose sand up there. Slid close to the edge of the cliff. That would've solved all my problems, wouldn't it?"

"Damn you for saying that!"

Johnny closed his eyes and tilted his head back. The sun warmed his face. Brian's voice, when angry, resonated with an even deeper and richer baritone. Johnny lowered his head and absently scanned the ground. He couldn't produce a positive thought. "Oh I'm not gonna kill myself, Brian. I'm going home to a wife I can't look in the eye anymore. It's not that I've changed. I realize that now. I just shouldn't be married. And I can't blame Cassandra or Julian. I'm who I am and it's choking me with guilt."

"You insist on feeling guilty over something you can't control."

"Easy enough for you to say. You don't have a wife putting up with all of your crap and loving you anyway, for nine years."

Brian laid back, exasperated. "You're depressed. And weary. Give it a little time. Think about the progress we made today. We found out they'll communicate with us."

"I'm talking about how I feel about you! Time makes it worse. It's real. It won't fade away when I come off some kind of drug. No drug has made me feel this way." A half laugh blew through his nose. "You know what occurred to me last night? I was thinking about my marriage, how we hardly ever made love. Nine years ... Marilee caught up in her life, me caught up in mine. It was more like an economic partnership. Now I know why it never bothered me much when weeks passed without any kind of intimacy. Nine years, night after night, I was more interested in a movie on TV or reading a book. She was perfectly content flipping through a magazine in her god-awful pajamas.

"I was subconsciously relieved. Relieved she didn't expect me to seduce her. Not that she's not desirable. She is. She's quite beautiful. But the dynamic wasn't there, the sexual dynamic that compliments your relationship. Intimacy makes the difference. If it's all you think about; if you can feel it in your hands, you know, don't you?" Johnny lowered his head and rubbed his forehead with the back of his fist.

"This conversation is taking us on thin ice, my friend," Brian said wistfully. He cleared his throat and added: "Things will look different after you get some rest. You'll soon be home with your wife, and on your way out of this mess."

"Back to what? Debt collectors? Foreclosure notices? My career's ruined. I've lost my ambition. I can't pretend these secret fantasies don't really mean anything. My wife thinks I need a psychiatrist." Johnny looked out across the valley and sighed. "Maybe I do, but where would the money to pay him come from?" He looked at his hands, rubbing the palm with a thumb. "I know I love her. She gives me something I need. I feel it even if I can't describe it. I love being around her, having breakfast with her. I miss her now."

"Of course you do. She's your wife," Brian insisted, wondering if Johnny had just described feelings for his wife or for his best friend. "And you said your physical relationship changed for the better, right? Sounds like your marriage has come full circle. Isn't that what counts?"

"Full circle. I'm not so sure. It's more like our newfound affection only gives me the means to go on pretending."

"That's nonsense," Brian huffed.

"We'll see. Tonight you and me will be in a hotel room in Nairobi. Think either one of us will get any sleep?"

"It's too late to leave for Nairobi today."

"Then tomorrow night."

Brian looked at him. "We'll get two rooms."

"Sure we will. Besides, my credit cards are maxed out."

Brian drew up his legs and released a long breath. "You seem determined to setup a no-win situation."

"What are you thinking about when you stare at that book every night, without ever turning a page? Same thing as me, no doubt. We're in the calm before the storm. We'll be working together on opposite sides of a barrier."

"My imagination has defeated that barrier a time or two," Brian said reflectively.

Johnny looked at Brian's bent leg. The khaki shorts we're gapping around his inner thigh. The image tingled on his skin. "I'll tell you Brian, I'm miserable with it."

Brian got to his feet. "We have a long walk ahead of us, my friend. Maybe you'll feel better by the time we get back to the settlement." He extended a hand. "Get up. Let's get started."

They trekked into the valley, zigzagging around rock formations and sparse flora, and then up into the rolling hills toward Pakopai's village. They had crossed the valley without a word spoken, their silent thoughts like leaves drifting side-by-side on a slow moving stream, their blissful fantasies accompanied by thumbscrews of guilt. It was as if the wilderness had conspired to enhance the torture of denial. All it would take to set the kindling ablaze was a glance at the right moment, or a pair of eyes falling upon a vulnerable expression.

Though Cassandra remained inside Johnny, her significance had receded behind the euphoria of sleeping with Brian. Her hold would come and go from day to day until she tired of him, when what he felt for Brian was enduring and relentless. Damn the world that would hold him in contempt for wanting it so, but their circumstances came with a hard truth. He and Brian were simply not to be. Their future seemed both clear and heartrending—there would be no physical affection, no making each other whole. They would explore the realm of those that never die, and the day would eventually come when their work was through and they would part ways, destined to live out their lives thinking about their short time together. Their conversations, their mutual glances, their sleeping within the close parameters of lovers—only a chapter destined to end, an adventure that would fade into an unfulfilled memory.

That night they ate beef and retired early, exhausted from the long hike and contemplating the revelations presented by Meramo. On his own bed, lying back, hands clasped behind his head, Brian stared at the dry mud ceiling. Johnny, his legs folded, had not yet settled enough to lie down.

He was staring at Brian. "What are you thinking about?"

"Julian. He doesn't age. He looks and feels human. Fascinating."

Johnny pondered his encounters with Julian for a moment. "That's right. You have to look close to realize something's different about him. He's too perfect. No flaws anywhere on his face or body. Even his fingernails. Always perfectly manicured. His face—perfect symmetry. You stare because he's so beautiful. It's when you look into his eyes you know he's not human."

"I saw that in the boy today, when he knelt in front of us. There's a void in them, like he's looking at you from behind them instead of through them."

"Yeah. Good way to put it," said Johnny.

"Ah," said Brian, tossing off the thought, "it's so damn perplexing." As he looked at Johnny his thoughts drifted elsewhere. "Hmm ..." He felt a shiver between his shoulders. "You feel any better?"

"Yeah. Sorry I was such a downer today. It all piles up sometimes."

"No problem. It's been a long day. We both need a good night's sleep. You ready?"

Johnny laid down on his side and felt Brian scooted up close, arm over his ribs, leg nestled between his, breath on the back of his neck, already a pattern, luxuriously pleasant, nourishing. Yes, it was nice. Yes, it made temptation more irresistible, but he would not deny himself this.

As he closed his eyes, he heard Brian's voice one more time before the house fell completely silent. "I'll miss sleeping with you."

After breakfast, lost among those going about their morning routines, their departure was uneventful. Johnny climbed into Brian's Jeep feeling oddly confined in his own clothes. Pakopai and his wife had walked with them to the Jeep, where she presented a memento of his visit, a length of cloth to be wrapped around his waist and worn like a skirt, just like those worn by the young Maasai warriors. At once it became a prized possession, and Johnny regretted not having a gift in return. He looked at it at length and then folded it on his lap, turning to Pakopai's wife with a grateful smile, that silent, well-received communication understood by people all over the world.

Brian said goodbye and backed the Jeep from the shade of the Acacia tree. Johnny craned his neck, surveying the compound one last time, as if he were collecting the final images of an adventure that was to last the rest of his days, aware this short encounter with the Maasai had forever changed his perspective. Somehow he believed it possible to get beyond his trials with Julian and Cassandra, beyond the conflicts of his sexuality, and settle down again with Marilee. He wanted a normal life, a life far less complicated than his had been in the past. Material concerns were less important than sharing life's small pleasures with the one he loved.

This trip gave him something else—Africa. His ancestral home was no longer a vague concept that might as well exist on the moon; rather a grand continent that had become very real to him and had taken a prominent place in his heart. He had breathed her air and had walked on her soil. He had taken food and had danced and had donned the clothes of her people; and though he may never return, this had definitely become a part of him.

As Brian grumbled and wrestled with the gears of the well-worn Jeep, the Maasai settlement fell behind. The great savannah expanded before them with its miles of listless hues and textures. Johnny felt a sense of solidarity as he brushed his fingers over the soft fabric of the red skirt. The whole of his stay was etched in his memory. He pictured himself back home, sitting in the garden, escaping, much like he was now, into one of the many scenes of daily life in the Maasai village, drawing on the contentment he had seen, making it his own.

An hour passed in silence, but for the gusts vibrating the windshield and the creaking steel frame and the occasional whine of the transmission. Bouncing and swaying over the uneven terrain, the old Jeep labored across dry creek beds and climbed out of ravines with little protest. The breeze billowed over the windshield and across their faces, fluttering their shirts. They glanced at each other from time to time, eyes expressing similar thoughts. What could be said, having resisted the want in their loins and the romance buoyed by Africa's moonlit nights, when what might have been owned most of their thoughts? What could displace these feelings, or make them go away, when each glance seemed only to enhance them?

"A warm shower. Clean sheets. We'll sleep like babies tonight," said Brian, his voice jarred by the ruts.

Johnny looked at his hand resting on the shifter, the same hand that had rested on his belly the past few night, the same hand that had cared for him after Julian's visit. "Don't forget that salad," he said, thinking about the bittersweet agony of the two of them being alone in a hotel room.

"Yeah. And bacon and eggs for breakfast. It's been a while."

"I could've stayed longer," said Johnny, shifting his eyes to the terrain beyond the windshield. He settled into the seat and propped a foot on the dash and rested his hand on his knee. "A shower will feel good, though."

"Be nice if you could come back next summer. Maybe a couple of weeks. I'd enjoy that, and could use your help."

"We should be lovers, Brian," said Johnny, his eyes trained straight ahead.

Brian glanced at him. His chest swelled and he released a frustrated breath as his eyes returned to the terrain ahead. "Looks like we're having trouble not thinking about that. That little taste we get sleeping together only whets the appetite." Brian moved his hand to the back of Johnny's neck. He looked at him and smiled. "I felt you on my hands yesterday, all day. Seems our fate is teetering on the edge of a cliff. So yeah, maybe we should push it off and see if it takes flight. But not here in Africa. You're a long way from home. Let's see if you can make that decision after you have another look in your wife's eyes." Brian reached for a small towel and blotted his neck. "You're vulnerable. You feel alone. I'm the only one who believes you and understands what it must be like. We can't make a mistake based on that." He paused and shook his head. "It's a real predicament for me, I can tell you. I'm long past due finding someone I'm compatible with. Why the Almighty sent me a married man, I'll never know. It's like I'm being punished."

Brian returned his hand to the wheel and gazed out over the savannah. "You came to Africa with your incredible story. I listened, thinking at long last I was going to find out exactly what these immortals are. After fifteen long years of research, I thought nothing could be more important. You proved that wrong. I listened and watched your lips as those bizarre tales spilled out, realizing I wanted to touch them. Then I realized I wanted more than that. I wanted to hold you. I wanted to see us together in the future. So, my friend, I realized what I've been missing. All those years of snatching bits and pieces of truth about our immortal friends, I grew lonely. Obviously, I became quite adept at keeping it buried. But it crawls out during the night. You ache to hold more than a pillow. When you're exhausted and feeling sorry for yourself, there's no one to talk to. Then you come along, a breath of fresh air. That first night in Pakopai's house, I wanted to devour you.

"What can I say? You've got those long fingers of yours wrapped around my heart. I first noticed an agreeable little stab soon after you arrived, even before we walked out of that hut together. Something to do with the way you stood your ground. Then you told me to get screwed when we walked outside." Brian smiled, nodding at the memory. "Funny, most people have little difficulty calling me an eccentric s.o.b. behind my back. Face-to-face, I intimidate the sons-of-bitches. Not you. There you stood, telling me to go to hell while I was getting lost in your beautiful brown eyes." Brian's chest swelled on a breath. "Want to hear it all?"

Johnny looked at him. "Yes."

"I like the way you smell. Your body drives me crazy. That first night you fell asleep in my arms, my nose was pressed against the back of your neck. God, I wanted you. I haven't felt that kind of desire in a long time." Brian glanced at him. "I wanted you. And I want you now. I want you for myself." Brian reached up and rubbed his jaw. "So here I am, driving into Nairobi with a man I feel a connection. We're compatible. We could be companions, lovers... but you're out of reach. That's tough, my friend. To ache for someone you can't have is one of life's greatest misfortunes."

"Brian ..."

"You don't have to say it. We'll have our moment, our secret affair, after you look into your wife's eyes one more time. After you see the smile that lights her face when you walk through the door. After you watch her bring your breakfast to the table the next morning. If you can come to me then, we'll get undressed together and we'll free our hands. We'll take a romp in that garden. And then, if I have to lay in bed night after night waiting for our next stolen moment, if that's all I can have, then I'll take it."

They rode in silence the rest of the way to Nairobi. The sun was well into the western sky when they entered the hotel room. For a moment, after being in the wild so long, it felt strange to both of them being confined within four walls. The pristine creature comforts seemed a bit disconcerting. Plopping their luggage on the bed, both men perused the room: Johnny went to the window to look out; Brian had a look at the bathroom.

The intimacy of the room settled over them almost immediately. At first, being together in a private room seemed a bit awkward, more so than they had imagined; not at all like the close confines of Pakopai's hut, where they felt more like boys with naughty ideas getting away with touching each other. Here, they had had entered a domain of adult distinctions, constrained by nothing more than their force of will. The possibilities hung in the silence while they explored the room, each with their own thoughts, and neither of them, for a while, said a word.

Johnny sat down in an armchair near the window and watched Brian rummage through his bag for a clean pair of shorts. The window faced west and was letting in the afternoon sun. Chilled air from the air conditioning vent settled on his arms and felt good, if not a little strange. Brian found his shorts and laid them on the bed and tried to smooth out the wrinkles.

"Washed these in the river two weeks ago. Guess I should've folded 'um better." He looked at Johnny. "Thought you were in a hurry to get a shower."

"I am."

"Looks like it," said Brian.

"I'll wait until after we eat. Why, you wanna go first?"

"No. I want to watch you undress."

Johnny smiled. "Are men supposed to say things like that to each other?"

"I wouldn't know or care what men are supposed to say, but I do know what I like." Brian held the shorts up to inspect them, and then gave them a sniff. "They're wrinkled, but they smell fresh enough."

Johnny liked Brian's casual attitude. It was tempered with a natural perception for what really mattered in life. He found it refreshing. Put to the test, he knew his own life lacked that kind of definable direction. He wanted to feel good about himself. He wanted life to feel warm in his belly. Even if the Globalcorp project had been successful, it wouldn't have mattered—he would be financially secure with something missing. "Guess most of us trudge through life carrying the baggage we were handed. I never knew how nice it would be to have a companion. You grow up thinking men aren't supposed to care about anything but making money, or getting their hands on a pair of tits and squirting their semen sixty seconds later."

"I know the type. They're bores."

Johnny continued: "We're supposed to get married, then beat our brains out to pay for bigger houses and cars." He stared at the floor for a moment, and then looked back at Brian. "Fact is I enjoy you looking at me. I like the way it makes me feel, especially when I know what you're thinking. I like being able to say I like it. That was missing in my life. It's kind of exciting."

Brian looked at him for a moment. "I've witnessed a metamorphosis. Your gay side seems to be gaining momentum."

"I've recognized it. I've admitted it. Now I'm gonna enjoy it, even if it's restricted to fantasies."

"I can see myself explaining your transition to Marilee: 'He put on a tank-top and headed for San Francisco to live out the rest of his days.'" Brian looked at the TV. "Too bad we don't have a good porn movie. Masturbation can cleanse the soul."

Johnny was staring at his companion, as if his imagination was confirming his thought. "I bet you're a good lover."

Brian smiled. "Maybe. At least I know how to enjoy a receptive partner. I suppose that's because it's been such a rare occurrence; but yes, I do like to take my time." Brian tossed the shorts on the bed. "You ready to eat?"

"Yeah."

Brian walked over and picked up the phone to order room service: two large salads and a bottle of wine. Then, from his bag, he took his black address book and pulled a chair closer to the telephone.

"Might as well make a few calls while we're waiting for dinner," he said, laying the address book on the table. "With a little luck, might just find somebody willing to come over here to take my place distributing those meds."

Relaxing in the armchair, Johnny watched him make half a dozen calls, one after another, each seemingly more frustrating than the last. Did he find Brian's temper amusing, he wondered, or endearing, with his cheeks turning red and the bark so much worse than the bite?

"Shit!" Brian yelled, slamming down the phone. He lowered his head and rubbed his temples.

A knock came on the door, room service. Johnny swung open the heavy door to allow the porter in. Sporting the weight of the tray on his shoulder, dressed in a traditional bellman's uniform, he set the food on the small table by the window. Six floors up gave them a good view of that part of Nairobi. Brian handed the bellman a crumpled bill as he passed on his way out of the room.

"Might be harder to find my replacement than I had hoped," Brian said as he approached the table and glanced over the dinner tray. "See any bleu cheese dressing?"

Johnny lifted a carafe to his nose and sniffed. "This smells like bleu cheese."

"Good." Brian sat down and spread a napkin on his lap. He looked around, sniffing the air. Then he raised his arm and sniffed his armpit. "I should've showered instead of waste that time on the phone." He grinned. "One overlooks hygiene in the field, but reek seems rather out of place in a ritzy hotel, doesn't it?"

Johnny glanced down at his open shirt. "Don't worry about me," he said without reserve. "Tell you the truth, my whole life's been too sterile. I've enjoyed letting go for a while."

Brian took a large bite of bread. Chewing it, he stared thoughtfully at his friend across the table.

Johnny pursed his lips and then smiled. "You're a fresh breath of fowl air," he ventured.

Brian swallowed what he had reduced to a wet lump. He continued to stare as if he were pondering something. Finally he said: "I think we have more in common than we know. I'm a heathen myself when it comes to the sense of smell. The size, not to mention the duration of my erections is usually determined by what passes through my nose." He reached down to adjust himself. "Hmm, seems just talking about it can have an effect."

Johnny took a bite of his salad. He was staring back. No matter how much effort he used to restrain it, the restlessness seemed to continually redouble. "We don't have to wait until we get back to Savannah. I can tell you right now that I'll come to you. Even after I look into my wife's eyes and feel her arms around me. I'll love her as much as the day I married her ... but I'll come. We can't go on pretending, no matter how much guilt is involved."

Brian stopped pouring the dressing over his salad, holding the carafe semi-consciously as he thought about what Johnny had just said. He looked at the forearm resting on the table, the black skin against the white linen the porter had spread over the table.

He shook his head and his eyes shifted to the wall below the window. "Shit, I'm eaten up with it," he said under his breath.

Johnny took another bite of his salad and looked over at the bed, then scanned the room. The sun had dipped below the horizon and the dim light from the single lamp made the room muted and shadowy. The walls separating them from the world created a small realm of privacy as they contemplated the path that was taking them into the night, both painfully disposed to free their hands and their imaginations. Johnny looked at the door, realizing they were fated to eventually leave the room with regrets, regrets yet to be determined: those emerging from an opportunity lost, or those born in guilt for giving in to the most relentless temptation he had ever known. When he looked back at his companion, he found him gazing out the window.

"Look at it out there. It's nearly impossible to believe a city could be so different from Boston. Savannah, too, for that matter. I never cease to be astounded by the diverse cultures of the world."

"It's still impossible to believe I'm here," said Johnny, though the diversion moved him no further away from surrender.

"Damn, this salad is delicious," said Brian, stabbing a tomato with his fork, continuing the struggle to escape emotions that would not let go.

"They're not very big. We'll probably still be hungry."

"I'll order desert later." Brian looked back out the window. "Think she's out there looking at us?"

"Cassandra?"

"Yes."

"I don't think so. I feel her presence when she's nearby. A kind of nervousness in my hands. It's not unpleasant; it's just there."

"Or is it there when Julian's nearby?" Brian asked, looking at him.

"Wouldn't make any difference. They're always together."

Brian turned back to the window. "They might make their presence known only when they want to. For all we know, she could be right on the other side of that glass, looking in on us right now."

"Julian maybe," said Johnny, looking at the glass. "I doubt Cassandra has the power to become invisible. But Julian, if he can turn himself into a snake, stands to reason he can make himself invisible."

In thought, Brian's eyes raked across the table. "If it's the last thing I do, I'll find out what Julian is." He reached for a dinner roll. "We also have to figure out why Cassandra is put out with you."

"I don't have a clue. She's as charming as she can be when I'm with her."

"Nevertheless, Meramo was quite specific. What he said about her anger keeps echoing in my mind. What it means, your guess is as good as mine."

Johnny looked out the window, wondering if Brian simply planned to avoid the issue.

Brian continued: "Out of the blue, she comes into your life, angry with you for some reason. It must have something to do with you being her old lover's grandson. Maybe something happened when you were a boy."

"If so, I've forgotten about it. I don't even remember ever seeing my grandmother."

"Whatever it is, strange she carried it from one lifetime to the next. That's frightening."

"I don't know, Brian. Meramo could've been wrong."

Brian looked at him, his brow furrowed with doubt. "Well, we'll sleep on it. Something might come to you sooner or later. Maybe something you remember your mother saying. Who knows? Right now I'm still keen on finding out more about Julian."

"Shame Meramo didn't tell us more." Johnny pondered for a moment, his forearm resting on the table, his eyes set distantly on the glass of wine he was about to lift to his lips. "When I'm with him, I sense he's not in his true form. An image of half man, half beast comes to mind, a man's torso and legs, very muscular, a long tail, hooves instead of feet, the head of a beast, a wolf or a fox. But that's a cultural image I've seen many times. Maybe it influenced me." He lifted the glass for a sip.

"Fascinating, isn't it? This kind of conjecture can take us anywhere. I liked your religious theory. I can picture some hapless ancient cleric running up against one of our immortal friends. He's got to explain it somehow, doesn't he? Like you said, he creates the concept of the devil. And where would his Satan come from? Where else but the mysterious depths of the earth? So now we have Hell. The cleric is relieved to have arrived at the only plausible answer. Word gets around and comes down through the ages as truth." Brian blotted the corners of his mouth, bemused by his portentous theory. "Now we have devils from hell scaring the crap out of us. We go scurrying off to church every Sunday morning."

Johnny smiled. "Sounds like we have theory number one. We'll call it our Mephistophelian theory."

"Why not? Why not put one reasonable theory under our belts?" Brian paused in thought for a moment, and then said: "On the cliff yesterday, the boy gave me chills."

"That whole episode gave me chills," said Johnny, stretching his legs out under the table and crossing them comfortably.

"You glance at him, you see a beautiful boy on the verge of manhood. You look closer, you look into his eyes, your breath stops. That's why I'm prepared to die."

Johnny looked at him sharply. "Why would you say that?"

"Because I now believe they could strike me dead where I stand, but that won't stop me from finding out what they are, or what their purpose is. That's what I was thinking about on the drive into Nairobi." He glanced at Johnny's shoulders. "Or should I say: one of the things I was thinking about."

"I won't let that happen," Johnny declared, drawing his feet back under the chair.

"You could stop them from killing me?"

"I'll stop you ... from doing something stupid. I won't let you back them against a wall. You heard what Meramo said. They fear us. They believe the human race would destroy them if they're discovered. You try marching them naked through the streets and you'll find yourself sleeping with a viper." Johnny paused, feeling a little anxious, hoping Brian was taking the danger seriously. "We'll take it one slow step at a time, encourage *them* to open the door, not try to kick it open."

Brian was staring at his empty salad bowl in thought. He ran his hand over his belly. "Chocolate. A Hershey bar. That's what I want. You like chocolate?"

"It's one of my addictions," said Johnny.

Brian stood up. "Maybe they have some in the lobby." He pulled out his money to see if he had enough cash for candy.

Johnny stood up and pushed his hand into his pocket.

"Keep your money, my friend."

"I was thinking about my share on the room."

"Forget it. I have an expense account."

Johnny pushed the money back into his pocket and followed him across the room. He locked the door when Brian left and went into the bathroom, where he got out of his clothes and stepped into the shower.

The steamy hot water felt good. He placed his hands high on the tile wall, arched his back and let the water cascade over his shoulders. Soothing it was as it ran down his back and between his legs, even sensual, fingers of warmth melting into his muscle. He looked down at his body and thought about the casual nudity so common in the Maasai settlement. He liked being naked, especially around Brian. Brian made him feel attractive and desirable, something he had never experienced before. He lathered up thinking about what it would be like to be in the shower with him. Standing trance-like for a long while, watching the soapy water swirl down the drain, he wondered what it would be like to kiss him. There had been several occasions he had wanted to, though it felt odd to contemplate kissing a man. He wanted to; that and use his hands without inhibition.

The bathroom had filled with steam. He stepped out of the shower with an erection, reached for a towel and stepped in front of the mirror. Wiping the steam from the glass, he saw Brian's reflection across the room, sitting in the armchair, staring at back him over the top of a newspaper.

"Don't bend over or I'll come over there and devour you where you stand," said Brian. His deep voice resonated with sincerity.

Johnny glanced at the bed. The red skirt Pakopai's wife had given him was draped over his suitcase. He went for it and stepped back in front of the mirror, watching his reflection as he wrapped it around his waist. Turning this and that, he pondered his profile and then craned his neck to see how it looked from behind, enlightened by the fact that he felt entirely comfortable primping in front of Brian. He was pleased with how he looked wearing it, even though he had put on an inch or two around the middle since college.

The rather obvious bulge in front gave the skirt, he thought, a masculine affect.

Johnny turned from the mirror and strode into the room. "What do you think?"

Brian's eyes shone with a glint of wonderment. "My God! Surely you know how sensuous you look in that thing." His chest heaved with a sigh and he reached up to lower his reading glasses a little further down his nose as he peered over them. His thoughts gave rise to certain changes taking place in his body, staring as he was like a man whose will to resist had gone down for the last time.

"Well?" Johnny inquired again.

"Damn you! I swear I'll not have a married man wearing me down," Brian mumbled in exasperation. "We're still in Africa, you know," he added, lifting his eyes from the skirt. "We have an agreement, remember? I'll be damned if I don't stick to it. I'll be damned if I become the source of your guilt before you've had time to think this over. I'll be damned if I expose myself to even more grief if you change your mind about us when we get home." He set the newspaper aside and got up and started toward the bathroom, pausing between Johnny and the bed, glancing again at the skirt. "No hundred-dollar whore could affect me this way. Damn you! You're making me feel like a love-struck teenager."

"I just asked what you think," Johnny protested. "Why the tirade?"

"Look at you, for chrissake! You're fucking beautiful. And we'll be sleeping in the same bed tonight."

Johnny stared at him a moment, not so sure they would be sleeping. He had never been desired before, not like this, and he liked it. He liked wearing the wrap, the airy, sensual feel of it, and he liked the way it affected Brian. "Don't worry about me changing my mind. What's between us is pretty clear to me. And you don't have to worry about making me feel guilty. It's too late. I already do. All the same, I can't spend the rest of my life trying to ignore who I am."

"You forget, we're waiting for you to confirm *who you are* when we get to Savannah," Brian shot back, starting toward the bathroom. "In the meantime, quit torturing me."

Johnny followed him into the bathroom. The room was split into two sections: the sink and counter area opened to the bedroom, a small second room for the shower and toilet. "Want to try it on," said Johnny, standing by the sink, goading him in an attempt to soften the sudden edge of tension.

"Good God, man," Brian protested as he stepped out of his grimy khaki shorts.

"Do you?" Johnny repeated.

"No! And quit talking," Brian shouted irritably as he turned on the water. "I want to concentrate while I'm masturbating."

The affect of seeing Brian naked in the hotel room caught Johnny off guard. Somehow it seemed more erotic, more compelling than it did in Pakopai's hut. He felt suddenly disoriented. An urge came over him to look, to step into the shower with him, to use the soap, which collided with the image of Marilee at the airport. How would she feel about him staring at a man in the shower, a man that might as well be his lover? He cringed. The guilt came in waves, relentless, with no sign of abating or becoming easier to bear.

Johnny approached the bed and sat down in the middle of it, folding his legs in front of him, feeling renewed shame for wrecking her life. He looked down at the wrap and lifted a corner of the durable fabric, absently running his thumb over the stitching. *Nine years.* All that time, it had never occurred to him to deceive Marilee; not once. Contemplating it now stabbed at his heart. He lowered his head and listened to the running water, picturing the soapy rivulets running over Brian's rugged body, plastering his body hair to his skin. Whatever the cause, whatever the consequences, he realized he loved two people. And just now, simmering across his skin, singing its sweet agony in every pore, lay an unbearable desire for Brian.

He heard the water stop. Brian came out with a towel wrapped around his waist. Johnny watched him as he stood before the sink to brush his teeth. Brian leaned forward to rinse his mouth, then turned and approached the bed. He removed the towel, flung it back toward the bathroom and sat down on the edge of the bed with his back to Johnny, who turned his bowed head sideways to look at him, consumed by the urges in his body.

Chapter 25

"Look at us," said Brian, "two mature, intelligent men, pining like adolescent girls."

Johnny was looking at the back of his head, the long wet hair combed back. "Brian," he said quietly, "no, we're not. We're acting like two men with something meaningful to share."

"Damn distracting, isn't it?"

"Yeah, it is," said Johnny. "Feels pretty good to be distracted." He drew in his feet and ran his hands up the back of his legs. "I shouldn't be married."

Brian turned and looked at him.

"I know we've only known each other for a short time, but sometimes you just know, don't you? It overwhelms you. We have more than a sexual attraction for each other." Johnny took a deep breath to buoy up his resolve to go on. "I like being with you ... waking up with you in the mornings. I like listening to you. I like looking at you and how it feels when you look at me. I like talking about the future with you." Johnny glanced down at his hands resting on the skirt. "I like just being with you."

Brian leaned toward him on his elbow. "Lay back," he said decisively.

Johnny looked at him for a moment and then complied. He closed his eyes, feeling lightheaded from a sudden rush of adrenaline when he felt Brian's fingertips on his skin. Then he opened his eyes in surprise. Brian had straddled him.

"Maybe we're making it more complicated than it needs to be," Brian said, watching his fingertips trail down Johnny's belly.

"Maybe."

"You gonna blame me for your guilt?"

"No."

"Even if I want to feel your long black cock in my ass?"

Johnny missed a breath. His chest swelled with a kind of euphoria that sang from every fiber of his body. The moment he had fantasized about since the first day they met was upon them. "I won't blame you."

Brian nodded. His hands moved up Johnny's arms, over his shoulders, down to his chest. He pulled at the nipples, turned them to hard, dark caramel peaks. He lowered his head and their lips came cautiously together. The kiss took hold of them, wet and lingering and purposeful. Their tongues explored the wet textures of the other's mouth as the hand moved further down Johnny's belly, pausing at the waistline of the skirt and then venturing further.

Brian lifted his weight and loosened the wrap. Johnny's hips rose so that Brian could pull it off. He felt his nakedness, felt Brian's eyes drink him in, then the fingers within the warm well of flesh behind his testicles. His heart quickened. His mind fell into a pleasant drift. This was it, two men offering themselves to each other, both primed for acts that would cosign them to society's loathsome fringes. This was the moment his life was to be redefined, when two like-minded men ignore social mores and find themselves in a wonderful Eden.

As the feel of mutual touch shimmered through their bodies, Brian positioned himself over his lover. He reached through his legs, took hold of the cock and rubbed the glans over his anus. A dribble of semen made it slippery, a fantasy made real, a breath of life for bodies starving for a physical and emotional bond. It was two minds in sync and two hearts beating fast and the pliant texture of male organs. It was the illicit act of two men coupling this way, and just that quickly everything else seemed vague and secondary.

Johnny felt the engulfing warmth. The firm diameter had pushed through, warm and forbidden, tight and gripping, intimate in a way that all other intimacies paled by comparison. He heard a groan and a long sigh. He lifted his head and looked down—his cock had disappeared inside another man, full of heat and hard and twitching. His head dropped and he closed his eyes, consumed by the sensations of Brian's rising and lowering hips.

Nothing had ever taken a hold of him like this. Yes, it was what he expected, to have his cock inside his lover, to know the clinging feel of a lover's forbidden gate, seeping into his consciousness with such weightless pleasure. He felt the slippery emollients glistening on his cock, acquainting the room with the smell of male sex. What could put forth his feelings for this man more effectively than this?

Eventually both men collapsed. Sweat filmed their bodies and dampened their underarms. Flights of fantasy floated like languid clouds in Johnny's mind: the feel of his testicles in a man's curious hands, the taste of a lover's semen, which happened just moments before when he got over him and sucked him like a newborn calf. For a while the spurting had seemed endless, the taste both salty and sweet, the swallowing of it yet another confirmation of his feelings for the man he had come to love.

How was it all to mesh with his life in Savannah?

Finally Brian lifted his head. He had reentered the world of wearisome thought. Johnny looked at him quietly, his shivers of anticipation now foundering in a pool of contentment. They had poorly resisted their urges and were destined for uncertainty; though Johnny remained determined that their impulsive emotions were to stand the test of their return home.

"There you have it, my friend," said Brian. "My surrender." He grazed his hand over Johnny's leg. "We made love in your wife's shadow. I've handed you my heart in hopes it won't be tossed aside." He looked at Johnny, who was looking back at him through dark eyes soft with both adoration and understanding. "It was my fault we slipped," Brian added, "me ... the one at risk of being left in the cold. No ... it was your fault. That talk of leaving this room without regrets. Then you put that wrap on. You must be determined to make a basket case of me, you beautiful son-of-a-bitch. You'd have me draw to an inside straight."

"I'd say you're holding better cards than that."

Brian sat up and ran his hand over his head. "I thought at first you were affecting me the same way as that Maasai princess I told you about. No. Not like that at all. You know what I'm saying, don't you?" He scanned Johnny's prone body. "This'll take some getting used to, sharing you like a smitten mistress. That's how I feel, you know." He looked at Johnny through ill-fated eyes. "You, your downside in this is far more tolerable. You have only to listen to me rant."

"Go on then, get it out. Maybe you'll sleep better tonight. I won't. I'm still quivering with what you did with your hands."

"Quivering? You just have a taste, my friend. We have the whole garden to explore, you and I." Brian took Johnny's hand and traced over the knuckles with his thumb. His eyes shifted to Johnny's genitals, resting with flaccid innocence in the crease between his legs. "So there's a word people use to sum all of this up, isn't there?"

"You mean the 'L' word?"

"It's like I'm tempted to say it, now that I'm beginning to believe in that *first sight* theory." Brian shifted his weight and reclined beside him, gazing distantly at the ceiling. "I'm going to like Marilee, I can feel it. Of course that'll make it even harder; but by God, it kills my soul she has you."

Johnny listened silently, his chest rising and falling on unhurried breaths. It seemed every moment they were together was a precious jewel soon to become a memory. It had so unexpectedly come out of the blue, so completely stolen them from their business with the supernatural, that his blood pulsed faster just thinking about it. The adultery had already played out in his heart. Still, in spite of the relentless grip, the underlying issue was clear—the choice they made seemed preordained. He would have, that moment, given himself in any way to Brian, had Brian's morale not hit the wall. He understood the posturing, nothing more than the last line of defense to prevent a broken heart. Even though they felt the same way, they faced many trials and complications back in Savannah.

Brian had quit muttering. He leaned over to turn off the light. The room softened with the glow of city lights twinkling through the window. Johnny moved closer and rested his head on the arm awaiting him. They were together for the night, weary and close, his arm draped across Brian's chest, breathing the fresh clean scent of his underarm. He stared across Brian's chest at the window, thinking about how different he felt. He pressed closer, losing himself in Brian's masculinity, aware of the day's fatigue in every muscle. They had given in and it was a part of him, a significant part. Nothing would ever be the same.

By the time Johnny awoke, Brian had stretched the phone cord across the room and had already made a half dozen calls. A basket of pastries and a carafe of juice rested on the table by the window. The morning sun spilled a pleasant warmth across the room. Brian sat naked in the chair, his muscular legs propped upon the windowsill, one crossed over the other, the back of his broad shoulders dwarfing the wooden chair, his long hair combed back over his head.

Johnny listened to his sonorous baritone. On the phone he sounded more like a sophisticate than an adventurer, though the tone was touched with a hint of frustration. Evidently it was someone from the university. Brian could not leave Kenya until the matter of distributing the antiviral medication had been resolved. When he leaned toward the table to hang up the phone, he turned and saw Johnny sitting against the headboard. A smile crossed his stoic lips and the corners of his eyes crinkled.

"You look rather appetizing in the morning, my friend."

"Kinda irresistible yourself."

"Hmm ..."

"Interesting waking up with a naked man across the room."

"We're a sad case, aren't we? A couple of hapless fucks lusting for something we shouldn't want."

Johnny nodded at the phone. "Any luck?"

"None. Looks like we're not flying to Savannah together. I'll get someone out here, but it might take a few days."

Johnny shifted his legs over the edge of the bed and got to his feet. Brian's eyes followed him to the window. Standing in the muted glare between Brian and the window, Johnny looked out over Nairobi, not at all wanting to leave without him.

"God, you're a beautiful man," said Brian, squinting at the male form darkened by the backlight of the window.

Johnny turned and looked at him. "She'll be waiting for me, Brian. Cassandra will try to come between us."

Brian considered Johnny's nervousness for a moment and then asked: "How much can you tell your wife about your experiences with Cassandra?"

"Not much. If I don't understand how I was drawn in—how could she?"

"I asked because, as it stands now, Marilee is another of your concerns, not an ally. I know it'd be difficult, but I think you should talk to her. Tell her as much as you can. You're a victim. Better to have her as a sympathetic partner."

"She refuses to believe they exist. When she went to the house alone, I hoped Cassandra would make herself known and demonstrate her power. It didn't happen. It never will."

"Then we'll have to make her believe. She's standing on the sideline while you're going through this. It's not fair keeping her in the dark, thinking her marriage is falling apart and not knowing why."

Johnny continued to stare out the window. "We're at square one with Marilee. She thinks you're some kind of a weirdo, writing books to make money off of basket cases like me. She thinks I need a psychiatrist."

"Ah, yes, of course, a psychiatrist. Well, isn't that to be expected? Everyone I know thinks I need one; and I obliged them a couple of years ago by sitting through a rather awkward one-hour session. Ended up with the poor bastard's collar in my grip after he handed me a prescription for a sedative."

Johnny turned and looked at him and smiled. His eyes traveled down a muscular body that nearly any man fifteen years his junior would envy, a body awash in a golden glow of morning light, comfortably prone in the chair, his hands folded over his belly, his genitals nestled in the crease between his crossed legs. "Not everyone you know thinks you need a psychiatrist," he said absently, lifting his eyes. "Me for example."

"Thanks for the vote of confidence, my friend. Maybe that's why I love you—you've become my link to sanity."

Johnny stepped out of the glare and looked at the pastries. "Have you eaten?"

"Had a couple of those rolls. Go ahead—eat something. There's coffee plugged in on the bathroom counter." Brian lowered his legs and sat up, then reached down to adjust himself. "About last night ..."

Johnny looked at him.

"I'm addicted to you."

Johnny thought about all the sensations that had stormed through his body, the sensations he had experienced with his hands, the feel of being inside a male lover, the emotions, the intimacy. He had thought about it during the night, when he woke up and stared at the man sleeping next to him. Even now, standing before him, it was like making love—he could feel Brian's eyes on his skin. They had crossed the bridge and there was no going back.

"I think that's a mutual problem," he said.

Brian smiled. "We'll have all afternoon. As soon as I finish making these calls. Maybe I'll get lucky and find someone who's available."

Johnny started across the room toward the coffee pot. Brian scooted the chair up to the table and opened his address book, looking at, instead of the names written in the book, the shudder and flex of two fleshy mounds. He had not lifted the phone by the time Johnny started back to the table with a full cup, his eyes this time drawn to the sway of a penis still flush with morning weight.

"So meet the man who could sit here all day and watch you walk across this room. Ever have anyone that addicted to you before?"

"Hardly," Johnny replied, taking a seat and choosing a pastry.

"You had me squirming last night. It's gonna be hard to think about anything else."

Johnny took a sip of coffee. He sighed. What he wanted to say had to stay inside—this affair would be difficult with his wife constantly in his thoughts. Difficult, yes, and essential.

Brian drew a breath and looked down at his address book. He turned a page and then picked up the phone.

Johnny took a bite of the pastry as he listened to Brian get an acquaintance in London on the phone, glad to be eating something other than beef for breakfast. He took a another sip of coffee and picked up the newspaper that Brian had been looking at the night before. It struck him that he was looking at an English translation of a Nairobi newspaper, and he wished again they had more time to spend in Kenya. He looked over a few articles reporting on the current debates in parliament while Brian cajoled an acquaintance over the phone. His eyes lifted when Brian hung up. The verbal arm-twisting had produced no results.

"Any one of them would love to do it," Brian said, exasperated. "They can't get away from prior commitments."

"Who are *they?*" Johnny asked.

"Doctors I know who work in Africa from time to time."

"Will you be able to find someone?"

"I don't give up that easy, my friend."

"So I figured," said Johnny, coming to his feet. "Think I'll get dressed and go for a walk while you're calling."

"Don't wear the wrap," Brian joked. "Don't need to add the boys of Nairobi to my competition."

"You'll have no more competition," Johnny said, swallowing the last bite of the pastry. "Two people in my life are more than enough for me."

A few minutes later Johnny stepped out of the elevator and strode across the lobby. He paused on the sidewalk in front of the hotel. Centered in the city, the hotel was located on a main thoroughfare. The cool of the night had yet to leave the morning air. Nairobi's higher elevation had provided a delightfully pleasant morning. He spotted a building that looked architecturally interesting down the way and started toward it. Walking with his hands in his pockets, he came to the structure, the Kenya National Theatre, a boastful and fine tribute to the arts; and as Johnny gazed across the façade, his thoughts drifted to the shaded, narrow streets of old Savannah. He would be home soon, dealing with the challenges on two fronts: Cassandra Mott and Marilee. Somehow, even with her enormous will and supernatural power, facing Cassandra and resisting her decadent temptations seemed inconsequential compared to facing his wife.

He had slept with a man, willingly. He had felt a man inside. Would Marilee know he was different, different from the man she married and the husband she had always known? Would she detect subtle changes in his sexual appetite, his distractions, his compulsion to spend time with Brian? He felt like a man struggling to push square pegs into round holes. It meant nothing less than facing a loss, which his heart could never be prepared for; that to avoid it, to have and love two people, he must setup a duplicitous world of deceit with the woman he loved, coupled with the thankless task of asking Brian to accept nothing more than an occasional stolen afternoon. This kind of plotting was anathema to him and time offered no solution, though he would grab all the time within reach with the hope that, somehow, he could step back into the light with three hearts still intact.

He walked on, this thoughts a hopeless collage of images and doubts, his brain a throbbing mass of questions with no answers. How does a man hand his wife a live grenade? *If I'm truthful about Cassandra, she'll despise what I've done. She'll hate me.* He walked past the University of Nairobi, wondering how it might differ from American universities, worrying about a future without Globalcorp. He would have to find a new client or lose everything they had worked for. Try as he may, he could not predict what might come by day's end, let alone predict the outcome of his return home. And there was the question of whether or not Cassandra would let Brian live in peace when he arrived in Savannah.

He came to what was known as the Municipal Market and sat down on a bench to watch the busy comings and goings, somewhat detached from this taste of how life differs in Nairobi. By the minute the weight of his return home grew heavier. How, he wondered, could he convince a new client to take him on with his life foundering in turmoil? How, racked with self-doubt, could he provide for Marilee? He realized it came down to finding a job, at least for a while; but even that meant the trials of an interview. No wonder he awoke during the night, wishing the blissful security of Brian's arms would never end.

He got up and walked on and eventually came to the elaborate Parliament Building, vaguely aware of its splendor and the bustle of auto and foot traffic around him. It occurred to him that the day might come when his life returned to normal. Then he would bring Marilee to Africa. Together they could explore this exotic human mosaic, where the modern is superimposed upon the primitive, where wealth and poverty mingle like strangers in a crowded room. That would be nice, he thought wistfully, to come and walk hand-in-hand through all of this as carefree tourists; even though, just now, he could hardly focus on any one of his tribulations, let alone the wonders of Nairobi.

It was time to go home.

He had not realized it, but his walk had lasted three hours. Brian, still sitting at the table, had finally made a successful call by the time Johnny got back to the room.

"One of my colleagues in Boston suggested his protégé," Brian explained as Johnny returned from the bathroom counter with a cup of coffee. "She's fresh out of her internship, and eager for an adventure in Africa. She'll be here in three days."

"Our problem is solved then," said Johnny, standing before the window, staring out, blowing the steam from his coffee.

"Yes, except I'll have to stay here to meet her, and then accompany her in the field for a couple of days. I'll get to Savannah within a week."

Brian stood and came up behind and placed his hands on Johnny's shoulders. He leaned forward and brushed his nose across the back of his neck. "It's your call, my friend. I can take you to the airport the first thing in the morning, or you can spend the week here with me."

Johnny continued staring out the window. It was a decision he did not want to make. Another week before having to face his problems at home seemed like a benign eternity. *Seven more nights with him in this room.* Seven more nights in those magnificent arms. The repeated thrill of that kiss. It was a dilemma, pulling him toward a fine garden mist just when he was about to take that first step into the fire. A week. The inclination to stay, to have all those nights with such a sensuous and passionate man was perhaps the most compelling temptation he ever had to deny; but deny it he would. Marilee was waiting for him to come home, that on top of the question of money. He simply could not afford another week in Africa. Despite the warm breath now falling upon his neck, despite the ache rising within his loins, his reasons for getting on that plane defeated the temptation.

He turned. His eyes were like those of a sailor watching a true love grow small on the shore.

Brian smiled. "You don't have to say it, my friend. I agree. You should go home tomorrow. That leaves us only one more night here in Africa." He reached up to touch Johnny's lips. "One night to savor you."

Johnny suddenly felt weak, or sleepy, he didn't know which. He wanted to lie down, to close his eyes and rest, to escape what seemed like demons stabbing at his brain with pointed forks. He brushed past Brian and moved to the bed and sat on the edge of the mattress. Lightheaded, he looked at his concerned companion.

"You all right?" Brain asked, approaching and sitting beside him. "You look faint," he said, pressing his palm against Johnny's forehead.

"I'm tired," Johnny said, rubbing his brow with his fingertips. "I just feel so tired."

"Then you should rest." Brian drew aside the bedding. "Here, let me take your sandals off."

When Johnny fell back, Brian reached down to remove his sandals. He unbuttoned the jeans and pulled them down Johnny's legs. He then lifted the sheet so Johnny could get his feet and legs under it, and he fluffed the pillow for Johnny's head. As a doctor, Brian recognized mental exhaustion and he knew he was seeing it now.

Having put the matter of his replacement to rest, thinking a nap seemed agreeable, Brian went to his backpack for a book before he lied down. The air conditioner had come on and had chilled the room. Brian, partially propped against the headboard, pulled the sheet up over his chest and opened the book to a dog-eared page.

"What're you reading?" Johnny asked hazily, lying beside him.

"*Crime and Punishment* ... Dostoevsky. Such strange brilliance. Here's an author still getting into people's minds the world over a hundred and fifty years after he wrote this novel. Wish I understood Russian so I could read the words exactly as he wrote them."

Comforted by the sound of his voice, Johnny moved closer and rested his hand on Brian's stomach. It came to him that this was the essence of having a male companion, being close, being there for each other, something subtle but substantial nevertheless. The moment gave rise to a unique sense of inner peace, a special kind of harmony, born in intimacy shared with another man, and he felt steeped in it now, lying heavy-eyed beside Brian beneath the cool sheet. Despite a world that would condemn them, he felt like one of the fortunate few, a gift that allowed him to enjoy his skin and see life's different colors.

His hand moved down Brian's stomach, past his navel. Until last night, he had taken no liberties with Brian; though now, in his hazy state of mind, now that their relationship had been christened, he wanted to savor him on their last day in Africa together. His fingers ventured into the silky mound of hair, thick and matted, that shadowy place on a man's body that invariably draws the eyes and arouses the imagination. His fingertips raked back and forth and then moved lower, and he contemplated the fleshy texture of the malleable organs, taking his time to ponder the workings of a man's genitals. An agreeable squeeze caused Brian to set aside the book and rest his hand on Johnny's shoulder.

Johnny pushed the sheet down with his foot and laid his head on Brian's belly, so close the hairs tickled his nose. As he drew the meaty end across his lips, the musky smell reaffirmed his inclination for another man. He took it into his mouth and sucked and teased it with his tongue, a taste that set his inner workings stirring. He worked the loose skin and watched the large pink testicles rise and fall as he listened to the sounds of passion rumbling within Brian's chest. Moments later, Brian's grip tightened on his shoulder.

He pointed the cock upward and watched it ejaculate, lying perfectly still, contended, contemplating the white rivulets running down the back of his hand. There were no laws, no moral codes, no fear of social tar and feathers that could prevent him from falling in love with this man. He had never felt this close to anyone, this intimate. His eyes fluttered as he breathed in the scent of semen and his hazy contentment moved closer to unconsciousness.

Brian felt Johnny's hand go limp. He tilted his head and smiled. Fate had been most generous to bring him this man, whose head now rested on his belly, so fragile, so vulnerable in the hands of the immortals. How unjust for them to toy with his life and threaten his sanity, this beautiful man that had fallen asleep like a small boy holding a forbidden possession. So yes—if he was to have no more than a slice of him, he would take it gladly, for the lonely nights would be easier to endure charged with sweet agony of anticipation.

It was a moment's escape, their sleeping away the afternoon, their mingling of arms and legs, their shared warmth and dreams. And when they awoke they hardly stirred, lying just that way in quiet, expanding discovery, contemplating the horizon that lay before them.

After a while, Brian got up and sat down in the armchair with his tattered copy of *Crime and Punishment*. Johnny took a place at the table to look through the newspaper. The mellow silence lasted the rest of the day, a kind of quiet and fertile evolving of their companionship. So little need be said when the simple luxury of being together in the room sufficed, when fate's next whim could wait just a while longer before emerging from the shadows.

In the early evening, when the city lights began to cast a soft glare on the window, Brian dog-eared the page he just read and set the novel aside. He pushed out of the armchair and strode toward the sink to splash his face with cold water.

"Let's go find something to eat," he said, blotting his face on a towel.

"I saw a couple of eateries when I walked this morning,"

"Good. I'm famished." He bent down and picked up the khaki shorts he had been wearing and began turning them right side out. "I liked being naked all day. We ought to go to one those nude resorts in Caribbean, where you loll around all day and go anywhere you want in the buff."

"Shall we leave tonight?" Johnny replied only half jokingly.

"I like you more by the minute, my friend," said Brian, sniffing the shorts. "Good God!" He flung them into the sink. "I must have smelled like a Neanderthal."

"We both did. Guess we got used to it."

Brian stopped the sink and turned on the water. "That explains how the Neanderthals managed to procreate—they got used to it."

"Bet the foreplay was short and sweet back then."

"They used their noses for foreplay ... like dogs do ... like I do." He swished the shorts around in the water. "My Maasai princess wasn't clean. Beautiful, but not clean. You could smell Mother Earth under her arms. I could bury my nose in her ass and be intoxicated on the first breath. I'm that way." He looked back over his shoulder. "Kinda like the way I am with you. Last night, when I pulled my finger out of your ass, I could've held it under my nose the rest of the night." He lifted the shorts, rang them and ran fresh water. "That ties me to those distant ancestors who took the first few steps out of the trees." He turned and looked at Johnny. "Wouldn't you say?"

"I'd say my ass is available anytime you have the urge."

"Ha!" He turned back to the sink. "I'll let these soak while we're out."

Fifteen minutes later, they stepped out on the sidewalk through the hotel's front entrance. Though tainted with exhaust fumes, the night air in Nairobi was cool and felt good on their skin. Invigorated, they started down the boulevard in search of a café.

The next day came touched with melancholy, which persisted through the repacking of Johnny's bag and the drive to the airport. They walked side-by-side through the terminal, both thinking about the coming week they would spend before seeing each other again. Brian paid a small bribe to be allowed to accompany Johnny to the gate. They were oblivious to the comings and goings around them.

"Funny how a grown man can be spoiled faster than a child," said Brian, pushing his hands into the pockets of his wrinkled shorts. "I'm not looking forward to sleeping alone tonight." He seemed a little more emotional than Johnny had expected. "But you ... no doubt you're feeling a little homesick for your wife." Brian wasn't really cynical about Johnny's marriage, just envious. It was difficult to hide.

"I feel torn. Miserable and exhilarated at the same time." Johnny turned his head for a moment and stared absently at a mother trying to rein in a promiscuous child. Then he looked directly into Brian's eyes. "I've quit trying to figure it out. Maybe it shouldn't have, but it happened. It just happened. All I know is I'd like you to get to Savannah as quick as you can."

"And then we'll take it one day at a time?"

"Yes," said Johnny. "One day at a time."

Brian looked around the waiting area, scarcely aware of the hundred or so passengers sitting and waiting to board the plane, their feet crowded by carry-on luggage. For him, the moment had grown awkward. He let out a long breath and looked back at Johnny. "A week," he said resolutely, taking a hold of his companion's arm and squeezing it. "Until then." He turned abruptly and walked away, leaving Johnny standing alone to wait for the plane. They had been together day and night for days. It saddened him to watch Brian vanish in the throngs of the busy corridor.

After two layovers, Johnny's final flight landed in Atlanta on the morning of the second day. With another hour's wait before the next shuttle departed for Savannah, he ambled through the terminal and went into a coffee shop for a sweet roll and coffee. It would take a while to readjust to Georgia's time zone, and being back home. When the hour passed, after climbing on board the small bus, he found it difficult to relax and settle in. Those taking seats around him cast occasional glances his way. It seemed they were staring at him: a black woman with two small children, a business man with a loosened tie, a white teenage boy in tattered jeans. *What are they looking at? Are my sins branded on my forehead?*

Not used to the man he had become, he felt irrationally self-conscious. With one foot in a supernatural world, he bore the shame of carnal dalliances that no married man should ever consider; plus he had willingly slept with another man. He was different from those around him; and with those eyes casting about, snatching glimpses, it felt as if they knew. It felt like they could see through his skin, right into his soul; though he realized these were ridiculous thoughts. Still, it made him uncomfortable.

He sat leaning against the window, staring out as the bus made its way through the maddening traffic of Atlanta. Anxious to see his wife, he hoped by then that the toxins of duplicity would settle in his stomach. Would his demeanor be the same? How does a man that's slept with another man keep it from tainting his eyes? The questions he anticipated made him nervous as the miles fell behind, as he stared through the tinted glass at the endless stands of pine whirring past, scenery which barely touched his conscious thoughts. What was to become of him? What could he tell her to justify a trip to Africa that had cost them so dearly? He feared losing her. He feared he had pushed her to wits end. Why would any woman cling to her love for a man whose life has turned into chaos, whose future promised only more frustration?

I'll give up Brian. It's the only way. I can't have them both. It's not fair to either one of them. I'll convince Marilee that Cassandra exists and tell her the whole truth. I'll find a job and get our bills caught up again. We'll deal with Cassandra together. His heart felt a cold hard grip. *Oh God ... how can I give up Brian? How? Just like that?*

The shuttle arrived in Savannah two hours later. The driver pulled out of the traffic at a small depot just outside of the historic district. Standing beside the bus in the parking lot, Johnny waited until the driver unloaded his suitcase and set it on the pavement. He picked it up and started home, wondering how long it would be before he had to confront Cassandra. Did she already know he was home, walking the familiar sidewalks of old Savannah? It was humid of course, and very warm, and he walked hurriedly, determined to close his mind to Cassandra's summons, at least today.

A chill of excitement ran through him when he turned a corner and his house came into view. Everything inside him that had enabled him to resist another week with Brian welled up like a volcano of joy. He picked up his pace and bounded up onto the front porch, fumbling with the key as he tried getting it into the lock. Dropping the suitcase in the entry, he went straight into the kitchen, wanting to surprise her and take her into his arms, to pretend for just a moment that the forces working against them did not exist.

She wasn't there. Calling out, he rushed to the bedroom, turning his head this way and that. The bed had been made; the lights were out—

everything comfortable and homey. He hurried through the rest of the house, then out into the back yard. Finally, standing in the middle of the garage, his heart raced with trepidation. The van was gone. Marilee was not home.

She left me!

The thought gripped him with dread. Breathing in quick, panicky gasps, he folded his arms over his chest, staring at the cavernous space where the van should be.

No, she went to the market. That's all. She's shopping.

He hurried back to the bedroom like a man touched with a delusional fever, opening one after another of Marilee's drawers, hurrying then to check the closet. All of her clothes appeared to be there. Her luggage was stacked on the top shelf. Had she left him intending to come back for her things, or perhaps send someone? His hands felt tight, useless. He rubbed them together as his eyes raked over Marilee's wardrobe. Irrational, he realized, but the fear of her leaving him had crawled through his body and left a wake of emptiness.

He suddenly needed fresh air, to go outside. No. He needed to sit down, to hide under the sheet, to sleep and not wake up until this awful foreboding went away. Wringing his hands, he went to the bed and sat on the edge, breathing in labored gasps. His eyes refused to settle, shifting uneasily about the room, scanning the four walls as if they formed a prison. He couldn't capture a rational thought. He wanted his wife. He wanted to see her, to be held, to have her nearby. He needed her. It wasn't good to be alone. Not just now. Not with this craziness crawling in and out of his brain like a centipede looking to hide.

An hour passed. He had wandered about the house trying to pass time, trying to fend off another wave of panic. He tried to read, to watch television, to somehow occupy his mind. Nothing worked. He thought of little chores to stay busy. The trash—he took it out. The dishwasher—he emptied it. His suitcase—he unpacked it. All the while the panic lay in wait, like something breathing, pulsing, just inside his head.

By mid-afternoon he was still alone.

He went into the garage to tidy it up, but where to begin? The van was gone. It was just a big empty space. He could think about nothing else.

She's at church. Something came up there. No, she wasn't going back. She told me that. ...Another church. No. She planned to wait before finding another church. ...Her mother. She's gone to see her mother. Oh God ... Marilee, where are you?

The panic resurfaced. Disconcerted, his eyes leapt about the garage like a caged animal's. Sweat came over his face and dampened his shirt. He paced, went back into the house, wandered through one room after another, trembling like a lost child. He ended up in the garden room, feeling the grasp of panic, desperate for fresh air, fearing to go outside, desperate to run ... to scream ... anything. Nothing seemed right. Nothing had purpose. Nothing stopped the phantoms from laughing and roiling inside his head.

His gaze settled on the drafting table. He stared impotently at the corner that had once been his haven, where he did the work he loved: the stool, the lamp, the table on which his creations had sprung to life, the untouched pens and inks that now multiplied the guilt of neglected responsibility. His knees weakened. He shrunk to the floor in the middle of the room. He reached helplessly for a cushion on the rocker and hugged it to his chest. The fear that Marilee had left him would not go away. He crouched forward, pressing his forehead to the floor, rocking quietly, trying to endure the acids churning in his belly, embraced by the relentless arms of madness.

There he waited. *Someone will come. They'll take me away. A sanitarium.* The thought comforted him. There he would be protected. The expectations of him would be small. His heart raced and his breath came in fits as he cowered on his knees and squeezed the pillow close to his chest.

Johnny did not hear the garage door creak open. Nor did he hear Marilee's footfall across the kitchen floor. She found him huddled on the garden room rug.

Shocked, she stopped abruptly in the doorway. To see her husband back home when she had expected him to be gone longer was surprise enough. To see him cowering on the floor horrified her. She stepped forward at once, knelt beside him and placed her hands on his shoulders, not at all certain of what to do.

Chapter 26

"Johnny ... what's wrong? Say something."

His head lifted, his eyes swollen from sobbing. She pulled his head into her chest and held tight, stroking the side of his damp face.

"What's happened to you? Johnny, please, tell me what's wrong."

"Help me, Marilee," he pleaded. Comforted by the warmth of her embrace, the panic began to recede.

Yearning to help him, she held him tighter. "Why are you on the floor like this?"

"I thought I lost you," he said in despair. "You weren't here."

She shifted her weight and sat down beside him. It killed her soul to see him like this, this on top of everything else. He shifted off of his knees and sat facing her, lifting his shirtsleeve to dry his eyes. She took a hold of his hand.

"Why you would think something like that? Why would I leave you?"

He stared at her for a long while, collecting his thoughts and assuring himself she had come home. "I couldn't think of a reason you shouldn't leave me." It was like the mere sight of her had sent the demons running. "I thought I was losing my mind."

Though seeing him so emotionally frail alarmed Marilee, she had never felt so loved and needed in her life. That her husband had fallen into despair by thinking she had left him filled her chest with an emotion she had never known. She hardly knew what to do, but to love him, love him with heart and soul and every part of her being.

"You were gone so long," he said, implying that had compounded his anxiety.

"Are you all right now?"

His eyes drifted across the room. The knot in his chest was gone. The feeling of helplessness had left him. Evidently he had suffered through it, though no remedy could have been better than having his wife at home.

He nodded, brushing his hand over the back of his head like someone dazed. He looked at her. "I never felt like that before. I couldn't cope. Thought I was gonna spend the rest of my life in an asylum."

"It was a panic attack, honey. Not surprising with what's going on in your life right now."

"I feel drained." A faint smile worked its way to his lips as he gazed at her. "God, I'm glad to see you."

Still overwhelmed by being loved that powerfully, she could not imagine leaving him, no matter how bleak their future seemed.

"Where were you?" he asked.

"I took a job. I was at work."

"What?"

"You can't be surprised about that. We have bills on the kitchen counter we can't pay."

"What kind of job?"

"At the florists shop where I worked before. Doesn't pay much, but it's enough the make the house payment and pay two or three other bills."

Johnny's heart sank. He had hoped she would never have to work again, unless she wanted to for her own reasons. That she had taken a job as a matter of survival was one more blow to his ego and peace of mind.

"They offered me quite a bit more money for the closing manager's position. I'd be working until nine at night. I'm thinking about taking it."

He closed his eyes and released a breath. *Maybe I'll find something before she has to do that.*

"I wasn't expecting you back this soon," she said. "You didn't call to let me know."

"Wanted to surprise you."

"You did, more than you realize."

"I'm sorry, Marilee. You don't deserve what I'm putting you through."

"I'll survive." Marilee looked down at his hand in hers. There was no doubt about her love, but she had not slept well at all since he announced his intent to go to Africa. Try as she might to understand, it had been difficult. His trip to Africa had sown the seeds that had come to feel very much like doubt; not for her love, but for their future, his future. For all she knew, he was indeed on his way to an asylum. She looked up at him. "Did you find the man you were looking for? What's his name?"

The question, of course, was inevitable. Nevertheless, talking about Brian made Johnny wary. Not that there wasn't a lot he wanted to tell her about, it was the emotion involved in talking about Brian, the emotion he would have to hide.

"Uh ... Brian Fowler. Yeah, I found him. He's also a medical doctor. I found him treating a young girl in a Maasai village in Kenya." He felt an eruption welling to tell her all about the trip; though, in view of her skepticism for his reason to go, he realized his approach required a certain tact. "He's coming here, to Savannah."

Marilee detected his enthusiasm right away. Not only did she feel relieved that his melancholy seemed to have evaporated, she was intrigued. A hundred questions began to form in her mind. "He's coming here?"

"Yes. He was fascinated by what I told him has happened in that house. He had planned to spend the rest of the summer in Kenya, distributing AIDS medication; but after I told him about the Mott house, he changed his plans. He'll come as soon as his replacement arrives in Kenya."

"So when you told him about the house, he believed it—all of it?"

Johnny reached out and took her by the shoulders. "I can't tell you how good it is to be home with you, but I still have to find a way to make you understand something that I'm only beginning to understand myself. Brian not only believed everything I said, he's coming here to see for himself, to make them part of his studies. He's gonna help me deal with them."

"Them?" she said.

"You know who I'm talking about. Cassandra and Julian Mott. I told you about them before I went to Africa."

"Brian Fowler believes they exist?"

"He *knows* they exist. Honey, you read his book. Cassandra is one of the entities he describes in that third section. She's immortal. Brian has researched beings like her for the last fifteen years. Julian's different. We don't know what he is, but Julian is another reason he's coming here; to find out."

Marilee was befuddled. She had hoped Johnny would travel to Africa, discover Brian Fowler was some kind of a nut, and then return home realizing he needed professional help. She sat listening as Johnny plowed on, telling her about their visit with an old man called Meramo and a naked boy that was like Julian. He told her his experiences with Cassandra Mott fascinated Brian because he had never known the entities to allow a human being into their secret realm. The story became more bizarre with every sentence, expanding in endless complexity. Aware of her growing bewilderment, he paused to let what he had said so far soak in.

It was too much for Marilee. After her last visit to the Mott house, she had come to believe in the possibility of ghosts, but lots of people believed in ghosts. Johnny was still talking about Cassandra Mott, describing her as flesh and blood, a beautiful young woman that had reincarnated time and again over some three thousand years with supernatural powers, who had, for some inexplicable reason, cast him into some kind of strange mystification; when Cassandra Mott to her was the old lady that died and left Johnny that Godforsaken house. The fact that Brian Fowler planned to come to Savannah convinced her of nothing. It was perfectly reasonable to believe the author of that book was a nut, that when Johnny found him and told him this story, he simply decided it would be a good opportunity to come to Savannah and write a sequel.

Yet, with all of her heart she wanted to believe her husband. She *did* believe his sincerity, for whatever had affected him was very real to him. How she wished he would agree to see a psychologists, and she figured he eventually would. In the meantime, it was a matter of being as supportive as possible, and taking the evening manager's position at the florist shop.

"You still can't believe it, can you?" Johnny said with a touch of disappointment.

"Oh Johnny, I love you so, and I know you believe these things, but ..."

"Meramo disclosed what he is. We heard it. The words came right from his lips. Fifteen lifetimes he told us."

Marilee forced a sympathetic smile. Meramo? Her mind conjured an image of a lunatic sitting cross-legged in a robe, espousing his ravings to anyone that would listen, his face mirroring his lunacy.

Johnny turned his head from her, hurting because she still didn't believe him. An awkward silence filled the garden room. Neither of them knew what to say.

Marilee finally broke the silence. "Are you hungry?"

"No."

She got to her feet and extended her hand. "C'mon, let's go into the kitchen. I missed lunch today and I'm starving. I'll put together a light snack and brew some coffee."

He sat at the table and watched her cut cheese and slice a couple of apples. She added a few cold cuts and then brought the plate to the table, then went back to the counter to pour two cups of coffee. She ate a few bites before she told him her decision.

"I'm going to take the evening position. That way we can to cover most of our bills. We still won't be able to make all the credit card payments. Our credit will be bad, but I don't care about that any more."

Johnny lowered his head and scratched the back of his neck, heartsick. "I'll go see Mr. Johansen tomorrow," he said somberly, speaking of his old boss at Artco Designs, the company he had resigned from to start his own firm.

"You're not going to look for a new client?" Marilee asked, disappointed to see her husband knocked down another notch.

"Not until we're back on our feet." He reached for a slice of ham. It seemed pointless telling her his situation with Cassandra would jeopardize a good working relationship with any new clients, even if he managed to find one. Besides, his heart wasn't in it.

Demoralized, Johnny had no idea how to bring himself and his wife together in the same place. It seemed they stood in the twilight on separate ice flows, drifting on a dark sea, reaching out in vain for one another as they drifted further apart. Though a few bites of cheese and fruit made him feel a bit better, he hardly spoke with enthusiasm when Marilee inquired about his experiences in Africa, aware his adventure meant little more to her than suffering years of minimum credit card payments. After half-heartedly describing the Maasai settlement, he went to the bedroom to shower. Then he paused in front of the mirror.

You don't know who you are anymore, do you?

He looked at himself, picturing those strong white arms wrapped around his black chest, and he wondered what Brian was doing just now, too weary to calculate what time of day it would be in Nairobi. He opened the medicine cabinet and took out a bottle of Pepto Bismol, taking a gulp before going in to recline on the bed. An hour passed before Marilee came into the room. She sat on the bed beside him. It looked like she had been crying.

"You know I'm trying, don't you?" she said with sincerity.

"Yes."

"I desperately want to believe what you've told me about Cassandra Mott. I ... I just can't. Reincarnation, mysticism; those things aren't real, Johnny. I went there myself, remember? Twice I've been inside that house. It seems to me, if Cassandra Mott is living there, or anyone for that matter, there'd be some sign of her. Johnny ... that house is empty. But you tell me it's full of furniture and she's there when you go without me. It doesn't make any sense."

"Brian said no one would believe any of this." It occurred to Johnny that this is why the immortals allow Brian to go unharmed—no one believes him.

"He's right, my love. It's impossible to believe."

"What about the woman in the foyer. You saw her yourself."

"That's true, I did. I still don't know what I saw for sure, but I admit it was eerie."

Johnny could see she had something else on her mind, and he knew what it was. "You want me to see a shrink. I can tell."

"Is that really such a bad thing?"

"Why? To confirm I'm having hallucinations or losing my mind?" He paused for a moment and caught his anger before he went on. "I'm sorry, Marilee, but we both know a psychologist would see it the same way you do, that somehow it's my imagination. We would accomplish nothing. A one-hour session would cost as much as you make working at the florist shop all day. For what? To hear what we already know? How much sense does that make?"

"Wish I knew what else to do," she said with a sense of lost hope. "But you're right; it'd be a waste of money unless you believe you need help." She knew he wasn't completely aware of how vulnerable she felt—she had worked so hard at hiding it, but that was getting harder to do. If only there was an end in sight, some flicker of light on the horizon.

"You'll eventually believe, Marilee. Something will happen to convince you. You'll know everything I've told you is real. For me, there's two ways it can go. I'll either defeat the hold she has on me, or I'll be destroyed by it. There's no middle ground."

This sounded morbid to her, frightening. "Don't put it that way."

"How would you like me to say it? Look at what's happened already. We lost our business just as it was beginning to take off. We're broke. I'm dreading tomorrow because I have to talk to a shithead about getting my old job back. I can't predict what'll happen from one day to the next."

She thought for a moment and then looked at him. "Why do you think Cassandra Mott ... what do you call her? An entity? Why is she interested in you?"

"We're not certain yet. Brian thinks she has a reason. A purpose he calls it. Something beyond me being related to her ex-lover's grandson. If so, and if we can find out what it is, I think I can find an end to it. We know they amuse themselves with human beings. They choose people randomly, but it's different in my case. She's taken me into her world. At first I thought she was curious about me because I'm Emily's grandson. But why have they revealed so much? Things like making the furniture disappear when you go there. Brian has never seen an entity do that before. He's convinced Cassandra has a specific purpose."

"Like using you to get her house back?"

"That could be part of it." Johnny squinted slightly and looked at her a little closer, realizing her question implied she was toying with the possibility of Cassandra's existence. "I wish Brian were here. I think he might convince you they really do exist."

Marilee was beginning to wonder about the man Johnny had met in Africa. If Brian Fowler was a college professor and a medical doctor, he couldn't be a heartless conniver ... could he? Plus, a man that sacrificed his summers to help those in need in Africa didn't seem like the kind of man that would exploit Johnny for the sake of another book. Maybe Brian Fowler *was* someone who could help them. She suddenly felt anxious to meet him.

"We became very close," Johnny said out of the blue.

Marilee looked at him quizzically. The statement and the way he said it sounded almost out of character to her.

"I've never had a friend like him before," Johnny went on to say, as if he were speaking his thoughts out loud. He looked at her for a long moment, aching to end the lies, to confess his sins and deal openly with her. "Marilee, could you still love me if ..." He stopped short of completing the question, realizing what he was about to say. Dumping his bisexuality in her lap would surely be the last straw.

"If what?" she asked.

"Nothing," he said, averting his eyes.

"I think you're emotionally exhausted," she said, getting off the bed. She lifted the sheet. "Here, let me cover you before I get in the shower."

He swung his legs under the sheet and she laid it over his chest, and then leaned in to kiss him. After she turned off the air conditioner and opened the window next to the headboard, he watched her walk into the bathroom, lifting her blouse off her shoulders just as she disappeared beyond the doorframe. His eyes shifted back to the ceiling. He was asleep by the time she crawled into the bed beside him.

Propped against the headboard, her reading lamp on, Marilee lowered the magazine she had been reading and looked at the outline of her husband's form under the sheet. How could such a perfect man have fallen into a state of uncertainty and despair? He looked troubled even in his sleep. She thought about their nine years together, all that time and all the things she had taken for granted. It had crushed her to see him cowering on the floor, broken, only because he thought she had left him. She had always loved him in some rather remote and undefined way, but never like the way she loved him now. Why hadn't she known how to love him before? Why, now that they could turn an afternoon together into a moment in paradise? Why, now that he had shown her how to feel like a woman, now that they shared a physical love she couldn't imagine sharing with any other man, why were their lives coming apart? Why did he seem different?

Her gaze shifted to the shadows across the room. From the river the distant sound of a ship's foghorn wafted through the window. The chirping crickets set alive the black void beyond the screen, and Savannah's sultry night air lavished velvety moisture over her chest and arms. Cassandra Mott. Real or imagined, the blame went to her, even if she was nothing more than the little old lady that died and had left them that awful house. But was she still that same little old lady, dead and buried? Not if Johnny's long history of almost maddening practicality was taken into account—he was simply too driven by the laws of logic to fall prey to witches and false apparitions. It had been her biggest obstacle in getting him to church, in that he would argue vehemently that Noah could have never built an arc big enough to hold all those animals, and that it was ludicrous to believe Adam and Eve could have populated the world with such diverse humanity.

Marilee contemplated the stoic sincerity on Johnny's face when he talked tonight about Cassandra Mott, which had turned to disappointment when he realized she was thinking about getting him professional help. So was Cassandra Mott no more than a figment of his imagination? Every fiber of her brain insisted it must be; yet, tangled within this logic there was doubt. There was more to it than what she had been able to discover when she went inside that house. This she was beginning to believe. But what? And what about Brian Fowler? What was really inside that house that would cause two grown men to believe these incredible things?

Marilee looked at him again in the small light. Her eyes drifted over the male contours she had become so conscious of. It wasn't the fact that, finally, after their nine years together, she felt glad to be a woman by just looking at him that touched her heart just then; but the fact that she finally realized he needed her. She wished they had made love before he fell asleep, but that had not been in him, not tonight, not after what he had put himself through. He had seen the face of insanity and touched those bedeviled lips. He had suffered that agony alone by reaching out for a wife that was not there. How could she love any man more? She lifted the magazine and opened it, hoping, this time, the blurry paragraphs would put her to sleep.

Johnny put extra effort in getting dressed the next morning. He took a dress shirt and a pair of slacks out of the closet and ironed them meticulously. He shined his best pair of black leather shoes. In the bathroom, he opened a cabinet and found a new bottle of mouthwash, thinking all the while about the Maasai. There, if he were one of them, if he were getting ready for an important occasion, he would be draping beads from his ears and covering his hair with ochre-tinted animal fat. While he shaved, Marilee, while putting away the jeans she had washed, found in the drawer the wrap he brought home from Africa.

"What's this," she asked, entering the bathroom, holding up the folded cloth.

"It's a Maasai skirt. The warriors wear them when they practice spear throwing and things like that. I told you about Pakopai. His wife gave it to me just before we left the village."

"You put it in the drawer before it was washed. It smells like cattle."

He had also detected the smell. "They keep their calves inside their houses. Probably everything they own smells like cattle."

He took it from her and unfolded it.

"Would you like me to wash it?" she asked.

"Thought I'd hand-wash it later," he said, and then smiled. "Since there's no label with laundering instructions."

He wrapped it around his waist and tucked the loose end into the waistband of his briefs. "What do you think?" he asked, holding his hands out to the side.

Struck by how sensual he looked in the red garment, she stared at him for a moment. She had no idea a man could look so masculine in a skirt. "I love it," she finally said.

"I'm glad. I'd like to wear it around the house now and then."

Her eyes lifted to his. "Just make sure you have plenty of energy when you do."

His lips pursed as he glanced her over, still not used to her sexual innuendo. The outfit she put on to wear to work did little to hide her enchanting hips, but he couldn't allow himself to become distracted from matters at hand. Marilee was due at her job in thirty minutes and he was anxious to see Mr. Johansen at Artco Designs—anxious to get it over with, that is. He turned for a look at himself in the mirror, noting a little pudgier belly than he remembered seeing on the warriors; though not bad, he surmised, for a man thirty-one.

They left the house together. Marilee took the van. Johnny declined a ride, thinking a brisk walk to the west side of the historic district, where the Artco Designs offices were located, would help psyche him up for the meeting. He also wanted time to eat an apple before squaring off with Mr. Johansen. He didn't expect to be kept waiting in the reception area for forty-five minutes.

He hated waiting. It seemed to dull him. Reading the magazines made him feel sleepy; and pacing, which he felt like doing, made him look over anxious. So he sat and fidgeted. It irked him to be here asking for his old job back, having only recently been in competition with Artco. Glad he had given Johansen three weeks notice before he left, he figured they had parted on good terms; though he doubted his old boss would hand him back his sixty-five thousand dollar salary, nor did he expect the annual thirty days paid vacation. Johansen would know he needed the job and the wily Swede was too shrewd to give away more than he needed to. Johnny assumed he could get fifty thousand out of him, which was more than enough to keep Marilee from having to work at night.

Finally, he was ushered into Johansen's office, an anti-climatic event that seemed a bit formal to him.

"Well, hello Johnny," said Johansen as Johnny entered the large room. "Long time, no see."

Johnny felt awkward and out of place. He regretted having to be there even more than he had anticipated. Preoccupied with the graphics strewn across his large oak desk, Johansen had barely looked up.

"What brings you here this morning?" Johansen asked, finally shifting his attention to Johnny, failing to invite him to sit down.

It was at once terribly awkward for Johnny. He felt like a beggar, pursuing a handout. He stepped in front of one of the chairs facing Johansen's desk and sat down.

"I've decided I'd rather be a part of a larger firm than owning my own," Johnny said, thinking that was a good way to present himself without looking like he had no choice.

"I see," said Johansen.

Johnny was not certain, but Johansen seemed to have a glimmer in his eye. Johansen picked up a graphic and looked at it in thought.

"I like what this company stands for and thought I'd see how things were going here before I started sending out resumes."

Johansen's eyes lifted from the graphic. Johnny felt increasingly antsy. He wished he had waited for a response before adding that second statement. Johansen was a cool one all right, his square jaw and sharp blue eyes rather intimidating. He had taken over at Artco just a few months before Johnny resigned. Though Johnny didn't get to know him very well, he never really cared much for his one-dimensional personality. Johansen was the kind of man that women referred to as a jerk—handsome to a fault, but totally lacking in depth or personality, and single-minded in his ambitious pursuits.

Johnny wished he would respond.

"Have you moved someone into my old job?" Johnny asked in frustration.

"You know, Johnny, this is a close-knit industry. News gets around quick. I hear Globalcorp was disappointed in your performance." Johansen pitched the graphic to the other side of his desk. "What was it? In over your head with that project?"

Johnny's blood ran cold. He wanted nothing more than to get up and walk out, but the thought of Marilee working at night kept him pinned to the chair. It killed his soul to hope that Johansen had started off by being so cocky just to negotiate a better deal for himself.

"Mr. Johansen, I had a personal problem to deal with. It interfered with the deadlines I had with Globalcorp."

"I heard about that, too. Savannah's a small town, you know. Some friends of mine go to your wife's church. Or should I say the church your wife used to go to?"

Johnny realized the Reverend Aragones must have instigated some gossip about the condition he came home in that night he had suffered the gang rape. "Fact is, I need the job and we parted on good terms. If my credibility has suffered, I'm willing to work for a smaller salary until I prove myself."

"I'm afraid not," said Johansen. "As a matter of fact, if I were you, I wouldn't waste my time looking for a job in the advertising industry in Savannah."

This pronouncement chilled Johnny to the bone. It was as if he had been blacklisted; and he had to hear it from a younger, less talented, less experienced yuppie. A rage of contempt flashed through him. It took a moment to gather the wherewithal to stand and walk out of Johansen's office. He wanted to tell the blond, holier-than-thou kiss-ass to get fucked, but he caught himself and got to his feet instead. Without another word said, he exited the office hurriedly. A sense of dread tightened his shoulders as he made his way back through the hallway, ignoring old colleagues in passing, determined to get through the front door without screaming.

A block down the street, he stopped to cool his emotions. His heart pounded with anger and frustration. He slumped against a building and rubbed his eyes. What could he do, if not work in the advertising industry? He couldn't move out of Savannah to find work, even if he wanted to, penniless. The reality of toiling at some kind of a low-level job loomed in his mind like a taunting bully. Picturing himself working in a grocery store, ringing up Johansen's groceries, he walked aimlessly another few blocks and ended up on Bay Street, the busy thoroughfare that ran along the river close to Factor's Row. The apple he ate earlier left him hungry, or was it the whole of his insides were empty? Maybe he should eat. Maybe if he walked down to the river he could find a restaurant not spilling over with tourists and have an omelet. Maybe that would quell the awful feeling of emptiness.

He started across Bay Street, pausing as an open-air tourist coach passed by, the operator reciting Savannah's points of interest through her microphone, for likely the millionth time. On board were a dozen neck-craning tourists. He pictured himself reciting into a similar microphone, on a similar coach. His stomach began to churn, making a bite of breakfast seem impossible.

It was a completely different kind of panic, this new level of rock-bottom, this unexpected slap of diminished self-worth. He reached the riverwalk, still dazed with reproach, and sat down on a bench and ran his hand down the back of his neck, an outcast in his own profession. It had been one thing to let go of his mores when he first lifted his legs for Julian, offering his very soul to contamination; but this, this involuntary exile from his own trade, this castration. How could he face Marilee, unable to provide for her, unable to look her in the eye, unable to offer her even a speck of truth? How much worthlessness can she accept in a man and still be willing to call him her husband?

His stomach began to settle as he gazed out over the river. A calm came over him, a familiar calm, like an invisible, electrified cloud had descended over him. It tingled down his arms and legs. A tightness came into his hands and he rubbed them together. This he recognized. This would dissolve the anguish and pain. It was that battle of two minds where but one action would prevail. He wanted to see Cassandra, to be close to her, to bathe in the security of her frivolous strength. Ah, her sweet beckoning, coiling around him like tentacles of pleasure, promising to free him from the perils and stresses of life. The ache moved from his hands, up his arms and settled pleasantly in the back of his neck. When had he needed her more?

Then that other voice inside his head, pleading, tightening the tendons of his neck, telling him to resist, to hold his ground. He leaned forward and propped his elbows on his knees, gazing out over the glinting ripples across the river's surface. It was that smaller voice, calling out with its dimming influence that kept him from standing and walking toward Confederate Square, calling out from the remotest corner of his mind, that voice inherent in most every man, pleading like a prisoner of a tainted mind. *Resist, Johnny Feelwater, resist her bewitching spell.*

The need Cassandra had planted equaled the need to breathe, a promise to nourish and soothe his troubled mind before he collapsed in irreversible ruin. He felt it strongly. His visit to Artco had been much like falling on his own sword. Nothing to date tore at him like that glimmer in Johansen's cold steel eyes, the blade that first punctured his belly.

Johnny stood, about to start for Confederate Square, but his feet held fast. The emotional war continued inside his head: the victor nodding toward a rainbow, the vanquished preaching the wisdom of second thoughts. It was maddening. The escape awaited a mere few blocks away, that sweet peace of mind which could be found on the other side of Cassandra's door. Drawn by the promise of one more fix, he started walking, making his way through knots of tourists enthralled by the shops and sights of Factor's Row. He turned into a steep, cobbled alleyway that took him back up to Bay Street.

There, on the sidewalk, he stopped. The traffic moved along bumper to bumper in both directions. The noise assaulted his ears, horns and loud engines and shouting. Swirling through his nostrils were the fumes. The traffic and city noises seemed louder today, more noxious. He couldn't cross the street, too many cars. Pacing a few feet here and a few feet there, he turned his head in one direction and then another. None of it looked familiar, though he knew every inch of historic Savannah as well as anyone. *Why are they staring at me?* he wondered, watching the people looking out from passing cars. His shirt felt damp—he pulled it away from his chest. From both directions came passers-by. An appeal arose in his eyes, shifting as they were from one small group to the next, glancing away when they looked at him. The activity around him melted into a blur of confusion, spinning and surreal. Coherent thought sank beyond reach in a quicksand of confusion.

Brian... What's happening to me? Where are you? Oh God, someone help me!

His knees buckled. The cars, the pedestrians, the buildings along Bay Street became a streaking blur. The sky flashed in his eyes just before his head hit the pavement.

Chapter 27

Johnny heard Cassandra's voice when his eyes fluttered an hour later.

"Have you decided to join us, darlin'?"

He was lying on her sofa. A dull ache throbbed at the back of his head. Dazed, he twisted his neck and saw Julian sitting on the opposite sofa, staring at him, his expression heartfelt and compassionate. A few feet behind Julian, by the wall, wearing a white cotton dress, stood Cassandra. She was adjusting a painting.

"Pierre Renoir gave me this painting," she said turning and casting her eyes gaily toward Johnny. "It's marvelous, don't you think?"

Johnny stared at her for a long while. He noticed for the first time a kind of aura about her, something vague, but ever so slightly visual, perhaps a glow of some kind from her accumulation of centuries. How distracting she was in her white dress, those fleshy contours so perfectly accentuated by the soft white fabric, such that would draw any man's eyes and momentarily rob his mind of his past and future.

Johnny's gaze shifted to Julian, who sat wearing his white linen pants, staring quietly, contentedly. Beside him, draped carefully over the back of the sofa, was his linen shirt. His sandals had been placed side-by-side under the low table. Julian sat comfortably with the ankle of one leg resting atop the knee of the other, one hand in his lap, the other limp across the sofa back. More than anything about him, his eyes set him apart from the humanity that he dwelled among, icy blue and beautiful, subtle in a disarming way, or terrifying to those who looked into them too long; for one sensed they seemed to have a purpose beyond seeing. And there was more, if one looked closely enough. Was it a shimmer of air around him, like heat rising off hot pavement? And did his beautiful skin have a slight translucence, a characteristic perhaps inherent in his kind?

"That was such a lovely day in Paris," said Cassandra. "Claude Monet was there, too. You've never met such temperamental men."

Johnny's gaze shifted to the painting. Indeed, it was a Renoir, a young woman in repose, painted in the nude.

Cassandra gazed at the painting as if she were reliving a speck of her past. "Do you remember that day, Julian? 1864 wasn't it? We went to Paris to get away from the war for a few weeks. Pierre was ranting about a review he had read in the paper." Cassandra lifted her chin and drew her fingertips down her neck. "He had just started his career. Can you imagine, not becoming instantly famous for his beautiful work? I remember it like it was yesterday." She turned to look at Johnny. "That was his first exhibition. He offered to paint me, but we wanted to get back to Savannah. I surely regret not making time to pose for him."

Johnny's eyes followed her as she approached. It was the first time she had offered specific acknowledgement of a past life. She knelt beside him, looking at him adoringly, placing her hand aside his face.

"You knew Renoir?" he asked.

"The dear man couldn't give his paintings away that day. Today they hang in museums all over the world." Her gaze crisscrossed his face as she stroked his cheek. "Welcome back to Savannah, darlin'."

He winced when he looked up at the chandelier.

"You hurt yourself when you fell," she said with concern. "There's a nasty bump on the back of your head."

"So it seems," said Johnny.

"Julian, come over here a minute and see if you can help him. Sit up darlin'. Let Julian take care of that for you."

Julian stepped around the low table and sat on the edge of the sofa and leaned over Johnny. He placed his hand on the back of Johnny's head when Johnny came up on his elbow. The hand felt warm. Like a poultice, it drew the pain and swelling from the wound. Intimately close, the muscular flesh of Julian's chest and outstretched arm were mere inches before Johnny's eyes. The scent of his underarms reached Johnny's nostrils. His body heat touched Johnny's face. Closing his eyes, a deep breath came through his nose as memories of their couplings entered his mind. Johnny reached up to touch his lips. He drew his fingertips along Julian's jaw and over his chin, smooth skin without the slightest trace of stubble. When Julian stood and returned to the other sofa, Johnny noticed at once that the pain at the back of his head had vanished.

"How'd I get here?" he asked, his eyes shifting from Julian to Cassandra, still kneeling beside him.

"You mean here, to my house?"

"Yes," he said, sitting up.

"You created quite a scene over on Bay Street, Johnny. People circled around you, whispering and pointing at you. You were fortunate Julian happened to be there when you passed out."

"Julian just *happened* to be there?"

"Yes. He carried you here so we could care for you."

"Carried me? All that way?"

"He's quite strong, but you know that, don't you?" She looked at him quizzically. "You seem angry with me. Why?"

"How did you know I went to Africa?"

Her expression turned a bit dire as she got off her knee. She sat down beside him and leaned toward the low table to pour a glass of wine. Taking the glass, Johnny looked at it, thinking about the consequences of eating or drinking anything in her house. He rested the glass in his lap.

"Are we never gonna talk to each other, Cassandra?"

"Of course we are, darlin'. We're talking now, aren't we? I was hoping you would tell me about your trip to Africa and your new friend."

"You mean Brian? Seems to me you already know him."

"Tell me about his intentions."

"Why? You want to test me, Cassandra? See if I'll lie to you?"

"You're being silly, darlin'."

"I'd rather talk about Meramo. Do you know him?"

Cassandra stiffened.

Johnny watched the fingers of her hands entwine and lock together. "Yes, of course you know him."

"An old man covered in dust, living in wretched obscurity," she seethed.

"He was kinder when he talked about you. He declined to tell us why you're angry with me."

Cassandra's eyes flared. "Angry? Am I angry with you, Johnny? Have you seen the slightest hint of anger? On the contrary—you are angry with me."

Johnny looked into her engaging eyes. His head dropped back on the sofa. Even without the benefit of whatever might be in the wine, he found it difficult to focus on a specific line of thought. Her beauty and sensuality had that effect. He had not yet ingested the wine, but that didn't stop his mouth from watering when his head lifted and his gaze fell to Cassandra's breasts, nipples protruding against the white cotton fabric, their bottom weight round and heavy with milk. Why bother with the wine, when she could simply lower the dress and offer him that? Why even that, when the deviltry of Julian's scent thrived in his nostrils, the presence of which was enough to set him fidgeting? Whatever Julian might be, his replication of a man comprised all facets of masculine beauty, and Johnny's perception of that was enough to make him squirm.

Angry? With Cassandra? How could he be? Put-off perhaps, momentarily, and just why he wasn't quiet sure, when their close proximity seemed to nourish the essence of his soul. By their strange methods they had become part of him, or he a part of them, and he knew he would go to any length to be with them, to protect them, to give them anything they might want of him. Yet he yearned to know more, to understand them, to be considered equal, even though this seemed impossible. He set the glass of wine on the low table, and then reached for Cassandra's wrist and held her hand before his eyes. Caressing her palm with his fingertips, he marveled at its velvety smooth perfection.

"Brian's coming here, Cassandra, to Savannah."

"Is he?" Her eyes narrowed, squeezing away her pleasant smile. "Tell me, Johnny, is he an uncommonly brave man, or just a simple fool?"

Johnny looked at her. "Would you hurt the man I love more than I could love a brother?"

"He would cause us harm," she said with a tone of sincerity that Johnny had not heard before.

"No. He loves you as I do. He knows who you are and he wants to know you better. He wishes to meet you, and Julian. Become friends."

"You're naïve, Johnny. Men like him have persecuted us throughout the ages when they learn we exist. They know we're different. They fear us. They see us as threats. They must be destroyed before they destroy us."

"Not Brian. He doesn't fear you. He only wants to know you."

"Brian Fowler pushes his luck. He will be watched."

Johnny released her hand, leaned forward and braced his elbows on his knees, worried about Brian's safety. It was clear that she didn't intend to harm Brian maliciously; but if she perceived it as a matter of self-preservation, Brian would very likely vanish from the face of the earth. Johnny would ponder this and find a way to allay her concerns, another time. For now, he wanted the balm of her companionship, not banter. He reached for the glass of wine and held it to the light for a moment before taking a sip.

370 / *The Strange Haunting of Johnny Feelwater*

It was delicious. He took a second sip. The effect spread through him immediately and warmly. Just that quickly, all that he and Cassandra had just discussed seemed vague and distant. He watched Julian stand and start toward the bathroom, stopping in the doorframe to look back at him. Johnny set the wine down and came to his feet and followed him into the opulent room.

Feeling lightheaded, he leaned on his haunches against the counter. After Julian turned on the faucet to fill the bathtub, he disrobed, pulling his linen pants over his feet as steam rose from the water filling the tub. Now standing naked, he watched a pair of soft brown submissive eyes drift over his golden body. Julian stepped forward and began undressing his compliant guest, rendering him nude and prepared for the exquisite pain certain to come. Julian then leaned over the tub and passed his fingers through the water and it turned at once into mud. Steam rose from its shimmering surface as Julian stepped in and lowered himself. Resting against the back of the tub, he slid down, submerged to his neck, and then he came up on his knees.

Mesmerized in a state of near disbelief, Johnny appraised the lines and contours of a man that looked like he had been dipped in chocolate. The mud flowed down Julian's body like slow moving molasses. Immediately aroused, Johnny had never imagined anything like it. Forgotten were his unpaid debts, his encounter with Borg Johansen, the madness that overwhelmed him the day before—everything outside the walls of this elegant room. He stood speechless, staring at Julian's outstretched hand, collecting his thoughts as he moved forward.

Stepping in, the mud squished between his toes. He found footing on the slippery porcelain bottom and went slowly down on his knees. Julian inched forward, glowing with enchantment, and wrapped his muddy arms around his mystified lover. The mud smeared onto Johnny from Julian's arms and chest, warm and sensuous, a few shades lighter than his skin, drawing him further into an erotic world of mystic sex. Julian took hold of his shoulders and guided him down into the mud, which felt like he was being swallowed as it closed over his chest. It oozed and squished between his legs, into his crack and around his genitals, a heavenly, engulfing warmth. It drew the knots and the last remnants of anxiety from his body.

Julian leaned back against the tub with an outstretched arm, summoning his lover to come closer. Johnny maneuvered closer, positioned himself between Julian's legs and leaned back against his chest. A breath upon his ear, two strong arms wrapped around his chest pulling him closer, two legs pressed against his hips. Sweat formed on his face from the rising steam and ran down his neck and chest. Utterly relaxed, he sat entwined with Julian, losing himself to sensations that felt like magic fingers reaching inside him and making his toes curl. They sat quietly, contemplating the experience, the luxurious intimacy shared by two men. Eventually, Johnny wondered what it would be like to do this with Brian.

"Julian, does Cassandra intend to harm Brian Fowler?"

Julian remained silent. His hands shifted to Johnny's shoulders and slid down his muddy arms. Johnny thought about all the things he'd like to discuss with Julian, to talk freely, to learn more about the polarity of their two worlds; but he assumed Julian did not intend to answer. He had never been willing to discuss anything ... until now.

Brian Fowler is a fool.

The voiceless statement surprised Johnny. He lifted his hands and rested them on Julian's knees. He had heard it clearly, though they weren't facing each other, and that surprised him, too. Perhaps Julian was letting him in. just perhaps the taboo had been lifted.

"He means you no harm," said Johnny. "He wants to know you. That's all. He understands your reasons for secrecy."

He decides his own destiny.

Johnny understood what Julian meant by this. He would talk to Brian, forcefully, make sure he understood it, too.

They lay together in the warm mud for a long while, their hearts pounding close, the warm mud drawing toxins from their pours.

Today you were insulted by a man called Borg Johansen.

Johnny's hands eased down Julian's legs and pressed them tighter against his hips, caught off-guard. Apparently there were no limits to Julian's awareness of such things. "I suppose I was. He handed me a rejection I could've lived without."

He insulted you. I hurt for you because of that.

Johnny leaned forward and turned his head to look at Julian. He had not expected such heartfelt, personal compassion.

Shall he become a eunuch?

Johnny smiled. Julian's proposal was clear enough, though Johnny was less astounded by his ability to turn Johansen into a eunuch than his offer to actually do it. He pictured Johansen's sudden alarm, standing over the toilet, realizing something that had been quite important to him was missing; that the only way he would ever empty his bladder again was to lower the seat and perch like a woman, his obnoxious ego reduced by the same proportion as his manhood. Amused by the notion, Johnny declined the revenge.

Then it occurred to him these were the musings of two men that had become close.

"Why me, Julian. Why have you and Cassandra chosen me?"

Cassandra chose you, not me.

"Yes, I've always assumed that, but why?"

In the silence, no communication came from Julian.

"Tell me, Julian. I'd like to know."

You are Emily's grandson.

Another silence followed. The reply confounded Johnny. Why, by reason of a grandmother he never knew, would they bring him into their world? It was confounding to be sure, and confronting it seemed at odds with Julian's mood. The two men sat quietly and close in the soothing warm mud and a few seconds passed before Johnny heard more of Julian's thoughts.

There are better things to think about, Johnny Feelwater. The pleasures of the ninth gate. Get on your hands and knees and know that pleasure again.

Johnny sat up. On the strength of Julian's suggestion, a familiar sensation passed through him. He suddenly felt like a parched traveler drawing closer to the splash of a fountain. His chest sank as the air in his lungs rushed through his nostrils. Not a word had been spoken, but Julian's desire came like a poem whispering in his mind's ear. Johnny complied. He flushed as he came up on his knees, sated in a heightened awareness of being naked, the mud a sensuous second skin. He felt giddy posing himself this way, his genitals coated with mud and dangling before another man's eyes. The consequences had escaped him. There was no need to fret over what was inside that allowed him to present himself this way, with such abandon. It was nothing more than the natural order of things.

Heat from the mud rose all around him. No longer by transference of thought, Julian's messages came through his hands, traveling as they were down between his legs, the mud glistening and warm and slippery. Johnny found himself breathless, impaled so suddenly and intimately by a finger, which worked its unique magic until Julian withdrew it and came up on his knees behind him. The slippery ooze heightened the sensation of two bodies pressed close together. Unhurried came the penetration, though deep and deliberate, accommodated agreeably by muscle relaxed and made pliable by the penetrating warmth of the mud.

Julian slumped back in the sumptuous mud a few moments later, exhausted, breathing like a man that had raced up a dozen flights of stairs. Still on his knees, Johnny folded his arms on the tiled edge of the tub and rested the side of his head on them. The submissiveness that had tingled through his body had evolved into a sweet harmony of mind and muscle. He stayed in that position for a long while, recharging his body with long, deep breaths. Then he looked back at Julian.

It was a moment of weakness for Julian as he sat gazing at Johnny, his eyes reflecting both gratification and a fleeting vulnerability. Johnny knew full well that he, Julian, this immortal in the form of a man, was the source of all of his tribulations—not Cassandra, though it was certainly Cassandra's whims that prompted Julian's mystifying power. It had crossed Johnny's mind more than once, if he were to ever have his life back, that he might have to kill Julian. That is, if Julian could be killed; and if so, it would have to be during a moment like this, though Johnny despised the thought, even if it were the only way to his own salvation. Beyond the risk of even thinking about it, how could he raise his hand against something he loved, something he would risk his own life to protect?

"Does having a man weaken you, Julian?"

Julian's eyes narrowed. *You can't kill me, Johnny Feelwater. Yes, it weakens me, but even then you are not strong enough to kill me.*

"Can you be killed?"

There is a way. Do you wish me dead?

"You already know the answer, don't you? You know your strength isn't what keeps me from trying to kill you."

Yes, I know.

Encouraged by the straightforwardness of the exchange, Johnny pressed further. "Julian ... are you of God ... or of Satan?"

I am of myself.

"Can I love you without being controlled by you?"

From Julian came no reply. In the silence, Johnny shifted his weight and lowered his hips into the mud and sat facing him.

"Will you not answer? Do you think you have to control me to have my love?"

I wish you no harm, Johnny Feelwater. I love you.

Johnny smiled at him. He sensed there would be no more communication.

A few minutes later, Julian passed his fingers through the surface of the mud and it turned back into water. He stood and turned on the showerhead. After the cascade rinsed the last remnants of mud from their bodies, Julian handed Johnny a white terry cloth robe. They walked together to Julian's bed, where they reclined. His head resting on Julian's chest, Johnny stared at the portrait of Cassandra on the opposite wall. With Julian stroking his hair, he fell asleep.

Johnny got home later that afternoon, an hour before Marilee was due in from her new job. She entered the kitchen at five-thirty and found Johnny sitting at the breakfast table. The mail was scattered across the table: advertisements, a couple of bills and a letter that Johnny had opened. He looked at her as she entered the room, despondent.

Ready to rest her weary legs, she sat down, prepared for more bad news. She glanced over the mail and her eyes lifted to meet his. "What came in the mail?"

"Some credit card bills and a letter from the bank. They declined our request for the mortgage extension."

She picked up the letter, glanced at it and tossed it aside. They had asked for only sixty days, but Marilee had expected the denial. It meant a few months of late fees and more of those miserable phone calls, at least nothing catastrophic. "How did it go at Artco Designs?"

His head turned and he looked down at the floor. It was the moment he dreaded as he sat there waiting for her to come home. If there had been only one way left to hold his head up with a spark of pride, it would have been by way of his career. But his career had been turned against him, used by a rival like the twisting of a knife. He faced telling his wife that he had been professionally castrated by his old boss.

Marilee sighed. He didn't have to say anything. The answer was in his eyes.

"Johnny, I took the evening position. Starting tomorrow. My salary will cover the mortgage payment, the utilities, and a limited grocery budget. We'll get by. We'll just have to be prepared for the credit card companies to start calling."

He shook his head, shamed by the devastating circumstance of being supported by his wife. He had never imagined such a day would come, but it was upon them now and it felt like a thorn in his heart.

"They're hiring at that new home improvement center on the highway," he said, implying he had come to believe that that was his only alternative, at least for now. "It won't pay much, but maybe it'll be enough to cover the rest of the bills."

"Don't you think your time would better spent if you looked for another advertising contract? It doesn't have to be a Globalcorp."

It was as if he couldn't look her in the eyes. His self-confidence had evaporated, the last of it snuffed out in Johansen's office that very morning. He couldn't imagine picking up a pencil to start a sketch, let alone summons the confidence to approach another company with a bid for their advertising work. Nor could he imagine more ways a man could disappoint his wife. He wondered how she stayed so strong. How did she persevere with such quiet determination?

"I'm sorry, Marilee. Right now, all I want is a job."

She nodded wearily. "Had anything to eat today?"

Johnny realized he was famished. "No."

She got back on her feet and started dinner. He watched as she moved between the refrigerator and stove, preparing spaghetti, a woman that had worked on her feet all day, still on her feet in the kitchen. The guilt was not something he could get used to. On the contrary, it was becoming more of a physical torment, pressing against his chest, often making it difficult to breathe.

They ate in silence. By the time Johnny pushed his empty plate aside, Marilee had eaten less than half of her pasta. She took the napkin from her lap to blot her lips.

"Don't worry about the dishes," he said. "I'll clean up the kitchen."

She managed a fragile smile. "Then I'll be in the shower." After getting up, she pecked him on the cheek with a kiss before leaving the room.

He wiped off the counter after placing the dishes in the dishwasher and then sat down at the table. Staring into space, he thought about Julian. He had had the strangest feeling from the moment of their exchange. Julian had revealed more than Johnny would have expected, and during their brief discourse he sensed Julian was at odds with Cassandra about something. It baffled him, unlikely as it seemed that the beautiful pair would be at odds about anything; but if they were, he wondered if it somehow involved him. Meramo certainly seemed put-off by Cassandra's motives of late. He had spoken of her anger, though Johnny had decided to discount that scenario— he had never seen Cassandra angry about anything. Brian was certain she harbored a purpose; and if so, could that be Julian's point of contention? But then, even the theory of some profound purpose was wearing thin. If she had one, would it not have been revealed by now? Johnny reached up to rub the back of his neck. It just seemed preposterous to think the beautiful pair could be at odds with each other for *any* reason, but he couldn't shake the suspicion that they were.

Twilight soon settled over the day. Johnny pushed his feet further under the table and slumped in the chair. He missed Brian. There was already much to tell him: more phenomena like how Julian had so freely revealed his thoughts, and how he had turned bath water into mud and healed a head injury by the touch of a hand. It made Johnny wonder if he had really fallen, or if that whole incident of hitting his head on the sidewalk had been planted in his mind. Yes, there was much to tell Brian, like how much he missed being with him, looking at him, sleeping with him; like how he'd been reduced to a malfeasant by an old adversary not vested with near his talent or credentials; like how he had been with Julian, indulging the desires of his body while Marilee toiled at her job all day; that it was getting to him like a carnivore pulling at the meat and gristle of his sanity.

Darkness settled over the kitchen as he sat mulling over his private menagerie of woe, suffering far too much guilt to enter the intimacy of the bedroom before Marilee was sound asleep, guilt compounded by a hunger that refused to be ignored. He longed to feel Brian's hand aside his face and be told everything's going to be okay. Then the Great Rift Valley formed in his mind's eye, awash in golden sun and air fragrant with eternally renewed hope, he and Brian sitting side-by-side on the trunk of that fallen tree. How it had soothed him, that island of time and having a sympathetic companion close by, with those endless hours to contemplate nothing more wearisome than the distant horizon. He sighed.

Finally Johnny got up from the table and walked quietly through the house and got into bed beside Marilee, intending to get up early the next morning. He would use the van to go to the home improvement center and get back before Marilee had to leave for work.

It was a sprawling complex, an institution mindful of every size and shape screw known to man, of materials and tools enough to ignite one's imagination with an endless calendar of home improvements. Comprising acres of concrete, the parking lot looked empty, though a hundred or more cars were parked in a cluster in front of the store. The cars belonged to those inside stocking the shelves, and those, like himself, that were there to fill out job applications. Johnny pulled in and parked among them. He sat behind the wheel for a long while and stared at the building, before swallowing his pride and stepping out of the van.

Inside, harried managers were in the process of hiring dozens of people for a variety of hourly positions. The simple process took less than two hours. Accepting one of the jobs still open in the lawn and garden department, Johnny would work in the open air, keeping the plants and shrubs watered. restocking and assisting customers with their purchases. With several pamphlets and an employee manual in hand, he stopped in the parking lot half way back to the van. Turning, he looked at the building once more, then closed his eyes and felt a whole new kind of angst tighten his shoulders.

By the end of the first week, Johnny was performing his tasks routinely. It had been a somber week for him and Marilee—no crushing events, just a melancholy acceptance a new life neither could identify with. They had estimated their income and had penciled out a budget, which, provided they made no more than minimum payments on their credit cards, would cover their expenses. With a little luck, maybe enough now and then for a movie.

Toward the end of the week, Johnny's supervisor asked him to stay late. A truck dispatched from a Florida nursery had been delayed. It broke down in route and they needed his help to unload it when it arrived. He agreed, though he had been restocking all day and lifting heavy bags of mulch and fertilizer. He went out front and sat down near the outdoor grills and leaned back against the building to rest a few minutes before the truck arrived. He sat motionless, watching people come and go, carrying their new garden tools and hoses. It was one of those times he felt utterly useless, like his previous taste of success had come his way for no other reason than to define his ultimate failure. He looked at his hands, turning them, wondering if his destiny was to be one day upon another of figuring out how to load these grills into the trunks of cars.

It was exhausting work on top of a long hard day, but finished in time for him to catch the last bus to the historic district. He got home at ten-thirty. Marilee was relaxing in the tub when Johnny entered the bathroom.

"They asked me to stay late tonight," he said. "Had to help unload a truck."

Locked in a state of calm, Marilee didn't open her eyes. "It's hard to picture you unloading a truck."

He sat down on the commode and looked at her for a moment, her head at rest on the porcelain rim, her neck and upper chest moist with a light sweat. In the globe of golden light from a single candle, she looked lovely in wet repose, one knee extended above the blanket of bubbles, as were her shoulders and upper arms. They would lie together momentarily, with hardly the energy for more than a smile and scooting close. It seemed the course of their marriage had shifted again.

Drawing down his last remnants of energy, Johnny got out his clothes and got into the shower. *At least we'll be able to keep our home.* He had told himself this all week to help get through the lowest moments. They were treading water now—better than slipping further beneath the surface. But something was different, even though they had crawled back up on square-one financially. It was something inside their home, something that hung in the silence between them, as if the many despairs of their emotional gauntlet had worn them down and had affected the perspective of their marriage. Johnny tilted his head back and let the water run over his face. It was confounding, this living partially in a supernatural world, apart from the rest of humanity, this knowledge of what no one else can see or believe; this, on top of his own demons pulling him in one direction and then another; such as now, even as he contemplated the pleasant image of his wife in the bath and still feel the urge to lay with Brian. He wondered, as hot water cascaded over his sore shoulders and back, if a man attracted to another man could hope to be a good husband. He wondered if Marilee had sensed that particular change in him, though their love was certainly there, just redefined in a way that wasn't yet clear.

He stepped out of the shower and dried off and made his way to the bed, where Marilee awaited him. He pulled the sheet over them and drew his wife close; trying, as he breathed the scent of her hair, to avoid questioning why Cassandra had not called for him all week.

Chapter 28

Brian knocked on the door a couple of days later. It was mid-morning, after Johnny had left the house to go to work, and a couple of hours before Marilee would leave to begin her day at the florist. She answered the door.

She knew at once who he was. His disheveled hair and crumpled shirt complimented, in some eccentric and characteristic way, his wayward sophistication and imposing presence. She stared at him for a moment, gathering up a first impression, and she found herself almost charmed, and certainly disarmed by the smile that brought crinkles to the corners of his eyes. He seemed taken, and a little fidgety, as a man often is when confronting a striking woman for the first time.

"No wonder he thought of you all the while he was in Africa," he said, reaching for Marilee's hand and placing upon it a gentlemanly kiss.

"Mr. Fowler, I assume," she said, enamored by his rich voice, wanting to like him, though finding it difficult to abandon her suspicions.

"Please call me Brian," he said with a slight bow.

"We've been expecting you. Johnny isn't here, but as you've guessed, I'm his wife, Marilee. Welcome to Savannah, and our home." She stared at him a moment longer and then said: "Please come in."

"Thank you, lovely lady," he said, stepping into the foyer and closing the door behind him. "May I call you Marilee?"

"Please do," she said, stepping aside, feeling a bit less comfortable than she'd like to feel wearing her green and white stripped uniform. "I have to leave shortly, but I have time for coffee if you'd like to join me."

"I'd be delighted."

Brian followed her into the kitchen and sat at the breakfast table while she started a new pot of coffee. As she measured the grind and filled the pot with water, she thought of the many questions that she intended to ask her visitor. While the coffee brewed, she joined him.

"I feel as though I know you," she said, not sure where to begin.

"Then no doubt you think I'm some kind of a superstitious nut."

She cocked her head and smiled at him, thinking he must wear that label like a second skin. "I'm not sure what I think just yet, Mr. Fowler ... Brian. I do know you've made an enormous impression on my husband."

"If you don't mind my asking, where are you at regarding his dilemma?"

She looked at his big hands clasped together on the table, and considered his question for a moment. "Actually, I'm trying to believe my husband doesn't need psychiatric care. It's like he's been backed into a corner and can't reemerge. You can't possibly imagine how worried I am about him."

Brian took a deep breath, looking at her analytically. "Let's say then, at least I understand what you're going through perhaps better than anyone else would."

"You believe what he says about Cassandra Mott, don't you?"

"Cassandra Mott is real, Marilee. Forgive me for saying so, but your skepticism is his most insurmountable handicap in dealing with her. Few men have ever needed their wife's support as desperately as Johnny needs yours."

Marilee eyes shifted to the table as she rubbed her shoulder in thought. Of course she felt guilty for doubting her husband, but how could she believe what seemed like such implausible hallucinations?

"You, my dear lady, are the starting place. Even if you think your husband and I are nothing more than a couple of nuts who happened upon each other, you're the first step to getting his life back. Reserve room for doubt if you must; but for now, believe what he's telling you on faith if nothing else. Your husband is one of the sanest, most normal men I've ever met. I should think it would be easier to believe he's been affected by the supernatural, than to believe a man like him has suddenly turned into an irrational basket case."

Marilee felt a twinge of anger. Must she now listen to someone come into her house and dictate her emotions? But then, her rather arrogant guest had said nothing offensive, she realized, and her quick anger began to evolve into remorse. As she thought about it, her eyes shifting back to Brian. Why not believe Johnny's story on faith? Why not try and see where it leads?

"Exactly what has he encountered in that house, Brian? What's there that I couldn't see when I went there myself?"

"That's what I'm here to find out. All I know with any certainty is Cassandra Mott is one of the entities I described in my book. Johnny told me you read it. I've learned, with Johnny's help, that they exist in pairs; in this case we're talking about Julian, a completely different, but very powerful creature. He's known as Cassandra's younger brother. They're both immortal. At this point, I'm assuming they're somehow mutually self-sustaining. Everything your husband has experienced has not only reconfirmed facts I've known for a long time, it's also opened up whole new aspects of who and what they are. But there's still much we must learn."

"What, so you can write another book?" Marilee shot back, her voice chilled with cynicism.

Brian smiled with understanding. "I certainly can't ask you to trust *me* on faith, can I?"

"I'm sorry. Guess I'm at wits-end." She stood, went to the counter to pour two cups of coffee and returned to the table. "Tell me, Brian, why doesn't the whole world know about these beings, *entities* as you call them?"

"Ah, a question I've asked myself a thousand times. I think after all these years, I finally know why. Because they would be destroyed, or at least they have good reason to think so. We humans have a way of destroying what we don't understand. Their destiny is to live among us, and interact with us, but they fear they'll be annihilated if they're discovered. The reason Cassandra didn't kill me when she came to Africa is because she knows no one believes my ranting."

This took Marilee by surprise. "Cassandra Mott was in Africa ... while Johnny was there?"

Brian feared he had inadvertently revealed something that perhaps he should not have. He looked at her with regret. It would be difficult to explain further without revealing what had happened to Johnny that night.

"You saw Cassandra Mott yourself?"

"Obviously he didn't tell you."

"No. Why should he have? He knows what I would say—more hallucinations."

Brian adjusted his weight in the chair and leaned in, folding his arms on the table. "Marilee, what makes your husband's case unique is that he's been taken into Cassandra Mott's confidence. My question is why? Why, when in all my years of observing them, they've shunned that kind of exposure? I think she has a specific reason and I hope to find out what it is. I don't know for sure if Johnny's in danger, but I can tell you that she, or her brother Julian, has the power to neutralize his will, and that makes him vulnerable to a woman whose whims are, uh, shall I say quite amazing. I've watched them indulge themselves with human beings, but they've always been discreet. With Johnny, it's overt."

Marilee's eyes again shifted to the table, her thoughts reeling. Her obviously intelligent visitor was confirming that her husband is a victim; and as confusing as it seemed, she found both comfort and alarm in that. Quite simply, if this were truly a matter of Johnny being victimized, it would be much easier to deal with. She could stand behind him and rally to his defense in anyway that might help.

"When you say, 'indulge themselves with human beings', what do you mean?"

Brian thought for a moment. He had to be careful here, lest he slip and divulge their sexual exploitation of Johnny. "It's a cat and mouse game with Cassandra Mott. She's the cat, in the form of a beautiful and very eccentric women. I've been calling them *entities*, but now I believe the true entities are their companions. Julian for example. I've come to believe creatures of his ilk are the supernatural entities, and their partners, Cassandra, are more closely related to humans. These creatures have extraordinary power, far more than I thought in the past. Johnny thinks they're demonic."

"My God! What are they doing to him? He's drawn to that house even though it seems it's against his will."

"That's exactly what they're doing, Marilee. You have here two incredibly powerful beings, Cassandra and Julian Mott, who are interested in Johnny for some reason. They can shut down his ability to resist them and have done so time and again. We must find out what they want from him and then somehow deal with it from that angle. Only then can he be set free."

A tear had formed in the corner of her eye. She wiped it away when it streaked down her face. There were so many questions. She felt as if she were being nudged into a glass box, in which she could see out but no one could see in. It had worn her down so, all the misfortune she and Johnny had endured during the last few weeks, and now the long hours of a job. She glanced at Brian, her eyes watery, embarrassed for breaking down when they hardly knew each other. Yet he had calming effect about him, and there was confidence in his deep, magnificent voice, and a spark of hope in his words. Marilee was grateful he had come by early enough for her to visit with him for a while. When she glanced at her watch and realized that her time was short, she reached across the table and took a hold of his big hand.

"Thank you, Brian. I'll be thinking about what we've talked about while I'm at work today. Johnny should be home shortly after five o'clock. You're welcome to stay here if you like."

He glanced down at her small hands wrapped around his, regretting that he and Johnny had not restrained themselves in Africa. What in Kenya had been an abstract notion of an awaiting wife was now a living, breathing woman; and clearly a woman that deserved to be treated with integrity. Brian knew his feelings for Johnny could not be abandoned easily, but abandon them he must. What could he do, but lock his feelings in his heart, lock them away forever. It saddened him, for he knew the compatibility he and Johnny had found came rarely in one's lifetime. Nevertheless, as he looked at Marilee Feelwater's appreciative face, he vowed silently to honor the sanctity of her marriage.

"Thank you, dear lady, but I rented a furnished room near here, so I think I'll spend the day putting it in order and maybe take a short nap. I'm anxious to see him though. Will it be all right if I come back this evening when he's home?"

"Of course. You're welcome anytime, Brian. It's refreshing to talk someone who doesn't think we're both losing our minds."

After showing Brian to the door, she wrote a note telling Johnny he had come by and left it on the table.

Johnny came home weary. He still wasn't used to the heavy lifting all day long. It wasn't a bad company or a bad job, but he regretted expending his time for so little, especially when it meant Marilee had to compensate by working into the late evening. He found the note on the breakfast table and sat down with it in his hand, feeling an immediate sense of relief. He had intended to shower, but decided against it, thinking Brian might show up any minute. Instead, he put on fresh coffee and opened the refrigerator to rummage for a snack. He placed some cheese and crackers on the table and then went into the bedroom to get out the clothes he had worked in all day. After changing into his shorts and sandals and a pullover shirt, he went back to the table for a bite of cheese, and waited for Brian.

Brian arrived shortly before seven o'clock. When Johnny opened the door the two men hesitated, struck by each other's sudden presence. It had been little more than a week, but it seemed longer. In their exchange of glances, that which sprang to life in Africa quickly promised to be just as vibrant in Savannah. A hapless smile formed on Brian's lips.

"How are you, my friend?"

Johnny returned the smile and pushed the door wide open, then stepped aside so Brian could come in. "I've missed you." He wrapped his arm around Brian's shoulders. "Let's go in the garden room."

Brian paused a few feet into the room and looked around. "I should have a room like this to write in," he said, perusing the casual furnishings and plants, warmed by Savannah's evening sun filtering through the towering oaks with soft shafts of light.

Nodding at the wicker chairs, Johnny said: "Have a seat and I'll get some coffee."

He returned a few minutes later and set the mugs on the small table between the chairs and then joined Brian. They smiled and allowed a comfortable silence to pass as they settled into their reunion.

"I've been worried about you, my friend. Tell me, have you seen Cassandra since you've been back?"

"Afraid so. Don't know what caused it, but I had a little problem one day last week. Blacked out on a public sidewalk and woke up in her parlor."

Brian thought about this for a second. "Did it seem like something our friends arranged?"

"Yeah. Plus it was a strange visit. Both of them openly communicated with me. Cassandra talked about Renoir and the painting he gave her in 1864 at his first exhibition. It hangs on the wall in her parlor. Then she asked about you and your intentions. She's afraid of you, Brian. I can't stop worrying about that."

Brian nodded thoughtfully. "I'm still surprised she even knows who I am." He looked at Johnny for a moment. "The two of you had a normal conversation?"

"Well, if normal's the right word, maybe for a minute or so. She usually just teases me with innuendo and half-statements, but there for a little while I think you could've called it a normal conversation." Johnny looked at him with concern. "She spoke about you straightforwardly. Don't take her lightly."

"Did she make a direct threat?"

"No."

"Then let's not be too concerned."

Johnny thought about the visit for a moment. "Something remarkable happened," he said distantly, then looked at Brian. "You probably already guessed I was there for Julian. We bathed together. When he filled the tub he turned the water into mud. Just swished his hand through it. I couldn't believe it."

"Yes, I'd call that remarkable, unless you ate or drank something while you were there. Could it have been a hallucination?"

"I drank some wine and I could tell it was drugged, but can you hallucinate warm mud squishing up your crack?"

Brian shifted his gaze in thought. He felt a twinge of jealousy. What he had fantasized from the first day he met Johnny, what he felt so guilty about, Julian, the one who could seduce near any man in Savannah, took gratuitously. Man or immortal, on this particular issue it didn't matter—it galled him.

"He still uses thought transferences," Johnny went on to say. "It's remarkable how clearly you understand what he's telling you. He opened up while we sat in tub together. You don't even notice you're not hearing speech; you're just having a conversation. He knew my old boss declined giving back my old job. He wanted to know if I wanted the guy turned into a eunuch."

Brian listened with fascination. He pondered Julian's offer for a moment, and then said: "I certainly hope that's not what he has in mind for me."

Johnny offered a sympathetic smile. "Something to think about, isn't it?"

"Let's just say I've become accustomed to my little friend in its present state."

"He warned me, too. They're watching you."

Brian seemed uninterested in this. He took a sip of coffee as he glanced over the room again. "These old houses are lovely, aren't they? You and Marilee have a wonderful place here."

"If we don't lose it," Johnny said soberly. "So you met her today?"

"Yes. She's an outstanding woman. I felt guilt ridden the moment I set eyes on her."

"*You* felt guilt ridden! I'm drowning in it, constantly." Johnny leaned back against the chair and looked up at the ceiling. "I really don't know why she continues to tolerate what I'm putting her through."

"It'll be different in the end. Soon as we figure out what Cassandra Mott is up to."

"Did Marilee tell you she thinks I'm losing my mind?"

"She's coming around. Down inside she knows you haven't lost your mind. Sooner or later she'll realize we're sharing this world with immortals."

Johnny took a deep, frustrated breath. "Where are you staying?"

"I took a one-room walkup over on Abercorn Street."

"Sounds cozy."

"Not as cozy as it could be," said Brian. His unspoken emotions had crawled out on his sleeve.

"Oh, Brian," Johnny sighed. "I was counting down the hours until you got here. I've been so depressed."

"Depressed?"

"Marilee was disappointed when I took an hourly job at a home improvement center. She thought I should look for a couple of new clients, smaller ones. I couldn't face more rejection in the advertising field, so I took an hourly job to help pay the bills. It got me down, punching that time clock and watching another day wasted. But I don't feel like executive material right now. There were a few times this week I would've given anything to have you here. I just wanted to be near you."

"So you took an hourly job to get away from the rat race for a while. So what? You're an artist, my friend. You're just going through a downtime right now. It'll pass. Your career will be back on track before you know it."

There was a short silence. Both of them, despite the issues that brought them together, were thinking forbidden thoughts.

"At night, I lay awake thinking about you. Now you'll be staying a couple of blocks from here. It's maddening having these feelings and not having a future with you. It's frustrating. Even when Cassandra is out of my life, I'll feel the same way. You'll be going back to Boston or Africa and I'll be here in Savannah, thinking about you constantly." Johnny rubbed his forehead with his fingertips. "Marilee deserves a more stable husband than that."

Brian studied him for a moment, thinking about Marilee and how her gentle smile of gratitude had stabbed his heart. It seemed he had spent his whole life dealing with hopeless situations and causes, but nothing had ever affected him like this. There was nothing he could possibly want more than to embrace a relationship that promised to bring his life full-circle. He, too, had lain awake at night, thinking about a companion that would end his loneliness and balance his remaining years—dreams simply beyond reach. "You love her, Johnny. Your feelings for me don't change that. If you left her, you'd end up longing for her and we'd both be miserable. We're dealing with something much like an alcohol addiction, my friend. We're painfully aware of our addiction, but we can never allow ourselves another drink."

"It's a shitty deal for all of us, including Marilee."

"You've built a life with her. I'm odd man out. We have to face that." Brian reached for his mug and took a sip of coffee. He thought about his apartment less than a mile away, a one-room bungalow perfect for creating a few memories to take back to Boston. At least he would have that. Then the image of Marilee's tormented expression formed in his mind and the unborn memories evaporated like thin fog.

The forbidden apple, like a silver thread sewn through their evolving thoughts, remained conspicuously in their minds as their conversation moved across the details of Johnny's recent encounter with Julian and Cassandra and on through the rest of his week. Marilee walked in at nine-thirty. Exhausted from being on her feet all day, seeing Brian invigorated her. He stood as she entered the room and charmed her with another kiss on the back of her hand. She had thought about him all day and decided he had the makings of a trusted friend, that he might be just the right man to help them pull their lives back together. She slipped off her shoes and joined them.

"If I didn't know better, you two look like an unlikely pair of African adventurers," she said lightheartedly.

"*Homesick* African adventurers was more like it. I lost count of the number of times your husband wished you were there. Perhaps one summer you and Johnny could join me in Kenya. Maybe a few days in a Maasai village. That's quite an experience for an American."

Marilee wasn't thinking about Africa. Her earlier conversation with Brian had convinced her there must be something going on in that house, that somehow Johnny had been drawn in. At work, she had been unable to think about anything else. To get her attention, two or three of her customers had to pull her from distraction. She wondered what these two men had been talking about before she got home; if they had discussed a course of action that might sever Johnny from his involvement with Cassandra Mott.

At first, seeing the two people he loved in the same room proved difficult for Johnny. He felt nervous and tried to avoid showing it. Plus it panged him to see Marilee coming home from work this late in the evening. Whereas her presence usually filled the room with a warm radiance, she simply looked weary. But they seemed comfortable with each other. He began to believe something positive might come from their newfound friendship.

"Brian thinks you're having second thoughts about Cassandra Mott's existence," he said.

"I *am* having second thoughts, and I'm not sure what scares me more: you suffering hallucinations, or you being possessed by a woman everyone thinks is dead."

"Except me," said Brian. "And possessed is a good way to describe it, my dear lady."

"I'd like to hear more. Who are they, Brian? You say they live forever. Why do they impose on people's lives?"

"A good place to start." Brian glanced at Johnny. "I'll tell you about Ken Wells first. When I got back to the States, I called my contact in New York to inquire about him."

"That name sounds familiar," said Marilee, searching her mind for where she had heard it before.

"He's the infamous stock trader who's in the news from time to time," said Johnny, adding: "He's one of them."

"What?" Marilee gasped, now picturing the man she had seen on television interviews. The more she heard the harder it was to fathom. This seemed preposterous and made it suddenly difficult to not regress into a state of disbelief; when, to her, it all seemed like an ever-expanding and impossible scenario, as if invisible fumes were secretly menacing the world and affecting no one but them.

Brian continued: "Ken Wells is one of three I've encountered over the years. Infamous is correct, and obscenely rich. I've followed him into New York's seediest neighborhoods and watched him disappear into abandoned buildings with male prostitutes, disguised as someone you'd never recognize. All the while his chauffeur is waiting in his limousine a couple of blocks away. Now I wonder about our great artists and musicians and writers, anyone who achieves far more than the rest of us. Even people like mob bosses and politicians. After learning Ken Wells is an immortal, I'm suspicious of them all." Brian continued to watch Marilee's reaction. He paused for a sip of coffee. "As we talked about earlier today, we believe they live and sustain themselves in pairs, a marriage of sorts, though they're two completely different kinds of creatures. Ken Wells' chauffeur, as it turns out, also serves as his private secretary. Always nearby. Rather obvious when you know, isn't it?"

"There's no other explanation," Johnny said to his wife, his excitement elevated. At last she seemed to be listening as if she were hearing the truth. "Meramo has the boy, Ken Wells has the chauffeur, and Cassandra has Julian."

Brian was nodding agreement and watching her. "The dominate one of these pairings—Cassandra opposed to Julian, Ken Wells opposed to his chauffeur—seems to be more or less human, aberrations perhaps in a long evolutionary chain. They're endowed with the power of self-determined and selective reincarnation. Like I said this morning, we have no idea what Julian and his kind are, but we know they have demonic power. My theories about them are unending. For example: What if Julian and his ilk are the original creatures? What if they come by their companions by mating with a human female, resulting in the birth of one like Cassandra? A parent/child relationship, incestuous as it may be, would certainly explain their incredible bond, I would think."

Johnny noticed Marilee's incredulous reaction to all of this. Sitting stiffly, her eyes shifted back and forth between them as they spoke. "Cassandra's become more open with me," Johnny explained. "The last time I saw her, she spoke openly about a past life. She has a Renoir painting hanging on the back wall in her parlor. Said he gave it to her himself, in Paris, 1864."

"I didn't see it," said Marilee.

"That's one more thing we haven't figured out, why they're keeping you from seeing these things."

The sun had gone down. In a small circle of wicker chairs, they sat in the soft glow of a single floor lamp. Marilee's eyes continued to shift between them. She saw the demeanor of two perfectly rational men. Their words had been succinct and to the point. Their eyes had been focused and thoughtful. How could she not believe them? Her life was in a state of change and it was wearing on her, but the real challenge lie in comprehending the source of Johnny's tribulations and why they had befallen him. She still found it difficult to join their enthusiasm, to acknowledge something unknown and apart from the rest of the world.

Marilee's befuddled gaze settled on Johnny. "I still don't understand why you can't resist or ignore whatever she's doing to you."

Brian responded before Johnny could attempt an answer. "It can be explained this way: Cassandra's mystification works like a drug. Deprived of his drug, an addict develops an ever-increasing need. That's the sort of thing your husband is dealing with. It appears they can reach out for him transcendentally, and thereby compel him to go to that house."

"That's truly frightening, Brian," said Marilee, pressing the edge of her fist against her lip.

"Yes, it is, and we have only one consolation. There's no evidence of malice toward us. They may manipulate us, but they don't harm us."

"So if they ruin our lives," Marilee objected, "we don't consider that harm?"

"Of course we do," Brian replied, "but the question is a matter of intent. They don't intend to ruin our lives, but obviously that can be a side-effect. That's one of the reasons it's important we find a way to communicate with them, to show them they can cause harm inadvertently. We must make them understand that. If they involve themselves in someone's life, as Cassandra has in Johnny's, they must do so straightforwardly instead of toying with us. They must understand that any relationship with a human should be consensual."

Marilee looked at her husband for a long while, and finally asked: "Why you, Johnny? What happens when you go there?"

Her question came at him like an anvil dropped from a high window. He averted his eyes, and then locked them shut as his heart started to race. The question was inevitable, though he had hoped dearly she would never ask it.

Brian felt awkward. He knew Johnny would have to lie to avoid giving her another emotional blow; or leave her assuming something perhaps even worse; though what that might be, from a wife's perspective, he couldn't say.

Johnny's jaw tightened when he turned his head to look at her. Her eyes were imploring, begging him to help her grasp what he himself did not fully understand. He realized that he could no longer leave her in the dark about Cassandra's excesses, not completely. His tone was unemotional when he spoke. "That night I didn't come home," he hesitated, shaking his head with the agony of making the confession. "...Cassandra took me to remote ally across town. There was a bar there, a hangout for the scum of the earth. They wore leather. They had pierced nipples and tongues and all kinds of tattoos. About thirty of them, mostly men. Heathens. They drugged me and stripped off my clothes, then put me on a pool table and gang raped me. I passed out and didn't wake up until the next morning. You and Reverend Aragones saw what I looked like when I got home."

Reacting to shock, Marilee came to her feet. "My God!" she cried, turning and walking toward the drafting table, dazed with the images Johnny had put in her mind.

Brian released a sigh. "That's the sort of thing the entities do to amuse themselves," he said sadly. "At least the one called Cassandra Mott."

"And you say she doesn't want to harm us?" Marilee shot at Brian, turning sharply to look at him.

"Marilee," said Johnny, "what he means is they have no desire to inflict pain or kill us. Cassandra didn't interpret what she was doing as harmful. And that's the scary part. They can put you through something like that unaware of how harmful it is. Scarier still that you're left wondering if you somehow belong to that sort of world."

Marilee was speechless. That morning had burned deeply into her memory, where it remained like a festering sore. Though it was the last thing she would have suspected, what Johnny had just described perfectly fit the condition he had come home in that morning. That he had endured it, that a man, particularly the man she was married to, could be made to avail that kind of thing was beyond her comprehension. Hatred for Cassandra Mott filled her heart. That woman, or entity, or whatever Cassandra Mott happened to be, had defiled her husband in a monstrous way. It wasn't a spell or a mystification—it was a curse. And what Marilee hated most of all were the conflicting emotions inside her husband's head. Was he an innocent in all of this, or just a man not fully determined to stop an exotic adventure?

She stepped over to the glass doors and looked out at the dark Savannah night. Moonlight fell softly on the garden, off and on shadowed by drifting clouds with bright edges and dark bellies. Through the glass she could almost hear the eerie quiet that seemed to have swallowed their home. Much of the back yard lie in shadows, black voids harboring who knows what. She wondered what might be out there looking back, perhaps sizing her up, a thought brought on by a newfound awareness that the world all around her was a far more mysterious and frightening place, inhabited by the unstated and the unseen.

"How do we get Cassandra Mott and her brother out of our lives?" she muttered, her face near its reflection in the glass. She turned and looked at the men who were staring at the floor, and the stress that gripped her voice rose from her belly. "I'm scared Johnny. Please tell me ... how do we fight this?"

Johnny lifted his head to look at her. "I'm not scheduled to work tomorrow. I'm taking Brian over there first thing in the morning."

"She might shut me out like she has you," Brian added. "I hope not. If Cassandra will allow me in, we might be able to start a dialogue, or at least find out why she's fixated on Johnny."

Marilee didn't like the idea of Johnny going back to that house, but for want of a better idea she kept quiet. Anything, anything at all was better than sitting on their hands.

Brian drained the last swallow of his third cup of coffee and stood up. Before leaving, he jotted down the phone number and address to his small apartment. Johnny walked with him to the door, and then returned to the garden room. Marilee still stood near the glass, looking out. He came up behind her and wrapped his arms around her waist.

"You're at wits-end with me, aren't you?" he said.

"I just wish I knew why she chose you, Johnny. Wish I could understand how they've existed so long and no one knows about them." She paused in thought, staring out into the darkness. "I can't understand why you went to that bar, the kind of place men like that go."

He pulled her closer to him and held her for a moment. "You've had a long day," he finally said. "Are you hungry?"

"I took a dinner break at six o'clock."

"Then let's go to bed."

In the bedroom, he undressed and waited atop the sheets while Marilee showered. He had not mentioned it to Marilee, but he had enormous reservations about taking Brian into that house. He had not had time to convince Cassandra that Brian meant her no harm, and he worried Julian might simply grow weary of Brian's aggressive pursuit. But Brian had insisted they go right away and no argument swayed him.

Marilee came out of the bathroom, blotting her arms and legs with a towel. Nearing the bed, she flung it aside and crawled in beside Johnny, pulling the sheet up over her chest. He turned on his side, facing her, prepared to move closer, but hesitated, aware intuitively that she wanted to be left alone.

"I've wondered the same thing, myself," he said.

"Wondered what?" she asked, staring at the ceiling.

"How they've existed for thousands of years without detection. Seems to me maybe they haven't." He shifted his weight and propped himself on his elbow. "Perhaps their existence has come down through the ages in lore and history books. Witches for example. Makes sense, doesn't it? There're references to witchcraft and sorcery all the way back to biblical times. If past generations witnessed their eccentric behavior and power, why wouldn't our ancestors conclude the entities were witches. It could've been a creature like Cassandra, or even Cassandra herself who stirred up Salem. She could've been responsible for the witch trials."

She turned to look at him. He seemed eager to put her mind to rest. A fragile smile formed on her lips and she reached over and placed her hand aside his face.

"Why didn't you tell me what happened to you that night?"

Johnny's expression sobered. "It's not something a man wants to tell his wife. I was emasculated that night. I just wanted to forget it happened."

"Why did she take you there? She must have known how damaging that would be to you."

"That's just it, Marilee. I don't believe for a minute she knows that. Her world is so bizarre. I believe she thinks that god-awful ordeal was a source of pleasure for me."

Marilee withdrew her hand, at odds with what he was saying. "You're defending her!"

"No. I'm trying to understand her motives."

Marilee's eyes shifted back to the ceiling. A silence fell over them for a few moments. He looked at her, scared to death their present course might spiral out of control; that she might eventually learn of the carnal acts he had been involved in with Julian. He felt tainted. He had failed to resist the urges he could feel inside, even now as he lay beside her. His acts of submission, his going to Cassandra's house for that purpose, Marilee could never forgive. He prayed that Brian, with his penchant for persuasion, might find a way to convince Cassandra to bring this nightmare to an end; for no matter what else may happen, he wanted to cling to their newfound closeness. Just now, he wanted nothing more than to be loved by his wife.

"Can I hold you?" he asked, his tone touched with unease, verging on a plea.

She lifted the sheet and he shifted his weight to get closer, moving in beside her with his arm across her ribs just beneath her breasts. He ventured a leg over hers and rested his head next to hers on her pillow, finding peace in the comforting scent of her hair. They lay quietly, a weary pair about to fall asleep as one. After a while, Marilee heard the long, deep breaths of sleep and she turned her head to look at her husband. Their time-honored bond had become frayed. How long, she wondered, could it hold them together?

Chapter 29

Brian arrived at seven A.M. the next morning. Marilee answered the door and invited him in for poached eggs and toast. Johnny had just gotten out of bed and was shaving. Brian sat the breakfast table and watched her move along the counter with the routine of her morning chore, wondering briefly if he himself might be suited to growing old with a wife. The thought evaporated. He had gone past that, the memories still vivid of a failed marriage, not to mention the weeks he had wallowed in bliss with his young Maasai lover. It had been bliss, to be sure; but now, at this stage in his life, his libido no longer awakened with vibrancy for the softer, more delicate curves of a woman; which, at the moment were reflecting delightfully from his eyes. Though the feminine half of humanity enchanted him and were often so easy on the eyes, he had long since reconciled his need for the companionship of another male.

"Johnny's afraid Cassandra will hurt you if she feels threatened by your research," Marilee said over her shoulder.

"I know. I suppose my unsolicited appearance over there will test that theory. Fact is, I'd give almost anything to be taken into her confidence."

"Showing up unexpected sounds like a risky way to test her."

"Well, I know better than to wait for an invitation. I think if she meant to harm me, she would've done so in Africa. Since she appeared while I was sleeping, I didn't see her. Have to say, I can hardly wait to set eyes on her."

"Hope you have better luck than I did," said Marilee, bringing a tray filled with toast and eggs to the table.

Johnny walked in, yawning. He had lain awake most of the night, much like he did every night, this time fretting over what could happen to Brian. But this was the first step toward salvaging what little was left of his life and he had gotten out of bed feeling slightly optimistic for the first time in a long while. It was like a resolution had been born in him during the night.

"Good morning, Professor Fowler," he said, giving Brian a squeeze on the shoulder as he passed. "Are you ready to be turned into a toad?"

Brian laughed, saying: "Please, if she decides to transform me into some kind of creature, use your influence with her to make it something other than a toad. Go for a bird ... a hawk perhaps, or even a crow. Anything but a toad."

Johnny sat down and scooted his chair up to the table. "I wouldn't count too heavily on my influence."

"Let's just hope she'll see me," said Brian, spooning two poached eggs onto his plate.

They ate and were walking out of the house twenty minutes later. Marilee, her neck and shoulders tight with worry, stood in the doorway and watched them get into Brian's rented car, hoping the queasiness in her stomach wasn't a dark premonition for their morning adventure.

Ten minutes later, Brian found a place to park on the far side of Confederate Square. When he got out and closed the car door, he stood looking at the imposing facade for a moment. Johnny came around from behind the car and stood beside him.

"Having second thoughts?" he asked.

"No. Just admiring it. I picture Cassandra as an exquisite Southern belle. The house fits that image perfectly."

Johnny scanned the front windows and saw no signs of the beautiful pair. Side-by-side, he and Brian started into the square. Everything but the house melted into vague blurs in their peripheral vision. It would be a while before the droves of tourists were walking about, the park-like square now sparsely inhabited only by a few students on their way to their first class. The air, already warm on their skin, lay motionless over the old city, promising damp collars and underarms well before noon. The sky above the graceful boughs looked like a creamy blue dome, interspersed with the dark and translucent greens of a million leaves.

Passing through the front gate, their necks craned and stiff, they scanned the windows and the door. Buoyed by the confidence of companionship, they walked with resolute strides and mounted the stairs. Johnny took from his pocket the key. Waiting with unease, Brian watched the door swing open and then followed Johnny inside.

"Son of a bitch!"

It was an outburst of indignation. Johnny turned this way and that, frustrated by the echo of his own voice. If Brian was to confront Cassandra Mott, if he was to be severely dealt with, it would not be today. The house was empty—not a stick of furniture to be seen. No wall table offering a serving dish of peanuts near the door. No beautiful woman gazing up at the balustrade. No chorus emanating from the wall. Nothing.

He turned to face Brian. The frustration had gathered on his face like a brewing storm.

"What's going on here?" Brian asked in confusion.

"Nothing's going on here! That's the problem! She's not here. Everything's gone, the furniture, everything."

Brian swiped his hand over his mouth, glancing about, feeling a sense of disappointment and maybe a small underlying bit of relief. Evidently he would not see Cassandra today, nor would be turned into a toad. He allowed himself a moment to reorder his thoughts, and then said: "At least you can show me the house."

Johnny twisted his head downward and reached up to rub the back of his neck. "She's driving me crazy. Next thing I know, you'll be doubting me, too, just like Marilee."

"Not likely, my friend. It's obvious Cassandra wants no part of me. Come on, show me the downstairs first."

They walked from room to room. Johnny remained alert, listening for any sound at all, scanning the nooks and shadows for the snake. The walls and cornices looked the same, the polished hardwood floors, the fine woodwork and plaster; but the feel was so very different—there was no feel at all. It was just a big, empty house. There were no tingles on his skin, no tightness in his chest. It could have been any abandoned house in Savannah.

Taking his time, Brian perused every detail of every room, every cornice and cabinet, almost as fascinated by the hundred year old architecture as he was by their reason for being there. The first floor tour ended back in the front foyer.

"I can tell this house is occupied," he said, looking up the stairway.

"Well, that evidence got past me," said Johnny, looking at him cynically.

"There isn't a spot of dust anywhere. Not even on the baseboards. It also smells fresh. Haven't you noticed? In this heat and humidity a house would smell stale if it had been sitting unoccupied."

"Thank God!" said Johnny. What would he do if Brian became hesitant to believe him?

"I'll never doubt you, my friend. I haven't from the first moment we met, and I never will. Don't forget I saw the confirmation Julian left behind in Africa. And as for this house? If he can turn water into mud, he should have no trouble making a houseful of furniture disappear. Our scheming little surprise visit simply didn't work, that's all. We'll have to think of another way to get me turned into a toad."

Johnny smiled, and the smile melted wistfully with a labored swallow as he stared at his companion. "I can't tell you how much I missed you."

Brian's shoulders dropped and he released a sigh. He turned from Johnny and strode to the window next to the front door. There he stood and looked out, not only disappointed by Cassandra's absence, but also desperate for Johnny to let that subject drop.

"She's gonna leave me," he heard Johnny say, his tone flat, as if he knew with certainty that his wife was destined to leave him, that he had already accepted it. "I sensed it last night, and again this morning."

Brian whipped around. "How the hell do you sense something like that?"

"I just know."

"That's ridiculous!"

"Not after living with her for nine years. When you know someone that well, they tell you things in subtle ways, whether they mean to or not. It can be the look in their eyes, or a distant silence, or maybe their body-language when they get in bed beside you."

Brian turned back toward the window.

"I'll always love her. I know I will. I think she'll always love me, or who I was, but I'm not the same man she's been married to for nine years, and she knows it. I held her last night. I felt the love between us, but I also felt something else. She was tense, like she was allowing herself to be held by a man she didn't really know. I think she and I both realize that I'll never be able to give back the life she's always known. I think you know that, too, and you know the reason why. Even if Cassandra leaves my life forever, and you go back to Boston or Africa, what I feel for you will still be inside me. I didn't ask for it, but it's there. I want to be naked, Brian. I want to feel your eyes on me, and that sort of thing makes me a poor husband. It's only surprising she's tolerated as much as she already has."

Brian continued to stare out the window. Johnny's emotional disclosure had come unexpectedly. He had just listened to words that set off a kind of euphoric confusion when his mindset had involved facing Cassandra Mott. His nervousness increased as Johnny stepped up behind him and stood a mere few inches away. The sunlight filtered in and felt warm on his face, and he closed his eyes to it, trying to collect his thoughts.

"What scares me is," Johnny went on to say, "when she leaves, what's left of me won't be enough to interest you."

Brian turned and looked at him with clear anger. "Don't you think I would be the best judge of that?" He drew in a deep breath and took Johnny by the shoulders. A life of companionship and bliss passed through his mind like a pleasant breeze; yet he resisted the impulse to kiss him because of his faltering moral code and the fact that this was the worst possible timing. "Listen to me. I have very quickly come to care for Marilee; but if it turns outs she decides she's better off starting a new life, so be it. For all you know, that may never happen. It's nothing more than conjecture. So quit torturing yourself, and me. We have another challenge here, within the walls of this house. We don't have the luxury of letting our focus be overshadowed by anything else."

A moment of weakness came over Johnny, brought on by his desire to be loved by the man now looking at him with such concern. The premonition of Marilee leaving him was too real to ignore, born in her weary and silent presence. His face weighted with futility, Brian took him into his arms and Johnny melted into the revitalizing warmth. He tilted back his head and stared into Brian's eyes; and then watched the hints of a vulnerable smile curled the corners of his pale lips.

Brian's heart raced as he looked at his companion. There was nothing preventing him from going to the floor with this man, except those strained sinews of willpower that keep a man from committing a wrong. He drew a deep breath.

"Let's take a look at the second floor," he said, releasing his arms, letting his hand slide down and rest on the small of Johnny's back. They turned toward the stairway.

Johnny paused half way up the stairs to press his ear against the wall. Dead quiet. He reared back his head and looked at it as if the wall had betrayed him.

"What're you doing?" Brian asked.

"The voices come from here, that chorus I told you about."

Brian's gaze lifted all the way up the wall and back down. He saw nothing other than a high span of expensive wallpaper.

Johnny paused again at the top of the stairs, staring down the hallway at Cassandra's door. It occurred to him, in spite of the fact the rest of the house was empty, that *that* door could open on just about anything. He felt anxious about entering the parlor, knowing Cassandra could be in there waiting.

"That's her door, isn't it?" said Brian, coming around beside him.

Johnny nodded as his eyes shifted to the knob. He stared at it, as if it were the muzzle of a vicious dog, ready to snap at any hand that reached for it.

"Shall we have a look in there first?" said Brian.

Johnny looked at him. "Are you as nonchalant about going in there as you sound?"

"Lord no, my friend. I could quite easily bolt back down those stairs and out the front door. But of course that would mean facing this hallway again, and walking down it for the first time. Might as well be done with it today."

Johnny returned his attention to the door, and then started toward it, listening carefully, hearing nothing but their creaking footfall across the ancient floor. Pausing at the door, he lifted his hand to take hold of the knob. The antique white porcelain felt cool and smooth against his palm. Then, without further thought, he turned the knob and pushed open the door. Brian heard a breath of relief.

The room was empty.

Brian stepped around him and stopped a few feet into the room and glanced around, nodding his approval of the elegant room.

"There you see, we were fretting over nothing," said Brian, perusing the room. "Well, you said it was a parlor and a magnificent parlor it is." He looked up into the ceiling alcove, at the chandelier. "Ah ... one might expect to see cobwebs on that fine chandelier if this house had been sitting vacant. It sparkles as if it had been polished yesterday."

Johnny's eyes narrowed with suspicion as he scanned every inch of the room. He felt disoriented—the room normally so well appointed now so empty. Gone were the luxurious sofas, the lamps, the mahogany furniture. It was no more than a large enclosure of beautiful bare walls, and doors that led to more empty space. He crossed the room and looked closely at the wall on which the Renoir hung a few days before. No discoloration where a painting had hung, no nail or wall hook. He ran his fingers over the plaster and couldn't find so much as a nail hole.

It was maddening. Sure, Julian had turned a bathtub full of water into mud, but it was still impossible to fathom the disappearance of an entire house full of furniture. And when did he do it, Johnny wondered? The moment he and Brian drove into Confederate Square? Or the moment they walked through the front gate? Were the beautiful pair in the house this very moment, in some secret room or passageway, watching and waiting? Or could Cassandra and Julian, like the furniture, simply vanish into thin air? It tormented him, this mysterious, unexplainable game, this toying with his mind.

Brian had stopped gazing up at the chandelier and was squinting at the cornicing and fretwork along the walls just under the ceiling. He followed Johnny into the bathroom, where Johnny stood trance-like, looking at the tub.

"So that's where you and Julian had your mud bath?" Brian said, stepping closer to the counter.

"Yeah," Johnny said, staring at the tub, picturing him and Julian covered in mud. It brought to mind the forgotten frolics of his youth, those few naïve episodes when he and a roommate explored each other's body, a far cry from his recent awakening to the profound hunger for male intimacy. That youthful curiosity had reemerged with undying energy, a need to couple with another man, precisely the man whose presence he could feel not three feet behind him.

Brian leaned over the marble counter to appraise the golden fixtures gracing the sink. He let out a small laugh. "Wonder what she'd do if I brought in a cot and camped out here until she and Julian returned?"

The tension had settled into Johnny's shoulders. He turned, rubbing his left arm. "Do you seriously think you could stay in this house alone, at night, and actually fall asleep?"

Brian turned to Johnny with a grin. "What happens if I do—I get turned into a *dead* toad?"

Johnny stepped over beside him. "Seems like this little adventure has charged your batteries."

"I find a bit of levity helpful when I'm scared shitless."

"You ready to see the rest of the upstairs?"

"My friend, I'm ready to get out of here."

Johnny smiled and nodded.

Following his companion back through the parlor, Brian looked toward the alcove at the front of the room. "Wait a minute. ...Does that window overlook the square?" Brian was looking at the small sitting area, a sunny space divided from the rest of the parlor by two pairs of columns. Johnny followed him in. "A perfect place to read and write," Brian said, approaching the window. "I suppose when you live in a house this big, you end up with a favorite room. This would be mine." He knifed his fingers through the center of the lace curtains and parted them and looked down at the square. There were more pedestrians on the sidewalks now. Kids were climbing on the bronze cannon in the center of the square. The sun had inched further into the morning sky and imposed a glare on the glass.

"She could see her guests as they arrived in carriages," Brain said, looking down toward the wrought-iron gate. "The old stepping-stone is still there. You can almost see the grand coaches pulling up to the curb one after another. Gentlemen in their top hats extending their hands to help the elegant ladies step down to the pavement. No wonder Cassandra wanted another lifetime in Savannah. I'm not surprised she longs for that era."

Brian suddenly felt something crawling on his forearm.

"My God!" he cried.

A centipede!

He stood paralyzed, staring at the long segmented insect that apparently came off the curtains, its countless legs in motion as it advanced toward the crook of his arm. Johnny stepped forward with a determined swoosh of his hand, sending the insect flying against a windowpane. It crawled into a crack in the corner of the sill. Brian stood there for a moment, staring at his arm. Then his eyes shifted with aversion to Johnny's.

"I hate those damn things" he said with a weakened voice. "Too many legs." There were tiny beads of sweat across his forehead.

"Why didn't you knock it off?"

"Guess I froze. Snakes don't bother me nearly as much."

"Yeah, well, I'm surprised we haven't seen one of those here today," Johnny said, taking Brian's forearm for a closer look. "It didn't sting you, did it?"

"Just felt it crawling up my arm."

Johnny released his arm and looked at him. "Interesting. Afraid of bugs, a man who spends so much time in Africa."

"We all have our weaknesses, my friend."

"And right now one of mine is fresh air. Let's get out of here."

Brian glanced at the windowsill and said: "I'm right behind you."

Johnny stopped briefly half way down the stairs to press his ear against the wall one more time. Nothing. He proceeded down the stairs and out the front door, frustrated. They crossed the street and took a seat on a shaded bench in the middle of Confederate Square.

"We didn't see a single sign of her," Johnny said, leaning back against the bench.

Brian folded his arms and turned to look at the house. "You saw her the first time you entered the house?"

"Yeah ... in the shower." Johnny recalled the image. "Naked," he said, staring across the square, remembering the hypnotic effect of her casual nudity. "God, she's beautiful. I was in the parlor and heard water running in the bathroom. I went in ... couldn't believe my eyes. There she was. When she asked my name, I couldn't remember it."

"A good way to slam you right into her world, sounds like."

"It worked. Just her beauty mystifies you." Johnny rubbed his hand over the top of his head. "What are you gonna do if she refuses to see you?"

"I'll find a way to see her eventually," Brian said, glancing at the tourists crossing the square with their cameras. He was thinking about Johnny's premonition about Marilee leaving him. "Right now I'm worried about you, my friend."

Johnny turned to look at him. "Oh really! Why? Just because I'm falling into a bottomless hole?"

"Actually, I was thinking about your wife. She didn't give me the impression she intends to leave you."

"She's changed, Brian. And why not? I've ruined her life. She thinks I'm losing my mind. She's working long hours because I lost the ambition to rebuild my career. If that's not enough, she'll never trust me again when she finds out what I've been involved in inside that house." Johnny looked at him. "Would you stay married to me if you were her? And there's you. Now she has a husband who wants to be with another man. Even if I could fix everything else, that'll eventually come between us. It feels inevitable."

Brian looked down at the small birds landing on the brick walkway near his feet.

Johnny drew a troubled breath and released it. "She's still young and pretty. I see men looking at her all the time. There's someone out there who deserves her more than I do. I've thought about it. Best thing I could do for her is be honest. Tell her everything. Tell her about you and me." Johnny sat upright and his head fell back as he looked up into the trees. "She'd be better off with Reverend Aragones. He certainly seemed interested."

"From what you told me about him, I got the impression he's a rather duplicitous character."

"He's stable. Well respected here in Savannah. He can offer a woman security. And the sonofabitch looks like an Italian count."

An elderly couple walked by in the warm morning air. The sparrows fluttered and returned one by one. Brian pondered Johnny's words with mixed emotions. The thought of ending his lonely nights with a companion and lover unfolded pleasantly in his mind, but the cost seemed so high. He felt like an intruder, an instigator of bad choices, though Johnny might not have a choice in the matter since the uncertainty of their future promised only to escalate. He wondered if Johnny, down deep inside, could ever stop loving the woman he had spent nine years with.

"Give it some time, my friend. Think about what you're saying. If the time comes to make a decision like that, it'll be clearer to you than it is now."

"I keep asking myself if it's wrong to keep her hanging on to something that's already lost," said Johnny, his voice strained with facts he never imagined he would have to face. "We haven't even had that much in common, not really. She's always been disappointed that I wouldn't share her religious beliefs or participate in her social activities. Just recently she gave all of that up to try to be the wife she thinks I want her to be. Shit. I feel like I could crawl in a hole and never come out." He glanced at Brian. The agony of his words had tightened his face. "I even thought about leaving Savannah," he said as his gaze drifted back out over the square. "Just disappear. California maybe. Work as a janitor or something. Sit on the beach and stare at the sea until I'm too old to live any longer."

Brian had not seen Johnny this depressed. It worried him. It worried him because Johnny was facing a transition, the kind of thing that sometimes made people look for an easier way out. He draped his arm around Johnny's shoulders and pulled him closer. In the fragrant morning air, they sat quietly for a while. Brian looked at the house and an idea began to incubate.

"C'mon," he said, squeezing Johnny's shoulder. "You've had a long week at that home improvement center. You could use a little rest. I'll drive you home so you can take a nap. We'll go out tonight for dinner."

Brian pulled into Johnny's driveway a few minutes later. Johnny noticed, as he got out of the car, a man sitting in a pick-up truck parked at the curb. As Brian backed out onto the street and drove away, the man got out of the truck and approached with a sheaf of papers.

"Are you Johnny Feelwater?" he asked cordially, indicating a purpose for being there.

Johnny looked him over, a tall thin, good ol' boy type, his clothes a size too small and dated twenty years, his hair oiled and combed back. He seemed harmless enough.

"Yes, I'm Johnny Feelwater."

"Now that's a piece of luck. I knocked on your door and no one answered. Just having a bite of lunch when you drove up."

Johnny knew that Marilee would have already left for work by now. "Is there something I could do for you?" he asked as the man looked through his papers.

"You can sign right here," he said, extending a clipboard.

"Sign? What is it?"

"A lawsuit, Mr. Feelwater. I'm a county deputy. Looks like you're being sued by an outfit called Globalcorp." The man attempted to hand Johnny the papers.

Johnny looked at them as if he were being presented a rabid skunk.

"Just sign here, sir, and I'll finish my lunch and be on my way. Got three more of these to take care of before the day's over."

Johnny took the pen absentmindedly. His thoughts reeled in a flurry of disbelief. *A lawsuit? Globalcorp? Why would they want to sue me?* He signed and looked at the cover page as the man turned and walked back to his truck. *Breach of Contract! What the hell...?*

Another little piece of his future had been snatched. In unexpected increments, his life had been dismantled. Walking dazed into the house, he thought of Marilee. One more thing to add to the heap, maybe the last straw. It reinforced his belief that he wasn't fit to be her husband. A lawsuit! He didn't have the money to hire a lawyer, let alone offer a settlement. Their hope for any kind of prosperity was being ground under the heel of a relentless boot.

He walked through the garden room and plopped the papers on his drafting table on the way out to the patio. After peeling off his shirt in the late morning heat, he slumped into one of the outdoor chairs, his eyes vacant as he stared across the yard at the garden. He didn't want to tell her about those papers. A lawsuit. Even a weak case against him was ruinous. With Globalcorp certain to come at him with the full clout of its legal department, he could scarcely afford even one hour of a lawyer's time.

California crept into his mind. That, at least, sounded better than the nearest asylum. He could live in obscurity. In one room. Do his laundry with the illegal immigrants. He could survive on warm cans of soup and spend hours walking the beach. His eyes flittered aimlessly across the back yard. Such a dismal existence seemed vastly more desirable than what he faced now. California. Three thousand miles away. He would miss her, certainly. At least she would have her life back. But could he abandon Brian, forever dreaming about their last day in Africa together, regretting perhaps the single most important lost opportunity of his lifetime? That would be tough. That kept him from packing a suitcase.

♦ ♦ ♦

Needing a few supplies for his small apartment, Brian drove to a super center a few miles outside of the historic district. He pushed a cart down one aisle after another, tossing in towels and detergent and frozen dinners, preoccupied with a single thought. By the time he got back to his room he was obsessed.

He gathered the three full bags he had purchased and got out of the rent car. Flooded with a growing sense of urgency, he climbed the wooden stairway that led to his room. Inside, he absently placed the supplies in various drawers and cabinets. He had noticed that Johnny had forgotten to lock the front door when they walked out of Cassandra's house. Now he was anxious to go back, to go inside and look around, alone, to challenge Cassandra to present herself.

This time, the house looked even more ominous as he drove into to Confederate Square. Brian parked and took a few deep breaths to steel his courage. After crossing the square, he approached the house as if it were a cave of hibernating bears. The front gate creaked open with a half-hearted nudge. He took the porch steps with leaded feet and paused for one more breath before turning the knob. The door then pushed open just as he had hoped. He stepped inside and closed it behind him.

Struck immediately, everywhere he looked, the house was fully furnished. Astonished, his heart at once beat faster. This visit, he quickly realized, would be much different than his first.

He looked in the dining room with a start. A dog!

It came to its feet, alert, a large mixed-breed of some kind, its head hyena-like, its chest broad. It stared intently, head lowered, horrific with its tattered black hair and menacing yellow eyes. Brian stepped back. Feeling his shoulders against the door, his hand went slowly for the knob, a cautious move but enough to provoke the dog. It bore fangs and quivering lips and from it came a low, guttural growl. Brian had never seen such a god-awful creature. It continued to step toward him, emitting that awful growl, as if it were sizing up its prey.

"Planning to do me in with a heart attack, Cassandra?" Brian called out, not taking his eyes off the dog.

His back pressed against the door, Brian found the knob and quickly let go. It was hot, like grabbing something metallic that had been placed near a flame. The dog slunk ever closer, its eyes locked on Brian's. He stood motionless, his breath erratic as the dog sniffed the cuff of his pants, feeling its hot breath through the fabric as its snout moved up the inside of his leg, all the way to his crotch. As he closed his eyes and rested the back of his head against the door, the fury of his heart made him doubt how much of this he could endure. He wished mightily he had not come. Desperate, just as he was about to try the doorknob again, he heard a woman's voice.

"You decided to come back, I see," Cassandra said from the balustrade.

His eyes opened and lifted and beheld a most exquisite woman. Her red hair was pulled back tight and tied in a ponytail. She wore a satiny black negligee that lay open down the front, under which he saw a pattern of black leather straps, crisscrossing over the feminine contours of her cream colored skin. Her makeup was harsh and heavy, her eyes glowering as she leaned into the railing, looking down at him. Brian swallowed dryly, staring at her for a moment before his first words labored from his cottony throat.

"You must be Cassandra," he said, still pressed against the door.

"Should I be flattered you know me, Mr. Fowler?"

"No, Madam. But please, I would be eternally grateful if you'd call off this dog."

"What dog, Mr. Fowler?"

Brian's eyes shifted downward. The pent-up tension left his body like air hissing from a balloon. His head snapped in every direction. The dog had disappeared. His gaze shot upward. Born in a squall of conflicting emotions, his instincts told him to excuse himself and get out of that house as quickly as possible. He hesitated. His curiosity would not let him reach for the knob. Though within her eyes he saw anger and contempt, he also saw a woman possessed by her own curiosity. He realized that this could be his one and only opportunity to win her over, to befriend her; that by failing to do so, he may never see her again.

Damp with perspiration, still trembling within, he took a few steps forward. "Are ... are we to become acquainted today, Miss Mott?"

"You must intend to write another book."

"Whatever I intend to do, it's not meant to offend or threaten you," Brian tried to assure her.

"Do you really believe you could threaten me, sir?"

"Do you *not* want me to write another book?"

Cassandra smiled. "On the contrary, I intend to give you something to write about. But I shall first introduce you to two of my friends," she said, nodding at the two men now standing directly behind him.

Brian turned slowly and looked at the men standing to his right and left. They had appeared out of thin air, large, muscular men, bare feet and naked chests, wearing canvas dungarees. They stood stoically, one with hands clasped on his hips, the other with tattooed arms folded over a rising and falling chest, as if they were awaiting Cassandra's directive. Brian, immediately nervous, vastly preferred them to the dog.

Sizing up her supernatural power as phenomenal, Brian glanced back up at her, wondering if these theatrics posed a real threat. It occurred to him that she had presented herself as a dominatrix, that perhaps the two men were servants or sex slaves. But why were they standing behind him, so close?

Cassandra nodded. Both men reached for Brian's arms. Directed toward the stairs, he offered no resistance as they began to ascend. They reached the landing. Cassandra turned and sauntered resolutely toward her parlor, the long black negligee flowing from side-to-side with her stride. She held open the door as the two men escorted Brian inside.

"Am I being kidnapped, Miss Mott?" he said in passing.

She ignored the question and took an intimidating stand beneath the chandelier, looking Brian over from head to toe. Still seized by both arms, he hesitated before asking another question. Loathe to divulge the ambiguity that tightened his chest, he glanced over the elaborate furnishings in the room, and then saw a third man sitting on one of the sofas. Not nearly as large or threatening as the two gripping his arms, this man was striking and seemingly oblivious to the goings-on in the room as he casually flipped through a magazine.

Julian, thought Brian. *My God, he's beautiful. He just sits there ignoring all of this.*

Distracted, Brian momentarily slipped from his state of apprehension. His gaze drifted from Julian to the back wall. There, he saw the Renoir, which returned his thoughts to the intrigues of Cassandra's parlor.

"Are you a fan of Renoir, Mr. Fowler?"

Brian looked at her. "An adoring fan, Miss Mott. Mind if I have a closer look?"

She nodded and the two brutes released Brian's arms. He walked past her and approached the painting, thoroughly mystified by the circumstances it so casually hung on this particular wall, when any museum in the world would covet it. He lost himself briefly in his love for Renoir's voluptuous interpretation of the female form, perusing the brush strokes and contrasts of light that formed such sensuous pleasure for the eye.

"So Renoir handed you this painting himself," Brian said, reaching out to lift the painting off the wall.

"Look on the back," said Cassandra. The hard edge in her tone had softened.

Brian turned the painting over, where he saw written on the canvas in red paint the words: *You enchant me, Cassie. You must pose for me, soon.*

Brian looked at her.

A wily gleam appeared in Cassandra's eyes. "You're a fool, Brian Fowler. You're thinking Renoir actually wrote those words to me."

Brian smiled, realizing it would take more than a little effort to win her confidence. His heart had settled, for the threat before him seemed less ominous than it had moments earlier. He believed, by virtue of this visit, he had found a way to put to rest a few of her suspicions.

After placing the painting back on the wall, he noticed the two men had closed in on him again.

"Are you ready to become a believer, Mr. Fowler?"

"A believer?" The way she said it made him suddenly lightheaded.

Her mood had reverted. She stood with her fists on her hips, feet wide apart and planted firmly, posturing with total authority. "Strip him naked," she demanded.

Once again in their clutches and now disoriented, Brian found himself being disrobed. He could not imagine what she had in mind. He looked down. His shirt and pants had been unbuttoned. From behind, one of the men had locked his arms around Brian's, while the other, kneeling in front of him, took a hold of the waistbands of his pants and underwear. Brian felt a rush of intoxication as his pants slid down his legs. The kneeling man unbuckled and removed his sandals and then lifted one leg at a time to pull the clothing over Brian's bare feet.

Adrenaline displaced his bewilderment. From the heat of his humiliation came a rebellious flash of rage. An explosion of violence knocked the man holding him off balance. Brian whipped around and threw a punch, landing it on a rock-hard jaw. Now steeled for a fight, he stood ready as both men came at him. The three of them collapsed in masse to the floor, a roiling maelstrom of arms and legs and fists. Holding his own, Brian broke free and got back on his feet, backing toward the sofas as his two foes approached for another attempt to subdue him. Panting, his shirt hung from his shoulders, torn down the front. His tense retreat halted when the back of his legs came up against the low table between the sofas. He turned and found himself standing face to face with Julian.

Julian looked at the two men, stopping them in their tracks; and then he looked up at Brian, who towered some three inches over him. His crystal blue eyes belied emotion, nor were they menacing as Brian stared at them as if they were rare jewels. There was an aura about him, like the air around him was charged with invisible particles that tingled across the hairs on Brian's forearms. Affected by such close proximity to one with untold strength, he realized the brawl had been put to an end. He could break and run, he presumed, but then realized he would never get past the door. He would not be allowed to leave this room without first hand knowledge of Cassandra's indoctrination.

Brian turned and glanced at the two men before his eyes shifted to Cassandra. "I'm quite capable of undressing myself, Madam," he said with withering indignation, slipping the shirt from his shoulders and letting it fall to the floor. As the chilled air settled over his skin, still moist from the brief moment of combat, he resisted the urge to squeeze his legs together and cup his hands over his genitals. Standing naked and humiliated before a beautiful woman and her cohorts brought on a level of mortification he had never experienced. Her eyes seemed to reduce him to a carnal whim, charging his fibers and pores with both sweet and shrinking sensations. To be displayed naked, though still suspended somewhat from the reality of his plight, he realized all too quickly that standing exposed before four pairs of eyes utterly extracted one's dignity. Cassandra stepped forward and combed her fingernails down through the salt and pepper hairs of his chest.

"My, my," she cooed with a sinister smile. "Our foolish guest has a temper."

Rubbing his sore knuckles, Brian all but cowered under the weight of her domineering presence. He nervously stated his argument again. "I'm not here to antagonize you, Cassandra. I want very much to be your friend."

"You're my enemy, Mr. Fowler."

"No," he said, for want of words to convince her.

"So you're a professor of antiquities. No doubt you know what the Roman armies did to their vanquished enemies after the battle," she said, removing her satin negligee, revealing a female form trussed in an intricate network of leather straps. The straps crisscrossed her upper body and cinched into her flesh. There was one strap over each shoulder and one that came up through her crotch, all joining a metal ring centered over her naval. Tightly trussed, her breasts stained against a web of narrower straps that joined a pair of similar but smaller rings, through which her nipples protruded. Rising to mid-thigh, her soft leather boots elevated her some three inches with rather dangerous looking spiked heels.

A sense of dread welled inside him and a chill rushed across his skin. Exposed to these unfamiliar and interested eyes, he feared the immanent unknown; yet he felt it drawing him into that world Johnny had so thoroughly described. His penis had taken on weight. Alive and aroused, he felt it twitching before her sensuous eyes, rendering him further exposed as it jutted outward. Was it her eyes that effected the chemical change, that bolted him to the here and now, which added a dimension to his nakedness that threatened to reduce him to begging for any degradation she might wish to impose?

From a drawer in the end table, Cassandra took out a leather harness of some kind. The two men again took a hold of his arms as she strapped it on. Wrapped around her small waist like a belt, she pulled a dangling lower piece through her legs, to which was attached a phallus. It was a monstrous thing, thick and upward curving with its veined rubbery length, now in place and protruding outward from her pubic mound. The two men forced Brian to bend over the back of the sofa. His heart was racing again. He felt confused by his own emotional conflicts, both drawn in to this series of events and terrified. An extreme unease strained the muscles of his neck and the back of his legs. Standing naked before her a moment earlier, he had heard and had begun to understand the sweet lyrics of the masochist's song, lyrics that now seemed bitter and frightening. He no longer felt the disarming calm that had lulled him, rather a menacing anticipation of what was to occur, a desperate wanting to get it over with; for nothing could be more obvious than Cassandra's intent. Brain glanced at Julian with a silent plea, who then returned to his magazine with no interest to intervene.

One of the brutes began to prepare him. Closing his eyes, Brian felt a rude parting of his gluteal cheeks and a gelatinous slathering. He could only hope that Cassandra would not damage him.

She stepped up behind him, directing the phallus with a crude nudge. As a prelude to his taming, she leaned forward to run her silky hands up both sides of his back, placing her bright red lips very near his ear. Brian felt the breath of her whisper.

"Now you shall have something to write about, my dear Mr. Fowler. You may tell the world that you were raped by a woman who's lived forty lifetimes over three thousand years. Tell them everything, my lovely man," she said, kneading his helpless shoulders. "Tell the whole world the woman that violated you once crossed a parched desert in an entourage behind Jesus Christ, just to hear His beautiful words." Dragging her fingernails down his back as she stood, her taunting continued. "Tell them everything ... and find out if they still put lunatics in asylums these days."

She rammed the phallus in.

Brian howled in pain. He tensed reflexively, enduring it with quivering lips and clenched fists. Sweat came over his entire body. His hands opened and his fingers scraped over the velvety sofa seeking something to grab. Impaled so rudely, the pain seared through him as if the thing had split him open. He had always believed a man's anus, that small gathering of pinched flesh, was designed to accommodate another man's cock—why else that implicit need? But not this, not the length and breadth of such a vile monster strapped to a taunting woman. He felt her soft hands take a hold of his hips as she thrust forward, grinding her pelvis against his flesh. He moaned and begged with incoherent words, squirming on the phallus to ease the pain. What had appeared to be soft rubber, felt like hot iron stabbing into unthinkable depths.

She backed out and then delivered another unmerciful thrust. Again his fingers turned into fists. His face ran with sweat as she thrust with the mastery of a man and fell into a masculine rhythm. The pain did not abate, nor did the agony turn into pleasure—it simply hurt, and he sought futilely to resign himself to the duration. And then, again like a man, Cassandra's rhythm became more intense. As if she had entered a carnal euphoria, she pounded with growing frenzy. He heard her moan and assumed the other end of the phallus must be pushing against the sensitive folds of her nether lips; for she released a scream and pushed ever harder against him.

Then it stopped.

She stepped back, pulling the behemoth from Brian's suffering flesh, unleashing the humid odors of his bowels. His jaw locked as he tried to stand, but his spent muscle gave way and he slumped onto the floor, a mass of weary flesh shuddering before the woman that did this to him.

"There, Mr. Fowler, you have another chapter," she said, removing the harness and letting it drop to the floor near his feet. His eyes made their way up to meet hers. "And of course you're welcome to come back anytime you run out of things to write about. I'm sure we can devise even more interesting episodes."

Brian got up on his elbow and watched her sweep across the room toward the bedroom, followed by her two male slaves. He lowered his head and rubbed his eyes with his fingers. The small movement shot painful messages to his brain. Finally getting to his feet, a dribble of watery mucus trickled down the back of his leg, and he reached back to find the horse-sized phallus had left his anus swollen and gaping. When he limped around the sofa to gather his clothes, Julian looked up from his magazine and watched his struggle to dress. Glancing at the beautiful creature, wondering what he might be thinking, Brian made no to attempt to communicate, wanting only to get out of their house. He fastened his pants, left his tattered shirt unbuttoned and then made his way across the room, glancing back once as he passed through the doorframe, questioning his nerve to ever come here again.

Outside, Brian crossed over to Confederate Square and paused at the first unoccupied bench. Taking a hold of the back of the bench, he wondered how much it would hurt to sit down. He looked back at the house and found Cassandra's window, certain he could see her standing behind the lace curtains, staring out at him. Why had she emasculated him? Had his humiliation been a warning or merely a test of his mettle? Painfully aware of the vibrant agony in his body, he wondered if perhaps it had been his initiation into her world; or instead, a sadistic admonition to stay away.

Chapter 30

After showering and lying on his stomach in bed the rest of the day, Brian arrived at Johnny's house at six o'clock as planned. Since Marilee was still at work, just the two of them would go out for dinner. Johnny answered the door and noticed right away something unspoken behind Brian's jovial but forced expression.

"You hungry?" Brian asked.

He seemed unusually withdrawn to Johnny. "Yeah. I forgot lunch."

Johnny stepped out onto the porch and turned to lock the door. When he got into the passenger side of the rent car, he watched Brian take a hold of the steering wheel and slowly lower himself onto the seat. After a few labored adjustments to his sitting position, Brian pulled the door closed.

"Something wrong?" Johnny asked.

"Rather obvious, isn't it?" Brian said regrettably, resting his forearms on the wheel. "I figured you'd recognize the after-effects of paying an impromptu visit to a certain nemesis of ours."

"What are you talking about?"

"I met your enchantress."

"You went to her house, alone!"

"Afraid my many years of higher education didn't provide an abundance of common sense."

"Brian," said Johnny, perturbed, "you didn't tell me you planned to go back by yourself."

"I came up with the idea after I took you home. Didn't call because you were tired. Didn't want you to try to talk me out of it, or feel obligated to go along."

Johnny's eyes swept along the dash. He wanted to explode, to chastise his companion for such a foolish maneuver, but refrained, knowing why Brian had taken the risk.

"You're a dumb-ass," he said out of frustration.

"I'm a sore-ass, my friend, real sore!"

Johnny looked at him. "So you saw her this time."

"Her, and Julian, and the two big bruisers who do her bidding ... oh yes, a Renoir properly hung on the back wall, a dog from hell, and a house full of wonderful furnishings. That was about it."

"What'd she do to you?"

Brian leaned forward and turned the ignition. The engine fired and he moved the shifter into reverse. "Where shall we go for dinner?"

"Do you know the way to the riverfront?"

"Factor's Row?"

"Yes."

"Believe so," said Brian, shifting into drive after backing into the street.

"Well?"

"You didn't tell me about her muscle-bound man-servants."

Johnny looked at him. "Man-servants?"

"She has two. They held me down while she raped me." Brian shifted his weight forward as much as possible. "It might have been a pleasant experience, if I'd been a female elephant."

Brian needed not say more. If it hurt him to sit, Johnny had little difficulty imagining Brian's ordeal. He stared through the windshield with concern, oblivious to the familiar neighborhoods falling behind.

"So what do you think?" Brian asked. "Did she have a reason to rape me other than a little mid-day entertainment?"

"It was a warning. She wouldn't have hurt you otherwise. She doesn't want you to expose their world—none of them do. It worries me. If your writing ever gains public acceptance, they'll feel backed into a corner. They won't let that happen, Brian."

"That's why I wanted to establish a dialog with them. I'm not so sure now."

"So Cassandra threw some water on your bed of coals?"

A wry breath of mirth came through Brian's nostrils. "He didn't touch me or say a word, but Julian influenced me more than Cassandra. I don't know. Maybe it was the way he looked at me, or what I felt standing close to him, but can't explain. What little time I've had to think about it, seems like I have a new perspective. It's like a feeling of respect for their privacy."

"Sounds like she got her point across," said Johnny.

"I wonder where her characters come from. Those two bruisers weren't a couple of boys from down the street. They were real, though. I could smell their body odor when they were holding me."

"That puzzles me, too. Those Confederate soldiers I ran into over there that day were real. It was like they just walked off the battlefield." Johnny looked at him. "Are you saying you're going to abandon your research?"

"Can't. For your sake if nothing else. That aside, my curiosity won't let me stop, no matter how sore my ass is right now. I'm thinking a new approach. I'll back off going public with what I learn, not that that made any difference anyway, but I still want to learn all I can. I still want to befriend them. I have to find a way to get past the brick wall."

"Let's hope the brick wall doesn't fall on you," Johnny said, pointing at a parking lot. "Pull in there. Might be a few empty spaces."

Brian found a place to park and then turned to look at his companion. "You look preoccupied. Something happen today?"

Shifting from his concern about Brian's safety, Johnny's peered through the windshield as he reflected on his most recent problem. "Globalcorp is suing me for breach of contract."

"Good Lord!" Brian looked out the side window. He closed his eyes and reached up to rub them. "How can so much bad luck happen to one man?" In view of the fact that earlier in the day Johnny sounded like a man on the verge of throwing in the towel, this news was particularly gloomy. "You sure you're in the mood for dinner?"

"Yeah. I haven't eaten since breakfast. There's a good seafood restaurant on the river."

"Sounds good to me," Brian said, reaching for the door handle.

Crossing the street, Johnny noticed Brian's stride significantly impaired. "Do you need to see a doctor for that?"

Brian scoffed. "Yeah, sure. Find myself trying to explain how something that big got shoved up my ass. I'll live with it."

Johnny smiled, though he was angry Cassandra had intentionally hurt him. "What if..."

"Don't worry about it," Brian interrupted. "I examined it with a mirror. Just bruised muscle."

They took the short walk to Factor's Row and turned down the steep, cobbled passageway between two of the old cotton exchange buildings. On the river side of the buildings, moving along with a tide of tourists, they walked another block to Johnny's favorite restaurant. Luckily, with just two or three parties ahead of them, a table by the window soon became available. After ordering dinner, Brian began thinking about Johnny's lawsuit.

"That's a raw deal, Globalcorp coming after you like that."

"I dread telling Marilee. Thought I'd wait until tomorrow. It's not in me to lay something else on her today. If I could just tell her when all of this was going to end, it wouldn't be so bad."

"If this was Boston, I could help you, but I don't know any lawyers here in Savannah."

"Doesn't matter. I don't have the money for a lawyer anyway. I'll have to plead my own case."

"You know what would be fascinating? Can you imagine Julian taking on this issue for you? I swear, when we stood eye-to-eye this afternoon, I could sense his power. It was almost like an electrical field surrounding him. He ended the fight just by standing up."

"Fight?"

"Wasn't much ... just a little tussle between me and Cassandra's male servants."

Johnny looked at his hand. "So that's what happened to your knuckles."

"Yeah. Hit one of um in the teeth. Didn't mean to. Going for the jaw."

Johnny's eyes lifted. "You're a born lunatic, Brian."

"No doubt I would've fared better ten years ago. I think Cassandra enjoyed it though." Brian adjusted his weight. "It's a whole different world, isn't it? I couldn't believe the sensations crawling all over me, getting stripped naked by two men while Cassandra watched. She looked incredible with that rubber dick strapped on."

Johnny shook his head. "You really got a taste, didn't you?"

"Yeah. It made the stories you told me about your experiences over there snap to life. Fascinating. Makes me want to know them all the more. Especially Julian. I can't imagine a sexual experience with him."

"It's not real," said Johnny.

"What do you mean?"

"It feels real ... nice I mean, but shallow. There's no real emotional attachment, not that that's important to a lot of guys." Johnny looked at Brian's forearm resting on the white linen tablecloth and said as a sort of quiet after-thought: "It is to me."

Brian was looking at him. The elements that comprised Johnny's personality came together like poetry for Brian. He thought about how much he enjoyed the simple things with him, how the last third of his life could be rounded out by the two of them sharing the meaningful pleasures in life, like this quiet dinner they were having together. He couldn't think of any place he'd rather be than sitting there and looking across the table at him, save the cozy little flat he would later be sleeping in alone. "Ah, well, like you said in Africa, we have to take it one day at a time, don't we, my friend?"

Johnny was in bed asleep by the time Marilee got home. He and Brian had spent a couple of hours walking along the riverfront, both of them thinking the same thing, both loathe to say it for fear of making it more difficult than it already was. Under other circumstances, it would have been natural for the two of them to go home together.

He awoke during the night staring into darkness, unable to get back to sleep. It wasn't the lawsuit keeping him awake—that had settled into his sub-consciousness like so many rotting leaves. He had awakened angry at Cassandra, wanting to confront her for what she did to Brian. But then, why bother to waste time being angry at her, when one glimpse of her smile could not only melt a man's anger, but his capacity for rational thought?

He turned his head and looked at Marilee, so lovely, sleeping peacefully beside him. Their love had been pushed onto a precipice. Though his love for her remained vibrant and strong, he was only now beginning to understand, as he lay quietly looking at her, that it had become the kind of love a man would feel for his sister.

He got out of bed and wandered around the house, ending up in the kitchen. Light spilled across the floor when he opened the refrigerator. Squinting into the brightness, he reached for an apple and carried it outside. Taking a bite, he looked up into the sky, a moonless black void splayed with a million stars. The night air felt like silk on his skin, the thick humidity still embracing the day's heat. Rolling his head over his weary shoulders, he looked back at the house, thinking it no longer seemed like his. It didn't seem possible. How could he and Marilee have been on the verge of losing the house they loved, saving it, at least for the time being, from certain foreclosure by virtue of accepting hourly jobs? Even without the negative impact of his growing list of secrets, it wasn't surprising their marriage had foundered on such numbing trials.

There was another question, one even more perplexing and far more complex: How had their marriage endured all those passionless years?

Johnny had been pondering that question a lot lately, and now he knew, now that passion had finally been introduced into their long marriage. A theory that seemed to firm up when he mentioned it to Brian. The answer was simple. What he felt in the beginning had faded. All that time he had not yearned for the pleasures of her body, not really. What stirred him had been set aside and ignored, displaced by ambition and that long crawl to the loftier heights in the advertising world. He recognized that his love for Marilee, then and now, included no real need for physical passion; rather their marriage had been more of a coming together to comprise a suitable whole, a union that would neatly fit in the overall social puzzle. Maybe it had taken a haunting to get him to understand, an instantaneous attraction to an immortal in the form of a perfect man to make him realize an important part of his life had been vacant.

Johnny reached up and rubbed a shoulder, staring into the shadows. An occasional insect whirred past his head. The premise was simple. The whole of his relationship with Marilee was a partnership to create a home, to build a career, to have the security of sharing life with another human being—not a union steeped in lust and the lathery smells of impassioned flesh. First Julian, then Brian had caused him to reach into his soul and reorder everything that had been the norm, everything he had taken for granted for so many years. Now there were consequences he had to face, rooted in the injustice to himself and Marilee brought on by their marriage. Was it a matter of direction and timing? Of when and how? They would eventually have to talk about these things. It was a vague recognition, but a recognition nevertheless, of himself, and it felt like chaos and enlightenment at the same time. He threw the half-eaten apple into the garden and stepped back into the house, his ambivalence in conflict with the tranquility of the night.

Unsettled despite his newborn conclusions, he slipped back into bed beside Marilee and pulled the sheet up to his waist, and there he lie with hands folded over his belly for the rest of the night, staring into nothingness. He felt an urge to do something, to once and for all put himself on the path to his true destiny. He felt determined to break free of Cassandra and Julian Mott.

Johnny seemed quiet as he sat the table waiting for breakfast. Her housecoat tied at the waist, Marilee glanced at him from time to time as she boiled water for oatmeal and buttered toast. Fidgeting with a napkin, his expression was distant. It seemed he didn't realize she was in the room. He had not made love with her all week, though she had not expected him to, not with the gloom that had settled over them both. He had walked into the room with that familiar distance that came when he was most unpredictable, the state of mind that made her feel helpless and lost. Whatever was in that house, could it be powerful enough to have taken him away from her, she wondered as she poured two glasses of juice, her hand trembling with the weight of the pitcher? Maybe she should have never abandoned the church.

Johnny had forgotten that he planned to tell Marilee about the Globalcorp lawsuit this morning, preoccupied by something entirely different. He had gotten out of bed thinking about Cassandra's parlor. It had come over him during the night, that hunger for Julian that sang from the lower muscles of his body; yet he had dressed for work, determined to resist.

Steam wafted up from the hot oatmeal when Marilee placed the bowl before him. After bringing butter and brown sugar to the table, she sat down opposite him. Moments later, staring at the table just beyond his bowl, Johnny had not made the first move to eat.

"What's on your mind this morning, Johnny?"

His eyes lifted. "Nothing."

Marilee hesitated, as if she had stepped out on thin ice. "Something's bothering you. I know you didn't sleep well last night."

An irrational anger flared in him. "Damn it, Marilee. Why are you always asking that?" he wanted to know. His voice was loud and impatient and demeaning. "Can't I just relax a few minutes before I leave for that godforsaken job?"

She looked at him for a moment, and then stood and hurried from the room. He cringed with self-contempt, looking at her empty chair and her untouched bowl of oatmeal. He had ruined her breakfast, her morning, her day. He wanted to scream. His anger roiled inside like a poison. How could he eat? He burst to his feet, knocking over the chair, and stormed toward the front door, slamming it behind him. Taking deep, unsettled breaths, he paced to the corner to await the bus that would take him to the home improvement center.

A ten-minute wait turned his hands into fists. It was maddening, this unwanted, all-consuming urge. The bus appeared six blocks down the street. His throat tight and dry, his breath coming faster, he watched it grow larger in the distance, then turned his gaze in the direction of Confederate Square. He stepped off the curb and in that direction he went. One block after another of Savannah's historic neighborhoods fell behind his quick pace. As he neared the familiar square, his heart quickened as he paused to look up at her window before crossing the street. A warm sensation passed through him, bringing a smile to his lips. And Cassandra returned the smile, holding aside the lace curtain as she peered down at him.

Johnny pushed his hands into his pockets, narrowed his shoulders and started for the wrought-iron gate. Inside the house, the chorus spilled from the wall midway up the staircase and filled the foyer with its woeful song. A chill came to the back of Johnny's neck, not unpleasant, but something familiar, something gratifying like a sip of hot cocoa after a cold walk. It seemed he was where he should be. On up the stairs he went and down the hallway, and he entered Cassandra's parlor feeling much like a desert wanderer entering an oasis. She had come back into the main room, wearing a floral summer dress, and had taken a seat on the sofa across from Julian. Between her forefinger and thumb she held a plump dried apricot close to her lips.

"Mmm, how wonderfully delicious these are," she said, plopping it into her mouth. "Come in and join us, Johnny. Try one of these wonderful apricots."

He strode with cautious enthusiasm across the room and sat down on the edge of the sofa beside her. From the crystal serving dish he took an apricot. Sitting directly across from Johnny, Julian leaned back and locked his fingers behind his head, watching him chew and swallow the fruit. It was moist and sweet, delicious indeed. He reached for another, permitting his eyes to roam Julian's body and rest upon the nuances between those muscled thighs. The sheer gauzy white linen with its creases and contours left little to the imagination. Johnny felt the stirrings of an erection.

His thoughts shifted as he looked back at Cassandra. "That chorus in the foyer. Where do those voices come from?" he asked after swallowing the second apricot.

Cassandra smiled. "My three girls, darlin'. I think of them as my daughters. They were one of the reasons I bought this house."

"Sounds like they're behind the wall next to the stairway."

"They are. Their mother hid their bodies there when she killed them."

"Killed them? They're ghosts?" Johnny's jaw yawed open as he listened to the story.

"Yes. They told Julian what happened that day. The poor dear mother simply lost her mind. She beat them to death with a small oar and then plastered them behind that wall. She hired a handyman to hang that beautiful wallpaper the next day."

Her words began to echo and run together in Johnny's head. He slouched back against the sofa and he glanced about the room as if his thoughts were dancing without order. "Uh, no one ... no one ever took them out of the wall and buried them?" he asked from his shapeless fog.

"No one knows they're there but Julian and I, and now you." She reached out to touch the side of his face. "Of course there was blood everywhere. The mother couldn't get the stains out of the carpet. That's why the authorities suspected her. They questioned her. She became hysterical and confessed, but never told anyone what she did with the bodies." Cassandra stroked his head, appraising the effect of the apricots in his eyes.

"What'd they do to her?" He closed his eyes, lightheaded and dreamy. The apricots made the story less appalling.

"They hung her. I was a young woman then, still living on our plantation. When I heard the story, I couldn't wait to see the house it happened in. I heard their voices the moment I walked in. I insisted my father buy this property for me."

"You had a father?"

"Yes, darlin'." She smiled, reading the confusion in his eyes. "Sometimes I enter the world through the womb. It's so much fun to be a little girl, to have a father and mother, don't you think? Julian arranged to be born next, so he could be my little brother."

"Cassandra ..." His head fell back with a kind of floating dizziness.

"What is it, darlin'?" he heard her say.

When his eyes opened, she had come up over him, straddling his legs on her knees and was smiling down at him. She untied the string behind her neck, allowing the floral fabric over her left breast to fall. The breast swayed before his eyes and his mouth watered as the nipple seized his thoughts. The swollen and supple peak beckoned as he reached out and took the breast in both hands. A milky stream spattered his chin and lips. The sinews of his neck tightened as he strained forward, pulling her closer, yearning for the warmth of her milk in his belly. How binding it was, this joining of lips and nipple, the warm wet texture flowing over his tongue and filling his mouth faster than he could swallow. He pressed his hands together, squirting the milk, which caused it to run in rivulets down his neck and dampen his collar.

When Cassandra withdrew the nipple, Johnny felt the effect: warm tendrils spreading through him from his belly. Inches before his eyes, the breast drooped slightly under its own weight. The loose flap of cotton cloth below it was wet. Beyond the seductress sat Julian, his head turned, his eyes fixed on something across the room. Johnny looked at Julian's hand resting on the cushion; its proportion and even the fine blonde hairs on the back of his fingers seemed to heighten the perception of perfect masculinity. Johnny's gaze dropped and he envisioned the darker shades and pendulous sway of a male organ, convoluted in obscurity behind the delicate fibers of linen. The hint of its shape moved the ache deeper in his loins.

Trying to sit up, Johnny reeled, then doubled over. He clutched his arms over his belly and rolled from the couch to the floor, pushing aside the low table. The milk set his mind swimming against the currents of a maddening bliss. He curled into a ball and locked his arms around his knees, rocking the floor. His thoughts, like an angry ox crashing through the woods, raged through his mind in torrents of nirvana interspersed with hints of revulsion and fleeting streaks of self-loathing. He reached back and took a hold of his haunches where the ache was acute.

"Here, darlin', let me help you."

Cassandra's voice. It came to his ears from a million miles away. It soothed him like an aural caress. He felt his hand in hers, her palm warm and smooth. At once he wanted to go with her, shifting drunkenly to his hands and knees, slowly lifting his upper body. His foot came forward and he stood, and it felt as if his body was a mass of floating particles that might spill back onto the floor like so many grains of sand.

Johnny followed Cassandra into the bedroom, his steps erratic and wobbly. He sat on the edge of the bed after she turned back the sheet, then watched her fingers find the buttons of his shirt. Gooseflesh raced across his arms when she lifted the shirt from his shoulders. He fell back on the bed and she unbuttoned his jeans and pulled them down his legs. He lifted his head when Julian came into the room, now lying naked before them on the cool sheet. Cassandra sat down beside him while Julian undressed, then watched her brother come between Johnny's legs and lift them to his shoulders.

The two men lay side-by-side on damp sheets moments later. Johnny opened his eyes and saw the calm beauty of a seductress smiling down at him, her red hair glistening and falling about her shoulders.

"Do you love me, Cassandra? Is that why you call me here?"

Her eyes narrowed. Her smile dissolved as she contemplated her depleted guest. *You'll know soon enough, my little man. You'll know why you're here.* "Do you believe I love you, darlin'? Do you believe I can do with you as I wish? Do you enjoy coming here where nothing else matters?"

◆ ◆ ◆

Brian had spent most of the day at the library plowing through an archive of old Savannah newspapers, looking for anything he might find on the Mott family. After coming across the name a few times in the social pages, he found a story about a Colonel Mott that dated back to the Civil War. The man had been a prominent local citizen, wounded in battle, returning then to his plantation just outside of the city. The names *Cassandra* and *Julian* appeared in the listing of the Colonel's eight offspring. Brian stared at the article, stricken by an alarming notion. If the two of them had been born into that family, it had happened by their choice. Did they somehow entered the mother's womb, he wondered? Did they displace the fetuses of Colonel Mott's own unborn children?

He left the library, weary with eye-strain and shaken by his discovery, and went home to warm a can of soup in his tiny kitchenette, planning to call Johnny after having a bite to eat. Instead, he fell asleep in the recliner, the television flickering with the daily news, the empty soup bowl resting in his lap. The phone awoke him at nine-thirty. He heard Marilee's voice when he answered it.

"Is Johnny with you, Brian?"

Concerned at once, Brian sat upright. "No, as a matter of fact, he's not."

"He's not here either."

Still groggy, Brian could imagine only one place Johnny might be.

"I'm worried about him," Marilee went on to say. "He didn't go to work today or call in. He left the house in one of those strange moods this morning." Brian heard a silence, and then Marilee added: "I think he's with her."

Brian rubbed the back of his neck, caught without a viable response that might alleviate her concern. "Marilee ..."

"I'm going over there to get him," she said.

"Don't go alone, Marilee. Give me a few minutes and I'll be over to pick you up."

"Thanks, Brian. That's the last place on earth I want to go alone."

Thirty minutes later, Brian parked the rent car at a curb on Confederate Square. Escorting Marilee through the wrought-iron gate and up the steps, they heard orchestral music as they neared the front door. They glanced at each other and then Brian's eyes shifted to the doorknob. He took a hold of it and found it unlocked. He pushed the door open and they stepped inside. Marilee gasped at the sight of a fully furnished house. They were both astonished by what certainly had to be a small live orchestra. Straight ahead, the anteroom opened on the right into the grand living room. From there the music came, along with the laughter and gaiety of many voices. Stepping forward cautiously, they entered the anteroom and ventured closer the archway of the grand living room, astounded further by what they saw.

Dressed in high-fashion 1860's Savannah finery, seventy or eighty people occupied the room in lively merriment. Arranged on the west side of the room, the small orchestra was performing a waltz. Butlers in elegantly tailored uniforms carried silver trays of hors d'oeuvres. Gloved hands held crystal champagne glasses, men in tails and starched collars, women in bustled gowns of lace and silken fabrics gathered in back and cascading in ruffled layers to the floor. Mingling among the crowd were a half dozen Confederate officers, men animated with stories of war and dressed in immaculate gray uniforms.

"Is it a costume party?" Marilee asked, staring with disbelief into the room, aware somehow it wasn't that at all.

"I think not, dear lady," said Brian. "But I believe I know what it is." He pointed across the room. "See that officer over there? I saw his picture at the library today, in the newspaper archives. He was killed in battle with Sherman's army during the fall of Atlanta in 1864. He's a native of Savannah, a hero at the time. That gentleman ... all these people were Cassandra's friends. She must call them from the grave so they can relive these festive occasions."

Marilee took Brian's arm as she gazed at the elegant crowd. She had come to believe this house was occupied by something she could not understand, but she had not been prepared for anything like this. Now everything was clear. Everything Johnny had been trying to convince her of was true. Her thoughts were weighted with trepidation, though resolutely charged with concern for her husband. "I don't see Johnny."

Nor did Brian. He didn't see Julian either. In linking their absence, he urgently wanted to get Marilee out of the house.

"He's not here. Shall we leave before we're discovered?"

"That's her next to the fireplace, isn't it?" Marilee asked, looking at the voluptuous redhead standing next to a Confederate officer, easily the most beautiful woman there.

Brian was anxious to leave. "Yes," he said reluctantly.

To his alarm, Marilee set off into the room, maneuvering through the crowd toward Cassandra. Drawing the powerful woman's attention, Marilee stood before her quietly, suppressing a nearly overwhelming dread.

"Who are you, my dear woman?" Cassandra asked, looking at Marilee with amused eyes.

"Marilee Feelwater. I'm looking for my husband."

Cassandra appeared to be delighted. "So you're Johnny's lovely little wife?"

"Is he here?"

"Why yes, he is. He's upstairs."

Marilee turned abruptly and strode back across the large room. Walking past Brian, she went directly into the foyer and turned toward the stairway.

Caught off guard, Brian collected himself and just as he started after her, Cassandra approached.

"What are *you* doing here?" she demanded, hurrying past him after Marilee.

He shuddered as he started up the stairs behind them. Looking up, he saw Marilee disappear into the hallway to the parlor, Cassandra close behind. A sense of dismay came over him as he mounted the stairs.

Standing in her elegant attire, Cassandra had stopped midway into the room and watched as if this were an unexpected source of amusement. There was no one in the room, or in the front alcove. The door to the darkened bathroom stood open. Marilee started toward the bedroom door at the back of the room.

Brian paused in the doorframe. He lowered his head and rubbed his eyes with regret just as Marilee opened the bedroom door. He heard her gasp.

Marilee froze, and then slumped against the doorframe.

Positioned on Julian's bed, naked, her husband was on his hands and knees. He and Julian had slept together during the afternoon, waking from time to time to indulge in what had become a carnal marathon. Julian had mounted him just before Marilee appeared at the door.

Johnny's heart sank when he looked at her. The effects of the apricots and breast milk had receded. He realized only then how long he had been there. Panicked, he pulled free of Julian when his wife turned and hurried from the room. He grabbed his jeans and stepped into them as fast as he could.

Marilee brushed past Brian and broke into a distraught run for the stairs. Brian turned and looked at Cassandra. He stepped forward and stared defiantly into her eyes, quite put off by the sly smile on her face.

"You've ruined him, Cassandra. Was that your goal, to dismantle his life one piece at a time? If so, you've succeeded."

Johnny came hurrying out of the bedroom. Brian rushed after him as he bounded down the stairs, catching up with Marilee just beyond the wrought-iron gate. As he approached, she stood resolutely and looked at him as she would being confronted by a stranger.

"You disgust me," she said with contempt.

"Marilee, I ..."

"So that's what you've been doing over here? With a man! I can't understand that, Johnny."

"I couldn't tell you. I wanted to. I wanted to make you understand what they're capable of."

Brian stood off to the side, his hands in his pockets, his heart going out to them both. He saw in this scene their undoing. Marilee was at wits end.

"You can't!" Marilee shouted with unconstrained anger.

Johnny closed his eyes with a helpless, sinking feeling. Had he told her, they might have worked through it. But she had walked in on them, seen with her own eyes what he was doing with Julian. The humiliation of getting caught that way was greater than any he had ever suffered. He knew the image would never leave her mind.

"Anything but infidelity, Johnny ... anything. Why did it have to be with a man? How could you betray me like that?"

"Please don't believe it was my choice," he pleaded, knowing it was a lie. He had slept with Brian, which had been by choice, and of little consequence they had tried to refrain.

"Not your choice, Johnny? You left this morning to go to work. You chose to come here instead. I believe what I saw with my own eyes."

He nodded sadly. He wanted to touch her, to hold her and again feel her love through his arms. But in the blink of an eye that too had disappeared from his life. She would never permit him to touch her again, not ever. He knew, he could see it in the way she looked at him. There was an awful distance between them, sudden and absolute, a distance that could not be measured. Marilee was no longer his foundation.

Staring at the pavement for a moment in anger, Marilee's eyes then lifted. "Stay away from the house until I pack my things. You can have what I leave behind after I go to Atlanta." She looked at Brian. "Will you drive me home?"

Brian nodded and stepped forward and took Johnny by the arms. "I'll take her home, Johnny. Then I'll come back for you. Where will you be?"

Johnny was watching Marilee get into the rent car. It had ended so abruptly, so decisively, he was overwhelmed. There was no going back, no truth or lie that could change her mind—it was simply over. Together they had planted the seeds for the future. Together they had hoed many weeds, hoping all the while their efforts would bear fruit. Now it seemed as if it never happened.

Brian gently shook him.

"What?" Johnny said distantly, his eyes locked on the woman that was walking out of his life.

"Where will you be when I come back for you?" Brian repeated.

Johnny looked at him with a glassy stare.

Brian tightened his grip on Johnny's arms. "Listen to me," he demanded. "I'm taking Marilee home. Wait for me over there in the square until I get back. Understand?"

Johnny nodded, which seemed to satisfy Brian, and then watched his companion get into the car. He knew it would end, but not like this, not with Marilee revolted by him. He watched them drive away, as if his past and all he had left was in the car. He stood for a long while, an empty shell, oblivious to everything but the pain gripping his heart.

Brian returned to Confederate Square like a madman on a mission. He ran the rent car into the curb and hopped out from behind the wheel after slamming the gearshift into park. As he scanned the square, his shoulders fell. Johnny was nowhere to be seen. Approaching the bronze Confederate soldiers, he scanned the benches along the brick walkway, then squinted across the shadows beneath the trees. He craned his neck and looked down the streets that led away from the square. Then he turned and looked at the house.

Cassandra had changed into a white summer dress and was sitting in a rocker on the porch. Brian stared at her for a moment before starting in her direction. His pace quickened as he steadfastly approached the wrought-iron gate, then pushed it open and climbed the steps.

"You're walking better today, I see," she said as he came to a stop in front of her.

"The party over already, Cassandra?"

"You are a bothersome man, aren't you, Mr. Fowler?"

"I went to the library this afternoon. Read about one of your guests in an old newspaper article. Captain Jacob Harris. He died in Atlanta in 1864."

"I hated those Yankees for what they did to Savannah."

"Savannah was spared, dear lady. What the Yankees did here was no more than spit on the sidewalk compared to what they did to Atlanta."

"A history lesson. How charmin'."

"Where is he?"

"Who might that be?" she asked. Her shrewd smile belied her feigned naiveté.

"You know who. Did he go back in the house with Julian?"

Her smile turned contemptuous. "He sulked away like a small boy."

"Where? What direction?"

"My, my. Curt aren't we?"

"Cassandra, please, just tell me which direction he went."

She nodded toward a side street off the northeast corner of the square.

Brian turned and rushed back to the rent car. He drove one block after another, doubling back on one street and then the next. He found Johnny fifteen minutes later, sitting on curb several blocks from Confederate Square. Screeching to a stop, Brian got out of the car and hurried to the curb. He sat down beside his companion and leaned forward, resting his forearms on his knees to let his heart calm.

He felt the weight of Johnny's sadness. He had never seen such deep despair. "Are you ready to go home?"

"Home?" Johnny said, turning to look at him.

"Yes. Home. It's small but comfortable, and right now it's the only place you and I have."

They stood and walked to the car. When they arrived at the flat, Brian followed his companion up the outside stairs that led to the door. Brian went into the bathroom and turned on the water in the tiny shower stall, returning to find Johnny on the edge of the bed, still wearing nothing more than his blue jeans, staring down at the floor.

"That water you hear is for you," said Brian.

After unfastening his jeans, Johnny leaned back to push them over his hips. Brian stepped forward, took a hold of the cuffs and pulled them down his legs, pausing to look at the man he would be sleeping with. It was different now. Brian sensed his life had just changed, that the man he was looking at, the fluid lines of his long slender body, the fleshy bulk of his shoulders and hips, was to be a significant part of his future. Such an interesting mind in such a beautiful package.

"Look at you," said Brian. "Dried semen on your chest. You're a mess."

Johnny looked down at himself. Brian flung the jeans into a corner and extended his hand and pulled Johnny off the bed. "Looks like you could use a little pampering," said Brian, walking with him to the bathroom and directing him into the stream of water. After soaping him head to toe and watching him rinse off, Brian reached for a towel and blotted him dry. He fully realized he was taking care of the man he wanted to spend the rest of his life with, though at the moment it was like taking care of someone who had lost his will to go on. He got Johnny into the bed and then undressed and got in beside him. They laid side-by-side staring up at the ceiling in silence.

"I told her it wasn't your choice," Brian eventually said. "I explained they have the power to make you do things against your will. Somewhere deep inside, she understands that, but your premonition was right. She's tired. Seeing you with Julian was more than she could deal with."

"I should've told her," Johnny said. "I never wanted her to see me like that. It would've been easier if I had just talked to her."

"What man has the balls to tell his wife he's fucking another man, no matter what the circumstances are?"

"She must hate me."

"No, she doesn't hate you, my friend. Women don't stop loving someone that easily. She just can't endure any more."

"Brian ... think I'm free of them now?"

Brian reached up and rubbed his face with his hands. "I suppose we'll find out soon enough, after you move to Boston with me."

Johnny looked at him.

A hapless smile formed on Brian's lips. "I hate being an opportunists, but looks like it's you and me now, doesn't it?"

Johnny looked back at the ceiling. In that he and Brian were together, a vague calm came over him, though this twist of fate left a significant part of his heart aching. But yes, his love for Brian had germinated in Africa. It had bloomed in his thoughts and dreams, and he found enormous comfort in lying beside him now.

"I have a bit of news to tell you," Brian said, moving his arm under Johnny's head. "I've had enough of it myself. My adventures with the immortal are over. They can have their secret world without interference from me." Brian released a sigh. "I'll tell you what did it, which is on top of the fact I'm scared to death of them. I found out today, in her last life Cassandra had a mother and father. She came back into the world through a mother's womb. Can you imagine that? She could have managed it only one way, and that horrifies me. So it seems, my friend, some things should be left alone."

Johnny turned onto his side and moved into the warmth of Brian's body, resting the side his face on Brian's shoulder.

"She entered a mother's womb and displaced a child to make way for herself." Brian paused to consider the enormity of such an act. "I tell you, I want no more of it. They've lived among us for countless centuries, and so be it. I never want to think on it again."

Johnny pondered what Brian had learned. He knew, if Cassandra had entered a mother's womb, it had been because Julian had somehow placed her there, that Julian was the catalyst for her many reincarnations, be they a discreet reappearance in adult form or the birth of a girl child. He, too, wanted to be rid of Cassandra's whims and Julian's devilry, which he intended to be after just one more visit. That visit would come in the morning. He intended to convince Cassandra to leave him alone, so that he could finally try to pick up the pieces, to deal with losing his wife, the one person on the face of the earth he trusted, who found out, in the end, couldn't trust him. He would convince her to stay away from him, so that he and Brian could attempt a new life in Boston.

They lay quietly for a while, contemplating the path their lives had taken, coming to realize that destiny had brought them together. For Johnny, it wasn't that he had lost his wife—he had recognized the inevitability of that even before he and Brian left Africa. It was losing a best friend, a lady he loved deeply; though Marilee obviously was not, and most likely could never be given over to forgive or accept what she had seen him doing.

As the silence grew long, the stealthy phantoms of sleep began to snatch at their consciousness. Johnny felt calm. It was as if an invisible hand had reached inside him and soothed his soul. He moved his hand down between Brian's legs, felt the dewy flesh of male organs, reminded that he and Brian were to be lovers. So that which was not meant to be had come to an end, and born in those ashes was this disposition of two men of one mind.

Brian, as his thoughts began fading into dreams, turned his head and kissed Johnny's hair, snuggling a bit closer and settling into the comfort of the bed. "I like laying with you," he said languidly. "I like it a lot."

Chapter 31

Sunrise came and passed. Warm light cascaded through the window of the small room, falling over a single man still asleep on the bed. Johnny had turned off the alarm clock before he slipped out the door, leaving his lover to awaken on his own. He would be back in time for lunch, at which time he would have some good news to share.

Brian awoke with a start, the morning sun on his face, realizing at once Johnny wasn't there, stricken by the same sense of dread that tightened his chest the day before.

It was nine o'clock; two hours after the alarm should have gone off. He swung his legs off the bed and sat up, all but certain Johnny had gone back to Cassandra's house for some reason. This time he was scared, genuinely scared of going back into that house after him. The thought of facing that dog ran down his spine like a cold chill. He stood and crossed the room to splash some water on his face, taking on faith that by the time he dressed and got over there, his knees or his heart wouldn't fail him.

Johnny first went to see Marilee. Hoping that she would let him in, hoping she would listen to what he had to say. He got there before she left for work.

Marilee stared at him for a long while when she opened the front door, standing in her housecoat, holding it together at her breasts, her eyes weary from crying and lack of sleep. Finally, wiping the wetness from her cheeks with her fingers, she stepped aside and allowed him in. He followed her into the kitchen where they sat silently for a moment on opposite sides of the kitchen table. Her demeanor had stiffened with resolve and defensiveness.

"I should've talked to you." His voice sounded out of place in the very kitchen they had shared so many meals. He felt like an intruder.

Marilee continued to stare. Her expression offered little more than permission to speak, cold in a way that made it clear no words could redirect their future.

"I was afraid I'd lose you." He let out an ironic half-laugh. "I lost you anyway." He fretted for a moment with a spoon that had been left on the table. "I want say you can have the house, and the van, and the bank accounts, but I don't have those things to give. I have nothing I can give you." A tear formed in his eye and he rubbed it away, looking at her with a plea. "Can I explain it to you now?"

"I'm listening," Marilee said flatly.

He nodded with a weak smile. "Guess I've always known I'm that way, but I thought it was wrong. I thought it was something college boys experiment with and then the curiosity goes away. I tried to convince myself of that. When I met you in the library that day, it seemed nothing else mattered. I wanted you. I wanted to be normal, you know, to lead a traditional life and be married to you."

He paused, hoping he was reaching some small part of her, hoping that one day she would forgive him. "...Marilee, Julian could seduce any man alive. If not consensually, he could use his power over the human mind. I admit, with me he had little difficulty drawing me into his bedroom. I understand it now. He merely introduced me to the ..." Johnny's forehead tilted onto the steeple formed by his index fingers as he struggled for the right words to say. Momentarily, he looked up. "Well, he *reintroduced* me to the urges in my body." Johnny shook his head sadly. "I should've told you. I hate that you found out that way."

"Me too, Johnny. Yes, you should've told me, and yes, I'd still be moving to Atlanta; but it would be a little bit different, wouldn't it, between you and I."

"You wouldn't have let me come in, and you wouldn't be sitting there listening if you hated me."

"Oh, lord, Johnny." She shook her head with frustration. "Looking back over the last few weeks, I realize worrying about you not coming back from Africa wasn't what I had to worry about at all. It was already too late. You never came back from your first visit to Cassandra Mott's house." She looked down at the half full cup of coffee she had been drinking, pressing her lips with her fingers to hold her emotions in check before going on. "It must be obvious I laid awake thinking about all of this last night. I don't hate you. I never will. I don't regret spending nine years with you, or regret you have nothing to give me. Right now I'm angry—just a little too weary to show it, but it's not regret. I'm angry, but I still believe you're a special man. And perhaps for reasons beyond your control or mine, you've been taken from me. Your character, your thoughtfulness and sensitivity, it's all those things. It's little things, and even if an important part of our marriage was missing for nine years, I loved you for who you are."

"Marilee ..."

"I have more to say, Johnny." He pressed his lips together and nodded. "It's been in the back of my mind for a while now, but I thought about it a lot last night. All these years we've slept together and rarely made love. I believe it was because you weren't that interested. I was part of it, too, because of my religion, but look what happened when you finally got angry about it. You acted like you wanted me and challenged me to be your wife. It made me feel desirable. It was there for us all along, wasn't it?"

Marilee drew a breath and stared at him for a moment before she continued. "I'm still religious. It's more spiritual now than something I seek from the church. I realize my beliefs weren't the reason I spent so much time on church events. I needed some kind of fulfillment, something for me personally, like what you were getting from your design work. The church occupied my time and my mind while you were busy in your own world. I see it as a little pathetic now, but I've changed. Today I'm giving the flower shop a two-week notice. I intend to move to Atlanta. Not because my mother is there, though I may stay with her a few weeks until I'm settled. I'm going because Atlanta offers more opportunities for someone willing to work hard to get ahead. That's me. I plan to start a new life there and build a career."

Struck without a word to say, Johnny's eyes, wet with both sadness and admiration, searched the tabletop. It was another side of Marilee he had never seen. On her own and in the face of despair, she had called upon her inner strength to face a new challenge. Johnny loved her perhaps even more, though it saddened him that she would be so far away. He wanted so much to take her hand and be forgiven.

"You've gotten rather quiet, Johnny."

Their eyes met, and another tear streaked down his face. His lower lip quivered as he realized his sadness had robbed him of words.

"I've listened to you, haven't I?" Marilee continued. "I may smash a few dishes on the floor before I get them all packed, but I'm sure I'll eventually get over this anger. I want you to leave me alone until I have that chance. For now, I have to finish getting ready to go to work, so I'll say good-bye from here instead of the front door."

He watched her get up and disappear through the den. The awful weight of sadness heightened as he walked back through the house to the front door.

A block away, an occasional tear still rolled down Johnny's cheek. He had not seen Marilee stronger than she appeared to be today. It dawned on him that she had stayed with him all those years, not because she was dependant on him, but because she wanted to, and the thought made the pain knifing at his heart go just a little deeper. He took solace in the fact that she had listened to him, that she had admitted to not hating him. He even hoped that she would eventually understand that his giving himself to another man was a thing some men were meant to do, that in the end, he might not have lost a best friend.

He sat down on the curb and looked down the tree-lined street, the gables and eves of fine old Savannah homes juxtaposed with limbs and leaves. He lifted his hands and looked at his palms, and then his eyes shifting down to the front of his shirt. What did he have left, other than the clothes on his back? But what did it matter? He raised his palm to his nose and smelled Brian, and then he thought of Boston. It was like he had been staring through a wall of ice, like he had seen through the crystalline haze another life calling out to him; and as he sat on the curb with the warm summer air on his skin, he realized the wall of ice had melted away.

Was it misgiving he felt in going to Cassandra's house this morning? He couldn't say. It was to be a morning of confrontation, a morning in which he would sever his tie to the beautiful pair. He rolled his head on his shoulders and drew a breath and then stood. One way or another, if he was to leave Savannah with his soul intact, or have a chance with Brian, he had no choice but to confront her.

Johnny entered the house and found Cassandra relaxing in the bathtub. Leaning back, her red hair cascading down into the fragrant water, she raised her left leg straight up into the air to rub on some lotion. Johnny sat down on the floor beside the tub and folded his legs before him.

"How nice of you to come by and see me this morning, Johnny."

He knew, in spite of everything, that he still could not be angry with her. He remembered getting out of Julian's bed in the late afternoon the day before, coming downstairs when he heard the music. Spellbound, he had watched the gala for a few moments before he noticed a few of the guests had spotted him. *A naked black man standing in the anteroom,* they were whispering, looking at him with amusement. He had hurried back to Julian's room before the humiliation expanded.

"Quite a lavish party yesterday," he said absently.

"I didn't see you come down. Why didn't you say something?"

"I was naked."

She looked at him and smiled. "Oh, my! I'm certain my guests would have been mortified by that."

"Marilee is leaving me. She's moving to Atlanta."

"My goodness! Whatever for? Is she upset with you about something?"

"Yeah. I ruined her life. Of course seeing me with Julian was the last straw." He was staring at the bubbles lapping gently about her shoulders. "I suppose it doesn't matter since it was gonna happen sooner or later, anyway." He looked at her. "I'm gay you know."

"We shan't be judgmental, not Julian and I."

"I lost my company and my reputation in advertising's been destroyed. Globalcorp's suing me for breach of contract." He mentioned all of this certain she already knew, certain she knew that she was the cause.

"For heaven's sake, you *are* havin' a run of bad luck." She raised the other leg to apply lotion. "I remember the awful tragedies people endured during the war. People are resilient though, aren't they, Johnny?"

"The bank will be foreclosing on my house soon. I'm broke. I've lost everything."

"You've come to see me for money. Of course. How much would you like?"

"I've come to say good-bye."

She turned and looked at him.

"I can never come back, Cassandra. I don't want you to call for me."

"This must have something to do with that man, what's his name ... oh yes, Mr. Fowler. What's he been putting in your head about me?"

"It has to do with me. It's my choice. Bryan doesn't know I'm here." He paused, looking at her, desperate for words that would inspire her to release him. "You've had your fun with me, Cassandra. I'm used up and very tired. It's time we move on."

She rose from the tub. The sudsy water cascaded and glistened down her sensuous body. She sat down on the edge of the porcelain and opened her legs before him.

"Are you sure you want to stay away, Johnny?"

The distraction had become easier to resist. His eyes lifted from the red tuft of pubic hair to hers. "Please, Cassandra ... let me go. Don't call for me again. Surely you understand."

A sympathetic smile crossed her lips. "I shall miss you terribly, Johnny Feelwater. You have Emily's eyes." The memory saddened her and she looked away. Then, as if the memory had been swept aside, her casual gaiety returned. She looked at him and said: "I know what we can do. Julian and I plan to go out for breakfast. You can join us. We'll have breakfast together to commemorate our parting friendship. I shall not interfere with your affair with Brian Fowler, now that he's given up writing his books."

Johnny cocked his head. "How did you know that?"

"Remember, darlin', he was here in my house yesterday. His mind reads like a gaudy road sign."

Johnny pondered her sincerity, thinking this was going down too easily. "Do I have your word?"

"Of course you do, my lovely man. I shall leave you alone forever."

Johnny stared at her for a moment. Maybe his appeal reached her heart. Maybe she had already decided she was through with him. He believed her. A smile formed on his lips. "Then I'd be delighted to have breakfast with you."

Near the garage behind the house, Johnny stood next to Cassandra while Julian backed the long car out onto the gravel driveway. The balloon-like tires crunched noisily over the crushed rock.

"He's never gotten used to driving an automobile," she said, leaning forward to see if her brother was going to scrape the side of the garage door. "Julian would rather communicate with a horse."

The heavy car made a jerking stop when Julian cleared the garage. Cassandra and Johnny got into the front seat with him, Cassandra in the middle. Julian backed the unwieldy car into the alley and from there the street, and on through the historic neighborhoods of Savannah they went.

It was a 1960 Cadillac convertible. But for its ponderous weight, its huge fins suggested the ability to rocket off into space. A breeze poured over the windshield and washed over their faces, fluttering their hair. Neither Cassandra nor Julian seemed aware that their lumbering, dated machine stuck out in the traffic like an ostrich among swans; Julian hunched over the wheel like a man under attack, Cassandra holding her face joyously to the wind.

Such an upbeat moment, Johnny thought, with the sunlight flickering through the overhead leaves. It seemed odd to him that these two could set out like ordinary people on a casual outing. A shame they weren't, really, for he loved them both. Aside from Cassandra's penchant for wrecking lives, he loved being around them, as would Brian, he was sure, if only it were practical. But it wasn't, no more than trying to befriend a pair of lions. So now a final breakfast together would end their misguided association forever.

Thinking about it, Johnny wished he had told Brian about his plans, knowing how concerned he had been the night before. But he knew that Brian would have thrown a great deal of resistance against his plan to see Cassandra, especially since she had made a believer out of him. He resolved to call him the moment they arrived at the restaurant.

"Oh look!" Cassandra suddenly cried out. "A bank. Julian, stop the car and we'll go inside."

Puzzled, Johnny looked at her. He couldn't imagine Cassandra's reason to go into a bank. "You have to cash a check or something?"

"It's a bank, darlin'. They can solve those money problems you were telling me about. Let's go in and see."

Johnny stared at her at a loss. It made no sense. *My money problems? What's she talking about? Maybe she's playing a joke.*

Julian steered the car out of the traffic. Johnny was looking at Cassandra, perplexed. Accustomed to her illogical interpretations and bizarre notions, this was somehow different. Inexplicably, she seemed determined to go inside the bank. A foreboding came over him. Why did she think this bank, or any bank, would be interested in solving his money problems, when he can't pay the debts he already has?

Julian stopped the car at the curb, Cassandra poised to open the door.

"Wait!" Johnny persisted as Cassandra opened the car door. "What do you mean, solve my ...?"

Ignoring his protest, Cassandra got out of the car, as did Julian. "Don't just sit there, darlin'," she said, calling back to him. "Come inside with us."

He stared at them, incredulous, watching the two of them approach the heavy glass doors and enter the bank. Maybe she thought he wanted a loan. If so, she wasn't well versed on creditworthiness—he couldn't get a loan if his life depended on it. It occurred to him to get in there and stop whatever she intended to do.

Hurrying inside, Johnny saw a dozen or so people in the lobby and Cassandra parading toward a teller's window. Where was Julian? The sudden turn of events had disoriented him. He watched her approach the counter with something in her hand, unable to determine what it was. Then, to Johnny's horror, she raised her arm. She had a gun and was aiming it directly at the teller.

"Get your hands up!" she shouted, positioned like a gun moll, her eyes alert and scanning the faces around her. "Hand over the money!" she demanded.

The buzz of conversation across the lobby fell silent. Like time had stopped, everyone in the bank froze. Johnny's horror-stricken eyes panned across the spacious lobby, alarmed by the frightened and stunned faces. Just that quickly, what had been a glorious morning had turned into a nightmare. He felt overwhelmed by a sensation of falling through space. Time ticked by in agonizing, dreamlike seconds.

The bank erupted in gunfire. Johnny's head jerked toward the sound and he saw Julian standing near the back of the lobby, firing yet another gun at the ceiling. There was instant chaos, screams, objects crashing to the floor, people shuffling, trying to get low on the floor. Cassandra stepped closer to the counter and snatched the bag the teller had stuffed with money. She turned in Johnny's direction and stepped quickly toward him, tossing him the bag with a smile.

"There, that should take care of your money problems."

He looked at the bag with disbelief.

She handed him the revolver and then looked back at the tellers. "We better get out of here. I think they're mad at us." She started for the door.

Too disoriented to move, Johnny turned and saw two-dozen pairs of eyes looking at him in mortal fear. Panic gripped as the reality of what had happened began to seep into his mind. Confused, he looked at the weapon in his hand, realizing the danger confronting him. A split second later, he bolted for the door, exploding out into the sunshine, looking madly for the car. Frantically scanning the intersection, he spotted the Cadillac across from the bank and down the next block. He started quickly toward it, stopped in his tracks in the middle of the wide street by a shout from behind.

"Stop where you are!" the bank guard shouted from the sidewalk.

Beating wildly, Johnny's heart sank. He turned to face the guard. In the same instant he heard the blast.

A thud impacted his chest. For a second or two it all seemed like a rude joke. His mind reflexively tried to reject what was happening—it was too bizarre, too impossible to believe. But something felt dreadfully wrong. Beset with a sudden dizziness, he dropped the bag and the gun and looked down. A red stain was expanding on his shirt. His knees weakened and gave way and he collapsed. A fog came into his head as he lay in an expanding pool of blood, staring into a surreal world of blue sky and glaring sun. Julian appeared and knelt over him. Their eyes met and Julian's were adoring. He knew there wasn't much time.

I regret this. Now I have eternity to think about you. That is my just reward.

Over the street noises that seemed a million miles away, Johnny heard Julian's thoughts, aware he was dying. Though he tried, he had no strength to reach out to Julian for help. A small crowd had collected on the sidewalk. Of those from inside the bank, none remembered Julian or Cassandra, only Johnny.

When Julian moved away, Johnny saw Cassandra standing over him, her expression harsh and uncaring.

"Why this way, Cassandra? Why didn't you just kill me in the beginning?"

"You took Emily from me. You killed her. I wanted you to suffer, the way your grandmother did ... the way I did when she died because of you."

"I know you don't hate me," Johnny whispered, holding his chest, gasping for air, reaching for understanding. "You love me. I've seen it in your eyes. Not even you can hide something like that."

She stared at him for a moment. "You bastard!" she blurted. "Even when you're dying you want me to suffer." In one breath her tone had turned to a whimper ringing with regret. She stared at him a moment longer before averting her eyes.

A few feet behind her, Julian stood looking at him; and as the world around him blurred, Johnny's last image was the sadness in Julian's gaze.

Johnny Feelwater's world then ceased.

No one was at Cassandra's house. Brian didn't know where to look next. Then he remembered, the day before, as they drove by, Johnny had pointed out the florist's shop where Marilee worked. Certain he could find the location again, he got back into the rent car. After thirty minutes of driving around, he found the florist and went inside, greeted by a matronly proprietor. She looked him over when he asked for Marilee.

"Are you a friend, young man?"

"Yes," Brian said, still not certain that approaching Marilee with Johnny's disappearance was a good idea.

"I'm afraid you just missed her," said the woman. "It appears her husband was shot. He's in the hospital."

The words came at Brian like a slap. "Shot!"

"All I know is the police department called and asked for Marilee. The poor dear was distraught when she got off the phone. I had no idea she was married to a bank robber. That poor dear."

Brian's brow furled. This news scattered his sensibilities. Thinking he must have misunderstood, Brian said: "I'm sorry, Madam, it sounded like you said *bank robber.*"

"I did. That's how he got shot, robbing a bank."

"My God!" Brian gasped, looking away from her, dazed.

"Do you know him?"

Brian was miles away in thought.

"Young man, do you know him?"

Brian looked at her, his mind spinning. "Something's wrong here. He's not a bank robber."

The woman's brows lifted as if she took issue at being doubted. "Mr. Feelwater was shot robbing a bank, young man. That's what the police told Marilee not thirty minutes ago."

"Please, how do I get to the hospital?"

The woman took a pad of paper from under the counter and sketched out a rudimentary map. Brian looked at it and recognized the intersection. He turned abruptly and hurried to his car.

Johnny had gone through the preliminary procedures in the ER by the time Brian arrived at the hospital. As a member of the medical fraternity, he had little difficulty arranging a few minutes with the surgeon that headed the team that had kept Johnny alive, barely alive.

The surgeon lowered her surgical mask and crossed her arms as she spoke. "The bullet just missed his heart, but it tore through his left lung. He lost a lot of blood before he got here. We brought him around with cardiac shock. He's hanging on, but it doesn't look good, Dr. Fowler."

Brain nodded and with welling emotion, his jaw clamped shut. His eyes closed and he tilted his head back to take a few breaths. A moment passed while the reality took hold in his heart and mind, and then he took the few steps to the small room. He paused in the doorway, next to a policeman that occupied a chair next to the door. Marilee was standing beside Johnny, sobbing. Hooked to life support and monitors, Johnny lay partially upright, unconscious, surrounded by a myriad of medical machines.

"Someone told me he was shot robbing a bank," Brian said to the policeman, staring sorrowfully at his dying companion.

"Yeah, that's right, Mister. A bank guard shot him in the street. Had the money and a gun in his hands."

Brian nodded, then stepped inside the room and sat down in a wooden chair near the foot of the bed. It was worse than any nightmare he had ever imagined. Why would Cassandra kill him? Why? What sense did it make to ruin his life and then do this? Brian felt a welling anger such as he had never felt. It seemed the entities were mankind's enemies after all. Maybe they should be destroyed, if that was possible.

A few moments later, when Marilee looked at him in grief, he stepped up beside her. Johnny, but for the tubes protruding from his nose and mouth, looked peaceful.

"He wasn't involved in robbing that bank," Brian said as he gazed at Johnny. "You know that, don't you?"

"I don't understand anything that's happened to us, Brian."

"Cassandra must have intended to do this all along. It must have been her purpose. I just can't figure out why. In spite of everything, Johnny thought she cared for him. I know that sounds odd, but he really thought she cared for him in her own way."

Marilee wiped away another tear with her fingertips. "I never thought I'd want to kill someone. God help me, I do. I could aim a gun and pull the trigger easily."

"Don't think about things like that, Marilee. They're finished with you and your husband. You need to go on with your life."

She reached out and pulled the sheet a little higher on Johnny's chest. "Is he dying?" she asked, though it seemed she already knew the answer.

"Yes," Brian said solemnly.

"I feel guilty for not believing him all that time. It's funny how your mind works in circumstances like this. Maddening really. I love him more now than I ever have. Just not in the way I loved my husband. I lost my husband weeks ago." She pressed her fingers against her lips. "I'll never forget him. He's very special and I love him deeply." She turned and looked at Brian for a few moments, and saw the great sadness in his eyes. "You loved him, too."

Brian looked at her. "Yes," he said, "I loved him."

They noticed a movement in Johnny's eyes. Then he stirred ever so slightly and his eyes opened. He saw them standing beside him, two people wanting terribly to take him into their arms.

Johnny's lips moved as he tried to make a sound. "Revenge," he said, laboring to speak with the tubes in his mouth. "Her purpose was revenge."

His eyes fluttered and went blank. The steady beeping sound behind Brian and Marilee stopped. The machine emitted a shrill buzzing sound. A nurse quickly appeared, but made no attempt to come to his aide. She looked over the body and turned to check the monitors. After flipping a switch that stopped the buzzing, she turned and faced Marilee.

"Mrs. Feelwater," she said gently, "I assume you know your husband had a living will."

"Yes, I knew," said Marilee.

"Then you know Mr. Feelwater left instructions to perform no heroic procedures to prolong his life."

Marilee nodded. The nurse's words made Johnny's death all too real.

"I'm very sorry there wasn't more we could do."

Marilee produced a weak smile.

"We'll be back in after a while to take care of him," the nurse said. "I'll be at the desk if you need my assistance." She turned and walked out of the room.

Brian and Marilee looked at Johnny again. Marilee lifted his hand and kissed it gently. A tear rolled down Brian's cheek as he straightened the sheet over Johnny's body. They stood in sorrow, not knowing what to do, not wanting to leave, their perspectives so opposed, yet remarkably similar. It was a matter of coming to terms with what neither of them could have anticipated; for Marilee, a life without the man she spent nine years with and loved dearly; for Brian, a thousand nights lying awake feeling hollow, wondering until his last day on earth what might have been.

Brian thought about the way they held each other in Africa, he and the lifeless man before him; how they tried to cling to the principles of right and wrong; how they had held each other the night before, weary, but finding a special kind of peace in each other's arms. Now what? If he were to find the resolve to leave this awful room, to go to his small apartment and pack his things and return to Boston, it wasn't in him now. He couldn't take his eyes from the peacefulness on Johnny's face.

A sudden feeling came on the back of Brian's neck, like the fine hairs had been raised by a static charge. Something about the room had changed. Was it the room or his imagination? The monitor behind him suddenly started beeping, the hum of the equipment returned. Brian's and Marilee's eyes fixed on the slight flaring of Johnny's nostrils. The feeling on Brian's neck persisted. He turned.

The policeman was sleeping. Next to him, framed by the doorway, stood Julian.

Beside himself, Brian's head whipped back around. What did it mean? Johnny was clearly breathing. The monitors were defining life by their hums and beeping. Marilee was staring at her husband with utter confusion as he opened his eyes. A gleam formed in them and a faint smile curled the corners of his lips. Jubilant, Brian turned again to look at Julian, whose eyes shifted from Johnny to him.

He is for you, Brian Fowler. Julian looked at Brian for a moment and then turned to walk away.

"Julian," Brian called out, his mind racing. "They'll put him in prison for robbing the bank."

Julian's eyes shifted to Johnny. *No one will remember what happened at the bank. The wound in his chest was accidental. He was cleaning his gun.*

"And Cassandra's vendetta?" Brian pressed.

My sister is in remorse. Johnny Feelwater is free of us both.

Brian heard the words. He heard Julian's thoughts as clearly as if they had been whispered in his ear. A joy rose in him and tightened his throat. He stared, his heart beating fast. Julian turned and quietly disappeared down the hallway.

Made in the USA